JAMES HERBERT

The Fog · The Spear · Sepulchre

CHANCELLOR PRESS

The Fog first published in Great Britain in 1975 by New English
Library
The Spear first published in Great Britain in 1978 by New English
Library
Sepulchre first published in Great Britain in 1987 by Hodder &
Stoughton Ltd

This collected volume first published in Great Britain in 1993 by
Chancellor Press an imprint of
Reed International Books Ltd
Michelin House, 81 Fulham Road
London SW3 6RB
and Auckland, Melbourne, Singapore and Toronto

by arrangement with Hodder & Stoughton Ltd

ISBN 185152 440 1

Reprinted 1993

A CIP catalogue record for this book is available from the British
Library

Typeset in the UK by ROM-Data Corporation, Falmouth, Cornwall
Printed in the UK by the Bath Press

Contents

THE FOG

Foreword

The Fog MADE ME A LOT OF ENEMIES. FORTUNATELY, IT ALSO MADE ME A LOT OF friends. It was first published in 1975 (written in 1974) when spy stories and historical romances were the vogue. In the United States, William Peter Blatty had made his definitive mark with the movie of *The Exorcist*, and word was going around about an interesting new writer by the name of Stephen King. In England a new kind of horror tale involving mutant rats on the loose in London's East End, a story that held scant regard for conventional moderation in its depiction of violence and the consequences, had created something of a stir. It was a book that (literally, you might say) went straight for the jugular. *The Rats* was my first attempt at a novel. *The Fog* was my second.

For better or worse, they were the initial part in a growing explicitness of narrative, stories that rarely balked at expressing horror's true physical reality. Judging by the genre's swift return to public attention, through both the novel and the screen, that reality had been suppressed far too long (whether or not the sudden healthy release has transmuted in an unhealthy fascination is another matter). Readers or movie-goers no longer wanted to be merely frightened, they wanted to be shocked rigid too.

Yet, for all that, is *The Fog*, a tale of murder, madness and mayhem, as graphically horrific as its longlasting notoriety would suggest? By comparison with today's standards, certainly not. But when it was first published in 1975? Well, even that's debatable. Ramsey Campbell, perhaps one of the most respected authors of the genre, has said in a reappraisal: '*The Fog* contains remarkably few graphic acts of violence, though two are so horrible and painful that they pervade the book. Herbert concentrates rather on painting a landscape of (occasionally comic) nightmare, and most of the episodes are of terror rather than explicit violence.' My point is – and this is an observation, not a defence – that much of the controversial extremism is in the mind of the beholder rather than on the page. I must confess, however, to being pleased with the effectiveness of its images.

Nevertheless, with this new edition, the temptation was to re-write, to smooth out the rougher edges, perhaps endow some of the characters with a little more depth. After all, a dozen novels on, and by the very nature of practice, I must have picked up a few more skills along the way.

But by so doing, would I detract from the original? To me, *The Fog* provides an honest reflection of the transient mood of the horror genre in the seventies, being in some ways a throwback to the fifties and much earlier, whereby due homage (albeit subconsciously) is paid to Wells, Wyndham and Kneale – *War of the Worlds, Day of the Triffids* and *Quatermass* respectively – while advancing very firmly towards the eighties. And it's sheer energy that carries the story through to the climactic finale; refinement might well sap its strength. I think change would be an unnecessary indulgence on my part.

Besides, I like the beast the way it is.

James Herbert
Sussex 1988

▪ 1 ▪

THE VILLAGE SLOWLY BEGAN TO SHAKE OFF ITS SLUMBER AND COME TO LIFE. Slowly because nothing ever happened with speed in that part of Wiltshire; a mood of timelessness carefully cultivated by the villagers over the centuries prevailed. Newcomers had soon fallen into the leisurely pace and welcomed the security it created. Restless youngsters never stayed long but always remembered, and many missed, the protective quiet of the village. The occasional tourist discovered it by accident and delighted in its weathered charm, but within minutes its quaintness would be explored to the full and the traveller would move on, sighing for the peace of it, but a little afraid of the boredom it might bring.

Jessie opened her grocery shop at precisely 8.30 as she had been doing for the past twenty years. Her first customer, Mrs Thackery, wouldn't be in till 8.45, but to break the routine of early opening would never be considered. Even when Tom, her late husband, had died, the shop had still been opened on the dot of 8.30 and two days later when he'd been buried it was only shut for an hour between 10.00 and 11.00. Jessie enjoyed her morning chat with Mrs Thackery, who always called whether she needed to buy something or not. She'd been a great comfort since Tom had died and never missed her morning cup of tea with Jessie. They never got bored by each other's gossip; one topic could last two weeks and a death in the village would get them through three.

She waved to Mr Papworth, the butcher across the street who was sweeping the pavement outside his shop. Nice man, Mr Papworth. Much nicer since his wife had left him. That had caused a stir in the village and no mistake, when she'd walked out after six years of marriage. She hadn't been his sort anyway. Much too young for him, too flighty; couldn't stand the quiet life. He'd brought her back from his holiday in Bournemouth and after all the years, when everybody had thought him a confirmed bachelor, had announced her as his bride. It could never have lasted, they all knew that at the outset, but he had tried. Still, all that was in the past. His visits from across the road were becoming more and more frequent and the whole village knew what was in the wind and that the butcher's and grocery shop would eventually become a combined family business. There was no rush; things would take their course.

'Good morning, Mrs Bundock!'

Her reverie was interrupted by two young voices in unison. She looked down and smiled at little Freddy Graves and his even smaller sister, Clara.

'Hello, you two. Just off to school?'

'Yep,' replied Freddy, craning his neck to look at the jars of sweets on the shelves behind her.

'And how are you, Clara?' Jessie beamed at the five-year-old who had only recently started school.

'Fine, thank you,' came the shy reply.

'I'm surprised to see you two today. Saturday's usually your pocket-money day, isn't it?'

'Yep. But we polished all Daddy's boots yesterday, so he gave us a special treat,' was Freddy's bright-faced reply. Their father was a policeman whose station was in the next town. He was a gruff-spoken but pleasant man who adored his two children, but dealt with them strictly.

'Well, what are you going to buy?' Jessie asked, knowing they wouldn't have much to spend. 'You'd better hurry or you'll miss your bus.'

Clara pointed at the penny-chews and Freddy nodded his head in agreement. 'Three each, please,' he said.

'Well now, penny-chews are cheaper on Mondays. You get four each for six p today.'

They beamed up at her as she reached for the jar and took out the sweets.

'Thank you,' said Clara as she put three in her pocket and began to unwrap the fourth. Freddy gave Jessie the money, took his four and followed his sister's example.

'Bye bye now. Have a nice day!' she called after them as they ran from the shop, Freddy clutching Clara's hand.

'Morning Jessie.' The postman was leaning his bike up outside the door.

'Hello, Tom. Something for me?'

'Airmail, 'spect it's from your boy,' he replied, entering the shop. 'S'going to be another lovely day today. Beautiful clear sky out.' He handed her the blue and red envelope, noticing the shadow of sadness that seemed to pass over her face. 'Been in the army nearly a year now, hasn't he?'

She nodded, studying the stamps on the envelope.

'Ah well, Jessie, it was only to be expected. Young boy like that. Couldn't stay cooped up in a village like this all his life, could he? Needed to see places, did Andy. Always liked to get about, always up to some mischief. Having the time of his life now, I reckon.'

She nodded again, sighing as she began to open the envelope.

'Yes, I suppose you're right. But I do miss him. He was a good boy.'

The postman shook his head once then shrugged his shoulders.

'Well, see you tomorrow, Jessie. Must be off.'

'Yes. Bye, Tom.' She unfolded the thin blue writing paper and began to read the letter, a smile spreading across her face as Andy's natural boisterousness shone through the written words.

Suddenly she felt giddy and lurched against the counter. She put her hand to her forehead, alarmed at the strange stomach-rising feeling. Then she heard a deep rumbling noise, a sound that came from below, under her feet. The floor began to quiver causing her to clutch at the counter again; the quiver became a trembling. Jars began to rattle on their shelves, cans began to tumble. The rumbling grew louder, deeper. It began to fill her head. She dropped her letter and clapped both hands to her ears. The ground shook. She lost her balance and fell to her knees. The whole shop seemed to be moving. The large glass window cracked and then fell in. Shelves collapsed. The noise became deafening. Jessie screamed and stumbled towards the doorway; every time she tried to rise she was thrown to her knees. She crawled to the entrance, terror of the building collapsing in on her forcing her on. Vibrations ran through her body, at times the shaking almost making her lose contact with the floor.

She reached the door, and looked out at the road that ran through the village. She couldn't believe what her eyes told her.

The postman stood in the middle of the road holding on to his bike. A huge crack appeared at his feet and suddenly, as the ground opened up, he disappeared. The crack snaked along the length of the street to where young Freddy and Clara stood transfixed, clutching one another, and on towards Mrs Thackery who had been making her way to Jessie's shop. Suddenly it seemed as though the whole village had been wrenched apart. The road disappeared as the ground opened up like a gigantic yawning mouth.

Jessie looked across the road and just caught sight of the terrified face of Mr Papworth as he and the whole row of shops and houses on his side were swallowed up by the earth.

▪ 2 ▪

JOHN HOLMAN WEARILY CHANGED GEAR TO TAKE THE CAR AROUND THE BEND IN the narrow country road. He was unshaven and his clothes were still damp from the morning dew. He'd spent half the night trying to sleep inside a thicket out of sight of the army patrols that practised their manoeuvres on a large but secluded part of Salisbury Plain. The area was owned by the Ministry of Defence and trespassers were severely dealt with if caught. The grounds could never be entered by accident; high fences and many warning notices took care of that. The fences travelled many miles around the territory's perimeter and a heavy screen of trees and undergrowth successfully concealed what lay beyond.

Holman shook his head in disgust at the danger and discomfort he'd had to go through to maintain secrecy when he himself worked for the same government.

It was idiotic that the two departments, the Ministry of Defence and the Department of the Environment, couldn't work hand in hand, but held back information, guarded against intrusion, as if they were two different countries. He had been recruited into a new office specially formed by the Department of the Environment, to investigate anything from polluted rivers to outbreaks of disease. It was a special unit because nearly all the investigations were carried out secretly. If a company was suspected of illegally dumping dangerous waste product, be it into the sea, into a river, or on to a tip, but no proof could be found by direct methods, then Holman was sent in to probe further.

He usually worked alone and often under a cover, more than once he'd taken on manual labour to get inside a factory to find the information needed. Hospitals, a mental home – even an experimental home-range factory farm; he'd worked in many places and, often as not, in government institutions to get at the source of suspected malpractice. His one big frustration was that the trangressions he unearthed were not always acted upon. When politics – business or governmental – became involved, he knew the chances of prosecution against the offenders were slim. At thirty-two, Holman was still young enough to be angered by the seeming lack of resolution shown by his superiors when he himself had taken great risks to ferret out the proof they had asked him to provide.

However, he could also be quite unscrupulous in achieving his aims and more than once had seriously infringed the law, causing alarm among the few superiors who knew about his activities. At the moment his project was to investigate land owned by the Ministry of Defence, used by them for military purposes and protected for them by the Official Secrets Act. Vast areas of land, much of it appropriated during the Napoleonic war and, more recently, World War II, was used as a training ground for the army. Most of it was in the south because of invasion fears. Holman knew that much of it was going to waste, areas of great natural beauty, rich arable soil being allowed to spoil. At a time when good land and open spaces were becoming more and more scarce, valuable country could not be allowed to be misused. The Ministry of Defence was holding tightly on to over 750,000 acres for training or test purposes and his department was demanding at least 30,000 of those acres be handed back to the people. There was every reason for the Ministry of Defence to retain a good part of this private land, but suspicions were that only a fraction of it was necessary.

The Ministry had been approached, but a tight security net had been drawn over any enquiries. So Holman had been given the job of seeing just how much land was being used and if for valid purposes. The war between different government departments was ridiculous in his eyes, but he accepted it as a fact of life.

He had spent two rigorous days dodging patrols, taking photographs, gathering information about the enormous woodland area owned by the Ministry on Salisbury Plain. Had he been caught the consequences could have been quite severe, but he knew the risk involved and even enjoyed it. His employers knew this and played on the streak in his character that demanded risk, an element of danger, a gamble.

Now, as he rounded the bend, he saw a village ahead. One of the small, barely known villages that dotted the Plain, he decided. Maybe he could get some breakfast here.

He drew nearer and suddenly became aware of a strange vibration running through the car, then of a deep rumbling noise as the vehicle began to shake. By the time he reached the main street running through the village his vision was becoming too blurred for him to travel further. And what he could see, he found hard to comprehend.

A gigantic crack appeared directly ahead of him then grew longer and wider, reaching towards him in a jagged, fast-moving line. His shocked brain just had time to register two children and a woman, and beyond them a man with a bicycle, before the ground opened up and they disappeared into the black chasm it created. The shops on his left began to collapse into the widening hole. The noise was deafening as the earth was wrenched apart, climaxing in a sound like an explosive thunderclap. Through his horror he realized that the ground below his car was beginning to split. He opened the door but too late – the car lurched forward and began to fall. The door was forced shut and Holman was trapped inside.

For a moment the car was stuck, but as the hole widened, it slid forward again. Panic seized him. He cried out in terror. Down it plunged at an acute angle, the rough sides of the earth preventing it from free-falling. After what must have been only a few sickening seconds, the car became wedged again and he found himself pressed up against the steering wheel, staring down into a frightening black void. His body was frozen, his mind almost paralysed with the horror of what was happening. Slowly, his brain began to function. He must be at the end of the opening, where the sides were narrowest. If it widened further, the car would plunge into the black depths below. He tried to look up towards ground level but couldn't see through the swirling dust.

Panic drove him into action. He frantically pushed himself away from the steering wheel but the sudden movement caused the car to slide a terrifying two feet further down. He forced himself to keep calm, his breath coming in short gasps, the sounds of falling masonry, glass and dislodged earth filling his ears. More cautiously, he began to edge himself over into the back seat. He froze as the car shifted again, but this time the movement was fractional. He kept his position for a few tense moments then started to ease himself back again.

Gaining the back seat, he turned round into a position where he could wind down a rear side window. He saw there was just sufficient gap between the car and the side of the chasm for him to squeeze through. Loose earth fell through the open window adding more weight to the precariously balanced vehicle.

Abandoning caution, he scrambled through and clung to the crumbling wall of rock and earth, expecting to hear the wrenching sound of the car tearing itself loose to fall into the depths below. For a full five minutes he stayed there, his head tight against the earth, clutching desperately to the treacherous surface.

The unsettled dust began to clear slightly and he looked around him fearfully. From the jagged outline above he guessed the eruption was at least five hundred yards long. The sides seemed steady now although shales of earth still showered down into what seemed a bottomless pit. He peered into the darkness below and shuddered at the awesome sight. It was as though the very bowels of the earth had opened up; the blackness seemed infinite.

A slight tremor made him bury his hands and face into the earth again, his heart pounding wildly, expecting at any moment to be dislodged from his insecure perch.

A sudden cry forced his eyes open once more. He peered through the disturbed dust and saw what looked like a tiny figure lying on a narrow sloping ledge about fifty feet away on the opposite wall of earth. With shock, he realized it was one of the children he'd seen in the street above. The little girl. Of the boy who'd been with her, there was no sign. She began to whimper piteously.

Holman knew he had to reach her or she would soon slide down the incline into the deep chasm. He called out to her, but she didn't seem to hear. He looked around, wondering how he would cross the gorge to get to her. She was about ten feet above him and thirty feet below ground level. Climbing to her shouldn't be too difficult providing he took great care; the sides were full of protuberances and old roots. The problem was to get across – and quickly.

Another thought struck him; what if the gap should close? The thought of being crushed to death as though in a giant nutcracker spurred him into action.

The car would have to act as a bridge. Two steps and he would be on the other side. It was dangerous but the only course of action he could take. Tentatively he placed a foot on the roof of the car. It held. He put his weight on it, still holding on to the wall on his side. The roof slanted downward and the thought of slipping on its smooth surface terrified him. Before he could allow himself to think further he took two bounds across the gap, almost willing himself to fly.

But the second step caused the car to lose its grip on the sides of the walls and it slipped forward and down, taking Holman with it. Desperately he grabbed at the side he had been making for and, with more luck than judgement, managed to grasp a dead tree root. It cracked and broke, but thin tendons held it together and swung him inwards.

The child looked up at the sound of the crashing car and screamed when she saw the man hanging there. Rivers of earth, disturbed by her feet, ran over the ledge and showered into the gaping hole. She buried her head in her hands and sobbed, calling for her lost brother.

Holman hung there, thin strands of rotted wood between him and death. His feet sought support from the crumbling earth and one hand grabbed at solid rock. He managed to find a handhold and eased his weight from the broken root. He raised his feet until they found a more solid rest. Gulping in lungfuls of dusty air he looked towards the little girl.

'It's all right,' he shouted across. 'Stay perfectly still and you'll be all right. I'm coming to get you!'

He didn't know if she heard him or not, but he knew she would not last long on the precarious ledge. Again the thought of the ground closing up drove him on. He inched forward, testing every handhold, every foothold, and gradually came within eight feet of her and found himself on a fairly solid outcrop of rock.

He didn't know how much time had elapsed; it could have been hours, but more likely it was no longer than minutes. Surely help would come soon, someone would try to see if anyone was trapped in the hole. He looked for a way to reach the girl.

There was a narrow crack running along the wall almost from where he stood to four feet below the ledge the girl was on. If he used it for footholds and used his hands to cling to the rock above his head, he should be able to reach the ledge, lean over it from the side and grab her. Her little body shook from the sobs but she didn't look up.

Carefully, he began to feel his way along, keeping his eyes on the girl, ready to warn her not to move. As he drew nearer, her sobbing stopped and she looked up at him, her tiny face a mask of sheer horror. God, what must he look like coming towards her like this? With all the terror she'd been through, now to see this shape, filthy with dust, eyes wide and staring, clambering towards her.

'It's okay, it's okay,' he said, softly but urgently. 'I'm coming to help you. Don't move.'

She began to back away.

'No, no, don't move!' he couldn't help but shout.

She began to slide down, and, realizing her predicament, dug her hands into the soft earth, crying out in fright.

Holman took a chance and lurched forward, hoping the side of the ledge would hold his weight. One foot stayed in the crack, the other dangled in space, one hand shot towards the girl, the other grabbed at the rock face. He managed to grab her outstretched hand and prevent her from sliding further. Her legs were over the edge now, her feet kicking at the empty air. His left hand found a crevice in the wall and he clung to it grimly, knowing if he lost his grip both he and the girl would plunge to their deaths. She was screaming now, but her hand grabbed his as she realized the danger behind her.

For a few moments, all he could do was cling there, looking into her frightened face, clutching her struggling limbs. He whispered to her to be still, kindly, trying to keep panic from his voice. Slowly, her struggles died down and her body went limp, as though she knew nothing more could happen to her, her young mind going blank to protect her. He began to pull her up, her slight body no weight, but difficult because of his awkward position. Finally, she was completely back on the ledge but still he dragged her towards his chest.

'Hold on to me, sweetheart,' he told her gently. 'Put your arms around my neck and hold tight.'

He pulled her down between the ledge and his body, telling her to put her legs around his waist. Numbly she complied, her short legs resting on his hips.

'Now don't let go and everything will be fine,' he whispered, easing himself back along the crack, the shape of the girl pushing him outwards. His arm and leg muscles were rigid with the strain, but endurance was one of his assets.

Finally, exhausted, he reached the more solid outcrop of rock. He sank to his knees, still holding the child close, his shoulders heaving with the exertion.

Turning slowly, still clutching the girl, he leaned back against the cliff wall and
rested his aching limbs.

For a few minutes his brain registered no more than the blessed relief from
exertion but, as his strength returned and his breathing grew more even, he
began to wonder at what had happened.

He remembered entering the village and then – and then the ground, the
very earth opening up. First the crack snaking its jagged way along the concrete,
then the noise, the deep rumble, the build-up to the cracking stone, and then
the incredible sight of the ground opening up, the enormous split in the earth.
The two sides moving apart, their edges crashing inwards, down, down into
God knows where. The sight of the two children, the man and his bike – had
he seen a woman too? – disappearing into the hole. The shops collapsing – he
remembered seeing the shops on one side collapsing – and then the ragged
mouth reaching towards him. The tilt of the car, the lurch as it slid forward.

It all seemed to have happened in slow motion. And yet it had all happened
so fast. He stroked the girl's head, trying to still her sobs, reassuring her that
they'd be all right, but the cries for her brother stung his heart.

He looked up towards the daylight, hoping he would see someone up there,
someone looking for survivors. Survivors? Survivors of what? The question
exploded in his brain. An earthquake? It was incredible. Earthquakes had
occurred in England before, and minor tremors were frequent. But an eruption
of this size? The incredible, the unbelievable, had happened. In a crazy world,
the most crazy thing had happened. Wiltshire had suffered an earthquake! He
laughed aloud at the thought, startling the child. He pulled her raised head
back to his chest, gently, and rocked her comfortingly.

What had caused it? It certainly wasn't any gas-mains explosion; not with
this devastation. The hole was too deep, too long. No, it had certainly been an
earth tremor, not as serious as those suffered in other countries of course, but
of just as great a magnitude because it had happened in England! Why? Had
the nearby military installation been testing some underground explosives? He
had evidence of some pretty strange goings-on from his discreet weekend visit,
but doubted they had anything to do with this. A chain reaction, perhaps, from
one of their experiments. But probably nothing to do with them for, after all,
they had vast areas of British-occupied wasteland in far off countries to carry
out their tests in. England was no place for experiments of this kind. It was more
likely a freak of nature, a disturbance below that had been building up for
centuries, probably thousands of years. And today had been the day for it to
erupt.

But still the doubt lingered.

Just then Holman noticed movement at his feet. At first he thought it was
dust caused by the disturbance, but then saw it was billowing up from below.
It was like a mist, slowly rising in a sluggish swirling motion, slightly yellowish
although he couldn't be sure in the gloom. It seemed to spread along the length
of the split, moving up towards his chest, covering the girl's head. She started
to cough, then looked up and her whimpers became stronger when she saw the
mist. He lifted her higher so that her head was level with his shoulder. Then

the mist reached his nostrils. It had a slightly acidy smell to it, unpleasant but not choking. He got to his knees, wondering what it could be. Gas? A ruptured main? He doubted it – gas was generally colourless, this had some substance to it. It was more like – well, a fog. It had body, the yellowish tinge, a slight but distinct odour. A vapour probably released by the eruption from deep underground, trapped for centuries, finally finding its way to the surface.

It was above his head now and he found it difficult to see through. He got to his feet, lifting the child with him. Once above the rising cloud, an immense fear overcame him. For some reason his horror of the swirling mist was more intense than the horror he'd just been through. Perhaps it was because this was happening slowly, whereas everything else had been so fast, leaving so little time for thought. This somehow seemed more evil, more sinister; he didn't know why, but it filled him with a great sense of foreboding.

'Help! Is there anybody up there? Can anyone hear me?' He called out urgently, no panic in his voice yet, but he could feel hysteria rising. There was no answer. Maybe it was too dangerous to approach the edge of the hole. Perhaps there were too many injured up there anyway.

'I want you to get on my back, darling, and put your arms around my neck,' he told the girl, lifting her chin so he could look at her face. 'We're going to climb up now.'

'I – I want my brother,' she whimpered, no longer afraid of him, but still not trusting.

'I know, darling, I know. But your Mummy and Daddy will be waiting for you up there.'

She burst into tears again, burying her head into his shoulder. The thick blanket of fog was now up to his chin. Moving her around to his back, he took off his belt and tied her wrists together just below his neck, tucking her legs around his waist. He began to climb.

The people above heard the cry for help coming from the huge hole that had wrecked the village. They'd assumed that anyone who had plunged into it must surely be dead, but now gained new heart at the sound of a voice, a chance to react against the tragedy. The policeman whose children were thought to have been lost in the eruption, was lowered over the edge of the crack. He would not give up. He had searched the rubble and still half-collapsed, potentially dangerous buildings, but hadn't found his youngsters yet. When they heard the cry for help, he was already tying a stout rope to his waist to be lowered into the hole to search for survivors.

When he emerged five minutes later, he held a small unconscious girl in his arms. He laid her on the ground to be taken care of by the elderly but competent doctor, he kissed her once, tears from his eyes falling on her face, then dashed back to the hole and was lowered again. This time, he brought up a man. A man covered from head to foot with dust and dirt. A man who gibbered and screamed, a man who had to be restrained by four others from running back and throwing himself into the black depths. A man who was insane.

The villagers watched the mist rise from the hole, not billowing over the edges, but rising in a densely-packed steady column, the centre of which seemed to glow faintly – or was it merely the strong sun shining through it? – rising high into the air to form a heavy, yellowish cloud. It looked like the aftermath of a hydrogen bomb, only a much smaller mushroom shape, the lower column finally ending and joining the cloud in the sky. It was soon forgotten when the winds blew it away; not dispersing it, but moving it in a huge, almost solid-looking mass, across the sky, away from the ruined village.

▪ 3 ▪

THE REVEREND MARTIN HURDLE TRUDGED ACROSS THE FIELDS WITH A HEAVY heart. His thoughts were on the nearby village that had suffered the great disaster, the peaceful little village that had virtually been demolished by the freak earthquake. It had been the main story in the newspapers all that week. The great shock was that it had happened in England, not some far off, remote country that people had scarcely heard of. This was on their own doorstep, the British people could relate to it, not viewing it distantly through the news media and the press, thereby finding true sympathy hard to arouse. This had happened to their own kind. For the people of his village, they were neighbours, relatives; for the people in the rest of Britain, they were countrymen. This would be the basis of his sermon today: that through this tragic event they could now perhaps truly understand and feel compassion for the plight of other nations all over the world who suffered misfortune as a normal part of their lives. People were concerned too much with their own mundane, day-to-day problems: money worries, job worries, affair-of-the-heart worries, disputes with family, with neighbours, with life itself – all petty, insulated, but only shown to be so when some major disaster happened.

This tragic event would force people to look outward, to see what was happening in the world around them, to realize just how insignificant their selfish, introverted problems were. If only he could use this distressing event to show his congregation just how big life was, that the world did not revolve around individuals but around the great mass of humanity itself. This was the very reason that one had to help *everybody*, help them to exist, to survive. That the catastrophe had happened to *their* neighbouring village proved it could strike anywhere at any time; no one, no community, no nation was immune.

The words ran vigorously through his mind. He knew just how he would tell his congregation that Sunday morning, just when his voice would soften almost to a whisper, to allow him to build up to a loud, heart-stirring climax. After thirty years as a clergyman he now knew the subtle inflections his voice could use, and the times he had to boom out to reach his parishioners. At fifty-two he had not yet quite despaired of human nature. There was good in the worst people, just as there was hypocrisy in the most devout, but some-times –

He shrugged his shoulders helplessly. He usually enjoyed his early Sunday morning walk across the fields, his pace brisk, his mind running through the sermon he would deliver that day, but he supposed the tragedy of the eruption still bore heavily on him. Having heard the news, he'd driven to the village to try to help, to administer the Last Rites to the dying, to comfort the injured. The last war had been the only experience he'd had of death and injury in these proportions and he had believed he'd got over the horror of it, but old memories had been resurrected, scars he'd thought healed were opened freshly.

He looked up from the ground abruptly, realizing he'd walked into a mist. Early morning mists were familiar to him but this seemed different. It had a yellowish tinge to it and was thick, suddenly very thick as it swept over him. Strange smell, too. Goodness, he thought, better retrace my steps and get clear of this. Wouldn't want to get lost and.be late for service.

He walked back in the direction he'd come, for some reason becoming nervous as his steps didn't bring him clear of the dense mist. No, this wasn't a mist, he thought. It was fog. How strange to run into fog on a summer morning as brilliant as it had been when he'd set out. This was as bad as some of the old London 'pea-soupers'. He looked skyward and could just make out the faint haze of the sun. He wondered now if he were walking in the right direction.

'Goodness,' he muttered aloud, 'I'm lost!' What was that? His heart pounded as a dark, nebulous shape approached him.

It was large, not as tall as him, but bulky. And silent.

It seemed to drift towards him suspended in mid-air, its size increasing as it drew nearer. Then, oh God! – another. Another joined it, seeming to dissolve into it, becoming one huge shape, still approaching, almost on top of him. It, whatever it was, knew he was there! He backed away steadily, his mouth opening and closing soundlessly. He began to move faster, not turning but walking backwards, afraid to take his eyes off the shapes that loomed larger before him.

Suddenly, he bumped into something solid. He whirled, falling to his knees in his fright. Another black shape hovered over him, menacingly silent.

And then, he laughed. Tears of relief ran down his face and he pounded the earth in near-hysterical amusement.

He had walked into a herd of cows. He laughed louder, occasionally choking as he breathed deep mouthfuls of the murky air, the cows observing him in dumb vacuity, an occasional restless ululation their only comment.

It took him a full five minutes to recover his wits and admonish himself for his foolishness. Frightened by a herd of cows! Old George Ross, who owned them, would roar with laughter when he told him the story. No wonder he thought the shapes had been floating above the ground. The fog was so thick one could hardly see the cows' legs!

Yes, he'd learned a lesson himself today. The unknown was always more fearful than the reality.

It took him another twenty minutes to find his way clear of the fog.

The man crouched low in the bushes when he heard a rustle of leaves to his left. Human or animal? Tom Abbot had to be careful. If he was caught poaching on the Colonel's land again he'd be in serious trouble. Colonel Meredith had caught him red-handed last time and given him a 'sound thrashing' as the Colonel liked to boast in the village pub, then warned him if it ever happened again he'd 'march him off to the police station, toute suite'. Toute suite! Him and his fancy language. Well, he'd never catch Tom again. Last time it had only been because he'd lingered too long into the morning on account of his poor catch in the early hours. The Colonel had spotted him hiding in the bushes and crept up on him, then used his thick walking stick to beat him about the head and shoulders. Too surprised and hurt to offer resistance, he'd been dragged along by his collar as though he were riff-raff and booted off the estate with the threat of police action and 'another bloody good hiding' if he set foot on that land again.

Well, Colonel Meredith, you won't get old Tom again, he repeated to himself. Too wily for the likes of you, with your fancy house and fancy cars and fancy friends. Nice little pheasant I've got here and I'll get myself another before I leave. It's still too early for you to be about, I've got a good hour before you're up and around. Three months I've laid off, fooled you into thinking you'd frightened me off, but oh no, old Tom don't give up that easy. Nice price I'll get for this pheasant and no questions asked.

The poacher crept forward again, still cursing the landowner in his mind, peering into the bushes ahead. He froze. Yes, there was something there and not a man. He kept perfectly still, not wanting to frighten it away, to let it come out in its own time, whatever it was. Another pheasant, I'll warrant, Tom told himself. Woods were full of them, all under the sanctuary of bloody Colonel Meredith. Well, Tom had patience. Tom would wait for it to show itself. Tom could wait for nearly an hour without so much as twitching a muscle. Come on, my beauty, take your time. Tom can wait.

He crouched there for a full ten minutes before he became aware of the yellow tentacles of mist creeping around his legs. My Gawd, that's all I need, he cursed silently. He looked behind him and was surprised to see a solid blanket of fog almost on top of him. Queer, he'd never experienced fog here before. Well, he'd wait a while longer in the hope that whatever was in the bushes would make a move and show itself before the fog grew too dense.

Soon, he was completely enveloped in it and began to curse, realizing if the bird or animal didn't make a move soon he wouldn't be able to see it anyway. Still nothing happened and the heavy mist crept forward till eventually he couldn't even see the bush. Only then did he hear a rustle and the sound of something scampering away. He cursed aloud this time and stood up, kicking at the ground in disgust.

Ah well, one was better than nothing at all. He turned back and walked deeper into the fog. It didn't bother him, he knew the area so well he could find his way back blindfold.

The Reverend Martin Hurdle prepared himself for his Sunday morning service. As he donned his cassock he smiled at the thought of the panic he'd been in earlier when he'd got lost in the fog. Usually one of the joys of the week, his early morning walk had almost turned into a nightmare. He couldn't explain the lift he'd felt when he'd emerged again into the sun, the sense of relief, the delight of being released from that sinister cloud. He had a slight headache now but otherwise he'd got over the unpleasant experience and no doubt would chuckle when he recounted the story to his friends.

The church was fairly full today, the pleasantness of the weather helping, but the tragedy of the neighbouring village accounting primarily for the large attendance. The vicar greeted his parishioners at the door of the church as they went in, chatting briefly with some, smiling and nodding at others. When it was time for the service to begin, he entered through a side door into the sacristy, hurried his altar boys along, and walked briskly with them into the church.

The service began as normal, pleasurable to some, boring to others, but today, because of the tragedy, meaningful for most. A few people near the front noticed the vicar occasionally put his hand to his forehead as though he were tired or had a headache, but the service continued smoothly enough.

They sat and looked up at him when he climbed the steps to his pulpit, anxious to be comforted by his words in their time of sadness. He looked down at their upturned, expectant faces, eyes focused on him, eager for him to speak.

Then the Reverend Martin Hurdle, Vicar of St Augustine's for eighteen years, lifted his cassock, undid his trousers, took out his penis, and urinated over his congregation.

'Now where have those blessed cows got to?' George Ross asked himself aloud, a frown wrinkling his already multi-wrinkled, weathered face even more. 'Bet they've got through that gap again.'

The farmer was used to his herd breaking through the fence of bushes and trees that surrounded their meadow and wandering off into the next. He plodded down towards the spot they'd most likely have broken through. 'As if I haven't got enough to do without chasing those silly creatures all mornin'. I'll give 'em what for!' he cursed angrily.

He reached the gap and pushed his way through. 'Now where are yer?' He stood looking around, then his mouth dropped open at the sight of the fog at the other end of his field. 'Well I'll be! Never noticed that.' He scratched his bristly chin, puzzled.

He began to walk towards the murky cloud and grinned as he saw his cows emerging from it. 'Trust you!' he shouted at them. 'Trust you to get yourselves lost in that. Stupid bloody creatures!'

Funny, having a fog down here, he pondered. Too heavy to be a mist. All this bloomin' p'lution. 'Come on, me beauties!' he called out as they trudged towards him. The fog, he noticed, was drifting off into the adjoining field. Strange that he could see the edges of it, like a solid block of smoke moving across the countryside, not at all like the normal widespread blanket of grey.

The cows were up to him now and the leaders passed him.

'Come on now, up to the sheds!' he bellowed at them, slapping one hard on the rump as it passed.

It stopped and turned its head towards him. 'Move yourself,' the farmer said gruffly, slapping it again. The cow stood silently watching him.

George cursed it more loudly, then turned to see what progress the rest of the herd was making. They had all stopped and were turned towards him, watching.

'What's this, then?' For some inexplicable reason, he had begun to feel nervous. There was a tension about his herd that he couldn't understand. 'Move yourselves. Get on 'ome!' He waved his arms at them, trying to startle them into movement. They watched him.

Then they began to close in on him.

He realized he was surrounded by the cows and the ring was drawing tighter around him. What was happening? He could not understand the menacing air these dumb, gentle animals had taken on. He felt himself jostled from behind. He turned and lashed out at the cow he'd slapped before. 'Get back!' he shouted, logic telling him his rising fear was unreasonable.

He heard a pounding of hooves and again felt himself pushed from behind, this time more violently. He fell to the ground.

'Get away, get away!' He scrambled about on his hands and knees trying to rise, but every time he raised himself, he was knocked off his feet again. Suddenly, one of the cows turned and kicked out with its hind legs, catching him an agonizing blow in the ribs, sending him flying forward.

He began to scream as he received more kicks. They seemed to be taking it in turns to run forward and lash out at him. One kick caught him full in the face, breaking his nose, blinding him for a few seconds. When he could see once more, it was like opening his eyes to a bad dream.

The cows were racing round him, their eyes bulging almost out of their sockets, froth and slime running from their mouths. They trampled over him. If he rose, they crushed him with their bodies. They used their heads to knock him off his knees. They began to bite him, snapping off his fingers as he raised his arms to protect himself. A scream ended in a gurgling, choking noise as a kick broke his jaw and blood ran down his throat.

When at last he lay sprawled semi-conscious on the muddied grass, they herded together, and crushed the life from his battered body with their hooves.

*

The poacher gazed at the house from his hiding place in the undergrowth. He'd emerged from the fog, but instead of returning to his ramshackle house on the outskirts of the village he'd walked along the main road towards the gates of the Colonel's huge country home. He'd skulked up the long, winding drive and hidden in the bushes, waiting and peering through the leaves at the house. After a while his eyes, strangely glazed, looked from left to right. He rose and crept stealthily towards the back of the building. He knew where to go for he'd done casual work for the Colonel's head gardener years before. That was how he knew the grounds so well, the best places to poach, the best places to hide. He walked down towards a wooden hut at the end of the long garden. He pushed open the door, his eyes now developing a fixed stare, no longer worrying about the noise he was making, his movements controlled, steady. He reached for an axe, rusted with time, but the blade still sharp. As he turned to leave the hut, his gaze fell on a box of three-inch nails used for fencing. He scooped up a handful and put them in his pocket.

He walked back up the garden, not bothering to hide, walking in a straight line towards the house. As he reached the back door, the Merediths' cook was just opening it to let the steam from her kitchen escape. She'd just cooked the Colonel and his wife breakfast and the maid had taken it up to them. Now it was time for her morning tea before she started to make preparations for their lunch. There were lots of guests coming, so there was much to do.

She had no chance to scream before the axe hit her, only a fleeting look into the eyes of a madman, a chance for fear to begin to rise but never to reach its peak, for in the next instant she was dead.

Tom Abbot entered the kitchen and climbed the stairs that led to the hall. He'd never been in the house before and only the sound of voices drew him towards the dining-room. He opened the first door he came to and went in, not stopping till he was in the middle of a large sitting-room, bigger than the whole of the ground floor of his tiny house. He stood there, gazing ahead.

The sound of footsteps passing the open door caused him to turn and retrace his steps. He heard the sound of voices again and walked towards another door.

The maid hummed to herself as she descended the stairs to the kitchen, holding her tray with half-eaten grapefruit and crusts of toast aloft so that she could see the steps beneath her.

'Put the kettle on, Mrs Peabody,' she called out as she approached the kitchen door. 'Let's have a nice cuppa' while they're noshing their bacon and eggs.'

Discovering the kitchen empty, she looked around curiously. The kettle was already steaming away. She put down her tray and walked over to the gas stove to turn the kettle off. The door to the garden was open so she assumed the cook had stepped outside for a breath of fresh air or to empty some food scraps into one of the dustbins. She walked around the large centre table to the door so she could call for her. A scream broke from her lips as she saw the body, lying there just outside the doorway, its skull cleaved open to the bridge of the nose. Before she fainted, she realized it was the cook, recognizable only because of her build and clothes, her face covered in blood, her features in a frozen grimace of terror, bearing no resemblance to the face it had once been. As she collapsed, the maid's brain just registered the other scream, the scream from upstairs that pierced the still air.

When she regained consciousness, she couldn't at first recollect what had happened. Then her body stiffened as she remembered. She saw the corpse, her foot almost touching it, and she backed away shuddering, trying to call for help but her vocal cords paralysed with fear. She somehow got to her feet and staggered towards the stairs, clambering up them, falling and sobbing, nothing preventing her from getting away from that kitchen. She gained the hallway and ran down it towards the dining-room, gasping for air, trying to call out.

She stumbled through the open door and stopped short at the sight confronting her.

Her mistress lay sprawled on the floor in a pool of blood, only a few tendons in her neck holding her head to her body. It lay parallel to her left shoulder, grinning up at her. The Colonel lay spreadeagled on the huge dining table, long nails through the palms of his hands and the flesh of his ankles to pin him there. A man stood over him, an axe dripping with blood in his hands.

As the maid watched, dumb-struck, unable to move with the horror of it, the man raised the axe above his head and brought it down with all his strength. It severed a hand and splintered the wood beneath. The man struggled to free the weapon from the table and raised it again. By the time he'd cut off the other hand, the Colonel was unconscious. By the time he'd hacked off both feet, the Colonel was dead.

The maid finally began to scream when the man with the axe turned his head and looked at her.

▪ 4 ▪

'HELLO, JOHN.'

John Holman looked at the girl and smiled. 'Hello, Casey.'

'How do you feel?'

'Okay.'

He was sitting on the steps of the hospital, unwilling to wait inside. He found hospitals depressing.

'They said you'd need at least another couple of weeks.' She sat next to him on the steps.

'No, I'm all right now. Any longer in there and I'd have gone mad again.'

She flinched at the words, remembering how he had been the first time she'd visited.

The news of the eruption had stunned the country, spreading alarm, causing dismay among geologists, panic in the neighbouring towns and villages. She hadn't even known Holman was in that area for he was very secretive about his job; she wasn't even sure of his department. All she knew was that he had an 'assignment' for the weekend, that no, he couldn't tell her where he was going, and *no*, she definitely could *not* go with him. Had she known he had been in the village that suffered the earthquake, she – she refused to think about it. It had been bad enough when she had rung his office the following day to find out why he hadn't called her on his return and had learnt of his involvement. The department knew he'd been in the area and as they hadn't heard from him since, assumed he either couldn't get back because the roads leading to the disaster were completely blocked by rescue and medical services and the hordes of curious sightseers – the usual ghoulish element that flocked to any disaster – or he had stayed to help. They didn't reveal to her that they were concerned that perhaps he was being held by the military on their Salisbury Plain base and they were now anxiously expecting the Ministry of Defence to come roaring down their necks. She was asked to ring back later when no doubt they would have some news and was advised not to make the trip down to Wiltshire because of the mounting traffic and the impossibility of finding him anyway.

The rest of the day had been spent in a fear-ridden daze. She rang her employer, an exclusive antique-dealer in one of the side streets off Bond Street, and told him she felt too ill to come in. A fussy little man, who considered women necessary only for business purposes, he brusquely hoped she would be well enough to do her job tomorrow. For the rest of the day she wandered listlessly around the house, afraid to go out in case the phone rang. She barely ate and listened to the radio only to find out more news of the earthquake.

Casey had known Holman for nearly a year now and was becoming more and more aware that if he ever left her, she would be lost. Her dependence on him was now stronger even than her dependence on her father had been. When her mother had divorced her father eight years ago, she had turned to him to provide the comfort and guidance every child needs from a mother, and he had coped extraordinarily well. Too well, in fact, for by overcompensating for the lack of his wife, he had tied the daughter almost irrevocably to him. Holman had begun to break the bonds between them, unconsciously at first, but when he realized just how strong the ties were he began to gently, but purposefully, draw Casey away from her father. He did this not so much out of love for her, but because he cared about her as a person. He knew she had a strong mind and a will of her own, but she was too tightly enmeshed in her father's domineering love. If the relationship developed any further then she would never be free to live her own life. Besides, the closeness between father and daughter made him feel uneasy.

Holman had tried to get Casey – her real name was Christine, but he had invented the nickname for reasons he hadn't told her of yet – to leave her father's house and get a flat of her own. This she would have done had he allowed her to live with him, but there he'd drawn the line. After two previous disastrous affairs he had resolved never to become too entangled with one person again. He had been near to it many times and even proposed marriage once, but the girl backed out because she knew, and realized she had always known, that he didn't love her. That had been years before, and now he wondered if he were really capable of love. He had gradually lost most of his cynicism on that topic during the months he had known Casey. He still resisted, but guessed he was fighting a losing battle. Maybe he was getting old, resigning himself to the fact he needed a companion, that although he'd never been quite alone, he hadn't shared for a long, long time.

Casey was breaking down that barrier just as he was breaking down the closeness between her and her father. The process was gradual, but inevitable. Still, each of them offered resistance. She would not leave her father without the assurance of someone taking his place; he refused to be that someone, the move had to come from her *before* she had the guarantee of someone to run to. Holman was older than Casey, but had no intention of becoming a father-figure. At the moment, it was deadlock.

Now, in her anxiety, as she waited for the phone to ring, Casey knew she would do as he asked. She understood his reasons. It would hurt her father terribly, but it wasn't as though she would never see him again. And perhaps when he realized she was determined, his iciness towards John would begin to thaw. If it didn't, then she knew she would have to go through the agony of choosing again, but this time for keeps. And she knew it would be her father who would lose.

She waited till 3.00 p.m., then rang Holman's office again. This time they had some news. They apologized for not having let her know sooner but all hell had broken loose in their department because of the earthquake. These things just weren't *meant* to happen in England! A man identified as John Holman, whose papers showed he worked for the Department of the Environment, had been taken to Salisbury General Hospital, where he was in an extreme state of shock. When Casey pressed them for details, her heart pounding, her thoughts racing, they became evasive, but assured her that John had suffered no physical damage. Again, they advised her to keep clear of the area and promised they would keep her informed of any developments.

Casey thanked them and replaced the receiver. Then she rang the hospital itself. The operator apologized, told her that the hospital was jammed with calls and suggested she try later.

Numbed, she scribbled a note to her father, looked for the town on a road-map, and hurried out to her bright yellow saloon car, a present from her father. She avoided driving through London by going north and then around on the North Circular.

She bypassed Basingstoke and Andover, taking minor roads, knowing the towns would be jammed with traffic. On the outskirts of Salisbury, she ran into heavy traffic being held up by the police. Drivers of cars were being cross-examined as to their destination, and unless their reasons for travel were genuine and not just to satisfy ghoulish curiosity about the earthquake, they were turned back. When it was Casey's turn, she explained about John and was allowed to continue her journey with the undertaking that on no account would she try to travel beyond the town to the disaster area. On their advice, she parked her car on the outskirts of the town and walked to the hospital which she found in a state of turmoil. Having enquired about Holman, she was asked to wait with the many other anxious relatives or friends who had come to the hospital for news of victims of the catastrophe.

It was not until 8.00 that evening and after several attempts to obtain news of Holman that a weary-looking doctor came down to see her. He took her aside and told her in a low voice that it would be better if she did not see John that night; he was suffering from shock and had sustained an injury that, although not too serious, required him to be given a blood transfusion and, at that moment, he was under heavy sedation. Observing the girl was in a highly emotional state, he chose not to explain the nature of Holman's sickness at that time. Tomorrow, when she'd calmed down, would be time enough to explain that her lover, boyfriend, whatever he was to her, had gone totally mad, and at that moment was strapped to the bed, even though he was under sedation, so he could not harm himself or anybody else. It was strange how the man had been bent on killing himself. He'd had to be tied down in the ambulance on the way to the hospital, and once there he'd broken free, smashed a glass window and tried to drive a long, knife-like shard of glass through his neck. Only the intervention of the burly ambulance driver who now suffered from a broken jaw caused in the ensuing struggle had saved him from cutting himself too deeply. Holman had gone completely berserk and two porters and a doctor had been injured before he could be restrained and finally sedated. Even then he was fitful and had to be strapped down. No, the doctor decided, now was not the time to tell her. Tomorrow she could see for herself.

Casey spent the night in an hotel crowded with journalists and also people who lived near the wrecked village and thought it wise to be a little further away from the area. By careful listening Casey learned more details of the earthquake. At least a third of the village's tiny population of four hundred had been killed, at least another third injured. Many of the old houses and cottages that were not even near the enormous split in the earth had been demolished, killing or maiming their occupants. The most remarkable story was of the little girl and the man who had been rescued from the very jaws of the eruption. They'd been discovered alive inside the gigantic hole and had been pulled to the surface, the girl unconscious, the man in a state of shock, but nevertheless, very much alive. Only much later did Casey realize they had been talking of John Holman.

The next morning she went back to the hospital and was told she would be able to see him later on in the day, but to be prepared for a shock. The doctor she'd seen the night before explained quietly to her that Holman was no longer the man she had known, that he had gone uncontrollably insane. When the girl broke down, the doctor hastened to add that the illness could be short-term, that the experience he'd suffered might have only temporarily snapped his mind and given time it could heal itself. She went back to the hotel and cried her way through the day until it was time to go back to the hospital. They advised her not to see him, but she insisted – and then regretted her insistence.

The doctor had been right – he wasn't the man she knew. And loved. He was an animal. A foul-mouthed, raging animal. Heavy leather straps tied him to a bed. A bed in a special room for it contained only the bed; there were no windows and the walls were covered in a soft, plastic-like material. Only his head, hands and feet could move, and this they did in a constant, violent motion, his head thrashing from side to side, his throat bandaged, thick wadding secured in his mouth to prevent him from biting off his own tongue, his hands clenching and unclenching, like claws. And his eyes. She would never forget the maniac look in those enlarged, staring eyes. He had worked the wadding in his mouth loose and began to scream. She couldn't believe the obscenity she heard, that any human being could harbour the thoughts that flowed verbally from his lips. Although his eyes looked at her, he didn't see her. A nurse ran forward and once again stuffed the wadding back into his mouth, carefully avoiding his snapping teeth.

Casey left in a wretched daze, tears blurring her vision. At first, she hadn't been sure if it even was John, his physical appearance had seemed so different, and now she wanted to tell herself that it hadn't been. But it was useless to pretend. She had to face up to the facts if she were to help him recover – and if he didn't? Could she go on loving the thing she'd just seen?

She returned to the hotel, her mind in a turmoil, her emotions confused. A conflict began deep inside her. After hours of weeping, of fighting the repulsion she felt for his madness, she began to lose the battle. She rang her father. He urged her to come home immediately and she had to resist the impulse to agree to it; she wanted his protection, his comforting words, the words that would take the responsibility away from her.

But no. She owed it to John to stay near him while there was a chance – the flimsiest chance. The illness couldn't destroy what had been, the closeness that had been theirs. She told her father she would stay until she knew about John one way or the other. She was adamant that he shouldn't come down, that she would come home only when satisfied John was beyond help.

Casey's wretchedness increased that evening when she visited Holman again. The doctor felt that she should know about the young child rescued with him who had died that afternoon without ever coming out of the unusual coma she'd been in since the eruption. They now thought she'd been affected by gas released from below the ground. It was possible that Holman also had been affected and this, in some strange way, was the cause of his madness. The next few days would tell if the brain damage was permanent or would pass. Or if the effects were fatal.

She hardly slept that night. Now that death had to be considered, her emotions had become clearer: if he lived, even if he were still insane, she would never leave him Reality told her that her love could not be the same as before, that it would be a different kind of love, a love born out of his need for her. If he died – she forced her mind to accept the words – if he died, then she would forget the creature she had seen these last two days and remember only what he'd been, what they'd shared. In the early hours of the morning she finally fell into an exhausted and dream-filled sleep.

When she returned to the hospital in the morning, dread in her heart but still hopeful, Holman was completely sane. Weak, ashen-faced, but totally sane. And one week later, he was ready to go home.

Sitting on the steps next to him, Casey took Holman's hand. He kissed her cheek and smiled at her. 'Thanks,' he said.

'For what?'

'For being here. For not running away.'

She was silent.

'The doctors told me how I was,' he continued. 'It must have been frightening for you.'

'It was. Very.'

'They're still trying to work out how a complete maniac could become normal again so quickly. They say the gas, whatever it was, must have been responsible. It temporarily affected the brain then wore off. I was lucky. It killed the little girl.' He stared at the ground, unable to hide his grief.

She squeezed his hand and asked, 'Are you sure it's all right for you to leave the hospital so soon?'

'Oh, they wanted me to stay. Wanted to do more tests, find out if there'd be any permanent damage. But I've had enough. Reporters, television interviewers – they've hounded the survivors that are well enough, and I've been a prime target. Even Spiers came down yesterday to interrogate me.'

Spiers was Holman's immediate boss at his Ministry, a man he both admired and hated. Their many disputes arose mainly after Holman's various assignments had been completed, when he had provided all the evidence he could lay his hands on, presented all the facts to Spiers who had engineered the assignment, and then the man would take no action against the offenders. 'It will go on file,' he would say. What Holman never knew was the battle his superior went through to get action taken, but his power was limited against the overriding strength of wealth and politics.

'What did he want to know?' asked Casey.

'Whether I'd completed my weekend's assignment.' He couldn't tell her Spiers had come to find out if he had found any evidence that could connect the earthquake with experiments being carried out on the military base. Holman thought it unlikely and had no such proof anyway.

'Fat little toad! I don't like him,' said Casey.

'He's not really too bad. Bit cold, a bit hard – but he can be okay. Anyway, I've got to report to him tomorrow –' he put up his hand at her protests, 'just to give him a debrief on the weekend job, then I'm on a week's leave.'

'I should think so too, after all you've been through.'

'Yes, but honestly, I feel fine now. Throat's still a little sore, but they tell me

I was lucky – the cut wasn't too deep – and God knows, I've had a good enough rest in here. Come on, let's leave before I go out of my mind again.'

He laughed at her frown.

It was just before Weyhill that they ran into the fog again. The roads had been fairly quiet, the weather fine. They kept to the smaller roads purposely, not wanting to rush back to London but to enjoy the passing countryside, the peaceful warmth of the summer morning.

When they saw the heavy cloud ahead of them it was about half-a-mile away, looking depressingly ominous. They could see its outermost edges quite clearly, but its top was more like the usual fuzzy-edged fog shape.

'Strange,' said Holman, stopping the car. 'Is it smoke or just a mist?'

'It's too heavy for mist,' replied Casey, staring ahead. 'It's fog. Let's go back, John, it's creepy.'

'It's too much of a detour to go back. Anyway, it isn't much of a fog, we'll soon pass through it. Funny, it's just like a wall, the sides are so straight.'

They both jumped at the sound of a horn as a coach sped past them heading towards Weyhill. Six small boys stuck their tongues out and waggled their hands at them from the back window as the school bus swung back into the proper lane.

'Bloody fool,' muttered Holman. 'He's heading right into it.' They watched it disappear down the road and then get swallowed up by the fog. 'He must be bloody blind!'

They suddenly realized the fog had crept much nearer to them. 'Christ, it moves fast,' said Holman. 'Come on then, let's go through it. It'll be okay if I take it easy.'

He put Casey's car into first and drove on, unaware that the girl at his side was becoming unnaturally nervous. She couldn't rationalize her apprehension, it was just that the black cloud somehow seemed pregnant with menace, like the heavy dark clouds just before a storm broke. She said nothing to Holman, but her hands gripped the sides of her seat tightly.

Very soon, they entered the fog.

It was much thicker than Holman had anticipated. He could barely see the road ahead. He drove cautiously, keeping in second, using dipped headlights. He leaned close to the windscreen for better vision, occasionally using his wipers to clear the heavy smog from the glass, keeping his side window open to look through now and again. The fog seemed to be tinged with yellow, or was it just the throwback glare from his headlights? As the slightly acrid smell reached his nostrils, a tiny nerve twitched in his memory cells. It was something to do with the earthquake the week before. He still couldn't remember much about it – the doctors informed him this was perfectly normal, a certain part of his mind was still in a state of shock – but somehow the smell, the yellowish colour, the very atmosphere stirred something inside him. He broke into a cold sweat and stopped the car.

'What's the matter, John?' Casey asked, alarm in her voice.

'I don't know. It's just a feeling. The fog – it seems familiar.'

'John, the papers said a cloud of dust or smoke came from the eruption; they thought it had been caused by a blast beneath the ground. This isn't a normal fog we're in. Could this be it?'

'No, surely not. It would have been dispersed by the wind by now, not hanging around in a great lump.'

'How do you know? If it came from deep underground, how do you know how it would act?'

'All right, maybe it is. Anyway, let's not sit here discussing it, let's try and get clear first.' He wound up the side window, hoping the action would not throw any fear into her 'At the rate it's moving, I reckon it will be easier to try and go on through it rather than turn back.'

'Okay,' she answered, 'but please be careful.'

He edged forward, his eyes peering ahead into the gloom. They had made a hundred yards' slow progress when they came upon the coach lying half in a ditch alongside the road. They had nearly run into a small group of boys who had been standing at the rear of the coach before Holman jammed on his brakes. Fortunately, they had been travelling so slowly they were able to stop almost immediately.

'Now come along, boys, I've already told you to keep to the side, away from the road,' they heard a voice bellow.

Holman opened his door and climbed out of the car, telling Casey to remain inside. The slight but distinct odour of the fog disturbed him again as he closed the door behind him.

'Is anyone hurt?' he asked the spectral shape of the man he assumed was the boys' master.

'A few bruises here and there among the boys,' came the reply as the figure approached him, 'but I'm afraid our driver has suffered a nasty blow on the head.'

When the teacher was only three feet away Holman saw he was a tall, gaunt-looking man, with a hooked nose and deep-set eyes. He had only one arm, his right ending just above the wrist. The teacher went on, in a lower tone of voice. 'Mind you, it was all his fault, the idiot. He was so busy joking with the boys he didn't even notice the fog until he was in it and then he hardly slowed down even though I warned him.' He looked down at the pupils who had now clustered around him. 'Boys! I told you to get to the side of the road. Now the next boy who disobeys me gets a flogging. Move yourselves!'

They scattered, enjoying the fun now that they'd got over their initial shock.

'Let's have a look at the driver,' said Holman, 'maybe I can help.'

They walked to the front of the coach where they found the driver sitting on the grass beside the ditch nursing his head in his hands. He held a bloody handkerchief to his forehead and occasionally moaned as he rocked backwards and forwards. A group of boys stood around him, watching him both anxiously and curiously.

'Now, Mr Hodges, how are we feeling?' asked the teacher, hardly a trace of sympathy in his tone.

'Fucking awful,' came the muffled reply.

The boys tittered and hid smiles of delight behind shaking hands.

The teacher cleared his throat and stiffly ordered his pupils to go to the back of the coach and stay out of the road. 'Yes, well, let's have a look at the cut, Mr Hodges, and perhaps we can do something about it.'

Holman bent down and brought the hand holding the blood-stained handkerchief away from the damaged forehead. The gash looked worse than it probably was. He took out his own handkerchief and pressed it to the cut telling the driver to hold it in place.

'I don't think it's serious, but we'd better get you to a hospital right away.'

'There's a doctor's surgery in the town ahead. I'm sure they'll look after Mr Hodges,' said the impatient teacher. 'The only problem is getting him there.'

'We'll take him and inform the police at the same time. They'll soon get a breakdown lorry to you and arrange other transport for the boys. Are you sure none of them are hurt badly?'

'Yes, quite sure, thank you. It's really very kind of you. I do hope we won't have to wait too long, this damp fog won't be good for the boys.'

As they helped the injured Hodges back to the car, the teacher explained the coach journey to Holman. 'We're from Redbrook House, a private boarding school in Andover. We were just on our way back from a nature ramble on the Plain, you know. It was a beautiful morning and the boys get so restless towards the end of term, I had to get them out into the fresh air. I cannot for the life of me imagine where this fog came from.'

Holman cast an anxious eye around him. The fog seemed as dense as ever.

'Of course, many of the boys' parents wanted me to send them home when that dreadful earth tremor occurred,' the master continued, 'but I was insistent that they remain and finish off the term. Freaks of nature, I told them, happen only rarely, perhaps once in a lifetime, and Redbrook certainly was not going to close down because of hysterical howling of over-anxious parents. A few of them persisted of course, and I had no choice but to let their offspring go – but I can tell you, they took a very stiff letter with them!'

Holman smiled to himself at the prattling of the one-armed teacher. The old die-hard, traditionalist teachers still flourished despite the new wave of long-haired, liberal-minded younger educationalists. Well, there was good and bad to be said for both sides.

As the trio approached the yellow car, easily visible in the murky fog, Holman saw Casey's white face apprehensively watching them through the windscreen. She opened her door and made as if to get out to help him.

'No, stay there, don't get out!' he shouted at her.

Puzzled, she remained where she was, half in, half out.

'Close the door,' he told her, less sharply. She complied, the puzzled expression still on her face.

He opened the door on his side, pulled the seat forward and helped the injured driver to climb through into the back. Then he turned back to the teacher.

'If I were you, I'd get all the boys back into the coach and keep the door and windows closed.'

'Whatever for?' the teacher asked.

'Let's just say the fog can't be good for them. I'll get someone back to you as soon as possible, so just sit tight.' He got into the car and turned the ignition. Before he closed the door he reiterated his advice. 'Keep them inside and close all the windows.'

'Very well, Mr, er ... ?'

'Holman.'

'... Holman, but I'm sure we'll be warm enough and a little fog can't do too much harm.' Oh can't it? thought Holman as he gunned the engine and cautiously moved off. I wonder? He still wasn't quite sure of his uneasiness about the fog. The doctors had said his breakdown could have been caused in some way by released gas from the cracked earth. It was a pretty far-fetched possibility, but that smell had seemed familiar somehow and he knew he'd never experienced it before the eruption. It was more instinct than judgement, but he had learned to trust his instincts implicitly. A groan from behind interrupted his thoughts.

'Ooh, 'ave I got a headache,' Hodges moaned loudly.

'We'll soon get you to a doctor,' Casey reassured him, reluctantly taking her eyes off the murky road ahead to examine the unfortunate coach driver.

'I'll get the blame for this,' he went on woefully. 'Summers'll make sure of that. Miserable bastard. Oh, sorry, miss,' he excused himself.

Summers, they assumed, was the teacher they'd just left with the boys.

'Never did like me. Didn't like the way I got on with the boys.'

'Is Redbrook his school?' asked Holman.

'Nah! 'e's only deputy head, but the way he carries on you'd think it was. The kids call him Captain Hook.' He laughed and winced at the effort. 'It was all his fault, any road.'

'What do you mean?'

'Wal', I was driving along, 'aving a bit of a laugh with the boys, y'know, showin' off a bit I suppose, and 'e starts snappin' at me like I was one of the kids. Wal', I turns round to give 'im the right answer, and wallop – we're in the ditch. Lucky I didn't go right through the windscreen, I can tell you. Anyway, I blacks out and the next thing I know, I wake up, blood pourin' down me face, and 'e's still going on at me. Ain't right, is it?'

Holman chuckled and said nothing. His amusement soon vanished when he realized the fog was becoming thicker. He slowed down to a crawling pace and leaned even further towards the windscreen.

'John, what's that?' Casey clutched his arm, her eyes staring across him at something to his right.

He looked through his side window but saw only the swirling mist. 'What? I can't see anything.'

'It's gone. It may have been nothing, but I thought I saw a glow. Something white, shining through the fog, but it vanished almost immediately. I think a heavier bank of fog must have swept by. I can't see it anymore.'

'It might have just been a clear patch, the sun getting through somewhere.'

'Yes, maybe.'

Their attention was drawn back to their passenger as he began cursing again.
'Bloody weather. Bright one minute, fog the next. Goes with the times, it does.'
'What d'you mean?' Holman asked.
'Nice peaceful summer we've had, couldn't 'ave been better. Then what happens? A bloody earthquake, of all things. Here in Wiltshire!' He rocked forward in pain as his voice rose. 'And then yesterday. Did you hear about yesterday?'
Holman shook his head, still concentrating on the road. Casey replied, 'You mean the axe murders?'
'Yeah. In all the papers this mornin'. 'Appened fairly near the earthquake village, an' all. Rich bloke, Colonel something-or-other, murdered with 'is wife and all 'is staff, cook and a maid, I think. Done in with an axe. And the bloke they reckon done it chopped at 'is own wrists 'till he bled to death. Party of people came over to see this Colonel and found all the bodies just lyin' around. I dunno what it's comin' to, one thing after another.'
'Yes,' said Holman, 'it's like you said. Sunny one minute, dark the next.'
'And now I suppose I'm goin' to lose me job over this.'
'No, I'm sure you won't,' Casey said sympathetically.
'Oh, you don't know old Captain Hook. Never 'as liked me. Still, I know a few little secrets about him.' Hodges groaned again. 'How much further?'
For another painfully slow fifteen minutes they were immersed in the dense fog then, suddenly, they were clear. It was like passing through a door, the change was so abrupt.
'Christ,' muttered Holman in surprise. He'd been squinting into the mist and just had time to register it becoming slightly lighter when at once they were driving in bright sunlight. He and Casey looked over their shoulders at the thick yellowish-grey blanket behind them. Hodges was too busy nursing his own pain and grievances to take any notice. As they watched, it seemed to move away from them like a dark shroud being drawn across the countryside. Casey shivered and Holman smiled at her with a reassurance he hardly felt.
'It isn't natural,' the girl whispered.
Holman shook his head, but had no answer to give. He switched off the car lights and moved forward again, picking up welcome speed as he went. The village was soon reached and Hodges directed him to the police station. He ran up the steps and quickly told them what had happened to the coach. The police sergeant couldn't quite understand Holman's anxiety when he learnt that none of the boys was seriously hurt. He was surprised and almost disbelieving about the fog, it certainly hadn't passed through the village and he'd had no reports of it from around the surrounding countryside. Nevertheless, he reassured Holman, he would get in touch with the garage and send one of his men out there right away. He gave him directions for the doctor's surgery and thanked him for the trouble he'd taken.
When Holman left the police station he had a faint feeling of dissatisfaction. Perhaps he was making more of it than the situation warranted, after all, fog in England certainly wasn't unusual although at this time of year it was a little strange. It was difficult to conjure up the menacing atmosphere of the cloudy

yellow-greyness in his mind now that he was in the bright sunshine. The fog seemed unreal, as though it had never really happened. Could it be he wasn't well yet? Was his mind still a bit 'disturbed'? He knew Casey had also been uneasy about the experience they'd been through, but was that merely the transference of his fears? He knew how easy it was for tension from one person to be passed on to another until a whole group of people were infected. He needed to relax. The strain of the past hour had already drained him, left him feeling agitated and restless. Why hadn't he wanted Casey to get out of the car? Did he really think this fog had something to do with his own recent illness? He wasn't at all sure of his motives, but hadn't wanted her to be subjected to too much of the smoke-like substance. Maybe the feeling of apprehension would pass once his body – and his mind – had fully rested.

They drove the still grumbling Hodges to the doctor's surgery, left him in capable and friendly hands, then drove on to London.

▪ 5 ▪

A FEW HOURS LATER, AFTER STOPPING FOR A PUB LUNCH ON THE WAY, THEY reached Holman's flat in St John's Wood Road, opposite Lord's cricket ground. He parked the car in the forecourt and wearily they took the lift to his flat at the top of the old but well-kept building. His flat was sparsely furnished, uncluttered and comfortable. A few original paintings hung on the walls, but otherwise the decorations were kept to a minimum. In one corner stood the tall, long stem of a plant, its length completely bare, but with thick rich foliage sprouting from its top. He claimed laughingly that it had climbed over the wall of the London Botanical Gardens and found its way to his flat because it was looking for someone to love. The truth was Holman had stolen it one night many years before on a drunken raid on the Gardens with some equally inebriated friends. He had no idea of the correct name for it so he called it George.

His bedroom window looked out on to a flat roof where he had spent many a peaceful summer's evening just gazing at the stars, a contrast to the side of him that demanded excitement, to be involved in trouble. The only big luxury he had allowed himself to indulge in was his bed. He liked to sleep, he liked to make love; when he slept he hated to feel cramped by a partner; when he made love, he hated to feel cramped by a bed. So it was logical his bed should take up most of the space in his medium-sized bedroom. On first seeing it, Casey had giggled; on sharing its luxury, she had become immensely jealous of

Holman's past. But in the time she had known him, she had matured enough to accept the life he had obviously once led.

She made him coffee while he slumped in a chair, pulling his shoes off for greater comfort. She brought the cups in and sat at his feet, placing the coffee on the floor.

'How do you feel now, John?' she asked gently.

'Oh, a little bit tired, that's all. Post-hospital depression I think it's called.'

She rubbed the soles of his feet abstractedly. 'I've decided to leave Theo.' She always called her father by his first name, another habit Holman unreasonably found irritating.

'Leave him?' He sat up in surprise, studying her face as if her expression would confirm or deny her statement.

'Yes. I discovered a lot of things about myself when you were in hospital, John, the most important being that I love you more than I could have imagined possible. More than Theo. More than anything. I nearly gave up, darling. I nearly left you there when I thought you were beyond help.'

He leaned closer to her, taking her face in his hands, saying nothing.

'The way you were,' she continued, 'things you said. It frightened me — I couldn't believe it was you.'

'It wasn't really me, Casey,' he said softly.

'I know, John. But it was like a nightmare. Not knowing if you'd ever recover, ever be close to me again – ever hold me like this. I went home and rang Theo. I was going to leave you, to go home. But as I spoke to him I realized I couldn't. And when I went back to the hospital the next day and they told me there was the possibility that you could die – I realized I'd be nothing without you. My father could never mean as much to me again, he could never take your place.'

'Casey …'

'Believe me, John.'

'Casey, listen. Give it a couple of weeks; don't decide now.'

'I don't need to. I know.'

'All right, do it for me then. You've been through too much recently. I want you to be absolutely certain of how you feel – for both our sakes.'

'And what about you, John? Are you certain of your feelings?'

He lay back heavily in the armchair. 'Don't ask me yet. Too much has happened for me to be sure of anything at the moment.'

'Is that why you want me to think about it – because you need more time?' She bit her lip, now uncertain of his love.

'Partly, yes. I need to sort myself out too.'

Tears began to form in her eyes as she rested her cheek on his knee, not wanting him to see her weeping. He stroked her hair and they sat in silence for a few moments, then she looked up at him and said, 'John, let me stay tonight.'

'What about your father?' he asked.

'I've told you, he doesn't matter. I still love him. I could never lose that, but it's you now. I don't want to leave you. Let me stay for at least tonight.'

'Okay, Casey, why should I fight you off?' he answered, trying to lighten the mood.

'I'll ring Theo later and explain.' She knelt, bringing her face close to his. 'I don't need more time, John, but I'll take it. I want you to be sure, too, and if you should decide you don't really want me that badly ...' she hesitated, forcing herself to say the next words, '... I'll go away.'

He kissed her lips, suddenly laughing at her sorrowful face. 'Okay, Casey,' he said, 'you've got a deal!'

They drank their coffee, both lost for a while in their own thoughts. Gradually, Holman began to relax. He pushed thoughts of the earthquake, the fog, and now Casey's decision from his mind. He never walked away from a problem, but occasionally liked to bury it and dig it up later. His moods changed as easily as traffic lights, a quality the girl sometimes adored, sometimes hated. This time, because she too needed some relief, she was gladly susceptible to it.

'You know, a week in that hospital, and not seeing you the weekend before ...' he looked down at her, a hint of a leer in his smile.

'Yes?' She smiled back at him.

'Well, I feel a bit like a monk. Celibate.'

'It's good for you.'

'I could go blind.'

She laughed and said, 'I thought you needed rest.'

'Quite right. Let's go to bed.'

'Promise me one thing.'

'Anything.' He began to unbutton her blouse, becoming impatient as the second button stuck. She undid it for him.

'Promise me you'll come back tomorrow after seeing Spiers. You won't get involved in another assignment.'

'You must be joking. I'm taking the rest of the week off even if the whole country cracks in half!'

He pulled her blouse free of her skirt and cupped her breast with his hand, sliding one finger inside the lacy material of her bra.

'What about you?' he asked. 'You won't be able to get any more time off, will you?'

'Oh, yes I will,' she answered, now unbuttoning his shirt. 'I've been sacked.'

His restless hand rested.

'What?'

'When I rang the boss and informed him I was staying near you for the week he politely told me not to come back, I would be replaced.'

'The little bastard,' Holman cursed.

'It's a relief,' she laughed. 'He was too jealous of my clothes anyway; I think he thought they'd look better on him.'

Holman got to his feet, discarding his unbuttoned shirt. 'I think you need comforting,' he said, taking her hand and leading her into the bedroom.

Holman strolled along Marsham Street enjoying the bustle, glad to be among normal, active people after the subdued confinement of the hospital. They flowed into their offices like ants into cracks beneath a stone, regretfully leaving the bright morning sun for the artificial glare of fluorescent tubes, allowing their personalities to emerge once again after brief hibernation during their journey to work. Holman entered the gloom of the large Environment building and took the lift to the eighth floor. He greeted Mrs Tribshaw, a middle-aged fluttery secretary he shared with a colleague, assuring her he was in the best of health after his misadventure with the earthquake, entered his office and closed the door on her excited queries as to the extent of his injuries.

'Hello, John,' his colleague, a cheerful Scot with only a trace of accent, looked up and greeted him with a quizzical grin. 'What the hell happened to you?'

'It's a long story, Mac, I'll tell you over a drink when we get the chance.'

McLellan continued to stare at Holman, still grinning inanely. They had often shared the same assignment and knew they could depend on each other in a tricky situation. He was slightly older than Holman, but a little more idealistic. Although he pretended to envy Holman's bachelor life-style, he secretly relished his own family life. Three kids – two boys, one girl – a fiery-tempered but good-natured red-headed wife, and a semi-detached in the better part of Wimbledon; not a lot he had to admit, but enough to keep him content. His one release was his job. Although Holman handled the more risky assignments, occasionally he was sent on one requiring subterfuge, a little deviousness. But on the whole, his tasks were fairly routine, yet even these he rarely found boring. He often laughingly explained to Holman it was the fact that he, a little Jock from Glasgow, could help to bring the arrogant, money-conscious, filth-disposing capitalists into line. Or that he, a modestly paid, under-privileged civil servant could find a flaw in the land-destroying schemes of his own government, his own bosses. True, his information was not always acted upon, in fact, he would grudgingly admit, in fifty per cent of the cases it was *not* acted upon, but he got a great kick on the occasions he succeeded. Holman called him a Communist infiltrator, and he would laughingly admit it was true, although both knew it was far from the truth. When they worked together they enjoyed each other's company immensely, McLellan because he had the chance to lead the bachelor life for a brief time, Holman because he liked the Scot's dry sense of humour.

'Spiers has been calling for you,' Mac finally said, having satisfied himself that physically, at least, Holman seemed okay. 'He rang down about half-nine wanting to know where the hell you were.'

Holman walked around his desk and sat down, quickly looking through the memos that had piled up during his absence.

'Nothing changes, does it,' he observed, sifting through a stack of grey report pages. 'You're away for a week and you think everything's altered in that time; you come back feeling a stranger and within five minutes you've caught up with everything and you're back in the old routine.'

'Yes, well, if I were you, I'd get back into the old routine of seeing Spiers right away.'

'Right. I'll see you later, Mac, then I'm off for the rest of the week.'

'Lucky bleeder,' Mac grinned, and then his smile faded for an instant. 'I'm glad you're okay, John. Spiers didn't say much about it, but I gather you went through a rough time. You take it easy.'

'Sure, Mac. Thanks.'

Holman winked at Mrs Tribshaw as he strode through the outer office, raising his hand to still her fretful questions, and climbed the stairs to the ninth floor to Spiers' office.

'Is he in?' he asked the secretary, who stopped typing and looked up startled.

'John! Are you better?' He felt slightly embarrassed at her obvious joy at seeing him.

'I'm fine. Is he in?'

'What? Oh, yes, you can go right in. What happened, John? We heard you were involved in that awful earthquake.'

'Tell you later.' He knocked on the door and entered the inner office.

Spiers looked up from his papers, peering at him through thick-lensed glasses. 'Ah, John. Feeling okay? Good. Take a seat, I'll be with you in a moment.'

Holman sat, studying the bald head his chief presented to him as he continued to read through his papers. Finally, Spiers shuffled them together and put them neatly to one side of his desk.

'Well, John,' he said, staring at Holman with eyes that penetrated yet seemed to see nothing. 'I've had your films processed and examined the contacts. There do seem to be a few strange items among them, but they really don't affect us in any way. Now, the shots of the countryside within the perimeter are very interesting, but we'll get to that later. First, I'd like you to tell me again about the earthquake, right from the beginning, leave nothing out.'

Holman told him as much as he could remember, but his mind went blank as he reached the point where he had rescued the girl.

Spiers leaned forward on his desk. 'John, try to think. Did you hear an explosion before the ground opened?'

'No, definitely not. I heard the rumble, that's all, and then the crack as the ground split, but I'm sure there wasn't an explosion.'

Spiers slumped back in his chair, taking off his glasses and polishing them with his handkerchief. He cleared his throat sharply and rubbed the bridge of his nose with finger and thumb, as though tired. He replaced his glasses and leaned forward again. 'You see,' he said, 'a cloud of smoke was reported rising out of the ground just after they'd brought you up.'

'You think there was an explosion then?'

'Possibly.'

'Connected with the military base?'

'No, no. We've absolutely no grounds to suspect anything like that. You said you thought it was unlikely yourself.'

'Yes, I know, but I'm beginning to wonder now. Who knows what they're doing out there? On the way back yesterday, I ran into fog. Fog – on a hot summer's day! Are they using some new kind of smoke-screen device that they've just let drift off their patch into the rest of the countryside?'

'Oh, come now. That could have been caused by anything – a change in temperature, a factory nearby. I ran into some fog myself when I came down to see you. Salisbury Plain is full of mists at any time of year; we can't blame the military for everything, you know.'

'But you think they had something to do with the eruption?'

'Certainly not. I know there are certain aspects of the Ministry of Defence which we both dislike, but you can be sure they would never be as irresponsible as to have caused a disaster like this.'

'What about the photographs? They show some pretty strange things. You saw the dome?'

'They prove nothing!' Spiers was becoming angry and realized it. Once again he slumped back in his chair and went on more quietly. 'Anyway, I've had them destroyed.'

'What?'

'Do you realize the trouble you could be in – the department could be in – if it was discovered we held photographs of secret military installations?'

'But what was the point of going down there?'

'To take photographs, yes! But not to be used by us. I merely wanted proof for myself, so that I knew there was rich land being wasted, acres of arable soil, beauty spots, so that I was in a stronger position to argue that the area should be given back to us. My God, we could be put away for years for the sort of photographs you took!'

A seed of suspicion was planted in Holman's mind. 'You suspect something, don't you?' he asked Spiers quietly.

Spiers spoke wearily: 'Look, I've been on to the Ministry of Defence. There is a massive clamp-down in security – I don't know if it means anything, and I'm powerless if it does. I have a meeting arranged for this afternoon with the Defence Minister and Sir Trevor Chambers, and we hope to get some answers.' Sir Trevor Chambers was their department's Parliamentary Under-Secretary, a gruff, forceful man, who indeed liked to get answers. 'Needless to say, this is strictly between you and me.'

'And if you do discover the army is involved?'

'We shall have to wait and see.'

'Oh yes, the usual answer. I suppose it'll go on file, will it?'

'Damn your belligerence! Just who do you think you are? I think ...' He began to falter and without thinking Holman took advantage of the break in his words.

'For once, let's slay them! If they are responsible, let's break their bloody arms, let's –'

Spiers seemed to regain his composure and said, 'Let's remain calm. There is nothing to gain ...' Once again, his voice trailed off in mid-sentence.

Still unaware in his anger of the change that seemed to be taking place in his chief, Holman raged on, until finally there was no ignoring the strange, vacant look that had come into the eyes of Spiers behind the heavy glasses.

'What's wrong?' Holman asked, concerned. 'What's –' He broke off as Spiers rose from his chair, staring over Holman's head. Spiers turned and walked to the window; Holman was still too puzzled to move. Spiers opened the window and turned again to look at the surprised young man, his eyes for a second almost losing their blankness, a flicker of recognition returning to them but lost again in an instant. Then he turned back to the window, climbed on to the sill, and before Holman could make a move towards him, jumped out.

Holman was stunned. He sat rigid, his mouth open, unable to take in what he had just witnessed. Then, shouting Spiers' name, he rushed to the window. He saw the crumpled figure lying on the pavement nine floors below, a pool of blood spreading swiftly from beneath the smashed head. From that distance, he could just make out one hand curiously raised in the air, the elbow resting on the ground, the fingers of the hand clenching and unclenching in a twitching, spasmodic motion. Then the whole body arched upwards in a violent jerk and just as suddenly collapsed again, this time to lie perfectly still, the twitching hand finally resting.

Holman drew in a long, uneven breath and leaned against the window frame. People were rushing towards the broken body, others keeping well away, averting their eyes. He turned back in towards the room and saw Spiers' secretary standing in the doorway, a frightened look on her face.

'He – he jumped,' Holman managed to say at last.

She backed away from him into her own office. The door burst open behind her and several people rushed in. 'What's happened?' one of the men demanded to know. 'Who was it?'

Holman sank into the chair Spiers had occupied only moments ago, strangely, perversely, noting it was still warm. He didn't answer the people who crowded around him; he just sat staring at the desk top. What had happened? Why had he jumped? What had unhinged his mind so suddenly? The feeling came over Holman again. The sense of skin crawling, the feeling he'd had when they'd entered the fog. It couldn't be, there was no reason to it. But his brain needed no reason, the feeling was enough. He sprang to his feet and pushed past the startled people crowding into the office. He had to get to Casey.

■ 6 ■

REDBROOK HOUSE STOOD IN ITS OWN GROUNDS IN ONE OF THE QUIETER ROADS in Andover. A long gravel drive with trees on either side separated it from the outside world, the large red-bricked building looming frighteningly for any young newcomer taking his first journey down to it. Though built long before, it was established in 1910 as a school for only the privileged classes. It flourished successfully until the 1930s when it suddenly fell out of favour with the very rich who had begun to notice that some of the boys admitted were not quite as well-bred as their own offspring, though the parents were obviously wealthy enough to afford the exorbitant fees the school demanded; but then, money was not just a matter of inheritance anymore. The school declined in stature over the next fifteen years until the arrival of an eager, energetic and young deputy headmaster who managed to sweep away the old traditions and teaching methods maintained from Lord Redbrook's days, and to introduce new, more exciting ways of training, more vigorous approaches to the old and often boring subjects. Within five years he had established himself as headmaster and rejuvenated the school into a modern, forward-looking college, still private, but not quite as exclusive. His name was Hayward, and now, after over thirty years, the very methods he had introduced were the old, tired ways.

Five years before, Hayward had taken on a deputy headmaster in the hope of breathing new life into the school, knowing his methods were out of date but loving the old place too much to leave it himself. And, after all those years, perhaps too afraid to leave. The governors of the school had, over the last few years, frequently urged him to retire, but felt too much compassion for the old man to make it a directive. It was they who had suggested he take on a new deputy head, the old one having died two years before and never been replaced. Hayward would have considered a much younger man for the job, a man perhaps in his late twenties as he had been when he had joined the school, fresh-minded and eager to experiment, but such teachers were hard to find for a school like this. The younger men were more ambitious. They sought the more outward-going establishments where they could reap the glory without a long, uphill struggle. And Mr Summers came highly recommended by one of the Governing Committee's members.

Summers had been a captain in the army during World War II and had lost an arm in the course of it. He never talked about his injury or how he had acquired it. Indeed, he rarely spoke of his war-time exploits at all, and even less of his career as a schoolmaster. Although Hayward was disappointed by his assistant's narrow-minded educational theories, he had to admit the man was generally very competent. Disliked by the boys, he was sure, but he did show an extreme interest in and devotion to the school and would no doubt take over his position as head eventually. But his constant carping was becoming increasingly irritating.

Summers had turned the business of the crashed coach into a major issue, condemning poor Hodges out of hand, demanding his instant dismissal. The blame belonged entirely to Hodges, he had informed the headmaster, for speeding in such dangerous weather, showing off in front of the boys. He was too friendly with the boys anyway.

When Hayward had confronted the wretched-looking driver, who acted as janitor, gardener, and performed countless other tasks around the school, he had admitted it was true, but had gone on in a surly tone to imply certain notions about the deputy head. It was because of these implications that Hayward had decided to sack Hodges, not because of the misadventure in the fog. He could not allow the man to go around spreading these allegations against one of the members of his staff, particularly as he could provide no proof of them. As for Summers, Hayward would not even question the man; it would be too embarrassing for both of them. But he would certainly keep an eye on him.

Tomorrow Hayward would send for Hodges and tell him of his decision to let him go and warn him, warn him forcefully, not to spread any malicious slander which would cause him to end up in court. He thanked God the crash itself hadn't been serious; none of the thirty-six boys taken along had been hurt badly, a few bruises here and there, nothing to worry about. Only the unfortunate Hodges had sustained a nasty knock on the head, but even he, after a good night's rest, seemed physically sound. It was such a pity he had to get rid of the man, thought Hayward with a sigh, but good teachers were harder to replace than odd-job men.

Hodges sat on the old broken armchair in the basement storeroom he called his office and sipped at his strongly brewed tea. He poured some Scotch into the tin mug, swirling it around to mix with the hot liquid. He grunted several times as he stared into the thick brew, shrugging his shoulders and clucking his tongue.

That's cooked his goose for 'im, he told himself with a grin. Thought 'e'd got me in trouble, did 'e? Oh, yes, well I soon turned the tables on 'im, didn't I? He sniggered aloud. He wasn't at all drunk; the whisky with his tea was his usual mid-morning break. Old Captain Hook is really goin' to pay for it this time. Didn't recognize me when 'e first came to the school, did 'e? But I recognized 'im all right. I was just a corporal then, 'e was a smart-arsed captain, but word gets around on an army camp. Oh, yes, we knew about 'im.

He thought back to the old days: to the huge army installation at Aldershot, the rough training ground for thousands of raw recruits. There had been tension in the air in those days; the war was in its third year, every week more and more soldiers were being shipped abroad, and each week they seemed younger, less experienced. Hodges was a corporal in the cookhouse and was content to idle away the war as such. He knew of Captain Summers, had heard the rumours about him, sniggered with his cronies each time they saw the thin, waspish figure march by, saluting but wriggling their little fingers at him when he had passed. But Summers hadn't been the only one; in a camp that size and with so many raw young men, homosexuality was not too unusual. It was sneered at, true, despised by most, but many had secretly indulged in its illicit pleasure. Hodges had even tried it himself once, but found it painful and 'too much like bloody hard work!' for his liking. The rumoured 'bromide in the tea' didn't seem to do much good. He used to chuckle to himself when on night duty at the thought of all those pricks raised secretly towards the stars, pumped up by thousands of hands all over the camp.

But Summers had propositioned the wrong new recruit one day. He had looked fresh-faced and girlish enough, but, too late, the Captain discovered he had been conscripted with a bunch of his mates from North London. The boy had told him what he could go and do with himself and then applied some threatening blackmail to gain himself and his friends special privileges as well as the odd quid or two.

After only a few months, when the boy learnt he was going to be shipped abroad and suspecting that Summers had something to do with the arrangement, he and three of his bunch had waited one night on a quiet stretch of road leading to the camp, knowing that Summers would be returning alone on his bike. He often had assignations with young men from the town or arranged to meet a soldier there, always returning alone, always using the second-hand bike he had bought himself rather than taking the bus or begging a lift from one of his motor-possessing fellow officers. The group waited patiently, drinking beer and giggling as they described what they would do to the Captain when they got hold of him.

And then, after an hour's wait, they caught sight of him coming towards them along the dark road. They waited for him to draw level and then pounced, restraining their shouts of glee and anger for fear of being heard by anyone else who might be coming along in the distance. They began to beat him viciously, giving him no chance to recognize any one of them. His cries of fright and pain were cut off by a vicious kick to the throat. He drew his legs up and covered his head with his arms to protect himself, but the constant kicks and punches forced him to try to crawl away. Suddenly, over the screams of the terrified man, they heard the roar of an approaching lorry and saw the side lights in the not-too-far distance.

Taking advantage of the sudden break in their assault, Summers scrambled to his feet and staggered across the road, falling rather than jumping over a fence before they realized what had happened. With a shout, two of them chased after him, the other two deeming it wiser to take the opposite direction and hide in the bushes until the lorry had passed. The aggrieved boy was one of the pursuers and he had no intention of allowing the officer to escape so lightly.

Summers stumbled across the open field, panic lending him speed, the dull thud of boots on grass behind him giving him strength. Without seeing where he was going, or caring, he ran headlong into a barbed-wire fence. He did not see the warning signs spaced at regular intervals along the cruel wire fence, nor would he have understood them if he had – his terror was greater than his rationality. His cry of pain as a barb gashed his cheek brought renewed shouting and cursing from behind. He climbed through the fence, ripping his uniform, wickedly tearing his flesh, and ran headlong into the minefield.

The boy behind, ignoring the warnings in his rage, followed him through, pulling a knife from his trouser pocket, knowing he would soon catch up with his quarry. His companion called after him, warning him of the danger, shouting for him to come back, but he was too close to Summers now. The Captain had fallen to his knees and had raised one arm towards the boy as though to ward him off, blubbering like a baby, pleading.

The boy grinned. It didn't matter that the queer had recognized him. He hadn't intended it to go this far, but now he decided. He would be overseas soon, probably killed in this fucking war, so the Captain was going to pay. No one would know who'd done it, he was a known proof. It could've been anyone. He raised the knife so the officer could see it clearly, enjoying the new paralytic fear in the other's eyes. He grinned nastily as he walked towards the officer.

The explosion killed the boy instantly, throwing his body into the air as though it was a leaf blown by the wind. The Captain was knocked back by the blast and when he tried to sit up, his right arm would not support him. When he tried to see why, he dully registered that part of his arm wasn't there any longer.

They found him a little later, sitting in the middle of the minefield, holding the bloody stump of his right arm, still wondering what had happened to the rest of it.

Everyone in camp knew what had happened all right, even though it had been hushed up. It had caused quite a stir and Hodges had relished every minute of it along with a thousand others. Summers had been discharged, of course, but on medical grounds; a one-armed captain was no use in a war. Hodges himself, to his regret, had been shipped off abroad a few months later and had soon forgotten the incident, his dim mind concentrating only on survival. It was not until five years ago when he'd shown the new deputy head into Mr Hayward's study that he'd remembered. Summers hadn't recognized him of course, but the one arm, the thin waspish figure, had brought it all back. He debated with himself whether he should inform the headmaster or not; a man like that shouldn't be around young boys. He decided not to, feeling that somehow the knowledge might be put to his advantage eventually. Well, he had been right about that – today had proven it. Occasionally, he had enjoyed himself by hinting to Summers that he knew of his past. Nothing direct, of course, just a seemingly casual remark about his army days, about the war, the 'queer' things that had happened. Hints as subtle as a kick in the groin, but Summers would merely look at him as though he were something the dog had neglected to bury.

He drained the brownish tea, took a swig from the whisky bottle for good measure, wiped his mouth with the back of his hand, and picked up the garden shears with the intention of trimming the hedges outside the front gate. He ignored the headache, blaming it on the blow on the head he'd received the day before. He went upstairs.

Summers sat in his study engaged in writing a full report of the coach incident for the school governors. He implicated Hodges, the driver, as wholly responsible because of reckless driving in extremely adverse weather. He finally put down his pen and sat back in his chair with a satisfied smile, quickly scanning the report then picking it up again to add a few words here and there, occasionally deleting a sentence, adding another, until he was sure that he was completely vindicated from any blame. After all, it was the headmaster's idea

that he should take his form out to the Plain in the first place. End-of-term
restlessness, indeed. If he had had his way, the boys would have had a
twenty-times-around-the-playing-fields trot to work off any restlessness they
might feel. He rubbed his eyes vigorously, blinking rapidly when he took his
hand away. Dratted headache! Throughout the morning, he'd felt a sharp pain
across his eyes, only lasting a few seconds at a time, but nevertheless, extremely
painful.

He shuffled the pages of his lengthy report together, now completely satisfied that it was ready to be typed by Miss Thorson, the school's secretary and
administrative clerk. Only the fact that it would be signed by the headmaster
as well as himself prevented him from adding a few derogatory comments
concerning other matters relating to the running of the school. However, he
could always filter these through verbally to the Board via his personal contact.

And that, my friend, he smiled to himself as he rose from his desk, is your
goose cooked at any rate. He walked to the window, thinking of the despicable
coach driver, Hodges. He was sure he had known the man years ago when he'd
been in the army, but could not remember from which camp. Something in the
man's manner disturbed him, the seemingly casual remark, the sly look that
crossed his face when he mentioned the war. Did he imagine he could intimidate him in some way? What exactly did Hodges know of his past? Well,
whatever the loathsome man knew or did not know, he was a reminder of the
past. And the past was something Summers wanted desperately to forget.

He raised the stump of his arm, the sight of it reviving memories of pain and
humiliation. Had Hodges known the full story? Had his crafty comments
alluded to the terrible incident and the reason for it? No, the army had been
discreet. The few brother officers that had known of his weakness, and indeed,
some of whom shared it, had covered up the affair as only the services could.
He, himself, could not remember much about that night, but even now, thirty-
odd years later, he could still feel the pain in his hand as though it were still
there. The nights he had lain awake because of the dull, throbbing ache in a
non-existent limb, the pain not coming from the healed-over stump, but from
below it, where there was nothing.

And the damage had been much greater than just the maiming of his body.
The maiming of his mind had caused him even greater suffering. Although the
desire had still been there for a while after the accident, he discovered his body could
no longer fulfil his needs. The discovery had frightened him, filling him with suicidal
despair. But to kill himself required more courage than he would ever possess, so
he had survived the mental torture and the physical wound, not because he was
courageous, defiant to adversity, but because he was afraid to die.

Then, mercifully, after a few years, even the desire began to fade as though
his mind had accepted the disability, not just compromised, but given in
completely to the impotence of his body. He felt no yearning towards the young
boys he taught, or attraction to the young men he came in contact with, although
he still liked to be around them. The sight of youthful bodies no longer stirred
him, but he could appreciate their beauty, like a man without sense of smell
could continue to appreciate the sight of a rose.

Out of the corner of his eye, Summers caught sight of a figure lumbering along the driveway towards the main gate. Hodges. The hunched, shuffling gait was unmistakable. Summers smiled to himself, feeling a sense of agreeable pleasure in the knowledge that soon the man would no longer be an annoyance to him. He noted the bandaged head, glad that the injury had been inflicted. You deserve worse, he thought to himself, and that's just what you are going to get. Old Hayward was too soft, but this time he would not be able to dismiss his recommendation that Hodges be sacked. The report would have to go before the Governing Committee and they certainly would not tolerate the irresponsible actions of the driver-cum-odd-job-man.

He abruptly turned from the window and glanced at his watch. Time to do a round of the school before his next lesson. He often did a quick tour of the school in his free period, feeling it was his duty as deputy head to make a regular inspection of the classes while lessons were in progress, even visiting the empty dormitories to ensure the boys had left them neat and tidy, beds made, side-lockers carefully packed. Many a boy had been punished for leaving a discarded sock under a bed. He secretly enjoyed going through their lockers, seeking out pornographic photographs or books, various items that could be confiscated, even sniffing at dirty handkerchiefs for signs of masturbation.

The boys, from bitter experience, knew of his quirks and were careful not to leave any incriminating evidence lying around. One had foolishly left a drawing of a one-armed man, crudely resembling Summers, on his knees peeping through a keyhole, the caption reading: 'Beware, beware, Captain Hook is always there – especially if you are bare.' The culprit had been severely dealt with by Summers personally, the headmaster not even being informed of the matter.

Summers left his study, ignoring the sudden pain again before his eyes, carrying the report under his arm. As he walked along the corridor he listened at each classroom door, almost wishing to hear the sounds of rowdiness. When he reached the headmaster's outer office he handed over the document to the busy Miss Thorson. Satisfied with her guarantee to type it before lunch, he continued his round of the school. His own form, he knew, would be in the gymnasium, a comparatively new addition to the old school, a building that stood across the small playground away from the main building itself. They had all fully recovered from their shake-up of the previous day, a few proudly displaying their bruises to the other boys in the school who had not been on the outing to the Plain, and all glorifying the event beyond the facts. As Summers crossed the playground, unconsciously eager to see the boys performing their physical exercises, he hummed a tune to himself.

Hodges had almost reached the main gate when he suddenly stopped. He stood there for several minutes before he sank to his knees, dropping the cutting shears, holding his hands to his face. He rocked backwards and forwards for a few moments then fell forward so that he was on all fours, staring at the ground. The shears lay beneath him, glowing dully in the shadow of his body. He crouched back on his knees and grasped the handles bringing the implement up before his eyes, staring at the shears without comprehension. He opened and closed them with one sharp snapping movement, then slowly rose to his feet. He turned and walked back towards the school, holding the shears before him with both hands as though they were a water diviner. He entered the main entrance to the old building and passed the open doorway to the headmaster's outer office. Miss Thorson barely gave him a glance as she busily tapped away at her typewriter. As he walked down the corridor towards the rear of the school he caught sight through the open doorway to the playground of a black-gowned figure walking briskly towards the gymnasium. The thin, waspish figure, the stump of one arm swinging at his side, told him who the figure belonged to. He followed.

The boys had stopped halfway through the PE exercises leaving Osborne, their burly physical training master, jumping on the spot alone, arms and legs snapping in-out, in-out. One boy had ceased jumping first, then all the others, as one, had followed suit. They stood rigid, staring at the energetic teacher, their arms at their sides, no words passing between them, but somehow mentally in tune with one another. Osborne finally stopped his prancing and glared at the boys.

'Who told you to stop?' he thundered at them. 'Well?'

The boys just stared.

'Get cracking right away!' He began jumping on the spot again but stopped as he realized they were not following his example. He marched angrily towards the boy nearest to him, unable to understand this sudden attitude, suspecting he might be the victim of some practical joke. Although a big bluff man who liked to shout and always reacted swiftly and roughly to any insolence, he was popular among the pupils and, to some, a kind of hero. His prowess at all forms of athletics and sports had won him the respect even of his fellow teachers.

'What's the game, Jenkins?' he demanded of the blank-faced boy before him. The boy's lips moved but no sound came from them. He pushed roughly past him to the next boy.

'Come on, Clark, what's all this about, eh?'

Clark, one of his personal favourites because of his promising ability as a sportsman, said nothing, but stared at the teacher as though he'd never seen him before.

'All right, all right, you've had your little prank, but I'm going to give you five seconds to get weaving again!' He strode into the middle of them. 'One ...'

He failed to notice Clark, now behind him, walk towards a cricket bat lying on one of the benches at the side of the gym.

'... two ... I'm warning you boys, you're all going to be punished for this! Three ...'

Clark picked up the bat and walked back with it towards the angry teacher.

'Four. This is your last chance ...'

As his lips formed the word 'five', Clark raised the bat high and brought it crashing down on the back of Osborne's head. The teacher staggered forward as the hall filled with the crack of the impact between wood and skull. Clutching the back of his head, bent double, almost blind with pain, he turned in time to see the heavy bat swinging down towards him again. He cried out in horror, the look of questioning on his face barely registering before it was erased under the impact of the second blow.

He sank to the ground, still conscious but painfully stunned. He sprawled forward as the bat landed again, blood now running down his neck, staining his blue track suit. The boys surged forward as one, shouting in a wild fury, stamping on the limp man with plimsoled feet. They tore the trousers of his track suit from his body and turned him over on to his back, grabbing and kicking at his exposed testicles. Several tore off their own shorts and vests and began rubbing at their own already enlarged penises. One of the smaller boys jumped on the teacher and tried to enter him as though he were a woman, but was dragged off and beaten to the ground by the others. They pulled the top half of the track suit off so Osborne was completely naked, then dragged him towards the wall bars. The bars were of the type that swung away from the wall when in use, so that climbing ropes hung from the tops of their frames.

The boys lifted Osborne and viciously pushed him back against the bars, two climbing either side of him to loop the hanging ropes through the wooden bars and lashing his wrists to them high above his head. Then his feet were pushed through the lower rungs so that they were trapped by the ankles.

While some spat, kicked, punched or just jeered at the hanging man, others ran towards the huge sports chest and brought out wicket stumps, skipping ropes, more bats. One boy struggled with a heavy medicine ball. Their laughter and shouting stopped as they formed a semi-circle around the moaning figure. Blood from Osborne's head wounds spread down his body as he writhed feebly in his agonizing position. Then, in turn they began to beat him with the wicket stumps, lashing him with the wooden ends of the skipping ropes, striking him with the bats. His genitals were crushed by one of the stronger boys who systematically hit at Osborne's knee caps and private parts. Clark took the medicine ball and aimed it at Osborne's head, making it crack back against the wall bars under the impact of the throw. The boys all bore the same animal look of madness on their faces, their eyes wide, their mouths slack and drooling, the insane excitement of their actions making them scarcely human. All except one. One small boy crouched shivering in a far corner, too terrified to run away, too paralysed to take his eyes off the incredible scene taking place. A boy who had not been allowed to accompany the others on their coach trip the day before because he was recovering from an illness. He crouched there in a tight ball, his legs drawn up, clutching them with his arms, his nose buried into his knees – hoping, praying that the others would not notice him.

Summers reached the entrance to the gymnasium and paused; the pain in his head was becoming more severe. He dabbed a handkerchief to his forehead, wiping away the beads of sweat that had broken out. Perhaps I'm coming down with something, he thought. Perhaps the crash yesterday had more effect on me than I imagined. Oh well, it will soon be end of term and then I'll have a couple of months to rest and forget about these wretched boys for a while.

He opened the door and stopped again, this time with shock. His mouth dropped open in a soundless scream, his legs almost gave way beneath him. The boys, most of them naked, were milling around something red and pink hanging from the wall bars. It looked like a carcass, a bloody, butcher's carcass – and then he realized it was Osborne. Surely dead; the head hung loosely down towards his chest, the hands hung limply from the ropes that bound them. He saw now that the body was a mass of bruises and contusions, blood flowing down from a head wound. He could see that some of the boys' feet were red from the pool that had formed on the ground. They turned to stare at him as he stepped forward, still unable to speak. He saw that some of the boys lay on the floor writhing in their own private ecstasy as they masturbated, and others were coupled together. He saw the damage they had done to the obscene-looking body, the beating they had dealt it. He saw the boys watching him, *his* boys, so pure in their innocence, so evil in their deviation. Standing before him, magnificent in their nakedness!

He suddenly felt a stirring. A stirring in a region that had lain dormant for so many years. He looked down, amazed at the thrusting bulge from between his legs. A cloud seemed to haze over his eyes and he shook his head jerkily. Then a smile formed on his lips.

He strode forward towards the silent boys.

'Yes,' he said urgently. 'Yes, yes!'

Hodges walked across the playground, still holding the shears before him, his eyes focused only on the door ahead. He reached it and pushed it open. There was no reaction on his face as his eyes fell upon the bizarre scene before him, and only a dull reaction in his brain. Two men were tied to the wall bars on the far wall; one hanging still and quiet, his body now hardly recognizable as that of a man, as the other writhed and squirmed and moaned, not with pain, but with the pleasure pain brought. One arm was tied by the wrist to the wooden struts of the wall bars, the other was tied between the shoulder and elbow because there was no wrist. His feet were trapped inside the lower rungs, bent slightly at the knees so that the pelvis was thrust forward. Both men were naked so Hodges could see the huge, erect penis of the one who appeared to be alive. The boys were beating at the organ with wooden sticks, while others were lashing at the man with ropes. The man was Summers. His eyes gleamed with the excitement, his head twisted with ecstasy.

'Captain Hook,' said Hodges aloud.

All eyes turned towards him. Even Summers stopped his squirming to look. He walked forward, brandishing the large garden shears, snapping them open and shut. 'Captain Hook, Captain Hook,' he repeated over and over again as he walked towards the helpless figure, an evil grin spread across his features.

Summers also smiled as Hodges stood before him, saliva running from his mouth. His breath came in short, sharp heaves as he looked expectantly at the odd-job man. Hodges' eyes travelled down the bare torso before him until they reached the huge, swollen penis. He grasped it with one hand and chuckled throatily, the laugh becoming insanely loud. Summers grinned back at him, his head nodding in a seemingly meaningless gesture.

Hodges released the throbbing member and slowly raised the shears, so that it was between the two sharp blades.

'Yes, yes,' Summers cried, his whole body now quivering with excitement.

The boys watched in silence as the two blades snapped together and the scream echoed around the gymnasium.

▪ 7 ▪

HOLMAN IMPATIENTLY STABBED AT THE LIFT BUTTON. HE WAS BREATHING HARD, having left the taxi in which he'd raced back to St John's Wood, trapped in the inevitable traffic jam. The taxi driver's look of astonishment had turned into one of delight as he clutched the couple of pound notes Holman had hastily thrust into his hand. Fortunately the snarl-up had not been far from Holman's flat, but the sprint down the road had left him breathless and with a painful stitch in his side. He jiggled with the button, knowing it wouldn't make the lift come any sooner, but unable to stand there inactive. It finally arrived just when he was considering using the stairs and he abruptly pushed past the middle-aged, blue-haired woman who emerged. She gave him a look of disgust as the door closed, telling the Pekinese at her heels that rude young men like that should be birched and made to sweep the streets.

Holman thumped the side of the lift with the soft underside of his fist as it began its slow ascent. Surely Casey would be all right. She had stayed in the car during the incident with the fog so it may have had no effect on her at all. And what about himself? He felt okay and he'd been fully exposed to it. But Spiers? He'd said he'd run into some fog when he'd been down to visit him. Could it have been the same fog? Then he remembered the slightly acrid smell, the tinge of yellow in the mist; it had seemed familiar at the time, and now he began to remember his experience in the fissure. The mist that had risen from the depths of the crevice – yellow, sharp smelling. Was it the same? Had it caused his madness? Or was he still mad?

The lift jerked to a stop and he gave the slow-moving door a helpful shove, sliding through when the opening was wide enough. He reached the door of his flat fumbling for the key, trying to calm himself, only too willing to appear foolish if she was perfectly all right. He opened the door and a chill ran through him as he saw the place was in darkness. Perhaps she was still sleeping and had not bothered to draw the curtains. No, he had drawn them open himself that morning. He stood in the doorway and called out her name, not too loudly, not wanting to alarm her. He walked to the half-open door to the lounge. Pushing the door wider, he reached in and switched on the light. The room was empty. Everything was as he'd left it except for the closed curtains. He tried the kitchen. Empty. He walked softly to the bedroom door, grasped the handle, and gently pushed it open.

'Casey?'

Silence.

He could see the bed through the gloom but could not tell if its ruffled blankets covered a sleeping body. He stepped into the room and walked towards it.

Only the harsh, dry chuckle he heard behind him saved his life. He whirled around at the sound, the movement causing the kitchen knife Casey was plunging down towards his back to miss and slew through the material of his coat sleeve. He gasped with pain as the blade cut a fine line across the muscle of his arm, but the shock caused him to fall back and so avoid the knife on its return journey. She stood before him, familiar, but a stranger. Her eyes were cold, her mouth was drawn back in a grimace that resembled the frozen smile he'd seen on dead animals. Her brown-blonde hair hung limply across her face as though she'd been caught in the rain, there were long scratch marks on her cheeks where she'd raked them with her fingernails. A stream of saliva glistened on her delicate chin. She held the knife above her head and the dry, harsh chuckle came again from her throat. She plunged down once more with the knife, but this time Holman was ready. He stepped back and tried to grab her wrist, but missed. As the knife swept up again, the long, wicked-looking blade aimed at his stomach, he caught her arm and moved in towards her, his other arm encircling her waist.

Their heads were close together, almost touching, and suddenly she sank her teeth into his cheek, biting deep and hard. He wrenched his head away, feeling the skin tear, but oblivious to any pain. They fell backwards, on to the bed. Snarling noises came from her lips as they struggled for the knife and the fingernails of her free hand tried to rake his face. He twisted her wrist, trying to make her release the weapon, but her strength was incredible. He got his other arm underneath her chin, not wanting to hurt her but knowing he had no choice. He pushed up, forcing her head back, stretching her neck, causing her to choke. As she emitted an almost animal whine, he almost released her, afraid to hurt her too much. Aware of the slight relaxation in his muscles, she brought her knee up full into his groin. He cried out at the sudden agonizing pain and doubled up, his grip on her wrist weakening considerably. She pulled it free and sprang away from him laughing triumphantly.

She knelt on the bed beside him as he gasped for air and raised the knife above her head again, holding it with both hands. The sight made him forget his pain and he kicked out at her stomach, viciously sending her crashing off the bed to land in a heap on the floor. He struggled up on one elbow, both of them now heaving, trying to draw air back into their bodies. The knife lay somewhere in the gloom, he couldn't see where. She raised herself to her knees, glaring maliciously at him, her teeth bared in a snarl of rage, then leapt towards him, her arms flailing, fingers clawing to tear at his eyes. He caught her arms as her full weight landed on him, then arched his body to try to throw her off, but was only partially successful. They rolled over on the bed, their bodies becoming entangled in the bedclothes, restricting their movements. She spat at him, her eyes gleaming with fury, muted growling noises coming from deep down in her throat. He fought back desperately, still afraid to hurt her but knowing he would have to if he were to prevent her harming him and possibly herself.

They fell to the floor, taking the bedclothes with them, landing in a struggling, mixed-up heap on the floor. She managed to free herself from his grasp and raise herself to one knee, the sheets from the bed impeding her efforts. He grabbed for her again and caught at her blouse. It tore as she pulled herself away, exposing her small breasts, the sight causing Holman to hesitate, to freeze momentarily, dangerously. It was as though her sudden nakedness, the sight of her soft defenceless flesh made her vulnerable. Helpless.

But her laugh quickly swept pity from his mind, and he struggled to free himself of the sheets. It was a laugh that chilled him; the empty cackle of a crazy woman. He sprang at her.

She dodged his outstretched arms and leapt across the bed with an agility that surprised him. He clumsily scrambled after her, his feet still caught in the sheets on the floor, and managed to roll to one side as she brought the bedside lamp crashing down towards his head. He gasped as it struck his already injured shoulder, crying out her name as though it would bring her to her senses. Swinging his feet round, dragging some of the bedclothes with them, he crouched on the floor beside her. She kicked him in the face, catching his jaw, stunning him. He fell back against the side of the bed, the restraint of not wanting to hurt her now completely gone from his mind. He would have to fight her as he would fight a man – or a mad dog. He saw her grab for something on the floor and realized it must be the knife. As she came towards him again he pushed himself off the bed and backed away, never taking his eyes off her, fighting down his emotion for her, regarding her as the crazed stranger she now was. She advanced slowly, no longer chuckling, but the smiling grimace still there on her face, the look of hatred still distorting her features. Their movements were slow, measured, the movements of a cat stalking a terrified mouse. Suddenly, she ran forward, raising the knife high for the death strike, a scream of anticipation escaping from her lips. He ducked beneath the descending arm and was behind her. As she whirled, he made for the bedroom door, feeling terror of the blade he knew was a few feet from his exposed back. He reached the door, grabbed the handle and twisted his body to slam it shut behind him. He heard the thunk of the knife as it sank into the wood then the thud of her body as it followed through and struck the door. He immediately pushed the door open again, all his strength behind the thrust, the whole action in one fluid movement. It slammed into the girl, knocking her back violently, causing her to lose her grip of the knife handle. She fell to the floor with a scream more of rage than hurt, her skirt rising high to her thighs, the sight exciting Holman despite his predicament. He leapt on to her, his whole weight pinning her to the floor, but still she struggled, her continuing strength amazing him. Her legs opened in her efforts to free herself and he lay between them, his face next to hers, his arms pinning hers above her head. He could feel himself growing stiff, the position of lovemaking and the excitement of his fright combining to distract his mind from the danger towards the more primitive urge of his body. 'Casey,' he breathed as he moved his body against her, 'Casey!'

She bit into his already wounded neck, deep and hard, drawing blood and savouring it. He cried out and tried to pull away, but she clung to him, her head rising with him. He could feel his flesh break again as her teeth sank deeper. He released one of her arms, which immediately clawed at his hair, and drew his fist back. He punched her hard in her ribs but still she would not let go. Desperately, ignoring the pain, he pulled one knee up so it rested high between her legs, causing his back to make a hole between their bodies. Then he raised his fist again and slammed it low into her stomach.

Her head fell back to the floor and she lay there gasping in air through blood-stained lips, her legs drawn up, her free hand clutching her stomach. Then he slapped her. A hard, cruel, swiping blow that threw her head to one side. He pulled her half to her feet and hit her again, knocking her to the floor once more. At the sight of her lying there, moaning, tiny whimpering noises coming through tears of pain, his rage vanished.

He knelt beside her and cradled her in his arms, tenderly rocking her to and fro.

'Oh, Casey, I'm sorry, darling,' he said softly, forgetting her madness, thinking only of the pain he had caused her. But even as he held her and her breathing became more even, he could feel her body stiffening, her whimpers becoming low murmurings. He looked around quickly and caught sight of the rumpled sheets on the floor. He lowered her body, praying she was still too helpless to move, and grabbed for them, pulling them towards him. Her shoulders began to heave now, not from breathlessness but from insane anger building up. She raised herself on one elbow. Hastily, he pushed her back down and rolled her over, pulling her hands behind her back. She began to kick out but he sat heavily on her to make her helpless. As he tied her hands with the rolled-up sheet, she thrashed her head from side to side, scraping it on the hard floor, oblivious to the pain. Then, without warning, her body went limp, her eyes became glazed as though she were in a deep cataleptic trance, and saliva, pink from Holman's blood, drooled from her once-sweet lips to the floor.

He turned her over and anxiously wiped away the thin layer of moisture from her brow. She stared ahead unseeingly. Lifting her gently, he took her over to the bed, and laid her on it, propping her head and shoulders up with two pillows. He drew the sides of her ripped blouse together, covering her breasts, the proud little breasts he had lovingly kissed so often, and arranged her skirt to cover her thighs, the soft thighs he had also lovingly kissed so many times before. Then he wiped the spittle and blood from around her mouth with the edge of a sheet, reminding himself of the wound she had re-opened with her sharp teeth. He put his handkerchief to his neck and winced at the pain now that he had become conscious of it. There was quite a lot of blood on the handkerchief when he drew it away, but he didn't think too much damage had been done.

He sat there in the gloom staring at the girl, one hand with the handkerchief to his throat, the other resting lightly on her knee. She was unresponsive when he quietly spoke her name. How much had the gas, the fog – whatever it was – how much had it affected her? Would she ever be normal again? Would she try to kill herself as Spiers had done? Even he, Holman, had tried to throw himself back down the fissure and later cut his own throat with glass. The little girl had died because of the fog. But she had been heavily subjected to it, as had he, inside the hole, and her young mind had been unable to cope with the effects. His only hope was that Casey had not been exposed to too much. She'd been inside the car most of the time. Did it make any difference though? Was such a short exposure still as lethal? The next few days would tell. His only hope was to get her to a hospital where they could keep her under restraint until she got over it, or – He pushed the thought from his mind. The doctors had told him there was little they had been able to do but keep him on drugs to pacify him while the struggle had gone on inside his brain, an area they could not enter unless they used drastic surgery which may have proved fatal anyway. Would her mind be strong enough to resist whatever was eating into it?

He was still sitting there in the semi-darkness when the police pounded on the door ten minutes later.

Holman went to the door quickly, afraid to leave Casey alone for too long. He was surprised to see the police and immediately assumed a neighbour had been concerned about the sounds of the struggle. There were two, one uniformed, the other in plain-clothes. He didn't know there was yet another guarding the stairs on the ground floor.

'John Holman?' the man in plain-clothes asked brusquely.

'Yes. Good thing you came …'

He was cut off as the detective pushed his way in, flashing a card in Holman's face and pocketing it immediately. 'Detective Inspector Barrow, we've been told to pick you up.'

'What? Oh, Spiers. Look, get an amb …'

'We understand that you were the only witness present at, er, an incident at the Department of the Environment building a short while ago.' The detective was young and very unlike Holman's idea of a detective. He wore a polo-neck jumper and a long suede jacket; his hair, though not exactly long, was certainly no 'short back and sides'. He glanced around the flat, visibly puzzled by the absence of daylight.

'Yes, that's right. My boss committed suicide, but ...'

'Why did you leave?' The detective was walking away from him, opening doors and looking in as he went. Holman turned towards the burly policeman standing in the doorway. 'Look we've got to get an ambulance right away,' he said, ignoring the detective's question.

'Christ!' he heard and turned again to see the plain-clothes policeman standing at the door to his bedroom, a look of astonishment on his face.

'Hold him, Turner!' the detective shouted over his shoulder as he disappeared into the room. A heavy hand clamped on to Holman's upper arm as he made towards the bedroom.

'You don't understand,' Holman said angrily. 'We've got to get her to a hospital immediately.' He wrenched his arm free and ran down the short passage. He saw the young detective sitting on the bed untying Casey's hands. 'No, wait! Don't release her – she's not sane!' The words hurt him to say, but he had to make them understand. A rough hand went around his neck and his right arm was yanked behind him and up.

'You don't understand!' he managed to gasp.

'Oh, we understand all right,' said the CID man, turning to eye him coolly. 'Your colleagues told us *you* hadn't been well. Don't give us any trouble, mate, I'm just in the mood for a bastard like you.' He spoke quietly, but the menace was unmistakable.

Holman relaxed his muscles, unafraid of the threat, but realizing there was nothing he could do for the moment.

'All right, let's take it easy. But you've got to get her to a hospital,' he said, trying to keep his voice calm. 'I was in the earthquake in Wiltshire last week. There was a gas released, it affects the brain ...'

'It certainly affected yours,' said the detective, helping the girl to her feet. 'I don't know what you've done to her, but look at her, look at those eyes ...'

'No, no. It wasn't me. It was the fog. Spiers was caught up in it too. It affects the brain.'

'As far as we know, there've been no reports of gas during any damage at the earthquake.'

'But I was inside it. Inside the eruption where the gas was!'

'Yes, we heard about a man and a child being rescued. The kid's dead, we'll take your word for it that you were the man. But there's been no mention of anybody else being down there.'

'They weren't down there.' Holman was beginning to lose his temper, but fought hard to control it knowing no good would come from a shouting match. 'This was later, at different times.'

'All right, Sergeant, get him out of here, we've got plenty of time for questions.'

'Wait a minute, there's something else!' Holman resisted the strong arms of the policeman holding him. 'The school! Listen to me. There was a bus-load of kids caught in the fog. I can't remember the name of the school, but it was in Andover. You've got to find it and quickly. God knows what's happened there by now!'

*

Holman impatiently drummed his fingers on the hard top of the bare table in one of New Scotland Yard's many 'interview' rooms. The stone-faced policeman who stood by the door watching him said nothing, bored by his duty, but ready to spring into action at the least sign of aggressiveness from his charge.

'What have they done with the girl?' Holman asked him for the third time. As before, there was no reply. 'You could at least tell me that!' Holman slumped back in his seat, knowing it was useless to argue with this zombie. He'd been kept at the police headquarters for well over three hours now, wearily answering the same questions over and over again. Their disbelief was evident and when he'd been left alone with his guard and given time to reflect, he realized he could not blame them. He had been the only other person in the office when Spiers had jumped and they had been heard arguing beforehand; the police had discovered him with a bound and beaten girl in his flat; he'd only just been released from hospital after suffering a mental breakdown. The facts spoke for themselves and his anger at their repeated questions had not improved their opinion of his sanity. The girl was in a state of shock it seemed, unable to tell them of her ordeal, but they were sure she would be able to answer their questions later. They had finally agreed to check on the schools in Andover; if there was some abnormality with the pupils then maybe his story could begin to take on some credence.

He looked up sharply as the door suddenly opened and two men walked briskly into the room. One was the young detective who had brought him in. He stood back, icily regarding Holman, as the other, an older, more genial-looking man, sat in the chair facing him on the other side of the table. Chief Superintendent Wreford had skilfully interrogated Holman, allowing his younger colleague to be antagonistic while he played the more sympathetic role. Holman had soon realized this was an act and that the mild-mannered, soft-spoken policeman was in fact a shrewd and perceptive interrogator. Wreford had tried to determine whether Holman was a dangerous lunatic or a clever liar with some obscure but sinister motive. So far, he wasn't sure.

'We've been checking on the schools in Andover ...' he paused to study Holman's reaction.

'Yes!' said Holman leaning forward.

'... and found nothing.'

Holman's look of frustration was too natural to be forced.

'However,' the Chief Superintendent went on, 'we've had a report of a serious fire in a school just on the outskirts of the town.'

'That must be it! It has to be!'

'Well, there's no way of knowing yet. Apparently the fire was in a gymnasium adjoining the school and they believe there could have been thirty-or-so boys trapped inside. The survivors are in a state of shock, and can't be questioned just yet. We haven't got all the facts, but at least we know the name of the school.' His gaze became imperceptibly more intense. 'It was Crayton's.'

Holman looked down at the table and frowned as he tried to remember. 'No, no, I don't think that was it. The teacher told me the name, but I just can't remember it. I do remember the teacher only had one arm, but that's not much use to you.'

The Chief Superintendent studied Holman's face for a few moments and then said, 'All right, that wasn't the real name. I'm going to show you a list – let's see if you recognize any of the names on it.'

He handed a sheet of paper to Holman who quickly scanned the typewritten list. He shook his head and read through it again, this time more slowly. 'It's no good,' he said finally, 'I don't recognize any. One or two sound familiar but ...' Again, he shook his head.

'The name of the school is Redbrook. Redbrook House, to be exact. Ring a bell?'

'It sounds right, but I couldn't honestly swear to it.'

'I bet you couldn't,' the younger policeman broke in harshly.

'Let me handle this, Barrow,' Wreford said sharply, becoming a little tired now of his subordinate's ruthlessness. Although he often used him as a balance against his assumed mildness, he had begun to wonder if Barrow didn't relish the role he played just a little too much.

'All right, Mr Holman,' he said, his voice quickly becoming more even, 'we'll have to hold you for a short time while we're making further investigations.'

'Are you arresting me?' Holman's tone was incredulous.

'Certainly not. But you must admit, the circumstances are suspicious, to say the least.'

'I suppose so. But what about Casey? She'll need me.'

'Miss Simmons will be well looked after.'

'Where is she?'

'At the moment, she's in the Middlesex Hospital under sedation. It seems she's still in a state of shock.'

'But don't you see, that's because of the fog. It's a reaction to it!'

'Whether it is or not, we'll soon find out. And tell me something, Mr Holman, if this fog is drifting around the country sending people mad, why haven't we had reports of it? Why aren't all the people living in that part of the country raving lunatics?' A slight edge of anger had appeared in the policeman's last question.

'I don't know! I suppose it's because the fog doesn't cover such a wide area. And don't forget, there's a lot of open land around there. It may be that not too many people have come in contact with it as yet. And there seems to be some sort of delayed reaction. We came in contact with it yesterday, Spiers the day before. It must take time to work its way into the system!'

'But you told us you were mad when they dragged you from the hole!' said Barrow, annoyed that his superior should even listen to such drivel.

'I was subjected to a massive dose of it! I was its first victim!' Holman angrily banged his hand on the table.

'Then tell us, Mr Holman,' said Wreford calmly, 'why you are not mad now. Or are you?'

There was an abrupt silence in the small room. Three pairs of eyes looked intently into Holman's, the three policemen waiting for his reply.

'Look,' he said wearily, 'I just don't know. I'm not a doctor, I'm not a scientist – maybe the Ministry of Defence can tell you.'

The two CID men looked at one another. 'What do you mean by that?' asked the Chief Superintendent quietly.

'They've got military installations down on Salisbury Plain. They conduct experiments – dangerous experiments – in the interest of the nation! Maybe they've got some answers.'

'Oh, come on ...' began Barrow, a sneering grin on his face, but he was cut off by the older man.

'Are you saying the Ministry of Defence is responsible for this? That they've released some sort of ...' Wreford paused, '... some sort of nerve gas?'

'For God's sake, I don't know! It's a possibility though!'

'Oh, sir, do we have to listen to this?' Barrow looked as though he were ready to pounce on Holman.

'No, we don't. If what you say is true, Mr Holman, then we should know very shortly. Until we do, I'm afraid we have to hold you.'

'Okay, okay. But see they look after Casey. She's got to be watched constantly.'

'She'll be in safe hands, Mr Holman, I can assure you of that.'

▪ 8 ▪

Herbert Brown was worried about his pigeons. He drained his whisky and stared at the empty glass for a few moments.

'Another one, Herby?' asked the barman, reaching for a new glass, knowing his customer would not drink from the old.

'Yes, Harry. Have another one y'self.'

Harry knew the offer would come, which was why he was always eager to serve Herbert.

'Ta. I'll have a small light,' he said, smiling through cigarette-stained teeth. He was a runt of a man, insignificant to most of his customers, but always treated well by Herbert Brown.

'Nah, have a short.'

'All right, Herby. I'll have a gin and tonic.' He poured the drinks and took the pound note from the bar where Herbert had nonchalantly laid it. He rang up the till and swiftly scraped out the change, a ten pence piece finding its way into his own pocket.

'Here you are, Herby. Cheers.' He raised his glass and sipped his gin. He was a good sort, Herby. Always ready to buy a drink. Never checked his change. He spent at least three evenings a week in the pub opposite his shop in Hackney Road, and most lunch-times. Herbert usually rose early, about 5.00 or 6.00, and went to the market to buy stock for his fruit shop. By 11.00, he considered his day was done and a trip to the betting shop was always followed by a visit to the pub, leaving his hard-working wife to cope with the selling of the fruit. She had long ago resigned herself to the fact that Herbert would never change, but this did not stop her acid-tongued beratement of him. And the more he was nagged, the more he drank. And the more he drank, the more he was nagged. The circle was never-ending, but neither of them could see it. It was a way of life.

'I shouldn't worry about them, Herb. They'll turn up.' Harry leaned forward on the bar, a false look of sympathy on his face. He couldn't understand how anyone could worry about bloody pigeons, let alone breed them. He'd once been up to Herby's coop, a dangerously perched hut built on a side roof at the back of his shop. The house itself was large, as were most of the houses along London's Hackney Road; their backyards dropped a floor below road level, providing extra habitable basement rooms and giving the houses concealed depth. An extension had been built by the shop's previous occupiers, extending most of the length of the backyard and reaching the second floor level. The roof, which was flat, could be reached from a landing window, and on it Herbert had built his pigeon coop.

The smell inside the hut made Harry feel nauseous, and Herbert's drunken clucking had filled him with barely concealed disgust. For the life of him he could not understand what Herby saw in the fat, cooing creatures. Puffing themselves up, messing all over the place. They weren't good for anything – even pigeon pie was out of style nowadays. Herby raced them, Harry knew that. But he'd never won anything from it. When he'd cautiously broached the subject to him, the only reply he'd got was, 'Have you ever watched them fly?' Just the silly sort of answer you'd expect from an old drunk. Still, apart from his stinking pigeons, Herby was all right. Always good for a drink, always good for a tap.

'They should've been back before now,' Herbert was saying mournfully. 'Only took them down to Salisbury in the van. Got some new ones, y'see, you've got to go easy on 'em at first. Mustn't take 'em too far or they'll never find their way home. Some of the older ones were with 'em so they should've been all right. And Claude never gets lost!'

Harry had to hide a grin as he thought of the ridiculously-named pigeon which was Herbert's favourite. He'd had it for many years, a scruffy old bird that always looked as though it had just escaped from the clutches of a cat. He treated it like a baby. The time Harry had been up there, Herby had held it to his cheek and spoken to it as though it could understand every word. Not baby-talk though, but sensibly, man-to-man. When Harry had held it, it had shat in his hand.

'Took 'em on Sunday,' Herbert continued, his words slurring slightly.

'Should be back by now. Trouble is, y'see, they need the sun to guide them.'

'Well, maybe they got back earlier this evening Herb, just after you got here. You wait, when you get home, they'll all be sitting up waiting for you.' He caught another customer's eye and looked heavenward, careful that Herbert didn't see. The man, who had been eavesdropping, winked back.

'You taking the piss, Harry?' Herbert's words were challenging.

Harry knew that after a few Scotches his friend could quickly turn nasty at the slightest hint of sarcasm. 'No, no,' he said hastily. 'I just mean they'll all be up there on the roof waiting for you. I'm sure they will. Here, it's about time you had one on me.' He turned to reach for a new glass and breathed a sigh of relief when he heard Herbert's voice droning on, now sentimental again. He didn't want to upset Herby.

'Thing is with birds, Harry, they don't demand nothing. You feed 'em, an' that's it, they're yours. They're not like dogs or cats that creep around you, begging. They're proud, y'see. They come to you for food and that's it. If you don't feed 'em, sod ya', they're off.' He leaned forward and pointed a rigid finger at the barman. 'But if you look after them right, they'll always come back to you. They're loyal, y'see. Independent, but loyal.'

He sat back as though satisfied with his statement. Harry placed the whisky on the bar before him, nodding his agreement, but annoyed that he'd been forced to buy him a drink. The landlord had eagle eyes so he couldn't take too many chances with the till. He'd have to pay for it.

'Claude'll bring 'em back, I know he will.' Herbert emptied the glass in two swift swallows, causing Harry to wince at the thought of the fiery liquid burning its way down his throat to eat away at the lining of his stomach. His insides must be made of cast-iron.

'Can't understand why they've been gone so long though.' Herbert stood up, swaying slightly. 'I'm off, Harry.'

'Okay, Herb, see you tomorrow,' grinned the barman and added maliciously, 'Give my love to the old lady.'

He almost regretted his words when Herbert turned back to the bar and eyed him for three long seconds, his befuddled brain unsure of the tone of the last remark.

'Fuck 'er,' Herbert finally said, and weaved his way unsteadily out of the pub.

Once outside, he leaned against the wall for a few moments. He'd taken the last drink too fast and could feel the bile rising inside him. It was the thought that his beloved birds might be waiting for him that had suddenly caused his haste. He fought down the sickness and lurched across the wide main road, stopping at its centre to allow a No 6 bus to crawl slowly by.

His wife watched him from their bedroom window above the shop.

She'd done it so many times before, had spent long, solitary hours gazing out at the busy main road from the darkened room, driven there not to watch for him coming home but by loneliness. She would study the people walking by, the young couples, the customers she knew, wondering where they were going, what they would do when they got there. The strangers, who were they, what were they doing in this neighbourhood? Sometimes her mind would go off into strange, often sordid, fantasies at the sight of them. There had been a time when the sight of one coloured person was enough to send her off into a frenzy of fancies, but now she was filled only with angry indignation. She could look directly into the brightly lit upper decks of the double-decker buses that regularly passed by her window. Although the glimpses were fleeting, they filled her mind with curiosity. And enhanced her loneliness.

Since the boys had left, she found she had too much time to herself, too much time to ponder over her marriage and the hard years it had brought her. They had their own lives to make, it was true, but you'd think they would visit more often even though they both lived a little way out now. She loved to see the babies, her grandchildren. It was Herbert who'd driven the boys away with his drinking, his belligerence. What affection had he shown them? What interest? But his pigeons were another matter. Oh yes, nothing was too good for his bloody pigeons! Look how worried he was when he thought they were lost, how anxious he'd been the last couple of days. What could he see in them?

Look at him now, standing in the middle of the road in a drunken stupor. God, how she wished that bus had knocked him down! She was the one who had made the business a success; it was all due to the hard work she'd put into it. All right, so he did get to the market very early in the mornings, but why should that excuse him for the rest of the day? They could have been well off if he didn't squander every penny they made on drink and gambling. And giving it away. Oh yes, all his cronies knew where to come when they were short of a few bob! Good old Herby – the paupers' friend. Well, she'd sifted a bit away out of the takings; she had to, otherwise they'd soon be out on the street if business suddenly went bad. It wasn't stealing – how could you steal money you earned yourself? But there was no reason he should know about it. Look at him, staggering across the road! I just hope none of the customers see him, the rotten bastard.

Tears glistened in Lena Brown's eyes, not tears of self-pity or sorrow, but tears of hate.

'I wish you'd die,' she said aloud, her breath causing the window-pane to mist up. 'I wish you'd fucking die.'

Herbert reached the side door to his shop and fumbled for his key. His wife had once bolted the door from the inside. Only once, never again. The police had been called because of the commotion he'd made, but she'd never dared to lock him out of his own house again. He found his key and had no difficulty in placing it in its metal womb, turning it viciously and pushing the door open. He closed it loudly behind him, not caring if he disturbed his wife upstairs. Not that she'd be asleep. Oh no, she'd be waiting for him no matter what time it was. You'd think she'd get sick at the sound of her own voice by now. Well, fuck 'er! She wasn't important.

He felt his way along the dark passageway and down the steps to the backyard, not bothering to turn on the lights. Unbolting the heavy back door, he stepped out into the cool night air, breathing in great mouthfuls of it. He unzipped his trousers and pissed on the hard concrete ground, enjoying the sound as the yellow stream spattered off it. He never knew why he did this, their toilet stood directly opposite him and it had cost him a small fortune to have the one upstairs put in. But it was one of life's little pleasures, he told himself. And it infuriated Lena.

As the stream of urine lost its impetus and retreated back towards his shoes, he became conscious of another sound. It was the sound of cooing.

He looked up towards the roof His pigeons – they'd come back, bless 'em! He laughed aloud and quickly zipped up his trousers, getting his fingers wet in the process. Wiping his hands on his jacket, he lurched back into the house, leaving the door wide open behind him. He staggered up the stairs, cursing as he tripped, using his hands on the stairs ahead of him. As he reached the landing window, he heard his wife's voice coming from the bedroom.

'You dirty bastard!' she called. 'You're a bloody animal! Why don't you use the lavatory like any normal man?'

'Shut your noise,' he shouted back, reaching one knee up to the window-sill. He had to be careful now. More than once he'd lost his grip and gone tumbling down the stairs. She always said he'd go walking off the roof one of these nights, and good riddance too. But he knew he'd never get that drunk because if he did, he would never be able to get out the bleedin' window.

He scrambled through, his hands resting on the floor of the roof, supporting his upper body. He could still hear her voice from inside the house, shrill, unpleasant. But he could also hear the cooing now, much louder, and the sounds of movement inside the coop as the birds shuffled on their perches, excited by the noise he was making.

'I'm coming, my darlings,' he called out, drunkenly conscious of the silly grin on his face. He was careful to keep well away from the edge of the flat roof; he didn't fancy the drop on to the concrete thirty feet below. 'I knew you'd get back, Claude. I knew I could depend on you. What happened, get lost, did you?'

He struggled with the latch on the door, noticing that some of the newer birds were still on the roof of the wooden hut. They always took a little while to learn how to get back inside the coop. They'd soon follow the example of the others. 'Claude, come on, darling, where are you?' He switched on the bicycle lamp he kept hanging up inside the hut, the sudden light causing several of the birds to flutter around in panic.

'It's all right, darlings, it's only me. I won't hurt you.' Herbert closed the door behind him so that none of the pigeons could escape. He had to crouch low as the sloping roof of the hut was not high enough to allow a grown man to stand. He quickly checked over the birds, counting them, making sure none had received any injuries. He finally spotted Claude, perched high in the corner of the hut, not moving, but a gentle cooing coming from its throat.

'Hello, old Claude. D'you miss me?' He lurched towards the older pigeon trying not to disturb the others. He was unaware of the sudden silence that had descended upon them, or that they were now all perfectly still.

'Well, Claude, what have you got to say for yourself, eh?' He reached for the pigeon and gently picked it up. Holding it close to his face, he began to stroke its breast, making soft clucking noises. 'You know who's boss, don't you? You know who'll look after you.'

The bird's head suddenly shot forward and its beak pecked at Herbert's bleary eye. He screamed out in pain and fell back among the perches, releasing his grip on his pet bird. The whole hut erupted into a whirlwind of screeching, fluttering bodies as the birds flew at him from all sides. He raised his arms to protect his face, but they pecked at his hands viciously, causing thin trickles of blood to run down them. He swiped at them wildly, sending their frail bodies crashing into the sides of the coop, several falling to the floor again, unable to rise, feebly fluttering their broken wings in a useless attempt to reach him. But still the others continued their attack, flapping their wings at his head, pecking at his crouched body, finding exposed flesh, drawing tiny dots of blood.

Suddenly, part in rage, part in panic, Herbert grabbed at one of the feathered bodies and, with a cry of anguish, crushed its tiny bones with his hands. But the movement had left his face exposed and three of the pigeons immediately flew at it, one clinging to his neck, the other two striking at his cheeks and eyes. He was already half-blinded and now felt his other eye pop as he released the dead bird and tried to protect his face again. The shock forced him to his feet, thrashing out violently, smashing the birds to the ground, crushing them with his feet as he staggered blindly towards the small doorway. But in the turmoil, in the confusion of flying bodies, beating wings, the shrieks of the birds, his own cries of fear, his pain, he had lost all sense of direction and crashed into the side of the hut, knocking himself to the ground.

As he lay there, arms outstretched, stunned by the fall, the pigeons flurried on to his heaving chest and continued their combined onslaught. He kicked out, sobbing with the horror of it, and managed to roll over in the confined space, squashing the birds that still clung to him. Raising himself to one knee, feeling the sharp pecks at his neck and shoulders, but now almost oblivious to the pain, he stretched out one hand towards the side of the coop. His fingers curled through and round the wire mesh of one of its windows and he slowly pulled himself to his feet, ignoring the pigeon that had settled on his hand and was biting at his raw knuckles. Some inner sense informed him of the direction of the door based on the position of the wire window he clung to. The pain now was on its second wave and it broke through the protective barrier his fear had set up.

He screamed aloud, shaking, shuddering his entire body, flailing his limbs, and lumbered towards the small exit, still covered in feathered, tormenting bodies. Unable to see the torch, he sent it flying as he stumbled through the door, his brain as well as his eyes blind now.

His wife stared at him from the landing window, her face white in the moonlight, her hands clutching the window-sill. She had heard the commotion from her bedroom, at first ignoring it, assuming her husband was in one of his fits of rage. But then the urgency, the terror in the screams had reached her and she had flung herself from the bed, fearful at what she might find when she reached the landing window. And what she'd found had left her in open-mouthed disbelief.

A figure had emerged from the coop at the end of the small roof, a figure that seemed scarcely human in the moonlight. It moved in crouched, lurching steps and was surrounded by wildly-beating wings. She drew in her breath in horror as she realized it was her husband, just recognizable, and he was being attacked by the pigeons he loved. She stood there, her mouth agape, for once in her life speechless, unable to move, unable to help him. His next cry broke the spell and she struggled to climb through the window, her heavy body hindering her progress. When she was halfway through, her hands on the roof, her buttocks high in the air on the window ledge, she looked up to see her husband stumble towards the edge. She opened her mouth to scream his name, but no sound came. Her lips silently opened and closed twice and only when he stepped off into space did any sound emerge.

'Herby!' she screamed, and the scream covered the squelching thud as his body hit the concrete thirty feet below.

She crawled towards the edge of the parapet, sobbing and calling his name over and over again. She lay flat and peered into the darkness below. His body was barely visible, a dark form lying perfectly still, legs twisted outwards at odd angles. A sudden movement gave her hope, but she saw it was the weak fluttering of a dying bird that had plunged to the ground with him. She knew he was dead.

'Oh, Herby, my poor darling. Oh Herby,' she wept.

Above her, on the roof of the coop, the pigeons had gathered. They gazed down at her and were still. The one called Claude cooed softly.

Much earlier, on that same day, Edward Smallwood had been fishing. He was a tall, nervous man, prematurely balding and, at the age of thirty-five, still living with his parents. His nervousness was largely due to his domineering father, a man much smaller than himself, but a man with strict principles and harsh ideals, who made no effort to hide his disappointment in his 'weakling' son. Edward's even smaller mother doted on her son and kindly, but misguidedly, tried to shield him from the discordances of life and the severity of his father. Nevertheless, both parents loved their gangling, stoop-shouldered 'boy' in different ways, and both as damagingly. They supervised his life to an intimidating degree so that any spark of initiative, any mood of impulsiveness had been carefully drained from his nature at a very early age, not maliciously, but in a kindly, patronizing way. And because it was done in kindness, albeit a stricter kindness from his father, the effects were more lasting. They had guided him into his first and only job at the age of sixteen, a job in the bank managed by a friend of the family; a good job, 'safe, respectable'. There he had stayed and worked his way up to the position of assistant manager through dogged perseverance rather than natural ability. He had refused any transfers that had cropped up from time to time, not wanting to move from the busy but pleasant enough town of Ringwood on the borders of the New Forest, and knowing his parents would not allow it anyway. He had not even felt disappointment when the manager, the friend of his family, had died two years before and he had not been offered the appointment. It hadn't even occurred to him that he should and he was puzzled by his father's beratement over the matter.

Edward had never really hated anyone before that; disliked, certainly, been afraid of, most definitely, but the feeling of hate had never before intruded upon his life. But Norman Symes, the new bank manager, had aroused passions in him that had never even been tickled before. Symes' philosophy in life seemed to be, if each day, I can bring a little unhappiness into the life of Edward Smallwood, then that day has not been in vain. Edward had mentioned it only once to his parents and the scolding of his father and the twittering sympathy of his mother had prevented him from ever doing so again. So he had borne the misery alone, a misery only experienced before in his school-days. He was well aware of how others on the staff enjoyed his discomfort in the presence of the manager, and so was Symes; that was half the trouble. The manager seemed to go out of his way to humiliate him in front of the others, as though his own prestige was enhanced by these spiteful remarks. Edward sighed at the thought of the little but nasty tribulations the day would bring. With a bit of luck, Symes would be on one of his 'get out and meet the local businessmen' exercises that day, and they would see little of one another.

Edward pushed back the bedclothes and groped for his glasses, hidden somewhere on the small bedside table. He tutted as he knocked over the half-drunk cup of weak tea his mother had brought up to him earlier. His day had already been ruined by the fog which had suddenly descended upon him while he was fishing on a remote bank of the River Avon at six o'clock that morning. Twice a week he cycled out to his favourite spot to fish, a pleasure of which even his parents approved. His doctor recommended early morning fresh air to help rid him of his constant catarrh, an ailment that caused him to snuffle most of his way through the day. He hadn't noticed the early morning fresh air relieving his congestion much, but had found great pleasure in the quiet solitude of the river bank and it helped him to steel himself against the oncoming day. He even regretted catching any fish and rarely baited his hook. Now and again he had to, to satisfy the serious enquiries of his father, but to pull a life from its watery existence left him with a feeling of sorrow.

But that particular morning, engrossed in his own thoughts, the yellow mist had stealthily crept around him and it was only when he suddenly realized he could hardly see the end of his line that he became aware of the fog surrounding him. A little frightened by the suddenness of it, he had quickly packed away his flask and fishing tackle and tried to find his way back to the main road. It had taken him a good ten minutes of bumping into trees, becoming entangled in low-lying bushes to do this. Fortunately, the fog did not extend as far as the main road and, more by luck than judgement, he found himself back in bright sunlight. His mother was, as usual, overly sympathetic when he reached home, and packed him off to bed for an extra hour's rest before he went off to work. He was surprised to find later that he'd actually dozed off for that hour, but the fog had left a nasty taste in his mouth which his mother's weak tea did little to dispel.

He found his glasses and rubbed his eyes before putting them on, frowning with a headache that he had just become aware of. He made his way to the bathroom, bidding his father good-morning as he passed his door, knowing the old man would be propped up in bed reading the *Telegraph*, munching toast, sipping tea.

'Good-morning, Edward!' came the brisk reply, and Edward repeated his 'Good-morning, Father.'

After a more thorough toilet than his earlier effort, he went back to his room and dressed, putting on the clothes his mother had carefully laid out for him the night before. He went downstairs, kissed his mother's proffered cheek, and sat down at the table, not feeling very hungry, despite his early morning exercise. He made an attempt to eat but had to push the plate away after a short while. His mother looked at the remnants of his bacon and eggs and then peered anxiously into his face.

'Aren't you feeling well, dear?' she asked.

'I'm all right, Mother, just not feeling very hungry, that's all.' He sipped his tea, looking down into his cup rather than at her concerned face.

'It's probably that nasty fog, got on to your chest.'

'No, I don't think so, Mother.'

'You know how weak your chest is,' she went on, ignoring him. 'Perhaps you shouldn't be out in the cold air first thing in the morning after all.'

He pulled away as she reached towards his forehead.

'No, really, Mother, it's nothing at all. I'm just not hungry, that's all.'

'Have you been to the toilet?'

'Yes, Mother.'

'Let me get you some of your father's laxative pills.'

'No, Mother, I've been.'

'Well, where does it hurt then, dear?'

'It doesn't hurt. I'm just not hungry!'

'There's no need to snap, Edward, I'm only trying ...'

'I'm not snapping, Mother.'

'Just because you're not feeling well, there's no need to take it out on Mother.'

'But I am feeling well, Mother. I don't feel like breakfast, that's all. I've got a bit of a headache.'

'Well, why didn't you say so? I'll get you some paracetamols, they'll soon shift it.'

'No, it's not that bad ...' But she was gone, returning seconds later with two white tablets in her hand.

'Now, take those with your tea. You'll soon feel better.' She would have actually popped them into his mouth had he not grabbed them and swallowed them quickly. 'Your father thinks it might be wise if you stayed home today in case you get worse.'

'Oh for goodness sake, Mother, it's only a slight headache!' Edward rose from the table, his face going a blotchy red from anger.

'Sit down, Edward.'

'Yes, Mother.' He sat down.

'You know how frightful you look when you lose your temper.'

'I didn't lose my temper,' he sulked.

'There's no need to make others suffer just because you're not well.'

He sat in broody silence now, knowing any further words from him would only prolong the conversation and his mother would begin to snuffle at his ingratitude.

'Very well, Edward. You may go off to work, but please don't come home complaining that you're worse at lunch-time.'

'No, Mother.'

'Try to eat something in your tea break.'

'Yes, Mother.'

'A biscuit or something.'

'Yes, Mother.'

Mrs Smallwood softened at the look of misery on her son's face. What would he do when they were no longer there to care for him? He was so dependent on them, needed them so much. She knew she would go first and Father really didn't understand the boy too well. Who would comfort Edward when his father scolded him? To whom would Edward turn? She bravely fought back the tears of pity and reached a hand kindly towards him and patted his head.

'Off you go now, Edward, or you'll be late.'

'Yes, Mother.' He rose again from the table and buttoned his jacket.

His mother looked up at him, forcing a smile, trying to hide the sorrow she felt. 'We love you, dear,' she said.

'Yes, Mother,' he answered.

The dull throbbing in his head increased as he walked through the town towards his branch of the Midland Bank. Several people who knew him wished him good-morning and he returned their nods with a polite but strained smile. He loved his parents dearly, but did wish they wouldn't fuss so, especially Mother. She would worry herself into an early grave if she didn't learn not to fret over him so much. He choked at the thought. Goodness, he must remember to buy her a box of chocolates on his way home to lunch to make up for this morning's rudeness. He knew she would be upset for the rest of the week if he didn't. He thought of his father and how, since his early retirement, he'd seemed to have become even more domineering, as though the running of their lives had replaced the running of his old office with the insurance company. Still, Edward knew his father had his interests at heart.

As he stepped off the kerb, the beep of a car startled him into reality. He jumped back, his heels catching on the kerb, and sat down heavily on the pavement, managing to cling to his briefcase. Edward stared up at the passing car and saw the driver's mouth moving vehemently through the closed window. The car's horn sounded angrily again as the vehicle sped onwards. He heard the sniggers of passers-by as he sat there, his knees together, ankles far-stretched, holding his briefcase into his lap. They turned away as he looked at them, none offering to help him to his feet. He stood up, brushing at the back of his trousers with his hand, a huge blush sweeping over his face to the top of his balding scalp. Making sure the road was clear, he crossed it, his embarrassment giving his stride added length.

Damn them, he cursed inwardly, years of bitter resentment welling up inside him. Damn them for laughing, damn the driver for swearing at him! Damn the whole town. Damn the Midland Bank! Damn Symes!

He saw a man ahead of him stoop to pat the upturned head of a friend's dog. Edward strode briskly up to him and gave the offered bottom a hearty kick. The man jumped up with an astonished yelp, the dog holding on to his hand with its teeth in fright. He yelped again and turned back to the dog, smacking its head with the palm of his other hand. Edward marched on, ignoring the confused barking and shouting he'd left behind. A trader came out of his shop to see what the disturbance was about and as Edward passed him, he whirled and dealt the inquisitive shopkeeper a swift kick to his seat.

The man turned, using both hands to rub his smarting bottom, and stared after the retreating assistant bank manager, not quite sure of what had happened. Edward made his way along the street kicking bottoms at random, his victims too astonished to do anything but stare after his tall, foot-thrusting figure. He rounded a corner and spotted the most enormous backside he'd ever seen trundling along ahead of him. It belonged to a neatly and, of course, expensively dressed businessman, whose wide neck bulged over a spotlessly white collar. He was the proprietor of one of the costlier hotels in Ringwood, a pompous man and a perfectionist in his trade; this morning he was on his way to complain about the quality of yesterday's lamb to the owner of the large wholesale butcher who supplied most of the hotels in the area with their fresh meat.

The sharp blow to his rear startled him from his irascible thoughts. He turned quickly to discover the source of his rude surprise, and to his amazement found a tall, bespectacled man glaring challengingly into his face.

The fat man was too dumbfounded to muster up much vehemence in his indignant demand. 'What do you think you're doing?' he asked.

Edward did not reply but raised his leg to kick the side of the fat man's thigh, his foot curling round in an attempt to reach the ample backside.

'Here, stop that!' The man backed away nervously.

Edward manoeuvred himself into a more favourable position for reaching the man's rear.

'Stop it!' But the blow had already landed. The hotel proprietor rubbed his reddening bottom with both hands, using friction to dull the smarting. 'I'll have the law on you! Who do you …?' He half-turned to trundle away, frightened by the gleam in the advancing Edward's eye. 'Get away!' he spluttered, his fat legs increasing their pace, finally breaking into a lumbering run. Edward followed, his longer legs easily enabling him to keep up and deal out more kicks to the large wobbling target before him.

They left a trail of bewildered onlookers behind them, who stared and then chuckled at one another in delight. It made a fine comedy, the contrasting figures of the two men – one tall and thin, the other, short and roly – adding to the ridiculousness of it.

The hotel proprietor was becoming winded, his bottom sore and bruised. His pleas for help from the people he passed met only with incredulity turning to amusement. Finally he saw what he had been praying for. A policeman was just emerging from a shop and striding across the pavement to his Panda patrol car.

'Help!' the fat man panted. 'Help me!'

Fortunately for Edward, he'd seen the policeman too and had slowed down to a casual stroll. The fat man grabbed the policeman by the arm and was stabbing an agitated finger towards the now-passing assistant bank manager.

'That man! That man has been chasing me!' The policeman calmly turned and looked down at the fat man tugging at his shirt sleeve then at the passer-by he was gesticulating towards. 'Stop him!' the fat man went on excitedly, fuming at the policeman's apparent casualness. 'He's been attacking me! Arrest him!'

The policeman had learned long ago never to accept anybody's word unless there were at least one or two unbiased witnesses to back up their story. There were plenty of nutcases around who loved to create a scene and involve perfectly innocent bystanders and this little fat man didn't seem at all right in the head. However, these matters had to be investigated and feelings soothed. 'Just a moment, sir,' he called to Edward.

'That's it, constable,' the proprietor said with some feeling of satisfaction. 'He's a madman. You lock him up.'

'Yes, officer?' Edward walked calmly over to the two men, a faint look of surprise on his face.

The policeman immediately became suspicious of the fat man still tugging at his elbow. It seemed pretty obvious who the madman was.

'Er, this man says you assaulted him, sir,' he said, almost apologetically.

'I beg your pardon?' Edward replied, slightly indignant, not ruffled, but as though curious about the insinuation.

'He says you attacked him, sir.'

'He did. He's been chasing me all the way down the street, kicking me.' The fat man stood immediately behind the policeman, as though expecting another kick at any moment.

'But officer, there must be some mistake,' said Edward. 'I've never seen this man before.'

The policeman tried to calm the fat man who was hopping up and down behind him. 'He's kicked my bottom black and blue. Do something, constable!'

'Kicked his –? Oh, really, officer.' Edward smiled benignly. 'I do have to be on my way or I'll be late for work, but if I can assist you in any way …?'

'Er, just a moment, sir.' The policeman turned to face the dismayed hotel proprietor. 'Have you any witnesses?'

'Well, of course, yes!' The fat man pointed at the onlookers. Unfortunately, they only chuckled and shook their heads at the policeman.

'I see,' the policeman said, putting away his notebook, a weary look on his face.

'But he did kick me!' wailed the fat man.

'I did not,' said Edward calmly.

'Well, I'm afraid, sir, there's nothing I can do unless you have witnesses,' said the policeman. 'Now why don't you go on about your business and let this gentleman go on about his.' He ignored the outraged spluttering of the proprietor and turned back to Edward, speaking in a confidential tone. 'I'm sorry about this, sir. It often happens with these people. They see a uniform and immediately use it to make themselves feel important. He's harmless enough.'

'I understand, officer,' said Edward, with concern. 'It's quite all right. Really.'

'They want to be noticed, that's all.' The policeman smiled. 'It's certainly original, though, saying you kicked his bottom all the way down the street.'

Edward smiled back. 'Yes, it certainly is.' Both men shook their heads in wonder.

'Well, good-day to you, sir,' the policeman half-saluted. 'He won't bother you again.'

'Thank you, officer. Good-day.'

As the policeman turned and walked towards his car Edward took two brisk steps after him, swung his foot back, and gave him a hefty kick in the seat of his pants.

Symes looked up at the clock on the wall for the fourth time that morning. Half-past ten and still Smallwood had not shown! The scowling bank manager expected the telephone to ring at any moment and Smallwood's distraught mother to pour out excuses about the condition of her son's ill-health as soon as he picked up the receiver. Well, he was coming to the end of his tether with that boy. Boy! He was a grown man, but he acted as though he were sixteen! True, he was conscientious enough, rarely made a mistake in his figures, but he was so godawful slow! And at the slightest sign of illness his mother kept him at home. He knew the previous manager had coddled the big, overgrown schoolboy because he knew the boy's father, but *he* certainly was not going to tolerate much more of his constant absenteeism, even though it was a treat not to have him snuffling around him all day. It was his irritating mannerisms more than his lack of initiative that annoyed Symes: the way he chewed on his fingers, the way he apologized for everything, the way he bowed and scraped to the customers. And the rest of the staff had no respect for him; they regarded him as a joke.

Anyway, his being away so often was a good excuse to get rid of him. Balmer could take his place, he was a good lad, always quick with an answer, always ready to take on more work. And with Symes getting out and about more, meeting the people as it were, he needed a good back-up man to handle the steady influx of routine work. It was a good policy to go out and contact the local businessmen and developers personally, rather than wait for them to come to him. See them in their offices, visit the sites, talk business over a good three-hour lunch – that was the way to treat good clients and drum up new ones. Now that the word had been whispered down from Head Office that the world of banking no longer sat on its backside and waited for the corporations to come to them, but went out and searched for promising enterprises themselves, they expected the managers of their local branches to do the same. He was sure that his own activities would soon come to their notice, and, unlike many of his counterparts in other branches, he relished the thought of being called to Head Office to build his reputation in the very fountain-head of the bank. Today he had some extremely important appointments to keep and the thought of Smallwood letting him down again filled him with annoyance.

There was a light tap on the door and his secretary poked her head through the smallest gap possible and said, 'Mr Smallwood's in, Mr Symes. I thought you might like to know.' She smiled smugly.

Symes looked up in surprise. It was usual for his assistant to be away, but very unusual for him to be late. 'Is he indeed? Well, would you inform him I'd like to see him right away, Mrs Platt.'

His secretary's head disappeared from view and seconds later, the door opened again to reveal Smallwood standing outside.

'Come in, come in. Don't just stand there,' said Symes, irritably. 'Why are you so late?'

Edward closed the door behind him and walked up to the manager's desk, not answering.

'Well, I asked you a question and I expect an answer.'

Edward rubbed his forehead with his hand and looked at Symes as though he'd never seen him before. 'I – I ran into a little trouble, sir.'

The little trouble had in fact amounted to being charged with causing a breach of the peace and assaulting an officer of the law, a charge he would have to answer to in court the following morning. A kindly police sergeant who knew his parents had advised him to return home and rest, knowing there was nothing malicious about him, and putting the morning's event down as 'nervous exhaustion or something like that'. But Edward hadn't gone home. He had something to do.

Symes studied his assistant's face and sighed resignedly. He supposed he was lucky that Smallwood had turned up at all – he certainly *looked* rather pale.

'All right, you know I've got a busy day on, tell me later. I've got an appointment at 11.00 and want to go down to the vault before I leave.' He gathered up some papers and put them away in his drawer. 'Reverend Peters made rather a large deposit today for his Restoration Fund. The man's an idiot – keeps his collections at the vicarage until he has a sizeable amount, then deposits it. Doesn't like to trouble me too often, he says.' He walked around his desk to the wall-safe. 'I've told him so many times he'll get robbed one day. Three hundred pounds he brought in today!' He dialled the combination and swung the safe door open, reaching inside for a brown envelope and the keys to the vault room. 'I don't want this lying around while I'm out all day, even though it's safe enough in here. You can never be too careful, Smallwood. Besides, as I told Mrs Platt, if all goes well, I may not even be back at all today.' He had arranged to meet his last client of the day on the golf course.

He closed the safe door again and twirled the dial. Walking towards the door of his office he glanced back over his shoulder at Edward who was watching him silently.

'Come along, man, I haven't got all day!'

They descended the steps to the basement room that contained the vault. Symes unlocked the heavy metal door and they entered the room full of small lockers, each containing confidential papers belonging to the bank's clients. The vault itself stood at one end, fairly small but large enough for a bank of this size. The bank manager hummed as he walked towards it, anticipating the pleasant day he had before him. Edward followed.

'Now, Smallwood,' said Symes, handing him the brown envelope containing the vicar's money, 'you've got a busy day ahead of you and I don't want to find any work left over till tomorrow. Get Balmer to give you a hand if you need it.' He was silent as he dialled the combination to the vault, concentrating on the figures, enjoying the position of trust he had. The last numeral clicked into place and he stood straight, a smile of satisfaction on his face. He swung the heavy, metal door open and turned to retrieve the envelope from his assistant. He frowned at the blank look on Edward's face.

'I want to have a word with you tomorrow, Smallwood. It concerns your future with the bank, so don't be away.'

He turned back and placed one foot inside the vault, crouching slightly because of its smallness, and reaching for a black box marked 'St Andrew's Vicarage, Rev Anthony Stephen Peters'.

'Did you hear me, Smallwood?' came his muffled voice. 'I don't know what's the matter with you today.'

Edward stepped forward and pushed at his employer's back violently. Symes fell forward, striking his head on the back wall of the vault, his legs buckling beneath him. He was just in time to turn over and through the daze in his head see the heavy door swing shut, leaving him in a frightening black void.

Edward twisted the dial several times then leaned his aching forehead against the cold metal. The air inside the vault would not last long. Certainly for not more than a night.

He walked from the room, locking the door behind him, and climbed the stairs to the ground floor. When he passed Mrs Platt's desk, she looked up enquiringly.

'Where's Mr Symes?' she asked.

'Oh, he's gone for the day,' answered Edward. 'He went out the back way to his car, said he was late.'

'But what about his briefcase?'

'Said he didn't need it.'

Mrs Platt clucked in annoyance. 'He kept me late yesterday typing those papers. He said they were important for today.' She banged her keyboard, huffily.

'Mrs Platt,' said Edward.

She looked up at him.

'I'm going home now. I don't feel well.' He walked away from her. 'I doubt if I'll be back.'

∎ 9 ∎

'It seems we may owe you an apology, Mr Holman.' Wreford looked across his desk at Holman, indicating that he should take the seat opposite.

'You mean you've had more news from the school?'

Chief Superintendent Wreford paused before he spoke, a worried frown on his face. 'Indeed, we have,' he said.

Holman let a weary sigh escape from his lips. It was 4.00 a.m. and he had spent a restless night in a small detention room, furnished only with a chair and a hard bed. He'd been woken from his fitful doze by Barrow who had brought him up to Wreford's office without saying a word. Both CID men looked tired for they had spent much of the night talking with various police stations around the Salisbury area in an effort to find out if any unusual incidents had occurred in their areas recently. And if anyone had reported fog.

The report from Andover concerning Redbrook House had spurred them into this activity.

'Tell me what's happened,' said Holman.

'From a class of thirty-seven, one boy managed to escape without any serious injury from the fire. He was in a state of shock – it was assumed that the fire was responsible – but later, he began to say some strange things.' Wreford swivelled his chair so he faced away from Holman. 'At first, the doctors thought he was hysterical, but certain peculiarities about the bodies brought out caused them to listen more closely to what the boy was saying.'

Barrow broke in. 'Some of the bodies were naked; although the fire would have burnt the clothes there would have still been bits of material charred into the skin.'

Wreford continued: 'It looks as though the fire had been deliberately started; a can of petrol was found near one of the bodies – the body of a man. The man had one arm. They're sure it was the deputy headmaster, a man named Summers.'

Holman felt sick; could *he* have prevented it?

'It also seems that many of the bodies had been mutilated,' said Barrow, grimly.

Wreford turned his chair back to Holman. 'From what they can gather from the boy, it started out as a normal PE lesson. Then the boys turned on their sports master and beat him unconscious. Then the other teacher – Summers – came in, and they attacked him. The boy gets hysterical at this point and it's not very clear what happened next, but apparently the other boys seemed to have gone completely berserk, beating and –' he paused. 'And mutilating each other.'

'Oh, Jesus. If only I'd got to you sooner.'

'You're not to blame, Mr Holman. It happened fairly early in the day. You couldn't have known.'

Holman shook his head. 'No, but it was in the back of my head. Something disturbed me when we were actually in the fog. But what about this boy – is he insane?'

'The doctors think not. Hysterical, yes, and who knows what effect this experience will have on him? But they're sure he's not mad. And so are we.'

'Why? What makes you think so?'

'Something that helps to confirm your story about the fog.'

Barrow, sitting on the edge of his Chief Superintendent's desk, spoke: 'He was ill on the day of the outing. The matron wouldn't let him go because he was just getting over a chill. He was in the gym yesterday, but wasn't taking part in the exercises because he wasn't considered well enough. He was sitting at the back, watching his friends. Luckily, they took no notice of him, but he witnessed the whole bizarre episode! Poor little sod.'

The room was quiet for a few moments before Holman asked, 'What happens now?'

'We've spent most of the night talking to police stations in the area, trying to trace the whereabouts of the fog now, enquiring about any unusual events occurring recently on their patches.' Wreford held up several sheets of paper containing scribbled notes. 'There are plenty of strange things that have been happening, but then there always are. Our problem is which of them we can attribute to the fog.'

'Then you do believe me?'

'Let's say we don't disbelieve you. We needed more evidence – '

'More evidence?' Holman exploded, but Wreford held up his hand.

'We think we have that evidence. A hatchet murder a few days ago: a man named Abbot chopped up a wealthy landowner, his wife and his two women staff, then he cut his own wrists. He had a slight grievance against the landowner, we understand, but hardly enough to account for this butchery. In the same area, a farmer was trampled to death by his cattle, a vicar ran amok in his church. A few other incidents, relatively minor, but nevertheless, they could all add up to the same thing. We've asked for any further reports to be sent directly to us and we're now trying to locate the fog.'

'But it could be anywhere.'

'We'll soon find it.'

'All right, so what's your next move?'

'We compile all the facts, then I contact the Commissioner with a view to presenting the evidence to the Home Secretary.'

'But in the meantime, half the countryside will have been affected!'

'No, Mr Holman. I intend to move fast.' He leaned towards Holman and said sternly, 'But I must have the evidence to show it.'

'You've got it!'

'I have a few scribbled notes and reports on their way to me.'

'Then make a verbal report!'

'I intend to. But I have to have a clear case to get to the Home Secretary!'

'A clear case? You're waiting for something else to happen, aren't you?'

'Frankly, yes.'

Holman was dismayed. His mouth dropped open in disbelief.

'But that doesn't mean I'm not taking any action,' Wreford added quickly. 'I've alerted all our forces in the West Country – '

'Telling them what?'

'Telling them to be on the lookout for a dangerous gas and to move in immediately they hear of any disturbances, big or small.'

'But the people should be warned. They should be cleared from the path of the fog!'

'First we have to locate the fog, Mr Holman. And then we have to make sure it *is* responsible for these outbreaks.'

'But you said you believed me!'

'And so I do, but I have no power to do as you ask. And to get any authorization at all, I have to convince my superiors of the danger.'

'So you're going to wait for more people to die.'

'Within the next few hours, the fog or gas – whatever it may be – will begin to take effect on the people it has already been in contact with and then we should be provided with insurmountable evidence. There would be nothing we could do about these particular people now, anyway.'

'Except lock them up for their own good!'

'Be your age, Mr Holman. What would we do? Broadcast a message for anyone who has been in contact with fog recently to please report to their nearest police station? At best, we'd be a laughing stock; at worst, there'd be panic throughout the country. And for what purpose? What if the fog has now dispersed? What if it is now ineffective? What if we find the fog is not to blame after all, that the things that have happened are only unrelated, freak occurrences? What then, Mr Holman? Will you take the responsibility?'

Holman sprang to his feet and thumped the desk with his hand. 'We can't sit around doing nothing!' he shouted.

'I've told you my course of action,' snapped Wreford. 'Now please sit down and try to be reasonable.' He spoke more soothingly. 'Think about it, Mr Holman. We only have your evidence about the fog, and let me be frank, you were only released from hospital the other day after what appeared to be a nervous breakdown. Bear with me, let me assemble the facts before I put forward a case. As it is, I've stretched my neck out by ordering a full alert in the West Country. There'll be all hell to pay when my chiefs hear about it in the morning.' He glanced at his watch. 'I mean later today. I'm just asking you to be a little more patient.'

'I don't have much choice, do I?' said Holman, resting his elbows on his knees and clenching his hands together. 'Very well. But now I want to see Casey. I want to go to the hospital.'

Wreford smiled kindly. 'Of course, but I'd rather you stayed here.'

'Like hell!' Holman sat up again.

'I need you here. Let me get Detective Inspector Barrow to ring the hospital and see how she is. They wouldn't let you see her at this time of the morning, anyway.' Wreford nodded to the young detective, who disappeared from the room.

'I'm sure you understand our position,' Wreford continued smoothly.

'I'm sure I don't,' answered Holman.

Barrow returned a few moments later, a look of concern on his face. He ignored Holman and walked round the Chief Superintendent's desk to whisper in his ear.

'Oh, for God's sake!' stormed Holman.

'It's all right, Mr Holman,' said Wreford, quickly, not wanting the man's temper to boil over again. 'Barrow has rung the hospital and they informed him Miss Simmons was discharged a few hours ago in the care of her father.'

Holman stared blankly at him.

Wreford looked embarrassed. 'I'm sorry. Apparently, there was nothing they could do. The girl seemed perfectly all right, if a little dazed, and her father insisted he took her home despite their protests. They would have liked to have kept her in under observation for a short while, but unfortunately they couldn't prevent her from leaving.'

The blue-green Rover sped through the quiet streets towards Highgate, its three occupants grim and silent. Holman stared blankly out of a window, his tired mind in a frenzy of concern for Casey, an empty, sick feeling in the pit of his stomach. Was she all right? Had the effects of the gas worn off? She really hadn't had too much exposure to it.

Barrow sat beside him in the darkness, his feelings a mixture of disbelief and curiosity. It certainly was an unusual case and he still did not know if he was sitting next to a lunatic or a crusader. The man was certainly hot-tempered, but not exactly raving. And his incredible story certainly had some cold logic to it. You had to take a step back because you found yourself accepting it, and then, when looking at the whole affair objectively, *that* was when you realized how ridiculous it was. He was glad it was Wreford who would be taking responsibility and he would only be carrying out orders. Too soft, was Wreford, always had been. Shrewd, though, no question of that. But he'd made a big mistake this time, trusting this prick! He'd stuck his neck out all right, but not as much as he'd led Holman to believe. Wreford had alerted the local police forces, certainly, but only to be on the lookout for any adverse weather conditions, *particularly* fog, and to report such to him direct. He'd persuaded a friend in the central control room, where information from all over the country was relayed, to keep him informed throughout the night if any reports of an unusual nature came in from Somerset, Wiltshire, Dorset or Hampshire. Unofficially, of course.

He'd have to explain his request for weather reports, and he'd better have a good reason ready, but that was as far as he'd risked his reputation. And if – just *if* – Holman's incredible theory was correct, Wreford was covered; he'd acted, with discretion, on the information he'd received.

Barrow glanced at his watch. Ten past five. Jesus, he was tired. A couple of hours kip in one of the detention rooms hadn't done him much good, and all for what? For the benefit of this creep. Still, it had been uncanny about the school. Maybe …? No, now he was falling for it! Holman's voice instructing the driver interrupted his thoughts.

'Straight to the top of Highgate Hill and turn left through the village. Then it's a side-road off to the left. I'll tell you where.'

The police car began its ascent up the long hill, the gradual dawn light giving the streets a lonely and chilly atmosphere. They reached the village and turned left towards Hampstead, Holman peering through the window, anxiously looking for the road Casey and her father lived in. He spotted it and told the driver to turn off, the tension inside him beginning to mount. Again, he asked himself: had the effects of the fog worn off? He would soon find out.

He tapped the driver's shoulder when he saw the house. 'That's it,' he pointed.

It was a large house, set close to the road, the small front garden only nominal, but compensated for by the huge landscaped garden to the rear. Casey's father was a wealthy man, deputy-chairman of one of Britain's biggest unit trust finance houses and with interests in many other commercial enterprises, not the least of which was property development. On the few occasions they'd met, they had taken a dislike to one another, because both knew they were vying for the same person – Casey. Holman had been surprised at the intensity of Simmons' hostility; he understood his possessiveness after losing his wife, but the affection he displayed towards Casey made Holman feel uncomfortable. It seemed a little too intimate for a father-daughter relationship. When he later questioned her about it, Casey had been genuinely amazed that he should think there was anything odd about her father's attitude. Amazed, then angry at his implication. Holman had backed off, realizing his own jealousy could be colouring his view of the situation. But Simmons had made it quite obvious that Holman's interest in his daughter was not at all welcome and on one occasion had gone to great lengths to tell him so while Casey was out of the room. Holman's icy response had done nothing to soothe the situation between the two men and, as a consequence, he'd never been back to the house again while her father was there.

Now as he stared up at the dark windows of the house, he cursed the older man's stupidity in insisting Casey be released from the hospital so soon. If she had harmed herself – He pushed the unwelcome thoughts from his mind.

'Looks like they're all in bed, doesn't it?' remarked Barrow caustically.

Holman ignored him and got out of the car.

'You wait here, Tom,' he heard Barrow behind him tell the driver. Holman walked towards the front gate to the house, then stopped to let the Detective Inspector catch up.

'Do you really want to wake them up?' Barrow asked.

'Yes,' answered Holman, and walked towards the impressive white front door. His sense of foreboding increased when he discovered it was open. He pushed at it with a trembling hand.

▪ 10 ▪

AT THAT PRECISE MOMENT, JUST OVER A HUNDRED MILES AWAY, MAVIS EVERS stood barefoot on Bournemouth beach and contemplated suicide. She had driven through the night from London, fighting the tears that welled up, obscuring her vision, threatening to send her red Mini crashing off the road. She did not want to die in the wreckage of a car so that her friends, her parents would never know whether it had been deliberate or accidental. She wanted them to know she had taken her own life. Her death, unlike her life, had to have some meaning. Even if it was only Ronnie who fully understood that reason.

Ronnie had destroyed her. Ronnie had made her fall in love. Ronnie had made her lose her innocence.

Twice she had to pull over to the side of the road and stop, unable to stem the flood of tears that had abruptly burst forth. Once she had to stop as fog drifted into her path, and she had wept as she waited for it to pass.

Why had her lover done this to her? After living together for two years, sharing each other's lives joyfully, excluding anyone else from their intimate happiness. Laughing at the world. Until Ronnie had suddenly, and irrevocably, drifted away. It had taken a mere two weeks, the first signs when Ronnie had sorrowfully but firmly rejected her caresses, then the arguments, the questions, the pleading, and finally, the terrible revelation. Ronnie had fallen in love with someone else. A man. She had fallen in love with a man.

The irony was that it had been Ronnie who had seduced Mavis. Seduced her and introduced her to a kind of love she'd never known. A private kind of love – the kind that can only be shared by two women. A love not acceptable to most, but more binding by those it touched because of its illicitness.

Mavis had known Ronnie years before when they were both children living in Basingstoke. Their parents had been friends and they would often all go off together at weekends to the coast. The times they spent at Bournemouth were the times Mavis treasured most for it was there, in a boarding house where the two young girls had to share a bed, that Ronnie first introduced her to the delights of her own body. She was eleven, Ronnie was twelve. Their parents had gone out for the evening, promising the girls crisps and lemonade if they were good, hoping, in fact, that they'd both be sound asleep when they returned. As the girls lay there, talking over the events of the day, whom they both liked, whom they mutually disliked, Ronnie had suddenly asked Mavis if she had ever touched herself. Perplexed, she had asked where?

Shyly, Ronnie had put her fingers between Mavis' legs, then quickly drew them away. Mavis had been surprised and excited by the strange tingle that had run through her, and touched herself in the same place again, giggling at first and enjoying the sensation. Ronnie had asked if she could feel her there again and she'd agreed, a flush now spreading through her body, but on the condition that she could also touch Ronnie. They'd spent the following two hours in exciting, girlishly innocent, mutual masturbation.

It only happened on two other occasions after that, neither girl placing any significance on the act, both enjoying it for what it was – a happy diversion. They'd seen little of one another in the subsequent years, Ronnie's parents having moved to London, visiting each other perhaps three or four times a year, neither mentioning their earlier intimacies, Mavis at least realizing it was just a stage in development they'd gone through together. Eventually, Ronnie had moved away from her parents, finding a flat for herself further into town, nearer to her job, nearer to her social life. They had corresponded for a while, but even this dwindled to cards on birthdays and at Christmas. And then, not long after her twenty-first birthday, bored by her job, bored by her parents, and bored by her lack of boyfriends, Mavis decided London might be the place for her too. She contacted Ronnie to see if she knew of any reasonably priced flats available, and her friend wrote back suggesting she stayed with her until she found something. So, a little nervous of the sprawling city, Mavis moved in with Ronnie. She was slightly in awe of her friend of long ago when they met at Euston, for Ronnie had developed into a beautiful, sophisticated young woman – on the surface, at any rate. Mavis was soon to learn that she assumed this pose for people she didn't know very well, and this, for a brief time, included Mavis.

Mavis was amazed by Ronnie's wide circle of friends, several of whom were actually *coloured*, and tried desperately to fall in with their cynical and blasé attitudes towards their lives, but after a few weeks, she realized she would never fit naturally into their set. She found their values phoney, their ideals superficial.

She disliked being an imposition on her friend whom she found, underneath the gloss, was the same understanding, lonely girl she'd once known, so she searched for a suitable flat of her own. Disappointed by the depressingly poor accommodation she had been offered, she finally broke down one night after she had returned from another fruitless expedition into gloomy bedsitter land. The flats she had liked were way above her price range; the ones she could afford were too run-down and seedy for words. She had got soaked to the skin in the steady London drizzle and at the first kind words of sympathy from her friend, her emotions had bubbled to the surface.

Ronnie had perched on the arm of the settee on which Mavis was sitting and put her arms round her distraught friend's shoulders, telling her not to worry, that they would work something out later. She told her to get out of her wet clothes and to take a quick hot bath, then to hop into bed and she would bring her a good stiff drink. After weeping a little while longer, with Ronnie gently stroking her damp hair, she pulled herself together, smiled her thanks through her tears, and went into the tiny room that was used as a dressing-room and spare bedroom. She changed into her dressing-gown as Ronnie ran the bath for her. She soaked for ten minutes, allowing the hot water to warm her body and soothe her distraught nerves. She scrubbed herself and washed her hair, then briskly dried off on one of Ronnie's luxuriously soft towels. Her friend had done well for herself since she'd moved up to London, working as a secretary to the chairman of an American tobacco company, later becoming his personal assistant. The rent for the flat must have been quite high if the prices of the humble flats Mavis had come across were anything to go by. And her clothes were expensive and plentiful, the extent and range of her wardrobe stunning Mavis into open-mouthed admiration. But she was still basically the same sweet friend Mavis had known all those years ago.

She went to her room and heard Ronnie's voice from the kitchen. 'You get into bed and I'll bring you in some hot chocolate and that stiff drink I promised you!'

'Thank you,' Mavis called back, taking the towel from her wet hair, rubbing her head with it vigorously. She brushed out the knots until it was long and straight, clinging closely to her neck and shoulders. Unwrapping her dressing-gown from her body, she caught sight of herself in the full-length mirror, her pink flesh looking round and pure in the soft glow of the reading lamp. She studied herself for a few seconds, content that her figure, although not stunning, was firm yet supple, curvy, but certainly not fat. She ran her hands along her sides and inwards, over her hips and across her soft midriff, then up towards her breasts. As they travelled over the gentle swells, she became aware of Ronnie watching her from the doorway.

She quickly dropped her hands and flushed when she realized her nipples had stiffened to tiny pink points.

'Your body is lovely,' said Ronnie quietly.

Mavis was embarrassed. 'Oh, I'm no Venus, but I suppose it's okay.'

'It's beautiful.' Ronnie moved into the room and set the tray with hot chocolate and two brandies on the small dresser by the side of the bed. She pulled back the blankets and patted the pillow. 'Come on, jump in before you catch cold,' she said, holding the blankets open and moving aside to allow Mavis past.

As Mavis slid between the sheets, Ronnie sat on the edge of the bed, only partially covering her friend's body with the blankets, leaving her breasts and most of her tummy bare. Mavis felt herself reddening even more as Ronnie unashamedly studied her, a faint smile on her lips.

'Remember when we were kids?' Ronnie asked.

Mavis remembered, only now the memory seemed to take on a special meaning. She nodded her head.

'Your body was nice even then,' Ronnie went on, her gaze lingering on the two tiny rosebuds of flesh that were now even more pronounced. Strangely, Mavis no longer felt embarrassed by her look, but began to take pleasure from it, feeling the same rising excitement she'd felt as a child. Her heart was thumping, her nerves trembling. She neither thought of what might happen next, nor denied the thought; her mind was peculiarly alive, yet numb.

Ronnie raised her hand to Mavis's cheek. 'I've missed having a friend,' she said, her fingertips barely touching the skin, but delicately sensual because of it.

'But I thought you had lots of friends here.' Mavis's voice was small and hesitant.

Ronnie's eyes flickered with sadness for an instant, but the look was barely perceptible. 'Yes, I've lots of friends. But not a real friend – as you were.'

Mavis looked down. 'I'm sorry.'

'Don't be,' Ronnie smiled. 'You're here now.'

Her hand lightly travelled down and rested on Mavis's neck. The grip tightened slightly, then relaxed again.

Mavis found her breath quickening, her small breasts beginning to rise and fall. She raised her own hand to the hand resting at her neck and squeezed the fingers gently, leaving it there.

Ronnie's eyes glistened with what could have been tears and she drew in her breath sharply. Then her hand began to travel down again, tracing the fine skin with feather-like fingers until it found the soft mound she was looking for. Mavis shivered as the palm closed over her breast, and her nipple was trapped between two fingers. Ronnie leaned forward and touched the pink tip with her lips, kissing it gently then moistening it with her tongue.

A glow was enveloping Mavis, starting at her breasts and spreading down to her stomach, then down, down till it was between her thighs. Even the extremities of her limbs were tingling pleasurably, a subdued kind of electricity running through her entire body. She shut her mind from any thoughts of what it all meant. It didn't matter, its meaning wasn't important.

Ronnie had now put her arm around Mavis's back and pulled herself towards her, her lips brushing the naked girl's neck, kissing and biting very, very gently. Mavis slid further down in the bed allowing both of them to lie side by side. As yet, she had not touched Ronnie, a little afraid to do so, a tiny part of her subconscious telling her this would be the final irrevocable relinquishment.

Ronnie's lips finally found hers and they kissed, still softly, all their movements soft, as though passion would make it ugly. Ronnie thrust her tongue between Mavis's lips and was answered by a hesitant counter-thrust. Her hand found Mavis's breast again and this time, its touch was more urgent, gliding from one to the other, not wanting to neglect either. Mavis began to moan slightly as Ronnie's hand began its slow descent down her body towards the place that was so ready – and yearning to receive it. It reached the flat tummy and Ronnie spread it for a moment, feeling Mavis's muscles quiver. Then she continued her unhurried but anxious journey until she reached the little curls of hair, the matted triangle that hid the path to the centre, and her fingertips worked their gentle way through it.

Mavis was disappointed when, instead of descending between her thighs, the hand passed on and stroked the fleshy tops of her legs. She realized it had been an exquisite tease when the fingers began their ascent, this time along the beautifully sensitive inner sides of the thighs. She opened her legs slightly, so that the journey would not be hindered – and then Ronnie was there.

Mavis moaned aloud as Ronnie's fingers crept into her vagina and spread her moistness upwards. She clutched at Ronnie fiercely, finally giving in fully to the passion that had been aroused in her, eager to be touched, to be fondled – even to be hurt. Her fingers pulled at Ronnie's blouse until she found the breasts that Ronnie had so patiently waited to have touched, now wanting her friend's body as much as she had wanted Ronnie to have her own.

Mavis found her hand moving down until it was between her friend's legs. Her lover's legs! The thought increased her desire so that it was almost unbearable, and soon their senses stretched to a frenzy, their cries of joy merged into one long shuddering moan.

They lay naked in the bed and talked into the early hours, each reluctant to sleep, both eager to explore the other's mind and body. They made love many more times that night, in many different ways, but now each way was gentle and had little to do with lust. They discussed the thought that they were lesbians, yet neither could feel any guilt or shame. Ronnie admitted sadly that she had had affairs with women before, but none had touched her emotions as this had, none had been anything other than a means to satisfy passion.

Mavis confessed she had only once been made love to by a man and although she had enjoyed the experience, it had meant nothing emotionally. Both were touched by the other's disclosures; and both realized they had found something unique.

For two years Ronnie and Mavis had been happy sharing a life, not living as man and wife, but just as lovers; neither had any inclination to adopt a masculine role, it wasn't that kind of relationship. Their lovemaking excluded any artificial contrivances; they attained satisfaction only from the other's body, both retaining femininity, both regarding their intimacy as pure.

But then, only two weeks ago, a change had come over Ronnie. It was rapid and alarming. She had rejected Mavis's caresses, falling into long brooding silences, unable to disclose the reason for her sullen moods. Several nights she stayed out, refusing to tell Mavis where she had been, until last night, after being away for three consecutive days, she had come back to the flat and brokenly told her friend that she no longer loved her, that she had met someone who had swept away hidden fears, made her see that the physical love she had always dreaded was a wonderful and deeply moving act. She had fallen in love with a man, and had allowed that man to make love to her.

Ronnie had wept bitterly as she explained that she hadn't wanted it to happen, but Philip had been so kind, so gentle, that her inhibitions about men had melted and, it seemed, her body cleansed. These last words hurt Mavis terribly. Cleansed! Had their love been dirty? Had their sleeping together, holding one another – had it all been revolting? She screamed at Ronnie, implored her not to leave, begged her on her knees. But she had been pushed away, violently, and it was the violence of it that stunned her most, penetrated the part of her that refused to accept her lover's rejection. Ronnie had never used physical force against her before; she had thrown her from her as though this physical action represented the breaking of their ties. Mavis had crawled towards her again, weeping in her own shame, and tried to put her arms around her, tried to bury her head in Ronnie's breasts. Ronnie had allowed her to do so for a moment, but when Mavis's hand reached further in a desperate effort to bring back their previous closeness, she had jumped up, knocking Mavis to the floor, screaming that she must never touch her again.

That was when Mavis knew she had lost. Her sorrow turned to rage when she thought of how she had been cheated. It was Ronnie who had led *her* into this way of life, seduced her! How could she now cast her aside as though it had meant nothing, a phase she had gone through? She had found a 'normal' love and left Mavis unwilling now for any other kind of love. What would she become? A lonely, embittered lesbian? She cried out in self-pity.

Ronnie had walked to the door and opened it. Before she left, she had said, 'I'm sorry, Mavis, I'm so sorry. But I have to go, Philip is waiting for me downstairs in his car. He doesn't know about us, and I never want him to. Perhaps someday, when I'm sure of him, I'll tell him. Believe me, Mavis, I didn't want this to happen – I didn't know it ever could – but it's the right thing. I think we were wrong. Forgive me, darling. I hope someday you'll find what I have.'

When Ronnie had left, Mavis remained in a heap on the floor, weeping bitter tears, shocked by her lover's cruelty, appalled at the fate she saw for herself. She finally recognized their affair for what it was – two women living together in an abnormal relationship. She had never accepted the fact that she was homosexual, but somehow, Ronnie's leaving took away all the sensitivity of their mutual inclinations and revealed Mavis in her true light. A lesbian!

It was a fact she now felt unable to live with. The guilt that had lain hidden deep in her mind came to the surface and for the first time she felt remorse. But still she cried for Ronnie, wanted her there in her arms, to be comforted by her, to be possessed by her, and her shame increased because of it. She rose from the floor, her face puffed and blotchy, and curled up on the sofa, her knees drawn up to her chin. She thought back over the two years, the intimacies they'd shared, the plans they'd made. She went back to when they were younger, friends who giggled over their innocent secret. She thought of the first time, in Bournemouth, where now, she realized, their union had been unknowingly sealed. Why had everything changed? What was it that caused people to destroy each other?

Then she had decided what she would do. Fighting back her tears, she went down to the little red Mini they had bought, never thinking there would come a day when their possessions would have to be divided as would a divorced couple's.

She drove through the night to Bournemouth, stopping occasionally when she could no longer stem her tears, her only consolation now in what she was going to do. And once, she was forced to stop because of heavy fog.

And now, Mavis stood barefooted on the beach, looking at the moody grey sea in the dawn light. She had stopped crying, her emotions not drained but held in check, because there was no point in tears if she were going to die. She still saw the image of Ronnie before her: her sad-smiling face, her soft brown eyes that reflected sorrow even when they were laughing.

Mavis walked towards the sea, leaving her shoes on the beach behind. The water chilled her with its coldness, but the chill in her spirit was greater. She waded in further, the water rising to her knees, the tide pushing against her as though urging her to go back. It reached her thighs, causing her thin skirt to cling to them, then touched the part of her body that Ronnie had adored and kissed so often. She sank deeper and now the sea seemed to be drawing her in instead of pushing her back, welcoming her into its enveloping, icy depths. She found it difficult to breathe because of the combination of cold and the pressure of the water now around her chest. And the fear she had begun to feel. She stopped, straining to keep her balance against the now unfriendly water.

Death. Death was so absolute. And would there be pain before her body succumbed to the final blackness? Would her body resist the pull of death in those last seconds, panicking to regain the breath of life she'd deliberately let escape? Would her body betray her and fight to preserve its fleeing spirit, causing lingering agony instead of swift and final oblivion? And the pain, the mental anguish she would cause Ronnie, making her responsible for her death. Did she want to destroy Ronnie as well as herself? She still loved Ronnie, she didn't want to hurt her as she had been hurt. Perhaps there was still a chance; perhaps Ronnie would find she wasn't meant for heterosexual love. Perhaps, after a few weeks, she would return to Mavis, disillusioned with his maleness, yearning for the understanding and physical comfort only her friend could give her. There *had* to be a chance! And Mavis would be waiting, ready to forgive her, eager to hold her close while Ronnie pleaded with her to take her back. And their love would be stronger than ever, because both of them would know they were irrevocably tied.

The black sea around her was so frightening!

She struggled to turn around in it, desperate to reach the shore, no longer wanting to die. She nearly lost her balance, and cried out in terror. She was not a good swimmer and if her feet were swept from beneath her she would find it difficult to make her way back to the beach. It would be so pointless to die now, now that she knew that she had not necessarily lost her lover, that their bond could bring them together again.

She staggered back, careful not to lose her footing, feeling as though she were in a nightmare where her legs had become lead and would not allow her to run from the death behind.

She gradually reached a point where the lapping water was only waist deep and stopped for a moment to regain her breath, relieved that she was safe, her mind taking on a curious lightness now that the burden of death had been lifted.

As her chest heaved with the effort, her eyes widened uncomprehendingly.

There were hundreds – could it be thousands? – of people climbing down the steps to the beach and walking towards her, towards the sea!

Was she dreaming? Had her mind become unbalanced because of the distress she had been through? The people of the town were marching in a solid wall out to the sea, making no sound, staring towards the horizon as though something was beckoning to them. Their faces were white, trance-like, barely human. And there were children among them; some walked along on their own, seeming to belong to no one; those who couldn't walk were being carried. Most of the people were in their nightclothes, some were naked, having risen from their beds as though answering a call that Mavis neither heard nor saw. She looked behind her, out towards the brightening horizon, but saw only the black, threatening sea.

They were advancing on her now, and she realized there *were* thousands of them, pouring from houses, hotels, side streets, in a huge moving mass, their footsteps the only sound they made, and these muffled for the majority were barefooted.

Mavis saw an old woman in the front line stumble and fall and she gasped in horror as the crowd passed over her, trampling her into the sand. Their pace did not slow as they entered the sea and they advanced in a solid human wall. She looked to the right then to the left and saw the wall extended for as far as she could see. The scene, its significance, was too enormous for her to understand. She thought only of getting away from the path of that crushing multitude.

She backed away, but the sea behind was just as threatening. She began to scream at the people as they drew nearer, like a child who is to be punished screaming at an advancing parent. But still they came on, oblivious to her cries, unseeing. She realized her danger and ran towards them in a vain attempt to break through, but they forced her back, heedless to her pleas as she strained and beat against them. She managed to push a short path through them, but the great numbers before her were unconquerable, pushing her back, back into the waiting sea.

Mavis fell and struggled desperately to regain her feet. In doing so, she knocked down a small boy and immediately went down again to pull him to his feet. He stared ahead, not seeing her, not even knowing he had just fallen.

She was knocked again, and this time went under, losing her grip on the boy, her lungs filling with salty water. She emerged fighting for breath, blinded by the salt water, screaming and kicking out in panic. What was happening? Had she killed herself and was this the hell all suicides entered? She fell to her knees again, and this time, as she attempted to rise, other bodies fell on top of her. She squirmed around beneath the water, becoming tangled in other arms and legs. Air escaped from her lungs as she tried to scream and then felt a tiredness beginning to overcome her. Her struggles became weaker and she finally lay there in the blackness, bodies stumbling over her, some falling on top of her, pinning her to the soft sea floor. Her eyes were open as the last bubbles of air escaped from her lips. The terror had gone. There was no pain. There was no recollection of her life, no memories to taunt her in her dying. Just a misty blankness. No thoughts of God. No questions why. Just a descending white veil. Not a veil of peace, nor one of horror. Not even one of emptiness. Nothingness. Free of emotion and free of coldness. She was dead.

*

The inhabitants and the holidaymakers of Bournemouth came from their homes, hotels and guest houses in their thousands and made for the sea, filling the streets, pouring on to the beach. The fog that had ruined their day yesterday was killing them that morning. They walked into the sea to drown like lemmings, the people behind them climbing over the dead bodies that were heaping up on the sea-bed. People who, for various reasons, could not walk, killed themselves in other ways. Hundreds could not reach the sea because it was too full of others who had already drowned, and these were later pulled back screaming from the beach by people who rushed to the seaside resort in a vain attempt to minimize the destruction.

The fog rejected the sea either because of its coldness or because the winds were too strong for it. It moved inland again, as though it were a living thing, leaving behind its evil, never settling in one place, always moving, as though searching for something.

▪ 11 ▪

HOLMAN ENTERED THE DARK HOUSE, TRYING TO MAKE AS LITTLE NOISE AS POSSIBLE.

'It would be a better idea to ring the bell and wake them up, wouldn't it?' came Barrow's voice from behind.

'No,' Holman whispered.

'Why the hell not?'

'I don't know. I just don't think it's a good idea.'

'All right. But this is breaking and entering, you know that, don't you?'

'You can wait outside if you want,' Holman whispered back fiercely.

'Oh, no, mate, I'm going to hang on to you.'

'Then keep quiet and follow me.'

'I'll keep quiet for now, but later – '

Holman turned away, ignoring the CID man, angered by his arrogance. He moved towards the lounge and quietly pushed the door open. It was empty. He closed the door again and made his way down the hall, towards the room he knew to be Simmons' study. He thought he heard a muffled sound as he turned the handle, but Barrow's urgent whisper distracted him.

'There's a light on upstairs.' Barrow had already begun to climb the stairs and Holman hurried after him. He took the steps two at a time in an effort to catch up with the swift-moving policeman.

'It's her father's bedroom,' he told Barrow as he reached him.

'We're going to look pretty silly when we find him getting dressed for work,' the Detective Inspector sneered.

'Better we look silly than end up with a knife in our throat.'

'My God, and she's *your* girlfriend.'

'I told you, she's not responsible. For the moment, she's out of her mind.'

'Huh!' Barrow snorted. 'Someone is.'

Holman frowned at him. 'You still don't believe me.'

'Listen, mate. I'm under orders from Wreford to play along with you. It doesn't mean I have to believe you!'

'Barrow, you're a bundle of charm.' Holman grinned without humour. 'But you've got your orders – so play along with me.'

He turned away from the fuming policeman, and mounted the rest of the stairs, pausing at the top to listen for any sound. Barrow joined him and they moved stealthily towards the thin bar of light coming from beneath the bedroom door.

Holman slowly turned the handle, involuntarily holding his breath, and gently pushed the door open.

The light came from a small bedside lamp, so its brightness did not hurt their eyes. A figure lay in the bed. All they could see was the head, the eyes looking up towards the ceiling; the face was grey and sunken, the pallor of death about it.

'Simmons!' Holman hurried over to the bed and stopped before the prone figure, his worst fears realized. The shocked eyes slowly turned towards him, and the pale lips moved as though to speak. Barrow pushed past him and leaned towards the older man.

'What's happened, sir? Where are you hurt?'

For a moment the eyes looked at the policeman then swivelled back towards Holman.

'Y-you did this to her,' he said in a weak voice. 'You m-made her do this.'

Holman was too stunned to say anything. Was he now to be blamed for this? He knelt beside the older man.

'Where's Casey – Christine?' he asked.

'Why, why did she do this?' Simmons' eyes looked down as though indicating at something near his stomach.

Barrow yanked back the bedclothes and both men gasped. The end of a pair of scissors protruded from Simmons' stomach, and his pyjamas and the bedsheets were stained with blood.

'Jesus, Jesus!' breathed Barrow. He turned towards Holman. 'I'm going to get Jennings to radio for an ambulance. There's still a chance we can save him if we're quick. Prop his head up with a pillow so he doesn't choke on his own blood. And don't touch those scissors. Don't try and pull them out!' He disappeared through the door and Holman heard him leaping down the stairs, recklessly, two or three at a time.

Holman pulled a blood-soaked sheet over the wound, feeling sick, not at the sight of the injury, but at the thought that it had been Casey who had perpetrated it. He bent his head towards her father as he tried to speak, his words only a whisper, barely audible.

'W-why did she do it? I loved her, she knew that.'

'She wasn't responsible,' Holman told him, speaking in a soft voice, as though words could cause the man further injury. 'She came in contact with a – a poisonous gas that affected her mind.' Simmons' eyes looked puzzled for a moment, his brain not understanding the words but then accepting them almost with relief. She had tried to kill him because she was ill – it hadn't been an act of hate; that was enough for his weakened senses for the moment. He began to speak again. 'I brought her home from the hospital. They told me what you'd done to her.' His face became almost fierce, but the effort was too much and its lines fell back into an expression of pain.

'No, I didn't do anything to her,' Holman assured him. 'It was the gas, it made her unwell.'

'I – I brought her home. She seemed dazed. She kept putting her hands to her head as though she were in pain. They didn't want to let her go, but I knew she'd be better off with me. I put her to bed and sat there talking to her. She didn't seem to hear me. I told her things I've never spoken to her about before, but she didn't seem to hear me.'

He began to choke and Holman became worried that blood was rising in his throat. He slid his hand beneath the older man's head in an effort to stop the blood reaching his mouth, not really knowing if it would prevent asphyxiation.

Simmons managed to stop coughing and lay there breathing heavily. 'I loved her,' he went on, 'perhaps too much.'

Holman said nothing.

'And – and I told her something I'd never told her before tonight.'

'Don't talk any more. Try to save your strength.' Holman was hardly listening for he'd noticed fresh blood seeping through the sheets.

'No, I must tell you, Holman. You've a right to know – you love her too.' His hands tried to reach the scissors beneath the sheet, but fell back limply to his sides. 'I – I'm not her father, Holman. Her bitch of a mother told me who her real father was just before we were divorced. But it made no difference to me, I loved the child too much. I fought tooth-and-nail for custody, and her mother could never claim in court Christine wasn't mine because she would be admitting her own infidelity. And she was too shrewd and greedy for that.' Holman could almost detect an embittered smile on the pain-wracked face.

That could explain certain things about the man's attitude towards Casey. He looked on her as his daughter, but because he knew she wasn't, another element had crept into their relationship. An element that Casey hadn't been aware of and Holman had only suspected. But it was still sickening, even though there were no real blood ties. Even in his injured state, Holman felt a loathing towards the man.

'I told her tonight – that's why she did this to me,' Simmons murmured, more to himself than Holman.

'No, it wasn't because of that. I told you, it was the gas.'

'It was too much for her I suppose in her shocked state.' He was too deep in his own remorse to listen to the younger man. 'I woke up, I don't know how long ago – a couple of hours, I suppose – and there she was, standing over me. I'd left on the lamp in case she needed me during the night, so I could see her plainly; she was just looking down at me, expressionless, her hands behind her back.' A tear trickled from the corner of his eye. 'I – I put out my arms for her to come to me.' His eyes that had been staring at the ceiling now looked guiltily at Holman. 'I misunderstood.'

Holman frowned. Misunderstood?'

'She came towards me, then,' he began to tremble uncontrollably, 'then she pulled back the bedclothes and I saw the scissors slashing down ...' His voice broke as he relived the experience.

The younger man's thoughts were not clear. Simmons seemed to be blaming himself. He'd said he'd misunderstood; had he though? Oh, no, not that. Surely he couldn't have thought Casey had come to him for that kind of love? How stupid, how blind could he be? Poor Casey, to go through that ... A cry from downstairs interrupted his thoughts. It had sounded like a man's cry, probably Barrow's.

He left the dying man and rushed to the top of the stairs. The sounds seemed to be coming from the study below, sounds of crashing furniture and shouts of alarm. He flew down the stairs and pushed open the study door. And then he stopped.

Barrow was on his hands and knees on the floor, blood oozing from a wound in his scalp. Casey stood above him, a wicked-looking shard of glass in her hand. The remnants of the large antique mirror lay shattered around her feet. She raised her arm, ready to plunge the pointed glass down into the back of Barrow's neck.

'Casey!' Holman cried.

She turned to look at him, for an instant a flicker of recognition showing on her face. Then she smiled and walked towards him. He stopped, still wary, and reached out a hand to her. 'Casey,' he said softly.

With a snarl that changed her smiling face into a grimace of pure hatred she threw herself at him, the weapon slashing for his face.

He ducked under her arm and slammed his elbow into her back knocking her into the wall. He knew from their previous struggle he would have to use force to subdue her. She sprang away from the wall, her clenched fist bleeding from the glass she held, and leapt at him again, the tip of the shard catching his cheek and drawing a thin line of blood. Catching her wrist, Holman smacked her face viciously, sending her to her knees, but still holding on to her. He increased the pressure on her wrist causing her to cry out in pain and to drop the glass. Swiftly pulling her to her feet again, he turned her back to him and pinned her arms behind her. She screamed and fought like the mad woman she was, but this time he showed no mercy and used all his strength to hold her there, bruising her arms with his tight grip.

Barrow had staggered to the door now and was watching them in amazement. 'Christ,' he gasped. 'And to think I didn't believe you.'

'Don't just stand there, you bloody fool!' Holman shouted at him. 'Get something to tie her up with!'

Barrow disappeared from the doorway and returned a moment later with a length of curtain rope. The driver of the police car came through the front door as they were tying the girl's hands.

'Ambulance is on its way, sir,' he said to Barrow, not raising an eyebrow at the scene before him.

'Right. There's an injured man upstairs. Go and stay with him – I think he's had it.' The young detective rubbed the back of his neck. 'Bloody cow,' he groaned. 'I was just coming back into the house when I saw the study door closing. I reckon she was just leaving the house when we drew up and she ducked into the study as we came in. She was probably trying to creep out again as I came back.'

'What happened?' asked Holman, leading the girl into the vast lounge where he sat her down on a long, leather settee. She seemed docile now.

Barrow followed them. 'I ran into the study and then she hit me. She must have been standing behind the door with that bloody mirror in her hands, waiting for me. She knocked me silly, anyway. All I can remember is crawling around the floor trying to get away from her. Bitch!'

'Watch your mouth, Barrow,' said Holman, angrily. He'd had enough of the policeman for one day and was prepared to take a swing at him himself if the man continued in his aggressiveness. He knelt before Casey, taking her pale face in his hands. She stared past him, over his shoulder, her eyes wide and unseeing.

'Casey, darling, can you hear me?' he asked tenderly. 'Can you understand me?'

Her eyes looked at him coldly. 'Bastard,' she said.

It was as though she had hit him. The word was said with such icy vehemence it shocked and hurt him deeply.

'She doesn't know you, Holman, can't you see that?' said Barrow, not unkindly.

'No, she doesn't.' Holman's eyes clouded. 'Will she ever know me again?'

This time, Holman went with Casey to the hospital. Her father was taken by ambulance to the Whittington Hospital on Highgate Hill, while she was returned in the squad car to the Middlesex Hospital. Detective Inspector Barrow left Holman anxiously discussing the girl with the doctor who had treated her previously, and went back to make his report to Chief Superintendent Wreford at New Scotland Yard.

Barrow found the complex building in an uproar and was staggered himself when he caught drift of the news. He hurried to Wreford's office, who confirmed his worst suspicions and sent him rushing back to the hospital to bring in Holman. Reluctantly, Holman agreed to accompany him again to the Yard on the understanding that Casey was to be kept under the strictest supervision and having advised the doctor to get in touch with the hospital in Salisbury where he had been treated. The doctor had agreed but wanted to know more of Holman's case. Barrow interrupted, telling him he would have to obtain all his information from Salisbury. Holman was needed urgently at New Scotland Yard in a matter which involved more than the well-being of one girl.

He would say no more as they drove back towards Westminster, telling Holman he would find out soon enough and that he himself had yet to hear a full report. Finally, seated in Wreford's office, Holman was told the astonishing and frightening facts.

Wreford wasted no time with preamble. 'We've little time for apologies, Mr Holman,' he began bluntly. 'I've heard briefly what happened to yourself and Detective Inspector Barrow earlier this morning and I sympathize with what you've been through, but events have taken on a greater significance.

'Reports have been flowing in through the night about certain strange occurrences. They weren't channelled through to me of course until I made a request for such reports. I must tell you now, that I did this unofficially.'

He held up his hand at Holman's look of surprise. 'We won't go into it now, but you must understand, I couldn't just take your word for it; I had to play safe.'

'All right,' said Holman bitterly. 'I suppose I should be grateful you even took an interest.'

Wreford cleared his throat and looked down, for a moment embarrassed, then the snap was back in his voice as he went on. 'Well, the reports began to accumulate and pretty soon, it wasn't just me, but the whole building involved. They seemed to be just individual incidents at first, some minor, others a deal more serious, but together they began to take on a pattern. They seemed to be happening in a ragged line between Wiltshire, Dorset and Hampshire. They're pretty curious in our control room of course as to why I had put in an unofficial request for reports around those areas. I'm saving my answer for the Commissioner for Police; we have a meeting in,' he looked at his watch, 'ten minutes. I want you to be there.'

Holman nodded his agreement.

Wreford's face became even more grave as he went on. 'Most of these incidents were isolated, usually concerning one person, occasionally two or three, certainly no more. But just under an hour ago, the most alarming news of all came through. We're all very much in the dark at the moment – we're getting a fuller picture by the minute – but it seems incredible, totally unbelievable.'

'For Christ's sake!' said Holman impatiently.

'At around 6.00 this morning, virtually the entire population of Bournemouth left their homes and walked into the sea in a mass suicide attempt.'

Silence filled the room. At last, Holman managed to say, 'It's impossible.'

'Impossible, yes, but it has happened. Over 148,820 people. And that's not counting the thousands that were on holiday there. Men, women, children – all drowned. They're still trying to drag those who couldn't reach the sea back from the beach. Poole Harbour is just crammed with floating bodies, the shores around Bournemouth are littered with corpses.'

Barrow, who had been quiet up to now, spoke. 'What about the fog, sir? Has it been sighted?'

'I've issued instructions to locate it but naturally the local towns have enough on their minds without worrying about fog. I couldn't give them the reason yet without causing a large-scale panic. I have to see the Commissioner before I do that. But one thing I did learn: Bournemouth was covered in a thick blanket of fog yesterday.'

The Commissioner of Police wasted no time in getting in contact with the Home Secretary and arranging an immediate meeting. He'd listened grimly to Holman's story, occasionally interrupting to ask a relevant question, but not once voicing a negative opinion. Holman asked that the Minister of State for Defence and his own chief, the Parliamentary Under-Secretary of State for the Department of the Environment, be present at their meeting with the Home Secretary, remembering the meeting Spiers had arranged before his death.

Twenty minutes later, he found himself relating his story again in a large, oak-panelled room in Whitehall surrounded by the Ministers and their chiefs-of-staff, having questions fired at him in rapid succession, the Parliamentary Under-Secretary of State for the Army angrily rejecting his insinuations that the military in Salisbury might have some answers as to the cause of the fog.

The Home Secretary banged his fist sharply on the heavy table before them. 'Gentlemen, we will not have arguments at this stage. James, I want a full report on your establishments on Salisbury,' he ordered the Under-Secretary for the Army. 'I want to know of all recent experiments carried out there, particularly the Broadmeyer Experiment.' Holman caught the troubled look that passed between the two men.

'Richard,' the Home Secretary turned to the Minister of State for Defence, 'we'll need troops to clear Bournemouth and to control any panic that is bound to break out in the surrounding area. Commissioner, have your men located the fog yet?'

'No sir, but they have orders to report directly to me as soon as they have.'

'I suggest you get on to the Met Office and find out shifts in air currents.'

'They're helping us locate the fog now, sir.'

'When you've found it, you'll want to know where it's going, won't you?' the Home Secretary said without a trace of sarcasm in his voice.

'And what do you intend to do once you've found it?' Sir Trevor Chambers, Parliamentary Under-Secretary of State for the Department of the Environment asked dryly. It was a question that had been on all their minds. What could be done against a drifting, insubstantial mass? How could it be confined? How could it be destroyed?

'There are methods,' replied the Minister for Defence. 'Some were developed in the war by the RAF, but the progress of radar has made it unnecessary for this day and age. But the old methods are still usable.'

'Let's find it first,' the Home Secretary said impatiently. 'I want to know in which direction it's heading and *I want its path cleared of people.'*

'My God,' said Sir Trevor, 'that's going to be a massive operation.'

'I'm well aware of that, but what would you suggest?' He allowed no time for an answer. 'Mr Holman, I want you to put yourself at the disposal of the Department of Health's Medical Research Department. You are one victim of the fog who has recovered. I want to know why. It could save the lives of countless others.'

'Er, might I suggest that our chaps from Porton Down work in collusion with the Research Department?' asked the Under-Secretary for the Army.

'Porton Down?' Sir Trevor Chambers raised an eyebrow.

'Yes, our Chemical Defence and Microbiological Research Establishments are based there.'

'Porton Down, Salisbury?' Sir Trevor persisted.

'Yes, that's right.'

'This whole thing is beginning to smell bloody fishy to me!'

The Home Secretary held up his hands to dispel any arguments that might take place. 'Gentlemen, I've asked James for a full report on his work in Salisbury and I will not tolerate any disputes amongst ourselves until I have read that report. For the moment, there are more urgent matters to be put in hand. Now then, we will use the Chemical Defence and the Microbiological Research boys – we'll use anyone who can be of the slightest help in our efforts to combat this menace. Is that understood?'

For the next forty minutes plans were made to deal with the extraordinary situation; plans of action were laid down for the evacuation of people in the path of the threat, and ways of dispersing the fog were discussed. Men left to carry out their urgent duties, others were called in to receive instructions that puzzled them, but which they carried out anyway. The Commissioner was handed a slip of paper and interrupted the proceedings.

'They've located the fog,' he announced sombrely. 'It's moving back north. Towards Winchester.'

▪ 12 ▪

Captain Joe Ennard took his seat in the cockpit of the giant Boeing 747, greeting his flight officers with a forced grin.

'How was your day off?' his Flight Engineer called out.

'Terrific,' Joe said without enthusiasm. He thought of his day with Sylvia, the day that had started so well and ended so miserably, while he ran through the checks before take-off. Pressing his transmit button, he asked Departure Control for permission to start his engines. He was acknowledged and permission granted. He began pulling switches with his First Officer and the jumbo jet rumbled into life. The noise increased the dull ache he had at a point just above his eyes.

He had spent the previous day in the New Forest with his wife in an attempt to recapture some of the zest they'd had for each other earlier in their marriage. She'd always known about his casual affairs over the past few years but had tried to accept them because of her own shortcomings. At thirty-eight his sexual drive had hardly diminished from the time he was twenty-five. Whether it would have been the same if their marriage had taken a normal course, he didn't know, but the fact that she was so repulsed by the sex act had seemed to strengthen his demand for fulfilment rather than diminish it, despite the fact that he still loved her, he had been forced to look elsewhere for the important missing part of their marriage.

The irony was that he felt the guilt. She never spoke of his unfaithfulness, never blamed him for his misconduct. Often he found her quietly weeping, but they were never tears of accusation; only tears of regret. It had started two years after their marriage when they'd lost the baby. It hadn't been her fault but nobody, not even the doctors, could convince her of that. Joe had been present at the birth and even now he could see the beautifully formed human being that had emerged from her womb, so tiny, so perfect – so dead. The doctors had all the answers, of course, but answers couldn't bring the baby back.

Afterwards she was afraid that if she ever became pregnant again, the same thing would happen, and this had led to her frigidity. Even the precautions he took could not allay her fears and it wasn't too long before he gave up trying. But they had still loved each other deeply and his casual affairs were just that. There was never any emotional involvement, just a physical act that offered him some release. Was it possible to be unfaithful yet still love your wife? He knew the answer, at least in his case, was yes.

And then yesterday. A day that was meant to bring them closer, to seal the gap that he felt was developing between them. The years of infidelity were finally beginning to take their toll and he had decided that he would no longer look outside his marriage for physical comfort. He had brought her down to the New Forest, where they'd spent so much time before they were married, to pledge his love and loyalty to her, that he would not let his body betray them any more, that there was still enough in their marriage to tie them together, to begin to build on again.

But in the fog that had suddenly enveloped them, she had told him she was leaving. She had found someone else who was prepared to live with her on her terms, who wouldn't need others to satisfy his desires, who would be content to love her for herself and not her body.

He had been too dismayed even to plead with her.

That morning, he had felt a strange relief, almost as if a heavy burden had been lifted from his shoulders. He was free. It wouldn't be him leaving her but the reverse. He didn't have to worry about her breaking down because of the parting, she would be happy now. Perhaps it had been this which had bound him to her all these years; not love, but fear of hurting her when she'd already suffered so much. He even found it in himself to ask about the man. Who was he? Did he know him? Was he married? What did he do? He asked with no malice, with no thoughts of righteous indignation and she sensed this and answered his questions. His name was Kevin – Joe couldn't remember the surname – no, he'd never met him, he was divorced, he was a radar engineer. She'd met him in London while Joe was away on one of his flights. They'd known each other years ago, before Joe, and hadn't seen each other since. She was on a shopping spree and had bumped into him outside Heal's in Tottenham Court Road. He was in his lunch break and he asked her to join him. She had.

Kevin had told her of his divorce three years before, but she'd said little of her relationship with Joe. At the end of the lunch, they both knew they'd felt a mutual contact with each other, reached out and been met as neither had been for years. He told her proudly of the new field he was helping to develop in radar and that at the moment he was based in London's giant GPO Tower, promising her if she met him the next day he would give her a private tour of the fantastic building.

She broke her promise, but six days later, when Joe was away again, she rang his office at the Tower and arranged to meet him. That had been six months ago, and their feeling for one another had grown till neither wanted to live apart any longer.

She was surprised when Joe smiled at her and wished them both happiness. Was it really so easy to end ten years of marriage?

Joe had left the house and driven to Heathrow Airport, the dull headache successfully excluding thoughts of his failed marriage from his mind. He didn't bother to report the headache to the medical officer, considering the dull pain only a minor discomfort.

The 747 trundled towards its appropriated runway, taking its place in the queue behind the other waiting aircraft. The jumbo, weighing over three hundred and fifty tons and, although not fully-loaded, carrying nearly three hundred passengers, quivered with unreleased power.

Joe wiped the moisture from his forehead as he waited for the command from the Control Tower to get his aircraft moving. As always, it was a relief when the order came. The thrust from the four giant engines pushed him back in his seat and the jumbo rolled down the runway, gathering speed by the second. After six thousand feet he was able to ease back on the stick and bring the nose up, allowing the four main bogies to take up all the weight. Then the huge, clumsy beast was off the ground, gaining height, an impossible spectacle, but a triumph to man's ingenuity.

The crew breathed their sighs of relief as the 747 circled the airport in an effort to increase height. There was always that tense moment when they wondered if the monster would rise or flop back to the ground, despite their years of experience that told them the former would inevitably be true.

Miller, Joe's First Officer, grinned across at him. 'New York City, here I come. And Beryl, my dear, am I going to fly you!' He laughed at his own joke. Beryl was an air hostess belonging to a rival airline he had met at the John F. Kennedy Airport. Her company's over-used slogan always tickled him.

He was surprised at his Captain's lack of response to his joke. 'You okay, Skip?' he asked.

Joe Ennard stared ahead, his hands tightly clutching the stick before him.

'Hey, Captain,' called the nervous young Flight Engineer. It was only his second flight with Captain Ennard and he was still slightly in awe of the man. 'Er, we're a little off course.'

Miller didn't even have to check his instruments. He could tell visually by merely looking down at the ground, still only ten thousand feet below. 'You should be going that way,' he said humorously, pointing over his shoulder with his thumb. 'Skip? Hey, Joe!'

He reached across and shook Ennard's arm. 'You okay? Come on, Joe, snap out of it!' He leaned forward anxiously to look into the rigid man's face. He shook him again.

The blow from the back of Joe Ennard's hand knocked him back into his seat and drew blood from the corner of his mouth. 'Terry, get him!' he yelled at the Second Officer as he turned to his own controls and tried to wrest them from the Captain's iron grip.

The Flight Engineer unbuckled his seat belt and hurried forward, not sure of what he was going to do, reluctant to lay his hands on the Captain.

'Pull him away from the controls!' Miller shouted at him, his efforts to gain control of the giant machine useless without the Captain's co-operation.

Terry grabbed at Joe's hands and tried to yank them away, but the grip was too strong. He put his arm around the Captain's neck and squeezed, pulling back at the same time. The First Officer tried to prise Joe's fingers away from the stick. None of them heard the discreet but urgent tapping on the locked cockpit door; the Chief Steward was also worried about the direction of their flight.

Suddenly, in a swift movement, Captain Ennard released himself from his safety belt and rose as much as his cramped position would allow. A powerful man, and more powerful because of the madness within him, he lashed out at his First Officer, blinding him with his fist, sending him into a heap back in his seat. He drove an elbow into the Flight Engineer's ribs, causing him to lose his grip and double up with pain. With another blow from his forearm, he sent him crashing back down the cockpit.

Miller was holding his head, rubbing his eyes so that he could see again. He screamed at the half-conscious Flight Engineer, 'Get the gun! For God's sake, shoot him!'

They kept the illegal gun hidden behind the transmit unit, a secret agreement among themselves and many other aeroplane crews, as a protection against the increasingly frequent hijackings.

His words were cut off as a two-fisted blow landed on the back of his exposed neck. He slumped forward on to his controls, unconscious.

Joe Ennard took his seat again and reached for the stick. The angry mechanical sound of the voice from Heathrow's Control Tower buzzed through his head, filling the cockpit, but he ignored it. He looked down at London, searching for the tall familiar landmark, his eyes glazed but still seeing.

A grin of satisfaction spread across his features, a strange grin that bared his teeth, made his face skull-like. He'd found what he'd been looking for.

Terry slowly became aware of the frantic banging on the door. The Chief Steward had heard the commotion and was anxiously demanding that the door be opened, oblivious now to the fact that some of the passengers would hear. The Flight Engineer pulled himself groggily to his knees and looked towards the front of the cockpit. He couldn't see Miller, but he could see the Captain hunched over the controls as though looking through the windows at something below.

He felt the aircraft go into a dive as the pilot pushed forward on his stick, felt all four engines being given full throttle and the great machine thrust forward with unbelievable power. Desperately, he reached for the hidden gun and fumbled with its safety catch. He crawled towards the pilot's seat, holding it before him in a trembling hand.

'Stop!' he called out futilely. 'Pull her out or I'll shoot!'

He staggered to his feet, using the back of Captain Ennard's seat to lever himself up. He raised the gun to the back of the Captain's head, imploring him to pull back on the stick. Then his eyes fell on the building that was rushing towards them. He screamed as he squeezed the trigger.

Before the sound of the gunshot, before the Captain's brains mixed with blood were spattered on to the instrument panel in front of him, Terry thought he heard him say something. It sounded like, 'Good-morning, Kevin,' but the Flight Engineer had no time or desire to reflect on the words for his head was filled with its own terror.

The 747 jumbo jet exploded into the tall GPO Tower with a mighty roar that echoed throughout London, over three hundred and fifty tons of crashing metal that toppled the building as though it were made of children's blocks.

▪ 13 ▪

HOLMAN WAS DRIVEN TO THE MIDDLESEX HOSPITAL TO PICK UP CASEY WITH Detective Inspector Barrow acting as escort. The Home Secretary had made him a valuable man; the one person they had so far who had recovered from the effects of the mysterious fog. He would have to be examined and his brain patterns studied to find out how he had recovered – and if he were now immune. Casey was necessary too, as the nearest person suffering from the effects. Corpses would be flown up from Bournemouth by helicopter for autopsies to be performed on them in an attempt to discover exactly what damage had been done to their brain. Others, still living but insane, would be selected and flown up for further tests. But at that precise moment, John Holman and Casey Simmons were the two most important people in England.

From the hospital, they were taken by ambulance to the Ministry of Health building that was strangely situated at the Elephant and Castle. Holman sat in the ambulance looking down at Casey, who was under sedation, holding her hand in both of his, worried over the paleness of her features. He looked at his watch: 9.45. God, he was tired! He had thought it would be at least around noon. People were still scurrying off to work, their day just beginning, just hearing of the devastating news from the seaside resort. Would they panic? They'd certainly have to be given some answers. Who would they blame? The government? The Russians? The Chinese? Maybe some other countries for a change. Were there any friendly countries left? Even America was becoming hostile.

What excuse would the government give? Pollution? Would that play its part? God knows, he'd found enough evidence of the damage pollution could do in his job, but nothing of this magnitude, obviously. And the public weren't that stupid any more. The media had broadened their minds, given them an insight, however vague, to things that years ago would have been completely unheard of, let alone believed. They would suspect a chemical, a poisonous gas, mistakenly unleashed by some scientific laboratory somewhere, and if they didn't, he felt sure the media would point them in this direction.

If it hadn't been so catastrophic, he might have enjoyed watching the officials trying to worm their way out from the responsibility. But then, there was always the doubt, the doubt that governments all over the world could so cleverly play on. Even he wasn't sure if it was a man-made or freak-of-nature phenomenon; the tiny doubt in the back of his mind would prevent him from going all out to lay the blame on the Ministry of Defence's doorstep. But if he ever found concrete proof…

A muffled explosion jerked him from his thoughts. The ambulance pulled to a halt and as he opened the back doors, he saw that all the other traffic crossing Waterloo Bridge had done the same. As he climbed down the steps, Barrow came running around from the police car that had been escorting them.

'Look,' he pointed, 'over there!'

Holman followed his gaze and saw a great ball of smoke and flames rising from the direction of the West End. It snaked up towards the blue sky, a black, billowing cloud, violently red at its base.

'What the hell is it?' Holman asked nobody in particular, his question echoed by the other drivers who had emerged from their cars and were standing perplexed, staring into the sky.

'I'm not sure,' said Barrow, evenly, 'but it's coming from around the area of

Tottenham Court Road. It might be just in front of the GPO Tower. If it isn't in front…' He left the sentence unfinished.

Holman turned to stare at him. More muffled explosions came from the same spot and they could see flames shooting into the air.

'It's beginning to happen here,' said Holman quietly.

'What? No; we've had no fog here!' Barrow retorted. 'There's no connection, can't be!'

'I wish we could be sure of that.'

Several groups of people had gathered and were talking excitedly, gesturing towards the black-stained sky. Barrow walked over towards one of the groups and asked some sharp questions. A minute later, he returned to Holman.

'There's your answer,' he said. 'The people over there saw a jumbo jet circling over London. They said it was very, very low so they realized it was in trouble. Then it went into a dive. They think it hit the Tower, one old boy swears it did.'

Holman shook his head in disbelief. 'It's incredible. The school, Bournemouth – and now this.'

'I just told you, it's probably got nothing to do with the fog!'

'I wish I could believe it, Barrow. I wish I could.'

Even in the bright sunlight, Holman felt a shiver run through him.

He was surprised at the vast basement area that was used for medical research beneath the Alexander Fleming House building. Even as a civil servant himself, he hadn't known of its existence. They were met by the Chief Medical Officer, a fat, jovial man who explained, 'I'm going to take you downstairs and hand you over to Mrs Janet Halstead, Principal Medical Officer for the Research Council. It's a completely different department from ours, but they occupy that part of the building for good reasons. Their divisions of research are spread all over the place, the majority in London, but many as far as Scotland. When they need to get together on a project – and it has happened quite a number of times in the past I can assure you – they get together here. Needless to say, you're bound by the Official Secrets Act to keep this to yourselves.' He laughed at their serious faces. 'It's not that secret, you understand, but there are reasons for not letting it become public knowledge.'

They entered a lift, Casey having been taken through a more private entrance to the rear of the building.

A plump middle-aged woman wearing a white coat greeted them when the doors opened again. She stepped forward and shook Holman's hand without waiting for an introduction.

'You must be Mr Holman,' she said, smiling. 'I've been reading about you from your file your department sent me. Your photograph doesn't do you justice.'

Holman smiled back weakly, completely disarmed.

The Chief Medical Officer spoke up. 'This is Mrs Janet Halstead. I'll leave you to it then, Jan?'

She nodded and asked Holman and Barrow to follow her as the lift doors closed on the grinning Ministry of Health man. This was the Principal Medical Officer? Holman couldn't help but smile. She was certainly sweet, but she looked no brighter than the average housewife. The day would prove her to be otherwise.

'I take it Sir Geoffrey has explained why we brought you to this building. There are quite a few people we want to examine you, and it's a bit more convenient to bring them here than to cart you all over the country. I don't know if you've heard yet, but a State of Emergency has been declared. We have to find some answers, very, very quickly.'

She led them into an office and asked them to sit. She perched on the edge of a desk. 'Now, the first thing. Have either of you eaten this morning?' She smiled at their shaking heads. 'Right, we'll soon fix that. Not much for you, I'm afraid, Mr Holman. We have a few tests to put you through that won't allow it. However, we'll give you enough to sustain you. We don't want you passing out on us, do we?'

Holman felt himself almost mesmerized by her words and began to relax, a combination of his own tiredness, the soft chair he was sitting in and the easy manner in which she was talking to him.

'While you're eating, you can tell me all that's happened to you – and I'd appreciate it if you tried to leave out nothing. The smallest thing could be of the greatest importance.' She picked up the telephone and pressed a button, then ordered breakfast for them both.

Holman snatched a glance at Barrow who seemed distinctly uneasy in his non-active role.

'Oh, please call me Jan, by the way,' she told them as she replaced the receiver. 'Now, as I've already said, we have an extremely busy day ahead of us here. We have every facility we need and the best medical brains are either already here or on their way. I can promise you, we've wasted no time in the past couple of hours.

'Let me tell you briefly who will examine you. I won't mention all the names because I can't remember half of them myself, but most of them are from these Units: Cellular Disorders; Infectious and Immune Diseases; Psychiatry and Nervous Disorders; Biochemical Parasitology; Neurobiological Studies; Brain Metabolism; Cell Mutation; Molecular Genetics; Immunochemistry and Cellular Immunology; Molecular Pharmacology; Neurological Prostheses and Neuropsychiatry.' She smiled at Holman. 'Two others: Environmental Radiation and I believe the Ministry of Defence is sending us some of their Chemical Defence and Microbiological researchers.'

He sat there stunned and frightened and she hastily tried to reassure him. 'As you can see a lot of these divisions won't even come into it, we just have to have them at hand in case they're necessary.' She smiled her disarming smile again.

Holman was silent for a moment, a troubled look on his face. Then, he spoke. 'Two Units stuck in my mind, one I think you tried to hide among the others.'

She still smiled. 'And they were?' she asked.

'The obvious one was Environmental Radiation. The other was Cell Mutation.'

She looked at him keenly and said without any hint of patronization: 'I can see you're very sharp, Mr Holman – may I call you John?'

He nodded.

'Yes, I did bury it among the others, I didn't want to alarm you. As I said, many of these divisions of investigation will be a waste of time. I think Cell Mutation will be one of these – but we have to be sure. You do see that? We can't leave anything to chance. As for Environmental Radiation – well, that's an obvious one in this day and age, isn't it?'

'But what exactly can you find out from me? I mean, I'm cured, aren't I?'

'First of all, information, John. I've already spoken on the phone to the doctors who treated you in Salisbury. Their description of your symptoms was helpful, but I'm afraid very inadequate. By examining you, we can find to what extent your brain was damaged – if it was your brain. I think you are cured, certainly, but we may still find lingering signs of what caused it. Like a blow would leave a bruise, a cut would leave a scar.'

'But wouldn't that necessitate surgery?'

She laughed. 'No, I don't think so, not in your case.' She became serious once more. 'We have plenty of dead bodies we can examine in that way.'

'And what about Casey?'

'Miss Simmons? We'll try to cure her.'

The door opened and their breakfast was wheeled in on a trolley. Janet Halstead reached behind her and switched on a tape recorder.

'Now, John,' she said. 'Take your time and tell us everything you know about this mysterious fog. Start at the beginning and try to leave nothing out.'

The rest of the day was just a blur to Holman. He was probed, tested, examined, interrogated. He was given an electrocardiograph to test his heart; his entire body was X-rayed; a radio-opaque substance was injected into the arterial system of his brain to show up any deformation of the normal pattern in order to trace any space-occupying lesion; electrodes were placed on the surface of his head over the occipital and frontal region to discover any evidence of a tumour; a small amount of cerebrospinal fluid was drained by a needle introduced into the subarachnoid space below the termination of his spinal cord and tested. All these, and many more tests, were carried out on his and Casey's bodies and by late afternoon he was allowed to fall into an exhausted sleep.

He awoke several hours later to find Barrow slumped in a chair by his bedside, soft snoring noises droning from him. As Holman sat up, the policeman stirred and quickly woke, casting an anxious eye towards the bed. He grinned and rubbed his face.

'You were out for the count,' he said to Holman.

'You weren't doing too bad yourself,' Holman answered flatly.

'Yeah, but I'm a light sleeper.' He looked at Holman ruefully. 'Look, what about calling a truce? I know I was a bit rough on you, but it was pretty fantastic, wasn't it?'

'Yes, it was.'

'Well, I'm sorry.'

'Okay, let's forget it. Actually, I'm surprised you're still around.'

'Special duty, mate. I'm your bodyguard. You're an important person. You've got another one outside.'

'Do they think somebody's going to assassinate me, or – do they think I'm going to run away?' His face took on an incredulous look as he hoisted himself up further in the bed.

Barrow was slightly flustered. With a sigh, he said, 'I'll be honest; they're playing safe. Don't forget the effect this gas has had on others; we don't *really* know if you've recovered yet, do we?'

'All right, I get it,' said Holman, resigned. 'Tell me what's been happening while I've been asleep.'

'Quite a lot. A couple of hours ago the doctors and researchers went into a confab. I don't know what it was all about but they were having a go at those blokes from Porton Down, the Microbiological Research scientists. They were being evasive and finally refused to answer any more questions until they'd seen their Minister.'

'It all seems to point in the same direction, doesn't it?' Holman commented.

'Yeah,' said Barrow dryly, 'you could say that. Anyway, they went off to the Ministry of Defence about an hour ago, leaving the others in quite a rage. They're carrying on with their work, but they're not very happy about it.'

'How's Casey?'

'I don't know, but I'll get the Medical Officer. She wanted to be informed when you woke.' He walked to the door and gave instructions to the uniformed policeman outside to find Janet Halstead.

'What's happened with the fog?' asked Holman as the Detective Inspector returned to his chair.

'They found it, you know that, and luckily the winds have died down so it's drifting along at a very slow rate. It's an incredible sight, apparently, about a mile wide and a mile high.'

'It's grown.' The fact disturbed Holman. 'When I saw it last, it was half that size.'

'Yeah, they know it's growing. It's becoming thicker in density, too, a sort of dingy yellow colour. They've been spraying it all day to get it to disperse, but I don't know if they've had any success. They're evacuating Winchester anyway, just to be on the safe side, and the Met Office is keeping a constant check on wind shifts.'

'And how has the public reacted?'

'As you'd expect. Panic. Fear. Accusations. The press are having a field day.'

'And what answer have they been given?'

'Nothing official yet. Just that a grand-scale investigation is taking place and a statement will be made by the Prime Minister later this evening. But they've implied a poisonous gas has drifted in from the sea and caused the disaster in

Bournemouth.'

'My God, are people falling for it? What about the eruption?'

'No connection. At least that's the official answer that's been given.'

'The school! What about the school?'

'Er, news of that hasn't been released.'

'But they can't hush something like that up! What have the parents got to say?'

'As far as they know, their sons were killed in an accidental fire. In three major disasters concerning the lives of thousands, the school incident has been easily swallowed up.'

'Three? What are the three?'

'The eruption, Bournemouth and the crash this morning of the 747 into the GPO Tower.'

'How many were killed in that?'

'It hasn't been ascertained yet. It's estimated at least a thousand. There were two hundred and eighty-six on the jumbo alone, God knows how many were in the Tower and the offices around it.'

The air hung heavily in the small hospital-like room for several moments as both men tried to grasp the magnitude of the tragic events that had taken place. It was completely beyond their comprehension, somehow unreal. And it was the unreality of the situation that enabled them to cope.

'Does the public know about the fog?' It was Holman who broke the silence.

'Yes, they're aware. It's hardly a thing that could be kept a secret – a mile wide, a mile high. They had to be informed anyway, to get them to move out of its path.'

'And how have they reacted to that?'

'General hyster – '

The door opened and Janet Halstead entered, interrupting Barrow's answer.

'Hello, John, how are you feeling?' Her smile was a little more strained than it had been that morning.

'I'm fine. Tell me about Casey.'

'Her condition is deteriorating, John. I have to be honest with you, there's been enough evasiveness in this place for one day.' She sat on the edge of his bed. 'But there is a chance.'

He looked up at her, hopefully.

'We are pretty sure we know what is happening. We've had some of the finest minds in the country working on it. The autopsies have provided us with the answers. But we need to know the cause, John. We can't be sure until we know the cause. And that's what I meant when I mentioned evasiveness.'

'Tell me *exactly* what you mean.'

'We all feel – that is, the members of the Medical Research Council – that the Chemical and Microbiological Researchers from the Ministry of Defence are holding out on us. You see, in their tests, they seemed to know exactly what it was they were looking for, as though they were not looking for an answer but for confirmation of an answer they already had.

'We began to realize this as their tests progressed. There was no trial and error in their methods – they knew exactly what they were doing. Well, we let them finish and then we confronted them. But they clammed up, wouldn't say a word. They demanded that they see their Minister as only he had the authority to allow them to reveal their discovery – or affirmation.'

'The bastards – they're covering up!' Holman leapt from the bed. 'Barrow, you get me Sir Trevor Chambers. He'll get some answers for us. If he doesn't, I'm going to blow this thing sky high!'

'I'll get him, Holman, but there's nothing you can do personally. They'll lock you away,' said Barrow in a matter-of-fact voice.

'Just get him! We'll see!'

'Okay, okay. But keep calm, eh?'

'Yes, John,' said Janet Halstead firmly. 'It's no good getting excited, it won't help anyone. The first thing you must do is eat. I think we've found all we need to know from you; some results have still to come in, but I think they'll only confirm our suspicions. Now, let me order you some food while Inspector Barrow gets in touch with Sir Trevor, then I can put you in the picture as to our findings today.'

▪ 14 ▪

TWO HOURS LATER, HOLMAN FOUND HIMSELF SITTING BETWEEN JANET HALSTEAD and Sir Trevor Chambers in one of the spacious conference rooms at the Ministry of Defence. Sir Trevor had heeded his call from the Research Centre in Alexander Fleming House and made suitable bellowing noises in the right ears. They were soon to learn that the fuss was unnecessary; the Ministry had adopted a new policy of honesty – to a limited few, anyway. And they hadn't exactly adopted the policy willingly. They had been instructed to do so by a higher authority.

As he waited for the meeting to begin, Holman looked down the length of the long oak table and studied the faces deep in murmured conversation with their immediate neighbours. He recognized some of them and had been introduced to others on his arrival. He tried to remember the names and titles while he waited: the Home Secretary, Charles Lyall-Smith, looking calm and unruffled as always; the Minister of State for Defence, Lord Gibbon, and his Principal Private Secretary, deep in conversation with the Parliamentary Under-Secretary of State for Defence for the Army, William Douglas-Glyne and his Principal Private Secretary; the big, bluff Chief of Defence Staff, Sir Hugh Dowling, bellowing good humouredly across the table at the Chief of the General Staff, General Sir Michael Reedman, and his Vice-Chief, Lieutenant-General Sir Keith Macklen; the Chief Scientific Adviser, Professor Hermann Ryker, silently studying a document in front of him, underlining certain points with a pencil. There were others seated away from the table whose function was not clear to Holman, but three were dressed in military uniforms.

The Home Secretary rapped the table with his fountain pen to bring the meeting to order. 'Gentlemen,' he began, 'and lady,' he smiled briefly at Janet Halstead, 'you all know the facts; this evening's meeting is to inform you of how it happened and then to discuss a plan of action. I've been in constant touch with the Prime Minister who is at this very moment flying back from Russia. He regrets not being with us in this crisis, but does not wish any action we may take to be delayed because of his absence. It's a great pity his visit to Russia had to be cut short so abruptly – any such trips are of the highest diplomatic importance – but obviously, the safety of the country takes priority over any other matter. He has asked me to inform you that any action we decide upon this evening, he will endorse on his arrival, so there is to be no delay in implementing our plans, whatever they may be.

'His prime instruction is this: there is to be no information withheld by *any* Ministry from the people in this room tonight. I have had private talks with Lord Gibbon and Douglas-Glyne and have passed the facts that emerged from our conversations on to the PM. He is quite explicit that there is to be no cover-up between ourselves. Tonight's meeting *will not* indulge in accusations or blame-shedding; we are here to find solutions! The safety of millions is at stake – let's be quite clear on that issue. The catastrophes that have taken place have not been unrelated incidents. You know of the major disasters, but I can assure you there have been many, many small incidents with the same tragic consequences.

'A few of us in this room now know the cause of these outbreaks; it is my intention that you all know, so that we can combine our various skills to combat this growing – and I mean that literally – threat.'

He looked along the table, allowing his words to take their effect. Then he turned to the Minister of State for Defence, seated on his left, and said, 'Richard, will you repeat the information you gave me earlier?'

Lord Gibbon leaned forward, his elbows on the table, his thick hands clasped tightly before him. 'Gentlemen, I'm afraid the Ministry of Defence has to take a large amount of responsibility for – '

'We are not here to apportion blame, Richard. Just tell us the facts,' the Home Secretary snapped irritably.

'Very well.' The big man straightened up as though relieved and proceeded in a brisk, business-like manner, throwing off his look of guilty admission completely. 'If we are to start at the beginning, we must go back fifteen years, to our Microbiological Research Establishment at Porton Down and a brilliant scientist named Broadmeyer. His speciality was bacteriological warfare.'

Holman felt a coldness grip him. He had been right! The stupid bastards *had* been responsible.

'Professor Broadmeyer was a brilliant man in many ways,' Lord Gibbon continued. 'Perhaps too brilliant. He discovered – or invented – an organism that could affect the brains of man or animal.'

'May we be more accurate than that.' A slightly accented voice interrupted. All eyes swung round towards Professor Hermann Ryker, the Chief Scientific Adviser.

'Yes, Professor Ryker?' said the Home Secretary.

'He did not invent, he did not discover,' Ryker said gravely. 'He mutated. He took an organism known as mycoplasma and mutated it.' He was silent again.

'Perhaps you would like to continue, Professor. You're more of an authority on this kind of thing than I am,' said the Defence Minister.

'Yes,' Ryker admitted dryly. He looked around at the assembly. 'Broadmeyer *was* a brilliant man – I studied under him for many years – but he was, what shall we say, a little irresponsible. He mutated the mycoplasma so that if it entered the bloodstream it would attack the healthy existing cells and travel as a parasite to the brain. I am sure Mrs Halstead knows of the Rhesus factor,' – she nodded in acknowledgement – 'where a mother produces a mental defect because of antigenic incompatibility between the mother and foetus. In analogical theory the same process takes place except that the disease is transmitted to the host's brain rather than a foetus.

'The micro-organisms cause inflammation of the brain substance and covering membranes, eventually leading to a breakdown of existing healthy brain cells and a build-up of new, parasitical cells. The stronger the parasites become, the more easily the healthy cells are 'devoured'. Hence the complete and utter mental breakdown of whoever contracts the disease. Eventually, the victim would become a vegetable, capable of no action at all.'

'But what about me?' Holman exclaimed, unable to hold back. 'Why didn't I become a vegetable?'

Professor Ryker regarded him with a faint smile. 'You have been a very fortunate young man,' he said, then looking at Janet Halstead again. 'I believe Mrs Halstead will have some idea of what saved you by now, but there is a little more to it.'

The Principal Medical Officer spoke up. 'Mr Holman was given a blood transfusion because of an injury he sustained during his attack. I assume this helped clear the bloodstream of the foreign cells.'

'Precisely, Mrs Halstead,' the Professor nodded. 'It helped the existing cells destroy the parasites, rather like a regiment that has been sent reinforcements. Luckily for Mr Holman, he received the transfusion before the parasitical cells had a chance to multiply. But he was also lucky in another respect.

'Like most organisms used in germ warfare, the Broadmeyer Mutation, as it was secretly called, was self-reproducing. All it needed was carbon dioxide, the simple element that is contained in the very air we breathe and it could grow and grow, or I should say, multiply itself. Mr Holman was exposed to it in the early stages of its process for it had just been released in its pure form, therefore it was comparatively weak. The vapour, or fog as you have called it, is a by-product of the process it goes through as it draws the carbon dioxide from the air. This in itself is strange, for normally an organism that lives on carbon dioxide and precious little else must be photosynthetic, and would require sunlight to live and multiply. Now, mycoplasmas lack a cell wall, the mycoplasma being bounded only by the delicate plasma membrane – which means they can only survive and grow in an osmotically protective environment – hence they live as a large group in order to protect their inner core from changes in osmotic pressure. So you see the contradiction: they should need sunlight to exist, yet they surrounded themselves with this strange mist. Only Broadmeyer, as the creator of this mutation, knew the answer. And unfortunately, he is dead, killed by the disease he made.

'As I have said, he was an irresponsible man. I consider him irresponsible for ever producing such a mutation, but he was also irresponsible in smaller ways. He was careless and allowed himself to be exposed to the mycoplasma. Naturally, he went mad. And in his madness he destroyed all his papers, notes, the work of years, not just on the mutated mycoplasma, but other projects, more admirable conceptions, completely and utterly wasted. He died a lunatic, a victim of his own creation, and with him, he took many secrets.

'The mutation was contained and, like many others produced in the name of germ warfare, was considered too dangerous to use. Perhaps Lieutenant-General Macklen would care to tell you what happened to it?' He raised his eyebrows towards the Vice-Chief of the General Staff.

'We can hardly wait to hear,' Sir Trevor Chambers said caustically.

'Sir Trevor,' warned the Home Secretary.

'Before we do,' Janet Halstead broke in hastily, 'may I ask Professor Ryker a question about the cure? I think it's more important than anything else at the moment, wouldn't you agree?'

The Home Secretary nodded and said, 'Carry on.'

'You confirm that blood transfusion is the answer then, Professor?' she asked Ryker.

'Yes, provided it is given in time. If the parasite cells have taken on too strong a hold in the brain, then new blood will be of no use at all. Mr Holman here was fortunate in that they hadn't been given time to develop; they were easily overcome by the stronger existing cells. But once they have a grip...' He spread his hands and shrugged in a gesture of futility.

'But what if we use radiology to burn out the bad cells?'

'Y-e-s. Yes.' He drew out the words, his mind absorbing the thought. 'It's a possibility. But it's always dangerous; other good cells can be damaged by this method. Extreme care would have to be taken. And remember, nothing can ever be done about healthy cells that have been damaged either by the parasites *or* the X-ray. They will never grow again.'

'No, but it's a chance worth taking,' she said.

'Of course, you could never expect to treat everybody who contracts the disease in this way. I mean to say, there just aren't the resources.' Lord Gibbon shook his head in despair.

'No, we could never treat everyone in this way.' Janet Halstead looked around the room. 'But now it's your job to see that we don't have to. You have to destroy the mycoplasma!'

She allowed no time for them to comment on her last statement. She turned to Holman. 'John, I'm going back to the Research Centre. I want to give Miss Simmons a blood transfusion and if necessary subject her to radiology and, as her father is unable to, I think I should seek permission to do so from you.'

'Go ahead,' Holman answered. 'Whatever she needs – do it!'

She patted his shoulder as she rose from the table. 'Excuse me, gentlemen, I have some lives to save. And a lot to organize. I trust you'll keep me informed?'

Professor Ryker suppressed an admiring grin as she marched from the room. The Home Secretary cleared his throat. 'There is another question that I would like to ask; it could have a bearing on something to be discussed later.' He looked at Ryker. 'Once a person has successfully overcome the disease, would that person then be immune from further attacks?'

The professor pondered over the question. Finally he said, 'It would seem likely, although I'd value Mrs Halstead's opinion on this. Once the body's system has beaten off a disease, it builds some, or often total, resistance against it, and in this case, where the mutated mycoplasma would be virtually flushed from the system in the early stages and the unwanted cells in the brain killed before they had a chance to form, as they have in Mr Holman's case, then, yes, I believe one could be made immune from further attacks. The theory would have to be tested, of course, but the body has an acute sense of self-preservation, you know. It builds its own defences.'

'And is this, er, disease infectious?' Sir Trevor Chambers asked, carefully avoiding Holman's eyes. 'Could Mr Holman pass it on to others?'

'Well, that doesn't appear to have happened, does it?' Ryker answered with a restrained smile. 'My opinion is that the DNA – the genetic material – of the organism immediately combines with the DNA of brain cells, in a manner similar to that in which cancer-causing viruses are believed to join up with cellular material. In the case of cancer-causing viruses, of course, the extra genetic material can lie dormant for years until something triggers it off. I suggest that in the case of Broadmeyer's mutated organism, the DNA produces extremely malignant cells almost at once, which cause the untoward effects which make the organism non-infective.

'Our problem is that we do not even know enough about mycoplasma in its normal state, let alone when it has been tampered with. I shall tell you briefly of what we do know. Also called PPLO – pleuropneumonia-like organisms – mycoplasmas include the smallest known cells able to multiply independently of other living cells, some being almost spherical and only 0.001 mm in diameter. The chromosome of many probably contains not more than 650 genes – about one-fifth the number found in common bacteria – and from the physiological and biochemical viewpoint microplasmas are similar to bacteria, with the one important exception I've already mentioned: they lack a cell wall.' Ryker paused to look around at the blank faces.

He continued, his next words cutting through the incomprehension like a knife. 'This means, because they are not restricted by this rigid wall, they can be deformed and are able to squeeze through narrow pores smaller than their own diameter. It also means they are completely resistant to penicillin and any other substances which act by disrupting the synthesis of bacterial cell walls!'

An uneasy silence followed, broken finally by Sir Trevor clearing his throat. 'Er, you mean there is no cure?' he asked.

'No, no. We will find one,' Ryker assured them all, 'but to produce a serum, we need to know exactly how the mycoplasma has been mutated.'

'But surely *you* must have some idea?' said the Defence Minister.

'Oh, I have an idea. But do we have the time to experiment with and develop ideas?' He spoke as though to a child who had asked a foolish question and was being given a kind answer. 'No. But we may draw off some of the organism from the living victims. Then we could analyse it, discover its contents, and then develop a serum. But of course, to manufacture it in bulk would take time. And we do not have too much time, do we?' He looked around at them, then added, 'Of course, if we had some of the mutated mycoplasma in its pure state, then it would be an enormous advantage.' 'Well, what's to prevent us from containing some of the fog?' Douglas-Glyne, the Defence Under-Secretary, asked impatiently.

'I said "in its pure state". The fog, apart from being a mutated organism, now contains carbon dioxide and various other impurities. I suspect the yellowish colour is due to the pollution in the air – our own man-made pollution. To sort out all these elements to find the mutated mycoplasma in its purest form would take time.'

'This is leading on to our next point, gentlemen,' said the Home Secretary. 'I'd like to get back to Lieutenant-General Macklen. Sir Keith, would you tell us how the virus had been contained?'

'And how it escaped!' snorted Sir Trevor Chambers.

Sir Keith Macklen rose to his feet as though to address the officers on his staff.

'The Broadmeyer Mycoplasma,' he began, purposely avoiding Professor Ryker's name for it, 'was contained in a sealed-off room in small glassed steel containers. Broadmeyer had disturbed one of the vials and dislodged its cap while carrying out experiments on an animal – a rabbit I think. Anyway, he noticed the dislodged cap, replaced it and left the sealed room. It took a while for him to become insane. As Professor Ryker said, it was in its purest form and he was only exposed for a few seconds, before it had time to strengthen itself from the air, but when he did, he went under very fast.

'He destroyed his work and killed a fellow scientist in the process. Then he became – a nothing. His brain hardly functioned, he neither saw nor heard anything. He died soon after by his own hand!

'We decided the mutation was too dangerous ever to be used so we had to get rid of it. There were three ways of doing this: destroy it, dump it in the sea, or bury it below ground.'

'My God!' said Sir Trevor, exhaling a long breath. 'And you decided to bury it!'

'Er, not me, Sir Trevor. My superiors at that time. It was fifteen years ago, remember.'

'Carry on, Sir Keith,' said the Home Secretary.

'Well, we couldn't destroy it; we didn't know what it was exactly. And we couldn't dump it in the sea; we considered that was too risky. So we buried it. Very, very deep below ground, in glassed steel vials inside a strong, lead container.'

'Under the village,' said Holman, not a question, but a statement.

'Certainly not! The exact location was a quarter of a mile away from the village.' He looked at Holman with annoyance.

'Go on, Sir Keith,' said the Home Secretary again, keeping a tight rein on the meeting, refusing to allow it to become heated in any way.

'Records were made concerning the mycoplasma's potential and its location, and filed away. Fifteen years ago, as I said. Er, now…' He hesitated, looking at the expressionless faces, reluctant to continue. 'Er, up until a few weeks ago, the army has been carrying out some underground explosive tests – '

'I knew it!' Sir Trevor exploded, leaping to his feet. 'Trust the bloody army! The whole of Salisbury Plain and you have to pick the bloody spot where you planted a deadly disease fifteen years before!'

'We most certainly did not! Our experiment was at least two miles from there!'

'Then how do you account for the eruption in the village?'

'Sir Trevor, please sit down!' the Home Secretary ordered sharply. 'I've already warned you. This meeting will not become a dispute. We are here to find a solution! Sir Keith – please continue.'

'We were experimenting with a powerful new explosive. It was one of many we have carried out below ground for the past twenty years now. Many countries use this method to test the power of their bombs. Would you rather we blew up the countryside?'

'I'd rather you didn't test bombs at all,' Sir Trevor retorted.

'Apparently, the bomb – I'm afraid I can't tell you the nature of the explosive – caused a running fissure below the earth. It was this that caused the eruption and released the mycoplasma.'

'Do you mean to tell me you have a bomb that can cause that sort of damage two miles away?' asked Sir Trevor incredulously.

'Yes. Although we didn't know it at the time,' answered the Vice-Chief of the General Staff, careful to keep any hint of pride from his voice. 'The earth was ruptured severely around the blast, but the fissure that caused most damage ran for several miles. It must have reached the point where the mycoplasma was housed in its lead case, the force of the earth crushed it open, the tremor continued on its way until it found its way to the surface under the village, the mycoplasma being pushed along with it. We assume it was the mutation, already polluted and creating its own gas that was seen emerging from the fissure.'

'Why do you assume that?' asked Holman.

'Because we have been checking through our records most of the day – since we heard a poisonous gas may have been involved – of all our deposited stocks.

We found that particular stock was directly in line with the fissure.'

'And you've known all this time it was *your* explosion that caused the earthquake?' asked Sir Trevor accusingly.

He nodded, avoiding the many eyes that glared at him as though he were solely responsible.

The Home Secretary spoke before anyone else had a chance to. '*We* knew and *we* decided no good could come of its disclosure. Until today, that is. Thank you, Sir Keith.' The Vice-Chief of the General Staff sat down, relieved that his statement was over, and the Home Secretary continued: 'Gentlemen, we know most of the facts now. This is not the time for reprisals, but let me stress that *human error* of this magnitude will *not* be tolerated. That is all that is going to be said on that particular issue at this time, but I can assure you,' he looked towards Sir Trevor, 'it will be looked into thoroughly *after* we have made progress in defeating the present threat. Now, let's get on with it.

'We have lost the battle to prevent the fog entering Winchester; fortunately all the residents have been evacuated in time.'

'How did you try to stop it?' Holman asked.

'Perhaps you will tell us, William?' The Home Secretary turned to the Under-Secretary of State for Defence for the Army, William Douglas-Glyne.

'Yes. There are four principal methods of dealing with fog. The method we've been using today, all day, is sprinkling calcium chloride from low-flying aircraft, a practice used in San Francisco regularly to clear their fogs. It's a chemical that actually dries up the air, but although we've used tons of the stuff it hasn't had much effect. Very expensive method too, I might add. Some of the vapour was cleared but, as we now know, the gas is self-producing; it just goes on manufacturing itself.'

'Have you tried the other methods?' asked Sir Trevor.

'Not yet, we've had little time. And anyway, the calcium chloride was the most favoured. Let me tell you about the other ways and you'll understand. During the war, our airfields had what was called the F100 system, another expensive process and little used since. With radar, fog isn't much of a problem nowadays, but this is what they used to do: they warmed the air around the airfield with petrol in special devices; as it became warmer it absorbed more moisture and the droplets of liquid turned to invisible water vapour, dispersing the fog and forming a hole above the airfield through which aircraft could land.

'Now, apart from not having enough time to set up such an elaborate system around the town, all we would have succeeded in doing is divert the fog – not get rid of it.

'Another method is to use ultrasonic waves. Rapid to and fro movements produced by vibrations in the air tend to cause the tiny water droplets to collect together, forming drops that are large enough to fall as rain. The disadvantage of this method is that the force of the sound waves we would have had to have used could have been harmful to living things. And again, now we know it would be useless because of the self-productive factor.'

He paused, looking down at his notes, reluctant to look at the troubled faces around him.

'And the last method?' the Home Secretary prodded.

'The last method is no good at all. It involves the use of carbon dioxide and, of course, the organism thrives on this. If sprinkled on fog, it causes the water droplets to freeze and join together, making them heavy enough to fall to the ground, but in this case the mycoplasma would just "feed" on it.'

'Are you telling us there's nothing we can do?' asked Sir Trevor incredulously.

'We are still looking at other methods,' came the somewhat feeble reply.

'I'm sure we have enough top brains in this country to find a solution,' said the Home Secretary. 'As well as our own, we also have scientific institutes in America, Russia and France searching for the answer. The major powers of the world are working for us. Even China has approached us with an offer of assistance. Remember, there is nothing to prevent the fog from drifting out to sea and reaching other countries; the threat is not with us alone, although we are in the most immediate danger.

'The fact that it could virtually depopulate a town the size of Bournemouth has made the danger clear to every country in the world. If it has done any good at all, it's in the fact that the major powers now have a common enemy.

'If we cannot disperse the fog, our only hope is to find the antidote to the disease, fast. And to make that serum, we need a quantity – however small – of the mutated mycoplasma itself, as Professor Ryker says, in its 'purest form".'

'But you know it would be impossible to get that,' Ryker said, a worried frown creasing his face.

'Impossible, why?' Sir Trevor looked at the scientist. 'Surely someone wearing some sort of protective clothing, breathing apparatus, that sort of thing, could get close enough to get a sample?'

'It's not a matter of getting close enough,' said Ryker, 'it means going to the very centre of the fog.'

'The centre?'

'Yes,' said the Home Secretary. 'Sensors in our aircraft have discovered a force in the centre of the fog. This is obviously the nucleus of the mycoplasma itself.'

'The glow!' said Holman, half to himself. 'When we were driving through it, Casey saw a glow!'

'Yes, Mr Holman,' the Professor nodded his head. 'It is possible that the organism has taken on a sort of incandescent quality because of the process it is going through.'

Sir Trevor Chambers broke in huffily. 'All right. So the "neat" stuff is in the centre. That still doesn't prevent someone with suitable protection going in to get it!'

Ryker looked towards the Home Secretary askance. He received a sharp nod of acquiescence.

'We said earlier that Broadmeyer was careless,' he said to Sir Trevor. 'But only in small ways. No scientist is careless enough to handle dangerous chemicals or substances without suitable protection. He was covered from head to foot in protective clothing.'

'Good God! You mean there *is* no protection from it?'

'Not the practical protection that would enable a man to move freely. It was one of the reasons it was considered so dangerous, the fact that it could pass through the special heavy material of these suits.'

'Lead-lined suits?' said Holman.

'Too clumsy and cumbersome for an operation of this sort. The wearer would have to travel half a mile to reach the fog's centre in virtual darkness and still have no guarantee he would be safe from the mutated mycoplasma at its strongest.'

A hint of suspicion began to creep into Holman's mind. 'This sort of brings us back to the point about immunity, doesn't it?' he said, looking directly at the Home Secretary.

'Yes, it does,' said the Home Secretary, quite unembarrassed. 'We need someone who is immune to the disease to go in and bring back a sample. You, Mr Holman, it would seem, are that person.'

▪ 15 ▪

FOUR SPECTRAL SHAPES MOVED THROUGH THE THICK YELLOW MIST. THREE WERE gross, misshapen versions of the human form, lumbering along at a slow, uneven pace, one leading a small trolley containing a dark, oblong box that had several strange attachments to it. The fourth figure was more representative of his species, yet seemed to have a peculiar hump on his back and a face that contained only a pair of eyes.

One of the heavily suited men tapped Holman on the shoulder. This was as far as they dared to go; the rest was up to him. His voice was muffled through the smog mask as he gave them the thumbs-up sign and said, 'okay'. The three scientists couldn't have heard him anyway through their glass-visored helmets. The aperture for vision was very small and they had to swivel their heads to see one another, and even then the fog was so thick it was difficult to see more than two yards ahead.

It was clearer for Holman who was not wearing a suit, but still the farthest he could see was about five yards. The heavily clad figure who had tapped him on the shoulder handed him the handle to the trolley. By pressing a button in the tip of the handle, the small but heavy motorized vehicle would propel itself along, restricted in its speed by the person who controlled its power.

Holman looked into the inscrutable mask of the scientist, trying at least to see the man's eyes, but gave up, unable to penetrate the dark interior of the reinforced glass visor. Instead, he patted the man's arm once in a gesture of thanks.

He watched the grotesque figures turn and disappear into the yellow mist, leaving him with a feeling of utter loneliness, so acute that he had to fight the urge to call after them. But they had taken a risk bringing him this far; they knew the outer fringes of the fog were weak but just how weak, they hadn't yet ascertained.

Holman turned away from the point where they had been swallowed up and faced the direction he himself had to take, remembering the street plan he'd studied during the night. He thought by now he could walk the streets blindfolded and still find his way.

The tiny oxygen tank on his back was uncomfortable but deemed necessary in case the mist became too choking. He pressed the button controlling the trolley and moved forward again, feeling ill at ease and claustrophobic. The test had been positive. They were fairly certain he was immune; certain enough to consider it worth the risk, at any rate. But they had left the choice to him; nobody could force him to enter the fog again.

Of course, there was no choice really. What else could he do? If they couldn't destroy the fog, then millions could die from it. The only answer was the serum. And he was the only suitable person available. It was no good damning the army for their stupidity, the crass stupidity he had suspected all along; now was the time for constructive action. But my God, would they know about it when it was over! If it was ever over.

The small amount of blood containing the disease they had drained from a still-living, but completely insane victim of Bournemouth, had been absolutely rejected and destroyed by his own blood cells when introduced into his system. Whether that small amount was enough to judge the test conclusively or not, they did not know, but in a crisis of this proportion, chances had to be taken. And it was he who had to take them.

He thought of Casey. She had looked so pale last night, so still, and incredibly beautiful in her trance-like state. He didn't want to lose her! He'd rather die himself now than be left without her. Was it just her illness that had brought his love to this crushing, fearful peak? No, he answered himself. It had just made him realize her value, his own incompleteness without her. To lose her now would be the ultimate irony.

He stopped. For a moment he thought he had seen a shadow moving in the fog. Or was it just the swirling mist playing tricks on his eyes? He started walking again, keeping close to the sides of the streets so he could see the buildings and where they ended to allow for other turnings, but he stayed off the pavements because of the contraption trailing behind.

The transfusion on Casey had been successful: this morning it would be the turn of therapeutic radiology, the radiation burning out the badness, the angle of the X-ray constantly being moved so as to damage as little as possible of the healthy tissues. He prayed that it would work, expelling from his mind the frightening thought that it might not.

He dreaded the moment he would have to tell her of the death of her 'father'. Simmons had passed away during the night, never having regained consciousness since leaving the house. He had died alone. Holman would never tell Casey she had killed the man she thought to be her father – it might destroy her. And he still wasn't sure if he would tell her of the man's dying confession to him. Would it help diminish her loss? He thought not. It would only confuse her emotions. He walked on through the fog that was becoming thicker, more yellow.

Now, let's see, he thought. This must be the shopping arcade. If I turn right now, it should lead me to the cathedral. He paused for a moment, breathing heavily. He was sure it was more psychological than the fact that the fog was restricting his breathing; he was involuntarily inhaling as little of the surrounding air as possible even though he knew he would be able to use the small oxygen tank strapped to his back if he really needed to. They had told him the source of energy seemed to be coming from somewhere near the old cathedral. The trolley that trailed along behind him like a faithful dog contained a lead-lined box that operated on the same principle as a vacuum cleaner. Attached to its side were several lengths of metal tubing that when assembled and joined to a tough flexible hose from the container could be probed into the nucleus of the mutated mycoplasma and a sample drawn back into the holder. It was a hastily conceived plan, but the only one available to them in so short a time.

Summoning up his courage, Holman turned into the street that would lead him into the lawns surrounding the cathedral. The street was narrow and as he passed by the shops he noticed the window of one had been smashed. Further along, he discovered another had been broken. Looters? Was it possible that there were still people in the town, an unscrupulous few who didn't realize the danger they were in? The public had had to be told of the consequences of contact with the fog; surely no one would risk entering it now for the sake of robbing the unoccupied shops? Perhaps it had been an accident; an army lorry unable to manoeuvre comfortably in the narrow street, or perhaps someone had fallen against it in the rush to leave the town. But two windows? He looked more closely at the shop. It was a jeweller's. Well, that confirmed it. Someone had stayed behind to scavenge, ignoring the risk, heedless of the warnings. Was he, or were they, still around or had they fled having accomplished their robbery? He shrugged; it wasn't his problem.

The yellowness was even more dense now as he drew nearer to the historic building and the extent of his vision became even more limited. He passed through the opening to the lawns which housed their few important gravestones and surrounded the cathedral, his eyes constantly narrowed, peering into the murk, trying to make out the path that led to the very doors of the ancient place of worship. Where was the glow? Surely he should have come upon it by now? He would have to make a circuit of the building, they'd insisted the centre was in this particular area. It could have moved on, of course, but there was very little breeze to stir it.

But as he approached the cathedral's entrance, he noticed a faint half-glow.

He stopped dead. Was it possible? Was the nucleus, the heart of the disease, housed within the great church? Could it have drifted into Winchester Cathedral and become trapped inside its ancient but solid stone walls?

Another, more disturbing, thought jarred Holman's mind.

What if it hadn't drifted in by accident? Could it possibly be self-motivated? It was an incredible idea and he tried to dismiss it from his mind. It was too fantastic, too much like science-fiction. But then everything that had happened was too fantastic.

The thought persisted.

He walked on, a coldness creeping through his body, his steps noiseless and cautious. He tried to fight the chill that enveloped him, reassuring himself with the thought that the sinister circumstances, the loneliness and the lack of clear vision were all working together, attacking his imagination, allies to fear.

He saw that the glow – or was it just a brighter tone of yellow? – was definitely coming from the open doorway. Had he the nerve to confront its source lurking inside?

'Fuck it!' It was a soft spoken war cry. He went on.

Lingering at the entrance, he peered into the brighter mist. The air was much harder to breathe in, the acidity burnt his nostrils and throat. He reached for the oxygen mask looped over his shoulder and was about to remove the smog mask when something flickered in the corner of his vision. He froze and studied the spot in the fog from where the movement had come. Imagination again? He saw nothing, only the patterns made by the swirls of the mist. He listened and heard nothing but the imagined beating of his own heart.

Holman looked towards the source of the glow. It was at its strongest at the centre of the cathedral's vast interior, near the altar. It seemed to have no definable shape, its outer edges constantly changing their line and only visible because of the sudden contrast in yellows: the apparently clear clean yellow of the nucleus itself, against the murkier, greyer yellow of its protective screen, the fog. It was impossible to tell the size of the strangely writhing shape, his vision was too impaired by the surrounding layers of fog, but its very existence seemed to exude a malignancy, a malevolent growth that was frightening, yet perversely fascinating.

It was only with an extreme effort of will that Holman tore his eyes away from the eerie spectacle and knelt down by the machine at his side. He remembered his oxygen mask and placed it over his mouth after removing the smog mask. He drew in several deep breaths and his head immediately became clearer, making him wonder if the fog itself also had a slight drugging effect. Detaching the metal tubes from the vacuum container, he began to screw them together, becoming even more nervous with the action he now had to take.

He still wasn't sure if he had the courage to approach the glowing mass, the mass that looked pure but was in fact made from the deadly, growing mutation, so he closed his mind to it. The moment of truth would be on him soon enough and he would either walk towards it or run like hell away from it. Either way, whichever direction, the movement would be spontaneous, not carefully considered. He concentrated on the rods.

He became aware of their presence more by sensing it than hearing or seeing them. They appeared as three dark shapes in the fog, standing about five feet apart, just beyond reasonably clear visual range, unmoving, silent. He looked from one hazy form to another, their stillness more frightening than if they had been moving, for mobility would have at least given them some form, something he could identify.

He rose, apprehensively clutching the section of rods he'd managed to put together before him. One of the shapes moved forward and with some sense of relief he realized it was the figure of a man. But the head was different.

Holman took a step back in horror and raised the metal tubing in defence. As the figure drew nearer, he almost laughed with relief. It was a man, and his head looked so strange because he was wearing a grotesque World War II gas-mask. He held in his hands a long, black candlestick, its wicked-looking point, the point on which the base of a candle should have been pressed, exposed and aimed towards Holman.

'What the hell are you doing here?' Holman asked uncertainly, removing his oxygen mask to make himself understood. There was no reply as the man stepped before him.

'This fog is dangerous, you should have cleared out with the rest,' Holman continued, his eyes not moving from the point aimed at his chest. He watched, almost mesmerized, as the candlestick was slowly raised and drawn back, ready to strike.

Holman waited no longer. He jabbed the metal rod hard into the man's stomach and as he doubled up, brought it swiftly down on his exposed head. The man collapsed in a heap.

Holman raised the rod again, ready for the other two. But they'd vanished.

He looked around, his head darting from left to right, the figure at his feet moaning and squirming on the hard, stone floor. He knelt beside him and turned him over on to his back. 'Poor bloody fool!' he muttered. He must have thought the gas-mask would be protection against the fog and seized the opportunity to help himself to some of the valuables of the deserted town. But what were he and his companions doing in the cathedral and why had the man attacked him? Had the disease affected them already? Or did they just see him as a threat to their freedom?

He pulled the ugly mask from the groaning man's face and saw that his eyes had the slightly glazed look he'd seen in Casey's; he *had* been infected.

The sound of a footstep warned him of the second man's approach from behind. He whirled around to face him but a glancing blow sent him sprawling back, causing him to lose his grip on the rod. The figure loomed over him and began to laugh, a cackling, hysterical laugh. The third man materialized from the mist and stood by his side and began to laugh with his companion. Suddenly, they reached down and grabbed Holman by his ankles and started to drag him along the stone floor towards the glow. He tried to kick his legs free, but their grips were firm and his efforts made them laugh even louder. His hands scrabbled for a grip but the old stone was smooth from centuries of wear. As he passed the injured man his body came in contact with the heavy candlestick. He snatched at it desperately and thought he'd lost it when it rolled away from him. Fortunately it was stopped by the prone man's foot and Holman was able to seize it. He drew it to him and was about to hurl it at one of his assailants when the man he thought he'd put out of action raised himself to his knees with a demented roar, saw Holman, and threw himself at him, his teeth bared to be used as a weapon.

Holman managed to get an elbow under the man's throat and keep the gnashing teeth away, twisting his own head away at the same time. There were cries of rage from the other two as their progress was halted. They dropped Holman's legs and began to kick at the two struggling bodies, oblivious to friend or foe. One of them grabbed at the first man's hair and yanked his head back, beating at his face with his other hand.

It gave Holman the chance he needed. He struck at the exposed throat with his heavy weapon and crushed the man's windpipe, instantly sickened by his own action. But there was only time for momentary regret, for the other two now directed their attention completely towards him again.

He pushed the injured man away and pulled at the ankle of one of the others, bringing the startled man crashing to the floor. The third man caught Holman from behind and put his arms around his neck, squeezing his throat, trying to choke him to death. Because of his higher position, his head was above Holman's and saliva from his wildly grinning mouth trickled down on to Holman's gasping face.

Holman felt as though his head was about to explode. As he weakened, he was conscious of the man's insane chuckle and as his vision began to swim, he saw the man he'd brought down raise himself on one elbow and lie there laughing at him. Vaguely, almost remotely, he realized he still held the candlestick. With both hands, he brought its wicked point swiftly up to the only vulnerable spot he could reach. The man's scream and the sudden spurt of blood that gushed down on to Holman's face added new horror to the nightmare. The pressure on his throat was released and he sucked in the foul air greedily as his attacker fell away from him.

The remaining man was pointing a shaking finger at them, laughing hysterically.

It was too much for Holman. He staggered to his feet and ran from the cathedral.

Once outside, he fell to his knees on the gravel path, but the pounding footsteps behind him made him stumble on again into the thick blanket of fog, thankful for its concealing refuge. He found himself running on grass, regardless of the danger of possible collision with hidden trees or gravestones. His only thought was to get away, away from those madmen, away from the mutation, away from the cathedral. To get away from the fog, to be with normal people again. His mission was forgotten, his instinct for self-survival his only driving force. He did not even feel the sudden gustiness of the wind or see that the swirls had become more vigorous in their movements.

He slipped on the wet grass and as he stumbled forward, desperately trying to keep his balance, he ran into a tree. His head struck it with a loud crack and he slowly crumpled against it, sinking to his knees and then sprawling on to the grass.

As his consciousness slipped away from him, he was aware of a shadowy figure appearing from the mist and standing over him. The deep-throated chuckle was the last sound he heard before he blacked out.

They found the lunatic trying to bury Holman alive. The fog had cleared from the town, swept away by a sudden unpredicted force of wind and rain, and the helicopters hovering around the fringes of the thick blanket swooped down to search for him. As one circled the cathedral, it came across the figure of a man digging. At least, that was what the pilot thought the man was doing, but as he swept over him, he realized he was, in fact, filling in a deep hole. A crew member slapped his shoulder vigorously.

'Get down there, quickly!' he shouted above the noise of the helicopter's engine. 'There was a body in that hole. That man's trying to bury it!'

As they landed, the small-time crook who had been amazed at the chance of having the whole town of Winchester to himself to plunder undisturbed with his two cronies, and was now insane because of this ill-seized opportunity, ignored the descending machine and happily continued filling in the pit he had dragged the unconscious man towards. The hole had been left by workmen who had just begun to dig a grave that was to house the remains of an important church dignitary whose last wishes were to be buried in the shadow of his beloved cathedral. The work had been interrupted by the sudden evacuation order and the burial that was to have taken place later on in the day was now replaced by a far less dignified ceremony.

Holman lay at the bottom of the open grave where he'd been roughly dumped. There was a large swelling on his forehead caused by his fall against the tree and only the earth falling on to his body prodded his unconscious state, making him stir, a low moan escaping from his lips. As he raised a hand to his head, his eyes still closed, and opened his mouth to groan even louder, a shovel full of damp earth landed on his face, making his eyes suddenly blink open only to close again instantly as the loose soil ran into them.

He spluttered and choked as the earth fell into his open mouth and ran down his throat. He tried to sit up, but his head was still not clear enough to allow it, so instead, he ran his hands over his face in order to clear off the dirt. He could feel the clumps of earth still landing on his body and his mind struggled to understand what was happening. It was only the chuckling sound that broke through his stupor and brought him fully to his senses.

He opened his eyes again, this time cautiously keeping them covered with his fingers. He saw the edges of the trench above him and then caught sight of the figure that was shovelling the dirt on to him. He suddenly realized where he was and what was happening. The man was burying him alive!

Panic-stricken, he clutched at the loose earth at the sides of the pit and pulled himself to an upright position. With a snarl of anger, the man above him raised his shovel to strike down at him to prevent him leaving his premature grave.

He raised an arm to ward off the blow, closing his eyes, knowing there was not room enough to allow him to dodge it. But it never came. He heard voices shouting and then scuffling noises. When he opened his eyes, all he could see through the open rectangle of earth above him was the grey, disturbed sky. He became aware of the rain that was beating down into the hole, its soothing wetness serving to revive his senses even more. He drew his knees up, preparing himself to fight off any further attack.

Suddenly, a face appeared, breaking into the rectangle of sky. It grinned, and its voice said, 'This is no time to lie down on the job, Mr Holman.'

A hand was extended to help him climb from his gruesome resting place.

▪ 16 ▪

HOLMAN WAS FILLED WITH APPREHENSION AS HE WALKED DOWN THE LONG corridor towards Observation Room 3 in which, he had been informed, Casey was now resting. He hadn't been able to see Janet Halstead on his return to the Research Centre for she'd been working through the night organizing her staff as well as hospitals throughout the country for the emergency and still finding time to supervise Casey's treatment, but now she was snatching a necessary few hours' sleep. Another doctor had told him the radiology treatment had gone well and now they were waiting for Casey to come out of a deep slumber before they could tell if it had been successful.

Holman needed sleep too. His experience that morning had left him drained; the memory of regaining consciousness and finding himself in a grave with a madman shovelling in earth to bury him almost outweighed the other horrors he'd been through. Being buried alive was surely a nightmare that most people had had at some time, but very few had actually experienced it.

The army had flown him back to London by helicopter, realizing he would not be persuaded to go back into the fog again that day. Professor Ryker, and of course, Barrow, who was still acting as his bodyguard, flew with him. Ryker had naturally been disappointed when he had returned without a sample of the mutated mycoplasma, but had understood the scare he'd been through and did not persist in urging Holman to try again. The unpredicted change of weather was moving the fog too rapidly anyway for him to be able to locate its centre.

Towns that lay ahead of it, directly in its path, were being evacuated, but fortunately the direction in which it was moving was not too densely populated. Police and army vehicles, guided by the watchdog helicopters, raced before the rolling grey mass, stopping at small villages and remote houses and bundling their occupants into the vans and trucks, and once full, veering off at a right angle, away from the danger. Then they would unload their human cargo and speed back, using a different route, to repeat the process. It was exhausting and harrowing, and already many serious accidents had occurred, but on the whole, it was proving successful.

Unfortunately, it was a process that could not be maintained indefinitely and the men controlling the operation dreaded the unavoidable moment it would reach a large town. They prayed that the wind would not change its easterly direction and carry the fog towards Basingstoke, Farnham, Aldershot. *London*.

The biggest worry at the moment was Haslemere, the largest town directly in the path of the fog, but already it was being emptied of its occupants, most of the people fleeing north, unwilling to go south because of the fear of being trapped by the sea, the fate of Bournemouth inhabitants influencing their choice. They could not be convinced that their fears were unwarranted – the fog was still only a mile wide and could easily be skirted – and the roads north were jammed with vehicles of every description as well as panic-stricken people on foot.

The Prime Minister had arrived back in London and was directing operations with the help of his chief military, scientific and medical advisers, from a special operational headquarters, a vast, impenetrable underground shelter, less than a mile from the House of Commons, its actual location kept a strict secret from the general public. It was already being prepared for occupation if the fog should head towards London. It had been built as a sanctuary from nuclear bombs, but now it would be used as a shelter from a totally unimagined threat, and its defences against radiation poisoning would serve just as well against the deadly man-made disease.

The proposal to build huge fires in London to disperse the fog if it entered the city was considered and the go-ahead for their preparation given on the understanding that they were only to be used as a last resort; the danger of the whole of London going up in uncontrollable flames was a frightening possibility that could not be ignored. But it was at least a positive action. The demoralizing chess game that was being played with the fog further south could not go on for ever and the public had to *see* they were being given some form of physical protection, however crude.

They, the public, were informed an antidote was being prepared and large quantities would soon be available; they were told the disease itself was weakening and would probably soon die or be so diluted with pure air it would be ineffective; it was confirmed that the experts believed the organism had mysteriously drifted in from the sea and a full inquiry into its source would be put into force as soon as the crisis was over.

They were lied to because the government thought it best; large-scale panic would only increase the danger to lives. The truth could be told – or at least some of it – when the threat had passed.

Those responsible would pay the penalty – but not publicly.

Steps would be taken so that a disaster of this nature and magnitude could never happen again.

Holman had discussed with Ryker the fact that the mutated mycoplasma had been trapped inside the cathedral. Or had it taken shelter? Was it feasible, was it remotely possible, that the mutation had some sort of driving force? Could it have – Holman had hesitated to say it – could it have intelligence? After all, it was a parasite that fed on the brain.

Professor Ryker had laughed, but it was without humour. 'Every living thing has some driving force, Mr Holman. Even plant life has some intelligence, it's a matter of degree. But to suggest this organism has a will, a brain? It has a motivation for survival perhaps, just as a flower reaches towards the sun, but a mind of its own? No, Mr Holman, don't let your harrowing experience this morning send you into the realms of fantasy. The mycoplasma does not control the fog; when the wind took the protective cloud away, the mycoplasma had to go too, trapped in its centre, caged by its own protection. It exercised no power over its cloak of fog, it gives no direction. It is a mindless, organic thing, incapable of action by thought.'

'But action by instinct?' Holman had interrupted.

'Yes, perhaps.'

'Maybe it amounts to the same thing.'

Ryker spent the rest of the journey in silence, deep in thought, occasionally shaking his head as though to dismiss a theory, then his forehead wrinkling in concentration as a new thought was processed and again rejected.

Barrow had accompanied Holman to the Research Centre after Holman had given his report to the Home Secretary in person, promising he would attempt to procure some of the mycoplasma as soon as conditions were favourable. They would be in constant radio contact until that moment arrived and when it did, he would be flown to the spot immediately. It was suggested that he be positioned in a place directly in line with the fog's centre so that it would pass right over him, but Holman had rejected the idea vehemently. If there was no other way, then he would do it, but he was damned if he would confront the mutation when it was moving swiftly, giving him little chance to manoeuvre around it.

At another time, he would probably have taken the risk, but at that moment, his nerves were somewhat taut, and he was in no mood to repeat that morning's performance. He was also anxious to see Casey, to find out whether the experiment had worked, to know if she would become a vegetable or return to her normal self.

The Home Secretary wisely but reluctantly refrained from ordering him to carry out his request knowing the man would be more useful in a better condition. In the meantime, gadgets could be set up in the fog's path, containers that could be operated by remote control to close when sensors relayed the message that the source was in the vicinity. It was a hit and miss method, but the only one available at that time.

The rising trepidation Holman felt reached its peak when he turned the handle of the door marked '3'. Through its glass upper portion he could see the pale figure lying still in the bed. A nurse sat at her bedside ready to call in Janet Halstead at the first signs of consciousness. She smiled as Holman entered.

'How is she?' he asked.

'She's been sleeping peacefully enough,' the nurse replied, 'but she had to be heavily drugged for the radiology and the blood transfusion. I'm afraid she was a bit violent.'

'Can I stay with her for a while?'

'Yes, of course.' The nurse rose from her seat, still smiling at him. 'I'll leave you for a little while but if she wakes, press this button. I can promise you, this room will be full of people in a flash. We're all rather anxious to find out the result of the radiology.'

'Are the signs good?'

'Oh, the signs are good, but frankly, Mr Holman, we just don't know. I'm sure Mrs Halstead has explained.'

Holman nodded and sat in the chair she had just vacated. The nurse left the room after checking the girl's pulse for the sixth time since she'd been on duty, her face noncommittal to Holman's stare.

He sat watching Casey's face for several minutes, her frailty causing him concern. She had been through so much it seemed impossible that she would ever be the same again even if the parasite had been vanquished. When her eyes opened, would she recognize him or would they still hold that lost, faraway glaze that was so haunting, so terrible? He knew her wrists were strapped to the sides of the bed beneath the white sheets and the knowledge made his own eyes fill with tears he was unable to shed. He wished it were possible for him to cry, to find release for his emotions, but tears were a luxury he hadn't enjoyed for many, many years.

He reached forward to stroke her face, the desire to weep not conquered, but unwillingly suppressed, the incapability a burden rather than a strength.

He touched her lips with his hands, then her cheek, then her throat. She stirred, a slight frown creasing her forehead, but her face relaxed again, and became peaceful. He spoke her name, not to wake her, but because he needed to say it, and for an instant, her eyelids flickered. And then they opened.

They found his, and for an instant, they gave no sign. He froze, and for that tiny second, nothing existed, nothing was real, and there was no time and there were no questions.

Then the eyes became a person's because emotion was filtering through them, feelings reflected what lay beyond, and they smiled and her lips smiled with them.

'Why do you call me Casey, John?' she asked, and fell back into a deep sleep again.

Janet Halstead was delighted when Holman told her of Casey's words. She couldn't be sure until Casey had recovered consciousness fully, but it seemed fairly certain that her brain would function normally once she had. Janet urged Holman to snatch a couple of hours' sleep, promising to wake him as soon as

Casey came out of her slumber. She found him a quiet room containing a couch and left him resting while she went back to study Casey's chart.

It was three hours later that Barrow shook his shoulder to wake him.

'She's awake, Holman, and she's fine,' he told him.

With a grin, Holman sat up and rubbed his face. 'Hell,' he said, 'I need a shave.'

'I don't think she'll mind.'

'Any new developments with the fog?' he asked the policeman as he hurriedly slipped on his jacket.

'Plenty, but I'll tell you after you've seen the girl.'

When Holman reached Observation Room 3, Casey was sitting up in bed talking to Janet Halstead. Her face lit up as he walked through the door and in a second they were in each other's arms, Holman smothering her face with kisses. Janet smiled at Barrow and they discreetly left the room.

'You're all right!' Holman laughed, breaking away from the tight embrace at last.

'Yes, yes, I'm all right.'

'Do,' he hesitated, 'do you remember anything?'

'A few things, John.' She became serious, her eyes averting his. 'I remember trying to kill you.'

He drew her towards him and said nothing.

'It's all so unclear,' she went on. 'Different images going through my mind, all mixed up, none of it real.' She clung to him, tighter.

'My father ...' Her voice drifted off.

'Casey,' Holman began.

'He's dead, isn't he?'

Holman was stunned into silence. She remembered that? Finally, he said, 'Yes, Casey. He's dead.'

'He wasn't my father.'

Again, Holman fell into inadequate silence.

'He told me, John, just before I killed him. He told me he loved me ... but it was more than a father's love. He ... he wanted me.' She began to weep now, her body trembling, but the tears were of sadness and not remorse. 'I don't feel it yet. I feel sorry for him, but for some reason it's not really affecting me the way it should. Why, John? Am I still mad?' She pulled away and looked at him imploringly. 'Tell me, John, am I still insane?'

'No, darling,' he said, cupping her face in his hands. 'It'll hit you later.' And God help you when it does, he thought. 'You've been through too much. Your mind's protecting you. The pain will find you soon enough. Don't go looking for it.'

She cried out then and buried her head against him, her body now convulsing with her sobs. He held her tightly to him, knowing the hurt was seeping through, his words had spurred it to.

'I loved him, I loved him so much! How can I ever live with what I've done?'

'It wasn't your fault, Casey, you weren't responsible.'

'And you, John, I tried to kill you. Can you forgive me?'

'I told you, darling, you weren't responsible.'

'Am I really all right now? Am I really better?'

'Yes, of course you are. And I'll help you forget, Casey. I promise I'll help you forget.'

It would take a long time to heal the wound she'd inflicted upon herself, but he knew she was strong enough to get over it. Maybe the fact that Simmons' motives were not entirely pure would help, or maybe it would make matters worse. There was no way of knowing. It would be up to Casey, and up to him to make up for part of that love she'd lost.

He talked to her quietly for a long time, the intensity of his words breaking through her barrier of regret, reaching, searching, until she began to respond with feelings other than self-pity. 'What's going to happen now?' she finally asked.

'They want me to go back into the fog for the mycoplasma.'

'Why? Why you? Janet told me about the mutation and how it's causing the madness. But who wants you to get it? And why does it have to be you?'

Briefly, he told her of the events that had passed, of the disasters, of his immunity, and the fact that she would now be immune. He told her of the disease, of its origin, of the blind foolishness that had freed it. He barely mentioned his experience that morning, not wanting to give her cause for even more concern, merely telling her he'd been unable to locate the source.

She listened in quiet horror, occasionally shaking her head in disbelief, the rising fear inside her only slightly quelled by the knowledge that she was presumably now immune.

They were interrupted by Janet Halstead who bustled into the room, a tight smile betraying her tiredness. 'We still have a few more tests to make on Miss Simmons, John, and then I think she should get some rest. Your policeman is anxious to have a word with you, I believe.'

Holman kissed Casey and promised to return as soon as he was allowed. Casey wanted to tell him not to go back to the fog, to stay nearby, to take her away as soon as she was strong enough, but she knew her words would be wasted. And she knew the lives of many others depended on him. Despite all the technological advances of science, it seemed survival still depended on the action of a man. One man.

Barrow was still waiting for him in the corridor outside. 'They want you to go in again,' he told Holman.

'But what about the contraptions they set up to contain it?'

'Didn't work. The mutation itself just didn't cross their paths. At the moment they're still spraying the fog with calcium chloride, hundreds of tons of it, and it seems to be receding. They want you out there and ready to go in when they've dispersed it as much as they can.'

'What about the wind? Has it dropped?'

'It's not as bad as it was.'

'All right. Since I have no choice, I'll choose to try again.'

The helicopter flew them to a point east of Haslemere where they were met by Hermann Ryker, William Douglas-Glyne and Lieutenant-General Sir Keith

Macklen. The men were standing among a group of vehicles that held a high vantage point overlooking the surrounding countryside. Holman was impressed by the constant stream of light aircraft that flew over the distant cloud of fog which looked even more ominous in the evening gloom.

Douglas-Glyne strode towards him, his hand outstretched. 'Valiant effort this morning, Mr Holman,' he said, grasping Holman's hand.

Holman grinned wryly at the insincerity of the words. 'Sorry I couldn't pull it off,' he said.

'Not to worry. Better luck next time, eh?'

Sir Keith Macklen joined them and said bluntly, 'You have to try again. It's absolutely vital that you bring us back some of the bloody stuff.'

'Yes,' said Douglas-Glyne. 'We sent two volunteers in a couple of hours ago out of desperation. They were well protected with suits and used an army scout vehicle to go in. We lost radio contact with them about an hour ago.'

'So it's up to you now,' said Sir Keith.

'Gentlemen,' broke in Professor Ryker's voice as he walked over at a leisurely pace, 'there is nothing Mr Holman can do for the moment. We do not want to stop the spraying now that it seems to be taking effect and Mr Holman could hardly walk into such a heavy concentration of calcium chloride. Unfortunately, we have not dispersed the fog as much as I thought we would and it will be dark shortly which would make his task even more hazardous.'

'But there are thousands of lives at stake,' said Sir Keith gruffly.

'Precisely. That is why Mr Holman is so valuable to us. We cannot take unnecessary risks with his life – particularly now we know there are definitely two lunatics wandering around out there.'

'But we don't know that – '

'Yes we do!' Ryker said angrily. 'It was on your insistence, Sir Keith, that they went in. I advised against it, I told you what would happen. I will not allow Mr Holman to risk his life because of your misjudgement! He means too much to the whole operation.'

'But we can't just stand by and do nothing,' Douglas-Glyne fumed.

'We are not doing nothing. We will spray the fog all night, for as long as our supplies last. By early morning, it should have depleted enough for us to see the actual mycoplasma – if it is still visible without its protective mist. In the meantime, Mr Holman, I suggest you try to sleep and we'll call you when the time is right.'

Once again, Holman found Barrow shaking him into reluctant consciousness in the early hours of the following morning. He had watched the fog for hours the previous night as the fleet of cars and army vehicles had slowly trundled after it like a funeral procession searching for a graveyard, and had finally fallen into a heavy, dreamless sleep in the back of the car he was travelling in, woken only once when shouts of alarm had passed down the convoy. The bodies of the two scientists who had gone into the fog earlier had been found; the signs indicated that they had killed each other with the guns they had carried for protection against attacks from any individuals who had not escaped the fog. Sleep had recaptured him almost immediately, but it had been filled with grotesque figures which his eyes were somehow never able to focus on.

He was confused at Barrow's statement and had to ask him to repeat it, rubbing his eyes in an effort to become fully awake.

'I said the fog has gone,' said Barrow slowly, emphasizing each word. 'It's disappeared.'

▪ 17 ▪

Corporal Wilcox cursed as he slid down the steep incline in the dark. The damp grass increased the speed of his descent and an unseen root caught his foot, spinning his body at an awkward angle. He heard the hoots of laughter from the two soldiers who had watched his uncontrolled progress from above as he came to an abrupt halt at the foot of the embankment.

'I'll bloody murder you two!' he shouted up at them as he crawled forward to retrieve his fallen torch. He shone it towards the two grinning figures. 'Now get down 'ere, the pair of you!'

'Comin', Corp,' they replied in unison and with a shout they jumped together, switching off their torches as they did so.

He heard their crashing, giggling descent, swinging his beam away from them so they would be in complete darkness. Let the mad fuckers break their necks, he grumbled to himself.

They arrived at his feet and he had to jump back hastily to avoid being knocked over by their kicking legs. They lay on their backs, breathing hard and grinning up at him.

'Come on, get up,' he ordered gruffly. 'I don't know what's the matter with you two. You're like a couple of gigglin' fairies on a night out.'

'Sorry, Eddie,' the smaller of the two apologized with a smirk, 'but my friend Bernard' – he over-emphasized the 'ard' – 'always gets this way when it's past his bedtime.'

'It's Corporal to you, Evans,' said Wilcox, his dislike for the little Cockney and his Mancunian companion evident in his tone. The pair of them were a constant thorn in his flesh, always taking the piss, but never quite overstepping the mark so he could put them on a charge – or belt one of them. They didn't even have to say anything, their stupid mocking faces were enough to make him feel a cunt.

They picked themselves up, brushing themselves down and groaning at imagined bruises.

'What we coom down 'ere for anyway, Corp?' asked Private Buswell, his droning accent a further irritant to Wilcox. 'It's only a bloomin' railway track.'

'Orders are that every square inch of ground is to be covered!' the Corporal snapped, swinging his torch along the lines that were no longer silver but dull and rusty.

'Anyway, it's gone, innit?' Evans stated disgustedly. 'I mean, we been lookin' for two bleedin' days now!'

'They think it's gone. We're lookin' to make sure.'

'Yeah, but that spray stuff cleared it, didn't it?' insisted Evans.

'I told you, they think so.'

'Well, they couldn't 'ave just lost it, could they?' drawled Buswell.

'No, but it was funny 'ow it just vanished,' said Wilcox. 'I mean, they'd been sprayin' it all day and the stuff was workin', but all of a sudden, it wasn't there anymore. The thing in the middle, I mean.'

'Yeah, well, what is it then, this thing in the middle? It's supposed to be a bug, innit?' Evans asked, switching on his own torch, pointing it at the sky to see how far its beam travelled.

'The disease, that's what it is. They want to make sure that's gone an' all.'

'Yeah, well I don't fancy findin' it.'

'Don't worry, we don't have to go near it,' Wilcox reassured him, then added disdainfully, 'Anyway, you two bleeders are potty enough. It wouldn't have any effect on you.'

'Quite right, Corp,' grinned Evans, 'me and Bernard are right nutters, so I'd watch us close seeing as we've got bullets for our rifles.'

'Yeah, Corp,' said Buswell, his smiling expression turning into one of puzzlement, 'why've we got ammunition?'

'Just in case, Buswell, just in case we run into real lunatics.'

'You don't mean we'd 'ave to shoot them?'

'If we found the glow and ran into any trouble that might prevent us reportin' its location, then we're to use our own discretion, of course.'

'Ooh, makes me feel all cold,' shivered Evans. 'Come on, let's 'ave a fag.'

'Always the fuckin' same, you two. It's me who cops it if the Sarge finds us. He's around 'ere somewhere,' Wilcox moaned.

'Nah, he's a long way off. Let's walk up a bit, find a nice secluded spot.'

Corporal Wilcox stepped into the centre of the lines and began to walk forward, playing his torch along the sleepers ahead of him. The other two fell in behind him, Evans whistling an off-key tune.

''Ere! We not gonna' get run down, are we?' He broke off his whistling to ask the question.

'Don't be bloody daft. This is a disused track. You can see by the grass it hasn't been used for years. And look at the rust on the lines.'

'Just checkin', Corp.'

Wilcox heard Buswell's snigger from behind and snorted with weary annoyance. 'Why the hell do I always get roped in with you two piss artists?'

They marched on to the accompaniment of Evans's tuneless whistle, searching the steep embankment on either side with their torches.

'How coom it glows then, this stuff?' asked Buswell after a while.

'Radiation, innit?' Evans told him.

'Who said it was radiation?' Wilcox stopped and turned to look at him.

'Stand to reason, dunnit?' The amusement never left his eyes. 'It glows, so they tell us. It eats away people's brains. It's driftin' around the country at its leisure and they can't stop it. All adds up.'

'Yeah, well how would radiation come from the sea?' asked the Corporal belligerently.

'Oh gawd! You don't believe that do you?' said Evans, his turn to be disgusted. 'They rely on pricks like you to believe the stories they put out.'

'Watch it, Evans, or you'll be on a charge.'

'All right, Corp, don't get nasty. Come on, let's keep going.'

They continued marching, Evans expounding on his theory. 'You see, they've done it, the scientists. They've 'ad an accident at one of their atomic power plants and now they're doin' a cover-up. This bloody fog, in actual fact, is a bloody radiation cloud, right, Bernard?'

'Right, Professor.'

'That earthquake, the other day. Now what d'you think that was?'

'An earthquake,' said Buswell brightly.

'Oh, shut up, turd-brain. That, Corp, was an underground explosion. And for all we know, it was an atomic explosion. And for all we know, that's where this radiation came from.' He nodded his head in appreciation of his own theory.

'You do talk rubbish, Evans,' said Wilcox, his attention now directed at the black shape looming ahead of them.

'Yeah,' muttered Evans under his breath, 'and it's silly sods like you that never learn.'

Wilcox stopped abruptly again, causing Evans to bump into him, and Buswell to bump into Evans.

'There's a tunnel up ahead,' he told them.

'Right, let's 'ave a fag now then,' said Evans, already unbuttoning his tunic.

'You'll get me shot, you two,' grumbled the Corporal, the other two interpreting his remark for one of assent. They squatted just inside the entrance to the tunnel, away from the searching eyes of the other soldiers that were heavily concentrated in the surrounding area.

Evans shielded the flare from his match with a cupped hand, lighting Buswell's cigarette first and then his own. 'Oh, sorry, Corp,' he apologized insincerely, offering the light towards Wilcox.

Wilcox ignored him and huffily lit his cigarette with his own matches. He sat on the rail opposite the two privates.

'All right, know-all,' he said acidly to Evans, 'tell me something: if this thing we're lookin' for is radiation, why can't they find it with detectors?' He leaned forward, a smile of satisfaction on his face.

'Because, my old fruit, they've already got rid of it,' said Evans returning the smile smugly.

'What, with a bloody spray?' Wilcox sat upright, shaking his head at the private's stupidity.

'That's right. We don't know what the spray was, do we? They said it was to clear the fog, but what they really meant was it was to clear the radiation.'

'Gawd 'elp us,' sighed Wilcox, looking towards the roof of the tunnel.

'No, no,' Evans insisted. 'We don't know, do we? We don't know what they've invented. Stands to reason they'd 'ave thought of something to get rid of radiation. They've 'ad enough time to.'

Wilcox snorted again and Buswell sniggered.

'We're the cannon fodder, mate,' Evans went on. 'They've sent us in to make sure it '*as* cleared up.'

'Without detectors?'

'Without detectors. They don't want people to *know* it's radiation, do they?'

'Christ!' Wilcox gave up. Evans's absurd logic had been a source of irritation and frustration to him for a long time now, but sometimes it became unbearable. 'I'm gonna 'ave a quick look up the tunnel then we'll be on our way.' He could have sent either of the two men but couldn't face the protests as to why they shouldn't and besides, he felt the need to be away from them even if it was only for a few seconds.

Bloody misfits, he cursed inwardly, as he trudged down into the blackness. They hadn't joined the army for a career as he had. They'd joined because they wanted an easy life – free food, free lodgings, and someone else to make the decisions for them. The Professionals! The Shirkers was more like it. Any chance they had to get out of doing their job, they'd grab at it. They'd got him into enough trouble in the past, these two, that's why he wasn't a sergeant yet. You'd think after six bloody years he'd have made sergeant! He'd been in line for it this year until these two monkeys had latched on to him. Why him? What was so fascinating about him that they had to make themselves a nuisance around him? The time they'd got him pissed in Germany while they were on guard duty. They'd started off by persuading him to have just a quick one, then another, then another, till he didn't care any more and had got so drunk he spewed up over the NCO's shiny boots when he'd come round on his inspection.

He'd almost got court-martialled over that: it was only the fact that the NCO was being returned to England the next day and didn't want to hang around for the trial that got him off. But he'd been made to pay for it in other ways.

Then there was the 'nice, clean, little tart' they'd introduced him to in Hamburg. She even had a medical certificate to prove she was clean. He'd got the pox from her and the British army frowned on soldiers who get the pox, even though it happened all the time.

In Northern Ireland, they'd taken him to a 'friendly little social club', not far from the barracks and where they'd be well received so long as they were in civvies. The three of them had nearly 'well received' bullets in the backs of their heads on that occasion. It was only his prompt action of hurling a chair through the window, the three soldiers quickly following it, that had saved their lives. Evans had laid out the bitch who had invited them with a bottle before he'd leapt through, and that had cost him a glancing bullet on the side of his arse. It was a pity it hadn't gone right up it! The army hadn't been too pleased about that little episode either.

He supposed he'd been lucky, considering. The incidents – there were many more of them – were never quite enough to cause drastic action against him, but they all served to keep him down at his present rank.

The trouble was, he fell for it every time. They either smarmed their way round him or offered him a challenge. And he always gave in or rose to the bait. He always had to prove he was one of the boys. Christ, this was a long tunnel!

He looked back and realized he must have rounded a bend for the torches of the two privates were no longer visible. He shone his torch ahead but all he could see was its bright reflection against the shiny damp wall. He must be at the centre of the bend, unable to see back or ahead – and unable to be seen. Right, this is far enough, he thought to himself, stepping out of the track and leaning his rifle against the wall. He began to unbutton his trousers, holding his torch between his upper arm and side. That was another thing! He couldn't even piss in front of them. Their mocking faces caused a mental block – or a block somewhere else. They knew the effect they had on him and sometimes would follow him out to the gents if they were in the Naafi or a club, and stand on either side of him, grinning, while his face grew redder and the cock in his hand more apologetic.

Even now, just the thought of them was preventing him from performing his body's natural function. Why did they have to make his life a misery? Just wait till he was made sergeant, then they'd pay for it. Maybe that was it. Maybe they knew that and were trying to stop his progress. Bastards!

As he stared blankly at the wall two feet away from him, his features eerily lit in the throwback from his torch, his legs apart, his hands on his penis, his mind engrossed in bitter thoughts, he failed to notice the thick tentacles of mist that crept around his ankles like a wispy grey vine. The tentacles thickened into a layer of fog as they began to rise and slowly engulf his body.

'Eddie's a long time,' Buswell commented, his cigarette beginning to burn the insides of his fingers in his effort to waste as little as possible.

'You'll get cancer doing that,' Evans remarked. 'It's the last bit that's got most of the nicotine.'

Buswell shrugged his shoulders. He should worry.

'Come on, Corp, what you doing? Having a wank?' Evans shouted into the darkness. There was no reply. 'He's probably sulking,' he said, once more resting his elbows on his knees and flicking his cigarette end into the gloom.

'Poor old Eddie. He takes it serious, doesn't he?' said Buswell.

'Yeah. He's all right though. Just 'asn't really got what it takes. He's good for a laugh though.'

'D'you think he'll'ever get to be sergeant?'

'Nah, no chance! Every time there's a possibility, he fucks it up. Every time!'

Evans smiled, his face looking evil in the torch-light. 'Don't know how he does it.'

'What d'you think this fog really was then, Ray?' Buswell asked him, knowing Evans always had several theories on any topic.

'Well, I tell you, Bernard, I don't fuckin' know. But I bet you one thing – it's man-made. It's got something to do with the pollution, I reckon. It's like those rivers where they've found thousands of dead fish, all because the bleedin' factories have dumped their rubbish into them. Well, this time, somebody's dumped somethin' into the air, y'see, gas or chemicals, I dunno what, but it's got out of 'and. Like one of those 'orror films.'

'Get away.'

'Nah, I mean it. Somethin' got into the air and it was spreadin'. It ain't really fog, y'know. It's like, er, like vapour ...'

As he embroidered on his new theory which was occurring to him while he spoke, the fog, unseen in the dark, curled its way along the tunnel towards them. Just inside its fringes walked the figure of a man. He held a loaded rifle thrust before him, as though it were bayoneted and he was advancing on a rioting crowd. He heard the voices that were coming from ahead and something stirred in his disturbed mind.

He saw the figures outlined in the glare of two torches. His own torch lay shattered between the railway lines far back inside the tunnel. He drew nearer to the two men and the words, 'Where you been?' meant nothing to him.

Slowly he raised the rifle and placed it against the forehead of one of the soldiers. Then he pulled the trigger.

The tunnel was filled with the roar from the gun and the scream of the other man. The brief flash lit the scene into a frozen moment that was impressed for seconds after it had vanished on the mind of the soldier who had screamed.

Buswell threw his torch at Corporal Wilcox, who still held the smoking rifle, his fixed gaze on the dead man who was slowly toppling backwards. Still screaming, Buswell ran from the tunnel, leaving his rifle leaning against the dark wall. In his panic he made the mistake of trying to climb the steep embankment just outside the tunnel's entrance, his hands pulling out clumps of grass as he endeavoured to pull himself up, his feet slipping on the damp earth.

His flailing arms caught at a small bush and, miraculously, it held his weight enabling him to scramble up several feet. He heard the sound of a bolt being shot, sharp and clear in the chill night air, and it drove him on to further exertion for he realized the gun was ready to be fired again.

By sheer brute strength and blind defiance of the laws of gravity he almost reached the top of the incline.

His second mistake was to look back.

He saw the still figure at the foot of the slope staring up at him, not moving, not even raising his rifle.

Buswell sobbed and made a desperate lunge upwards, stretching his arm in a vain effort to reach the top of the embankment, as though there was another arm ready to grip his and pull him to safety. His hand closed over grass which was instantly torn from the soft earth and his boots were dislodged from their precarious footholds. He began to slither down, his scrabbling hands finding no purchase to halt his descent, his body pressed flat against the damp grass.

Slowly, slowly he slid down until his feet touched the bottom and carried on at right angles to his body so that he was almost in a kneeling position. The Corporal stood over him and raised the butt of his rifle.

The fog flowed from the tunnel, wispy and hesitant at first, but soon thickly and swift. It swirled around the two soldiers and quickly enveloped them.

▪ 18 ▪

HOLMAN OPENED HIS EYES, HIS BRAIN TAKING A FEW SECONDS TO BEGIN functioning normally. He stared up at the ceiling and allowed his thoughts to gather and settle, then turned towards the figure lying in his bed next to him. In the grey light that filtered through the drawn curtains her face looked as it used to be, calm, and hardly touched by life, but he knew, in harsh daylight, the faint beginnings of lines would be there, for she could not possibly have escaped the rigours of the past few days without their leaving some visible mark. And the wound left inside her would be much worse than any physical scar.

How different she looked from the last time she had been in his flat. Would he ever forget that deranged look of hatred on her face, the violence of her attack on him? Would he always be waiting for that look to return, unable to close his mind to visions of the past, dreading that the disease was only lying dormant, lurking deep in the recesses of her brain, waiting for the moment to begin its evil, parasitical journey once again?

Janet Halstead had assured him Casey was completely cured, as was he, and there was no chance of the malignancy ever returning, but it was difficult to rid himself of all his fears. Only time would do that.

He was grateful to the doctor for allowing him to bring Casey home. Although all the tests had been completed, both on himself and the girl, and their usefulness in that particular area had been diminished, she could have insisted that they both remain at the Research Centre in case of any eventuality that might arise. But provided they reported in every day, Janet was happy to let them go, recognizing the need for them to retreat into their own privacy, to lick their wounds, to comfort one another. Medical treatment could only reach a certain point; after that, it was up to each individual's natural protective instinct to complete the cure.

Holman was on call at any time although they had found no trace of the fog for two days now. The trail of havoc it had left behind it was appalling, for not everybody had been cleared from its path in time. The consequences of the fog were still occurring, for reaction to it took longer to manifest itself in some than in others. For many, the effect was immediate, causing instant madness, their brain cells crumbling rapidly against the onslaught of the mutated parasite. Many people were killed; many killed themselves.

On the first day of quiet, when the fog had inexplicably disappeared, the country had been left in a state of numbness. Then a stirring seemed to ripple through the land as the public demanded answers. What was the fog? Where had it come from? If it had come from the sea, what was its source? Had it really gone, and if so, could it possibly return? Were there still lunatics at large and what were the first symptoms? Had the government acted swiftly enough and what steps were being taken to ensure that a disaster of this kind and magnitude would never happen again? Had a foreign power secretly experimented on Britain and was the country now being held to ransom by that power?

All these questions and many more had been asked and the government had to provide answers – and quickly. Today was the day of answers and reassurances. Even the truth had been considered by the special inner Cabinet who had full knowledge of the source, but the consideration was easily rejected.

Holman's hand found the soft curve of Casey's waist and he dreaded the telephone call that might take him away from her. The thought of going back into the fog was repugnant to him and he prayed it had been finally vanquished.

She stirred and snuggled towards him, a low murmur of peace escaping from slightly parted lips. His hand slid up her back and he pulled her farther towards him until their bodies touched. Still half asleep, she pushed her leg between his and her arm encircled his waist, reaching down until her hand spread out over a buttock. He grew hard against her, softly and sweetly, his penis pressed between her soft flesh and his own.

Awake now, but her mind still comfortably dulled, her senses racing ahead of it, her hand reached down and casually stroked the back of his leg. She sighed and spoke his name and he whispered his love to her, kissing her hair and forehead. She raised her head and her lips met his, moist, gently demanding. He parted their bodies so he could touch her breasts and her nipples were hard beneath his fingertips, eager to be awakened and risen from their small surrounding islands of flesh. His head came down to take one in his mouth, his lips closing over it, his tongue moistening its tip.

She moaned and her body stretched, her lower limbs pressing tight against him, his thigh filling her inner thighs. There had been no desire for lovemaking for either of them the night before: the memory of her father's death was too dominant in their minds. Their bodies had needed contact, but only to gain each other's warmth and solace, and they had soon fallen asleep, both wearied in body and spirit by the week's events.

Now the tiredness had gone from their bodies and their spirits were on the first step towards recovery, although for Casey, the step was small. She pulled her breast away from him, the very act of its withdrawal heightening her sensuality, and her teeth bit gently at his neck, then harder, drawing his blood towards the spot without breaking the skin.

A flicker of fear passed swiftly through his thoughts but was instantly subdued as her lips moved on, murmuring sounds of love, kissing his chest, closing over his own rigid nipple then moving over to its jealous companion. Her tongue traced a line between the muscles of his stomach, a tiny damp stream that ended in the well of his navel.

His penis rose quivering to meet her parted lips and suddenly it was engulfed in a warm cavern, the soft entrance concealing a sharp ridge of teeth, but its interior containing a silky, ever-moving animal that smothered it in its welcome. Her lips moved down the length of him and back again in a steady, regular motion, her tongue always active, her teeth barely making contact. He shuddered at the sensation and his hands gripped her shoulders, moving with her, controlling her timing.

Before the shudders became frantic and the pleasure too exquisite, he withdrew himself from her and gently pulled her smiling face up to his, kissing her lips hard and passionately, the faint taste of his own body on her tongue exciting him even more.

His hand reached flatly towards her stomach and he ran his fingers downwards through the small, tidy forest of hair until he found her other even more moist cave, silky smooth with its aroused lubricity. Her hips rose slightly and her thighs tautened as her knees bent and her heels dug into the bed. She relaxed then tightened her muscles again, moaning as she twisted her head to one side. His fingers stayed near her entrance and teased her most sensual part, then stroking more firmly, understanding her body's demands.

This time it was Casey who drew him away before the ecstasy became too overwhelming. She pulled at his hip and he slid over her, entering her with measured ease, resisting his own urgency. The passage was smooth and he stopped only when his penis had travelled its full length, her hands tightly clenched on his buttocks, drawing him into her, desperate to claim every inch of him. She cried out as he began to move rhythmically, her lips frenziedly seeking his, then twisting her head away again into the pillow as the pleasure began its swift ascent. Her legs bent but did not close around him, unwilling to restrict his movements or her own upward thrusts. One of his hands reached up for her breast and crushed it cruelly, but the cruelty was derived from passion, and was understood and welcomed.

Her body-stretching release came seconds before his, but the warm fluid that finally flowed from him into her deepened her own satisfaction and she was pleased to receive the heavy weight of his body as it slumped against her, when his movements had ceased. They lay still until their breathing had become steady and their hearts had slowed their pace, she stroking the back of his head, he using his elbows to help ease his weight.

After a short while, he lifted himself from her, kissing her chest flushed from her orgasm, and rolled on to his back. She turned sideways towards him, one arm across his chest to clasp his shoulder, one leg raised to rest on his.

She gazed at his relaxed face and drew a finger down his profile, stopping to run the length of his mouth, then down again over his chin, past his neck to come to rest on his chest where it nestled amongst dark hairs.

'You still haven't told me,' she said after a while.

'What?' He looked down at her in surprise.

'You haven't told me.'

'Told you what?'

'Why you call me Casey.'

He began to chuckle. 'You really want to know, do you?'

'Yes.'

'No. You'll only get angry.'

'Angry? You'd better tell me now!' She raised her head to look down at him.

'You're sure you want to know?'

'Yes!' Indignant.

'Well,' he began, smiling and looking at her from the corner of his eyes, 'when I was a kid, I used to have a dog ...'

'A dog?'

'... and I used to call it Casey ...'

'You called it ...'

'... and when I saw you ...'

'... Casey! You – '

'... you had the same sad little eyes ...'

'... you ...'

'... and they made me fall in love with you ... and I knew I'd found something that would be precious again to me ... and that's why I called you Casey.'

She fell against him, half-laughing but ready to cry. He hugged her, still grinning, but strangely near to sadness himself.

'Imagine my delight when I found you were house-trained, too.'

And now, she did cry. She cried from happiness, sadness, and relief that they were together.

'Is it over now?'

'The fog? The nightmare? I just hope so. If it isn't, well, I just don't know what else they can do about it.'

'Surely they could find an answer.'

'The calcium chloride must have been the answer. They just needed a lot of it.'

'Why are they so reticent about announcing it?'

'Because they don't understand how the chemical could have destroyed the mycoplasma. On Ryker's advice, they've decided to play it cautiously, to wait until they're absolutely certain.'

'And when will that be?'

'Who knows? When they've covered the area thoroughly, I suppose.'

She shuddered and pressed closer to him. 'Or when people stop going insane.'

'They've got the cure now. Provided it doesn't happen again on a massive scale, they can cure anyone they find with the illness.'

'Unless the victims kill themselves first.'

He was silent. They'd been lucky, both of them, but the price they had to pay in memories was harsh. He knew there would be many silences between them now as they both remembered. It would take years for them to detach themselves from the dream, but because of their own personal experiences, they would be able to understand and help each other.

He looked down at her and her eyes met his. She too, had been lost in her own thoughts. She smiled.

'I'm okay,' she said.

He sat up then, resolving never to allow either of them to sink too far into the quicksands of their memories. 'I'll get some coffee.'

'No,' she pulled him down again, 'you stay there. Let me do it.'

He lay back and watched her naked figure slip into his discarded shirt. The shirt flapped large and seductively around her as she bent forward to kiss him, the glimpse of her small breasts beginning to excite him again. She walked around the bed towards the drawn curtains and once more the image of the last time he'd seen her in the darkened room leapt into his mind. But even now, the thought was becoming easier to push away.

She reached up and began to draw the curtains, but she stopped midway and he saw her body stiffen.

'John ...' he heard her say, half turning her head towards him but unable to tear her eyes away from the strangely subdued light that came from outside.

He leapt from the bed, already feeling the familiar coldness chilling his body. Reaching her side, he drew the curtain back at one side in a violent sweep, then stopped to stare at the scene that lay beyond.

'Oh God!' he gasped.

For there was no scene beyond. Just a grey blankness. A heavy, still blankness, tinged with yellow.

They stood in awe and dread of its obscuring density and were only dimly aware of the telephone that rang persistently from the room next door.

They had tried to warn the city of the approaching doom. It had appeared suddenly, a small cloud swept onwards by a strong wind. After two days of searching, just when they had begun to relax, it appeared, at first hidden by the pre-dawn mists, but then rising as though it had been lying in wait, mustering its forces, waiting for its new ally, the north-east wind. Many had panicked, for they were directly in the path of the fast-moving cloud, and had scattered in three directions. The bravest remembered to radio their mobile operations base before and as they fled, but the majority were concerned only with self-preservation.

As the fog swept over the countryside, it grew larger. It passed through the smaller towns, then through industrial estates which belched out their filthy fumes even during the night, and it welcomed the polluted air, drawing it to its poisonous womb, growing with it. It reached the suburbs and its size began to make the wind less effective. It drifted inwards towards the city.

The scattered army was regathered and the troops sped ahead of the fog, loudspeakers blaring out their ill-timed warning. They realized it was virtually useless, that by the time the people had rubbed their blurry eyes and the message registered, it would be too late, the growing fog would already be on them.

But they tried. Or at least, two-thirds of the forces tried. The remaining third raced into London to perform other tasks.

Janet Halstead was aroused from her sleep by one of her assistants. She slipped on her robe and went through to the office adjoining her private sleeping quarters. Picking up the phone, she asked the switchboard to put through the call that had been waiting for her. She listened in silence, her expression never changing, only her eyes betraying a sad weariness.

When she finally put down the phone, she stared at it for a few seconds longer. Then her body seemed to draw itself together and she began to snap instructions at her bewildered assistant for the immediate evacuation of the Research Centre. All equipment, notes – anything useful that could be dismantled – were to be moved to another location. A secret location. Transport was already on its way to take them there.

Stan Reynolds, a middle-aged security guard, strolled along the lush carpeted corridor towards his favourite room at the very top of the giant oil company building that towered over the black River Thames. It contained the largest boardroom table he'd ever seen, and he'd seen a few over the years in the various companies he'd been employed in as a guard. It was made of the deepest oak and was reputed to have cost over six thousand pounds; sixty people could be comfortably seated round it. He opened the heavy boardroom doors that reached the ceiling and stepped into the room, switching on the lights as he did so.

Walking the length of the table, he stopped behind the magnificent leather chair that belonged to the chairman. He sank into it, removed his boots and placed his feet on the table. With a contented sigh, he lost himself in a colourful reverie of big business deals and boardroom power games.

His nightly dream fulfilled, he swung his legs off the table, put his boots back on and strolled towards the huge windows that looked south across London. It was a view that always filled him with immense pride in the vast city, the lights shining like star clusters on a black velvet universe.

But on this occasion, the view was different. There was an orange glow in the sky and he drew in his breath as he realized the cause of it. He saw a line of fires stretching across South London, huge fires at regular intervals, their flames red and frightening. For a moment, his mind travelled back in time and it was the war and the blitz, the fires caused by the bombs of the enemy.

Then the flames seemed to lose their brightness as though they were being covered, one by one, by a semi-transparent blanket, leaving only a red glow shining dully through.

He thought he heard the sound of a loudspeaker coming from somewhere in the distance, but it was too indistinct and he was too puzzled by the phenomenon before him to concentrate on its message.

He stood and watched the approaching fog as it gradually obscured the million lights, crawling forward, swallowing the town, piece by piece, until it reached the river just below him.

And then the river was gone and the fog was brushing against the large plate-glass window in front of him.

Dawn. McLellan, Holman's colleague at the Ministry of the Environment, stared from his bedroom window out at the fog. His eyes were heavy from unshed tears. He knew it was *the* fog, its yellowish tinge told him that. And he had been expecting it; his faith in his own government in times of crisis had never been great and he had expected them to bungle this.

He was much more aware of the danger than most of the general public for he had been closer to the strange occurrences through Holman and the dead Spiers, and many people still did not understand that it was not the fog that killed, but the madness it caused that drove people to their deaths.

He turned to look at his wife still snugly curled up beneath the bedclothes, asleep and vulnerable. As he thought of his children in the adjoining bedrooms, the tears of bitterness and frustration broke. How long would it take for the poison to work on their minds, to make them insane? What would it do to him? Would he be the one to take the lives of his own family? He struck out at the air blindly. There must be a way to protect them.

Sitting on the edge of the bed, taking care not to wake his wife, he tried to calm himself. There had to be an answer! Could he tie them up, or lock them in their rooms? But what about himself? What would protect them from him? Could he make sure they were protected from themselves and then go out and hopefully lose himself in the fog? No, he couldn't leave them; it would seem like desertion. He had to think fast; God knows how long it took for the poison to take effect. For Spiers it had taken a day, for Holman, it was almost immediate.

Then he had the answer! It wasn't ideal, but it could give them a little time; time enough perhaps for the authorities to take some kind of action, time for them to start saving lives.

He went into his daughter's room and took the small toy blackboard from its easel, together with some chalk, carefully closing the door as he left so as not to disturb her. He went downstairs and, sitting on the bottom step, he chalked a message in large capitals on the board. Opening the front door, he placed the message on the doorstep, praying that it would serve its purpose. Then he went back upstairs and into the bathroom, taking the bottle of sleeping pills from the top shelf of the cabinet, the pills his wife sometimes found necessary to calm her from the rigours of raising three lively children. He filled a glass full of water and returned to his daughter's bedroom. He lifted her forward on the bed, ignoring her feeble, half-asleep protests, and forced her to take five of the pills. Kissing her forehead, he laid her down again and tucked her in, then repeated the same operation on the boys next door. Paul had been awkward, but at the promise of a staggering reward, he'd complied. The next part would be more difficult. He would have to wake his wife, Joan, and explain why he was doing this. Was it his imagination, or could he really feel the beginnings of a headache?

Joan wept and at first refused to take the pills, but after much persuasion and then pleading, she agreed. For himself, he took eight, not knowing what the fatal dose would be, sure that the amount he had given to his family and himself was not too dangerous. Besides, under the circumstances, the risk had to be taken.

He climbed back into the warm bed and drew his weeping wife to him. They lay there, waiting for sleep to come.

Irma Bidmead always rose early. At seventy-three, her days were too short to be wasted on slumber. And her cats would be hungry.

She had thirteen cats, all of them strays that she had adopted. Or perhaps they'd adopted her. She would often roam the streets late at night with a bagful of morsels and scraps for the cats she found in the back streets of Kennington. The cats knew her and recognized her tiny ragbag figure and hissing call as she trundled down the darkened streets and they would follow her until she decided she had a large enough gathering and stopped. Then she would feed them, talking to them, admonishing them for their greed, cackling at their antics to be the first to be fed.

Every few months there would be a van waiting at a prearranged spot, and a dozen or so of the cats would be piled into it and driven off to a South London hospital. The man who drove the van, the man she had the arrangement with, took the lion's share of the money paid by the hospital for the animals, but she still earned a nice little sum from it. Animals for vivisection had always been a profitable business even though the RSPCA had got massive support behind their outcry against it, but because it was necessary, and the authorities knew it, they turned a blind eye.

And the money she earned from the deal went towards feeding her own cats. Because she loved her cats.

Irma was oblivious to the smell that leapt from the room as she opened the door; after a lifetime of living with the creatures, their odour was part of her own, and the fact that thirteen of them had been locked up together in a room all night had no effect on her insensitive nostrils at all.

'Hello, lovelies,' she greeted them, expecting them to run towards her, nuzzling against her ragged dressing-gown in which she slept, as they normally did each morning. But this morning, they remained aloof, neither moving nor making any sound.

In her annoyance, she failed to notice the yellowish mist that drifted in through the thin crack of the slightly opened window.

'Now what's the matter with you today?' she demanded to know, her irritation growing. 'Showing off, are you? Well, you can feed yourselves!'

She stamped from the room and into the kitchen where she retrieved two stiff and pungent kippers from the sink. Muttering to herself, she flounced back to the cats' room and threw the kippers in.

"Ere,' she shouted, 'an' don't choke on the bones, you're lucky to get 'em!' She trundled back into her room and climbed into bed, pushing the comfortably curled-up cat that always slept with her away from the warm spot. It bristled in annoyance, but soon settled down again. Irma called out to the other cats again: 'Don't you come crawlin' 'round me when you've finished your fish! I don't want to know, I've got an 'eadache,' and then to herself as she pulled the covers up to her chin, 'Ungrateful pigs! I should take them all up the 'ospital, that's what I should do! Except you, Mogs, you love your old lady, don't yuh.' She turned her head and smiled at the cat that purred next to her. 'You're a good old girl, you are. Not like them others – all they want is feedin'! Ooh, my 'ead does ache today!' She closed her eyes to concentrate on the pain.

The cats ignored the fish and silently padded from their room and into Irma's where they waited at the foot of her bed as she began to doze off.

Chief Superintendent Wreford slumped down the stairs and entered the kitchen. Yawning freely, he filled the electric kettle with water and switched it on. God, he was tired! He'd worked long hours because of this wretched fog business and last night was the first he'd been able to take off. Hopefully, it was all over now and he'd be able to take a spot of leave. He congratulated himself on covering himself in the Holman affair. He could have chosen to dismiss the man as a crank, but experience had told him never to ignore warnings, no matter from what source. He'd played it right, not making his enquiries official; at least not until he'd found out there was some truth to the story, and then he'd jumped in feet first, claiming credit for precipitating proceedings before the terrible Bournemouth disaster.

I bet Barrow was choked, he smiled to himself as he emptied stale tea leaves from the pot into the sink. A bit *too* ambitious, that lad, he'd like to see me come unstuck.

He stood with one hand on the kettle and one hand on the pot as he waited for the water to boil, smiling at the wall before him. Still, he's not a bad lad. Bit brutal at times, but he'll mellow with experience and he's useful as he is for the moment. The emergence of steam from the kettle interrupted his thoughts and he poured the boiling water into the teapot, turning the switch off as he did so.

He went to the front door to collect the milk, eager for his first deep lungful of fresh morning air. It was a habit he'd acquired over the years, telling his wife it was the only time one could get a decent breath of fresh air living in London. By 9.00 the streets would be filled with fumes so he always made the most of his 7.30 deep breathing routine, standing on his doorstep for a full five minutes, taking in great gasps of air, while the tea in the kitchen brewed.

As he opened the door he was already drawing in his breath, and before he saw the fog, his lungs were half full of it.

*

Detective Inspector Barrow slept. He'd had a heavy week and this had been his first break. Playing nursemaid to Holman hadn't suited him at all; there were better things for him to do in a crisis such as this, chances to prove himself, to make himself felt. Hadn't it been he who had brought Holman in in the first place? The man irritated him. True, Barrow had been rough on him at first, but as soon as he'd realized his mistake, he had tried to make it up to him. He'd protected the man when he'd been assigned as his bodyguard, had worried about him, tried to start up a more friendly relationship with him. After all, as a man immune to the disease, he was quite important, and if anything *had* happened to him while under Barrow's protection, it would have been Barrow who copped it in the neck. But Holman hadn't wanted to be friendly; he'd kept a distance between them, unwilling to forgive him for his past treatment.

Well, it probably didn't matter any more, the scare seemed to be over. It had done a lot of damage but at least now it was under control – or so they said.

The thoughts had buzzed around his head the night before, a sure sign of extreme weariness, and he had gratefully sunk into his bed, for once unaccompanied by a girl. He had been too tired even for that.

He had immediately gone into a deep sleep and still slept as the sombre grey light filtered through the fog into his bedroom.

Samson King made his way blindly through the fog. He'd lived in London since he was fifteen, but he'd never experienced fog like this before. It was a good thing he did not live too far from the bus depot or he would never have been able to find it. As it was, he wasn't too sure he was going in the right direction. He did not miss the sun of Jamaica as much as his old folks did for he could hardly remember the warm beaches and the deep green sea they described. No, he was used to the watery sun of England and even found the few days of intense heat that the country sometimes had uncomfortable.

Surely they wouldn't expect him to take the bus out in weather like this. Bernice hadn't even wanted him to report for work but he was afraid it might look bad on his record. He did not want to lose this job as he had many others; it suited him being up there behind the wheel of the big red monster, totally in control, dwarfing and bullying the other traffic on the road.

Now, where was he? 'Goddam' fuckin' weather!' he cursed aloud, needing to hear the sound of his own voice. He hadn't passed anyone in the fog and it gave him a peculiar feeling of not being flesh and bone, of being a wandering spirit in a murky void.

The depot should be across the road. The zebra-crossing in front of him ran out halfway across the road, but he knew the bus station would be about fifty yards to the right of it. The crossing often helped him to get his bus out into the busy street for the flow of traffic often had to stop to allow people to cross.

He started forward, keeping a wary eye out for any approaching traffic and using the black and white stripes as a guide to the other side. His head ached, from eye strain he thought, from squinting into the fog, trying to catch glimpses of familiar sights. At least the roads should be clearer today. He giggled, not knowing why he did, and was still giggling when he reached the opposite pavement. He turned right, keeping close to the shops on his left, using them as a guide.

Soon he reached the garage and turned into it, an occasional giggle jerking his body. He didn't ask himself why the depot was empty, why there was no inspector to check him out, why there were no cleaners preparing to leave, why there was no crew-mate waiting impatiently for him. He asked himself no questions.

He just climbed up into his cabin, still grinning, occasionally giggling, and started his engine. Then he moved the bus slowly forward and out of the depot.

Throughout London, people were waking to discover the yellow-grey fog surrounding their homes, some realizing its meaning, some not; many already too insane to care. Thousands had fled during the night, fortunate to have heard the warnings of the loudspeakers or the radio broadcasts. Those had, in turn; informed relatives, friends or loved ones, either by telephone (which, because of the chaos, was the least reliable) or by hurried visits.

But it was a big city, and the thousands who had time to flee were a small proportion compared to the millions who received no warning at all. The huge beacons were lit, but the rolling fog swept right over them, rising from the heat, but immediately descending once it was cleared.

The panic of the night before was nothing compared to the tragic and bizarre pandemonium that was to follow during the ensuing day.

▪ 19 ▪

HOLMAN STEERED THE DEVASTATION VEHICLE CAUTIOUSLY UP THE RAMP OUT into the fog and away from the huge underground shelter. A man called Mason, gross and misshapen because of his protective clothing, sat in the seat next to him peering through the small, heavy lead-reinforced window, his face intense with concentration.

'It doesn't seem to be quite as thick as it was,' said Holman, still looking directly ahead.

'It's probably settled in the London basin and now it's spreading out a bit,' Mason replied.

Holman nodded; it seemed logical. London was in a dip, a saucer-shaped bowl, surrounded by hills. The fog would have drifted into it and come to rest at its base, then sprawled out, filling the town. Its probable way out, unless there was a strong wind, was east along the Thames, through the flat country of Essex.

'Go left along the Embankment,' said Mason, checking the instruments on a panel before him. 'If we follow the road into the City, it'll take us towards it.'

Holman turned left, using the pavement as a guideline. He could just about see the opposite pavement now, something he hadn't been able to do earlier that morning as he had made his way to the secret shelter. He shuddered inwardly, remembering the eerie journey through the fog-filled streets.

Even as he and Casey had been looking out at the fog, still in a state of shock and dismay, tentacles of despair spreading through them, the telephone had begun its persistent, strident ringing. He'd broken away from the mesmeric spell the fog was casting to answer it, as though it were some sort of lifeline, a straw to be clutched at.

It had been Douglas-Glyne, the Defence Under-Secretary, at the other end and he'd snapped out instructions, not allowing Holman to argue or dissent. He was to make his way to Westminster Bridge where he would be picked up by a vehicle resembling an army scout car, only larger and much heavier and fitted with various antennae.

From there he would be brought to a secret rendezvous, the whereabouts of which could not be revealed to him just yet. He was to avoid becoming involved in any incidents that might occur on the way; his sole purpose was to get to the rendezvous point unharmed and as quickly as possible. He was to protect himself even if it meant killing or hurting others to do so; one or two lives were nothing compared to the millions he could help save if he himself remained unhurt. The girl was to remain where she was for now; it was too risky for both of them to make the journey across town. If anything happened to Holman then they would find a way to reach her. They could have sent their 'special' vehicle to fetch him but this would have taken hours, for it was virtually blind in the fog because of its own restricted vision. If he did not make it, they would have to use this method to bring back the girl.

The phone went dead as soon as Holman said he understood and would carry out the instructions. He told Casey what was happening as he quickly dressed, doing his best to keep his voice calm and assured. She did not cry, nor protest, knowing circumstances were directing their actions, that they could no longer control their own destinies, that they had to move as events dictated. He told her to bolt the door behind him and then lock herself in his bedroom. They wasted little time in saying goodbye for the temptation to lock themselves in, away from the outside world and its madness, was too great; the slightest hint from either one of them would all too easily be succumbed to. Instead, they kissed and, without a word, he left.

He used the stairs to get to the ground, not daring to chance the lift which was unreliable at the best of times. The nightmare took on a new dimension once he was in the street.

It was the feeling of emptiness that was most frightening. A feeling of complete hollowness. Nothing was substantial, nothing quite real. He stayed close to the walls, dreading bumping into anyone, but, at the same time, eager to meet someone of his kind, of flesh and blood. He heard a strange wailing noise and realized it was human. He heard a car pass by, travelling fast, fading into the distance, then a crash, followed by cold silence. He heard a scream, a woman's scream, mingled with a laugh. Hysterical laughter. A madman's laugh. But it was all remote and unreal, the phony rantings of a fairground ghost house.

He was thankful it was still early morning and most people were either asleep or just stirring. In his mind's eye he saw a picture of the bedlam that would come later that day, and he quickened his step almost into a trot. He guessed what the task before him would be, but in a strange way he now welcomed it. At least it would be positive action and not just stumbling around in the mist waiting for something to happen. And he would be among people again, hopefully normal people. Thank God Casey was immune. If the plan failed, whatever they had in mind (and he had a shrewd idea), he would go back to her and get her away. To hell with them; they'd made the mess, let them deal with it. He'd done enough already.

Too late he saw the dark shadow before him and they collided, the impact sending the other man to the ground. Without thinking, Holman stooped down to help the sprawled figure to his feet. The man reached up and held on to Holman's shoulders and it was only then, when their faces were no more than a foot apart, that Holman noticed the strange grin on the man's face. He backed away, but the man clung to him, a low growling, chuckling noise coming from his wide grinning mouth. Holman tried to push him off, but an arm reached around his neck and his head was forced forward. He struck out in panic and the man's chuckle turned into a snarl of rage as he retaliated with a savage kick at Holman's ankle. Holman ducked forward, releasing himself from the tenacious grasp, then brought the flat of his hand up underneath the man's chin and pushed it back and back, swiftly, moving with it until the back of the man's head connected with the brick wall behind him. There was a loud crack and the man went down on his knees, one hand reaching for the back of his head, a pathetic whining sob coming from him. His other hand groped blindly for Holman's leg, but Holman stepped back out of reach then turned and began to run.

When he stopped, he found himself completely isolated. He must have run into the road for he could see nothing on either side of him. He walked forward briskly, but alert for any danger, hoping he was heading in the right direction. He heard a scream on his left, a long piercing scream that ended in a sickening, squelching thud. Something wet brushed his face and he put his hand to it. When he looked at his fingers, they were smeared with blood. He wiped his cheek vigorously with his coat sleeve, repulsed by the thought of what had happened. Someone, a man or woman, had jumped from a window, and their body had splattered blood for some distance as it broke on the concrete.

His pace quickened. The longer it took him to reach Westminster, the more people there would be out on the streets. He had to move faster. Dare he chance a car? It was risky, he would be driving virtually blind, but it might be worth it. He heard singing, not far away and drawing nearer. It was a man's voice, loud and clear. And happy. He saw the dark shape that suddenly became clearly defined; it was a man on a bicycle, weaving left and right, pedalling slowly, oblivious to anything but his own song. He saw Holman and rode round him in a tight circle, smiling and singing, his eyes never leaving Holman's, neither challenging nor belligerent. Placid.

As the cyclist completed a second circuit, Holman considered relieving him of his vehicle and using it himself, but decided against the idea, for it could be more dangerous than just walking. With a wave of his hand, the man disappeared into the mist again and Holman listened to the voice as it receded into the vacuous distance, leaving him feeling even more isolated.

He whirled as he heard running footsteps, but they carried on right past him without his catching anything more than a glimpse of a shadowy figure. He realized it was no good at all going on like this. His nerves were taut and his progress was slow; it would take him hours to reach Westminster at this rate and long before then the streets would be crowded. He would have to take a car; it wouldn't be too difficult to find one and he knew how to start one without a key. He found his way back to the kerb and used it as a guide. He was bound to run into a parked car soon.

He passed a woman who was pushing an ordinary house broom along the gutter, tutting at the piled-up dirt and cursing at the world in general.

He passed a body that lay sprawled across his path. He didn't stop to see whether it was male or female, dead or alive.

He passed a dog feeding on the carcass of another. It looked up and growled menacingly, saliva and blood drooling from its jaws, not attacking, but watching him intently until he'd been swallowed up by the fog again.

Holman's breath was coming in short gasps now and he wasn't quite sure if it was because of the impure air or the tenseness of the situation. He had to find a car soon.

Then, he saw the soft light ahead of him which grew brighter as he approached. He thought it might be a fire at first, then perhaps a shop front because of its steady glare, but, as he drew nearer, he realized its source. It gave him the answer; the way to get across London fast, and with far less risk. It would be frightening, he knew, but not as frightening as it would have been by car. He broke into a run.

Holman emerged from the underground station in Trafalgar Square just over an hour later, his hands and face black with dirt, a torch still glowing in his hand. The dark journey through the tunnels had been without incident. The station at St John's Wood had been deserted even though all the lights were still working. He had assumed it had been abandoned during the night and nobody had bothered to lock its gates or switch off the power. A door marked 'Private' had been left open and he had soon found a heavy-duty-type rubber torch. As he descended the staircase to the platform, he had wondered if the current had been switched off, but there would be no way of knowing. It was his intention to keep well clear of the lines, but he would have felt better in his own mind if he had known whether they contained their deadly electricity.

Fortunately, the single low-watt lights along the tunnels had been left on too, ready for the night cleaners and maintenance men, but on several stretches further on between stations he had been in total darkness. He had noticed the station itself had been full of the fog although less thick, and even the lower regions of the platforms contained some wispy clouds of it. On one occasion, he had heard muffled voices coming from the tunnel parallel to his and he'd switched off his torch and waited in the dark until they had faded into the distance. His main worry was that a train would come roaring down the tunnel at him, a notion he had a hard time shaking off. Even the black, scuttling shapes of disturbed rats did not bother him as much as that thought.

But he'd made it. The joy of once again emerging into the daylight, grey though it was, was immense and made him feel quite light headed. The fog seemed slightly less dense, but he wasn't sure if it wasn't because he'd come from the blackness of the tunnels and the contrast between total darkness and murky grey was deceiving his eyes.

He paused for a moment to get his bearings, switching the torch off and placing it on the ground. He became aware of a puzzling sound off to his right, a curious cooing noise echoing from the mists, continuous and monotonous and, somehow, haunting. He realized its source: pigeons. The thousands of pigeons that belonged to Trafalgar Square. Would they be affected by the fog? Their unified call was strange and hypnotic and aroused his curiosity. Forgetting his instructions to avoid any trouble, he walked towards the compulsive ululation, keeping a wary eye out for any sudden shadows that might appear. He crossed the broad road and reached the inner square where he stopped and peered into the mist.

The pigeons were spread like a deep grey carpet before him, disappearing into the mist, but giving the impression that the mass of small bodies covered the rest of the square completely. Occasionally, one would flutter a few feet into the air but would soon settle on to the backs of the others and snuggle its way in between them. Although they huddled together, they did not seem afraid; there was no nervousness about them, no sudden movements among them except for those that were squeezed from their positions and had to manoeuvre their way in again. And all the while, the deep-throated cooing penetrating the poisoned air, sinister and compelling. Holman suddenly noticed there were taller shadows rising from them; the ghostly shapes of people, quite motionless, silent and inhuman.

He backed away. Something was going to happen. He could sense it.

His eyes never left the birds until they had been obscured from his vision by the other enemy, the fog, and only then did he turn and begin to walk away at a brisk pace. He knew that a sudden movement from any of the people who stood among them – and there must have been many others for he had counted at least five within range of himself – and the pigeons would be galvanized into action. Whether or not they would attack he did not know for sure, but instinct had told him to get away; the menace that pervaded from them was an almost tangible thing.

Hoping he was headed in the right direction, he hurried on. The fact that he now appeared to be in a sort of no man's land, without a kerb or building to guide him, caused him even more anxiety. If his sense of direction was correct, Whitehall would be ahead of him, the Strand to the left and the Mall just off to the right; he was at the junction of all the roads.

He heard the car before he saw it. Its engine was roaring, the tyres screeching which, fortunately for Holman, gave him plenty of warning of its approach. Standing perfectly still, he tried to judge with his ears exactly where the car would appear. The noise was coming from the direction of the Strand, but seemed to be alternating from left to right; the screeching of tyres told him the driver was weaving some crazy pattern from one side of the road to the other. And then it was no more than twenty yards from him, sweeping through the mist like a demon from hell.

He was rigid from the shock of it for even though he had been expecting its emergence from the fog, the suddenness of its appearance had an almost paralysing effect on his limbs. His keen instinct for survival took command and moved his legs just in time as the vehicle, a bright red sports car, sped past, just catching the side of his leg, sending him spinning into the road. He had caught sight of its driver just as the car bore down on him: it had been a middle-aged man, naked – at least from the waist up – and gross, a maniacal grin on his face; beside him was an equally naked woman, also middle-aged, also gross, and she stood with her large breasts flopping over the windscreen, shrieking and laughing.

Holman lay in the road, not hurt but stunned, watching the car as it disappeared into the mist again. As he got to one knee, he heard one elongated screech of tortured tyres, silence, and then the awful sound of impact as the car struck something immovable. This was followed at once by the beating of thousands of wings, the cooing now becoming a shrill cry as the pigeons rose en masse into the fog-laden air. Human screams mingled with those of the birds and Holman knew he had been right; the pigeons were attacking.

He rose to his feet and pulled up his trousers to check his leg. He would have a nasty bruise later but the skin hadn't broken. All too conscious of the danger just beyond his vision, he ran away from the noise, limping only slightly, sure that if just one bird found him, others would soon follow.

He thanked God when he found the pavement and thanked Him again aloud when he discovered he was in Whitehall. The rest of the journey to Westminster Bridge was hazy and unreal, a fantasy of sounds and sudden visions that appeared briefly and vanished just as abruptly. He later remembered many people rushing past him towards the noise, like lemmings seeking destruction; a huge fire to his right (he had no idea of which building it had been, famous or otherwise); two more cars racing neck and neck, smashing into each other's sides as they went; a group of people engaged in a scuffle beneath the War Memorial. It had meant nothing to him as he fled; his only thoughts were to reach safety of some kind and the only safety he would find would be with sane people.

Finally he found the turn-off he sought. The bridge was just ahead. And so were the religious freaks.

He was among them before he'd had a chance to retreat. He had often seen them around London, dressed in long, brightly coloured saffron robes, the men's heads shaved, chanting their monotonous litany to the discordant accompaniment of crashing tambourines, shuffling along in a peculiar hopping-dance motion. Secretly, he had always been fondly amused by them, for there was an engaging freshness about them, and their religion seemed harmless and happy. But now, their appearance took on a more sinister aspect.

They were seated on the ground in a wide circle which he had unwittingly broken into.

'Welcome, Brother!' One of them, who had been standing in the centre leading the chant, spread his arms wide in greeting. 'Today is the Beginning! Join us in our thanks.'

Holman warily looked around; the others were on their feet now and advancing on him with their hopping gait, the gaps between them closing as they drew nearer.

'Come, Brother. Now is the time!' The man before him was only two feet away and Holman was impressed and a little intimidated by his size. He placed two huge hands on Holman's shoulders while the dirge coming from the others grew louder. He tried to pull away but the grip on his shoulders tightened.

The man leaned forward until his pointed face was touching Holman's and whispered, 'If you try to run, I'll break your fucking back.'

Holman was transfixed more by the harsh words than by the hold on him.

'To your knees, Brother. Humble yourself so that you might be saved.'

Holman tried to resist but more hands clasped his shoulders and forced him down. The big man stayed with him so they were both on their knees facing one another, the immense hands still holding him. He looked into the big-boned face and saw dark brown eyes that looked glazed yet cruel. A thin stream of saliva drooled from the corner of the man's mouth. His voice boomed out, 'I love you, Brother! We love you!' And then a whisper, 'I'm going to kill you, you fucking creep.'

He grinned at Holman, bringing his forehead down and kissing it.

'Today is your Beginning. And to Begin, you must first die,' he said, as others leaned forward to kiss Holman. Now they were all kneeling, packed tightly up against the two men in the centre.

'You – you've got to let me go,' Holman said, looking around anxiously. 'I'm the only one who can do something about the fog.'

'The fog, Brother? There is no fog. All you see around us is the spirit of mankind. Today is the Beginning. The mist is only the *Being*, the souls who have already begun the journey.'

'Let me go!'

'Peace! The bridge you are about to cross is short, and the brief pain you will feel will be nothing compared to the eternal happiness that waits beyond.' And again, the whispered words, 'You'll be the fifth today, bastard. I'll snap your neck like a fucking matchstick.'

His hands closed on Holman's neck, but before the thick fingers could form into a stranglehold, Holman brought his fist up into the man's lower stomach. The blow had no other effect than to tighten the religious leader's smile into a grimace. He rose to his feet bringing his victim up with him, held by the neck. The fingers began to squeeze.

In a desperate move, Holman went limp so that his body dropped, then pushed forward. It was fortunate for him that the other followers were still kneeling around them for the momentum forced the leader to step back thus tripping over the bowed head of one of his flock. They went down in a heap of struggling arms and legs, Holman managing to break free of the grip around his throat. He lashed out again with his fist, and with some satisfaction, drew blood from the big man's nose.

The long robes of the religious sect hampered their movements and put Holman at an advantage. Instead of trying to rise above the clutching leader, he rolled forward over him, his shoulder cracking the man's head hard against the pavement. His feet accidently kicked into the chest of one of the female members, sending her backwards and gaining him a free area to rise. Hands grabbed for him, voices screamed in dismay, but he was moving through them, slapping the hands away, pushing half-risen bodies back down. He heard the roar of the big man behind him and redoubled his efforts to get away. Just as he thought he was clear, a hand closed on his ankle, tripping him and sending him rolling across the pavement to crash against a restaurant front.

He rose as quickly as he could, but already the big man was coming for him, lifting his legs high to stride through the startled bodies as though wading through a stream, mouthing obscenities at Holman, the blood from his nose covering his face, giving him a red mask of pure hatred. Most of his confused followers were trying to gain their feet, and just as he was nearly through, one rose up in front of him. The big man pushed him viciously, sending him sprawling across the pavement to land at Holman's feet.

Holman's back was pressed up against the large window of a restaurant, the palms of his hands flat against it, ready to give him leverage to push himself away. The big man was only a few feet from him and still rushing forward, his arms outstretched to embrace him in a hug of death. But the frightened man at Holman's feet was now scrabbling around on hands and knees, and the leader's eyes were so intent on their prey that they failed to see him. Holman sprang to one side as the big man pitched forward, tripped by his follower on the ground.

Holman heard the scream and crash of shattered glass as the big man's bare head and upper body fell through the window, scattering the fancy cakes and expensive confectionery that lay just inside. The heavy glass descended on him like a guillotine, cutting into his neck and breaking across his back.

Splinters and shards of glass flew out at Holman, but they did little damage for he was already running away, now using the fog as an ally, trying to hide in it, seeking refuge in its murkiness. But the religious fanatics came after him, several picking up long slivers of glass to be used as weapons against him. Heedless of what lay ahead, he ran blindly on, spurred by their cries of vengeance, but unable to find the speed that would take him out of their vision.

He knew the bridge was near by and prayed that the government vehicle would be there waiting for him. His chest heaving, he reached the corner where the road branched off along the Embankment. My God, he suddenly thought, on which side would the vehicle be? Could it be on this corner, just out of sight in the mist, or would it be on the other side, the bridge corner? Without hesitating, he ran off the kerb and into the road, hoping his judgement was correct. He didn't much like the idea of dashing around in the fog trying to locate the car with the crowd of lunatics so close on his heels.

He reached the island in the middle of the road and kept going, trusting luck and his instinct for survival to pull him through. To have stopped to look around would have been more than pointless; it would have meant his death.

And then, two bright circles lit up before him, behind the circles, the shadowy shape of an odd-looking machine. He heard the roar of its engine and suddenly it was coming towards him. It must be the one! It had to be.

But to his dismay, it curved around him, gathering speed, going past. With a sickening feeling, he realized the driver's intention. The heavy, bulky vehicle ploughed into the following pack of bodies, sending them flying, crushing some beneath its broad wheels, scattering the luckier ones. Then it reversed and came back towards Holman. It didn't have the appearance of having speed, but the tyres screeched as they tried to grip the ground when the driver braked. He had to move fast to avoid being run down himself.

A small door at its side sprang open and a strange metallic voice said: 'Sorry, sir. But you're a bit more important than those people at the moment. I had to do it, it was your only chance. Now please get in, we haven't got much time!'

Crouching low, he clambered into the vehicle and was confronted by a heavily garbed figure, the suit similar to those worn by the men in Winchester, but much bulkier and more clumsy looking. The man wore a large helmet and Holman failed to see his eyes through the dark, narrow visor. The metallic voice came from a small mouthpiece positioned in the centre of his helmet.

'Close the door, sir. We don't want any of those lunatics or any more of the fog getting in.'

Holman did as he was told and turned to face the figure again.

'Where are you taking me?' he asked.

'You'll see, sir,' came the reply. 'My name is Mason – can't really shake hands, these gloves don't allow for it. I must say, you had me worried. I've been waiting ages.'

'I had a few problems on the way,' said Holman dryly, slumping back breathlessly in his seat. 'Where are we going?'

'Just a moment, sir. Must let them know I've picked you up.' He pressed a switch and spoke without the use of a hand speaker, reporting that his mission had so far been successful and they would soon be returning to base. He turned back to Holman.

'Now, sir. I'd like you to drive. These vehicles aren't really meant for travelling in thick fog as you can see by the tiny apertures. And my wearing this suit doesn't help much, either. Had a devil of a time reaching this spot even though I wasn't wearing a helmet then. Now that I've had the door open, I daren't risk taking it off again because some of the fog is bound to have got in.'

'The suit's lead-lined?'

'Yes, sir. That's what makes it so bloody cumbersome. Meant to be protection against radiation, y'see. The whole car is.'

'Radiation?'

'Yes. We call it the Devastation Vehicle. You'll find out why, later.'

Glancing around, Holman saw it was fitted with a mass of instruments, gauges and switches.

'I'm not sure I *can* drive it,' he said.

'Oh, don't let all those gadgets put you off,' Mason assured him. 'They're nothing to do with the running of the thing. In fact, it couldn't be simpler, just like driving a dodgem. The whole thing's operated on electricity, y'see: you push down on one pedal to go, another to stop, that's all there is to it. C'mon, there're a lot of people rather anxious to see you!'

Holman had followed Mason's instructions and driven slowly along the Embankment, turning left on command into what appeared to be an underground car park belonging to one of the large government office buildings. It was in darkness, but Holman had seen many cars crammed together in the glare of the vehicle's headlights. A lane had been left clear, and this he followed, going deeper and deeper below ground. It ended in a solid, concrete wall. Mason pressed a switch and began saying several words that sounded senseless to Holman; he realized they must have been in code. The wall before them suddenly rose into the ceiling and he saw a long box-shaped room beyond.

Mason touched his arm and the huge helmet nodded towards the opening. Holman drove forward and stopped once inside. The wall behind was lowered again and they sat in silence for a full minute until, quite abruptly, the wall before them swung open and they were faced with a long, dimly-lit corridor which again seemed to end in a blank wall. As they passed through, Holman saw that the wall which had just opened was in fact made of grey metal and was at least eighteen inches thick.

The corridor sloped downwards and they passed through two more doors before they entered a large, open area. Holman estimated they had travelled at least a quarter of a mile to reach this point. He noticed another vehicle looking identical to the one he had been travelling in parked in a far corner. A group of grey-suited men who had been waiting for them, each holding a long canister which was connected to a central box, stepped forward, pointing the canisters' nozzles at the vehicle, and then began to spray it with an almost invisible substance.

'Sit tight just a moment longer, sir,' said Mason. 'We were decontaminated when we first entered the tunnel, but this is a final going over. As a further precaution, they'll spray us as we get out.'

'Spray us against what?'

'The whole complex is sterile; there's not a germ down here. Everyone and everything that comes in is decontaminated. You see, it's built to contain at least three hundred people for anything up to ten years. If any bug got loose in such a confined space, well, it'd spread like wildfire.'

'Ten years?' Holman looked incredulously at the hooded figure. 'Just what the hell is this place?'

'I thought you knew. I thought you'd been told.'

Holman shook his head slowly.

'This,' said Mason, 'is a fallout shelter. A government fallout shelter.'

Mason waited for a comment from Holman, but none came so he continued. 'They started building it in the early 1960s and are still adding to it. If the country were ever to reach the point of crisis – the point where atomic war was inevitable – this is where the most important VIPs will come. There's a tunnel that leads directly to the Houses of Parliament, another that leads to the Palace.'

Holman's smile was cynical. 'Are there any others like it? For the ordinary people, I mean.'

'Er, I don't know about that, sir. These things are kept pretty much a secret. I know there isn't another in London, but I've visited one in Manchester and I assume some of the other major towns have them.'

'But all for 'special' people.'

'Well, they could hardly cope with the whole population of Great Britain, could they, sir?'

Holman sighed. 'No, I suppose not. But I wonder how you qualify to be a "special" person.'

Mason changed the subject. 'Time to get out now,' he said.

Holman was led along more corridors by a young, unexcited man, who, despite the crisis, was dressed immaculately and tastefully in a dark blue pin-stripe suit, deep red tie and spotlessly white collar. He spoke quietly and efficiently, explaining to Holman exactly what had happened during the night and how it was now being coped with. The Prime Minister was there, together with most of his Cabinet; they had been the first to be warned, along with the Royal Family who were now safe in Scotland. The PM had decided to stay in London and direct operations from there, for the shelter was ideal for that purpose: it was impenetrable, contained virtually unlimited resources, had contact with any point on the globe, and had a large and well-equipped 'war' room. It had its own source of power, even its own telephone exchange which had proved invaluable when London's had broken down (Holman realized now that that was how they had been able to contact him). The army was mustered just outside London, mobile and ready for whatever action was demanded of them, but most of the Chiefs of Staff were inside the shelter helping the PM draw up a plan of campaign. Professor Ryker was there along with many other notable scientists and they were already hard at work on a new theory of Ryker's regarding the rapid growth of the fog – a possible clue to its make-up. Janet Halstead was there with her research team and some of the victims of the fog whom she'd been treating. Many people skilled in various aspects of life had been brought into the vast underground shelter, from doctors to religious ministers, from naturalists to carpenters and plumbers; all had been previously earmarked for survival (mostly unknown to themselves) and their names and current addresses were kept on a list which was reviewed every three months.

As they walked, Holman recognized many familiar faces, familiar only because he'd seen them in the media. He was puzzled as to what possible value most of them could have in this situation. The fact that most were very wealthy made him extremely suspicious. Had they bought their way in? Or had they done certain favours for government officials, their price a ticket for survival on the Doomsday?

A lot of the people, both men and women, seemed to be in a daze. Ashen faced, many of the women in tears, they looked at him uncomprehendingly as he passed, some hoping to recognize a friend or relative, others envying him because he seemed to be going somewhere, had a task to perform, something positive, something active.

'How did you manage to get so many people in here in time?' he asked the young man he was following, walking briskly to keep up.

'A decision was made,' came the curt reply.

'What decision?'

'It was seen that the whole population of London could not possibly be saved and even if it was tried, the panic that would have ensued would have seriously disrupted rescue operations for certain key people.'

Holman caught his arm and brought him to a halt. 'You mean they didn't try? They just let people lie in their beds while the fog...?'

'Of course they tried!' the young man snapped. 'But they used common sense. A third of the force was deployed to warn certain people and bring them here, the rest did as much as they could. Thousands escaped into the surrounding suburbs because of the army, but London is a big place, you know. Common sense had to prevail!' He pulled his arm away and marched on, leaving Holman staring open-mouthed after him. Grimly, he followed.

They entered a large hall thriving with people, each of whom had some particular task to perform, and filled with electronic equipment, brightly lit maps, television screens. Despite the activity, there was an air of calm throughout the hall as though whatever turmoil was now taking place above ground was a world away, unreal because it was largely unseen, for the television screens showed only a grey blankness, an occasional shadowy figure appearing to be quickly swallowed up again.

They don't know, Holman thought. They don't know what it's like up there: the complete madness that would have now gripped the town, the chaos that lay beyond those mists shown on the screens. They felt shock, he was sure, but not true, deep-felt sorrow, for how could they? It was an unreal situation. They knew of the tragedy of Bournemouth of course, and of the aeroplane crash; but how could minds possibly accept the fact of one of the world's largest cities gone mad? Only he could realize its full horror because he had seen it at first-hand, had even experienced it. But perhaps they would have still acted in the same way if it had been the holocaust the shelter had originally been intended for. It was those who had nothing to do who were affected, those who could only watch and wait. And wonder.

'This way, Mr Holman,' the young man's voice cut through his thoughts. He was standing by a doorway guarded by an armed soldier. Holman walked towards them, a questioning look on his face.

'This is the Planning Room,' the young man told him. 'The Minister is waiting to brief you himself.' As he guided the Devastation Vehicle along the fog-bound street, Holman kept a wary eye out for groups of people. These would be the most dangerous; the ones that travelled in packs, like wolves searching for lone and defenceless victims. Most of the people ignored the strangely shaped car, for today everything was strange. Mason was now helmetless because the vehicle hadn't yet been opened above ground. They were using the reserve vehicle while the interior of the other was being carefully decontaminated. Mason grinned nervously at Holman. 'How are you feeling?' he asked, more to make conversation than out of actual curiosity.

'Sick,' replied Holman. 'I feel like driving on till we reach open country, away from this.'

'I know what you mean,' said Mason. 'But a lot depends on us, sir. I need you to guide me. I won't be able to see a thing once I get out there, not with this gear on.'

'The fog doesn't seem to be as bad now.'

'No. As I said, it's spreading out, thinning. But our reports say it isn't moving on yet. Look, we won't be out in it for long; just time enough for me to suction some of the bastard into our container and then we'll be off. If I didn't need your eyes, I'd do it on my own.'

Christ, you don't know the half of it, brooded Holman. He was armed with a revolver carried in a concealed shoulder holster and his instructions from the Prime Minister himself were that he was to protect his own life at all costs, even if it meant killing his companion to do so. It wasn't known yet if the protective suit was adequate against the mutated mycoplasma which was still an unknown entity and if Mason began to behave in the least threatening way, he was to be disposed of immediately and Holman was to carry out the mission on his own. He had balked at the order, but the PM had talked long and hard at him, telling him the choice was not his, that one life meant little compared to the millions that were in danger. A promise that he would carry out the order in the event was extracted from Holman, but he knew that only when the moment presented itself – if it presented itself – would he be able to decide.

Ryker had been present at the meeting and had assured Holman that the danger was getting worse. Because of the fog's rapid growth overnight, he now suspected that this was Broadmeyer's intention for the mycoplasma: to feed and grow on polluted air, thus the bigger the city, the more industrial, the more effective the disease was. The fog itself was a mere side effect of the gathering of impure air, deadly only because of the microbes that floated within it. It had given Ryker a clue to its source, but it would take time to investigate and come up with answers. In the meantime, the quickest way to probe the mutation was still to obtain a large sample of it. He had every faith in Holman that this time he would succeed. Holman wished he had as much faith in himself.

On his way back to the vehicle he had met Janet Halstead. Her cheeriness had gone, her face showed rigid lines of strain: she looked old. She, too, had urged him to succeed this time; only if he did could they begin to undo some of the terrible damage that had already been perpetrated. If she could inoculate against the disease, then men would be free to go into the disaster area and prevent others from destroying themselves and each other. He had left her without saying a word. How could he promise to succeed? There were too many other forces involved; he had thrived on risks before, but they had never been of this nature nor so numerous. All he could do was try.

'My God, look at that!' Mason was pointing ahead at four blazing cars that had piled up in the centre of the road. The flames were too thick to see if anybody occupied them, but a large crowd of people had gathered round the blaze, silently watching. As Holman and Mason drew nearer, the blood froze in their veins at the horror of what was happening. As the crowd watched, individuals would break from the ring and rush forward to throw themselves into the fire. The crowd cheered and then fell silent until another repeated the action.

'We've got to stop them!' Holman shouted, unable to take his eyes from the scene.

'No, we've got our orders,' said Mason firmly. 'We're not to interfere in any way. We *mustn't* get involved!'

Holman knew it was useless to argue. And Mason was right; they were not to jeopardize the mission. If they were to involve themselves in every incident that occurred along the way, then the odds were that they would never reach their destination.

'All right,' he said evenly, 'if there's nothing we can do, let's get away from it as quickly as possible.'

Mason was relieved. 'We'll go around,' he said. 'Back up, there's a turning to the left – goes towards the Strand. We'll go that way.'

Holman reversed the vehicle, narrowly missing a heavy truck that thundered past them, headed directly towards the burning cars and people. They heard the crash, for although the vehicle itself was soundproof, it was equipped with receivers on its exterior to pick up noise, a function that was necessary because of the lack of vision.

'Oh, Jesus,' breathed Mason, 'this is terrible.'

'It's only just beginning,' Holman told him cruelly. 'It'll get worse.'

And it did get worse. They passed many burning buildings, more blazing cars; scores of people roaming the streets, insanity evident in their faces; individuals curled up in corners, occasionally staring around with wide, fearful eyes. They passed bodies that had obviously fallen or jumped from the surrounding tall buildings; they heard screams, laughter, chanting; they saw people on their knees praying. And, strangest of all, they saw people behaving normally: queuing at bus stops, walking along briskly as though on their way to work, swinging umbrellas or carrying briefcases, entering the buildings that were open, waiting patiently outside others whose doors had not yet been unlocked, chatting to one another as though it were an ordinary working day, ignoring the chaos that was taking place around them. But that was *their* abnormality.

They drove slowly on down Fleet Street towards Ludgate Circus, steeling themselves against the sights, resisting the almost overwhelming urge to stop the vehicle and help those in particularly perilous plights. Holman was thankful they had passed no children. He realized they probably would later on when they passed through the more residential districts, but he hoped they would remain hidden from his eyes behind the veiling mist, for he doubted whether he could prevent himself helping a child in distress.

Suddenly they found themselves surrounded by a mob of workmen at the bottom of Fleet Street. The men began banging on the sides of the vehicle, trying to peer into the small but wide windows. They rapped on the glass, trying to break it. Holman and Mason heard heavy footsteps clunking overhead as some of the men scrambled on to the roof.

'Christ! Must be all the bloody printers in Fleet Street!' said Mason.

'Yes, they must have been working through the night,' Holman agreed. 'But surely they would have been warned?'

Mason shrugged his shoulders. 'We'll have to drive through them!' he said.

Just then the vehicle began to rock from side to side.

'They're trying to turn us over!' shouted Holman above the noise.

'Drive!' Mason commanded, leaning forward to switch off the sound. He didn't want Holman to hear the screams as they mowed their way through the crowd.

Holman pressed his foot down hard on the accelerator, sorry for the action he had to take but knowing it had to be done. He remembered Winchester and had less sympathy for the men and more interest in his own survival.

The car leapt forward and the startled men jumped back. Others were slower and disappeared beneath the wheels. Holman felt the car bump as it passed over their bodies, but he kept his foot down hard on the pedal, gathering speed, sending the men on the roof flying off. It ploughed through the thronging mass and Holman closed his mind from thoughts of his unfortunate victims. Perhaps it was because he regarded them as a threat rather than human beings. Perhaps he thought they were less human because of their madness. Or perhaps it was because he didn't have time to think at all that enabled him to carry on.

At last, they were clear of the mob and travelling up the hill towards St Paul's. Only then did Holman's hands begin to shake.

Mason noticed and said, 'Here, let me take over. You've had enough.'

'No,' said Holman, 'I'll be all right. I'd rather drive than sit and think. You check your instruments; make sure we're still going in the right direction.'

Mason clapped a steadying hand on his shoulder then turned his attention towards the panel of instruments in front of him. He reported their position back to the underground base and related some of the incidents they had run into and the fact that the fog seemed much thinner. Holman glanced at his watch and saw that they had only been out for thirty-odd minutes. It seemed like hours.

He heard over the speaker a voice telling Mason that people were fleeing from the town in their thousands; large internment camps had been set up and police and troops from all over the country had surrounded London with blockades, and were trying to hold everyone who was leaving, imprisoning them for their own protection. It was an impossible task, of course, to save everyone, but fortunately, most of those that had fled were unaffected as yet by the disease and willingly turnèd themselves over to the authorities in the hope they would be protected when the madness struck them.

Helicopters above the cloud had reported that the fog seemed thickest around the river and thickest of all around the dockside area past the Tower of London. Although it had spread further, they confirmed that it did seem to be thinning, particularly on its outer fringes. They could also see the glow of many large fires all over London.

The voice informed them that aircraft from all over the country were already on their way, loaded with calcium chloride in an attempt to avalanche the city with the chemical, but it would take hours for the operation to be put into effect.

It promised to send any further information that would help them and wished them both good luck.

Mason switched off and said to Holman, 'It all checks. We're going the right way – it's somewhere down by the docks.'

They were now passing St Paul's Cathedral and were amazed to see scores of people sitting on its steps, their faces expressionless, their lips unmoving.

'Switch on the sound again,' said Holman.

Mason did so but they heard no noise from the gathering.

'They remind me of a flock of birds,' said Mason. 'One loud noise and they'll be fluttering all over the place.'

Holman remembered the pigeons in Trafalgar Square and told Mason of it.

'Christ!' said Mason. 'It gives me the creeps – let's move a bit faster.'

He increased the speed as much as he dared and they soon left the historic building behind.

'You notice how they seem to be mostly grouping together,' observed Mason.

'Yes. It's as though with the breaking down of their brain cells, they're losing their individuality, flocking together the way animals do. Look how they're gathering at bus stops, a natural grouping place for people. At first, I thought in their shocked state they were queuing, but now I realize they're grouping together at spots that are familiar to that idea.'

'Look at him!' Mason was pointing at a figure that had suddenly emerged from the fog ahead of them. The man was completely naked and was brandishing a long, curved sword. He advanced on the vehicle.

Holman turned the wheel sharply and swerved around him, narrowly avoiding running him down. Mason swung his head around to watch him through the rear windows, but he had disappeared into the mists again.

'It seems, even in total madness, there are a few individuals though,' he commented.

They passed fewer people as they drove through the City, but when they left its grey canyons behind they were faced with a spectacular scene.

Across the road in front of them was a mass of white-pink bodies, a sea of writhing limbs. As their eyes narrowed to focus, they saw it was made up of small groups of people, but packed so tightly together they represented a solid mass. All were engaged in copulation.

'Jesus!' said Mason slowly. 'Look at them! A bloody street orgy!'

'It probably started with one couple and others just joined in,' said Holman.

'But there's some there that must be in their sixties.'

'And others not more than kids.'

'What do we do?' asked Mason, tearing his eyes away from the scene to look at Holman.

Holman smiled thinly, a faint feeling of satisfaction at his companion's sudden perplexity causing the smile. Mason's calm throughout had bothered him.

'Well, we don't join them,' he said, and then, more grimly, 'we go around, of course.'

He turned the vehicle and found a narrow side street. As he drove away, Mason craned his neck to keep the spectacle in sight for as long as possible, cursing at the fog when it obliterated it.

'Incredible,' was all he could say.

Holman turned into another, wider street to get them back on their original course. They had travelled no more than fifty yards when he stopped the vehicle with a sudden jerk.

'What's wrong?' asked the startled Mason who had been checking his instruments.

'Look,' said Holman, pointing ahead.

Mason narrowed his eyes and peered into the fog. He heard her screams before he actually saw the girl. She looked to be no more than fifteen and she was backed into a doorway. Even at that distance, they could see her eyes were wide with terror and her screams echoed round the cramped interior of the vehicle.

Advancing on her were two men, both heavy set, both wearing clothes that were in tatters, both grinning at the girl. Their faces and hands were black with filth giving them an even more menacing appearance. But most frightening of all was their actions upon themselves for it made their intent obvious. Each had unbuttoned his trousers and was slowly stroking his penis, calling out to the girl, mouthing obscenities, informing her of their intentions upon her small body. She crouched in the doorway – whether she, herself, was mad yet was not apparent – whimpering, holding her hands up to her face as if to hide the sight from her mind.

'Oh God,' said Holman.

'Look, we can't go out there. In this suit, I'd be no help to you at all. And you're too valuable to risk your life. And if we stopped to help everybody we see in trouble, we'd never get to the nucleus!'

'Shut up,' said Holman quietly. He stabbed his foot down hard on the accelerator and the vehicle leapt forward with a jolt. As it gathered speed it mounted the kerb and sped towards the two men, two wheels on the pavement, two wheels in the road. The two men just had time to see it coming, their grinning faces barely registering the fear that had begun its swift climb, before the vehicle hit them. One disappeared beneath the wheels, the other was tossed into the air to slam against the merciless concrete of a building. Their short screams, and the longer, more shrill scream of the girl, spun around in Holman's head even when the sound had stopped. He brought the vehicle to a screeching halt, throwing the astonished Mason forward on to his instruments. Holman swung around in his seat and looked through the rear apertures just in time to see the girl running into the fog, her face still hidden in her hands in an effort to block the horror.

He saw the crumpled figure of one of the men lying in the road, lifeless and somehow withered. The other lay propped up against the foot of the wall he'd smashed into, his neck twisted so that his open eyes seemed to be staring after the vehicle which had inflicted such a terrible death upon him.

Holman turned away from the sight and leaned forward on the steering wheel, rubbing a hand across his eyes then staring blankly downwards.

Mason pushed himself upright and silently placed a hand on Holman's shoulder, giving it a little shake of comfort. Without a word, Holman looked up and started the vehicle rolling forward again, guiding it back into the roadway and slowly building up a steady speed.

As they continued their journey, their minds became more numbed to each new incident, whether horrifying or just bizarre: the sight of an elderly woman pushing the obviously dead body of a man in a pram, leaving a stream of blood trickling from the carriage on to the road behind her, barely penetrated their consciousness; three men sitting by the roadside drinking from what looked like a can of paraffin, waving dirty handkerchiefs at the vehicle as it passed, meant nothing to them. For Holman, it was probably the fact that he had just killed other human beings; nothing could surpass the horror of deliberately taking the lives of other men, whether they were mad or not. Remorse had not yet set in, but repulsion for the act had and, because he had been forced to take such measures, his resolution to find the means of destroying the disease was stronger than ever. For Mason, it was the mere consistency of the strange happenings, consistency being the steadiest ally to acceptance.

The scenes had not become unreal to them, but they, in their enclosed mobile compartment, had become remote from the scenes, observers moving through a strange, cloudy world, like explorers in a diving capsule on a sea-bed.

From time to time, Mason reported back to the underground base, coldly describing the scenes around them: the fires, the havoc, the waste of human life. Suddenly, he asked Holman to stop the vehicle. Holman had no idea of their exact location, but he guessed they must be somewhere near the East London docks by now. He look askance towards his companion.

'We've lost it,' said Mason. He checked his instruments again then reported back to base speaking sharply and urgently.

'How could we have lost it?' asked Holman.

'We're being guided by a helicopter above the fog,' Mason told him. 'They have sensors that have been keeping track of the mycoplasma's centre; they relay the information back to headquarters who operate our directional finders from there. It has to be that complicated because obviously the chopper can't see which area it's over through the fog. But now, nothing's happening; our finder's just gone loose.'

A voice came over the speaker and echoed round the small apartment: 'Hello, D.V.1. Base here again. Do you read?' Mason acknowledged and the metallic voice went on, 'Trouble I'm afraid. D.V.1 Charlie 2 says they've lost the nucleus. Nothing at all shows on their instruments but they're going to scout around the area until they find it again. We don't understand how it's happened unless the bloody thing's gone into the river – you're near it – but that's hardly likely. Anyhow, sit tight for a while until you receive further instructions. Won't be long, I'm sure. Over and out.'

Mason sat back in his seat. 'Sod it!' he said, then added, 'We were close.'

'D'you think they'll find it again?' Holman asked.

'Who knows? They lost it before.' He glanced nervously around, looking through the apertures out at the fog-shrouded streets. 'Must say I don't much like sitting around in the open like this.'

'Nor me,' said Holman. 'It's too vulnerable. Let's get over against a building. It'll give us some shelter, at least.'

He moved the vehicle forward more slowly this time, angling it across the wide road, looking for a building that might give it some protection.

It was just then that the bus emerged from the fog like a huge red monster, its lights appearing a split second before it like two glaring, searching eyes. Its front was splattered with a darker red, the bloodstains of the many victims it had struck down in the course of its frantic journey. It swerved towards their vehicle and, guessing the driver's intention, Holman pressed down hard on the accelerator in an effort to get clear, but he was too late.

The bus struck their vehicle side on, towards the rear. They felt themselves lifted violently as the vehicle was pushed into the air and then over on to its back. The grey world became suddenly black.

For the second time that morning, Janet Halstead felt the room spin dizzily around her. She was beyond the point of exhaustion, she knew. What little sleep she had had during the past few days had been fitful and disturbed and last night's had been interrupted by the fresh, major crisis. But she had to keep going; countless lives depended on the work she and her colleagues were involved in. She realized Professor Ryker and his team of scientists, microbiologists and virologists were close to the answer and wondered if it had really been necessary to send Holman out into the fog once again. She sighed wearily, wondering if it was just her concern for the man himself that caused these thoughts; she had grown fond of him in a maternal way and it made her uneasy to see him used as a pawn, an instrument, by the great body of officials that ruled the country.

It was they who had made the mistake. The great, faceless *they* and now they were using one man, one man who had had nothing to do with their mistake, to help rectify it.

But, she supposed, it was necessary. There was a chance he could save them valuable time, be it hours, or days, and his life was expendable because of it.

She tried to focus her attention on the report before her: the latest patient they had treated was responding immediately to the blood transfusion and the radiology. Fortunately, they had got to him in time; others would not be so lucky. And this was just the beginning, the first few of the thousands, probably millions, to come. The world was standing by to give assistance, for Britain was no primitive, backwater country inhabited by people dying because they lacked civilization. Because it was a country populated by educated Westerners, other countries were eager to help, not just because of a kinship with another race, but because if it could happen to Great Britain, it could happen anywhere, on any continent, to any country. And if it, or something equal to it, ever did happen to another country, the country concerned wanted to be sure they would receive such help as they were now giving.

Still, Janet thought, the help, from whatever source and for whatever reason, would be sorely needed over the next few weeks.

Stan Reynolds, the security guard for the giant oil company building that stood towering over the Thames, again sat with his huge boots on the oak boardroom table smoking a fat cigar, sipping an expensive brand of Scotch.

'If it's good enough for the Chairman, it's good enough for me,' he chuckled, puffing away at the cigar while the flames from the room directly below heated the floor beneath him.

Earlier, he had visited many offices in the vast, complex building and emptied their desks and filing cabinets of paper on to the floor. He hated the building because it represented a life-style he had never experienced himself, nor ever would. He was expected to protect the executives' offices, to guard them with his life if necessary, and for what? A pittance of a salary and the privilege of having snot-nosed execs bidding him 'Good-morning' or 'Good-night' when they felt like it. That was why he had set fire to their 'confidential' papers, their 'strictly private' files. Besides, he liked fires; they reminded him of the blitz. He'd been something in those days; a sergeant in the army, respected by privates and snot-nosed young officers alike. And when he'd been home on leave during some of the worst bombing of the war, his neighbours had come to *him* for help. He'd been respected then.

By now, half the bottle of Scotch had gone and he took a long, stiff swallow of the remainder. As the heavy boardroom doors burst into flames, he rose unsteadily to his feet.

'Gen'men,' he said, looking along the table at the two rows of empty seats. 'I wish to perprose a toast.' He climbed on to the black leather chair, then on to the table, his boots making ugly scratch marks on its smooth surface. He raised the bottle high. 'Fuck the Chairman!' he shouted and took another swig from the bottle, nearly choking when he began to cackle with laughter.

Looking down, he saw the deep impressions his boots had made on the table and again went into fits of laughter. He dug a heel hard into the wood and was pleased with the result. He did it again with his other heel then clomped his way to the end of the table, stopping and turning to study his trail of scars. He lifted the bottle to his lips and drank, then threw it at the picture of the previous chairman which hung nearby, and, with one final whoop of exhilaration, ran back down the length of the oak table and jumped over the leather chair towards the huge window behind it.

He was well past his prime and his jump did not have much momentum, but half his body went through the glass and its weight toppled the rest over the edge behind him. He couldn't see the ground as he fell; all he could see was a soft, yellowish-grey blanket ready to receive him.

McLellan and his family slept soundly. Outside his house, in the normally quiet Wimbledon street where he lived, was pandemonium. His neighbours were in combat, using bottles, pokers, anything that came to hand; scratching at each other's eyes, tearing at each other's throats. They kicked, they punched, they pulled the clothes from one another. No one knew why and no one bothered to ask themselves; they were too far gone with the madness.

McLellan was lucky for they ignored the sign he'd left on his doorstep which said: PLEASE HELP. HAVE GIVEN FAMILY OVERDOSE TO KEEP FROM HARM. PLEASE HELP. He knew when he'd chalked the message on to his child's toy blackboard it was a slim chance, but there had been little choice anyway. Better to die in their sleep than be at the mercy of a dreadful madness.

So far, they had been left undisturbed and their neighbours were too intent on killing each other to break in and search them out. They slept on.

Irma Bidmead, the old woman who had loved cats yet sold their bodies for vivisection, was already dead. The cats she had fed and housed still gnawed away at her cold flesh mixed with bits of material from the garments she had worn. They had clawed and scratched at her eyes first, then when she had been blinded and weakened, they had sat on her face and smothered her. When her feeble struggles had ceased, they had begun to eat her.

Now they were full, eating out of greed, not hunger, but later they would go out and seek younger, more tender flesh. It wouldn't be hard to find.

Chief Superintendent Wreford laughed at the rantings of his wife. He had locked her in a bedroom cupboard and sat on the end of their bed watching the door as it bulged when she tried to force it open from inside. Her moans had a peculiar rasping tone to them, for earlier that morning he had climbed the stairs from the kitchen holding a kettle full of boiling water in one hand. He had stood over his wife and poured the contents of the kettle into her upturned, open mouth. Her snoring had always sickened him.

Then, as she had screamed and screamed, he had bundled her up in the bedclothes and locked her away in the cupboard.

Soon now, her struggles would grow weaker and he would let her out. She would see the joke when he explained it to her and if she didn't, if she began to nag at him like she had in the past, well, he would show her the kitchen knife he held in his lap. He had seen what you could do to a person with a kitchen knife; he had seen many pictures of victims at the Yard. They were funny those pictures; fascinating what you could do to a human face. You could make the lips smile permanently if you wanted to. He would show her when he let her out – if she whined at him.

He waited patiently, smiling at the cupboard door.

Detective Inspector Barrow had only just woken. He stood by the window, wearing a loose-fitting bathrobe, and gazed out at the fog. Abruptly, he turned away and walked towards the wardrobe. He took out his best suit and laid it carefully on the bed. Then he opened a drawer and took out a clean shirt which he laid on top of the suit. He walked back to the wardrobe again and reached up into the high shelf inside and brought down a wide cardboard box. It was his own private, and strictly against regulations, 'Black Museum' of weapons used in various cases in which he had been involved. He studied its contents for a while, then removed one particular object. He replaced the lid, and returned the box to its resting place.

He went into the bathroom and turned on the bath taps. While it was filling, he carefully shaved.

Samson King had enjoyed his bus ride immensely. He didn't know where he was for he had left his normal route, but it didn't matter. He felt free as a bird and a million times more powerful. He had smashed down anything that had got in the way of his charging red beast. People, cars – anything that had stood before him. The passengers on his bus had enjoyed it too; even now they were laughing gleefully, pointing out of the windows, calling out at the blank faces that stared after them. There were at least fifty people on his bus now for he had stopped twice at bus stops to let them on.

Samson giggled as he remembered the bus stop he hadn't stopped at. Instead, he had driven into the queue, encouraged by his passengers, fascinated by the bodies that disappeared like skittles beneath his wheels.

He couldn't see too far in the fog, and had crashed into quite a few traffic islands and signs. He had been using the kerb as a guide but occasionally he would switch to the other side of the road, and for a brief time would be driving blind in a no-man's-land. He had enjoyed that. He had also enjoyed the moments when he had found himself at a broad junction and had sent the bus spinning round and round, almost toppling it over.

But most of all, he had enjoyed crossing the river over Tower Bridge. There had been quite a few people on the bridge and he had swerved the bus from side to side, making them run before him, chasing them to the very edge where they had been forced to climb the parapet and jump into the filthy water. That had been best!

And now he raced down the wide road, not knowing where he was going and not caring, picking up speed, the excitement rising inside him, heedless to his lack of clear vision, regardless of anything that got in his way.

Then he saw the vehicle. It was an odd-looking thing, grey-coloured with strange-looking objects sticking out from its sides. He ignored its oddity for his mind had already determined to ram it. It was moving directly across his path and it suddenly gave a spurt of speed as though the driver had spotted him and was trying to get clear.

Samson laughed aloud. It couldn't escape him! He pressed down even harder on the accelerator and two seconds later the bus was on the vehicle, catching it at its rear, lifting it up and over, pushing it on to its back, knocking it aside. He lost control of the bus for a moment but didn't try to regain it. He was too busy laughing.

The bus sped across the road and ploughed into a shop-front.

■ 20 ■

HOLMAN SHOOK HIS HEAD TO TRY TO CLEAR THE HAZE. IT MADE IT WORSE SO HE stopped.

He lay there for several moments longer, giving his body time for feeling to return again, for the shock of the crash to wear off. Slowly, he opened his eyes and was surprised to find himself in daylight, grey though it was. He could hear a strange voice speaking from a distance. Unreal as it sounded, it managed to convey urgency, anxiety.

Lifting his head slightly, he tried to look around to find out where it was coming from, and, to his surprise, discovered he was lying in the road with the Devastation Vehicle on its back a few yards away from him. The voice was coming from the open doorway to its cabin and he realized it was the voice of the radio. Base was demanding to know what had happened.

He must have been thrown clear from the vehicle, but as yet could not ascertain whether he had been fortunate or not. The door must have been smashed by the bus as it had hit it, and then swung open as it turned over, spilling him out into the road. He didn't feel as though anything was broken: his face felt raw as if he had skidded along the road on it and both his knees hurt like hell, but apart from that, he seemed to be all right. He tried to lift himself and found he could, although it made him feel a little giddy.

Mason! Where was Mason? Holman's senses were returning rapidly now and he sat up, turning his body towards the vehicle, using one hand for support. He must be still inside, he told himself. God, he mustn't be hurt too badly! Trembling, he got to his feet, then staggered forward to the open doorway.

'Mason!' he called out, poking his head into the dim interior. It was empty. Holman spun round, leaning back against the vehicle for support. 'Mason!' he called out again, this time louder. Then he saw the grey-clad figure.

Mason was stumbling away from the vehicle, leaning forward at the waist, both hands to his face as though in pain. He was making for the red bus, whether by intent or because he was walking blind, there was no way of knowing, and as he drew nearer, several people were alighting from its platform and staring silently at him. One of them pointed at him and began to giggle.

'Mason, come back!' Holman shouted, realizing that without his helmet, his companion was exposed to the fog.

But Mason hadn't heard him. He fell to one knee as he reached the crowd that was still climbing off the bus. Several of them began to laugh now, pointing down at him, calling out to their fellow passengers to come and see the ridiculous-looking man. The front of the bus was embedded in a shop window, but now a figure was emerging from the wreckage, crunching through the shattered glass, leaning against the side of the bus to steady himself. He was wearing the uniform of a London Transport driver and blood trickled in a thin line from his crinkly scalp down his brown face. He was grinning broadly.

Holman started forward to warn Mason, but he was still unsteady on his feet and fell painfully on to his knees. He called out again, one hand reaching outward towards the crowd, but nobody seemed to hear him.

The driver was now standing over Mason, who was still on one knee, rocking his body backwards and forwards in pain, low moans coming from deep down in his throat. The black man swung a foot at him then stepped back and roared with laughter as the clumsy figure toppled. Someone else stepped forward and aimed a kick, retreating when the blow had been accomplished. The rest of the crowd joined in the laughter. At once, as if by some silent, mutual agreement, they all gathered around the prone body and began to kick at it.

'Don't, don't!' Holman screamed at them, but they took no notice, absorbed in their own violence. To his amazement, he saw the figure of Mason emerge from the tangle of legs, crawling on all fours protected from the worst of the blows by the heavy suit he wore. His eyes met Holman's and they registered recognition, but his hands were kicked from beneath him even as he opened his mouth to cry out. His exposed head hit the pavement with a loud thud and he lay motionless in the road. The crowd's laughter took on a new, more hysterical pitch as they leapt upon his body, using their feet to stomp the life from him.

With a shout of pure rage, Holman gained his feet and staggered towards them, his anger pumping adrenalin through his body, helping his strength to return. He leapt into the throng, taking several people down with him and was on his feet again instantly, swinging punches, kicking out at them. For a moment they cowered away from him, afraid of his anger, afraid because they sensed he wasn't like them.

All except the driver. He wasn't afraid of anybody. He roared at Holman for spoiling the fun and threw himself at him. Holman went down under the weight and found his face pressed hard against the road's surface and his eyes staring into those of a dead man.

Mason's face lay a foot away from his own and it was turned towards him, the eyes unseeing, the expression rigid. A thread of blood came from one corner of his mouth, an indication that some of his ribs had torn into his lungs. Whether it had been caused by the accident or the cruel kicks of the lunatic mob, Holman would never know; all he felt was despair and the urge to lie there on the ground until the crowd left him alone. But he knew they would not leave him alone until he too was dead. The heavy weight was suddenly released from his body as the black man stood up and a boot kicked Holman viciously over on to his back. He saw nothing but the greyness above him at first, the eddying, drifting clouds of fog, tinged with yellow, filled with man-made impurities. A ring of grinning, evil-looking heads intruded upon the periphery of the soft grey picture as the crowd gathered round him, looking down at him as though he were an animal about to be slaughtered for the sheer fun of it. They reminded him of the faces of his school friends when, many, so many years ago, they had trapped a wasp in a jam-jar and had begun to fill the jar with water through a small hole in the top. The ring of expectant faces had smiled gleefully at the wasp's struggles to get free as the water rose, frantically buzzing around the inside of the jar, its circuit becoming smaller and smaller, its tiny legs beating against the smooth glass in an effort to grip it, all to no avail. To Holman, the smiles had seemed to turn into sadistic leers as the water crept up, inch by inch, the space between the top of the water and the roof of the jar physically encapsulating the wasp's remaining lifetime. The grinning lunatics reminded him of the incident, for their expressions were not unlike those of the schoolboys and the circumstances now were not dissimilar. But this time there would be no one to save his life as he had done for the wasp by stepping forward and knocking the jar from the ringleader's hands so it shattered upon the ground, giving the insect its small existence back. He had paid for that action with a beating, but it had been worth it for the astonished, cheated looks on his companions' faces alone.

One head came closer to his, bringing his fleeing mind back to the present, and he saw it was the black man's. The bus driver's hand shot forward and grabbed him by the hair, pulling his head up and forward, the large brown eyes looking into his own. Holman recognized the slightly glazed look of the madness, even though the eyes were filled with cruel amusement. He remembered the revolver.

Carefully, he reached for the shoulder holster beneath his coat, flicked the gun's hammer free of its retaining loop, drew it out steadily, clicking off the safety catch as he did so, put the short barrel under the man's chin, and pulled the trigger.

The driver's head exploded, spattering the crowd with blood and brains, tiny bone fragments flying into the air acting as shrapnel. The force of the blast sent the body reeling back away from Holman, the grip on his hair tightening so some of it came away at the roots. He jumped to his feet, holding the gun forward, ready to use it again, but the mob was too stunned to attack him. They stood looking at the twitching body on the ground, their crazed minds unable to understand exactly what had happened.

Holman began slowly to back away, his eyes never leaving the faces of the crowd, waiting for the first sign of hostility towards him to resume. Several were wiping blood from their faces and looking at their hands in amazement. He saw one middle-aged woman, a woman who normally would have probably fainted at the sight of blood, lick the red stains from the fingers of one hand, then repeat the process with the other. Her glazed eyes looked around her at her companions, then at the bodies on the ground, then over towards the cautiously retreating Holman. A snarl broke from her lips.

Holman turned and fled. Away from the bus, away from the crowd, away from the dead bodies, away from the vehicle. Into the fog.

He heard a cry from behind and knew they were following. His legs hurt and still felt unsteady as a result of the crash, but he refused to succumb for if he stopped running, he would have to kill again. And then they would kill him.

From nowhere, a car appeared, screeching to a halt in front of him, pitching him forward on to the bonnet although it hadn't actually hit him; it was the momentum of his own pace that had sent him sprawling. The car was an old Ford Anglia, rusty with age but obviously still having some life in it. Holman rolled off the bonnet and ran round to the driver's door. He yanked it open and was about to haul its occupant out when the startled man said: 'Please let me go. I've got to get away from these lunatics!'

Holman hesitated and then bent forward to get a closer look at the man behind the wheel. He appeared to be in his early forties, fairly well dressed and most important of all, his eyes, although frightened, did not appear to have the glazed look that was a symptom of the disease. He looked up at Holman, a pleading expression on his face and said, again, 'Please let me go.'

'Get over!' Holman commanded, pushing his way in, using his weight to get the trembling man into the passenger seat. He revved up the engine and engaged first gear, pulling the door shut as the car shot forward. He was just in time, for outstretched hands clutched at the windows but were knocked aside by the sudden jerk of the car. A figure ran into their path and was sent spinning back into the road. He swerved to avoid another and skidded violently when he was confronted with the overturned Devastation Vehicle. The Anglia did a screeching U-turn, mounted the kerb on one side of the road and sped on along the broad pavement for fifty yards or so, leaving it with a resounding thump only when Holman saw he would not get through the gap ahead caused by a concrete street light and its neighbouring wall. When he considered he was far enough from the pursuing crowd, he reduced speed, afraid that he might run into another vehicle in the fog. He became aware he was still holding the revolver in one hand and the man he had pushed roughly into the passenger seat was staring at it apprehensively. He shoved it back into its holster and heard the man breathe a sigh of relief.

'You're not the same as the rest, are you?' the man asked nervously.

Holman took his eyes off the road for a moment to look at him. He was backed away as far as he could get against the door, one hand on the dashboard, the other holding on to the back of his seat to steady himself. He looked white and frightened.

'As the rest?' Holman asked cautiously.

'You know, not mad. Everyone's gone mad. It's the fog. Please tell me you're not, you're okay. Like me.'

Was it possible? Holman stole another quick glance at the man; was it possible the disease hadn't affected him? He seemed normal enough. Scared, his eyes were frightened, but he seemed rational under the circumstances.

'I'm sane,' Holman said, but wondering if he still was. Could anyone remain sane after all he'd been through?

The man smiled. 'Thank God for that,' he said. 'I've been living through a bad dream. I thought I was the only one left. You've no idea what I've been through.' He rubbed a hand across his eyes that were becoming moist with self-pity. 'My – my wife tried to kill me. We were having breakfast; we didn't realize what the fog was, what it meant. I don't know why, we just didn't associate it with the fog we'd heard about, the Bournemouth fog. I looked up and she was just sitting there, staring at me, a sort of smile on her face. I asked her what she was smiling about and she didn't answer. Just smiled even more. Her eyes – her eyes were different somehow. Wide. Not really seeing.' He began to sob quietly. 'It was horrible,' he said brokenly. Taking a deep breath, he continued: 'She got up from the table and walked around it until she was behind me. I didn't know she'd picked up the bread-knife. I turned around to ask her what was wrong and saw her bringing the knife down. I – I was lucky: it caught my shoulder and the blade snapped. It was only then I realized what was happening. The fog. I realized it was *the fog*! I jumped up and we struggled. I didn't want to hurt her but, God, she was so strong. She, she's only a tiny thing, my wife, you know, but suddenly, she was so strong. She pushed me back across the table and we fought there, over the breakfast things, until we rolled off on to the floor. She cracked her head, knocked herself out. I didn't know what to do.' His body began to shake and once more he had to stop talking until he had calmed himself.

'Take it easy,' said Holman soothingly, feeling pity for the man. How many countless others had gone through the same thing that morning? How many loved ones had turned on one another, tried to kill, to maim the people that meant most to them? How many had killed themselves so far? Was this man lucky because the disease had not affected him or was he unlucky because he'd had to witness what had happened to his wife, to watch her go insane, to fight her to save his own life? 'Don't talk about it anymore,' he said. 'I'll try to get you to a safe place.'

The man looked up at Holman, his tears under control again. 'No, I want to talk about it. You're the only normal person I've spoken to. I tried to get help from others, but they're all the same; they're all mad. Why not us, why haven't we gone mad? Why hasn't it done anything to us?'

Holman hesitated. Should he tell him the chances were that eventually the disease would destroy his brain cells and he, too, would become insane; that the time varied from person to person, that the parasite cells took longer to multiply in some than they did in others? Perhaps he could get him back to base in time for Janet Halstead to go to work on him. He was only one, one life, but at least it was something positive amongst all this carnage. The mission was scrapped now, there was nothing he could do on his own; perhaps he could come back in the other vehicle once they'd located the nucleus again, but in the meantime he could try to save this one life.

Fortunately, he did not have to answer the man's question, for he was talking again, reliving the horror of that morning. 'I tied her up. I didn't know what else to do. I was afraid of her, afraid of my own wife. She came out of her daze as I was tying her. She didn't struggle, didn't say anything at first – just stared at me with those eyes. Those terrible eyes. I was afraid to look at them; they were so – so hate filled!' He shook his head as though to erase the memory. 'And then she began to speak. Such filth! I couldn't believe it. I'd never known her even to swear before, but the filth, the obscenities that came from her! I couldn't believe such thoughts could exist in someone, especially not her! She's always been so good, so gentle. I couldn't stand it; I couldn't stand to listen to her, I couldn't stand to look at her eyes! Oh God, I didn't know what I should do!

'I knew I had to get away, to get out of London, and I knew my only chance would be in the car, I didn't know what it would be like out on the streets, but I knew I couldn't stay there. The drive was terrible. I couldn't go too fast in the fog, I was afraid of crashing, and the people that I saw ... lunatics. Some were like vegetables; just standing by the roadside, not moving. I saw people crawling along the gutters. I saw some sitting in burning cars, others making love in the streets. One man I saw was stabbing himself; standing in a doorway stabbing his own body with a knife. Oh thank God I met you! I think I would have gone mad myself if I hadn't. I got lost, you see. I didn't know where I was going and things just seemed to be getting worse and worse.'

'Did you make sure your wife was securely tied before you left her?' asked Holman, still keeping a wary eye on the road ahead, knowing he would have to make a turn soon if he were to go in the right direction back towards the underground base. 'Did you make sure she wouldn't be able to harm herself?'

'Oh, I didn't leave her,' the man replied. 'I couldn't have left Louise. I love her too much to have left her there alone at the mercy of anyone who might break in. But it was her eyes, you see, and the things she was saying. I couldn't stand it. I had to stop her from looking at me like that and saying those horrible things. And I couldn't leave her, not Louise, she's too precious to me. So I brought her with me; she's in the back. I stopped her saying those foul things and stopped her looking at me that way and put her in the back seat. There she is, my Louise, behind you, in the back.'

Holman quickly glanced over his shoulder and found himself transfixed, the car moving ahead unguided, picking up speed as his foot involuntarily pressed down on the accelerator.

On the back seat was slumped the bound figure of a woman, recognizable as a woman only by her clothes, for the body ended in a bloody stump at the neck. She had been decapitated.

'I couldn't leave her, you see,' the man went on, 'and I couldn't stand the things she was saying and the way she was looking so I used a saw. It was terribly messy, I must say. The kitchen was in a terrible state and I had to change my clothes. And, you know, she kept talking, even while I was doing it, but she had to stop in the end.' His voice grew sad. 'But I couldn't stop her eyes looking at me like that, even when the head came right off. She just kept glaring at me in that lunatic way. Look, she still does.'

He reached behind him, half kneeling on his seat, stretching for something that lay on the floor at the back. He brought his hand up again, his face looking seriously into Holman's. 'Look,' he said.

He held the blood-dripping head by the hair, pushing it towards Holman's face. He was right – the eyes *were* still staring.

A cry of horror escaped from Holman's lips as he backed away, the hairs on his body stiffening, the vertebrae of his spine seeming to contract and lock together. He thrashed out with his hand knocking the disembodied head aside, causing the car to swerve violently across the road. His fight to control it gave his mind a brief respite from the shock it had just received.

The man beside him was astonished that Holman had smashed his wife's head aside. 'Don't do that to Louise, you bastard!' he shouted, placing it gently on his lap. He reached behind him again, careful not to dislodge the head between his legs, and this time, his hand came up with a bloodstained saw. 'I'll kill you!' he screamed. 'You're the same as all the rest!'

He tried to bring the sharp-toothed blade down on the back of Holman's neck, but the car bumped over a kerb, mounting a narrow pavement which ran along the centre of the broad road, knocking him back against the door on his side, the saw falling harmlessly against Holman's shoulder blades. Even as he tried to control the car's skid when it thumped down on to the other lane of the road, Holman struck out with his fist at the figure beside him, catching the man on the side of the jaw. His foot was jammed down hard on the brake pedal and the tyres burnt into the road, struggling for a grip. He thought the car was bound to smash into a building on the other side of the road, but to his surprise and relief he found the way clear, there was a side road dead ahead. The road dipped and the car skidded down its incline, finally stopping broadside across it, the sudden jolt throwing the man forward against the windscreen. Before he had a chance to recover, Holman had leaned across his back and pushed the doorcatch down and shoved the door open. Still in one motion, he pushed the man's rising figure out of the car and into the road, raising his foot and using it to clear the man's legs. His efforts were helped because the car was slightly angled on the slope of the road, and the man's body easily fell forward. Holman saw the woman's head, with its ghastly staring eyes, begin a slow roll down the incline.

Not bothering to pull the door shut again, he restarted the stalled engine and swung the car round, heading down the slope, narrowly missing the head that had come to rest in the middle of the road. He corrected his turn and held the car steady, the door on his other side swinging shut with the momentum. He didn't want to stop; he didn't want to think. He just wanted to get away.

A black hole opened up ahead of him and he suddenly found himself swallowed up by darkness. Once again, his foot hit the brakes, and the car screeched to a halt. He looked around in panic but could see only blackness ahead and to his sides. He remembered the decapitated body behind him and turned swiftly as though to assure himself that it was still lying prone. Grey light flowed in from a high square arch about thirty yards back and he saw that the body had slumped to the floor behind the front seats. He looked up again at the light and then he realized what had happened. He had driven into a tunnel! He should have realized it instantly, but because of circumstances, everything that happened seemed abnormal.

A tunnel! And suddenly it came to him which tunnel.

'The Blackwall Tunnel,' he said aloud. It had to be; they'd been driving in that direction, into the City, through Aldgate, down Commercial Road towards Poplar. The road he had just driven down must have been a ramp leading into the tunnel from the main road. The long winding tunnel stretched beneath the Thames to the south side of London, cutting out miles of snarled up roads for motorists who would otherwise have had to use distant bridges. There were two tunnels in fact, running parallel to one another but completely separated; the old, built in the 1890s, and the new, completed in the late 1960s, one for the northbound traffic, the other for southbound. Holman was in the old tunnel, used for access to the north. He would use it himself now and get back to Westminster by following the river along its southern side. For a full minute he debated whether to go back to his flat, collect Casey, and get the hell out of London, but he finally dismissed the thought because he knew really there was no choice.

Before he made his way back, there was one thing he would have to do: get rid of the grotesque figure on the floor behind him. He opened the side door and got out, pulling the driving seat forward so he could reach the body, the old car being a two-door model. He could have switched the car's headlights on to give him more light, but he had no desire to see too clearly what he was doing; the dim light from the opening further back would suffice for his purposes. He groped around until he found the tied ankles and gave the body a tug, finding it surprisingly light as it came out smoothly. He avoided touching anything but the woman's ankles; the thought of coming in contact with her headless shoulders made him feel nauseous. He pulled the body to the side of the tunnel then straightened up and wiped his hands down the sides of his jacket to rid himself of the feel of her cold flesh. Looking down into the depths of the tunnel as he did so, he was forced to blink his eyes to clear them.

Was it his imagination, or was it lighter down there? The underground passage was filled with fog but much less than there was above ground so his vision was not seriously hindered, and his eyes had become fairly accustomed to the gloom. He was sure, there was light coming from ahead, from around a bend, but it couldn't be daylight, for the exit would be at least a quarter of a mile away on the other side of the river and there were more bends that would diminish any daylight coming from that source. The only other possibility was that there was another car down there with its headlights full on. Before he drove any further into the tunnel, he would have to investigate; he was reluctant to run into more trouble again. Cautiously, quietly, he began to walk down the tunnel towards the eerie light.

It grew brighter at his approach, a strange yellowish light, reminding him of the light he'd come across before, in Winchester. The familiar dread crept through him again; he began to suspect the source of the light. His heart seemed to be pounding almost painfully as he neared the bend and he had to take short, shallow breaths to combat the acrid smell that was growing stronger. He kept close to the wall, one hand touching its rough surface with every step he took, and then he was at the first curve of the tunnel

The bend was casual, not sharp, and there was no need to go to its apex to see what lay beyond. The whole tunnel further ahead was filled with the glow, the strange incandescence peculiar to the mutated mycoplasma. He had found it! Now he knew why the instruments of the helicopter above had lost it: it had literally gone to ground, slunk into a hole beneath the ground almost as though it remembered the hole it had been buried in for so many years. Could it be possible? Had it actually sought shelter like an animal searching for a lair? No, it was too ridiculous. And yet he *had* found it lurking inside the cathedral, and they *had* lost it once before. Could it really have drifted accidentally into these enclosures, into these man-made shelters?

He stood gazing into its hypnotic shine for several minutes, leaning back against the tunnel's wall, suddenly realizing he was actually resisting walking towards it, that it seemed to be pulling him forward, that a small part of his mind was urging him to envelop his body in the glow, but the fact that he had become conscious of its mesmeric influence made him back away. He felt certain his immunity would not hold if he were to enter the mycoplasma in its strongest form.

As soon as it was out of vision, the magnetic pull on his mind was broken and suddenly he wasn't sure if it had been his imagination or not. He hurried back towards the car, his brain racing with new thoughts and, by the time he had reached the car, an idea had formed in his mind.

He jumped into the Anglia, switched on the engine and, without turning on its lights, he began to reverse it towards the entrance. Looking over his shoulder through the rear window, he saw a shadowy figure silhouetted in the cloudy entrance and, as he drew nearer, he saw it was the man he'd thrown from the car. In his arms he cradled the head of his dead wife.

▪ 21 ▪

HOLMAN CROUCHED IN THE DARK INTERIOR OF THE SHOP AWAY FROM THE EYES of the groups of lunatics roaming the streets, but positioned so that he could see the overturned Devastation Vehicle lying in the middle of the road. The fog seemed much clearer now, although there were still thick pockets of it drifting through and the very air seemed to carry the yellow tinge to it. Holman had taken extreme care in driving back to the vehicle for everything depended on his reaching the radio; he needed help from the base if he were to carry out his plan. And certain materials.

He had driven slowly and every time he came across a menacing individual or mob, he had speeded up until he was a safe distance away from them. Twice he had to mount the pavement to avoid recklessly driven cars and once he'd deliberately run over a dog that was running amok attacking people, but that was the only time he'd allowed himself to interfere in the surrounding chaos and only because the dog had presented itself directly in the path of the car. If he had had to chase it, he wouldn't have bothered. He had detached himself from the nightmare and had become a mere observer. He knew it was the self-protection of his own mind: he'd always had that ability (or perhaps misfortune) to allow his feelings to go cold, remote, whenever circumstances became intolerable. He could either bury himself in action or retreat into insensitive logic; it wasn't callousness, for emotion always flooded through him after the event. It was a natural ability to survive.

He no longer felt any strong sympathy for the people out there; his feelings were more akin to fear. It was strange how madness, which, after all, was only an illness of the mind, was so repulsive to the 'normal'. Was it due to fear? Even with Casey when she had been under restraint, he'd felt the tension, the urge to get away from her, to shut her from his mind, and she must have experienced the same feelings when it had been he who was insane. That was what made madness so cruel for the relatives or friends of its victim: the fear of the person they loved. And now, there was a whole city full of the insane.

And yet, his detachment wasn't complete: it was the sight of the children, infants some of them, who were walking the streets, many on their own, still clad in pyjamas and nightclothes, that lost dazed look on their tiny faces. It was this that stirred his emotions most. He wanted to help them, to gather them up and lead them to safety, to keep them from harm until help was at hand, but he knew the best way he could help them was to carry out his plan.

The idea was simple: the mutated mycoplasma had been locked away below ground for many years, trapped and contained by tons of earth; now it had returned to another underground sanctuary, a man-made open womb that could be made into a prison if both ends were sealed. So he had returned to the vehicle and, with relief, found it untampered with; the radio was still buzzing (a voice had been calling in every ten minutes, desperate for a reply from the two passengers of the vehicle) and he'd used it to tell headquarters of his plan. There had been great excitement and relief at the sound of his voice, but the men on the other end were professionals and had soon acknowledged his instructions. He asked for explosives, the 'brisant' kind, the type used for quarrying and demolition work because of its shattering power. He asked for as much as could be loaded into the second Devastation Vehicle in case the first attempts failed, and an explosives expert because his own knowledge was extremely limited in that field. He gave them directions as to his exact location, for he had checked on the names of the streets on his way back to the vehicle: they would find him and the overturned vehicle at a point along the East India Dock Road close to a turning called Hale Street. He told them to hurry.

The voice at the other end urged him to sit tight and wait, no matter how long it took them to get there, and to avoid any trouble. If he were to be attacked, he was to use the gun without hesitation.

He had smiled grimly. He had little compunction about killing now, for he thought of the people out there as hardly human any more, their hostility helping to negate his compassion. He had remembered the demented man clutching his wife's disembodied head at the entrance to the tunnel; he had backed the car right into him, repugnance at what the man had done filling him with hatred – unreasonable hatred, he knew, for the man could not help the actions of a sick mind. The impact had killed him, Holman was sure, and he felt no regret. Perhaps later, when he had time to reflect, he would feel pity, but now he had become quite ruthless; partly because of fear of the illness, but mostly because he had a mission that he couldn't allow to be jeopardized.

Two hours went by before he saw the other vehicle appear from the fog and halt beside its ill-fortuned twin. He rose from his hiding place behind the shop's counter, amid shelves filled with confectionery, and walked towards the door, unbolting it and stepping outside into the misty street. He had found the door wide open when he'd arrived and assumed the owner had left it so on leaving the premises. He walked over to the second vehicle just as one of its side doors began to open. A heavy-suited figure clambered out carrying what appeared to be an ordinary rifle except that its trigger was at least three inches long and had a wide, looping guard to accommodate it. The figure wore a helmet fitted with a dark, narrow visor for vision, and he had to swing his whole body around from the waist in order to see about him. The black visor came to rest in the direction of Holman as he walked forward, his arm slightly raised in a gesture of greeting turning into one of apprehensive placation as the rifle swung up to meet him. The four fingers of the clumsy glove tightened on the long trigger and a voice with its familiar metallic tone said sharply, 'Stay there!'

'It's all right,' said Holman wearily, 'it's me, Holman.' He stopped nevertheless.

Another grey-suited figure was now climbing from the car. 'Yes, Captain, it's Holman. Put your gun down.'

'Sorry, sir,' the man holding the gun said, 'but I'm a bit jumpy after what we've seen coming here.'

'It's okay,' said Holman, 'I know what you mean.'

The second figure pushed by the Captain and advanced on Holman. 'Well done, Mr Holman,' said a voice, familiar although distorted by the helmet's speaker. 'Let us hope we are in time to carry out your plan, eh?'

He recognized the slight German accent. 'Professor Ryker?' he asked.

'Yes,' came the reply. 'I decided to see the mutation firsthand before we sealed it off. Once it is trapped, the fog itself should be easy to disperse. Later, we will be able to drill holes and draw the mycoplasma off into containers. It should in itself provide us with enough vaccine to cure a large majority of the people we catch in time. But first, I must have that sample for I'm afraid we still do not know exactly what the mutation is.'

'But you must have some idea by now,' said Holman.

'Brain cells perhaps, broken down, crystallized in some way, infected with the mycoplasma, multiplying, somehow feeding on impurities and carbon dioxide from the air. Yes, we have some idea,' said Ryker, 'but that is not enough. We still need the thing itself. And soon, if it is to be of any use.' He pointed towards the vehicle he'd just arrived in. 'Now please, let us go to this place, this tunnel. We must not waste any more time.'

He walked back to the vehicle, pulling Holman gently by the arm along with him. 'This is Captain Peters, our explosives expert,' he said as they passed the figure still clutching the gun.

'Sir,' the Captain said to Holman, 'you didn't say what had happened to Mason when you reported back.'

Holman pointed towards the two dead figures lying beside the bus across the road. 'One of them's Mason. He was – injured in the crash and ran into a mob. They kicked him to death.'

He thought he heard the Captain cursing softly as he climbed into the vehicle. Inside, he was surprised to find the figure of another man, also clad in the usual grotesque garb.

'This is Sergeant Stanton,' the Captain introduced him as he squeezed in behind Holman. The Sergeant's helmet nodded towards him.

'Did you find room for the explosives?' Holman asked, quite seriously. The small cabin was fairly cramped with all four of them, especially with the other three's suits making their bodies even more bulky.

'I think you'll find we have enough, sir,' the Sergeant replied, equally seriously. They had all seen enough distressing sights that day to dismiss any joviality they might normally have. 'Blasting gelatine we brought. Enough to blow up the houses of Parly. You're sitting on most of it!'

Holman shifted in his seat uncomfortably.

'Don't worry, sir,' the Captain said, 'it's quite safe for the moment.'

'So long as nobody bashes into us,' Stanton remarked dryly.

'Yes,' agreed the Captain. 'I think it might be better if Mr Holman drives providing he feels up to it; he'll have a clearer view than any of us. We daren't take off these helmets now that the door has been opened.'

Holman struggled forward into the driver's seat and the Sergeant squeezed back into the place he had vacated.

'Of course, we still do not know if these suits are strong enough to resist the mycoplasma,' said Ryker. 'At least not near its centre, in its purest form. That is why it is still you, Mr Holman, who will have to draw off the sample.'

As Holman shuddered, Ryker went on reassuringly, 'Don't worry, my friend. You will not have to go too near, we have long tubing which you will only have to direct into the nucleus. And one of us will come as far as possible with you to see that you come to no harm.'

The vehicle moved on and once again the four men were subjected to the wretched sight of fellow human beings in the depths of degradation. Holman noticed they were banding together more now, solitary figures becoming less and less frequent. He remarked on it.

'Yes, we have seen it too as we drove here,' said Ryker. 'There were thousands of them by the river. We had to take an alternative route to get through.'

'Oh, God, you don't think –' Holman began, remembering Bournemouth.

'It's possible,' said Ryker gravely, guessing Holman's meaning. 'That's why it is essential that we are successful this time and can clear the fog.'

'Why, what can you do? Thousands, millions more likely, are going to commit mass suicide. They'll throw themselves into the river. The Thames will be full of bodies – there'll be so many you'll be able to walk across it!'

'Calm yourself, please, Mr Holman,' Ryker placed a gentle hand on Holman's arm. 'We are going to spray the city, the whole town, with sleeping gas.'

'What? That's impossible!'

'No, it isn't,' Ryker answered quietly. 'Ever since the crisis began in London, small aircraft and helicopters – commercial as well as military – have been loading up with two things: calcium chloride and nitrous oxide, a gas you might describe as a knock-out gas. The intention is to send the city to sleep for as long as it takes to find and administer a serum. And remember: many will not have been affected by the disease yet for it varies from body to body as to how long it takes for the infection to begin its work; these people will have the best chance of all. Hundreds will still die, of course – thousands, perhaps – but we will save the majority. *Provided we have a serum and provided we are in time!*'

Holman picked up speed. It was plausible, countless lives could be saved! They had to succeed, no matter what they came up against, they had to succeed this time.

Soon, by carefully skirting likely trouble spots, they arrived at the black entrance to the twin tunnels. He stopped the vehicle and they clambered out, the two soldiers going first, each clutching their rifles, ready to use them if necessary.

'There's a body over there just inside the tunnel,' the Sergeant said flatly, pointing towards the recumbent figure of the man Holman had knocked down.

'I killed him,' he told them, and they accepted it without comment, as though he had told them he'd stepped on a bug.

'Now,' said Ryker, who was emerging last from the vehicle, 'we have to make sure the nucleus is still there and if it is, then you know what you must do, Mr Holman.' And then he added, in surprise, 'But there are two tunnels!'

Holman nodded. 'Yes, one is the old tunnel – the right-hand one – used by northbound traffic; the other, more recent one, is the south. The nucleus is in the old one.' He indicated with his hand, adding, 'At least, I hope to God it's still there.'

The four men walked into the entrance, three lumbering along, small oxygen tanks strapped to their backs, one, unencumbered, but looking humanly frail beside the others.

'It's pretty solid,' the Captain remarked, peering up at the roof of the entrance. 'Lovely solid chunks of concrete to come down and fill up the hole. Yes, should do very nicely.'

'Fuck me,' said the Sergeant through clenched lips, 'there's a bloody 'ead lyin' over there.'

'Forget it,' said Holman coldly.

He walked into the blackness for about six yards, then stood there, allowing his eyes to grow accustomed to the darkness. 'It's there,' he said after a while.

The two soldiers returned to the vehicle and unloaded a lead container mounted on wheels from its side, similar to the one Holman had used in Winchester, only bigger. The Sergeant unstrapped a long length of flexible steel tubing, narrower at one end. He coiled it over his shoulder and followed the Captain who was leading the motorized container back towards the tunnel's entrance.

'You know how to use the machine, Mr Holman,' Ryker said, facing him and placing one hand on his shoulder as though contact would make his words more intelligible. 'As I told you, there is no need to go too near the nucleus. You have sixty yards of steel tubing that is just stiff enough for you to push into the mycoplasma and by switching on the machine it will be sucked back into the container. I will come with you myself; I want to get a closer look at this monster.'

'Take this with you, sir,' the Captain said, handing Holman a small oxygen tank, 'you may find you need it. And there's a torch.'

Holman thanked him and put his arm through the strap of the tank, sliding it on to his shoulder. Switching on the torch, he took the arm of the mobile container in his other hand and said, 'I'm ready, Professor.'

They walked down the slope of the tunnel towards the first curve and Ryker stiffened as for the first time he became aware of the light shining from ahead.

'I can see it now,' he said to Holman.

Holman didn't bother to reply; he could feel his nerves tensing at every step nearer to the bend and the now-familiar clammy coldness creeping up his back. He kept the torch shining on to the ground just ahead of him, knowing it would only reflect back at him if he shone it directly at the fog in the tunnel. He moved to the side of the tunnel as if to keep out of vision from the brightness ahead, as if it were a seeing thing. Strangely, Professor Ryker followed suit.

They reached the bend and stopped for a moment, Holman turning to look at the scientist as though seeking reassurance. Ryker nodded and pointed ahead. 'I'll come with you around the curve so I can get a better look at it, but that's as far as I think I should go.'

Holman took a deep breath, then was forced to cough to clear his throat from the fumes. It wasn't too bad yet, but he would soon have to use the breathing apparatus as he went deeper into the tunnel. He moved on, Ryker following.

They were a long way down the next straight run before Holman said, 'You'd better stop here, Professor, the light's getting much stronger.'

'Yes, yes, I think you're right,' came the reply. 'I cannot see too well through this visor, but I think we must be very close to the main body of the myco-plasma.'

'The worst of it seems to be around the next bend; I can see the light shining brilliantly at its corner. I'm going forward, you stay here. I won't go out of your sight around the curve if I can help it.'

Once again, he felt the compulsion to approach it, but he did so only because he had to. The fog seemed thicker but he guessed it was only because of the light bouncing off its particles that made it more difficult to see. He turned his head to make sure Ryker was still in view; he didn't want the Professor to lose sight of him! He soon reached the next gently sweeping curve, this one bending to the right as opposed to the first which had bent to the left, but he stayed on the same side of the tunnel, hoping he would be able to reach the nucleus from as far back in the curve as possible.

The light was dazzling as he reached the point of the bend that allowed him to see further up the tunnel. Either it was just the confined space creating an illusion or the nucleus was growing larger; he was sure it hadn't been as bright as this in Winchester. True, he hadn't been as close as this there, but because of the old cathedral's vastness, he had been afforded an unhindered view. He began hastily to assemble the machinery, pushing the end of the steel tubing into its cavity and clicking the switch to release grips that would hold it securely; the sooner he had completed this task and could get away, the better he would like it. Before he began to push the tubing towards its goal, he placed the mouthpiece of the oxygen cylinder over his mouth for the acrid smell was becoming stronger. Then he began unwinding the coil of steel, placing its rigid end on the ground and slowly sliding it along the centre of the tunnel's flat surface. It began to go off course after a while, but that didn't matter; the side wall would guide it forward into the glowing mass ahead. Beads of perspiration broke out on Holman's forehead, due to the clammy heat inside the cavernous tunnel and the tension that had gripped him.

Finally the tubing began to disappear into the light, meeting no resistance, a fact that surprised Holman; he had almost expected the nucleus to have some substance, at least some kind of resilience, but he realized again it was an organism he was probing, millions of tiny microbes. He pushed the steel tube to the limit of its extension then pressed the switch on the container which would operate the suction unit. The machine began to buzz and draw off the deadly mutation into its reinforced container, the snaking coil of steel stiffening and straightening out as it did so. Previously, at Winchester, he had been instructed to leave the machine on for at least two minutes to allow the container to fill itself with the mutated microbes, but as this container was larger, he decided to leave it on for at least three minutes. He crouched on one knee, bathed in the yellow glow, studying the phenomenon before him.

He had come to regard it almost as a living, thinking thing. Ryker had called it a monster. It seemed apt. The feeling that it was protesting in some way against this violation against it still persisted but, of course, it was only the high-pitched humming of the machinery, the quivering stiffness of the steel tubing combining with his imagination that produced and heightened the effect. At least, that was what he told himself.

The urge to go closer to the source was becoming stronger and several times during that long three minutes he found himself staring blankly into the bright mass. At last, with a sigh of relief, he switched off the machine, pushed another button to effectively seal the container, then detached the tubing, leaving it lying limply along the ground. He stood up and once again looked into the radiance. Perhaps he *should* get a closer look at it. Perhaps behind the veiling mists that swirled in front of it he would find some clue to its beginnings; some idea of its structure he could inform Ryker of, who would perhaps recognize a vital factor in the progress of his theory. He was immune, after all; it wouldn't harm him.

He began to walk towards it.

A gloved hand clamped down heavily on his shoulder, when he had only gone ten yards, spinning him round roughly.

'What do you think you are doing?' Ryker demanded to know, his body heaving with the exertion of running in the cumbersome suit.

Holman could only stare at the darkened visor.

'I could barely make out your figure through the fog,' Ryker went on, 'and when it disappeared altogether, I knew something was wrong. It has been a long time since I have run so fast. Now tell me: what are you up to?'

Holman rubbed a hand across his forehead. 'Christ,' he said, 'I don't know. I was walking into it. I just had a compulsion to get nearer to it.'

'Yes,' said Ryker slowly and thoughtfully. 'Well, do not look at it again. Turn your back on it and let us return to the machine. Did you complete your task?'

'Y-yes. Yes, it should be full. But you shouldn't be this close – your suit may not be enough protection.'

'I know, I know, but you had to be stopped. Come along, let us get away from here.'

They collected the machine and made their way back to the tunnel's entrance, much to the relief of the two soldiers who had been growing more anxious by the minute.

'Everything okay, sir?' enquired the Captain, stepping forward to take the machine.

'Everything is fine,' Ryker told him. 'Now, we will not waste any more time; we must seal the tunnel entrance immediately. Take the container back out of harm's way–we will worry about loading it on to the vehicle later, when our next job is done.' He looked up at the arch of the tunnel and smiled inside his helmet.

'It is very fortunate that they thought of building another tunnel. Captain Peters and I will take explosives through the southbound passage and plant them at the other end. We must seal both openings at the same time so that the mycoplasma will be trapped; we will time our blasts so they occur simultaneously.'

They went over to the vehicle and the Sergeant began to unload three cases of explosives. 'This will be more than enough,' he told them. 'If we fail the first time, we've plenty more for as many goes as we like.' He reached in and brought out another box, smaller than the others. 'Detonators,' he explained.

They turned as they heard the lumbering figure of the Captain returning. 'I've put the container halfway up the incline,' he said, 'where the road branches off to the ramp we've just come down. It'll be quite safe there for now; it's virtually indestructible and nobody can move it unless they know how to operate it.'

He poked his head inside the cabin of the vehicle and emerged again holding a small two-way radio. 'We'll keep in touch constantly,' he said. 'You take this, Mr Holman. It's simple to operate, and you can speak to us while Sergeant Stanton is setting up his explosives.' He handed the radio to Holman who examined it briefly, then nodded.

'It should take us about twenty minutes to get through the tunnel and set ourselves up, providing we don't run into trouble on the way,' the Captain went on, glancing at his watch. 'But we'll radio through and synchronize our blasts that way. All set?' he turned towards Ryker.

The figure nodded and clambered into the vehicle. Before he was completely through, he turned and said, 'Good luck to all of us. And may God help us.'

Holman stood well back while the Sergeant went about setting his explosives thirty feet inside the tunnel, even though he was assured it was quite harmless until it had been 'primed'. 'In fact,' Sergeant Stanton had explained, 'it's the blasting caps that are more dangerous. Highly explosive, they are.' He had shown him the small metal tube that was the primer. 'There's a little bit of lead aside in there, with a larger amount of trinitrotoluene – TNT to you. Very sensitive.' He had grinned through his mask at Holman, enjoying the man's discomfort. 'Don't worry, sir, you'll be all right with me.' He had gone into the tunnel whistling tunelessly, happy now that he was at last doing something positive, something he was an expert at.

Holman dragged clear of the entrance the dead body of the man he'd thrown from the car, for some illogical reason not wanting it to be buried beneath tons of concrete. After a short while, the Sergeant came out of the tunnel, unwinding a long thin cable from a spindle behind him. 'That should do it,' he said, almost cheerfully now.

The radio crackled in Holman's hand. 'Hello, can you hear me, Mr Holman?' It was Ryker's voice sounding distant and even less human than it had through the mask's speaker. Holman acknowledged. 'The Captain is inside the tunnel now,' the voice went on. 'The south-bound passage was clear. Filled with fog of course, but not the nucleus. We had to take it steady – our vision was not too good – but we used dipped headlights and stayed close to the wall. As yet, we've seen no people over this side and I must admit, we have no desire to. The exit – or should I say entrance – at this end is perfect for our purposes. It is enclosed by heavy concrete slabs all the way along the incline leading from the tunnel. We have parked our vehicle on the opposite road of the other tunnel which is much higher than its sister road. That is where I am perched at this moment, looking straight down into the exit; we will move back to a safer position as soon as we are ready. How are things at your end?'

'Sergeant Stanton is just running out the fuse. We should be ready at any time.'

'Good. Captain Peters asked me to tell the Sergeant he will place one charge as near to the roof as possible, another at the bottom of the opposite wall. Could you pass that on to Sergeant Stanton please.'

Holman shouted the message after Stanton who was now some distance away up the incline. He looked up at Holman, nodded, pointed to his chest and gave the thumbs-up sign.

'The Sergeant's done the same,' Holman said into the mouthpiece.

'Good, good. Now I suggest we find cover. The Captain is coming out of the tunnel now so we should soon be ready to proceed. I will speak to you again in a few moments.'

The radio went dead and Holman walked back towards Sergeant Stanton who had now climbed the parapet on to the small side road that overlooked the incline leading down to the black hole.

'We'll be all right up here, sir,' the soldier said as Holman scrambled up after him. 'I've set it so that the tunnel will come down causing very little to come our way – but we'll have to be wary of a few flying rocks.'

'What about the container?' Holman pointed towards the mobile box that stood further down, closer to the entrance.

'Oh, that'll be all right, sir. There's not much that can harm that thing.' He connected the plastic-sheathed fuse to a small handbox. 'One twist of this knob here, sir, and we'll have that entrance down in no time.'

'No plunger?' asked Holman, feeling naive.

'Not for this.' The Sergeant grinned, his enjoyment increasing as the time for his blast grew nearer.

The radio crackled into life again and a voice said, 'Captain Peters here. Can you hear me, Sergeant?'

The Sergeant leaned towards the speaker. 'I can hear you, sir.'

'Right. We're in position here. We'll give it a countdown of one minute. Check your timer.'

Holman saw the soldier look at a small clockface on the detonation box he held in his hand. His gloved finger poised above a catch at its side. The voice from the radio said, 'Start it after three.' The seconds were counted and the Sergeant's clumsy finger pushed the catch down, starting a tiny red second hand on its circular course.

'All right, Sergeant. I'm handing the radio back to Professor Ryker now,' the Captain's voice said. 'Be ready on the stroke of sixty. Good luck and keep your bloody heads down.' The radio went silent again.

Holman watched in fascination as the red hand crept round the dial. Several times he thought it had stopped but realized it was only an optical illusion. As it reached the forty-five-second mark, he felt the urge to blow his nose, but he knew it was only nerves and rubbed it with a shaking finger instead. Ten. His throat felt dry. Seven. He cleared it. Five. He remembered to breathe. Three. Would the blast be powerful enough to completely block the entrance? Two. It had to be. One.

He buried his head in his hands as he sensed rather than saw the Sergeant briskly turn the knob.

He felt the whooshing of air before he heard the explosion, sweeping his hair back, dragging at his clothes. He thought the ground had actually trembled beneath him. Then he heard the roar, a split second behind the actual blast, muffled at first then developing into a loud, rumbling crack of thunder.

He kept his head down close to the concrete surface, expecting to feel fragments of rubble descending upon them, but none came. Still, he lay there, covering his head until the Sergeant's hand prodded him on the shoulder.

'It's all right now, sir. A nice clean one, that.'

The Sergeant was on his knees looking towards the tunnel's entrance, nodding his head in self-admiration. Holman looked up, deafened by the blast, but anxious to see its results.

Dust was swirling around the entrance, mixed with the fog, but after a few seconds, it began to drift away. Holman managed to smile at what he saw.

Tons of broken concrete and rubble had completely filled the high entrance – if one could call it an entrance any more. For some inexplicable reason, he had expected just to see the entrance blocked up, but of course, the beginning of the hole had now moved back forty feet or so and a steep slope of broken rock led up to its broken roof.

He clapped the grinning Sergeant on the arm and picked up the radio. 'Hello, Professor Ryker,' he said into it and was puzzled as to why he couldn't hear his own voice. Then he realized his head was still ringing with the blast so he placed the radio on the ground while he studied the wreckage more thoroughly. The Sergeant had already dropped down on to the incline and was now walking towards it. He reached its foot and stood there, examining the damage. At last satisfied, he turned and waved at Holman and once more gave him the thumbs-up sign.

By now, Holman's head was clearing so he picked up the radio again and spoke into it. 'Hello, Ryker, can you hear me?'

There were a few moments of static then the Professor's voice came through. 'Hello, hello, Mr Holman. Can you hear me?'

'Yes, I can, Professor.'

'Quite a blast, eh? Well, it seems to have done the job at this end. Captain Peters has just gone for a closer look, but from here it looks fine. How about your side?'

'It's completely sealed at this end. Sergeant Stanton is just climbing the slope to the top, but he's already indicated everything's fine.'

'Excellent, excellent. I shall move forward myself now along the top road, and examine the damage from there. The dust is settling and the air over here seems to be clearer than on your side, so I am getting a pretty clear picture of the results of our little blast. Yes, yes, the nearer I get the better it looks. I can see Captain Peters directly below me; I think he will be satisfied with his work. He is looking round for me – ah, yes, he sees me. He is waving. Good, good, I think he is happy – he is shaking hands with himself.' Holman heard a strange metallic rasping through the receiver which could only have been the Professor chuckling to himself. The voice went on: 'I am moving past the blockage now and I must say it looks very, very solid to me. There is one enormous concrete slab at an angle at the top, it must be at least twenty feet across, that is –' the radio went silent for a few moments, then the voice continued, and Holman could sense a sudden tension in it, even through its distortion. 'There is something wrong. There – there is dust spewing from the top of the concrete – no, from behind it. Is it dust?' There was a long pause. 'Or is it just the disturbed fog? No, the fog is clearer over here, it must be dust. I will look closer. It seemed to be coming out rapidly, like steam. I am near to it now, I can see behind the con –' again his voice broke off. 'There is a gap!' Holman started at the sudden exclamation. 'There is a gap in the roof! The fog – it is escaping from it! But this is impossible. It must be the force of the blast. The air inside the tunnel must be forcing the fog out. It must be that, surely the fog couldn't – God! There is a light! The hole is beginning to glow. The light is coming out. It is the light we saw in the tunnel, the yellow light. No, no, the mycoplasma is escaping. It is emerging with the fog! I must get away from here! I must get away.'

The radio went dead, except for the sharp crackle of static, and Holman, for the first time in many years, broke down and wept.

'Holman! Sergeant Stanton! Can you hear me?' Holman raised his head at the sound of the voice and made a grab for the radio. He had no idea of how much time had elapsed since the receiver had gone dead: it might only have been seconds, but more likely it had been several minutes for his tears of frustration had blotted out all sense of time. Was there no answer to this nightmare? Was there no way to succeed in destroying it?

'Hello, this is Holman,' he said hastily into the speaker. 'Ryker?'

'No, this is Captain Peters. Professor Ryker is beside me in the vehicle; I don't think he's too good.'

'What happened?'

'The mycoplasma; it got loose. I heard Professor Ryker shouting and scrambled up to the top of the slope to see what was wrong. He was down the road a piece, near the vehicle, lying in the road. Ahead of him, I could see a – I can only describe it as a solid mass of light, although that hardly fits. It seemed to be drifting away with the fog; *it must have passed right over him!*'

Holman drew in his breath slowly. 'Is he all right?'

'1 don't know, he seems sort of dazed. I dragged him into the vehicle, but couldn't risk taking his helmet off to examine him. I think it's more fright than anything; the sight of that thing escaping and coming towards him. Anyway, he seemed to come out of it a minute ago; he told me to follow it, said we mustn't lose sight of it this time, and then he just slumped back and seemed to black out. I think he's coming round a bit now.'

'Peters, be careful,', Holman urged. 'He may have been infected.'

'No, I don't think so; these suits are pretty bloody tough. I think it's just shock. Anyway, I'm following the thing, the nucleus, whatever it is, just keeping it within visual range. We haven't got far yet, but it seems to be heading due east towards –' again, the agonizing silence. 'Holman, there're two enormous buildings rising up ahead of us in the fog,' the voice broke in again. 'They look like yes, they are. Gas holders. Giant gas holders!'

Holman's mind raced back to the occasions he had used the three-lane motorway leading from the Blackwall Tunnel. He remembered the last time had been late at night, and on his left, just as he'd emerged from the southbound tunnel, he'd seen a fantastic sight that had resembled a scene from a science-fiction movie. It had been a vast gas refinery, its silver towers and tanks floodlit at night giving it an awesome and spectacular appearance. There were two main gas holders (those Peters had just seen presumably) and rows of smaller tanks farther back. The refinery had been built on the river bank to give it easy access for the coal that was brought up the Thames in barges to be processed for the manufacture of town gas. He knew it was one of the largest plants of its kind in England, for it helped serve a vast area of the South East.

'Holman, what is this place?' It had sounded like Ryker's voice.

'Professor, is that you?' he asked anxiously. 'Are you okay?'

'Yes, yes, I'm a little bit dizzy, but otherwise fine. Now, quickly tell me, what is this place ahead?'

Holman told him all he knew of the huge gasworks and how, if necessary, they could get into it.

'I think it is necessary,' the voice came back. 'The nucleus is making straight for it. How strange: it is the large quantities of carbon dioxide and sulphur dioxide that are formed in the combustion of gas that add greatly to the pollution of our atmosphere; and now, the mutated mycoplasma is seeking it out, going to it as if it knows it is under threat and needs replenishment, needs to grow stronger.

'Ah, Captain Peters has seen the side-road you spoke of; we are turning into it. We are close to the holders now, they are looming above us. There is a gate ahead; we will go through. I can see the nucleus.'

'Where is it, where is it now?' Holman shouted into the receiver.

He thought he heard a dry laugh at the other end. 'Why, where you would expect it to be, Mr Holman, nestled between the two gas holders, like a tiny child between two monstrous parents.'

Holman stared at the receiver. Ryker's voice had sounded almost whimsical. 'Ryker?' he said.

The voice that returned was brisker, sharper. 'Do you know what town gas is comprised of, Mr Holman? Let me tell you: it is a toxic mixture comprising fifty per cent hydrogen, twenty to thirty per cent methane, seven to seventeen per cent carbon monoxide, three per cent carbon dioxide, eight per cent nitrogen and two per cent hydrocarbons. Furthermore,' Ryker went on, as though lecturing an inquisitive student, 'it contains ammonia, sulphur, hydrocyanic acid, benzene and other substances. In other words, a highly combustible mixture. I think the mutation has provided us with another answer, don't you agree, Mr Holman?'

The radio went frustratingly dead again before he had time to answer. My God, he thought, he means to blow the tanks up and the mutated mycoplasma with them! But what sort of damage would an explosion of that force do to the surrounding area? But he was right; it was worth the risk!

Holman scrambled to his feet, intending to cross the river through the tunnel that was still intact and give help to the two on the other side. Hanging the radio over his shoulder by its strap, he raised a hand to his mouth to call the Sergeant, who was still unaware of what had happened. It was then that he discovered he had problems of his own.

Before he could utter a sound, Holman became conscious of the fact that he was not alone. A crowd, attracted by the noise of the explosion, had gathered behind him; there seemed to be a couple of hundred of them, filling the road leading to the tunnel. Whether the crowd had already assembled before and were mindlessly roaming the streets en masse, he had no way of knowing, but their complete silence was more disturbing than if they had been yelling and screaming. Somehow, he knew, they sensed he was different.

He backed cautiously away from their cold, staring eyes, not wanting to make any sudden movement that would alarm them and jerk them into action. But there was a stirring in the crowd and a small boy of about fourteen pushed his way through and said in a quavering voice: 'Please tell me what's happening, mister?'

Holman looked down at him in surprise. The poor kid, he thought. He hadn't been affected yet. He's wandering around with the pack wondering what the hell's going on. He stepped towards the boy and said, leaning forward, 'Listen, son –' He got no further. The crowd suddenly surged forward like a human tidal wave at the sound of his voice. The boy went down instantly, and Holman knew he was lost. Hands grabbed for him and he was swept backward with the motion of the people; striking out at them, trying to break their grips on him. He felled one man directly in front of him with his knee, backhanded a woman who was grabbing for his hair, struck another man who was trying to choke him with a hefty blow from his elbow. But there were too many of them. He felt himself going down, his breath crushed from his body.

Then a shot rang out. A body close to him screamed and fell forward. He couldn't tell by the scream if a man or a woman had been hit, but at that stage he couldn't have cared less. The crowd froze, then fell back, scrambling over one another to get clear. It was the noise of the rifle shot that had frightened them more than anything else.

'Quick, sir, make a break for it!' he heard the mechanical voice of Sergeant Stanton call out.

In a flash Holman was on his feet and, using one hand for support, feared the iron balustrade that ran along the road overlooking the ramp, dropping six feet on to the incline. He fell forward on to his knees, but the Sergeant allowed him no time to pause. 'This way, sir, quickly,' he shouted, and another shot rang out.

Holman sprang to his feet and ran towards the grey-suited soldier. 'Thank God you hung on to your gun,' he gasped.

'After what I've seen today, mate, I wouldn't go anywhere without it.' He fired into the crowd again. 'Not very accurate in this get-up, but with this mob, who needs accuracy.' He raised it again and fired. 'Quick now, into the tunnel. I won't be able to keep up with you, so you go ahead, get to the Captain. I'll be able to hold them as I beat a slow retreat.'

It was pointless to tell him what had happened at the other end of the tunnel so he said, 'I'll stay with you, I'll help you.'

'What you gonna do, spit at them?'

'I've got a gun.' Holman showed him the revolver.

'They'd have to be on top of you for that squirt to work, and if they're on top of you, well, that's not going to help much, is it? No, you go on, sir, I can hold 'em. Look at 'em now, cowering like animals. They won't come any nearer.' To show Holman what he meant he raised the rifle and shot at the nearest figure, a woman who was crawling forward towards them on all fours. As she screamed, the crowd moved several feet back. 'You be on your way, mate,' he said, and Holman could almost imagine him grinning beneath the mask.

He was staggered by the soldier's cruelty: he knew they were in a dangerous predicament and his feelings for the demented people were becoming less and less sympathetic by degree, but he could not understand the Sergeant's inhumanity. He was taking pot-shots at the mob as if they were diseased sheep that had to be slaughtered. Had the madness touched him, too?

'What about the container?' was all he could manage to say.

'That'll be all right. They can't harm it and they can't move it. We'll collect it later when we come back in the vehicle. Now for the last time: *will you get into that fucking tunnel ... sir?*'

Holman turned, and with one last look at the intimidated, but still slowly advancing crowd, he disappeared into the tunnel leaving the Sergeant at the foot of the broken concrete slope he had created. As his running footsteps echoed around the walls of the tunnel, and he sank deeper into the blackness of its interior, he heard two shots ring out in rapid succession. He hoped the Sergeant would retreat into the tunnel where he would be safer; the crowd might not even follow him into the darkness.

But Sergeant Stanton had been foolhardy in his contempt for the crowd, for as he had shot at them, taking his time, picking off the more dangerous looking of them, one had climbed around behind him to the top of the twin tunnels; madmen have a special kind of cunning. The man picked up a solid rock of concrete from the many scattered around the top of the bridging structure of the tunnels, and, almost nonchalantly, hurled it down at the unsuspecting Sergeant. Even the tough helmet could not prevent Sergeant Stanton's head from caving in under the impact. The grey-clad figure crumpled and the mob surged forward again, screeching with delight, grabbing the dead body and holding it aloft, throwing it high into the air and letting it drop to the ground with bone-shattering thuds. Then they stripped it of its clothing and ran into the tunnel with it, holding it high above their heads.

Holman heard the noise of the crowd behind him. He listened for gunshots but when none came, he knew what had happened; they'd got the Sergeant.

He was in total, frightening darkness now, halfway down the tunnel he guessed, but both ends out of sight because of its many curves. How he prayed to see that patch of grey light ahead that would mean the tunnel's exit, for the blackness made him feel as though he were in a void, without a body, inside his own mind, his fears intensified because his imagination had no barriers of vision now. At least earlier that day (God, had it been the same day, it seemed like an eternity away) in the Underground tunnel, he'd had a torch; he had been able to relate to what he actually saw, but now he only had the touch of the rough concrete wall and the feel of the road beneath his feet to tell him he still existed as a living person. He barely took his groping fingers off the wall for fear of it not being there when he reached for it again. He moved along at a careless speed, trusting to chance that he would not meet an unexpected obstacle in the dark. Ryker had said the tunnel was clear, but then he had been travelling in the vehicle.

He could hear the frenzied mob behind him, sounding much closer than he knew they actually were because of the confined space, but, nevertheless, he increased his pace. He felt the wall curve gently and the road begin a subtle ascent. Were his eyes playing tricks, or was the blackness really less solid to the right of his vision? He blinked his eyes, knowing he had only by the flexing of his small eye muscles. Yes, there was definitely a greyness ahead. There would be another bend, the incline would become steeper, and there, at the end, would be daylight! He was breathing heavily and the muscles of his thighs ached abominably, but the effect of the dull light and anticipation of the brighter light to follow gave him new stamina. His fatigue wasn't overcome; it was just ignored.

It took him another five minutes to emerge from the tunnel, the cries of the demented mob behind and the promise of daylight ahead continuing to keep his weary legs pumping away, refusing to slacken their cruel pace. The fresh air, fog-filled though it was, managed to revive him a little, which was fortunate, for the final slope leading on to the motorway above ground was the most exhausting. He was almost at the top when the radio hanging from his shoulder began to crackle into life again. Several times, in the tunnel, he had been tempted to dump it as an unnecessary encumbrance, but now he was glad he hadn't.

'Can you hear me, can you hear me?' a voice asked urgently.

He pressed the transmit switch. 'Hello, yes. This is Holman! I can hear you. Ryker? Peters?'

'Thank God,' the voice said. 'It's Captain Peters here.'

He slumped down against the wall which sloped down towards the tunnel. 'Have you planted the explosives yet?' he asked, trying to make his words intelligible through gasping breath.

'Yes, I've done that. As much as I could beneath each gas holder. They're made of steel those things, but they'll crack like eggs with the amount of gelignite I've used. I'm going to set the timer for five minutes which will give us plenty of time to get back into that tunnel. We're going to need all the shelter we can get.' Before Holman could tell him of the mob in the tunnel, the Captain went on, 'Here comes Ryker now. He was just getting a last look at the bloody thing while I was setting up the wires here. I think he's still in a state of shock, you know. One minute he's quite rational, the next he seems to go off into – my God! *He isn't wearing his helmet!*'

Holman heard the Captain calling out Professor Ryker's name, then the radio went dead. He raised himself and looked over the top of the wedge-shaped wall, narrow at his end, but deep by the tunnel's exit. He could just about make out the huge structures of the gasworks through the fog which, he noticed, was thinning out considerably.

'Peters, Peters!' he shouted into the receiver. 'What's happening? For Christ's sake answer!'

He was still shouting into the speaker when he realized it was answering. Again, it was the Captain's voice, but his words sounded even more distant. The brisk, military coolness had gone, and the words carried an edge of panic to them. 'H-he's taken the detonator box from me. He's become infected by the fog, I'm sure and yet …' The voice struggled to control itself, 'He seemed quite rational. He said we couldn't wait for five minutes, the risk of the nucleus moving away was too great – it had to be destroyed now while we had the chance. I refused, but h-he pushed me back and grabbed the box. I didn't dare struggle with him in case the mechanism was jolted and it went off there and then. He's – he's walking back now, into the fog, into the nucleus! Holman, wherever you are now, try and find shelter. Get into the tunnel if you can. I'm coming out! I'm beside the vehicle – I may just have a chance!' Static, then silence.

Holman knew better than to try to call the Captain again; the poor bastard needed all the time he could get! He looked towards the vast refinery, shaking at the thought of what was about to happen and then he thought he saw movement. He couldn't be sure because of the drifting fog, but yes, it looked like the Devastation Vehicle! He might *just* make it!

Then two things happened at the same time: the mob poured from the tunnel below, carrying what looked like a bloodied naked carcass above their heads, and, as he turned their way, a searing flash, followed by a deafening explosion, and then in turn followed by a thunderous whoosh of exploding gas, rocked the very earth.

Holman curled up into a tight ball, trying to make himself as small as possible. He could feel the hot air burning into his back, his hair crackling as it was singed from his scalp; he thought his eardrums would burst with the noise, he could feel the trickle of blood as it ran from his nose. The roar seemed to be going on forever, the concrete was cracking beneath him. Although he could not hear them with his deafened ears he could feel fresh blast-waves sweeping over him, more violent tremblings of the ground, and he knew the other smaller tanks were going up one by one. He was afraid to look even had it been possible, for he knew the world above him was now a blazing inferno and if he raised himself, the heat would scorch his eyes. He was luckier than most of the people below at the tunnel's exit; he was tight up against the solid wall which was reinforced by the width of the road running along its top, but they, although sheltered from the worst of the blast, were relatively exposed. Many were burnt to death instantly by the scorching blast of dry air; others were swept back into the tunnel, the bodies shattered by fragments of flying steel and masonry; and many more were crushed to death by the falling concrete slabs as parts of the tunnel caved in.

It was a long, long time before Holman had the courage to uncover his head from his blistered hands and look up. He saw that the ramp he had crouched in was littered with debris, much of it solid pieces of rock and metal that, if they had struck him, would have killed him instantly. He did not look down towards the tunnel for he had no desire to see the carnage to human bodies the explosion would have wreaked; instead, he slowly and painfully raised himself to his knees and cautiously, inch by inch, lifted his head so that he could see what lay beyond the wall.

The whole area before him seemed to be a gigantic ball of flame. He could no longer see the structures of the gas plant or any buildings at all for that matter; anything that had been left standing – *if* anything had been left standing – was completely obscured by the billowing fire. He couldn't hear the rumble of new, smaller explosions, but he could see the sudden bursts of yellow flame among the deeper orange and red billowing fire. He ducked down again for his eyes were already becoming sore with the heat and he blinked rapidly to moisten them. After a minute had passed, he looked over the top again.

The fire seemed to stretch from the river for at least a quarter of a mile to his right, covering the whole of the plant and most of the smaller factories nearby. He turned his head and saw that even the buildings across the wide motorway had been completely gutted. The devastation was appalling: the gas holders had obviously been full, the steel containers raised to the limits of their height for the use of gas that day would obviously have been small, and the two explosions beneath them had cracked them both wide open, igniting the highly combustible gas they held, setting off a chain reaction among the surrounding refining tanks, spreading the destruction with rebounding swiftness.

A few hundred yards away he could see what must have been the broken shell of the Devastation Vehicle lying on its side, almost completely burnt out now. He sank back down, his head against the wall, and closed his aching eyes. What a terrible price to pay. His thoughts were no longer angry – not even at those who had first instigated the malignancy then set it free by their stupidity – nor were his thoughts filled with fear of the madness it had caused. He was drained of feelings of that extremity; all he felt now was a deep, wearying sadness. He knew the mutation was gone, destroyed by the intense heat, the enemy and the ally of mankind. Nothing could have withstood that destructive but purifying inferno, not even the man-inspired disease, the mutated myco-plasma that seemed somehow more than just a formation of malignant and parasitical cells. Had its deviousness been imagined? Had it really possessed the power to evade its would-be destroyers, or had its movements been controlled merely by the drifting air currents? Had its mesmerizing quality only been the imagination of man, part of the subconscious will for self-destruction every mind possesses, hidden deep down in the darkest recesses of the brain, but always ready to be brought to the surface? Had Ryker really gone mad, or had he seen it was the only sure way? Perhaps he had known the disease had already got a grip on his brain and was steadily duplicating itself, destroying his healthy brain cells one by one, gaining control of his mind. Perhaps he had known this and decided in his last rational thoughts to end it both for himself and the disease. Or perhaps his suicide had been a combination of the madness and the compulsive drawing power of the nucleus itself. There was no way of knowing the answers to any of these questions now, and at that moment, Holman had no wish to know. All he wanted was to rest.

A sudden rush of colder air stirred him from his apathy. His hand stretched to the top of the wall and he pulled himself up once again. The fire was rising, drawing itself together in a great mushroom shape, spreading out with fire and black smoke at its head, the flames at its base almost white in their intensity. As it rose into the air, terrifyingly awesome in its furious beauty, the warm air rose with it, drawing in the cooler surrounding air, the heat repeating the process, creating an ascending maelstrom, reaching into the sky. He could see the fog being drawn in and sucked up, the streaking yellow-grey vapour making the fast currents of air visible, sweeping over him in swirling drifts, soaring upwards with the flames to be dispersed into the sky. Holman knew all the fog would not be cleared in this way, but at least a vast area would be free of it; the rest would be thinned and then dispersed by the wind now that its core, its nucleus, the mutation that had been creating and feeding from it, had been destroyed.

He sat, back against the wall, his hands hanging loosely over his raised knees, staring into the sky, waiting for the first clear blue patch to appear.

▪ 22 ▪

HOLMAN HAD MOORED THE SMALL LAUNCH BESIDE THE JETTY NEAR WESTMINSTER pier. He had left the lead container in the boat; they could send men in protective suits from the underground headquarters to collect it, he was too exhausted to attempt bringing it to dry land. He had waited by the tunnel exit for more than an hour before summoning up his reserves of power to make the journey back. He'd gone through the tunnel again, this time using the narrow catwalk at its side, slightly above the level of the road, intended for motorists whose cars had broken down, using its rail as a guide, ignoring the moans of torment and pain from the people in the darkness below him. On the other side he had found the trampled body of the boy who had come forward from the crowd, lost and afraid, wondering what had happened to the world around him. Holman's mind had gone back to the beginning to the little girl he had rescued from the earthquake in the village, the first victim to die from the disease. He tried to contain the sorrow for there was more for him to do.

He had found the container where they had left it and he led it towards the river. There, he had soon found a small row-boat which he had used to reach a motor launch moored further down. Starting the launch had caused no great problem for it had a self starter and by the simple trick of touching wires and completing the circuit, the engine had soon been running. With satisfaction he had noted its tanks were half full, more than enough for his purpose. He had run the mobile container off the dockside on to the deck and it lay there on its side, undamaged and, for him at least, immovable.

As he had guided the launch out into midstream and begun his journey up the long, winding river, the sun had been breaking through the patchy grey sky above, its rays, where they managed to strike the brownish water, reflecting schools of bobbing silver light shards. He could see both banks of the river and knew an enormous hole was being created in the fog. The fire behind him raged, its blazing column still rising and its base spreading outwards. The fire would last for days, consuming more lives, more property but, most important, the fog. Then it would burn itself out, finally subdued by its own ferocity.

All along the river banks, he could see people staring towards it, white-faced, shocked by its enormity, the sight filling their sick minds to the exclusion of all else. The blaze would be seen for miles and he hoped it had the same paralysing effect on many more; at least this way they had no thoughts of harming themselves or others. He avoided the floating bodies in the water where he could, but others were knocked aside by the launch, their stiff, puffed-up limbs turning lazily in the water.

The fog had been thicker near Westminster, but not as thick as before. He had left the launch and found his way back to the underground car park. They had seen him coming through their television scanners, but had not recognized him at first because of his scorched hair, his blackened and bruised face, his tattered and bloody clothes, but when he began pounding on the blank concrete wall at the back of the basement car park, they had realized who he was and immediately opened the massive door.

He had told them of all that had happened: of the journey through the city; the death of Mason; the sealing off of the Blackwall Tunnel; the final destruction of the mycoplasma with the destruction of the gas plant. They had fired questions rapidly at him and he did his weary best to answer them all. Finally, they had congratulated him, praised him, but he had told them it was Professor Ryker and Captain Peters who deserved the thanks; it had been their combined efforts that had finally destroyed the disease.

Janet Halstead had examined him quickly, but not before she had smothered his grimy face with kisses of relief. She had found nothing seriously wrong, although many of his cuts and the burns on his hands would need special attention, and the enormous bruise on the side of his face, caused when he had been thrown from the overturned vehicle, would give him a lot of pain in the days to follow. She had urged him to rest, insisting he was in a state of near collapse, but he had refused, telling her there was one more thing he had to do before they began spraying the town with sleeping gas: he had to reach Casey.

He had begged her for a shot of something that would keep his fatigued body going and seeing that he was determined to leave anyway, she agreed, warning him she did not know how long the effects of the drug would last in his exhausted condition. He had assured her they would last long enough for him to get to Casey and that he would then gladly lie down and sleep while the city was sprayed with gas. His resolve had been strengthened and his anxiety aroused when they had tried to reach his flat on their internal switchboard, but power throughout London had finally gone dead and their only communication with the waiting outside world was through their transmitters. They had promised him the spraying operation would begin in the southwest and the northeast areas, the aircraft working their way in sections across London, leaving the area in which he lived till last. To help him, they had given him the use of a military vehicle, a stocky, solid army scout car, but obviously, and to their regret, they could not risk sending anybody with him; the fog might still contain enough of the disease to penetrate the protective suits. As it was, they would need volunteers to collect the container, but that was a justifiable risk.

Finally, after Janet Halstead had quickly cleaned his face and hands up and he had borrowed a leather jacket from someone to cover the gun and shoulder holster he still wore, he had driven from the underground shelter, feeling the drug already beginning to revitalize his exhausted system.

He climbed the stairs and by the fourth flight, he could feel the weariness creeping back through his limbs; the drug was wearing off already. It must have been the drive back that had begun to drain him again, for the horror was still going on. Somehow he had half expected it to be all over with the destruction of the nucleus, but he soon realized the trail of misery it had left in its wake. There were still many of the individually gruesome and macabre incidents, but now the majority of the people had formed themselves into large marching crowds. Marching towards the river! It seemed that there would be a recurrence of the Bournemouth tragedy unless the gas reached them first. He had used the car's transmitter to inform the base of what was happening and they reported back they would now concentrate the dropping of the gas along the river's edge, on both sides, before dealing with the rest of London. Where he could, he had skirted the main groups of people, but several times he had had to drive carefully through them. Fortunately they ignored him, their minds filled now with only one thought. Self-destruction.

Even as he climbed the stairs, he could hear the low-flying aircraft in the distance, swooping down, spewing out their life-saving and hopefully for many, mind-saving gas. In other parts of the town, where the fog seemed fairly low, helicopters were being used, their pilots breathing through oxygen tanks in case gas from the aeroplanes drifted their way.

When he reached his floor, he breathed a sigh of relief to see the door to his flat was still firmly closed. As he pounded on it with his fist, calling out Casey's name, he failed to see the shadowy figure sitting on the stairs leading to the roof where it had been patiently waiting for most of the day.

Holman heard her muffled voice from behind the door, 'John, is that you?'

'Yes, darling,' he shouted back, managing to coax his aching face into a wide grin, 'it's me. Everything's going to be okay. Open up.'

He heard the scraping of furniture, the heavy bolt being shot back, the latch clicking, then her face appeared in the small gap governed by the safety chain, strained with dried-up tears, fresh ones about to flow.

'Oh, John,' she cried, 'I didn't know what had happened to you. I've been so worr –' her words were cut off as she fumbled with the safety chain. 'Somebody's been trying to get in all –' but again her words were cut off as he pushed the door wide and pulled her towards him, enveloping her with his arms, relaxing his grip slightly only to kiss her face.

She was crying with relief and happiness as he pushed her back into the hall and kicked the door with the heel of his foot.

She broke away to look into his face and her eyes instantly clouded with anxiety. 'John, what's happened to you? What have they done to you?' she asked.

He smiled wearily. 'It's a long story,' he said. 'First, you and I are going to have a stiff drink. Then we're going to bed and I'll tell you all about it. And then, we're going to sleep. We're going to go into a long and glorious sleep.'

She smiled back at him, her expression curious but full of happiness. And then it froze into rigid lines of fear as she saw something over his shoulder, something that had prevented the door from closing fully. Puzzled by her frightened look, Holman turned to see what had caused it. He caught his breath.

Barrow was standing in the doorway, a strange grin on his face.

Holman turned his body so that he was facing the detective and Casey was behind him.

'Hello, Barrow,' he said warily.

There was no reply, no movement.

Casey touched his shoulder and said in an urgent, hushed voice, 'John, it must have been him. Somebody's been trying to get in all day. Banging on the door, trying to force it. When I called out, there was never any answer but the pounding would stop then start again an hour or so later. He must have been out there all this time.'

Holman tried to get an answer from him again. 'What do you want, Barrow?' he said.

Again, there was no reply, just the odd, disturbing grin. Strangely, Holman noticed, he was immaculately dressed: dark brown three-piece suit, white stiff-collared shirt, deep green tie. It was only his distant eyes and the humourless smile that gave any signs of his demented state. Holman tensed as Barrow suddenly put his hand into the right-hand pocket of his jacket and drew something out. He couldn't make out what it was at first, but as Barrow began to unwind it, he saw it was a length of thin wire, two small wooden handles attached to each end.

'Get into the bedroom, Casey, and lock the door,' he said quietly, keeping his eyes on the figure in front of him.

'No, John, I'm not leaving you,' she said.

'Do as you're bloody told,' he said evenly through clenched teeth. He sensed her move away from him and heard the click as the bedroom door closed.

'What do you want, Barrow?' he said again, not expecting a reply but this time receiving one.

'You,' Barrow said. 'You, you bastard.'

He had the handles of the wire in either hand now, holding it up at chest level, drawing it out so that the wire was taut. Holman knew how the macabre weapon was meant to be used: as a garrotte. Twisted around the victim's neck, it would cut into the windpipe and jugular vein, killing within seconds.

Barrow took a step towards him.

Holman had been through too much that day to waste time trying to appease him and Barrow was already too near for him to risk reaching for the gun – so he attacked first.

He flew at the detective, charging low, ducking under the threatening wire, and both men went crashing back through the open doorway, falling in a struggling heap in the hall outside. Holman had landed on top but found himself being lifted completely off his opponent and then thrown to one side. The policeman's strength was incredible and, as he rolled over in an effort to get to one knee, Holman knew he would not stand much chance against him, especially in his own weakened condition. He saw Casey suddenly appear in the doorway, a hand to her open mouth as she saw the weapon Barrow held. The policeman was on his feet, moving in for the kill, a dry chuckling noise coming from his throat, but he turned his head when Casey screamed.

It gave Holman the fraction of time he needed to get to one knee and launch himself forward again from that position. His head struck Barrow in the midriff, knocking the wind from him, sending him reeling back along the hall. Holman found himself lying on Barrow's legs and he received a vicious kick under his chin from the detective's knee. He fell back against the wall, his senses spinning for precious moments. He tried to push himself up by using the wall for support, but he was too late. He felt the icy sharp wire go around his neck and just managed to get an arm up to prevent it closing completely. Barrow had crossed the two handles and was kneeling in front of Holman pulling them in opposite directions with all his strength.

Holman could feel the wire cutting into the back of his neck, and his arm, fortunately protected by the borrowed leather jacket, which was preventing him from being choked, although he was near to it. His hand was pressed up against the side of his face, held there by the wire at his wrist, and he tried to push it away, resisting the tremendous pressure Barrow was exerting, but it was no use; he could feel his strength deserting him. His vision seemed to be dimming, the excruciating pain was sending waves of white heat through his head. He began to lose consciousness.

Then, by some miracle, the pressure was released slightly. His eyes began to clear as he fought his way up from the deep well of unconsciousness, but it seemed an age before he could focus them, and when he could, he saw that Casey had Barrow by the hair and was pulling his head back, tears streaming down her face, her body trembling with the effort. Barrow was forced to let go of one of the handles to use a hand to free himself. He reached up and grabbed one of her wrists, trying to break her grip, but she hung on grimly, pulling him backwards, forcing him to lose his balance.

He came up again with an enraged roar, turning on her, forgetting Holman for the moment. He lashed out at her viciously with the back of his hand, sending her flying back against the opposite wall, bringing blood to her lips. She stood there sobbing, a hand to her face where he had hit her and he stepped towards her and slapped her again, knocking her body upright, her eyes blazing into his. He looked down at her, breathing heavily, his gaze completely blank for a few seconds. Then he began to grin again. He reached out and gripped the top of her flimsy blouse then pulled down with one swift motion, ripping it open, the sight of her small, exposed breasts causing him to pause, his smile becoming wider, his eyes more cruel.

He stared at Holman almost incomprehendingly when he was roughly swung round by his shoulder, his expression barely having time to change into one of fury before the fist smashed into his face. He went crashing back against the girl, but retaliated instantly, using his feet as he had been taught to – as weapons – catching Holman a painful blow on his thigh. He lashed out with his fist, catching Holman only a glancing blow on the forehead, but enough to send him spinning across the hallway. He made as if to follow, but Casey courageously hooked an arm around his neck and tried to pull him back. He whirled around in her grip and pushed her back against the wall, his body tight against hers, pressing into her. One hand reached up for her shoulder, ripping the blouse from it, then groping towards her breasts, his other hand sliding down towards her thighs. His head was close against hers, and she could feel the wetness of his lips on her cheek. She tried to cry out but found she couldn't, her terror paralysing her vocal cords.

Holman staggered towards him again, knowing he had to finish it soon or Barrow would kill them both. His anger when he saw the detective's intention gave him just the added strength he needed to launch another attack. His fingers encircled Barrow's head and found his eyes. He dug his fingers in and pulled back with all his might.

Barrow screamed and came away from the girl, his hands flying to his face, trying to break Holman's merciless grip. He pushed himself back, crushing Holman against the opposite wall but even though the grip was released, he found he couldn't see through his bruised eyeballs. He struck out blindly but Holman easily dodged the blow, using the opportunity himself to send a vicious hook into Barrow's stomach, doubling him up. He kicked him in the face, the back of Barrow's head taking the worst of the blow, but nevertheless, the force of it sending him staggering back down the corridor.

Even as Holman went after him, the detective was straightening his body, shaking his head, his sight returning. A smile was just beginning to spread across his face again when Holman charged into him, using his shoulder in an attempt to knock him flat. Barrow almost avoided the attack by twisting his body, but Holman just caught him, spinning him round, both of them falling to the floor again. Both men raised themselves to their knees at the same time and faced one another, but it was Barrow who reacted first. He used the hardened edge of his hand on the side of Holman's neck, bringing it down in a short sharp chopping motion. Again if it hadn't been for the collar of the leather jacket, Holman would have been seriously injured; as it was he fell forward on to his face, the whole of his left shoulder and the top of his arm completely numbed with pain.

He lay there gasping, his body heaving with the exertion, and he heard the dry insane chuckle of Barrow as he got to his feet.

The Detective Inspector looked down at his weakened opponent, his face a mask of sadistic pleasure. Casey was further down the hall, collapsed on her knees, leaning against the wall, her blouse hanging in tatters around her. She wept for Holman, but knew she could do no more to help him, the madman was too strong. Barrow raised a foot to bring it crushing down on the back of Holman's head.

As he did, Holman looked up and their eyes met: gloating victory showed through Barrow's crazed glare; defeat showed in Holman's. But the detective hesitated a moment too long in relishing his triumph and the defeat in Holman's eyes was replaced by a look of hope.

They had moved so far down the hall that Barrow now stood with his back to the stairs. Holman's right hand snaked out and grabbed for Barrow's foot, the one that supported his weight. He gripped the ankle and yanked it forward, using the last of his remaining strength to do so. The detective fell back and crashed down the stone stairs, over and over until he reached the bottom and bounced off the facing wall.

Holman's head sank to the floor and he lay there, his body heaving, too exhausted to move. He could hear Casey sobbing farther down the hall, but he could not summon the strength to go to her just yet. She called his name and slowly began to crawl towards him.

He lay there, his mind buzzing with thoughts as it does when too tired to concentrate on anything specific. He had been through so much in the last few days: his mind had had to adapt to so many strange factors; he'd had to accept death, not just individual but multiple death; *he'd had to accept killing*.

He heard a scraping noise coming from the stairs; a slithering, dragging noise. He looked up and saw that Casey had heard it too; she had frozen against the wall, her eyes looking at him in terror. He turned his head towards the stairs. The slithering noise continued, growing louder, now coupled with the sound of breathing. Holman stared at the empty space at the top of the stairs, unable to move, transfixed by the sounds, dreading what he would see. A hand appeared on the top stair, the fingers whitening as they pressed against the floor to grip and pull. Holman looked at them in disbelief, his head only two feet away from them. And then suddenly, he was staring into the evil, grinning face of Barrow! Blood was flowing from his nose and a deep cut above his eyebrow, giving his face an even more frightening aspect, but he grinned at Holman, his broken body shaking with exertion. He began to chuckle, his mouth opening in a wide grimace, the sound rasping from the back of his throat. He began to pull himself forward, over the top step. He wanted to reach Holman.

Holman slowly lifted his body, reached for the gun in his shoulder holster and clicked off the safety catch with his thumb. Then he put the barrel inside Barrow's grinning mouth, and pulled the trigger.

He knelt beside Casey, pulling her away from the wall and cradling her in his arms. Overhead, he could hear the hum of the low-flying aircraft and he knew they had reached his sector.

'The worst is over for us now, darling,' he told her, holding her close, rocking her gently back and forth. 'We'll never be the same, too much has happened to both of us, but we can help each other. I love you so much, Casey.'

He pulled her to her feet, and she wept against him.

'When this is finally finished, when they've done all they can for those who've been harmed, the people are going to find out exactly how it happened. I'm going to make sure of it and, I think, there are others who will too. But now,

Casey, we're going to sleep. We're going to lie down together, and drift into a long, long sleep.'

She managed to smile up at him and they walked towards his flat, his tired and aching body leaning on hers for support.

He closed the door behind them.

THE SPEAR

'A deathly cry! I rushed in:
Klingsor, laughing, was vanishing from there,
having stolen the holy Spear.'

RICHARD WAGNER: *PARSIFAL*

'For myself, I have the most intimate familiarity with Wagner's mental processes.
At every stage in my life I come back to him. Only a new nobility can introduce
the new civilization for us. If we strip "Parsifal" of every poetic element, we learn
from it that selection and renewal are possible only amid the continuous tension
of a lasting struggle. A world-wide process of segregation is going on before our
eyes. Those who see in struggle the meaning of life, gradually mount the steps of
a new nobility. Those who are in search of peace and order through dependence,
sink, whatever their origin, to the inert masses. The masses, however, are doomed
to decay and self-destruction. In our world-revolutionary turning-point the
masses are the sum total of the sinking civilization and its dying representatives.
We must allow them to die with their kings, like Amfortas.'

ADOLF HITLER

'You realize now what anxieties I have. The world regards Adolf Hitler as a
strongman – and that's how his name must go down in history. The greater
German Reich will stretch from the Urals to the North Sea after the war. That
will be the Führer's greatest achievement. He's the greatest man who ever lived
and without him it would never have been possible. So what does it matter that
he should be ill now, when his work is almost complete.'

HEINRICH HIMMLER

33 AD

... So the soldiers came and broke the legs of the first, and of the other who had been crucified with him; but when they came to Jesus and saw that he was already dead, they did not break his legs. But one of the soldiers pierced his side with a spear, and at once there came out blood and water ...

John 19:32 (RSV)

23rd May, 1945

Sergeant-Major Edwin Austin almost smiled in pity for the pathetic figure who sat huddled on the couch, with a blanket wrapped round his trembling body. Almost, but not quite, for they said this innocuous little man had caused the deaths of millions in the vicious war that had just ended. His persecution of the Jews in his own country, then in other captured territories, had horrified the world, and even now, more atrocities were coming to light. Could this be the man who had instigated such evil, this timid creature wearing only shirt, pants and socks beneath the army blanket? Was he really the person he claimed to be? Without the moustache, weak chin and bloated neck unshaven, without the military uniform, without the arrogance of his kind, it was difficult to tell. When he'd been captured, the German had been wearing a black eye-patch and a uniform with all the insignia removed. He'd claimed to be a member of the Secret Field Police, but under interrogation had announced a different – a more sinister – identity.

When he'd torn off the eye-patch and donned a pair of rimless spectacles, the likeness was evident, despite his bearing, his nervous affability.

Colonel Murphy, the Chief of Intelligence on Montgomery's staff, had accepted the German's claimed identity, so why should he, a mere sergeant-major, doubt it? They had insisted the prisoner be watched every moment of the day; that's how seriously they were treating the matter. The sergeant had already lost one prisoner who'd been put in his charge: SS General Pruetzmann had crushed a cyanide capsule between his teeth. He'd make no mistakes with this one.

Through the German's interpreter, the sergeant informed him the couch was to be his bed, and he was to undress and lie down. The prisoner began to protest but became silent when he saw the resolution on the Englishman's face. He unwrapped the blanket from his shoulders and began to take off his underpants.

It was at that moment that Colonel Murphy, followed by another uniformed officer, entered the room. The Intelligence Chief brusquely introduced his companion as Captain Wells, an army doctor, then ordered the German to strip completely.

The sergeant knew what was about to happen, for a small phial had been found hidden in the lining of the prisoner's jacket two days before and they suspected he had another secreted somewhere on his person. They were taking no chances with a prisoner of this importance.

They began to search him, running their fingers through the hair on his head and pubic regions; they examined his ears and the cracks between each toe; they spread his buttocks and checked his anal passage. Nothing was found but there was still one area unsearched, and this was the most obvious hiding place. The doctor ordered the prisoner to open his mouth.

Captain Wells saw the black phial immediately, between a gap in the German's teeth on the right-hand side of his lower jaw, and with a shout of alarm thrust his fingers into the open mouth. But the German was too quick. He wrenched his head to one side biting down hard on the medic's fingers as he did so. Colonel Murphy and Sergeant-Major Austin leapt forward and threw the struggling prisoner to the floor, the doctor holding him by the throat, squeezing with both hands, trying to force him to spit the capsule out. It was too late though; the phial had been cracked and the poison was already finding its way into the man's system. His death was inevitable but still they fought to prevent it.

Colonel Murphy told the sergeant to find a needle and cotton as quickly as possible and valuable minutes were lost as the interrogation centre was turned upside down in the search for such trivial articles. The doctor kept his pressure on the prisoner's throat, but the death spasms were already beginning. The sergeant soon returned and it was the steady hands of the Intelligence Chief that had to thread the needle and cotton. While Sergeant-Major Austin forced the dying man's mouth open, the colonel grasped the slippery tongue and pierced it with the needle; by pulling on the thread they were able to hold the tongue out from the mouth, preventing it from blocking the throat. For fifteen minutes they used emetics, a stomach-pump and every method of artificial respiration. It was no use; the three men had prevented the cyanide from killing with its usual swiftness, but they had only delayed death.

The prisoner's body contorted into one last spasm of agony, his face hideous in its torment, then his body slumped into stillness.

Two days later, Sergeant-Major Austin wrapped the corpse in army blankets, wound camouflage netting tied with telephone wire around it, and buried the body in an unmarked grave near Lüneburg. The final resting place of Reichsführer SS Heinrich Himmler was never recorded.

'The struggle for world domination will be fought entirely between us, between German and Jew. All else is façade and illusion. Behind England stands Israel, and behind France, and behind the United States. Even when we have driven the Jew out of Germany, he remains our world enemy.'

ADOLF HITLER

HARRY STEADMAN LOCKED THE DOOR OF HIS GREY CELICA AND GLANCED AROUND the wide, grass-middled square. The majority of other parking spaces were filled, forming a many-coloured, machine fringe around the green lawns. Most of the square's working inhabitants of solicitors and accountants had arrived, and were already easing their mental gears into the Monday morning pace. He'd noticed the couple sitting in their Cortina when he had driven towards his allocated parking space and would have paid them no mind had not the man's eyes snapped to attention on seeing Steadman; the forced casualness as the eyes glanced away again had not deceived the investigator. The man had recognized him, but Steadman had not recognized the man. Nor his female companion.

Both appeared to be in deep conversation as he looked across the roof of his car towards them. It was a small thing, for there was nothing unusual about clients waiting in their cars until their appointment with solicitor, accountant – or even private investigator – in Gray's Inn Square, but Steadman felt an unease he hadn't experienced for a long time. A throwback from the time he'd lived with that unease for weeks, sometimes months, on end. And it had been triggered off just by the meeting of eyes.

He crossed the smooth roadway and entered the gloomy interior of the red-bricked terraced building that contained his small agency, along with three company accountants' offices. It was a prime position for an enquiry agency, in the midst of the legal 'ghetto', Lincoln's Inn and Bloomsbury on the doorstep, the law courts and the Old Bailey ten minutes away. The address gave respectability to a profession that was often looked upon as seedy, even sordid. Harry Steadman, along with his partner, Maggie Wyeth, had worked long and hard to establish an agency of high repute, beginning with the principle that no case, provided there were no illegalities involved, was too big or too small. Fortunately, over the past two years, because of their growing reputation, most of their cases were for big companies, involving anything from industrial espionage to fraud or embezzlement within a company, though they still handled matrimonial enquiries, traced missing persons and carried out the service of legal process, delivering writs or warnings of prosecution to debtors. Their staff consisted of three: a retired police officer named Blake, whom they naturally called Sexton; a young trainee detective, Steve, who would leave them soon to set up on his own; and Sue, their receptionist/typist and general runaround, twenty-nine, plump, unmarried and an absolute godsend.

Steadman ignored the small and generally unreliable lift, and climbed the three flights of stairs to the agency, his breathing becoming sharper and his strides less agile as he neared the top. At thirty-eight, his condition could be described as 'fair but wearing'.

The clatter of Sue's typing met him in the hallway, and her smile greeted him when he pushed open the office door.

'Hello, Sue,' he said, returning her smile.

'Morning, Mr Steadman. Good trip?'

'Good enough. One more week should cover it.'

Steadman had spent the previous week in the North, setting up a complete security system for a manufacturer of electrical goods. The company's innovations in refining communications systems had a nasty habit of being 'innovated' by a rival company just weeks ahead of their own; coincidence was one thing, but almost identical patents over a period of eighteen months stretched credibility too far.

'Is Maggie in yet?' Steadman asked, taking the letters Sue slid towards him.

'Yes, she's got someone with her at the moment. I'll let her know you're back as soon as she's free.'

'Fine. I'll have to leave again about eleven so we'll need to talk soon.' He headed towards his office, waving a hand towards Steve who was frowning over a booklet outlining the Laws of Evidence and Procedure.

'Stick with it, Steve,' Steadman grinned. 'In ten years it will all be crystal clear.'

Steve smiled weakly back.

Steadman paused in the doorway of his office. 'Is Sexton around?' he asked Sue. 'I may need him this week to help find me some good security people.' As an ex-policeman, his employee still had good connections with the Force and knew who was soon to retire, or sick of the job and considering leaving. These men usually made excellent security staff.

'He's Process Server for Collins and Tullis this morning,' Sue replied.

'Okay, I'll ring him from Salford if I miss him.' Before he could close the door, Sue stopped him by waving a piece of paper in her hand.

'This gentleman wants to see you this morning, Mr Steadman,' she said apologetically.

'Oh, come on, Sue. You know I won't have time,' Steadman said in an exasperated tone. 'Can't he see Maggie?'

'I tried to get him to, but he insisted on seeing you. He rang last week and wanted to get in touch with you up North when I told him you were away. I didn't let him know where you were, of course, but he said it was very important that he saw you personally the moment you got back. He wouldn't even *talk* to Mrs Wyeth.'

Steadman walked back to the reception desk and took the folded piece of paper from the girl's fleshy hand. His stomach muscles tightened when he unfolded the paper and read the message. His earlier unease had been instinctively correct.

'Dark hair, dark complexion? In his early thirties?' he asked, still looking at the handwritten message.

'Yes,' Sue replied, puzzled by her employer's reaction. 'Goldblatt, he said his name was. I can put him off when he arrives, if you like? He did make it sound important, though, so I thought you might just fit him in before you went back to Salford.'

'No, it's all right, Sue. He's already downstairs sitting in his car. I'll give him ten minutes.'

As Steadman went into his office Sue stared across at Steve, who had been watching the brief exchange with interest. He shrugged his shoulders and turned his attention back to the intricacies of the Law.

Steadman sat at his desk and reread the message on the piece of paper. 'Zwi sends his regards' was all it said, but it stirred up memories of emotions and actions governed by a passionate vengeance. 'Zwi Zamir,' he said softly, – then screwed the paper into a tight ball on his desk. He swivelled his chair and gazed at the grey autumn sky outside his window, the image of Zwi Zamir, ex-Director of Mossad Aliyah Beth, the Israeli Secret Service, clear in his mind.

Ten minutes later, Sue buzzed him on the intercom. 'Mr Goldblatt for you, Mr Steadman.'

With a weary sigh, Steadman said, 'Send him in.'

He reached forward and picked up the crinkled ball of paper still lying on his desk and tossed it into the waste-bin, just as the door opened and Sue ushered in the man he had spotted earlier in the car. Goldblatt was alone, his companion presumably still waiting below.

'Mr Goldblatt,' Steadman acknowledged, standing and stretching his hand forward across the desk.

Goldblatt shook it, his grip hard and dry. He was a short, stocky man, his hair black and crinkly, cut short, his features not as dark as Steadman had at first thought. It must have been the darkness of the car deepening the man's natural swarthiness.

'David Goldblatt, Mr Steadman. Thank you for seeing me.' There was barely a trace of accent, except for a slight American inflection on certain words. His eyes searched Steadman's as though looking for some sign of recognition, not personal; perhaps a recognition of shared beliefs.

Steadman's eyes remained cold.

'I'll bring you some coffee.' Sue's words interrupted the awkward silence. She closed the door, nervous of the coldness she felt emanating from her employer. He seemed angry at this little Jewish man.

'You saw the note?' Goldblatt asked, taking the seat the investigator had indicated.

Steadman nodded, sitting himself and lounging back in his chair to study the other man. 'How is Zwi?'

Goldblatt smiled across at him. 'He's well. He retired from the Service, you know. He's Chairman of a big construction company now. It's owned by the Israeli confederation of trade unions, so his interests are still for the good of our country – as are the interests of all of us. They used to be yours too, even though you're not a Jew.'

Steadman dropped his gaze. 'Things change,' he said.

There was a silence between them. Goldblatt broke it by saying softly, 'We need your help again.'

'Forget it,' Steadman snapped. 'I told you, things change. Mossad changed. Ideals were replaced by vengeance.'

'Only by revenge can we achieve our ideals!' Goldblatt's voice was angry now. 'We have to avenge the persecution of our people. There must be retaliation for every Israeli man, woman and child killed by terrorists! Only then can they respect our strength. Only then will they realize we will never be beaten. You know that!'

'And I know you've murdered innocent people.' Steadman's anger matched the Jew's, but his voice was quieter, more steady.

'Innocent people? And the massacre at Lod Airport? Munich? Entebbe? Every time the PFLP or PLO guerrillas strike, innocent people are murdered.'

'Does that give you cause to act in the same way?'

'We have made mistakes, Mr Steadman. But they *were* mistakes, not deliberate acts of aggression against innocent bystanders! We have never hijacked a plane, nor planted bombs in crowded airports. How can you compare us with these animals?'

Steadman's voice had lost its anger now. 'I don't, Mr Goldblatt,' he said wearily. 'But I'd had enough of The Institute. I had to get out or be tainted by what we were doing. As you said, we made mistakes.'

A gentle tapping at the door brought a brief halt to their exchange. Sue entered bearing a tray containing two cups of coffee. She smiled nervously at Goldblatt and placed the coffee and sugar on the table between them. The two men were quiet until she'd left the room again. Goldblatt sipped his coffee and, as an afterthought, added sugar. Steadman ignored his.

'I'm sorry, Mr Steadman,' Goldblatt began again. 'I did not come here to argue with you. Israeli feelings run high, but then you understand that. Mossad needs your help again, and so far I have only succeeded in making you angry. Please accept my apology.'

'Accept mine too, Mr Goldblatt. I meant no disrespect to you, or your cause, but Zwi Zamir must have explained why I left the Israeli Intelligence Organization.'

Goldblatt nodded. 'Yes, he did. He also said you probably would not help us. But you did before; you left the British Army to join us. Perhaps you will find that sympathy for our cause once again.'

'No, I don't think so. I had a stronger reason then.'

'Lilla Kanaan?'

Her name, after so many years, still caused the old grief to flood through him, its intensity almost causing a panic within him. He said nothing.

'Listen to me first, then if you still will not help us, so be it. We'll find other ways.'

Goldblatt took Steadman's silence as approval for him to go on. 'Everyone is well aware of the escalation of terrorism throughout the world. At first, we Israelis defended our country from the inside but, as you well know, we were forced to fight our war beyond our own boundaries. We did not wish it, but we had no choice ...'

Steadman's thoughts were racing back to that blood-filled night, Tuesday, May 30th, 1972. Lod International Airport. He and Lilla had been waiting for the flight that would take him back to England, his assignment in the Middle East over – his orders now to return to his regiment. Gunshots had startled them from the sadness of parting, and exploding grenades had made him hurl Lilla to the floor and push her beneath a row of seats. When he saw the three Japanese with their Kalashnikov carbines and laden with hand-grenades, he covered her body with his, pulling a discarded suitcase in front of them as feeble protection against the hail of bullets and shrapnel. People were screaming, running in terror from the lethal fire; others threw themselves to the floor, too frightened to move, praying they would be spared. Steadman had looked up to see if there was any way to reach the gunmen and he had seen a grenade explode in the hand of one of the Japanese, tearing off the terrorist's head.

A second died as he carelessly strayed into his companion's line of fire. The third then seemed to lose his nerve and had begun to run; Steadman saw him disappear under a crush of border police and civilian police officers.

He pulled Lilla to him and they had sat there stunned at the violence and the carnage it had caused. The wailing began and the hall came alive with the dying.

Twenty-eight people had been slaughtered, most of them innocent Puerto Rican pilgrims, and seventy had been wounded. The surviving terrorist, Kozo Okamoto, later confessed he was a member of the Japanese Red Army and had been trained for the suicide mission by the Black September group.

Three months later, Steadman had returned to Israel and the Central Institute for Information and Espionage, no longer as an adviser on loan from British Military Intelligence, but as a member of the organization ...

'It was not long before we realized we were not fighting just one terrorist group but many.' Steadman's attention was drawn back to Goldblatt. 'In Ireland, the IRA; in Spain, the Basque; in South America, the Tupamaros; in Turkey, the Turkish Liberation Army; in Japan, the Red Army; in West Germany, the Baader-Meinhof. All are now aiding and abetting each other, a terrorist alliance brought about by the Russian KGB. They have even narrowed the split between the Arab factions, the PFLP and PLO. But the people we least expected to give succour to our enemies were the British.'

Steadman raised his eyebrows in surprise. 'The British? How are we helping such people?' he asked.

'By supplying them with arms; new, advanced weapons. Training the terrorists to use them effectively.'

'Nonsense. Sure, the Middle East and Iran are big customers of the British Government itself, but it doesn't deal with terrorist groups. Nor does it allow private armament companies to. Licences are strictly controlled.'

Goldblatt smiled without humour. 'Come now, Mr Steadman. As an ex-military man and as one who has negotiated the sale of arms to Israel yourself, you know just how far the arms business can be "strictly controlled".' He drew out the last two words scornfully. 'It's no longer just Russian weapons we find in the hands of our assassins. There are certain highly sophisticated weapons we have traced back to your country.'

'They may have been paid for and passed on by another source.'

'Having worked for Israeli Intelligence yourself, do you doubt our efficiency in these matters?'

Steadman had to shake his head, for he knew Israel had one of the most respected and feared Intelligence organizations in the world. On his return to that country he had joined Mossad, which was responsible for external Intelligence, and he soon appreciated the strength of Shin Beth, which was responsible for internal security and counter-espionage. No, he didn't doubt their efficiency.

'We know for certain that the PLO bought direct from a British company. Unfortunately, our source of information died under interrogation so we have no proof, no first-person confession.'

Steadman also knew how ruthless Israeli interrogations could be and shuddered inwardly.

'What do you know of Edward Gant?' the Mossad agent asked.

'Gant? You think he's the supplier?'

Goldblatt nodded.

'He's not one of the big dealers, but his weapons are of the sophisticated kind. Did your informant tell you it was him?'

'No, our informant didn't know. We believed him.'

I'll bet you did, Steadman thought. Torture has a way of making people want to be honest. 'So what makes you think he's your man?' he said.

'Let's just say several roads lead back to him. Now, what do you know of him?'

'Not much – he keeps out of the limelight. I know he's wealthy, respectable and, as I said, deals in the sale of arms on a small scale. He seems to move in high circles.'

'Appeared on the scene in the United States around the late fifties,' Goldblatt continued. 'His record shows he was an emigrant from Canada. He married a wealthy American widow and began his activity in the armament field, his innovations in light weaponry outstanding at that time. His wife's connections and money helped him approach top-ranking Army personnel as well as the odd senator here and there, and he soon became a steady supplier to the US Forces. He seemed to have some influence himself at the time, even though he was new to the country, and he was by no means a *poor* immigrant. He came to England in 1963 after his wife's death and opened up a weapons development plant here, warding off any state control when he became successful. He's now a considerable force in the industry and, like many arms dealers, has kept away from publicity – until recently, that is.

'By all accounts he is a remarkable man, hardly looking his age, extremely fit, shrewd and quite ruthless in business. Three weeks ago, one of our agents investigating Edward Gant's activities in this country disappeared. We have not heard from him since.'

The last words were made to sound as though they were part of the arms dealer's biography. Steadman leaned forward across the desk. 'You want me to find your man,' he said as a statement.

Goldblatt nodded.

'And if I can dig up some evidence against Gant at the same time, that would be useful.'

'Yes. Very.'

'And what would you do with that evidence?'

'Turn it over to your government, of course.'

Steadman sat back in his chair and stared coldly into the Mossad agent's eyes. 'Goodbye, Mr Goldblatt.'

The Israeli sighed deeply. 'Do you have no feelings for us any more?'

'None.'

'What changed you? What turned you against us?'

'Zwi Zamir knows. I'm sure he told you.'

'Did Lilla's death mean nothing to you?'

Steadman's hands clenched into fists on the desk-top. 'It meant everything to me,' he said evenly.

'And would her brother's death mean anything?'

Puzzlement showed in the investigator's eyes. 'What do you mean?'

'Her brother, Baruch, was the agent sent in to contact Gant.'

Baruch. Young. Anxious to serve his country. Even more so after the death of Lilla. They'd used him, just as they'd used his sister. Just as they used up the lives of so many of their young.

'I had no idea he'd joined the Institute.'

'Our country needs such fine young men to survive, Mr Steadman. Baruch Kanaan was conscripted into the Air Force and flew helicopter missions into enemy territory, giving support to GHQ assault groups on the ground, covering their retreat from Arab strongholds. I understand you, yourself, were recipient of such cover on several occasions when you were with us.'

Steadman nodded and thought of the nightmare raids into Beirut, the hasty retreats through hostile streets, silenced Parabellums, hot from use, burning their hands. The welcoming sound of rotor blades, the huge dragonflies dropping from the night sky with guns blazing to disrupt enemy pursuit. Grenades and spikes dropped into the roads to thwart enemy vehicles. It all seemed a long time ago.

'Baruch eventually became a member of the GHQ, himself,' Goldblatt continued, and allowed himself a brief smile. 'He walked to Petra twice.'

Steadman raised his eyebrows. The GHQ was a secret paramilitary outfit of the Israeli Defence Forces, its members specially chosen officers or sergeants from other units, an ability to fight in small groups against heavy odds an essential requirement. One of the initiation rites into the unit was a voluntary trip by foot from the Israeli border, across a stretch of the Jordanian desert to the abandoned city of Petra, only cunning and endurance keeping the lone traveller out of the hands of the prowling Bedouin battalion guarding the area. Some initiates declined to take the trip and these were considered unfit for future highly dangerous or solitary missions, while many others who accepted the challenge were never seen again. 'He must be very special,' the investigator said.

'Very special,' the Israeli agreed. 'It was not long before he became an agent for Mossad. He speaks French, German, and his English is particularly good. He is cool and resourceful under pressure, and quite ruthless where our enemies are concerned. He also has an excellent knowledge of the armaments market, much of it learnt from you, I gather.'

'Baruch liked to know everything about everything.'

'You were a good teacher. Baruch Kanaan was chosen for this mission because of these qualities and because his face was unknown to our enemies. He hoped to contact you, by the way, to enlist your help. We forbade it. We did not want to involve you in any way, but now I am afraid we have little choice.'

'What was his cover?'

'He contacted Gant as a representative of our government. He was to buy arms for us.'

'And?'

'He made the contact and reported back that Gant was interested. Then we heard no more from him. We learned he had checked out of his hotel and left no forwarding address. Baruch left no message for us, nor did he try to contact any of our 'safe' houses. He just disappeared.'

'Three weeks ago.'

'Yes.'

'And you've heard nothing since?'

'Nothing.'

It was Steadman's turn to sigh. 'Just how did you expect me to find him?'

'You could approach Gant in the same way, as a buyer for a Middle East power. You would not have to reveal your employer's identity at first – not until negotiations were underway.'

'But Baruch let Gant know he was working for Israel.'

'Yes. A mistake, we think.'

Steadman smiled wryly. 'Some mistake. If Gant is supplying arms to Arab terrorists, he may have some sympathy for their cause.'

'It is not unusual for an arms dealer to supply both sides in a war.'

'No. It can be an embarrassment sometimes though.'

'An embarrassed arms dealer? An amusing thought.' Goldblatt's smile was cynical. 'However, our point was this: if Gant showed any reluctance to deal with us, that would at least give some indication our information was correct.'

'Indicate, but hardly prove.'

'No, but that would only have been our first step. Surveillance, enquiries, bribery here and there would have confirmed the rest. Proof would have followed.'

'And if it hadn't? If you couldn't get the proof to hand to my government, what then? Eliminate Gant?'

'Probably.' There was no hesitation.

'But you can't fight your war in this country.' Steadman's anger was rising again.

'We have no choice.'

'I have. I won't help you.'

'We are not asking you to take any risks, Mr Steadman. We merely want you to get close to Gant, to find out if Baruch saw him again. If not, then trace Baruch's movements from the last time he contacted us. That's all we ask: a straightforward investigator's commission. No involvement with Mossad.'

'Why don't you go to the police?'

'That could prove rather embarrassing. Besides, we have no faith in the co-operation of foreign governments in Israeli affairs. You remember how France let the assassin Abu Daoud go free after arresting him in Paris in 1977? The French were worried that their sale of two hundred Mirage jets to Egypt would fall through because of it. No, justice is governed by self-interest in all countries. I think your government would not be too concerned with the whereabouts of one missing Israeli spy.'

'Then why not use another private investigator? Why me?'

'Because of your connections. You were with the military, you dealt in arms. You negotiated deals for arms for Israel in the past, and there is no reason why you should not be believed as a freelance now. You have the perfect cover; and you also know Baruch. You are suited for the job in every way.'

'Except one.'

'And that is?'

'I'm not interested.'

'Not even for Baruch's sake?'

'No.'

There was disgust in Goldblatt's eyes now. 'Will nothing I say persuade you?'

'Nothing. Find another agency, or do your own dirty work.'

The Mossad agent stood and looked coldly down at Steadman. 'You've lost your beliefs,' he said.

'No, they're just different now.' Steadman sat back in his chair, his face expressionless. 'I hope you find Baruch.'

With a shake of his head, Goldblatt turned and walked to the door. He stood there as if to say something further, then walked out, closing the door quietly behind him.

Steadman sighed deeply and drummed his fingers on the desk-top. The past never wants to let go, he mused. He wondered about Lilla's younger brother,

Baruch: always smiling, so easily excited, yet so intense when conversation turned to the political struggles of his nation. Had he been sacrificed now like his sister, all in the cause of his country's fight for freedom? The gentle tap at the door was a welcome relief from his brooding thoughts.

'Hello, Harry. That sounded heavy.' Maggie Wyeth's head peered round the door.

He grinned. 'Listening at keyholes again?'

Maggie entered the room and perched herself on the corner of his desk. Forty, elegant, she was attractive in the special way older women can be. A certain firmness in her lips and jawline gave her a slightly intimidating aura, and Steadman had frequently seen this turned to good use in many of the cases they had handled. Her husband had owned the agency and Maggie had helped run it, until a heart attack had killed him five years before. She had continued to run the business, having learned much from her late husband, but the prejudices of clients against a woman handling their affairs were difficult to overcome. Although not unusual for a woman to be a private investigator, she soon realized the agency needed a masculine influence and image, so 'feelers' were put out for the right man. Steadman had just returned to England having resigned from Mossad, and a mutual acquaintance had brought the two together. They were cautious of each other at first, but a reciprocal respect had soon grown between them. They had both lost something, but they were determined not to wallow in self-pity. They recognized the need in each other.

After a three-month trial, Steadman bought himself in as a full partner and the agency's client list had steadily begun to grow again. It was inevitable their relationship should develop beyond that of a business partnership, but their affair was brief, both realizing they could only offer each other a shallow comfort. There was genuine fondness between them, but love was something they'd used up on others. It had lasted for three months, then, by mutual consent, they'd reverted to their business relationship, although a strong bond of friendship had grown between them.

Steadman glanced appreciatively at the smooth line of Maggie's thigh and felt some of the tension drain from him. They hadn't seen each other for a week and both found it good to be in contact again.

'Who was he?' Maggie asked.

'A voice from the past, you could say,' Steadman replied casually.

'From Israel?'

'Yes.'

'Mossad?' She knew of Steadman's past associations.

He nodded.

'Do they want you to work for them again?'

'In a way. They wanted to commission the agency to find a man.'

'He wouldn't speak to me last week when you were away.'

'I have special connections, it seems.'

'But you didn't take the job on.'

'No. I want nothing to do with them.'

'But if it was just a straightforward case we could have handled it. We're not that busy that we can turn down work.'

Steadman frowned. 'With Mossad it's never that straightforward. We don't need it.'

'We could have discussed it first.' Maggie's tone was soft, but he recognized the firmness behind it. 'We could have given it to Sexton, or I could have handled it.'

'I told you, Maggie, they wanted me. Let's drop it, eh?'

This time Maggie recognized the firmness in *his* tone.

'Sorry, Harry. It's the businesswoman in me. I hate to let one get away.'

'Okay.' He smiled and patted her thigh. 'Now, what's been happening?'

'Well, we've still got a few cases on the go, nothing that Sexton and Steve can't handle, though. Sexton has a couple of writs to serve this week although we'll probably let Steve have a go at one of them – he can run faster than Sexton. I'm in court giving evidence tomorrow and Thursday, and a client I've just seen this morning wants to investigate pilfering in his chain of hardware stores. He's losing several hundred a week and suspects it's an organized ring working in his shops.'

'Is he losing stock or money from the till?'

'Oh, it's straight from the till. We'll check receipt books and till rolls in the evening and if we find too many "No Sale" marks we'll try some test purchases.'

Steadman nodded. Test purchases were an easy way of checking the honesty of suspect shop salesmen.

'You'll check on regular tradesmen to the shop, too?'

'Naturally. There might just be conspiracy involved. It shouldn't take too long to find the culprits, but after that, we're pretty clear for work. That's why I was interested in your visitor.'

'Oh come on, Maggie. You know what happens when we begin to slack off. People go missing, couples want a divorce after twenty years of marriage, debtors do a bunk, blackmailers start blackmailing – we're up to our ears in it again. And they're just the little cases. We've always our main diet of company jobs: industrial espionage, embezzlement, security.'

Maggie laughed aloud. 'It's my insecurity showing. There's no reason why things should suddenly go bad for us – not now.'

'Right. Look, I've got to get back up to Salford and there's a few things to tidy up before I go.'

Maggie stood. 'Is it going well?'

'The usual problem of old Joe retiring soon so why can't we put him in charge of security? Fortunately, they're seeing it my way and I want Sexton to select some good men and send them up to see me this week. Then it's just a matter of setting up systems and hiring and training the security.'

'All right, Harry, I'll let you get on. I'll give you a ring if anything important crops up while you're away.' She gave him an affectionate smile and walked to the door. 'Maggie,' he called after her. She turned, the door half-open. 'Forget about our Israeli friend,' he said.

'Forgotten.' She blew him a kiss, then left the office.

Sue looked up from her typewriter as Maggie approached.

Maggie's voice was low when she said, 'Sue, did Harry's visitor leave an address where he could be contacted?'

■ 2 ■

'... it is the tragedy of the élite to have to participate in acts of violence for the glory of the Fatherland.'

HEINRICH HIMMLER

'The world can only be ruled by fear.'

ADOLF HITLER

STEADMAN THREW HIS SUITCASE ON THE FLOOR AND SLUMPED ON TO THE BED. The night drive from Salford had been long and wearing, but he'd wanted to be home on Sunday evening. That way, he could be in the office the following day after a good night's sleep. His client had insisted he stay over for the weekend as his guest, after the long hours he'd put in during the week. Steadman had accepted gladly, for there were still a few loose ends to be tied up before he returned to London and these would be more easily concluded with his client in a congenial and relaxed mood.

Steadman was pleased with the way things had gone. Over the past two weeks he'd thoroughly screened all of the company's employees and had found nothing amiss; but from now on, every member of the firm would possess a Works Pass, numerically marked and containing a photograph of the employee over-stamped with the company name. A daily report would be submitted by security on any unusual happenings during the day or any early or late visits to the company by employees (even if the reports were negative they would still be submitted). All documents would be classified, the more important of which would receive special markings and closer attention. A better system of floodlighting was already being installed, and in future no windows or doors would be left in shadows; even the roof was to be illuminated. All locks and safe combinations had been changed, and ground-floor windows had been fitted with thin but sturdy bars. Steadman had been in favour of a silent alarm system so that the security guards and police could be alerted of illegal entry without actually warning the trespasser; he wanted the intruder to be caught, not merely frightened away. His client had wanted clanging bells and sirens at first, to show the power of his alarm system to would-be thieves so that they would be deterred from ever attempting a break-in again, but he had given way to Steadman's argument that the best deterrent to them, and any other villains who might have their eyes on the plant, was for them to be caught and made an example of. Steadman had also argued against the manufacturer's request for guard dogs; correctly trained dogs were expensive and required handlers. He also had a personal abhorrence of any animal being trained to attack a man. Besides which they could easily be drugged.

He had spent the weekend coaxing a higher salary for the Chief of Security out of the manufacturer, for Sexton had provided Steadman with the ideal man for the job. A soon-to-retire police officer, the man needed more persuading to move from London up to Salford, and only a good wage and financial help in moving would do it. The manufacturer argued that there were plenty of suitable men locally, but Steadman had not been totally happy with any he'd interviewed; they would be fine as guards, but were not sufficiently qualified in the key role of Chief of Security. The client finally succumbed to Steadman's wishes and the investigator pressed home his advantage by persuading him to employ his own maintenance men and even his own window cleaners rather than use outside tradesmen. It was a smaller issue, but as far as Steadman was concerned, of vital importance if strict security were to be maintained, so he was particularly pleased at the outcome and had allowed himself to relax for the rest of the weekend.

He flexed his shoulder blades against the softness of the bed and eased his shoes off with his toes. He had enjoyed the last two weeks' work even though it had been arduous and frustrating at times. If his client stuck to the agreed plan for security, then the plant should become thief-proof and, hopefully, spy-proof, which would be good for the agency's reputation and could lead on to similar commissions from other companies. Steadman had set up four such security systems in the past, with variations for the particular needs of each individual company, and it had proved to be highly lucrative work. It beat the hell out of runaway debtors or stay-away husbands.

He briefly considered ringing Maggie to let her know he was back, but on glancing at his watch and seeing it was well after eleven, he dismissed the thought. He had spoken to her a few times during the week and there had been no crises at the office, so there was little point in disturbing her at such a late hour. Tomorrow morning would be time enough to catch up on any news.

Steadman stretched his limbs but resisted the urge to let himself sink into sleep. He was hungry and a stiff drink would do wonders for his metabolism. The investigator rolled off the bed and padded over to the window. He peered into the darkness, seeing little of the small church grounds opposite, a dark reflection of himself in the glass obscuring the view.

Steadman lived in a small terraced house in a quiet mews off Knightsbridge. It had cost a small fortune, but the cul-de-sac was central and its peaceful position in the thriving city was something to be relished. The tiny park that surrounded the church across the narrow road made an ideal spot to relax over the Sunday papers during the summer months; even the occasional gravestones, grey and white with age and bird droppings, gave the grounds a peaceful stability. A few benches were scattered at random in the grounds and his neighbours all seemed to have their allocated spot, their dogs their allocated trees. The money Steadman had acquired through working for Mossad, and the commissions he had received on negotiating arms deals for the Israelis, had been enough to pay for the house as well as buy himself into Maggie's business, and now his earnings came purely from the agency. It gave him a comfortable life and a busy one which, he reflected, was the most one could expect. You had more, once, he told himself, and you foolishly expected it to last. Foolishly, because danger was all around you both then, but you still thought it couldn't touch you. It had though, and it had killed Lilla. So never expect too much again. That way, you'll never be disappointed. He closed the curtains on his dark, brooding image.

He went downstairs, his stockinged feet silent on the heavy carpets, and along the short hallway to the tiny kitchen, where he poured himself a large vodka with a small tonic. Deciding it was too late to eat out, he took a pizza from the fridge, unwrapped it and put it into the oven. His cleaning-lady, who came in twice a week, had thoughtfully stocked up his food supply during his absence, but he rarely cooked elaborate meals for himself – women friends could be relied on for that.

Steadman padded back down the hallway to the front door and retrieved the week's mail that was lying there. He took the letters and his drink into the lounge and settled into the armchair. He sipped at his vodka tonic, then began to open the envelopes on his lap. The only bills he paid any attention to were the red ones; the others he crumpled and dropped on the floor. A letter from an ex-girlfriend made him groan aloud. She had grown tired of being an ex-just as quickly as she had of being current and now thought it would be 'super' if they got together again. That letter, too, soon lay crumpled at his feet. An invitation to a security exhibition followed by a series of lectures on the subject interested him and he placed this one with the Final Demands resting on the arm of his chair. The rest were advertising circulars and these found their rightful place on the floor.

He ate his supper at the breakfast bar in his kitchen, the cool voice and records of a late-night DJ keeping him company. A hot shower and another large vodka eased the remaining stiffness from his muscles and left him pleasantly drowsy. He fell naked into his bed and was asleep within seconds.

The hammering woke him with a start. He lay on his back staring up into the darkness wondering what had dragged him from his slumber with such suddenness. Then the banging came again. It came from downstairs – his front door. Who the hell could want him at this time of night? And why not use the doorbell? But this was hammering, not knocking. With a curse, he leapt from the bed and pulled back the curtains, pressing his face close to the glass of the window in order to see directly below. The banging stopped almost immediately.

Steadman blinked his eyes as he tried to see into the gloom. He thought he saw movement in the shadows below, but couldn't be sure. As he turned from the window, about to find his discarded trousers and dash downstairs, he thought he saw a black shape scurry across the narrow road into the darkness of the churchyard opposite. Again, he couldn't be sure, nothing was distinct in the poor light.

As he pulled on his trousers, he snatched a quick look at the luminous digital clock by his bedside. Two twenty-three. If someone was playing a joke, he'd kill them. He ran down the stairs, angry now, but when he reached the hallway, he halted. Something made him hesitate. He stared at the door, for some reason reluctant to open it. There was a stillness in the air. A chill. And he could hear a strange muffled sound coming from the other side of the door.

He moved slowly along the hallway, his breathing held in check, his footsteps quiet and deliberate. He pressed his ear against the wood and listened.

Something was scraping itself against the door and he thought he heard a low murmuring. The sound wasn't human; it was like the whimpering of an animal in pain. He considered going back for his gun which was locked away upstairs, but dismissed the thought as being over-dramatic. A sudden thump against the door made him draw away.

Then he realized how ridiculously he was behaving, standing there in the dark like an old woman, afraid to open the front door. He reached for the latch and swung the door inwards with a jerk.

A figure stood spread-eagled in the doorway, arms out-stretched, holding on to the doorframe. The head hung down and a dark liquid seemed to be drooling from its mouth. The figure seemed strangely slumped, for the knees were bent as if giving no support to the body. A low moaning noise came from it, occasionally rising to the animal-like whimper Steadman had heard from the other side of the door; but the noise had a strange gurgling to it, as though blood were running down the person's throat.

Steadman could see nothing beyond the feebly twisting body except blackness. He reached for the hallway light switch and flicked it down, blinking his eyes rapidly against the sudden light. When he finally focused them, he saw that the figure in the doorway was that of a woman. And there was something familiar about the slumped head.

'Maggie.' The name came from Steadman's lips in a whisper. He reached forward and raised her head; blood ran from her mouth on to his hand. Her eyes were glazed and red-rimmed but he thought he saw a flicker of recognition there.

'Maggie, what's happened to you?' He moved forward to take her in his arms. For some reason, her arms remained stretched outwards as though unwilling to let go of the doorframe. Her head moved and she tried to speak, but the blood in her throat choked her words.

'Oh God, Maggie! Who did this?' He pulled her forward, wanting to carry her to the sofa in the lounge, but a weak scream came from her.

'Maggie, let go of the door. Let me take you in,' he pleaded.

She tried to speak again and her head slumped forward as she lost consciousness. This time Steadman tugged a little more firmly, but still she clung to the doorframe. Then he noticed the trails of blood running down from her arms. He pushed his head past her shoulder and his eyes widened in horror as he saw the nail protruding from the back of her hand.

He grabbed her to support her weight and saw her other hand also had been nailed to the doorframe. 'Maggie, Maggie,' he said over and over again, holding her close, lifting her to prevent her hands from tearing. He called out, hoping a neighbour would hear, but no lights came on from the other houses. It was the dead of night; they were either in deep sleep or just didn't want to hear. He made up his mind quickly, sensing he had no time to lose. Someone would come eventually if he kept shouting, but by then it might be too late.

He eased Maggie's body down as gently as he could, then ran into the kitchen and threw open a cupboard where he kept his work tools. He found a hammer and raced back down the hallway, his heart pounding, his fear rising. Her torn clothes were covered in blood, most of which seemed to have come from her mouth. Steadman eased himself past her and with one arm around her body, pushed the forked end of the hammer underneath the nailhead with his free hand. He tried to pull the nail out without using the back of her hand as a lever, but it was deeply embedded. He had to let her go and use both hands. Maggie's body slumped again and he pulled at the hammer with all his strength, a cry of relief escaping him as he finally wrenched the bloody nail clear. He tried to catch her as her body fell sideways, prevented from falling completely to the ground by the nail in her other hand. Steadman let her go and again gave all his energy to yanking out the other nail. It was embedded deep into her hand and he had to push the hammer's fork into the skin to gain a grip. It made him nauseous to do so but he knew he had no choice; he had to get her free as quickly as possible.

The three-inch nail loosened, then came out smoothly and clinked into the road. Steadman dropped the hammer and carried the still figure into the house, gently laying it on the sofa in his lounge. He snapped on the light, then knelt beside her, wondering if there was anything he could do before he called an ambulance. Her head lolled to one side and her open, unseeing eyes told him the worst. Frantically, he ripped open her jacket and placed his hand over her heart. He couldn't trust his trembling hand to give him an answer so he put his ear to her breast and listened. There was no heartbeat.

He cried out her name again and took her head in his hands, looking at her still face, pleading with her to be alive. Her mouth had dropped open and he saw it was thick with blood. Perhaps she was choking, perhaps if he laid her with her head down. Then his muscles froze as he stared into the blood-filled cavity. He fought against the sudden upheaval in his stomach and, as steadily as possible, rested her head back against the arm of the sofa.

He knew that she was dead. But he wondered why her tongue had been ripped out.

■ 3 ■

*'This time our sacred soil will not be spared. But I am not afraid of this. We shall
clench our teeth and go on fighting. Germany will emerge from those ruins lovelier
and greater than any country in the world has ever been.'*

ADOLF HITLER

STEADMAN SAT AT MAGGIE'S DESK AND COVERED HIS FACE WITH TREMBLING
hands. There were no tears in him, just a great weariness, a feeling of hopelessness. He thought he had banished violence as savage as this from his life once
and for all, but now it had searched him out again like an old enemy who
refused a truce. Why Maggie? Who could have done this to her?

The police, summoned by a neighbour in the mews who was not quite brave
enough to answer Steadman's call for help, but alarmed enough to call in the
law, had burst into the investigator's house finding him cradling the dead body
of his partner in his arms, his bare chest soaked in her blood. They had regarded
him warily, listening gravely to his story, but ready to pounce at the slightest
indication of aggression.

An ambulance had taken away the mutilated body and the hours that
followed were filled with questions, questions, questions. Who was the dead
person? What had been her relationship to him? Had they quarrelled? Was the
business going well? Were they lovers? Describe exactly what had happened.
Again. Again. What had their quarrel been about? Had there *never* been
disagreements in their partnership? What had their *latest* conflict been over?
What cases were they currently working on? When was the last time he'd seen
her before tonight? Describe again what had happened. What time had he
woken? Why hadn't he phoned for the police? Was she alive when he had found
her? Start at the beginning again.

His temper had flared then subsided. He was still in shock and the questions
– the situation – seemed unreal. The small house appeared to be filled with
moving figures, hostile, disbelieving faces. Their attitude towards him seemed
to change imperceptibly as the hours wore on and answers he gave them
matched answers he'd given earlier. They allowed him to shower and dress,
then two detectives accompanied him to the agency in Gray's Inn Square where
all three searched through recent files, looking for any clue in recent cases that
might shed some light on the gruesome murder. One of the questions uppermost in their minds was why Maggie Wyeth's murderer should crucify her to
her partner's front door. Could their agency have helped convict someone in

the past, and now this lunatic was taking his revenge? Other policemen were going over Maggie's Highgate home with a fine-tooth comb at the same time, looking for such evidence, but they, like the two detectives with Steadman, found no leads.

Business hours were approaching when they finally left Steadman alone in Maggie's office, his mind weary with fatigue and his senses still dulled by shock. They asked him to come to New Scotland Yard to make a statement later on in the day, and warned him not to say too much to the Press at this stage of the investigation, who they felt sure would soon be on to him. And they warned him not to leave the city without telling them of his destination first.

Sue found him there when she arrived for work. The door to Maggie's office was open and, still in her coat and shaking the rain from her umbrella, Sue put her head around the door, expecting to see Maggie. She looked at Steadman's dishevelled figure in bewilderment.

'Oh, I thought it was Mrs Wyeth. Would you ...'

'Come in, Sue.' Steadman cut off her words, barely glancing at the girl.

Sue was puzzled, then concerned, as she entered the room and drew nearer to the investigator. His eyes had an unfocused look to them.

'Are you all right, Mr Steadman? You look ...'

'What case did Maggie have on last week, Sue?' His eyes now became clearer and fastened on the secretary's.

The question – and its intensity – surprised her. 'Er, it should be in her book. She was in court twice – er, Tuesday and Thursday, I think – and she investigated some suspected pilfering in the Myer's chain store. That was about it, I think. It's in the book.' She pointed towards the red diary lying on the desk in front of Steadman.

'Yes, I've been through it,' he said, picking up the diary and flicking through the pages again. 'Was there anything nasty going on with this pilfering business?'

'No. No, I don't think so. Mrs Wyeth had only just started on the investigation. But she should be in soon, she'll be able to tell ...'

'Sue.' She stopped at his quiet tone. 'Mrs Wyeth won't be coming in.'

Sue stood in the centre of the room, the dripping umbrella still in her hand creating a pool of rainwater on the wood floor, her face suddenly pale. The look on Steadman's face told her she was about to hear something terrible, but she couldn't find the words to prompt him.

Steadman decided not to tell her until he'd learned as much as possible about Maggie's activities during the last week or so, for he knew the shock to his secretary would prevent further questioning. 'Try and think, Sue. Was Maggie involved in anything else while I was away?'

She shook her head, then froze. 'Well, there was another case, but ...'

Steadman waited, but the girl seemed reluctant to go on. 'You've got to tell me, Sue. It could be important.'

'She wanted to tell you herself when you got back. She asked me not to say anything.'

'Please tell me, Sue.' There was frustration in Steadman's voice.

'The man ... the man who came to see you last week. Mr Goldblatt? I think Mrs Wyeth was working on something for him.'

'Christ!' The girl jumped as Steadman's fist hit the desk. 'I told her I didn't want to handle that!' he shouted.

'She ... she said we weren't busy, that we could easily fit it in. It was only tracing a missing person.' Sue felt uncomfortable for she felt a strong loyalty towards both her employers.

'I'm sure Mrs Wyeth will explain ...'

'She won't though. She's dead!' The investigator regretted his anger immediately as Sue's face broke into lines of distress. He stood up and walked around the desk to her. 'I'm sorry, I shouldn't have told you like that.' He put two hands on her shoulders and guided her towards a chair.

'How did it happen?' she asked as she searched for a handkerchief in her pocket. 'She was fine on Thursday morning after court. There didn't seem to be anything wrong at all.'

'Was that the last time you saw her?' His voice was gentle now.

'Yes, Thursday morning.' She dabbed at her eyes with the handkerchief. 'She told me she would be out that afternoon and probably most of Friday. What happened, Mr Steadman? How did she die?'

Steadman hesitated, but realized the newspapers would carry the story even if the more grisly details were left out. 'She was murdered. Last night. That's why I have to know her movements last week.'

'Murdered? But who ... ?'

'We don't know, Sue. The police will probably want to question you later today.'

Steadman tried to comfort the girl as her shoulders shook with sudden grief.

'When did Mrs Wyeth see Goldblatt?' he asked after her sobs had become more controlled.

'On the same day you did. She arranged to see him at his hotel that afternoon.'

'Which hotel, Sue? Have you got the name?'

She nodded. 'It's in my pad. I'll get it for you.' Sue rose from the chair, still holding the crumpled handkerchief to her nose.

'Who would do it, Mr Steadman? Who would murder her?'

Steadman could give her no answer. He doubted if he even wanted to find out. Somehow he knew it would lead to even more death.

The hotel was in North-West London, close to Belsize Park, a modern, motor motel, the kind favoured by businessmen who spent only a week or so in town, then moved on to other parts of the country. It was central to London and anonymous – ideal for members of organizations such as Mossad.

Steadman paid the cabbie and strode purposefully through the swing-doors into the hotel's reception area. He had left Sue in the capable hands of Sexton. The older detective had arrived with Steve just as Sue had been finding Goldblatt's address for him, and Steadman had explained to all three exactly what had happened to Maggie. There had been more hysterics from Sue and Steve had gone deathly white, but Sexton had taken it all in his stride. He had been stunned, of that there was no doubt, but experience and acceptance of the ills of the world had enabled him to cast emotion to one side for the moment, for he was needed to calm the others. The retired policeman had wanted to accompany Steadman to the Mossad agent's hotel, but his employer had insisted he stay behind and do his best, under the circumstances, to carry on the business as normal. His firmness would also be needed to keep the Press at bay. Sexton had accepted his role without argument.

The hotel receptionist eyed Steadman coolly. The investigator realized his appearance was unkempt, the stubble of an unshaven chin, the open-necked shirt, and the signs of a sleepless night apparent in his face, making him an unwelcome guest; but he was in no mood for offended hotel receptionists.

'You have a Mr Goldblatt staying here. What room is he in?'

The authority in Steadman's voice allowed no dissent from the man behind the desk. The receptionist quickly ran a finger down the guest list.

'Room 314, sir. Third floor. I'll give Mr Goldblatt a call and let him know you're here. What name shall I say?'

'Don't bother,' Steadman told him as he turned away and walked towards the lifts.

'Just a minute, sir,' the receptionist called out, but the lift doors were already opening, disgorging a group of businessmen, and Steadman had stepped in behind them. The receptionist hastily picked up the phone and dialled a number.

The lift reached the third floor and the doors opened smoothly. Steadman stepped into the carpeted corridor and looked for room numbers. A door further down opened and the Mossad agent's figure appeared. He raised an arm in surprise towards Steadman.

The detective walked towards him, his eyes fixed firmly on the Israeli's. The Mossad agent was still in shirt-sleeves and clearly had not expected a visitor so early in the morning.

'I'm pleased you have come, Mr ...' His voice wavered as he recognized the look in Steadman's eyes. It reminded him of his old instructor's look when one of Goldblatt's companions had shot a fellow trainee in the throat with a machine-gun through carelessness; the veteran instructor had beaten his pupil to a pulp for wasting a badly needed Israeli life. That same cold look was now in Steadman's eyes.

He felt strangely powerless to prevent Steadman striking him, for the look held him rigid. The blow sent him reeling back into the room. He rolled over on his back and came to his knees, but Steadman's foot sent him over again. Goldblatt sprawled on his back then felt himself lifted by his shirt-front. 'Steadman, don't ...' he cried out, but his words were cut off by a vicious slap in the face. His head shot to one side, then to the other, as Steadman brought his hand sharply back.

'You used her, you bastard!' Steadman shouted down into the agent's face. 'You used Lilla and you used me. Now you've killed Maggie, too!'

'Steadman, what are you saying?'

'Maggie!' Steadman screamed. 'You killed her!'

The Israeli agent was thrown to the floor again and Steadman raised his fist to bring it down into the upturned face.

'Enough, Steadman. Please do not move!' The command came from the bedroom doorway.

Steadman swung his head round and saw the woman standing there, a small but long-barrelled Beretta in her hand and aimed at his chest. He recognized her as the woman he had seen with Goldblatt in the car the week before.

'Please don't make me shoot you,' she pleaded, her eyes nervously glancing at Goldblatt. Steadman knew she meant it, for the gunfire would make little noise: it was Mossad's custom to use bullets carrying light powder loadings to reduce their blast. The only problem for them would be the disposal of his corpse, but with the help of others, that could be arranged without too much difficulty. He stepped away from the recumbent Mossad agent and towards the woman, ready to pounce at her slightest distraction.

Her long, black hair falling to her shoulders and dark skin gave her a seductive attractiveness. The man's bathrobe she wore – obviously Goldblatt's – somehow heightened that attractiveness.

'It's all right, Hannah,' Goldblatt said hastily, wiping blood from the corner of his mouth. 'Don't shoot him. Yet.'

The Israeli staggered to his feet and went to the door, looking into the hallway before he closed it. No one had been disturbed. He walked back to Steadman, keeping behind him. He ran skilful, searching hands down the investigator's body, then straightened when satisfied there were no concealed weapons. He walked around to the woman called Hannah and took the gun from her hand, keeping it pointed at Steadman.

'Now, explain. Why did you do this?' he said.

'Don't you know what you've done?' Steadman asked angrily.

Goldblatt shook his head. 'Please explain.'

'You used my partner to find your missing agent, didn't you?'

'She came to us.'

'But I refused to work for you!'

'That was your choice, not hers. She wanted to take the job on. She said you could be persuaded once you saw it was just another routine commission.'

'Routine? With Mossad?' Steadman shook his head in disgust.

'What has happened to your partner, Mr Steadman?' It was the woman who spoke.

Steadman's eyes shifted to her. 'She was murdered last night. I found her nailed to my door. Her tongue had been torn out.' He said the words coldly, stifling the emotion he felt.

The woman closed her eyes and seemed to sway. Goldblatt reached out a hand to steady her, but he was too experienced to let the gun drift away from the investigator's direction.

'Why was this done to her?' he said to Steadman.

'You tell me,' came the bitter reply.

'But did they leave no message? Have they not contacted you?'

'They? Who would *they* be, Goldblatt?'

'It must have been Gant.'

'Why should he have done this to Maggie?'

'Perhaps she got too close, found out too much.'

'But why do that to her?'

'As a warning, Mr Steadman.'

'To me? But I wanted nothing to do with it!'

'Gant must know of your past association with Mossad.' The Israeli lowered his eyes briefly. 'Your partner must have told him.'

The realization hit Steadman hard. Maggie must have been frightened or tortured into disclosing that information. He clenched his fist and would have leapt at Goldblatt at that moment, gun or no gun, had not the woman suddenly burst into tears.

'That poor woman. Oh God, forgive us!' She slumped down on to one of the room's armchairs. Goldblatt lowered the gun.

'You see the evil of these people, Mr Steadman? You see what they will do to achieve their ends?'

'And what about you bastards? What do you do to achieve yours?'

'Not this. We do not make war on innocents.'

'But they get killed anyway.'

Goldblatt walked over to the room's other armchair and sat, no longer caring if the investigator attacked him again.

'Forgive us, Mr Steadman. We did not think they would harm a British citizen,' he said.

The anger had drained from Steadman. He had known people like these Mossad agents. They were mostly decent, dedicated people; their one common fault – to him – was their fanaticism towards Israel's cause.

He walked to the window and looked down on the busy street below. The drizzle had stopped and already fumes from the traffic were filling the air. 'Tell me exactly what happened when she contacted you,' he said quietly.

Goldblatt glanced at Hannah and an agreement seemed to pass between them. 'She came here to the hotel and we told her of Baruch's disappearance,' Goldblatt said. 'We were doubtful of using your agency after our meeting, Mr Steadman, but Mrs Wyeth convinced us you would see reason once the case was underway. And she thought perhaps you would not even have to know of it if Baruch could be found quickly. She said you were busy in the North.'

'But I'd have seen the books eventually,' said Steadman.

'By then – hopefully – it wouldn't have mattered.'

Goldblatt paused, but Steadman's expression urged him on. 'We told her of Baruch's contact with Edward Gant and how he had disappeared shortly after. She said she could start by making enquiries at Gant's London office to see if Baruch had visited him that day. A commissionaire, a receptionist – anyone in the building might recognize him if we could provide her with a photograph. It would be somewhere to start, anyway. She said she would check out the staff at the hotel where he had been staying. They might have seen something on that day and a few pound notes here and there would probably help them remember. She left after we had given her a thorough description of Baruch and an agenda of his activities since he'd been in this country. We told her as much as we could but, of course, not everything. Within twenty-four hours we had a photograph of Baruch – it was flown over from Israel – and this we gave to her on Wednesday. Since then, we have heard nothing.'

'Just how much did you tell her, Goldblatt?'

'We told her Baruch's mission was to make an arms deal with Gant.'

'And not that Gant is on your assassination list!'

'But he is not! We are merely investigating his dealings with terrorists.'

'My God,' Steadman scoffed, 'I could almost believe you.'

'Mr Steadman.' It was Hannah who spoke now. 'We did not realize the danger to your friend. We were desperate. It is not easy for our agents to operate in this country and we had used up all our resources to find Baruch. We thought her neutrality would protect her.'

'You were wrong!'

'Yes, we know that now. But doesn't this murder make you want to help us?'

'Help you?' Steadman shook his head in wonder. 'If – and I mean *if* – Maggie was killed by Gant, then the whole point of nailing her to my door was to serve as a warning for me to keep my nose out. And it worked!'

'But surely you will avenge her death?' Goldblatt was on his feet. 'Surely you will help us now?'

'Oh no. I've had my share of bloodletting in the name of revenge. Those days are over for me.'

The two Israeli agents stared at him in disbelief. 'You will let him get away with this murder?' Goldblatt said. 'What has happened to you, Steadman? How can a man be this way?'

'In this country we have a police force to find murderers,' Steadman told him evenly.

'You will tell the police of us?' The gun in Goldblatt's hand was raised towards the investigator again.

'I'll tell them everything I know.' Steadman saw the knuckles on the hand whiten.

'David. It would be wrong.' Hannah reached up and placed a gentle hand on Goldblatt's arm. After a few seconds' hesitation, the gun was lowered again.

'You are right,' Goldblatt said. 'Go then, Steadman. You are wrong about us, but we will never convince you of that now. I have pity for you.'

Steadman stood in silence, a tight smile on his face. It was ironic, he thought. A battle was going on inside him. These people didn't understand that he *wanted* to help them. Old fires had been rekindled, Maggie's death had stirred up feelings he had thought of as long buried; and now the struggle was to quench those fires, to remember the tragedies these feelings had led to in the past.

'You would do well not to mock us, Mr Steadman.' Goldblatt had mistaken the meaning behind the investigator's smile. His voice was menacing and his grip on the gun was rigid.

With a sigh, Steadman walked from the room. 'Go to hell,' he said mildly as he closed the door.

▪ 4 ▪

'It is becoming more and more obvious that a rift in public opinion is gradually widening, each individual going to the Right or Left as it suits them.'

'We shall have friends who will help us in all the enemy countries.'

ADOLF HITLER

POPE WAS WAITING FOR STEADMAN WHEN HE RETURNED TO HIS HOUSE. THE investigator had decided not to go back to the agency; he needed sleep and time to think.

He was surprised there were no reporters loitering as he pushed the key into the latch and twisted. A crucifixion in a London street was just the story to whet their ghoulish appetites. He went straight to the kitchen, poured himself a large vodka, and carried it through to the lounge. He had taken off his jacket and slumped into an armchair before he noticed the overcoated figure sitting on the sofa.

'Good morning, Mr Steadman. May I call you Harry?' The voice was gruff but contained a mixture of politeness and amusement. The man looked powerful, but in a gross way – the muscles had long been covered by layers of fat.

'My name is Nigel Pope.' The big man leaned forward with effort and proffered an open wallet towards Steadman. 'British Intelligence,' he said, almost apologetically.

Steadman barely glanced at the perspex-covered identity card in its frame of leather, wondering how they had got on to Mossad so quickly.

The wallet was flicked shut and returned to an inside breast pocket of the man's suit. 'I let myself in, I hope you don't mind.'

Steadman settled resignedly back in his chair and sipped his vodka. 'What has my partner's death got to do with Security?'

Pope gave the investigator a reproving look. 'What has Israeli Intelligence got to do with Mrs Wyeth's death?'

'How did you find out about that?'

'Why didn't you tell the police about your agency's connections with Mossad?' Pope countered.

'We don't have any connections with them! I only found out this morning that Maggie had accepted a commission from Mossad! I was going to tell the police that.'

'A man named Goldblatt came to your office and saw you, in particular, a week ago. We know he is a Mossad agent.'

'He wanted me to trace a missing agent, Baruch Kanaan. I turned the job down.'

'Harry, let me tell you what we know of you. Perhaps that way we can avoid unnecessary time-wasting between us.' Pope rose and stood with his back to the mantel, closed his eyes for a few moments, and then proceeded as though giving a lecture. 'You were born in Chichester in 1940 and had a perfectly normal childhood until your father died when you were thirteen. Your mother took in another man a year later, whom she subsequently married. But you didn't like him and he didn't much like you. You left home at fifteen much to your mother's distress and, lying about your age, worked in restaurants around London. You joined the Army in 1956 – perhaps the Suez Crisis aroused the fighting man in you – as a Junior soldier, and were trained in The Junior Infantrymen's Company in Bassingbourn. You were soon transferred into a Junior Leader's Regiment when it was realized you had some potential as an NCO but, although you later reached the rank of captain, there was something of a – what shall I say – "rebel" would be too romantic, "oddball" not quite correct. Let's just say team spirit was not one of your finer points.' Pope smiled and wagged a finger at Steadman. 'Er, yes. Ironically enough, at the age of nineteen, you were diverted into the Corps of Royal Military Police – I believe the British Army enjoys ironies, don't you? – and you became more disciplined. You spent some time in Germany and Hong Kong and, while you were there, your mother died after a long illness.' He looked at the investigator as if for affirmation.

Steadman nodded, wondering how long it had taken the fat man to memorize all this.

'Let's see, that would be in 1959?'

'Sixty,' Steadman corrected him.

'Oh yes, you were twenty then. Four years of service behind you. In '62 you married a German girl, but that lasted barely two years. It seemed she didn't like army life. Fortunately, there were no children. In '65 you joined the Intelligence Corps and there, I think, you found your niche. Leastways, you seemed contented enough for a few years. You were loaned to Israeli Intelligence in 1970, more as a means of keeping an eye on their activities than anything else, I shouldn't wonder, and you were with them for quite some time.'

'Two years,' Steadman informed the fat man needlessly.

'Yes, two years. Just about. It was while you were there that you formed an attachment with one of their operatives, a young lady by the name of Lilla Kanaan – the sister of this missing Mossad agent, Baruch.'

Attachment? The word was hardly adequate for a relationship that had run as deep as theirs.

'Correct so far, eh?' Pope enquired, a smile of satisfaction on his broad face. There was no answer from the investigator and the fat man went on. 'Well, we know you were very close. You more or less moved into her apartment in Tel Aviv, in fact. You spent a lot of time with her and her family, who lived in Anabta, and they became the family you had been denied. I think Israeli Intelligence probably tried to persuade you to leave British Intelligence long before you witnessed the massacre at Lod Airport.' He looked questioningly at Steadman, but still received no response. He shrugged his huge shoulders, then went on, 'You were on your way back to England, recalled to London. Whether or not it was already on your mind to return to Israel I don't know, but it seems the incident at Lod was the turning point for you. Within a few months, you had bought yourself out of the army and were back in Israel as a member of Mossad, and in time to become part of the new "revenge squad" set up by Golda Meir at the encouragement of Major-General Zwi Zamir. The killing of their athletes at the Munich Olympics had set the final seal of approval on this new outward-going organization within Israeli Intelligence and they knew your background would help them in taking their war outside the boundaries of their own country.

'You were not easily accepted by your Jewish colleagues, but your part in the attack on the Palestine Liberation Organization's quarters in Beirut in April '73 overcame their qualms, and you more than proved your physical abilities in the training camp at Caesarea.

'You and your friend, Lilla, became part of the squad known as Heth. Your role was to set up a cover in other countries which would help the rest of the group to operate as a whole. You set up communications, rented apartments, arranged hotel reservations, provided hire cars and supplied any information concerning the local area your group was to operate in. As an Englishman, your cover was ideal, and Lilla easily passed as a European. You worked together as man and wife.

'We're fairly certain of three killings you were involved in. Abdel Hamid Shibi and Abdel Hadi Nakaa, two known PLO terrorists who were living in Rome, were blown to pieces in their Mercedes. The same happened to Mohammad Boudia, a key organizer of Black September; he was blown up in his Renault in Paris.

'Oh, I don't say you actually carried out the killings yourself, but you and your woman friend certainly smoothed the way for Aleph, the assassins of your little liquidation group. There are other "incidents" we're not too sure of, but it seems it was a busy year for you.'

Pope sat down again, as though his bulk had suddenly become too heavy for his legs. He looked thoughtfully at Steadman, then continued: 'Apart from these missions, you were also involved in certain arms deals for the Israelis, working from Brussels and using your old army connections for contacts. You were, indeed, valuable to The Institute – as the Central Institute for Information and Espionage is known – and to the Israeli army itself. No wonder they were sad to see you go.'

Still Steadman was silent. He wasn't surprised that British Intelligence had this information – he was impressed more by Pope's memory than knowledge – but he was growing increasingly apprehensive as to the purpose of the fat man's visit.

'It was in August that, for you, tragedy struck. Mossad was suffering from a loss of morale due to the killing of an innocent man in Lillehammer, Norway, and the capture by the authorities there of the group involved. Lilla Kanaan and yourself were not part of that misguided mission. You were both exhausted by now and your nerve needed rest. The Israelis thought they had finally located the.man behind the Munich massacre, Ali Hassan Salemeh, but in fact the man they killed turned out to be a harmless waiter. In a way, it was unfortunate you hadn't been included in the mission because you might have been safely tucked away in a Norwegian prison at that time. An explosion in your Brussels' apartment injured you and killed the girl.'

The memory no longer caused Steadman's hands to shake uncontrollably, but it still seemed to drain him of any strength.

Pope quickly went on: 'When you had recovered – your health, that is – it seems you went on the rampage. At least, you appeared to be everywhere at once: Paris, Rome, Oslo, as well as Benghazi and Beirut, and in all these places, violence occurred prior to your departure. Even the Yom Kippur war in October of that year hardly seemed to contain your energies. But then, in January '74, it all stopped.'

Pope sat back in his chair and entwined his fingers across his huge paunch. He regarded Steadman quizzically. 'Why did you leave Mossad at that point, Harry?'

'I thought you knew all the answers,' came the reply.

'Not all, Harry. We have two conjectures: one, that you were suddenly sick of all the violence around you; two, that you didn't wash your hands of Mossad at all.'

Steadman raised his eyebrows.

'No, you see, we think perhaps it was meant to look that way, severing all ties with Israel, returning to England and joining Mrs Wyeth's enquiry agency. Perhaps it was all a new cover for you.'

'For nearly five years?' said Steadman incredulously.

' "Sleeper" agents are valuable assets to any espionage organization. Adopt a role, carry on as a normal member of a community for as long as five, ten, fifteen years even, until the occasion to be used comes along. It's far from rare in these uneasy times.'

Steadman laughed aloud, but he felt little humour in the situation. 'Why here? There's no hostilities between Britain and Israel,' he said.

'No, there's no open aggression. But Israel knows it has to spread its net, it has to fight its country's battles in other countries. With worldwide terrorism as it is now, the Israelis have to meet it on neutral territory. They can't afford to sit back and wait for it to hit their own country! Do you think I might have a cup of tea?'

Steadman was taken aback by the sudden innocuous request.

'Tea might do you some good too, Harry. It really is awfully early to be drinking vodka, you know,' Pope said reprovingly.

Steadman placed his glass on the carpet and rose from his seat. Bemused, he walked through to the kitchen.

'What use to Mossad would I be in this country?' he called back down the hallway as he waited for the kettle to boil. Pope's massive body appeared in the small hallway, almost blocking it completely. He leaned his bulk against a wall.

'Oh, keeping an eye on the scene,' he said casually. 'Maybe keeping an eye on the arms dealings, who's trading with whom, that sort of thing. Perhaps doing a little trading yourself.'

'Why would I need a cover for that?'

'Convenience? It's not unusual for a buyer to remain anonymous to the seller in such matters. You would be the link, the go-between.'

Steadman poured boiling water into the teapot and stirred it vigorously.

'Or maybe you were merely here to observe any terrorist activities,' Pope suggested. 'London, with its great foreign student population, makes a wonderful hive for such groups. Milk but no sugar for me, Harry. And do have one yourself. You look all in.'

Steadman poured two cups and carried them down the hallway. Pope backed into the lounge before him.

'It's awfully cold in here.' Pope took his seat again, shuddering inside his huge overcoat.

'I've been away,' Steadman said and added, 'as you probably know.' He went back into the kitchen and flicked down the switch that operated the central heating. 'It'll take a while to warm up,' he said, returning to the lounge. He sat facing the fat man once again. 'Do you really believe that?' he asked Pope. 'That I'm still with The Institute, I mean.'

Pope gulped his tea and watched Steadman over the rim of his cup. After a few moments' hesitation, he said, 'Actually, no, I don't. But that's just a personal judgement, neither here nor there. As a matter of fact, I rather admire the Israelis' cause, so it wouldn't matter that much to me anyway. However, we are not going to allow the wars of other nations to be fought in our country. We've kept a close eye on you, Harry, ever since your return to England and nothing you've done has given us grounds for suspicion of any sort. Until last week, that is.'

'Look, that was the first contact I've had with Mossad for nearly five years!'

'Drink your tea, Harry, it'll get cold.'

Steadman drank until the cup was empty, then he put it aside. 'Okay, Pope,' he said abruptly. 'My partner – who was also a close friend – has been murdered. I've been interrogated by the police for most of the night, I've had to organize the office, and now I'm beat. I just want to lie down and sleep. So let's get to the point. What do you want from me?'

'Why, Harry, you left out your visit to Mr Goldblatt this morning,' Pope said smoothly.

Steadman groaned aloud. 'I wanted to beat his brains in! For getting Maggie killed!'

'Of course, Harry.'

'I told him I wasn't interested last week. He hired Maggie in spite of that.'

'Yes, we know. I spoke to your staff this morning myself after you'd left. Your secretary told me you practically threw our Mr Goldblatt out of your office last week. It could have been an act, but I don't see that there would have been much point to it. I told you, Harry, I believe you – personally.'

'Then what the hell do you want?'

'Some help from you,' the big man said mildly.

'From me? How can I help you?'

Well, you want to find your partner's murderer, don't you?'

'No, I bloody don't!'

Pope looked at Steadman in surprise. 'Dear me, Harry! You don't really mean that.'

'Listen to me, Pope. I've seen enough killing for revenge to last me a lifetime. I've had enough. It's all burned out of me. Can you understand that?'

'But Mrs Wyeth was an innocent bystander. Surely you can't let her death go unaccounted for?'

'Can't I?'

'I think you're trying to convince yourself you can. But it won't work, Harry, I can assure you. You've had five years to get over your last bout of bloodletting, five years for that passion inside you to simmer. It's still there, make no mistake.'

'You're wrong.'

Pope smiled coldly. 'It makes no difference. You're still going to help us.' Steadman shook his head, but the big man held up a hand. 'Just hear me out first,' he said to the investigator. 'You said Goldblatt only wanted you to find out what had happened to their missing agent, Baruch Kanaan. Correct?'

Steadman nodded.

'And did they tell you his mission in England?'

'He was to contact an arms dealer to place an order for weapons,' Steadman said tiredly.

'The arms dealer was Edward Gant.'

'Yes. How did you know?'

'Gant is a man we've been watching for a very long time now. Unfortunately, he's influential, and not a man to intimidate.'

'The Israelis think he's supplying weapons to terrorists, as well as training them.'

'Oh, he is. Has been for some years.'

'You know that? And you've done nothing about it?'

'Nothing we could do. Never been caught red-handed.'

'You couldn't have warned him not to?'

Pope scoffed. 'He would have laughed in our faces, Harry. He's a very unusual man, our Mr Gant. The outrage last night is a mark of his manic confidence.'

'You *know* he killed Maggie?'

'No proof. We've put the lid on this murder for now, Harry. You won't be bothered by police, or reporters for the moment.'

'But how ...'

'It needed to be done – just for now. Publicity is the last thing we want at the moment. Apart from finding the missing agent, did Goldblatt want you to do any other investigating?'

'He wanted me to dig up any evidence on Gant that I could.'

'What sort of evidence?'

'His dealings with terrorists.'

'Nothing else?'

Steadman shrugged his shoulders. 'Anything I could get on him, I suppose.'

Pope took a deep breath, then quickly let the air escape. 'I don't think our friend Goldblatt has been entirely honest with you, Harry,' he said. 'True, the Israelis would like to provide proof to the British Government of Gant's clandestine dealings, but their interest goes beyond that.' The big man paused and drained the last of his cold tea. He placed the cup and saucer at his feet and dabbed at his moist lips with a neatly folded handkerchief from his overcoat pocket.

'Are you aware of the growing revival of Nazism throughout the world, Harry? Perhaps not, because it goes under many different names and guises. You may imagine such fanaticism could never become a threat again after the last World War, but you'd be wrong. It's a cancer spreading throughout the world, a parasite feeding on political unrest, poverty – and terrorist activity. Do you know, for example, that an extreme right-wing group from Belgium known as the Flemish New Order are fighting with the UDA in Ireland? They are not alone. You'll find other right-wing groups encouraging wars and becoming involved in them in many countries, supplying money, *supplying arms*'.

Steadman looked sharply at Pope. 'Gant?'

'In this country, and in America, we have several such organizations, the National Front here and the National Socialist Party in America being the more obvious. But lurking beneath these, and well in the shadows, are the more sinister factions such as Column 88, and these Hitlerite movements are growing, many joining in the common cause. I hardly need tell you of these organizations' detestation for everything Jewish. We believe Gant is at the head of one of the most powerful, but shadowy, Nazi organizations, right here in Britain. The Thule Gesellschaft.'

'That's why Mossad are interested in Gant? Not because he deals with terrorists?'

'Oh no, no. Both. One goes with the other.'

'But why this story about Baruch?'

'Because it's true. They wanted to hire you to find him – anything else was incidental. But Baruch's purpose was not to find proof of Gant's dealings with Arab terrorists, but to find out more of this Thule Society, this Thule Gesellschaft. It would seem he found out too much.'

'As did Maggie.'

'Yes, we think so. Only this kind of fanaticism could breed such killers as these. She must have unearthed something they weren't prepared to let become common knowledge.'

The investigator's shoulders slumped. 'My God, in this day and age ...' he said wearily.

'Especially in this day and age.'

'But why didn't Goldblatt tell me the whole story? Why would he let me walk into a set-up like that without warning?'

'I should imagine he thought it safer for you not to know. He wanted to hire you for a fairly routine investigation job, not to get you involved in this Hitlerite movement.'

'It didn't protect Maggie.'

'No, they underestimated the fanatical dedication of this group. I suppose they thought using her was even safer than your becoming involved. It's all very regrettable.'

'Regrettable? What do you intend to do about it?'

'What do you intend to do, Harry?'

'Me? You're Security. It's up to you to do something.'

'We will. With your help!'

'Sorry. I want nothing to do with it.'

'Did I offer you a choice, Harry?' Pope's tone was pleasant, but there was a sinister intent to the words. 'We could get you in so many ways. Suspicion of spying for Israel would do for a start. Coupled with suspicion of murder, of course.'

'Murder? You can't ...'

'We can, Harry, and make no mistake – we will.' All hint of pleasantness was suddenly gone. 'We'd have to let you go eventually on those counts, of course, but then we'd ruin your business in this country for you, and in most other countries as well. Law forces of the world like to co-operate nowadays, Harry. It's in all our interests.'

'Bastard!'

With an effort, the fat man leaned forward, elbows on knees, and the pleasantness came back to his features. 'Look,' he said, his voice gentle, 'I know you're just stubborn enough to resist, even if you bankrupted yourself. But take a good look at yourself. Inside, I mean. You want your partner's killers to pay, don't you? You can't ignore that old feeling inside you. You've suppressed it for years, but you can never lose it. You fought for Israel because you didn't like the way it was being oppressed. You fought because you hated to see the innocent hurt. You'll help us not because we'll force you to, but because you'll want to. You haven't lost that aggressiveness, Harry, you've just kept it smothered for some time.'

And Steadman realized the fat man was right; the urge to strike back was still in him. He wanted this man Gant to pay for Maggie's death just as he had wanted the Arab terrorists to pay for Lilla's. Maybe Pope's blackmail played some part in it, but he realized the old anger in him was the deciding factor.

'But why me?' he asked. 'You must have plenty more qualified.'

'None of our chaps fit in as nicely as you, Harry. You're a link, you see. A link between Mossad, Edward Gant – and now us. It gives us an advantage.'

'How can I help anyway? Gant knows who I am,' he said.

Pope settled back in his chair once again. 'Yes, he knows who you are, but that doesn't matter. He'll play out the game.'

'Game? This is just a game?' Steadman said incredulously.

'To someone like Gant, everything is a game. He enjoys subterfuge, enjoys testing his cunning against others.'

'And what's to stop him giving me the same treatment as Maggie?'

'Nothing. Except we'll be keeping an eye on you.'

'That fills me with confidence.'

Pope gave a small laugh. 'Well, you see, if he does make a move against you, we'll have him for that, won't we?'

The fat man laughed once again at the expression on Steadman's face, his stomach quivering with enjoyment. 'No, no Harry. I don't think even our Mr Gant can risk another murder so soon. Look, we need you because there's something in the wind. Something's about to happen and we don't know what. You'll be just a small part of this. Any information you come up with will just fit into a larger picture.'

'I feel like the sacrificial goat.'

'Nonsense. I told you, you'll be under surveillance all the time – we won't let any harm come to you. We want you to go back to your Mr Goldblatt and tell him you've changed your mind. You want Mrs Wyeth's murderers to be punished. He'll believe you because he needs you. You'll contact Gant on the grounds that you have a client who wishes to buy Gant's particular kind of weapons.'

'And if he refuses to deal with me?'

'He won't. He's an arms dealer and it would be too unprofessional not to enter discussions at least with a prospective client. He'll be curious about you too; I told you he is an arrogant man.

'Get close to him. He'll invite you to his private testing-grounds – it's his usual custom – and that's what we want to know about. Find out as much about the place as possible and what's going on there. That's all you need to do.'

'That's all?'

Pope pushed himself to his feet, his weight making the movement an effort. 'Yes,' he said. 'For the moment. Oh, you might find time to read this.' Pope reached for a green-covered file that had been lying unnoticed by Steadman on the sideboard. He handed it to the investigator. 'Not much in there I'm afraid, mostly recent stuff. Something of a mystery, our Mr Gant, but the file will provide you with some information on the man, mainly his recent dealings with the Arabs. Don't lose it, will you?'

Steadman regarded him with suspicion. None of it made sense. It just didn't add up.

'I'll see myself out, Harry. You get some rest now,' Pope said, walking to the door. His parting question gave the investigator even more cause for puzzlement.

'Just a small thing, Harry,' the big man said. 'Have you ever heard of the Heilige Lance?'

▪ 5 ▪

'It is not arms that decide, but the man behind them – always.'

ADOLF HITLER

'Only the loyal in blood can be loyal in spirit.'

HEINRICH HIMMLER

STEADMAN SLOUCHED LOW IN THE PASSENGER SEAT OF THE JAGUAR AND FLEXED his shoulder muscles against its soft back. He let his head loll slightly to one side and gazed up into the clear blue sky. It was one of those bright winter days, the air crisp and cold, hinting at the chill months to come, but invigorating with its keen-edged freshness.

As the car sped through country roads and busy towns, he reflected on Pope's last words to him. He had shaken his head – no, he'd never heard of the Heilige Lance, but what had that got to do with this Gant affair? The big man told him not to worry about it, it was just that the arms dealer seemed to have an interest in the Heilige Lance, which was in fact an ancient spearhead and he, Pope, had merely wondered if Steadman had any knowledge of the relic. With a wave of his hand as if to dismiss the subject, Pope had left Steadman with an even greater feeling of unease. Yet he felt a familiar excitement running through him, an old excitement that had been lying dormant for so many years. Now that he had no choice but to be involved, his reluctance had vanished, and increased adrenalin had sharpened his senses in the way it had years before when he had been a Mossad agent. Steadman appeared to be relaxed, but his thoughts and reflexes had become acute.

David Goldblatt and his companion, Hannah, had seemed relieved but not that surprised at his return, for it had been beyond their comprehension that he could walk away from the bizarre murder of his friend and business partner. The new Israelis no longer believed in turning the other cheek; in fact, they considered it cowardice and not humility to do so, and Steadman's past record showed him to be far from cowardly. His fire had been rekindled just as a cold blast would stir dying embers. His prior rejection of them had been due to shock and his passion had now overcome that shock. They understood. They needed him.

Peppercorn, a solicitor who had handled arms contracts for Steadman in the past, had arranged the meeting between him and Gant, and it was the solicitor's Jaguar in which they were travelling now. An arms exhibition was being held by the Ministry of Defence at their military range in Aldershot and Edward Gant, along with other private arms companies, would be present with his own weapons display. It was there that Gant and Steadman would meet.

'It was surprisingly smooth, you know,' Peppercorn's words broke into Steadman's thoughts. The investigator allowed his head to incline towards the solicitor.

'What was that?' he asked.

'Getting you the pass for the exhibition. Usually takes a while with these Ministry people, wanting to know who you are, what you've got your eye on, what country is it for? That sort of thing. They got you cleared in no time at all. Have you been pulling strings with your old military chums behind my back?'

'Old connections never die, Martin,' Steadman said. He guessed Pope had smoothed the way.

'Very opportune, really. Not an easy man to get hold of, this Gant. Better for you too, to meet him on neutral ground among his competitors. Should help your bargaining power psychologically.' He pulled out to overtake a heavy goods vehicle, then gently eased back into the stream of traffic. 'Why Gant's outfit in particular, Harry? Looking for something special?'

'Very special.' Steadman straightened from his slouched position knowing they would soon be at their destination.

'Well, Gant deals in specialities, all right. For Israel, is it?'

Steadman gave the solicitor a sharp look.

'Sorry, Harry. Shouldn't have asked at this stage,' Peppercorn grinned. 'I'll bet items like Swingfires and Blowpipes are on your shopping list though.'

It was an easy enough assumption for the solicitor to make, for not only did Gant deal specifically in these kinds of wire-controlled and hand-launched missiles, but Israel had suffered heavy losses when their tanks and jets had been attacked by such weapons in the 1973 conflict with the Egyptians. The Russian Strella shoulder-launched, infra-red-seeking anti-aircraft missile, for instance, had wreaked havoc on their air force, and if Steadman was representing the Israelis as Peppercorn more than suspected, then they would naturally regard such weapons as a priority for themselves.

'You'll know soon enough, Martin, when the deal is under way,' Steadman lied. The investigator hated to use his acquaintance in this way, but the deal had to look fairly legitimate so both parties could play out their deceptions without too much embarrassment. It was a game often utilized by politically opposite governments when superficial detente was not allowed to be harmed by private knowledge on both sides; undercurrents too dangerous to be acknowledged, but nevertheless secretly acted upon. He and Gant would play out the game until either one had reached the moment to strike. Steadman prayed the advantage would be his.

The car swung off the road and halted before tall, wire-mesh gates. An army sergeant stepped from an office built to one side of the gates and peered into the car. The two men showed their passes and the soldier gave a signal for the gates to be opened. The car swept through, making towards Long Valley where the solicitor knew they would find Gant.

Steadman mentally identified the various military vehicles they passed along the route: Chieftain and Scorpion tanks; Chieftain Bridge Layers; Spartan carriers; AT105 carriers; Fox armoured cars; Shorland SB301 troop carriers. Overhead, Gazelle helicopters hovered, occasionally swooping low. He was pleased he still had some knowledge of army hardware, but knew the progress made in other areas would leave him completely bemused. Computers were used to wage wars nowadays: microwave systems to detect the enemy, lasers to beam in on them, missiles to destroy. And the enemy had its own systems to counter every phase of an attack. The human brain could no longer react swiftly enough to cope in complex electronic warfare; computers had become the generals.

Muffled sounds of explosions came to their ears as they passed through a wooded area, which had warning signs of a quarry at intervals on their left.

'The Army showing off its Chobham armour, shouldn't wonder,' Pepper-corn said.

Steadman nodded. The tank armour had been a British breakthrough which provided three times greater protection than conventional steel armour. It had regenerated the life of the tank throughout the world, for missiles had all but made the vulnerable vehicle obsolescent; the new armour, a honeycomb of materials such as steel, ceramics and aluminium, added little to the weight or the cost of the tank. He could imagine the smug smiles on the faces of the British in the deep quarry below, as their armour was blasted with rockets and mortar shells for the benefit of their prospective foreign buyers.

The car soon arrived at a huge area filled with exhibition stands proudly displaying military hardware, ranging from laser rangefinders to barbed tape, from the multi-role MRCA combat aircraft to a set of webbing, from an AR18 rifle to pralidoxime mesylate counter-nerve-gas tablets.

Peppercorn drove the Jaguar into the allocated parking area and the two men stepped out. The noon sun was high and harsh in the sky, feebly trying to warm the autumn air but succeeding only in stealing the dampness from it. The solicitor reached back inside the car and pulled out an overcoat which he quickly donned.

'Deceptive, this weather,' he muttered. 'Catch a cold without knowing it.'

Steadman smiled. If Peppercorn knew the true nature of the man they were about to meet, his blood would run even colder.

They trudged across the field and past a long stand where foreign officers, diplomats and civil servants sat on wooden chairs, observing the antics of Strikers, Spartans, Scimitars and Scorpions as they paraded before them. As they walked, Peppercorn asked, 'Tell me, Harry, why Gant in particular? There are plenty of other dealers who sell similar weapons and, as far as I know, Gant has never dealt with the Israelis before.' He smiled at Steadman and added,

'Assuming your client is from Israel, of course. The contracts I've been involved in personally as far as Gant is concerned have been for Iran and some of the African states. To my knowledge, he's never been interested in selling to Israel.'

'Gant manufactures a wider range of more specialized items than most,' Steadman answered, 'from missiles to anti-terrorist devices. My client requires both and thinks he'll get a better deal by buying from the same source.' A little too pat, Steadman thought, but the solicitor seemed satisfied.

Peppercorn was too professional to press for the identity of Steadman's client any further, for that would soon be made clear the moment negotiations began; and besides, Steadman had virtually confirmed his suspicions in his last statement. Who else would he be buying for – the Arabs? Hardly, with his past associations.

'Ah, there he is,' Peppercorn said, pointing ahead.

The investigator's gaze followed the pointing finger and he saw a group of men gathered around a green-uniformed figure demonstrating a shoulder rocket-launcher. The uniform was unfamiliar to Steadman and he assumed it was merely worn by Gant's demonstrators to give individuality to his company.

'Which one is Gant?' he asked Peppercorn.

'The tall one in the middle. The one talking to the girl.'

Steadman had not noticed the girl in his eagerness to catch sight of the arms dealer, but now he briefly wondered what connections she could possibly have with someone like Gant. His eyes quickly flicked to the man beside her.

Gant was tall, even taller than Steadman, towering over the assembled group, who must have been foreign buyers judging by their dark-skinned features. His body was thin and seemed stiff, as though having little flexibility. The assumption was wrong, for as Gant turned to answer a question from one of the group, his body swivelled with a controlled grace. It was a small movement, but Steadman was a professional observer and the action revealed the man's hidden suppleness. As they advanced, Gant's attention became focused on them. He stood without moving for several moments and Steadman could feel himself being scrutinized with cold efficiency. He returned the stare and suddenly a chill ran through him. It was inexplicable, but he felt as though he were being drawn into a spider's web; and the man before him was well aware of the thought.

The visual link was broken when Gant turned to his prospective clients and excused himself. He broke away from the group and came forward to meet Steadman and the solicitor. Their eyes locked again and Steadman was only vaguely aware of the man in military uniform who followed the arms dealer.

Gant stopped two yards away from them so they had to keep walking to meet him. Steadman saw his eyes were light grey and he thought he detected a mocking amusement in them. The tall man's face was long and angular, high cheek-bones and hollowed cheeks giving it a slightly cadaverous appearance; his nose was strong with a firm bridge, and his high forehead, with short, light-brown hair swept back from it, held few wrinkles. He seemed younger than his years and emanated a strength that belied his gaunt frame. Only his neck gave an indication of the ravage the years had taken. It was long, therefore not easy to disguise with collar and tie, and its hollowed and wrinkled flesh caused a faint revulsion in Steadman.

'Good morning, Peppercorn,' Gant said, his eyes not leaving Steadman's. 'And this is Mr Steadman?' He raised a hand towards the investigator and once again, Steadman noticed the amusement flicker in them.

Reluctantly, Steadman grasped the proffered hand and returned the hardness of Gant's grip. The investigator loosened his hold, but the arms dealer held it firm and he was forced to resume his own pressure. There were no secrets between them as they stood that way for several seconds. Gant seemed to see into him and mocked what he saw; Steadman returned the unspoken challenge and even allowed his own glint of amusement to show. He noticed there were many tiny scars around the arms dealer's cheeks and mouth, only visible at such close range, and he briefly wondered what kind of accident would cause such a proliferation.

His hand was abruptly released and the investigator was uncertain if he hadn't imagined the whole exchange.

'This is Major Brannigan,' Gant said, inclining his body towards the soldier who had followed him. The major leaned forward and gave a swift handshake to Steadman and Peppercorn. He was a few inches shorter than Gant, and Steadman judged him to be in his early forties. Whereas he had detected the mockery in the arms dealer's eyes, Brannigan's showed an unrelenting hardness.

'And this is Miss Holly Miles who is taking advantage of her distant relationship to my late wife,' Gant said, stepping aside to allow a view of the girl who had followed both men and had been hidden by their tall figures.

'Louise Gant and my mother were cousins – of sorts,' she smiled apologetically and Steadman was surprised to hear her American accent, but then he remembered Gant's wife had come from the United States. He nodded at her and she acknowledged with a broader smile, flicking her long yellow hair to one side and behind an ear with delicate fingers. He noticed the Pentax draped around her neck.

'Pictures? Here?' he said quizzically.

'I'm a freelance writer,' she explained with a grin. 'I'm doing a feature on arms dealers for one of the Sunday magazines.'

'She used her flimsy connections with my family to persuade the magazine to give her the commission,' Gant interrupted, but his mocking tones now had more amusement in them than malice. Nevertheless there was a disquieting quality to his voice, a rasping sibilance that was slight, but seemed to create unease in the people around him. 'Major Brannigan is keeping an eye on her, making sure she doesn't photograph the wrong things.'

Brannigan did not seem in the least amused.

'Now, Mr Steadman,' Gant said, his voice suddenly becoming brusque. 'Peppercorn tells me you have a client who is in the market for certain types of weapons which I have a reputation for producing rather well.'

'That's right,' Steadman answered, his attention now diverted back to the arms dealer.

'May we establish from the start who your client is?'

'I'm afraid that will have to wait until I'm satisfied you can meet all our requirements,' Steadman countered.

'Very well, that's not unusual. Can you tell me specifically what you are looking for?'

'There's quite a list. I have our broad order for you here.' Steadman produced an envelope containing a detailed list, compiled by himself and Goldblatt, of armaments and defensive equipment that Israel would logically need but were, at the moment, obtained from other sources. It had a bias towards the type of weapons produced in Gant's factories. He handed it to the arms dealer. 'I believe you manufacture most of these items.'

Gant scrutinized the list, nodding occasionally. 'Yes, most of these are in our range,' he said, and Steadman suddenly found it difficult to believe it was all a charade. The arms dealer appeared to be perfectly sincere. 'I have a few other items, in fact, that you might also be interested in. Our new laser sniper rifle, for example, accurate up to a distance of half-a-mile. Our submachine-gun, similar to the Ingram but far more accurate, made with many plastic components and very cheaply mass-produced.' The mockery seemed to return to Gant's eyes then, and he said, 'I also have certain kinds of missiles, small and convenient to launch, but with enough power to bring down a Jumbo jet.'

There seemed to be some special significance to the words, for Gant said them slowly and deliberately, his gaze fixed steadily on Steadman and throwing out some kind of challenge.

'Sounds interesting,' he said, and was suddenly aware that the exchange had not gone unnoticed among the other members of the small group. There was a tenseness in their silence. Even the girl had a puzzled expression on her face.

'You think your client could have a use for such a weapon?' Gant asked, raising his eyebrows.

'Possibly. It would depend on the price,' Steadman answered.

'Of course. Would you like to see it?'

'Yes, I would.'

'Difficult to demonstrate, of course.' Gant gave a small laugh and Steadman smiled back agreeably. 'But I think we can show you its range and power. Why don't you ring me at my office tomorrow and we'll fix something. Peppercorn has the number.'

'That would be fine.'

'In the meantime, I'll go through your list and work out some figures for you. I take it your client isn't too frightened of figures, is he?' Again the mocking tones.

'It takes more than that,' said Steadman, still smiling.

'Yes, I'm sure. You must excuse me now. I'm afraid our visitors from Latin America are rather demanding today,' he gestured towards the gathering he had just left, 'and I think they're in a buying mood. And you, too, Miss Miles, will have to forgive my rudeness. I'm afraid business transactions of this nature might embarrass your magazine. If not, perhaps our government, if they saw it in print. Why not take the time to tell Mr Steadman the nature of your article on armament sales and show him some of the nasty weapons you've discovered here today. He may have a view on the subject.'

With one last glance at Steadman, he turned and walked back to his group of impatient foreign buyers.

'Er, yes, I'm afraid I have certain duties to perform, too,' Major Brannigan suddenly said. 'I'll have to take your camera with me, though. I'm sure you've got enough shots for today, anyway.' He held a hand out and, with a shrug, the girl lifted the Pentax from her neck and gave it to the major. 'Thank you,' Brannigan said. 'I'll send it down to the sergeant on the gate and you can collect it when you leave.' With that, he strode briskly away.

'Well, that was short and sweet,' said Peppercorn turning to Steadman and the girl. 'I think Gant will show you some things that'll surprise you, Harry.'

'I don't doubt it,' the investigator said wryly.

'Now then, Miss Miles,' the solicitor said, turning on the charm. 'It's very rare to find such blue-denimed beauty at these functions. Makes a welcome change from khaki. Why don't we all wander down to the big top and have a little drink?'

The girl glanced at Steadman and he said, 'I could use one.'

'Okay, so could I. Lead on.'

Once inside the large tent, Peppercorn threw himself in quest of drinks into the crowd that pressed itself to the bar, leaving Steadman and the American journalist alone.

'Are you really a distant relative of Gant's?' Steadman asked her, finding her face an agreeable distraction from the tension before.

She laughed. 'Well, let's say my mother was a distant cousin to Mr Gant's late wife. I'm surprised he still allowed me to interview him, though. These arms dealers are usually shy people.'

'Yes, publicity is one thing they don't need. I'm surprised he did.'

'It took a long, long time, I can tell you. Then suddenly, last week, right out of the blue, he agreed.'

'What changed his mind?' Steadman asked, puzzled.

'I've no idea. Perhaps his wife's memory stirred his conscience; he had little enough to do with her relatives when she was alive.'

'Do you know what she died of.'

'Yes. She was killed in a car crash.'

'Have you found out much about him. He seems a very private man.'

'He is. But I've spent some days with him and he's let me photograph most of what I want. He suddenly seems to want to exploit his name – well maybe not quite his name, but the new weapons he's producing, at least.' She frowned and bit the nail on the small finger of her right hand. 'I don't know, it's as if he's suddenly emerging from his dark shell, and actively seeking publicity.'

The idea somehow worried Steadman. Why should a man like Edward Gant, whose business transactions had always been kept in the shadows, suddenly emerge into the public eye? It made little sense.

He decided to change the subject. 'How long have you been in England?' he asked.

'Oh, about six months now. I used to roam the world before that, writing stories, taking pictures to go with them. I used to work for a syndicate, but now I prefer to find my own commissions. It makes me feel more free to come and go as I like.'

Peppercorn returned at that moment, carrying a Campari for the girl, vodka for Steadman and a gin drowned in tonic for himself, all precariously held in two hands.

'Look, Harry,' he said urgently. 'I've just bumped into a couple of people I know. It could lead to a nice little bit of business for me so I've rather selfishly arranged to have a spot of lunch with them. I hope you don't mind?'

Steadman shook his head, taking the Campari and vodka from his friend's outstretched fingers. 'Don't worry about it.'

'I could meet you back here afterwards and take you back to town?' the solicitor said anxiously.

'It's okay. I'll catch a train.'

'I could give you a lift,' said the girl.

'Ah, there you are, all settled.' Peppercorn grinned with satisfaction.

'Fine,' said Steadman, taking a swallow of his drink. The vodka scorched his throat, but it felt good.

'Right, must get back to them, Harry,' said the solicitor. 'I'll get my secretary to give you Gant's telephone number.' He was already moving away. 'Let me know how you get on and when you want me to do my bit. 'Bye for now, er, Miss Miles. Hope to see you again.'

The girl chuckled at the solicitor's retreating figure as it backed into a black-skinned dignatory who eyed him with wide-eyed alarm.

'Thanks for the lift,' Steadman said as her attention returned to him.

'I have to report back to the magazine, anyway. They'll want to know my progress.' She looked directly into Steadman's eyes. 'Tell me about yourself. Have you always been involved in the sale of weapons?'

'No, not always. I've spent a good portion of my life in the army.'

Holly raised her eyebrows. 'You don't look the military type,' she said.

Steadman grinned, presuming the girl meant it as a compliment.

'What made you leave?' she asked, sipping at the Campari.

'Oh, I decided I'd had enough of the British Army. There were other things to do.'

'Like buying and selling arms?'

'Among other things. I eventually joined an enquiry agency.'

'An enquiry agency? You're a gumshoe?'

Steadman laughed. 'It's a long time since I've been called that.'

Holly laughed with him. 'Sorry. You don't look like Sam Spade either.'

'Not many of us do. As a matter of fact, my partner ...' He suddenly broke off and Holly saw the pain in his eyes.

'Is something wrong?' she asked.

Steadman took a large swallow of vodka, then answered, 'I was going to say my partner is a woman. She's dead now.'

'I'm sorry, Harry.'

He shrugged.

'Was it recent?' she asked, then was puzzled by the strange smile on his face and the hardness in his eyes.

'Very,' he replied. 'Let's drop it, eh? Tell me more about your article. Any startling discoveries about Gant?' The question was put lightly, but Holly sensed its seriousness.

'Oh, I haven't got that close. Everything I've seen, everything he's told me, all seems studied, as though he's only revealing a top layer. I get the feeling there's plenty more layers underneath. Usually, when you do this kind of in-depth study of a person, you find out certain things by accident – a slip of the tongue, or maybe they get carried away with their own reminiscences. But Edward Gant's information has been guarded all along. I just can't get under the surface.'

'You've been to his home?'

'The one near Guildford, yes. I spent two days there and he's invited me back again. It's a small mansion in about six or seven acres of grounds; very quiet, very private.'

'Does he have another place?'

'Well, it seems so. When I was there he seemed to have a constant stream of visitors – some were important people, too – and I did hear them making arrangements for some kind of get-together in his home on the west coast. Gant was deliberately vague when I asked him about it though, but he did say it was a testing-ground for some of his more powerful weapons.'

'Do you know exactly where it is?'

'No. I asked directly, but he told me that in the arms business and especially with innovatory weapons, testing-sites were strictly private and their locations, as far as possible, kept secret. He clammed up after that.'

'These visitors. You said some were important.'

'You're kind of curious, aren't you? I guess that goes with the job, huh?'

'I guess it does,' Steadman said. 'Really, it's just that I want to know as much about Gant as possible so I can make sure I get a good deal for my clients. It might help to know his connections, that's all.'

'Okay. 'Nough said. A couple of them were politicians – minor ones, I may add. The others I recognized as industrialists and a few of your City guys. I can't put names to their faces, though.'

'Never mind. Would you like another?' Steadman pointed to the girl's empty glass.

'Er, no. I think I'd like to get back to town now. Are you ready to leave?'

Steadman drained his glass, then nodded. As he took Holly's arm and guided her through the crowded tent, the morning's displays over, the preliminary discussions having taken place, he caught sight of Major Brannigan listening politely to a foreign visitor. The major caught his eye, but gave no acknowledgement.

Steadman and the girl left the tent and the major's eyes followed them until they had disappeared from view.

Holly led the investigator towards her car, a bright yellow Mini. They climbed in and Holly snapped on her seat-belt. The car threaded its way through the other parked vehicles and turned into the gravelled roadway. It picked up speed and they left the display area with its business-like stands and array of sophisticated machinery of death.

'Tell me, Harry,' Holly said. 'Do you ever get a conscience about the weapons you buy?'

'Occasionally,' he replied, 'but greed generally manages to overcome it.'

She looked at him quickly, surprised at his rancour.

'I'm sorry,' she apologized. 'I didn't mean to sound high-minded.'

He studied her profile for a few moments, then said, 'I'm sorry, too. I didn't mean to snap. It's really a question of who you're buying for. There are certain countries and groups I would have nothing to do with, while there are others I have every sympathy for. Of course, dealers aren't supposed to have sympathy for any particular cause, it should be strictly business, but there are laws governing just who they can sell to.'

'And do you have a sympathy for the cause of the people you are negotiating for?'

'I used to,' was all he would say.

The road was winding through the wooded area now and the ground on either side was thick with fallen leaves. Steadman turned to the girl again and could not help glancing down at her body, her long legs bent to accommodate the slightly cramped space of the Mini. Her wrists were slender, yet handled the wheel firmly, and there was a quiet strength about her that had not been apparent on first sight. She suddenly turned her head towards him, feeling his gaze on her, and for a brief moment, something passed between them. Her attention went back to the road and he wondered if he had only imagined the understanding in her look.

He, too, turned his head back towards the road, and it was at that moment that the tank roared from the trees on their left.

▪ 6 ▪

'Brutality is respected. *Brutality and physical strength. The plain man in the street respects nothing but brutal strength and ruthlessness – women, too, for that matter, women and children. The people need wholesome fear. They want to fear something. They want someone to frighten them and make them shudderingly submissive. Haven't you seen everywhere that after boxing-matches, the beaten ones are the first to join the party as new members? Why babble about brutality and be indignant about tortures? The masses want that. They need something that will give them a thrill of horror.'*

ADOLF HITLER

The girl saw the Chieftain emerging from the trees a fraction of a second later than Steadman. Instinctively, her foot jammed down on the accelerator and the little car surged forward in an effort to escape the fifty-two tons of crushing metal.

Steadman automatically pushed himself away from his side of the car, thankful that he wasn't restricted by a seat-belt, and taking care not to crowd the girl. Their lives depended on her reaction. The tank loomed larger in his window-framed vision until it filled the rectangular shape completely, and the investigator clenched his teeth against the anticipated impact. But the blackness left the window nearest to him and he knew there might just be a chance to squeeze by the cumbersome monster.

The Chieftain had been too close, though, and it smashed into the back of the Mini, slewing the car round, mercifully pushing rather than crushing. The screaming of tearing metal and shattered glass filled their ears as the girl fought to control the car's spin. It slid across the road and spun into a tree, almost facing the way they had just come.

Again it was Steadman's side which took the brunt of the crash, but he had steadied himself by pushing one hand against the dashboard and the other around the back of the driver's seat. His head snapped back with the impact, but the car's buckled metal failed to touch him.

He reached for the girl whose head hung low on her chest. She still clutched the steering-wheel, her seat-belt preventing her from being tossed around. He took her chin and her head came up and turned towards him. With relief, he saw she had not been hurt, but was stunned by the impact. Her eyes were wide and looked questioningly at him.

'Bloody fools!' Steadman shouted, the anger in him now rising over the shock. He looked through the windscreen at the green goliath completely blocking the road in front of them. 'Why didn't they check to see if the road was clear before they tried to cross!' He was about to push the passenger door of the Mini open when the tank began moving backwards, the pin-jointed links of its tracks spitting up gravel from the roadway. The movement puzzled Steadman into immobility for a moment, then he saw the tank stop. Its far-side track gripped the road and began to go forward once again, the near-side track rotating at a slower pace. The Chieftain was turning towards them.

'Holly, I think …' he began to say, but the tank's objective became frighteningly clear. 'He's going to ram us again!'

The girl's face was horror-struck and Steadman knew he would never have time to release her from the seat-belt and get her out of the car before the tank crushed it to pieces.

'Drive!' he screamed at her. 'Into the trees!'

Fortunately, the engine was still running, for she had dipped the clutch as she had braked, and her feet still had both pedals pressed to the floor. Her eyes suddenly seemed to focus as she realized the further danger, and she reacted to Steadman's command. Pushing the gear-lever into first, she gunned the engine and the car leapt forward. Steadman prayed the back wheel hadn't been damaged in the crash, then once again clenched his teeth as the tank loomed up ahead of them.

It seemed there would be no escaping the mountain of metal this time as it rushed towards them, completely blocking their path, but Holly wrenched the wheel hard to her left and the Mini passed beneath the long 120mm gun of the Chieftain, scraping its side against the front of the tank's right-hand tracks. Metal clanged and buckled once more as the car was knocked to one side, but Holly managed to control the sideways deflection and the car skidded into the trees, its wheels tearing at the damp earth and leaves to maintain a grip. She turned the wheel to the right to avoid a tree which was directly in their path, but it was too late, and again Steadman's side of the car took a vicious blow against its metalwork.

The Mini stopped and Holly declutched to prevent the engine stalling. Steadman glanced back through the rear window and saw that the Chieftain was swiftly turning towards them.

'For Christ's sake, move it!' Steadman knew that even if the girl got clear, his door was jammed up against the side of the tree which would mean he'd have to try and scramble out on her side. The odds weren't promising.

The girl must have realized the same, and he was thankful for her courage in staying with him. The car moved forward a few inches, then sank back into the grooves it had dug for itself. Once again, the tank completely filled Steadman's view from the rear window and seemed poised to overwhelm them.

Then the car lurched forward, the wheels spinning but gaining a small grip, enough to draw them from the crushing belly of the Chieftain. It gathered speed as the wheels found firmer ground and Steadman saw the tank hit the tree they had skidded into, tilting it as though it were on a swivel, then coming on, chasing them as an armadillo would chase a millipede.

The car's speed was limited, for Holly had to steer a careful path through the trees and undergrowth, whereas the tank had only to avoid the stoutest trees, the other less firm trees and undergrowth easily succumbing to its massive weight. Steadman urged the girl on, his eyes constantly switching from the path ahead to the tank behind. He was shocked at the audacity of the attack, at Gant's – it *had* to be Gant behind it – arrogant confidence that he could get away with two outrageous murders within just a few days. First Maggie, now him. And the girl. Three murders.

Holly's eyes were narrowed in concentration as she struggled to keep the car under control on the slippery surface of leaves, and he saw that although there was fear in her there was no panic.

The Mini suddenly bumped over a fallen branch hidden by leaves and it rose into the air, throwing the passengers forward and up. Holly's seat-belt and her grip on the wheel checked her movement, but Steadman was tossed towards the windscreen. His arm struck the window first and fortunately the glass held. His head hit the roof of the car and he was thrown back into his seat, dazed but still conscious.

The car spun round as it landed and this time Holly lost control completely. It bounced off a tree and came to rest sideways on to the advancing tank. Steadman saw that the ground sloped down into a dip on his side of the car. The engine had stalled and for a few valuable seconds, Holly was too numbed by the sudden jolt to move. Steadman shook the haze from his head and looked at the girl. Beyond her profile, he saw the Chieftain looming larger and larger. Holly quickly looked to her right and saw that the tank was only a few yards from them and she desperately reached forward for the keys in the ignition. She twisted them viciously and depressed the accelerator to the floor. The engine roared and the car lurched forward and stalled again; in her haste she had left it still in gear. The tank was only a yard away.

Steadman knew they wouldn't make it and was reaching for the release on the girl's seat-belt in a vain attempt to pull her from the car on his side, when the Chieftain tank ploughed into them.

The noise of crunching metal, the rumbling of the tank's engines, and Holly's scream combined into a terrifying sound. The car on her side rose into the air and Steadman was thrown back against the passenger door. The world outside the small windows spun round crazily as the car was pushed completely over, first on to its side, then on to its back. The trees and the sky began to spin even faster as the Mini rolled over the brink of the dip it had come to rest on. Steadman threw one arm around the back of his seat and pushed the other against the dashboard in an attempt to wedge himself as the car rolled over and over down the slope. The dip had saved their lives for that moment, for if the car hadn't plunged into it, then it would have been crushed completely under the massive bulk of the tank.

For those few nauseating seconds as the car rolled down, Steadman lost his senses. He still managed to keep his grip on the seat and the dashboard through sheer reaction, only losing that hold when the car crashed to a halt on its back. He found himself lying bundled on the upturned roof of the car when he opened his eyes. He wasn't sure if he had blacked out or his mind had just gone blank for a few moments, but instinct told him he had no time to lose. From his curled-up position inside the overturned Mini, he could see back up the slope, and the tank poised at the top, a huge metallic predator making ready to plunge for the kill.

He pulled himself around on the buckled metal and saw Holly hanging upside down, her head and shoulders against the roof, her lower body still trapped by the seat-belt. Her eyes were closed, but when he called her name, they opened and looked towards him.

'Jesus Christ!' she said.

He scrambled into a better position to reach her, barely registering the fact that no sudden pain bespoke broken bones. He pressed the button to release her, taking her weight with his arm. She slid to the roof which was now the floor.

'We've got to get out!' he told her urgently. 'The tank'll be coming down after us.' He reached past her and tried to push open the driver's door. It opened two inches then jammed solidly into the hard earth.

He quickly turned around and tried the door on his side and it opened easily. He pushed it wide and to his horror saw the Chieftain had begun its descent. This time, the Mini would be squashed flat under the impact. Steadman reached back for the girl and yanked her towards him, heedless of any harm she might have suffered in the crash. She gasped at his roughness, but threw herself forward, realizing their danger. They scrambled from the car together and the tank towered above them, its speed increased by the angle of the slope.

Holly tried to scramble to one side, but Steadman knew it was already too late. The sheer width of the tank allowed them no room for escape – they would be crushed by either of its two-foot-wide set of tracks. He grabbed her arm and threw her upwards towards the onrushing monster. She screamed in fright, not understanding his motives. He pushed her down hard into the earth, throwing a protective arm over her head, holding her there, trying to make them both as flat as possible.

Everything went black as the Chieftain rumbled over them, and Steadman pressed his face close to Holly's, exerting pressure on her with his arm to make sure she didn't try to rise in panic. The underbelly of the tank was only inches from their bodies and the smell of diesel fumes and oil was overpowering. The investigator prayed that the angle of the slope would not alter before the vehicle had passed completely over them, for if it did, the tank's rear end would become lower as the main body righted its angle, and their bodies would be scraped into the earth.

They felt the tank shudder as it ploughed into the Mini, and the screech of grinding metal threw fresh terror into them.

'Try to move upwards!' he screamed at her over the noise. 'Keep moving up, but keep low!'

They inched forward as the tank sped over them, for any distance they gained could save their lives. He saw the rectangle of daylight ahead and realized the angle was narrowing; the juddering tank was beginning to level. He closed his eyes and stopped moving forward, knowing there was nothing they could do to save themselves now. He pressed himself close to Holly, holding her head against his, his lips against her cheek.

The noise of the car being crushed rose to a crescendo and suddenly he felt all movement around them judder to a halt. The tank's engine still roared on, but the clanking links of its tracks had ceased to move. The small car's tough little body had halted the tank's progress momentarily and Steadman realized they had been granted a few seconds' grace.

'Quick, move!' he yelled at the girl, and began to pull her up with him. With relief, he felt her body begin to worm its way up; she hadn't frozen.

The Chieftain's engine began to whine and suddenly it lurched forward again, demolishing the yellow car completely. But they were clear. Steadman reached safety first, then dragged the girl after him just as the tank's rear dropped and almost brushed the soil of the slope.

Holly fell against him and they stood drawing in deep breaths, their bodies heaving. Steadman looked back at the tank and could see nothing of the flattened Mini. The Chieftain was motionless and, irrationally, Steadman had the feeling the battle vehicle was a living thing, a mechanical beast that had somehow come to life to destroy them. It seemed to be watching them.

The tracks began to clank into life once again, but this time they had changed direction. The tank was coming back for them.

'Run!' he shouted, pushing the girl forward but keeping a grip on her arm in case she should fall. The slope would have been too treacherous to have attempted to climb, so they ran along the side of it, stumbling once and rolling down into the gully created by the dip. Steadman pulled the girl to her feet and looked into her face anxiously and again he felt an understanding pass between them. The Chieftain had turned its huge bulk towards them and now it made its destructive way along the gully, picking up speed as it came. They fled from it.

Leafless branches tore at their clothes and skin as they stumbled through the undergrowth, their throats raw with the effort of breathing. The gully took on a gentle slope and soon they were free of the dip, running towards an area of dense bracken and bramble. Steadman glanced back over his shoulder and saw they were out of the tank's vision.

'In there,' he gasped, pointing at the thick canopy, and they plunged into the bracken, wading deep, ignoring the stings of resisting bramble. They heard the rumbling of the tank behind them as it cleared the rise, and Steadman pulled the girl to the ground, the foliage closing around them. He lost sight of the tank but could still hear its engine. They tried to control their breathing as though the mechanical dinosaur might hear and seek them out.

'Why?' Holly whispered, desperation in her voice. 'Why are they trying to kill us?'

Steadman put a finger to her lips and shook his head. The Chieftain's engine seemed to be getting louder and they could hear the crashing of broken undergrowth. The investigator raised his head slightly to catch sight of the approaching vehicle and nearly cried out when he saw it was heading straight towards them. It was as if it could sense their presence.

They ran again, away from their relentless pursuer, lost in the woodland, not knowing in which direction lay the road. Bursting free of the bracken they discovered the ground was rising slightly, but they couldn't see what lay beyond the incline. Their muscles were aching now, their bodies bruised. Steadman dragged the girl forward, knowing she could not carry on much further. Her legs were dragging and she leaned heavily against him. They heard a muffled explosion and something vaguely registered in Steadman's head.

He put one arm around Holly's waist and helped her up, pulling her towards the incline. The tank, now relatively unimpeded by trees, was gaining on them. They staggered on and finally reached the top of the gentle slope. The ground dropped away dramatically into a vast quarry.

'It's the explosives' testing-ground,' said Steadman, realizing now why the muffled explosion moments earlier had registered in his mind. Deep below, they could see the long slabs of concrete, shelters for observers in the man-made valley, as they witnessed the damage caused by rockets, mortars and shell-fire.

Battered skeletal frames of army vehicles lay scattered around the grey plain, victims of weapons turned against them to demonstrate their destroyers' deadliness. As they watched, they saw a rocket leave the muzzle of a launcher held on a soldier's shoulder, and strike what must have been a sheet of Chobham armour three hundred yards away; the rocket exploded on impact but the metal sheet appeared to remain undented.

'We're trapped!' the girl cried and seemed to be about to sink to her knees in despair.

Steadman held her steady and pointed towards a clump of gorse that ran along the rim of the huge pit. 'In there!' he yelled at her. 'We may be able to hide from them!'

They stumbled towards the gorse patch and threw themselves into it, keeping as far away from the cliff edge as possible. They buried themselves in the waist-high spiky bushes, but Steadman forced them on, crawling on hands and knees until they were in the centre of the patch. They lay there panting and the investigator put an arm around the frightened girl's shoulders, pulling her towards him. He felt her trembling against his chest and tightened his grip on her. Her confusion was adding to her fear.

He decided he had to risk seeing if the men – or man – in the tank had observed their desperate run for cover. The rumble of the Chieftain was close and their position too vulnerable if their location was known.

He raised his head above the gorse and was dismayed when he saw the close proximity of the armoured vehicle. And it was headed straight towards them, increasing speed as it came, knowing where they were as if by instinct. He dragged the girl up and she screamed when she saw the approaching tank. She began to move away but he held her tight, to prevent her from backing towards the quarry's edge. He pulled her through the gorse, running to their left in a desperate attempt to dodge their uncanny and unerring pursuer; but a stout root, hidden from his view, tripped him and they both went down in a heap, the winter foliage cruelly ripping at their faces and hands. Holly lay slumped against him, unwilling or unable to move any more, giving in to their relentless hunter, too exhausted, too despairing to go on.

The tank was above them, the long phallic muzzle of its gun barrel passing over their heads like an antenna sensing their presence. In one last hopeless gesture of defiance, Steadman picked up the girl bodily, and with all the strength he could gather, leapt to one side, afraid to go under the tank again in case it stopped above them to grind its tracks backwards and forwards until their bodies had been crushed into the ground.

He almost made it, but the right-hand track caught his shoulder and he went down. The girl was clear, thrown forward by his rush, and she saw his body fall beneath the tank's wheels. Fortunately for Steadman, he had fallen into the angled space between the upper and lower wheels of the Chieftain, and it was enough to save the investigator from being dragged beneath the vehicle: he kept rolling, pushing himself away from the deadly moving links. He was inches clear, then suddenly found his movement checked. The back of his jacket was caught beneath the grinding track. He tried desperately to prevent his weight being pulled back under and his hands reached out to clutch roots – anything to hold on to.

Holly clamped her hands around his wrists and pulled with all her strength, her eyes tightly closed against the effort. Steadman felt his jacket tear, then suddenly he was free and moving forward into her arms. They clutched at each other as the tank lumbered by.

Steadman twisted his head, ready to pull the girl up and begin running again.

His eyes widened when he saw the Chieftain had not decreased its speed, but was trundling onwards towards the quarry's edge only feet away. The tracks spun in free air and screeched when the huge vehicle tilted forward, the edge of the cliff breaking away under its weight. The tank gave Steadman a view of its metal underbelly before sliding forward, the bare tracks now spinning in the air. Then it was gone, careering down towards the grey plain two hundred feet below.

Steadman scrambled forward, carefully avoiding the freshly broken earth at the cliff's edge, and was in time to see the Chieftain bounce off the limestone wall of the cliff and turn over, its gun pointing towards the sky. It bounced again, and again, then the tank seemed to disintegrate. Its tracks tore loose, and ran as streamers behind the main body; its gun caught against the rock-face as the tank turned over, and the turret was ripped from the hull. The fuel tank must have been punctured, for suddenly a bright flame flowered from the body and the blast of the explosion swept back up against the cliff face and hot air seared Steadman's face. A large, more powerful explosion joined the first almost immediately, and he realized the Chieftain had been carrying live ammunition.

The Chieftain reached the bottom of the quarry in many separate pieces.

Steadman blinked his eyes, moistening them against the scorching heat of the blast, and he saw figures emerging from behind concrete shelters. They were too far away for him to see their expressions, their faces just white blobs, but their shock was apparent in their stance.

He pushed himself away from the edge and scrambled back through the rough gorse towards the sobbing girl.

▪ 7 ▪

STEADMAN DREW BACK THE COVERS OF THE BED AND GAZED DOWN AT HOLLY'S golden body. The tips of her breasts were pink and alive, protruding from their soft mounds, erect and excited. His eyes followed the curve of her waist and reached the rise of her hip, then travelled inwards along the triangle that dipped into her smooth thighs. Her stomach was flat and had a firmness that told of muscles developed just beneath the skin; her whole body had that firmness to it, soft to look at and to touch, but conditioned to a surprising toughness.

'Please,' she said, looking up at him, 'just hold me.'

He was aware of his hardness as her eyes searched his body too, and he slid in beside her, pulling the sheets up to their shoulders, encircling an arm around her waist, drawing her to him. They stayed that way, their bodies pressed together, enjoying each other's warmth, relaxing into one another.

The girl had surprised Steadman earlier that day. Army vehicles had arrived at the top of the quarry within seconds of the tank's descent and questions had been fired at them mercilessly. Holly had recovered from her tear-shedding and remained calm at the barrage, whereas Steadman had soon lost his temper and flayed the curious officers with his tongue. They had been taken into the Aldershot HQ and the questioning had continued. Why had they wandered off the road towards the quarry? Hadn't they seen the warning signs? Why should a Chieftain chase them? Hadn't they just driven into the woods into the path of the tank? What had made the Chieftain plunge into the quarry? Had they spoken to the crew at any time?

All through the interrogation, the girl had answered quietly and firmly, showing no sign of the ordeal she had been through, apart from the physical aspect – her clothes were torn in places and scratches showed on her hands and face. Then she had turned the interview about, demanding to know why there was not stronger security on the site, and why they were being treated like offenders when it was *they* who would be suing the British Army.

The Lieutenant-Colonel in charge of the questioning was taken aback by the sudden onslaught and Steadman had smiled at his confusion. The arrival of

Major Brannigan, who vouched for their identities, had brought the hasty inquisition to a close. Reserved apologies and assurances were given that the matter would be fully investigated – the fully implying that they were most definitely still under suspicion.

Major Brannigan had organized a limousine to take them back into London and, after they had picked up Holly's Pentax from the Long Valley guard post, Steadman suggested she return with him to his house for a nerve-steadying drink and to clean herself up after her ordeal. She readily agreed for, at the moment, she was living and working out of an address in North London and felt she could not face the trip across the busy town just yet.

She was quiet on the trip back to London, and the moment of closeness their mutual danger had brought about seemed to have been lost. But when he had settled her in an armchair in his lounge, and before she had even sipped the brandy he had offered her, the tears broke through and she had buried her head into his shoulder. He'd held her and tried to soothe her, knowing it was merely the relief of having survived the nightmare, the fear having gone.

After a while, her trembling had stopped and again he forced the brandy on her, urging her to drink. He saw the tension begin to drain away. He drank with her, for she was not alone in having been shaken by the experience. The worst moment for him had been when the tracks of the Chieftain had tried to drag him back by his jacket and crush him. He remembered her hands clutching his wrists, her closed eyes and the effort on her face as she had struggled to pull him towards her. The brandy warmed them both, their senses acute and vulnerable after the shock, and as they looked into each other's eyes, the understanding – the intangible closeness – returned.

Steadman wasn't surprised when she asked him to take her to bed and, somehow, both knew the prime purpose was not to make love, but to share physically this closeness they were both feeling. For Steadman it was a feeling he hadn't experienced for a long, long time; not since Lilla. Strangely, the memory of her gave him no sense of guilt. He had felt it and rejected it when he had made love to other women – even Maggie – but now, when his emotions were beginning to run deep, the guilt hadn't even appeared. Who was she, this Holly Miles? And why were they reacting so strangely towards each other?

He led her upstairs and watched her undress. She had showered and reappeared, her hair now darkly wet and clinging. Her legs were long and the curve of her calves graceful, her thighs swelling just enough to give them shape. Her shoulders were wide for a girl, but only noticeably so when they were compared to her slim hips. Her breasts were full, and firm with youth.

She had climbed into bed, water from her hair dampening the pillow and, resting-on one elbow, had watched him undress. His body was still lean and well-muscled enough to be pleasing; he felt no self-consciousness under her gaze. He caught her look of concern when she saw the old scars scattered across his back, but she made no comment. He showered, then returned to the bedroom, finding a peacefulness in her he wanted to share.

Now he held her close and, for a fleeting second as her eyes opened, he thought he glimpsed something. Not fear, not confusion, but anguish. It was gone in a moment, yet he knew it wasn't imagined.

'Why did they try to kill us, Harry?' she asked, drawing slightly away so she could see more of his face. 'Why would the men in the tank want to do that?'

'I don't know, Holly,' he lied. 'You make enemies in this business. Maybe someone was trying to get at me. We don't know that there was a complete crew in the tank.'

'Hijack a tank just to kill you?'

Steadman shrugged. 'Like I said: you make enemies.'

'Unless whoever it was was trying to kill me.'

Steadman looked at her sharply. 'Kill you? Why should anyone want to do that?'

'I don't know. I just felt the menace there. Didn't you feel it? It was somehow – evil. As if the tank were a living thing.'

She had experienced it too. It had been uncanny.

Her body shivered and he drew her close again.

'Put it out of your mind for now,' he told her. 'They'll find the bodies – or body – in the tank and maybe their identities will tell us why they were trying to kill us.'

She pressed against him. 'There's more isn't there? You're not telling me everything.'

He suddenly felt the overwhelming desire to tell her all – about Maggie, Mossad, British Intelligence, this man Edward Gant. He wanted to confide. After all these years of introversion, he now felt the need to talk to someone, maybe not to share in the problems he faced, but at least to know of them. But something held him back.

Was it years of discretion as a private detective, as a Mossad agent, as a member of Military Intelligence? Had years of never trusting anyone been ingrained into his character? He felt he knew the girl so well, yet common sense told him she was still a stranger. Maybe it was that which held him back.

'Yes,' he said to her, 'there is more, but it's better that you're not involved.'

She was silent for a while, then said, 'Who are you really, Harry? Why are you involved in weapons? Can't you tell me that?'

'I've told you who I am.'

'You've told me what you are.'

He grinned at her. 'What I am is who I am.'

She shook her head. 'No, that's too easy. It doesn't explain anything. Why do you deal in armaments, Harry?'

'If it wasn't me, it'd be somebody else,' came the stock reply.

'You're still evading.'

His hand touched her cheek. 'Give it time, Holly,' he said quietly. 'We've been thrown together by mutual danger. Tomorrow, our feelings could be different. So let's be patient, eh?'

She nodded and silently reached behind his neck to touch his damp hair. 'You feel it too, then?' she asked.

He smiled back, then kissed her softly. 'I feel it,' he said.

'Then let it happen.'

She kissed him fiercely and quietened nerves became alive again, this time responding to a far different sensation than fear. His hand swept down her back and found her buttocks. Pulling her tight against him, he grew erect once more against the softness of her stomach.

He heard her sigh as their bodies filled each other's, their skin joining, its coolness turning to heat. His fingers fondled the sensitive base of her spine, and her long fingers reached down to touch him in the same place, then travelled further to the back of his legs. He could feel her stretching against him and suddenly her legs parted and his thigh filled the gap. He ran his hand down the smoothness of her skin and pulled her leg up slightly so that it rested over his own; then he caressed the back of her leg from the top to the sensitive area behind her knee.

Holly reached up again, laying her hand flatly against his back, exerting pressure so that his lips bore down hard against hers. The softness of her mouth aroused him further and her teeth bit down gently on his probing tongue. He felt her hand reach around to his chest and their bodies parted slightly to give it access. She touched him easily at first, then squeezed the firm skin of his chest hard, not to hurt, but to excite. Her fingers slid down towards his stomach and the muscles there quivered at her touch. He pushed himself towards her searching hand, demanding to be touched at his most sensitive area. Her fingers ignored his demands and passed that point, reaching below and encircling his testicles. She squeezed them and he groaned aloud at the warmth of the touch.

His own hand swept back upwards, never losing contact with her body, heightening her sensations as it journeyed towards her breasts. He covered a breast with his hand and moved his fingers gently to find her nipple, stroking it delicately, controlling the passion he felt.

They paused in their movements for a moment and kissed softly, both afraid to talk of love for it was too soon, but allowing their kiss to express feelings that ran deep, feelings that surprised them both. Only then did they allow their passions to rise uncontrolled.

He reached down, still keeping his fingers against her skin, tantalizing her with the direction his hand was taking. Over her stomach, staying there briefly to explore and awaken, then down into her hair, stroking and kneading, firm enough to reach deeper nerve cells, but soft enough to excite rather than fulfil. She could wait no longer and grabbed his wrist, forcing his hand lower, down between her thighs, into the aroused wetness there.

Her moan of pleasure mingled with his, for the sensation of probing her sweet dampness was almost as great as the exhilaration she felt at his touch. His fingers entered her, careful not to hurt, but she pushed against him and her wildness incited him further. His touch was hard now and her motion was rapid. Her whole body squirmed as she reached for his penis, reluctant to lose the excitement of his hand, but eager for something more fulfilling, more satisfying.

She turned on to her back and he rose above her, kissing her face and neck, her closed eyes. Her smile was inward, but she suddenly put an arm around his neck to pull his cheek against hers, to let him know she was sharing their pleasure, not retreating into her own. Her other hand was gently insistent, drawing him into her. He paused, then advanced slowly so there would be no pain, no sharpness; he sank further, pausing again when she gasped. But pain meant little to her now and she urged him on, pushing upwards with her hips to help him complete his journey.

His weight bore down on her and their mutual desire became exquisitely intolerable. It was no time to linger, no time to tease; that could come later when they were used to each other. Now they needed to climb and reach their peak, to find release for screaming sensations. He thrust into her and she met and countered his movements with equal force, her fingers crooked and pressing into his skin, her knees raised slightly, her thighs squeezing against him.

She surprised him by reaching down between their bodies, her hand desperately feeling underneath him, finding the area between his legs and pulling upwards as though to force him further into her. His passion grew even more and he felt the nerve-tingling tension begin its ascent, all the senses in his body drawn to that one region as though through a vortex. The same was happening to Holly. Her mouth was open, lips drawn back from her teeth. Her eyes were tightly shut and short gasps escaped her as she twisted her head against the pillow. Her muscles stiffened and juices inside her began to flow as though being squeezed through tiny apertures, faster, faster, until they burst through and flowed freely.

And Steadman's juices flowed to mingle with Holly's at the same time.

Even as the sensations subsided they still murmured their delight, Steadman resting against her, unwilling to relinquish the physical closeness. Holly kissed his neck, slowly stroking his back with gentle fingertips, happy at what had passed, but confused at the strength of her feelings for him. She was giving too much too soon.

She was unaware that the same confusion was running through Steadman. When he finally withdrew and lay by her side, they regarded each other with curious eyes.

'What's happening to us?' she asked, and she seemed nervous.

He put a finger to her lips. 'It's too uncertain to say.'

Holly seemed about to speak again, then changed her mind. She pulled her head away, but not before Steadman had seen the troubled look on her face. He turned her head back towards him and kissed her lips. 'Don't worry about it, eh?'

Her eyes were misted and damp as she pulled his head down and kissed his lips.

'I don't want to be involved with you,' she said.

'What are you afraid of, Holly? Are you really that scared of giving yourself to someone?'

'You don't understand ...'

Her words were cut off by the insistent ringing of the telephone downstairs. She suddenly felt Steadman's whole body go rigid and a distant look came into his eyes.

'Harry, what's wrong?'

There was no recognition when he looked at her; his mind had travelled back to another time, in another country. The phone had rung there too, in their apartment in Brussels, when he and Lilla had just finished making love. It was to be the last time for them.

Lilla had urged him to ignore the ringing, had clung to him, demanding more, more love. Laughing, he'd smothered her face with a pillow, telling her the call might be important, perhaps a new mission. He was becoming too used to the inactivity, getting to like it. All the more reason to let it ring, she had called after him as he leapt away from her and went through to the lounge.

The pillow had sailed through the air after him and struck the side of the open door, her pretended anger making him smile as he headed towards the phone. As he picked up the receiver he saw she had followed him and was standing in the doorway, a mischievous grin on her face, one hand cupping her breast, the other reaching between her legs, as if to say if he wouldn't stay to please her, she would amuse herself.

He turned his eyes away from the provocative sight and said hello into the mouthpiece.

A voice, in French, asked if it was Monsieur Clement speaking, and he had answered yes – Clement was the name he used at that time.

He knew immediately what the high-pitched whine from the earpiece meant, for the Israelis had used the same device against the Chief PLO representative in France, Dr Mahmoud Hamshari. The sound was an electronic signal transmitted through the telephone, to trigger off a bomb hidden somewhere in the apartment, probably near the phone itself.

As he dived towards Lilla he knew he was already too late.

The sudden searing flash which lit up the horror on her face told him there was no escape.

Not for Lilla. But he had survived.

They told him later it must have been the angle of his body as he had dived for Lilla. Shrapnel had imbedded itself in his feet and legs, but the rest of his body had been spared from the worst of the blast. A miracle they had called it, but for him there was no mercy in his salvation. He had no desire to live if Lilla was to die.

It had taken her three days to do so, this young, once vivacious, Israeli, her face torn away and her body lacerated and burnt. Three hideously pain-filled days. Never fully conscious, but her shredded lips constantly moving in her agony.

Steadman had prayed for her death, had begged the doctors to end the torture for her; but their job was to preserve life no matter how shattered or painful, and they paid no mind to his entreaties, finally sedating him against his own pain and anguish.

When he had finally recovered and she was long dead, there had been a blackness in him that had taken many other deaths to purge.

Now, in circumstances so similar to that time before, the telephone was ringing, calling to him, reminding him, telling him the past was always present.

'Harry?' Her hand shook his shoulder. 'What is it? You look so pale.'

His eyes snapped back into focus and he looked down into the anxious face of Holly.

'Aren't you going to answer it? It keeps ringing,' she said.

He eased himself from the bed without a word, and picked up a bathrobe lying over the back of a chair. He moved as though automated, but the concern in Holly's voice finally sank through.

'Stay there,' he ordered, and she saw the somnambulic quality of his movements change to one of alertness. He shrugged on the robe and disappeared through the doorway. She heard his footsteps padding lightly down the stairs.

Steadman reached the lounge and quickly glanced around, ignoring the shrilling phone for the moment. Nothing seemed out of place, but he quickly checked on the few places where a bomb could have been concealed, carefully lifting the settee and armchair to check beneath, peering behind the books on their shelves, examining the back of the television to see if it had been tampered with. Reasonably satisfied that everything was in order, he turned his attention to the telephone itself, the caller's persistence arousing his suspicions even more. There was nothing underneath the small coffee-table it rested on, but he knew the telephone itself could contain a bomb. He picked it up to feel its weight: it seemed normal enough. He took the gamble and lifted the receiver to his ear.

'Steadman, is that you?'

With a sigh of relief, he recognized Pope's voice.

'For Christ's sake, Steadman, answer!'

'It's me,' he said quietly.

There was a pause at the other end, then Pope said gruffly, 'It took you long enough to answer.'

'How did you know I was here?' Steadman countered.

'It's my business to know,' came the curt reply. The tone changed as the fat man relaxed. 'I heard what happened to you down at Long Valley. Tell me your end of it.'

Steadman told him flatly, without emotion, as though making a report to a client. He mentioned the invitation from Gant to arrange a further meeting.

'Good,' said Pope. 'Do so. Who's this girl, this, er, Holly Miles?'

'She's a writer – freelance. She's doing an article on the arms trade for one of the Sundays.'

'And Gant's obliging her?'

'It seems so.'

'Hm. Peculiar. Not like him to want publicity.'

'Maybe he wants to come out of the shadows.' Steadman whirled as he felt a presence in the room. Holly stood in the doorway, his shirt covering her small body seductively. She smiled at him and he relaxed. Pope's voice drew his attention back to their conversation.

'You say this tank was definitely chasing you,' he was saying.

'Yes, it was trying to ram us.'

'You're sure it wasn't just a runaway?'

'Look, we've been through all this with the military. The bloody thing wrecked the car, then tried to squash us flat when we ran for it! It chased us for at least five minutes.'

'Yes, yes. Very strange.'

Steadman's impatience grew. 'Is that all you can say? We know it was strange, but you and I ...' He cut off his words, remembering Holly was still in the doorway. 'Look, who was in the tank? Were they working for him?' He was careful not to mention Gant's name.

There was a long silence on the other end of the line.

'Pope? Did you hear me?'

'Er, yes, dear boy,' came the reply eventually. 'The tank was a complete wreck, of course, by the time it reached the bottom of the quarry. Its fuel tank exploded, you know, then its ammo.'

'I know that. Were the bodies badly burnt?'

'That's just it, Harry.' Again, Pope paused, as though considering his words. 'There were no bodies. The tank was empty.'

'But that's impossible! They must have escaped or been destroyed completely.' There was alarm in Steadman's voice and a chilling sensation in the pit of his stomach.

'No chance of escape. And there would have been some trace of human bodies, no matter how bad the damage. No, Harry. The tank was empty. There was no one driving it.'

Steadman stared at the receiver, unable to believe the words. Then he turned towards Holly and she saw the confusion in his eyes.

■ 8 ■

'*The eternal life granted by the grail is only for the truly pure and noble.*'

ADOLF HITLER

'*And many of them that sleep in the dust of the earth shall awake, some to everlasting life, and some to shame and everlasting contempt.*'

DANIEL 12:2 (RSV)

SMITH SHIVERED AND TIGHTENED HIS SCARF, SILENTLY CURSING THE COLDNESS of the night. It was morbid too, sitting in the churchyard in the dark, ancient gravestones scattered around, black and weathered, some tilting at odd angles suggesting their occupants had become restless. He wondered briefly if he should risk lighting a cigarette, but decided against it. Although the bench on which he sat was well-hidden in the darkness, there was just a chance that the cigarette's glow would be seen from the small road opposite. It wouldn't do to have any passer-by getting curious about someone sitting in a graveyard in the dead of night smoking a fag. Not that there *were* any passers-by at this time of bloody night!

He glanced at his watch, the luminous dial telling him he still had two hours to go before he came off shift. Two more hours in this stinking burial ground, he grumbled to himself. Two more hours of watching the stinking house opposite! And for what? They wouldn't be stupid enough to try anything like the other night. God, what kind of bastards would nail a woman to a door? He wondered if there were any other eyes watching the house. The police, maybe? It was strange they hadn't made more of the business, it wasn't the normal everyday kind of murder. And they'd managed to keep it out of the news, too. That must have taken some doing. Probably didn't want to encourage any similar types of crime. Unusual murders were always followed by other unusual murders. All the nuts around read about the first, got a kick out of it, and tried it out themselves. Same with bomb freaks.

What kind of man was this Steadman? He'd heard the detective was reluctant to help them at first, but the killing of his partner had persuaded him. Goldblatt had been furious at the investigator's previous refusal, even though he, Smith, had told the Mossad chief it would probably be so. He had kept an eye on Steadman over the years, it was part of his job as a 'sleeper' in this country, and he had seen how the agency had begun to flourish, how Steadman had settled down to live a relatively peaceful existence in England. The man had left wars and violence behind. Why should he become involved again? The brutal murder of Mrs Wyeth was the answer to that!

How *he* would like to be free of the organization. Joseph Solomon Smith, aged fifty-eight, jeweller in Walthamstow. Known as Solly to his friends. *Schmuck* to his wife, Sadie. Solly had fled to England along with thousands of other Jewish refugees just before the outbreak of the last World War, when Hitler's purge of Germany's and Austria's Jewish population was in full swing. It had been either flee or be interned in those days, not many realizing it was actually flee or die. The mass name-changing that had taken place, as the refugees had arrived in England and gone through the far from friendly formalities of entering the country, had been almost comical. The group in front of him had told the official their family name was Harris, for they had heard the people in front of them use the name. It sounded English. If the officials receiving the immigrants had been surprised at the amount of Harrises, Kanes and Golds among the arrivals, they'd given no indication of it. Perhaps they understood the stigma attached to names ending with 'berg', or 'stein', or 'baum', the danger such names threatened in the world at that terrible time. Perhaps they couldn't have cared less; there were too many to check.

He had chosen Smith because he knew it was indisputably British and he'd heard one of the customs officers call his companion by that name. It was a safe name. In fact, he'd nearly wet himself at the official's suspicious look and feared he'd been too blatant with his choice. However, the moment had passed and with a resigned smile, the man had cleared him.

Many of his compatriots had reclaimed their original names when the threat had died years later, but he had found no need to go to that trouble. Smith suited him fine.

He had escaped from Germany alone, his parents, two brothers and one sister having been rounded up by Hitler's thugs on the very eve of their departure from the country. He would have been taken with them, but he was young, and young men, when about to leave a place forever, often have bittersweet goodbyes to say, undying love to pledge. His farewell had taken most of the night and the girl had used his body as though there would never be any others for her.

He watched in horror from the shadows as the SS dragged his screaming family from their house, and he shrank back deeper into those shadows. He'd wept at his own cowardice then, and had wept with that same shame for many years after. Even the sight of his father falling into the gutter, his white beard now black in the moonlight – black because it was matted with blood – and the old man's screams as the rifle butts battered his frail body into unconsciousness, had not overcome his own terror. The brutality had only increased it. He had sunk to a squatting position, pressing himself hard against the rough wall, afraid to run lest the Gestapo hear his footsteps, stifling sobs with both hands against his mouth, unable to look away from the dreadful scene and unable to help his family. Even when his younger brother had been kicked senseless when he tried to go to the aid of his aged father. Even when his mother had been dragged by her hair into the waiting van. Even when his sister's young body had been bared and pawed by the uniformed thugs. Even when his older brother had been shot through the throat as he'd tried to escape. The terror had only been compounded.

The nightmares had finally ceased twenty years later, the horror gradually diminishing through repetition. The shame, too, had become numbed, for his spirit had grown weary of it and now kept it contained in a remote part of him. But the memory remained. And two faces burned within that memory: the faces of those who had caused the holocaust, the evil countenances of the two men responsible for the genocide, the decimation of his race, the murder of his family. Adolf Hitler and his henchman, Heinrich Himmler!

Their faces haunted him still because they were the cause of his terror, the source of his shame. And because he was aware their evil could so easily rise again.

After the war, when he learned the rest of his family had died in Auschwitz, he had tried to join the remnants of his race in Palestine, desperate to atone for his cowardice, yearning to take part in the rebirth of his nation. But the new Israelis now had a different way of thinking. For them, the centuries of oppression were over. They had returned to their home country and there they would either be free or perish fighting for that freedom. No longer would they accept persecution.

Defiance had to be tempered with cunning if they were to survive. They were a small nation in a small country; the world stood outside their boundaries, a giant wolf outside the door. The Israelis would never trust another nation again: they would work with them, they would trade with them, they would even encourage social intercourse. But they would never trust another race, another country.

Because they were surrounded by enemies on all sides, their strength would have to reach beyond their own boundaries so they would always be fore-warned of enemy action against them, enabling them to strike from behind when necessary.

They had persuaded Smith to remain in England, to build an identity there, to become British. And to be ready.

He had worked in a small jewellers in the Hatton Garden area of London at first, for that had been the family business, a trade he had been taught by his father. His claim against the German government for the restoration of his family's wealth had taken years to materialize, for there were many others like him claiming compensation for losses they had suffered under the Nazi regime, and each claim had to be carefully checked. Very few received compensation from the then impoverished country, but Smith was lucky enough to receive a small settlement. This, plus the marriage to Sadie which brought in some extra capital, enabled him to set up his own shop in Walthamstow.

Another source of income which Sadie never knew about were the regular amounts of money he received from the Shin Beth. The payments were small, but the work he carried out for his country was minimal and irregular. When he was younger, he had become impatient with the menial tasks they asked of him, but they had begged him to wait, to stay calm and serve his nation in the way they asked. His day would come.

It hadn't though, and gradually the fires in him dimmed and almost burnt out. He carried out the minor tasks asked of him with a sense of resigned duty and no passion. One of his 'duties' had been to keep an eye on the man Harry Steadman when he had returned to England from Israel and joined an enquiry agency. Smith had done this by employing the agency to check on the back-ground of his one and only employee, an innocent little countryman of his, whom he knew to be completely trustworthy, but who provided a good excuse for making contact with the investigator. The ex-policeman, Blake, had carried out the investigation, providing Smith with a clean bill of health for his shop assistant, but complimenting the jeweller on his wisdom in checking out his staff. One could never be too careful where goods of such value were involved. Smith had cultivated a friendship with the ex-policeman and engaged him privately in other concocted matters to do with his business. In that way, he was able to hear of the agency's progress and catch odd bits of information relating to Harry Steadman without becoming directly involved himself. He had skilfully avoided his curiosity about the investigator from becoming overt in any way, and most of the information had been volunteered by Blake without direct questioning. After all, they were good friends, they and their wives sometimes dined out together or visited the theatre. Hadn't he, Smith, introduced his friend into his own golf club at Chingford? If the very-British ex-policeman ever wondered about the beginnings of his friendship with the very-Jewish dealer in precious stones, then he would put it down to an obvious desire for the jeweller to have some connections with the law.

Smith blew on his hands to try and warm them, then pushed them deep into the pockets of his overcoat. I'm becoming too old for this sort of thing, he told himself. Surveillance in this kind of weather was no good for a man of his health. His heart wasn't as strong as it used to be, his constitution no longer robust. It seemed a waste of time anyway. Surely Steadman wouldn't be touched in his own home? Why was he so important to Israeli Intelligence? Smith cursed the secrecy his employers maintained. Why couldn't their own people be informed of what was going on? And what do I tell Sadie who knows nothing of Mossad and my little jobs for them, when she asks what kind of business deals keep me out till the early hours of the morning? The woman is becoming tiresome. Becoming? She always was. You got a loose woman, she'll tell me. Chance would be a fine thing, I'll tell her. You got … His body stiffened as something caught his eye.

Did I see something? he asked himself. Or was it my imagination? The street lighting is bad there over the road. Was it something moving?

Smith peered into the darkness, his eyes narrowed and his breath held. There it was again, a movement among the shadows!

He rose to his feet, his limbs stiff with cold, and bent his body forward as though it would help him see more clearly. He thought he saw movement again, but it somehow seemed unreal, his imagination playing tricks on him. The air around him was still, no wind to cause the stirring of tree branches which might create mysteriously moving shadows.

He moved forward, careful to make no sound, his breathing now thin and uneven. He had a number to call if anything suspicious occurred, but the nearest phone-box was two streets away. How stupid of them! If anything were to happen it would all be over by the time he reached the phone-box and they got here. But then, he had been told nothing had been expected to happen; he was only being used as an extra precaution.

He silently cursed the men who employed him, the silly little Jewish boys playing at cloak-and-dagger. Then he forced himself to relax. It's probably nothing at all. I've been in the dark too long – and in creepy surroundings at that. My eyes are tired and small wonder! My God, what time is it now? The luminous dial told him it was 1.35 a.m.

The jeweller stood and stared at the terraced house for a few seconds more and was about to return to his bench when he noticed something odd. His mind couldn't register just what that oddness was for a few moments, and then he focused his vision on the door of the house. There was a long, dark shadow at one side. It may just have been a shadow cast by the half-moon against the door's frame, but then he realized the moon was on the other side; the shadow – if there had been one caused by the frame on that side – should have been cast on the left and not the right. He moved forward for a closer look, keeping to the hard earth and grass of the churchyard so his footsteps would not be heard. He pushed his way through the sparse shrubbery at the perimeter and peered over the iron fence. Only then did he see that the front door to Steadman's house was partially open.

What to do now? Phone his contact or investigate further? If Steadman were sleeping – and he undoubtedly was – he could be in serious danger. But what could he, an old man, do to help the detective? Warn him, at least.

Perhaps it was the memory of having done nothing so many years before, or perhaps it was just the thought of it being a false alarm and his looking foolish in the eyes of the young Israelis who employed him. He decided to investigate further before calling in help.

He reached the gateless exit to the churchyard and stealthily crossed the road, welcoming the concealing shadows on that side. The jeweller, one hand on the wall as if to steady himself, moved along towards Steadman's house. He reached the open door and hesitated.

All the muscles in his ageing body had become tense, making his movements awkward and stiff. He felt a strange fear, as though someone – something – was waiting for him inside that house. Something that compelled him to enter.

He tried to break the spell, tried to tell himself he was being a foolish old man. He should try to get away, now, while there was still time. But there was something in there he had to see. Something there waiting just for him.

He pushed the door open further, his fingers trembling. His breathing had become heavier and he tried to suppress small whimpers escaping from his throat. Even then, he tried to turn and run, but his body – or was it his mind? – refused to obey. The door swung open and the hallway was a black, ominous tunnel.

Smith stepped over the threshold and felt his way along the passage, his eyes becoming more accustomed to the darkness. He stopped when he thought he heard breathing. Breathing that wasn't his own. But no other sounds came as he listened, although he felt that the beating of his own heart would surely drown out any other noise. He moved on and suddenly stumbled against the base of the stairway.

His hands took his weight, holding on to the high stairs for support, one knee resting on a lower step, and he grunted with the sudden jarring. Then he felt its presence.

His gaze travelled up the stairway, step by step, until it reached the bend. It was darker just there, a black hole in the general gloom, but there was someone – something – lurking in that pool of darkness. His whole body began to shake now, for he felt its evil; it seemed to emanate from that dark area, to flow down the stairs in a vaporous cloud, sweeping over him and chilling his mind.

A movement. A shape began to descend the stairs.

Smith moaned and tried to break away, but his limbs were locked rigid, paralysed by a fear that was even greater than the night of his family's abduction in Berlin. His eyes widened as the dark shape emerged from the total blackness of the bend in the stairs, and his mouth opened to form a scream as the figure became more discernible. And yet, the image still wasn't clear. It was just a black shape against the overall darkness of the hallway; but his mind saw more than his eyes. It came closer and stopped just before him. He tried to pull his hands away, for they were almost touching the shadow, but he found they would not obey him. The smell of decay pervaded the air, assailing his nostrils and almost causing him to vomit. He slowly looked up, searching the length of the figure towering over him and when he reached its head, a face came floating down at him as though the shape was bending.

'Oh, dear God.' Smith's moan rose to a wail. 'You! Oh God, it can't be!'

It was then he screamed.

The scream hadn't roused Steadman, for he'd been awake minutes before. He had lain there in the dark, unsure of what had dragged him from his deep slumber. He listened for any noises, and none came. He had become aware of the iciness of the room. It was a still coldness, penetrating the blankets of his bed, and not the normal chill of autumn. It was as though the temperature of the room had taken an abrupt downward plunge. He was aware of being very much alone.

Steadman had taken Holly home to her flat earlier that evening, both of them shaken by the revelation that the Chieftain tank which had tried to crush them that day had been empty. They were halfway to Holly's flat when the thought struck Steadman of how it could have been managed, and he had difficulty in keeping his sudden theory from the girl. There was no point in involving her, it would have meant telling her everything, better it remain a mystery to her.

He ran the idea through his mind as he drove and it seemed to fit; at least, there were no *other* possible explanations. Gant dealt in sophisticated armaments, the advanced technology of his weapons renowned and respected. It would not have been impossible for him to rig up remote-controlled operating machinery inside the tank, a mechanical driver which would obey instructions from afar. But from where? The operator had to be able to see them to send the Chieftain on their track. He had to be in close visual proximity. Weight was added to his theory when he realized how: helicopters had been buzzing over the testing-grounds all morning. They had been too busy trying to escape the tank to be aware of any helicopter hovering above them, but that must have been the answer! How else could their hiding places have been found so easily? The searching eyes had been above them! For a moment his theory floundered: whoever had been guiding the tank from the helicopter must have seen the quarry and would have taken avoiding action. But then he had been close to the quarry's edge; maybe the controller had not been quick enough to change the Chieftain's direction, maybe his eagerness to crush the detective had distracted his judgement. It had to be the answer! Steadman relaxed a little: he liked his mysteries to have some solution.

He had kissed Holly goodbye in his car when they reached her home, neither invited inside nor wanting to be. They were both curious about each other, both disturbed by the strength of their feelings; but both had had enough for one day. It was time for them to be alone, to lick their wounds and digest the events of the day. An unease showed in her eyes as she promised to see him soon. Then she was gone.

Steadman had driven to the agency, luckily catching Sexton and their young trainee, Steve, before they left for the night. He briefed them on two specific jobs they were to carry out during the following few days – current assignments would have to be slotted in somehow even if it meant spreading their load on to another agency. After warning them their investigations would require the utmost caution, he returned to his home in the back streets of Knightsbridge.

He made coffee, then settled down to reread the file on Edward Gant. Five cigarettes and three cups of coffee later he lay the document down by his feet, rubbing his eyes in weariness, his mind buzzing with unformed thoughts. There was still a smell about the whole business he didn't like. Why should British Intelligence, with all their resources, use him to get at Gant? Pope's explanation that he was a link with all the parties concerned didn't quite ring true. He was even more certain he was being set up as the sacrificial goat, the bait to draw out the tiger. Mossad's use of him seemed more genuine, but just as ruthless. Their resources in England were limited and he was in a good position to find their missing agent. But was that all there was to it? They had admitted they wanted to nail Gant, but then why not just eliminate him? They'd done so with their enemies in the past, so why balk at it this time? There was much more to it than either intelligence organizations were letting on and that was why he was taking out extra insurance. Sexton's task was to find out more about Gant, hearsay matters that might not be entered in official documents; young Steve's task was to keep an eye on the hotel near Belsize Park, to follow the movements of Goldblatt and Hannah. Steadman had decided not to tell the two men any more than they would need to know, but he warned them there would be danger involved. Steve's eyes had lit up at the idea and Sexton had accepted it with a weary grin. If it had something to do with Mrs Wyeth's death, then they were only too pleased to put in as many extra hours as it would take to help find the murderer or murderers. And that *was* what it was all about, wasn't it?

He had nodded and both men had resisted asking further questions. Before Steadman left the office, Sexton had promised to begin his investigation of the arms dealer the following morning when he had sorted out their current jobs, and Steve was already on the phone to Goldblatt's hotel, booking a room for an indefinite period beginning the following day. It would work out expensive for the agency, but Steadman was determined to recoup any losses from both Mossad and British Intelligence, whatever the outcome. He prayed he would still be around to forward the bills himself.

He had prepared a simple meal for himself, then phoned Holly, dialling the number she had given him earlier. He had been disappointed when there was no reply. She hadn't relaxed even after their lovemaking that afternoon, and who could blame her after what she'd been through? He replaced the receiver with a shrug. Perhaps she was in a dead sleep. Or visiting friends. What did he really know about her anyway? He had climbed the stairs, thrown off his clothes, and slumped wearily into bed. But first he had made sure all the doors were locked.

He lay there listening, his breath held. The coldness of the room made him shudder. What had made him wake so abruptly? Light from the street filtered through the open curtains, but was no match for the room's darker shadows and gave little comfort. No sounds came to his ears, yet the tension inside him mounted. His impulse was to leap from the bed and draw out the revolver he kept in the top of his wardrobe, but something held his body in check. Somehow he knew there was someone downstairs. The atmosphere seemed heavy with menace and he trusted his instincts too much to ignore the feeling. Then he sensed that the stairs leading to the bedroom were being mounted. The approach was slow, deliberate, its only physical warning a breathing sound, a sound which grew louder and more urgent as it drew nearer. The smell drifted under the door then. It was vile, choking, the smell of defecation and ... he struggled to remember where he had experienced it before. It came to him. Years ago, when one of Israel's border towns had been heavily mortared by their enemy, he had helped clear the rubble and search for bodies. A family had hidden in the cellar of their house, a cellar specially dug for such emergencies, and the building had collapsed around them, burying them alive. It had taken days to find them, and when they had, the flesh had decomposed. This was the same smell, only far stronger, more putrid: the stink of long-rotted flesh.

Steadman forced himself to sit upright, using every ounce of willpower he had. He felt his strength was being inexplicably drained away, drawn from his body, leaving him lifeless. He had to reach the gun. He moved as though deep beneath the ocean, pressure all around him, his breathing harsh and quickened. He staggered and fell to the side of the bed, forcing himself up again, moving towards the wardrobe, his naked body bent, walking like an arthritic old man. His eyes never left the door to the bedroom even though he was moving towards the wardrobe. He was afraid to look away. He thanked God it was locked. But then he had locked the front door downstairs.

A sudden bump stopped him. The sound had come from outside. Everything had become still.

He thought he heard a moan, then words, but he couldn't understand them. The scream snapped him into action.

It was as though a spell had been broken; the heaviness was gone, the fear overcome for the moment. Steadman jerked open the wardrobe door, reached up for the metal case containing his .38, pulled open the lid and snatched the gun out. He was thankful his old habit of always keeping it loaded was still with him. He leapt towards the bedroom door and fumbled with the key, the screams from downstairs still ringing in his ears.

The sounds stopped as he pulled open the door.

He jumped into the bend of the stairs, sure of his footing even in the dark, the gun held before him, the hammer ready to cock. He saw a dark shape lying at the bottom of the stairs and for a moment he thought he saw another shape moving away from it along the hallway, towards the open door. It could have been a trick of light, though, or imagination, for it seemed to have no form and was gone in an instant.

Steadman descended the stairs, moving cautiously, his senses alive and jumping. In the darkness, he could just make out the shape of a man lying at the foot of the stairs, his eyes white and staring. He leapt over the figure and ran to the open front door, quickly looking into the street beyond, oblivious of his own nakedness. The street was empty, although it would have been easy for someone to disappear into the churchyard opposite.

He slammed the door shut and flicked on the hall light all in one movement. Still keeping the gun poised before him, he quickly checked the lounge and then the kitchen, ignoring for the moment the still figure on the floor. Only when all the downstairs lights were on and he was sure no one was lurking in any of the rooms did he return to the collapsed body.

The man's eyes stared at the ceiling, the eyelids pulled back revealing their whites, the pupils dilating under the sudden glare. His lips were moving, but Steadman could hardly hear the words; they were soft and rambling. Spittle bubbled at the side of the man's mouth. His body was stiff and the investigator could see he was in a catatonic state. He had the look of someone who had seen a creature from hell.

▪ 9 ▪

'The hierarchical organization and the initiation through symbolic rites, that is to say without bothering the brains but by working on the imagination through magic and the symbols of a cult – all this is the dangerous element that I have taken over. Don't you see that our party must be of this character?'

'An Order, that is what it had to be – an Order, the hierarchical Order of a secular priesthood.'

ADOLF HITLER

Steadman brought his car to a halt outside the large wrought-iron gates and waited for the guard to step from his hut on the other side. The two Alsatians accompanying the guard looked menacingly towards him.

'Mr Steadman?' the guard called out and the investigator nodded.

'Identification?' There was neither belief nor disbelief in the guard's voice; it was all a matter of routine.

Steadman was forced to leave the car and walk over to the gate, pulling his licence from his wallet as he did so.

The guard, dressed in green tunic-like overalls, took the licence from him and said, 'Won't keep you a moment, sir.' He disappeared into the tiny hut, leaving the dogs glaring through the bars at the investigator. Steadman glared back but decided he couldn't outstare them. He walked back to his car and leaned on the bonnet, hands in his pockets. He wondered if the Mossad agent had come out of shock yet.

As he'd crouched over the trembling form the night before, he had been puzzled by the absolute terror on the man's face. What had put that look there? And why had he broken into his house? Steadman had tried to shake the man into awareness, but the eyes never lost their glaze and the lips never stopped their burbling. He had tried to catch the words, but they were incoherent. He quickly searched the shaking body and found no weapons. His driving licence revealed the man to be Joseph Solomon Smith and it was then that Steadman remembered him; Smith's features had altered so drastically in his horrified state that the investigator hadn't been able to recognize him, but the name had jolted his memory. Smith had come to the agency some time ago and had become one of their smaller clients. He was – what was it? – a jeweller. That's right, he'd wanted the background of one of his staff checked, a job Sexton had handled. There had been a few minor assignments for him over the last couple of years, but Steadman had had no call to see the jeweller again after the initial visit. It was only his particular ability to remember names, places and events, that helped him place the man at all. The obvious connection soon hit him. Smith, despite his English-sounding surname, was Jewish. It didn't take much to realize he was a hireling – or perhaps even an agent – of Mossad. Steadman shook his head in disgust. That was why the little jeweller had come to the agency in the first place, to keep an eye on him for The Institute. Sexton had been Smith's contact. How much had the ex-policeman told the jeweller over the years? There wasn't much to tell anyway, and Steadman was confident that his employee would have committed no serious indiscretions. But to use an old man like this, even for just a routine and periodic check! Look at him now. If the little Jew's heart didn't give way under the strain, then he would be fortunate.

It was the sudden draught rather than any sound which had caused Steadman to throw himself against the wall and point the .38 towards the slowly opening front door. Whoever was entering had silently used a key and was now stealthily pushing the door to one side. It suddenly opened all the way, still quietly, but very swiftly. Two men stood on either side in crouched positions, their bodies partially hidden, and two revolvers were levelled at Steadman's naked figure.

'Don't shoot, Steadman!' a voice commanded, and the investigator's finger froze on the trigger. 'MI5,' the voice came again, low but urgent. An open wallet was tossed down the hallway coming to a halt against the head of the prostrate jeweller. Without taking his eyes off the two men, Steadman reached forward for the wallet. He quickly checked the credentials framed inside the wallet and then stood up, waving for the two men to enter.

They did, the second man closing the door quietly behind them.

'What the hell's been going on?' the first asked, staring down at Smith.

'Let me get something on,' said Steadman, suddenly aware of his nakedness.

'Leave the gun,' the first man ordered as the detective turned to climb the stairs.

'Go fuck yourself,' Steadman said over his shoulder as he climbed.

The two MI5 agents looked at each other and the second shrugged his shoulders.

When Steadman returned, his heavy gun tucked into the deep pocket of his bathrobe, the two men were kneeling over the little Jew.

'What's been going on, Steadman?' the first man asked again, rising. 'What's happened to him?' There seemed to be some disgust in his tone as he pointed down at the figure lying on the floor.

'You tell me,' Steadman replied, irritated by the agent's abrupt manner. 'I heard a noise, then a scream. I came down to find him lying at the bottom of the stairs.' Had he heard a noise at first? He was already casting aside the unreasoning fear he had felt while lying in his bed.

'Did you see anyone? Did anyone get out the back way?' the second agent asked as he searched through Smith's pockets.

'No, it's still locked. I thought I saw someone going out of the front door though. It was just a shadow, I couldn't make much out in the dark.'

The two agents regarded him with puzzled expressions. 'No one came out, we'd have seen 'em,' the first said.

'But I'm sure ...' Steadman's voice trailed off.

'He's an old man,' the MI5 agent said. 'He's been sitting out there in the cold, in the churchyard over the road for hours. Maybe it was too much for him. He came over to see you and collapsed on the stairs.'

'How do you know he was over there? And why should he come over to see me at this time of night?'

'He was there watching you. And we were watching him. Your Mossad friends seem to want to keep an eye on you. They must be bloody desperate to use old men like him, though.'

'But why were you there?' Steadman asked.

'To keep an eye on you, of course. Compliments of Mr Pope. As to why the old man came over – who knows? Maybe he thought he saw something.'

'How did he get in? The door was locked.'

'Same way as us, Mr Steadman.' The agent held a Yale key aloft. 'I'm afraid we had it made during your absence. It was for your own protection,' he added by way of an apology, then looked back at the figure huddled on the floor. 'He's probably got a key on him somewhere or maybe he picked the lock. We'll find out later.'

Steadman shook his head resignedly. 'What do we do about him?' he said, kneeling once again by the old man whose body was still shaking. 'He needs to go to hospital.'

'We'll get him to one. Don't mention any of this to your Mossad friends or they'll want to know how MI5 got involved. They've got to think you're working on your own.'

'Aren't I?' Steadman asked caustically.

The two agents ignored the question. 'As far as you're concerned, you never saw this man tonight. Let them worry about his disappearance.'

They had carried the old man out, assuring Steadman that one of them would maintain the vigil outside the house through the night. Steadman made sure the door was locked, then poured himself a stiff drink. He spent the rest of the night dozing fitfully in an armchair, the .38 near at hand on a coffee-table. The next morning, after shaving, showering, and eating, he had rung Holly. Again, there had been no answer but, although a little concerned, he told himself she was a working girl and was probably at the magazine which had commissioned her current feature. Besides, she had nothing to do with this business, so why should she be in any danger? Yesterday's incident with the tank was because of him and nothing to do with any involvement on her part. Later, he had rung Edward Gant's company, using the number supplied by Peppercorn, and had been told the arms dealer would like him to visit his home that day where their business might be better dealt with. With some trepidation, Steadman had agreed and had been given instructions on how to get there. He had rung Pope immediately after and the fat man had been delighted with the invitation. 'Do be careful, dear boy,' had been his only hint at the risk Steadman was running. They had briefly discussed the incident of the night before and Pope had questioned the investigator on exactly what he had seen. Steadman detected a keen interest in the large man's voice and had almost told him of his own uncanny feelings towards the incident, but in the cold light of day, it all seemed very much a part of his own imagination.

After a quick call to his office and checking with Sue that everything was in order as far as their clients were concerned, he set out in his car towards Guildford, a nervousness in him and yet, an excitement. Maybe Pope was right: he had only smothered the flames inside him, the fire not completely put out.

The guard came back to the gate and held Steadman's licence through the bars. The investigator took it and climbed back into his car.

The gates were opened and he drove through, the Alsatians silent, but their eyes never leaving him. The gravel road curved through a small cluster of trees, then the house loomed up before him. It was a large house but by no means as grand as Steadman had expected, for Gant was, reportedly, a wealthy man. He remembered that this was not the arms dealer's only property: hadn't Holly mentioned a place on the west coast?

The grounds appeared to be perfectly normal for an English country house, and showed little evidence of the nature of the man's business. But surely there must be a testing-range somewhere on the estate, otherwise why would Gant have invited him there? Why indeed? he asked himself. There were several other cars parked outside the house and a BMW was just pulling away. The two men inside glanced around at Steadman, then quickly turned their heads, the passenger looking through the window on his side so only the back of his head was visible. But in the brief instant before, Steadman had recognized him: he was a Tory MP, well-known for his right-wing views and the brilliant but incitative speeches he made in support of those views. He seemed appropriate company for Gant, Steadman thought wryly, as he parked beside a silver

Mercedes. His door was already being pulled open by a man wearing a dark suit, as he turned off the ignition.

'Mr Gant is in the house waiting for you, sir,' the man said. 'Can I take your briefcase?'

'I don't have one,' said Steadman, climbing from the car.

'Follow me then, sir.' The man's voice and movements were brisk, and his words were more like an order than an invitation. Steadman followed him.

'Won't keep you a moment, sir,' the dark-suited man said, leaving him standing in a wide, gloomy hallway, and disappearing into one of the high-doored rooms leading off from it. Steadman began to wander down the hallway, studying the gilt-framed portraits hanging on either side, portraits of men he'd never heard of, but all dressed military style, when the door opened again and Gant stepped into the hall.

'Ah, Mr Steadman. Glad you could come,' the arms dealer said, smiling.

Steadman's eyes widened in shock, but he quickly recovered and strode towards Gant. The arms dealer did not offer his hand and his eyes glittered with some inner amusement.

'Did I ... surprise you?' he said. 'It is a shock at first, but you'll soon get used to it.'

Steadman found it hard to take his eyes away from the large, square sticking-plaster, punctured by two small holes, which covered the area where Gant's nose had been only the day before. He cleared his throat and said, 'Sorry, I didn't mean to ...'

'No need for apologies,' Gant raised a hand as if to ward off the sentiment. 'This happened many years ago. Fortunately my nasal passages function quite normally. It is unsightly at first, I know, but it's very uncomfortable wearing an artificial nose all the time. When I'm at home, I like to dispense with such vanities. Now do come in, there are some people I'd like you to meet.'

The room was large, the ceiling high, the furniture tastefully traditional. The four people in the room, two seated, two standing, looked towards Steadman as he entered and their conversations stopped. He was surprised to see that one of the men was Major Brannigan, this time out of uniform but still looking very much the military type, open hostility on his face. The other faces showed interest – perhaps curiosity would have been more accurate. Steadman felt uncomfortable under their gaze.

One of the seated occupants was a woman and Steadman found his eyes drawn towards her, to be held by her own deep gaze. She had extraordinary beauty: her hair was dark and lush, cascading down to her shoulders, her skin smooth and sallow in an exotic way; her nose was strong but well-formed and her lips full, half-smiling, slightly arrogant. It was her eyes that mesmerized him though, for they were dark, almost black from this distance, and seemed to draw him into her. And there was a shining expectancy about them that puzzled yet attracted him.

'Let me introduce everybody.' Gant's words broke the contact and Steadman swiftly took in the other two members of the group. The man seated next to the woman was aged and wizened, his skin full of deep creases and his eyes set back in shadows cast by a prominent forehead and brows. His wispy white hair was long, straggling over his ears, and his body seemed frail, ready to crumble at the slightest pressure. He held a thin, black cane before him, his gnarled yellow hands resting on its metal top.

The other man was much younger, probably in his early thirties. His short hair was sleeked back, cut in old-fashioned style, his face pale and unblemished, the sneer on his lips part of his features rather than an assumed expression. He wore a suit of darkest grey, elegantly cut and accentuating the slimness of his body. His eyes, though showing curiosity, were heavy-lidded, giving that curiosity a disdainful insolence.

'Kristina, this is Harry Steadman,' Gant said, presenting the investigator to the seated woman. Her lips widened into a full smile as she rose and walked towards him, a hand outstretched.

He took the hand and was surprised at its firmness.

'I'm very pleased to see you, Harry.' Her voice had a sensual huskiness to it. She was tall, at least five-nine, and wore a deep green velvet suit, the jacket thrust open by high breasts beneath a beige blouse. He recognized the same amusement in her look that he had noticed in Gant's the day before, and his feeling of taking part in a charade heightened. He smiled back, the hardness in his eyes causing her a brief moment of unease.

'Dr Franz Scheuer,' said Gant, indicating towards the old man still seated. Steadman nodded, making no attempt to go over. There was no reaction from the old man.

'Felix Köhner,' Gant looked towards the slim, young man who raised a hand in acknowledgement, 'and of course, you've already met Major Brannigan.'

The soldier glared at Steadman.

Nice to be among friends, the investigator told himself, and the thought helped him keep the amused defiance in his own eyes.

'Mr Steadman is here for preliminary discussions in arranging an arms contract for an overseas client,' Gant said, leading the detective towards an armchair and indicating that he should sit. 'Would you like a drink, Mr Steadman? Sherry? Martini? Something stronger for a man like you, I suspect.' That same mocking tone to his voice.

Steadman noticed that the man who had ushered him into the house was poised at a large cabinet containing an array of drinks.

'Vodka would be fine,' he said. Steadman was aware he was under scrutiny while other glasses around the room were being replenished. The old man leaned forward and whispered something to the woman and she hid a smile behind her hand.

'Now then, Mr Steadman,' said Gant, placing himself with his back towards the huge fireplace, 'can you tell us who this mysterious client of yours is, yet? Or must I make wild guesses?'

'No need to,' Steadman replied. 'I'm working for the Israelis.'

If Gant was surprised at the investigator's frankness, he hid it well. 'I see. You know I've never made any arrangements with the Jews before, don't you?' The word 'Jews' seemed to carry all kinds of insinuations.

'I was aware of it. I wondered why?'

'Because they've never approached me before,' Gant said, and laughed aloud. 'Until a few weeks ago, that is.'

Steadman raised his eyebrows in surprise.

'Yes, a young Jew approached me with a request for arms. I told him I was sure something could be arranged, but unfortunately ...' he smiled down at Steadman '... he never returned. I wonder why he suddenly lost interest?'

Bastard, Steadman thought, tired of the cat-and-mouse game. 'I wouldn't know, Mr Gant. What was his name, this ... Israeli?'

'Oh, Kanaan, something like that. Something very Jewish. It's not important now, is it?' His voice taunting.

Steadman grinned, wanting to smash the glass in the arms dealer's disfigured face. 'Not to me,' he said. 'I'd like to inspect some of your weapons.'

'Naturally. I've studied your list and I think I can accommodate you on all counts. Felix will show you the more moderate weapons we keep here, then perhaps you would like to visit our other testing-grounds for further demonstrations of our more powerful weapons.'

'And where is that?' Steadman asked mildly.

Gant chuckled. 'All in good time, Mr Steadman. Our Wewelsburg is not for your eyes yet.'

Heads turned sharply towards Gant, and Steadman saw the surprise – or alarm – in their eyes.

'I'm sorry. Your ... ?' he prompted.

But Gant only laughed again. 'Never mind, Mr Steadman. All in good time. Felix, will you go through the list and tell our guest of the weapons we can provide his clients with? These are weapons developed only by my company, Mr Steadman, weapons far superior to any of those of our competitors – government or otherwise.'

For the next hour, he was lectured by the man called Felix Köhner, who, as his name implied, was a German, while the others silently looked on as though studying him, only Gant sometimes expounding on the merits of certain weapons mentioned. Steadman felt his every movement was being watched, his every question analysed and filed in their minds. It was unnerving, yet the sense of challenge appealed to him. He felt a brooding malevolence emanating from the group, almost a force, and the old man with the shadowed eyes was at its centre.

Even Kristina's beauty seemed to conceal something corrupt, yet he found it difficult to keep his eyes from straying in her direction. She returned his looks with meaningful smiles and twice he caught a look of annoyance on Brannigan's face at those smiles. Was there something between them? What was a major in the British Army doing in such company anyway? What were his ties with Gant? Come to that, what had a Member of Parliament to do with the arms dealer? He had been told Gant had influential friends, but he had not realized they were in government.

Later, he was taken by Köhner and Brannigan through to the rear of the house where he was surprised to find a firing range and a long, brick building in which many kinds of weapons and their machinery were housed. A Gazelle helicopter rested lifelessly on a circular launching pad a hundred yards from the house, and Steadman wondered if the same machine had been used to guide the Chieftain the day before. Thoughts of danger were cast aside for the moment when he became absorbed in the new weapons demonstrated to him by green-uniformed teams. Most of the demonstrations were in principle only – it was hardly practical for the effects to be shown, but the effects *could* be shown on film and in the next two hours, the lethality of the weapons was projected on screen for his benefit.

It was early evening by the time the demonstrations were completed and Steadman was weary of the deadly machinery, the sharpness of Köhner's voice, and the open hostility of Major Brannigan. They returned to the house to find Gant waiting for them, the usual mocking smile on his face.

'Do you like what you've seen, Mr Steadman? Will your friends be interested?' he asked.

'Yes, I think so,' said Steadman, playing the game. 'But it's all pretty soft stuff so far. There are bigger items on my list. When do I get to see them in action?'

'We have, as I've already mentioned, more suitable testing-grounds for the weapons you have in mind. Today we wanted to whet your appetite. We've done that, haven't we?'

'Yes, you've done that. Where are these testing-grounds?'

Gant laughed aloud and turned to the woman, Kristina. *'Unser Parsifal ist neugierig – und ungeduldig.'*

She gave the arms dealer a sharp look and quickly covered it with a smile at Steadman. 'Would you like to see some other demonstrations, Harry?'

He was puzzled. Gant's relish in the game he was playing was obviously not shared by his companions. That had been the second remark of Gant's that had made them nervous. Why had he spoken in German? And why had he called him Parsifal? 'Yes, I'd like to see more,' he answered.

'And so you shall,' said Gant taking him by the shoulder. 'Instantly. Please come with me, Mr Steadman.' The flattened face made his grin seem all the more sinister.

'Edward! Is this the way?'

All eyes turned towards the old man who was now on his feet, his cane supporting him. His voice was thickly accented, and had a strength which belied his feeble frame.

Gant's eyes were cold as he appraised Dr Scheuer. *'Bezweifelst du jetzt die Wörter des Propheten? Alles be wahrheitet sich doch?'*

The old man returned the cold stare. *'Dazu zwingen Sie es,'* he said with suppressed anger.

Now Steadman knew the game was drawing to a close, the pretence coming to an end. And he had achieved nothing apart from putting his head inside the lion's mouth. He tensed, waiting for the right moment to make a break. The advantage was all theirs, but he felt disinclined to wait for them to make their final move. The arms dealer's grip on his shoulder tightened.

'Please come with me, Mr Steadman.' All humour had gone from his eyes as they bore into Steadman's. 'I promise you what I have to show you will be of great interest.'

The moment, for the investigator, had gone. Curiosity had replaced resistance. It could also be a chance to buy more time. He nodded and followed the arms dealer from the room, Major Brannigan and Köhner falling in close behind as an undisguised escort.

Gant led the way into the hall and up a broad staircase. They turned into a long corridor and marched its length to a room at the far end. Gant pushed open the door and motioned Steadman to go through. With some trepidation, he did so.

The sight confronting him wrenched at his gut, dragging it down and his spirits with it. The two slumped figures tied to chairs in the centre of the room were barely recognizable, their faces distorted by swelling and covered in blood. He went to them, knowing instinctively who they were, but lifting the sagging heads to make sure. The woman first, then the man.

David Goldblatt and Hannah.

▪ 10 ▪

'Follow Hitler! He will dance, but it is I who have called the tune!'

'I have initiated him into the "Secret Doctrine", opened his centres in vision and given him the means to communicate with the Powers.

'Do not mourn for me: I shall have influenced history more than any other German.'

DIETRICH ECKART

'Thule members were the people to whom Hitler first turned and who first allied themselves with Hitler.'

RUDOLF VON SEBOTTENDORFF

'The legend of Thule is as old as the Germanic race.'

LOUIS PAUWELS AND JACQUES BERGIER

'What should we do, Mr Blake? Shall we follow them or go in?' Steve looked towards the ex-policeman, trying to discern his features in the darkness of the Cortina's interior.

Sexton shivered, wanting to be on the move, but his training curbed his impatience. 'No, boy. We'll just wait a bit longer and see what happens.'

The car was parked off the road and invisible in the darkness to anyone emerging from the gates further down. Steve had spent half the day within sight of the entrance to the house and his boredom was hard to contain. His only break had been his hasty dash to the nearest phone-box to contact Sexton and let him know what had happened and why he was there. The older man had arrived shortly after dusk and found Steve lurking in the undergrowth not far from the spot where they were now parked. He'd had to drive slowly along the quiet stretch of road twice before the apprentice detective had emerged from the trees; he had felt pleased the boy was so cautious.

'Do you think Mr Steadman's all right?' Steve asked, blowing into his hands to create some warmth. 'Maybe he was in one of those cars that left.'

'I dunno, Steve. There's something very funny going on. I just wish Harry had taken me into his confidence.' Very funny indeed, Sexton thought. All starting with Mrs Wyeth's terrible murder. Was this man Gant connected with that? Sexton had spent the best part of the day probing the few old friends he still had in Special Branch, but they couldn't tell him much about Gant. A bit of an enigma all round, it seemed. Quietly supplying arms to governments abroad – and our own – for years, then suddenly coming to the fore, becoming one of the most important dealers in the country. His dubious association with the Arabs had worried them at first and they'd taken great pains to investigate his background, only to find he was vouched for by men of considerable power and influence. There were certain details they could give Sexton, but nothing that would reveal any deeper insight into the man. The phone call from Steve had sent him racing through town and down into the country where the boy had explained his reason for being there in greater detail.

Steve had taken a room as instructed in the same hotel as Goldblatt and his woman friend. Unable to get a room on the same floor as the two Israelis, he had spent most of his time in the reception area reading newspapers and magazines, situated close to the lifts and stairway so that neither Goldblatt nor the woman would be able to leave without his seeing them. It was a busy hotel and people – mostly businessmen, it seemed – were coming and going all day. But Steve had had trouble keeping the newspaper he was holding from shaking violently when the lift doors had opened and the two Israelis had emerged with three men pressed close to their sides, hemming them in, forming a tight group. He had seen the other three enter the lobby fifteen minutes earlier and disregarded them as they had waited for the lift; they looked like normal businessmen to him. But now, because of the nervousness on the faces of the two Israelis, the woman in particular looking quite agitated, and the rigidity of the tightly packed group, they took on an altogether more sinister aspect. He watched them walk to the reception desk, one of the men breaking off from the group, leading the woman with a hand on her arm towards the swing-doors. With the other two on either side of him, the Israeli asked for his bill, informing the clerk he was checking out and that his luggage would be collected later that day.

Steve was both nervous and excited. To him, this was real detective work, the kind he had read about. There was obviously something dangerous going on – you didn't have to be a super-sleuth to see that – but what to do about it? He didn't have time to ring the office or Steadman at his home, for the men would soon be leaving the hotel and he might lose them. He had to move fast. His Mini was parked in the hotel's underground garage; if he were to follow them, he had better be ready. He folded the newspaper with trembling hands, making a great effort to look outwardly calm. Then he strolled nonchalantly towards the swing-doors and out into the open. He saw the man who had left first with the woman, sitting in a car opposite, a grey Daimler and he gulped anxiously; he hoped his Mini would be able to keep up with it. When he was out of sight of the vehicle, he dashed down the ramp leading to the under-ground parking area and jumped into his little car. He dropped the keys once and then tried to use his front-door key in the ignition by mistake before he finally gunned the engine into life, and he emerged just in time to see the other three men climbing into the Daimler. Hands were taken from pockets and he realized that the two strangers must have been holding guns inside their overcoats. His bowels felt loose at the thought.

The car moved slowly out of the forecourt and nosed its way into the stream of main-road traffic, Steve following and checking his mileage indicator before he, too, eased into the flow. He would have to charge for mileage, of course, and Sexton insisted on accurate figures and no rounding off. The Daimler was easy to follow through London, but once they were past the busy roads of the southern suburbs the pace increased, and Steve broke into a sweat trying to keep the fast-moving car in sight. He managed to, though, more than once due to opportune traffic lights halting the Daimler's progress, and it was with relief that he saw the car turn off the road to stop outside a pair of ornate wrought-iron gates. He drove by slowly, glancing quickly to his right as he drew level with the opening gates, and just having time to see the guard and two vicious-looking Alsatian dogs. He parked his car further down the road and round a bend where it couldn't be seen from the gates, then he crept back through the trees on that side of the road. A high wall enclosed the property, the only break being the iron gate itself. He settled down behind a tree when he was opposite the gate and wondered what his next course of action should be. The words of his tutor came to him. 'When in doubt,' old Sexton would say, 'sit and wait for something to happen. Remember, you're an observer, not a partaker in the action.'

So he settled down to wait, checking the time and making a note of the morning's events in his notebook. He felt pleased with himself, but soon the cold dampness in the air and the increasing boredom of the observation began to depress him. He had just made up his mind to find a pub and have a beer and a sandwich – after all, he was entitled to have lunch – when a familiar car slowed down and pulled over into the gate's entrance. It was Harry Steadman's grey Celica! He almost called out, but ducked down when he saw the guard emerge from his wooden hut on the other side of the gates. Steve watched as the detective left his car and walked over to the guard, passing something through the bars. The temptation again to call out when Steadman strolled back and rested against the bonnet of the Celica was overpowering and he had a hand cupped to his mouth ready to shout when the guard was back at the gate.

He stilled his voice and swore under his breath. There was nothing he could do.

Dismally, he watched the car drive into the grounds and disappear down a road leading into a clump of trees. Only a few moments later, a BMW emerged from the drive and stopped before the gates for them to be swung open. He thought he recognized the passenger as the car swept into the road, but he couldn't quite place the face. Steve waited another twenty minutes before he made up his mind. He would have to get in touch with Sexton – he would know what to do.

He found the phone-box a few miles further down the road and fortunately the ex-policeman was still at the agency. Steve returned to his lonely vigil, happy in the knowledge that Sexton would soon join him and glowing with the praise that had been bestowed upon him. An hour or so later, Sexton's Cortina had slowly driven by, but he had waited until he was sure it really was the ex-policeman, before he'd run further down through the undergrowth and stood by the roadside waiting for the car to pass again.

'Do you think Mr Steadman's in trouble?' he asked Sexton for the third time. 'He's been in there a long time.'

The old man pondered over the question again. Finally, he said, 'Let's give it another hour. Then we'll go and find out.'

'Have you heard of the Thule Gesellschaft, Mr Steadman?' Gant stood over the investigator, his hands tucked neatly into his jacket pockets, his body straight, the smile on his face now arrogant rather than mocking.

Steadman tried to clear his thoughts. He wasn't tied, but the .38 Webley, pressed into his neck by Major Brannigan, bound him to the chair more securely than any ropes. He saw the hate in Goldblatt's eyes as the Israeli glared at the arms dealer. Hannah's body was still slumped, held to the chair by restraining ropes. Goldblatt had recovered consciousness minutes before and had groaned aloud when he saw Steadman, utter despair filling his face. He had tried to speak, but a vicious slap from Köhner had quickly silenced him.

Flickering shadows, cast by a blazing fire, played on the room's high ceiling, creating sinister patterns which were never still. The room itself was large and lit only by the red flames and a single corner lamp. The only furniture was the straight-back chairs on which Steadman, the woman and the old man and the two Israelis sat, and a long table at the far end. Gant, Brannigan and Köhner stood over them all; their very stance seemed threatening.

'The Thule Gesellschaft, Mr Steadman. The Thule Society. Surely, in your years in Military Intelligence and with the Israelis you learned something of our organization?'

Steadman tried to clear the clouding fear from his mind. There was a coldness around him: a coldness that shouldn't have been, for the fire was fierce, its flames high. The chill made his limbs tremble and he consciously fought to keep them still. He vaguely remembered mention of the Thules in the many lectures on the Second World War he'd had to attend as part of his training in Intelligence. They were some kind of occult society which had come into prominence just before the war, but had faded since.

'Ah, I see you have heard of us.' There was some satisfaction in Gant's voice. 'But obviously, our part in the events leading to the last war has not been emphasized to you enough.' He looked around at the assembled group. 'It seems our knight needs some education if he is to know his enemy.'

Köhner, standing over the Mossad agent, chuckled and looked at Steadman with contempt. 'I think our *knight* will soon shit himself,' he said.

Gant joined in the laughter but the remark, if anything, helped steady the investigator's nerves. His fear gave way to anger and Steadman had learned a long time ago to control that anger and channel it into a single-minded strength. And curiosity helped too. Why had they referred to him as a knight? Just what *was* his part in this whole bizarre affair?

'I'm sure you've heard, read – perhaps studied – the allegations that Adolf Hitler was involved in Black Magic, Satanic Rites and such like, in his rise to power, haven't you, Mr Steadman?' Gant raised his eyebrows and waited for a reply, his flat face even more repulsive now that it was bathed in a red glow from the fire, almost shadowless because of the absence of any prominent feature.

'I've heard the theories,' Steadman answered, 'but nothing's ever been proved conclusively.'

'Not proved? Hah! The refusal of men to accept such things is astounding! Keep such things away in the shadows, don't examine them too closely, don't bring them into the light. We might find it's true; then what? We might decide we like the joys such worship brings.' His sarcasm bit through the air. 'And that might mean the rejection of everything we've achieved since the Dark Ages. And look at those achievements: poverty, starvation, continual wars! What has happened to our spiritual quest? We believe we are advancing, mankind, aided by science, moving further away from his primitive beginnings; but just the reverse is happening, Mr Steadman. We are moving further away from our spiritual – our ethereal – beginnings! That was our sin, don't you see! Our Original Sin! Mankind's bestiality! His lust for the physical. And Hitler's great crime against mankind – in the eyes of mankind – was trying to lead us away from that evolvement, back to the spiritual. That's why he was rejected, that's why he had to die. *They killed your Christ for the same reason!*'

Steadman shuddered at the madness in Gant's eyes. He had seen that same madness in the eyes of fanatics all over the world – that same blind reasoning, that same passion for a belief that was based on perverted logic. And he knew the hypnotic effect it had on others, men who looked to a leader because of their own inadequacies, who yearned for someone to give a greater meaning to their own existence. He looked around the room and saw that yearning on their faces, their eyes shining with the emotion that the words had instilled. Only Goldblatt's eyes were filled with loathing.

'Hitler tried to purify his race from the breeds that had infiltrated it, mingled and brought it down to their own animal level, away from its natural Germanic heritage. That he failed meant a step backwards in man's national evolution – I might say reversion, for Thulists believe we need to *return* to our beginnings, not progress away from it. Hitler's plans for the Master Race were based on *völkish occultism,* and it was there the Thulists were able to help and guide him, for we were the roots of National Socialism! Even in those early days, our arms was the swastika with a curved sword and a wreath. A Thulist even designed the Nazi flag for Hitler! A swastika on a white circle against a red background, a symbol of the movement's ideology: the white its nationalism, the red its social ideal – and the swastika, itself, the struggle for victory of Aryan man.' Gant turned away from the group, his hands tucked deep into his jacket pockets, and walked towards the huge fireplace. He gazed into the flames for a few moments then spun round to face them again. 'Do you know the meaning of the swastika, Mr Steadman?' he said harshly.

With the blaze behind him, Gant's body was thrown into silhouette, the outline tinged red. Without waiting for a reply he said, 'It's a symbol of the sun, light, life itself; and for thousands of years, among many races, it's been used as such. The Buddhists believe it to be an accumulation of luck signs possessing ten thousand virtues. For the Thulists – and for Hitler – it was a symbolic link with our own esoteric prehistory, when we were not as we are now, but energy patterns existing on the lost island of Thule. Ethereal shadows, Mr Steadman. You might call them spirits.'

Steadman shivered again. The temperature of the room had dropped even more – or was it only his imagination? The air seemed charged and the arms dealer's silhouette had grown more dense, blacker.

'Signs, symbols, rituals – all are used by occultists to evoke power, just as the Eucharist and the Mass are used in the Church to evoke power. Whether that power is used for good or bad is up to whoever calls on it. Think of how the Catholic Church has abused its use over recent centuries, the crimes committed in God's name. But there is a direct way to tap evil forces and Hitler was advanced spiritually enough to know the Christian Good was evil, the Christian Evil was good! His reading of Nietzsche, the man who claimed God was dead, had convinced him of this. Hitler sought to draw from those evil powers and to do this he used the knowledge he had been given by men like Dietrich Eckart, the Thule propagandist, a dedicated satanist; Karl Haushofer, the astrologer, who later persuaded Hess to defect to England; Heilscher, the spiritual teacher to many of the Nazis. Even Wagner played his part in Hitler's spiritual ascension. Men like the Englishman, Houston Stewart Chamberlain, who had written the *Foundations of the Nineteenth Century,* the inspiration of the Third Reich, while possessed by demons. And Friedrich Nietzsche, who had announced that the time was right for the Übermensch – the Superman, the Élite of the Race. They had helped form Hitler's ideologies. But it was the magicians who initiated him into the practices that would enable him to draw on the forces he needed to reach total power.

'And one of those practices was the reversal of magic symbols. As the Black Mass is a reversal of the Holy Mass in order to evoke powers of evil – the ceremony performed by an unfrocked priest, feasting rather than fasting takes place as a preparation, lust replaces chastity, the altar is the body of a naked woman, preferably a prostitute, the Crucifix is reversed and broken, and the Host becomes a black turnip which is consecrated in the whore's vagina – so symbols are reversed to do the same. The swastika, as a solar symbol, spins clockwise to attract the Powers of Light, the trailing arms indicating the direction of the spin. Hitler ordered that *his* swastika be reversed, to spin anti-clockwise, to attract the Powers of Darkness! And the whole world was witness to his meteoric rise!'

Gant was still speaking in low tones, but the words were hissed, sibilant, as they carried round the room. His audience was rapt and Steadman considered tackling Brannigan, who stood behind him, but the pressure from the gun on his neck never ceased for a moment. He glanced over at Goldblatt and flinched at the desperation on the man's face.

'But Hitler rejected all occult societies, didn't he?' he suddenly shouted at the arms dealer. 'He banned them from the Party.'

All heads swung towards Steadman as though he had suddenly roused them from a dream. A thin laugh came from Gant as he moved away from the fire and approached the investigator, his steps slow and deliberate. He stopped before Steadman, hands still inside his jacket pockets. One hand suddenly snaked out and grabbed the investigator's hair, forcing his head back, and he brought his own forward so that his flat face was only inches away.

'He did not reject *us*, Mr Steadman,' he said, his voice tight. 'In the end, *we* rejected *him*.' He pulled Steadman's head forward again, released it, then slapped him viciously. The investigator tried to heave himself from the chair, but the restraining arm of Brannigan encircled his neck and the gun pressed even deeper into his skin.

'I wouldn't do that, Steadman,' the major warned. 'Just sit quietly, will you?'

Steadman allowed himself to relax back into the chair and his neck was released. Gant smiled, then turned away, returning to the fireplace as though it were a stage for his oratory.

'When Adolf Hitler's ideals were still unformed – perhaps that is a bad word – "unchannelled" might be better, the Thule Society and the German Order Walvater of the Holy Grail were practising Nordic freemasonry, to counter the orthodox Jewish freemasonry which was slowly strangling the German economy in the years after the First World War. We were strongly opposed to the Republican government in Berlin at that time because of their sinister alliance with the rabble of the land: Jews, Slavs, Marxists. These – these degenerates – were gradually seizing control of the state and industry, crippling the country with their demands and their greedy conniving ways, and had created a situation that is not too unlike the situation in Britain today. You would agree with the similarity, wouldn't you Mr Steadman?'

Gant waited for a reply, but when none was forthcoming his voice suddenly shrieked through the stillness of the room. '*You would agree?*'

'The comparison's a little extreme,' Steadman said blandly.

'You think so, do you?' There was malicious sarcasm in Gant's voice now. 'You think the elected government still rules this country? You think management still runs industry? You think the pure Anglo-Saxon still owns the country? Look around you, Mr Steadman, with your eyes open. Not just at this country, but throughout the world. It's happening everywhere, just as it happened in Germany so many years ago: *the upsurgence of the lower races*! The African states, the Arabs – look how fast they're growing. Latin America. China. Japan. *Russia*! And, of course, Israel.

'The comparison is too extreme, you say. Let me assure you: today, the threat is even greater!'

Steadman knew there was no point in arguing. Men like Gant were too obsessed with their own bigotry to see reason.

'The Aryan people needed a strong leader then, just as they need one now. Hitler knew this and he saw we could help him be that leader. We were already creating the climate of feeling against the Jewish-Bolshevik infiltration. We, the Thules, and the members of the German Order Walvater, had already formed a new party within our own – the Deutsche Arbeiterpartei, later to become known as the National Socialist German Workers Party. The Nazi Party.'

Gant paused as if for effect, and Steadman wondered if his audience was going to break into applause. They didn't, but there was a lustre in both Köhner's and Kristina's eyes. The old man sat rock-like, unmoving, his eyes hidden beneath deep shadows. Steadman's attention was drawn back to the arms dealer as he went on.

'Hitler, who was still in the army at that time, had been selected by his commanding officer for a course in political instruction and one of his duties was to attend meetings such as ours. It wasn't too long before he had joined us in our cause! And it was with us that men like Eckart and Guthbertlet initiated him into the study of Teutonic mysticism. It was with us he found his destiny.

'After years of struggle, after persecution and bloodshed, we conquered the enemy within our own country. In 1933, Hitler was made Chancellor of Germany – a great day for the Thules! And a tragic day for Hitler. For it was then he turned against us. He endeavoured to purge Germany of all mystical societies, and on the surface, we suffered with the rest. To the world it appeared he had rejected such cults, but in fact he had found a new source of power. A symbol. A weapon that had been wielded by glorious conquerors of the past! And he set in motion his plans to obtain it.'

▪ 11 ▪

'This modern (British) Empire shows all the marks of decay and inexorable breakdown because there is nowhere in it the courage of firm leadership. If you no longer have the strength to give orders to rule by means of force, and are too humane

to give orders, then it's time to resign. Britain will yet regret her softness. It will cost her her Empire.'

'For England, the First World War was a Pyrrhic victory.'

'To maintain their empire, they need a strong continental power at their side. Only Germany can be this power.'

ADOLF HITLER

'One thing is certain – Hitler has the spirit of the prophet.'

HERMANN RAUSCHNING

'HITLER DID NOT REJECT OCCULTISM, AS YOU SEEM TO BELIEVE, MR STEADMAN. Even the historians who dismiss such ideas as cheap fantasy cannot explain the many indications of Hitler's deep faith in all things occult. The Russians, when they finally overran Berlin, found a thousand corpses of Tibetan monks, all wearing the Nazi uniform – but without any insignia. Every one had committed suicide. Why would Hitler have such men drafted into his army and why should they have finally killed themselves? Why the bizarre experiments carried out on the degenerates of his concentration camps? The deep-freezing of living bodies; the scattering of the ashes from the gas ovens across the land; the thousands of severed skulls the Allies found when they invaded. Hitler held up experiments on the V2 rocket – the weapon that could have won the war for Germany – because he believed they might disintegrate an etheric structure he believed encircled the earth. Were these the acts of a man who had rejected occultism? The SS symbol of the Schutzstaffeln was derived from the ancient Sig rune; the black uniform itself, with its black cap and necromantic death's head insignia – would a man who no longer believed in the Black Arts place such importance on regalia of this kind? Even British Intelligence made use of an occult department as a counter-measure to the Nazi Occult Bureau.'

Although Gant's face was in darkness, Steadman could feel his eyes boring into him. 'You said Hitler had found a source of power. Some kind of symbol.' He remembered Pope's mention of an ancient spearhead. 'Would it have been the Heilige Lance?'

'Why yes, Mr Steadman.' There was a malicious satisfaction in Gant's smile. 'The spear that was believed to be the weapon that pierced the side of Christ as he died on the cross. The Spear of Longinus the Centurion. Adolf Hitler found the spearhead in Vienna's Hofburg Museum when he was little more than a vagrant in the city and made an extensive search into its history. Even at that time his head was filled with the past glories of the German people – and the glories yet to come. He also had visions of other battles, those fought in another dimension, mystical wars between the forces of God and the forces of the Devil.

'Richard Wagner portrayed these conflicts in many of his finest works and

Hitler believed Wagner was the true prophet of his race! It was in *Parsifal*, Wagner's last and most inspired opera, that Hitler discovered the true significance of the Holy Grail, the search for mankind's spiritual fulfilment. The kings, the emperors – the tyrants – who had claimed the holy relic throughout the centuries also knew its secret. It had caused Christ's blood to flow into the ground, to replenish, regenerate the very earth. Its spiritual powers were regarded as the symbolic manifestation of the constant cosmic struggle. It was a symbol of the conflicting powers and only the bearer could choose which it represented. Hitler's knowledge of both history and mysticism made him realize that he had found the link between earthly and spiritual forces. That link, in its material form, was the Spear of Longinus, for it was the weapon, in the hands of a Roman soldier, that had spilled Christ's very spirit into the ground. Hitler vowed he would one day possess the weapon. That day came when he annexed Austria!

'Churchill himself ordered the true facts to be kept secret from the public. The Nuremberg Trials did not even try to explain why such "atrocities" took place. The world had been frightened enough without bringing demonic significance to its attention. Oh no, Mr Steadman, the Führer did not give up his beliefs; far from it. He banned such secret societies because he believed them to be a threat to his own occult power. But the Thule Group continued. We had already become integrated into the SS thanks to the vision of another man, a man far greater than the failure who deigned to be Führer! The man who never gave up even when his beloved country had been betrayed by Hitler. I mean, of course, the Reichsführer, Heinrich Himmler!'

Steadman almost laughed aloud, but he knew Gant was deadly serious. The arms dealer's hands were held clasped together before him, almost in a gesture of prayer.

'Himmler knew the power of the Spear. He had pleaded with his Führer to allow him to take it from Vienna to his Wewelsburg, his shrine of the new Holy Order. But Hitler refused. He had other plans for the sacred relic. The Spear, along with all the other regalia of the Hofburg Treasure House, would be removed legally – not plundered – and taken to St Katherine's Church, Nuremberg, where it would remain until he had attained world dominance. *He failed because he ignored Himmler.*'

Gant was silent now, his shoulders heaving slightly as though he were finding it difficult to breathe. Vapour escaped from his mouth and Steadman realized just how cold the room had become. Unnaturally cold. The fire roared behind the arms dealer, yet no heat seemed to come from it. Gant would never have been able to stand so close otherwise. The arms dealer approached Steadman once again and the investigator tensed, knowing he would not accept another slap without some resistance. But Gant returned his hands to his pockets and stood over Steadman, his attitude menacing.

'But that is the past, Mr Steadman,' he said. 'Let us concern ourselves with the present. As you see – ' he nodded towards Goldblatt and Hannah ' – your two colleagues are of no use to you now. But we would like to know more about you, about your feeble plans to destroy our organization. I'm afraid your friends are not very good talkers. I wonder if your other Mossad associate is?'

'My other associate?' Steadman was perplexed. 'Wait. You mean Baruch Kanaan. You have him ...'

'No, Mr Steadman.' Gant spat out the words. 'I mean your colleague, Holly Miles.'

'Holly? No, you've got it wrong! She's got nothing to do with Mossad.'

'Really? I must say, she had a perfect cover. Even her credentials checked out. It seems she really is some distant relative of my late wife. But then Mossad is known for its thoroughness. As for the other one – this Baruch – I think he regrets the day he ever visited my Wewelsburg.'

'He's alive?'

Gant grinned maliciously. 'Almost,' he said.

Steadman wondered what 'almost' meant. 'Look, the girl – Holly – she has nothing to do with all this. She really is a journalist.'

'Of course.'

'No, I mean it. I don't belong to Mossad either. I finished with The Institute years ago. They hired me for a job, that's all, to find their missing agent, Baruch Kanaan.'

'I haven't got time for all this, Mr Steadman,' Gant said with an air of weariness. 'Köhner will find out all we need to know from you when we're gone. We have more important things to attend to, you see. I'll give your love to Miss Miles. I shall enjoy speaking to her.'

'Where is she, Gant? What have you done with her?' Steadman began to rise, but Brannigan pressed a heavy hand down on his shoulder. 'For Christ's sake, Brannigan, why are you involved with this madman? You're in the bloody British Army!'

Gant's hand cracked across his face again, snapping it to one side and drawing blood from the corner of his mouth.

'Please don't be so impolite, Mr Steadman,' Gant said quietly. 'I am not mad. It's the leaders of this country who are mad, allowing it to sink to these depths.'

'But your sympathies were with the Germans, weren't they,' Steadman said through his clenched teeth. 'You kept saying we – we helped Hitler, we, the Thules.'

'I am a German, Mr Steadman. And a loyal friend to Heinrich Himmler. But we never hated the British. We wanted them as allies. We even admired the British aristocracy, for their views were much in line with ours. Unfortunately, your country chose to condemn us. The ironic part is that many see their error now – not just in this country but in others, too. They've witnessed the rise of the lower races and are suffering because of it! It isn't too late, though. Powerful men are behind us now that the climate is right for the counter-revolution. It will be slow at first, but various "happenings" will cause its escalation. And these "happenings" will be engineered by us, the Thule Gesellschaft. Our first major strike will be tomorrow, which is why we have to leave you in the hands of Mr Köhner. He rather enjoys gathering information from people, you know. He especially enjoyed his conversation with your partner, Mrs Wyeth.'

Steadman ignored the restraining hand on his shoulder and the gun at his neck. His hands found Gant's throat and he began to squeeze with all his strength, the blind fury in him overcoming any fear. His head spun wildly as the gun barrel glanced off his skull, but still he clung to the arms dealer, still he tried to choke the life from him. Gant's fingers clenched around Steadman's wrists and tried to pull his hands away, but incredibly strong though the arms dealer's grip was, Steadman's hate was stronger. Only another blow from the gun barrel weakened his hold. The weapon struck yet again and he slowly sank to his knees, grasping at his victim's body as he went down. Gant's knee sent him keeling over on to the floor. He tried to rise, dazed and hurt, succeeding only in getting his knees under him, his hands flat against the floor. Brannigan stepped forward and kicked his ribs viciously, sending him rolling over on to his back. He tried to clear his head and open his eyes. Through the spinning haze, he saw the withered face of the old man peering down at him, the eyes still hidden inside the two dark caverns. A shriek made him twist his head and though the room tilted and turned, he could see it was Goldblatt who was screaming, straining at his ropes, his hands tied to the arms of the chair, like claws, pointing towards the tall figure of Gant as though wanting to tear him to shreds.

'You bastards,' he was screaming. 'You're still Gestapo filth! You're still the animals you always were. Assassins. You were called the Society of Assassins! And that's all you are!'

Everything took on a dream-like quality as his vision slowly began to fade. He saw Köhner draw something from his inside pocket, saw it gleam redly in the light from the fire, saw Gant slowly nod his head, saw Goldblatt's head pulled back by the hair, saw the knife's blade sweep across the exposed neck as if in slow motion, saw the blood spurt out in a great flood, turning the Israeli's shirt a deep crimson, soaking the floor at his feet. He saw the body stiffen then go into a spasmodic twitching dance.

And he felt the terrible coldness enveloping him as he lost consciousness.

▪ 12 ▪

'A great deal of potentially useful information can be extracted from suspects. Even if suspicion of their treasonable activities proves to be unfounded they can often be persuaded to give the SD information that will lead to other suspects. Such information is usually given under duress, threat, or promise of release.'

HEINRICH HIMMLER

'Bloody hell, a helicopter!' Steve looked anxiously at the older detective, then ducked his head towards the windscreen so he could see the red tail-light of the helicopter as it rose above the treetops and into the air. 'It's come from the house, I'm sure!'

Blake squinted into the night. 'It must be Gant's own private helicopter. Now I wonder where he's off to?'

'If he's in it. I can't see it too well in the dark, but it looks big enough to carry four or five people. D'you think Mr Steadman's there?'

'God knows. It doesn't make me feel any easier, though. I think we're going to have to do something soon.'

Steve nodded in agreement. He was cold, tired and bored. Cramped, too. Sexton hadn't let him leave the car to exercise his stiff limbs. 'What do we do? Drive up to the gate and demand to see him? Or shall we get the police?'

'Get the police? What for? As far as we know, everything's in order. The governor's doing a bit of business with the arms merchant. What could we tell the police?'

'Sorry. Just feeling a bit twitchy, that's all.'

'All right, son, I feel the same. Harry's been in there a long time. I think the first thing we'll do is get nearer the gates, see if anything . . .'

'Hold it!' Steve's hand closed over his arm in the dark. 'Something's happening. Look, headlights!'

Bright beams of light swung into view, shining through the gates and lighting up the dense forest opposite. Their movement stopped for a few seconds, the vehicle presumably waiting for the gates to be opened. Then they were in motion again, swinging away from the two hidden men, moving off down the road towards the west. They had just made out the shape of a large truck before it had turned fully away from them. They watched the tail-lights disappear down the road and were aware of the helicopter's drone fading into the distance.

'Looks like an exodus,' mused Sexton.

'What, Mr Blake?'

'Nothing. Come on, let's have a closer look.'

They left the Cortina and crept as quietly as possible through the undergrowth towards the entrance to the grounds. When they were opposite and still well-hidden, they waited, shivering against the chill night air.

Steadman brought a hand up to the back of his head, wincing at the sudden sharp pain. He was still lying on the floor where he had fallen, the hazy red shadows dancing on the ceiling confusing him for a few seconds. His head began to clear slowly, but when he tried to raise himself on one elbow, the room spun crazily and he sank back, both hands covering his eyes. Hearing movements, he lowered his hands again and blinked. Still not rising, he swung his head round, careful not to move too fast. He saw the hunched figure of a man – the same man who had shown him into the house that afternoon – dragging something along the floor, something that left a dark, liquid trail behind. It hit him suddenly, the memory tearing into his numbed brain. He tried to rise again, turning himself over on to his side, pushing against the floor with his hands, and this time he was partially successful. He was able to support himself with an elbow and get a clear view of the room. Dimly, in the background of his awareness, he heard the fading sounds of what could only have been a helicopter.

'You bastard!' he yelled, seeing Köhner at the far end of the room standing by the long table. He tried to stagger to his feet, but it was too soon and he fell to the floor again.

'Ah, Steadman. So glad you are awake again.' Köhner walked towards him, hands behind his back, a pleasant smile on his face. The man who had been dragging Goldblatt's bloodied body along the floor continued his journey after a curious glance at Steadman. When he reached a far corner of the room, he bundled the body up and pushed it as close to the wall as possible until it was just a black shape in the shadows. Köhner stopped just before Steadman and the investigator stared at the immaculately polished shoes, their highlights hued red in the glow from the fire. The room was no longer so cold, but now Steadman shivered with the rage building up inside him. What kind of man would kill as cold-bloodedly as this one had?

'We are just a small group now, Steadman. You and me, Craven – ' he indicated towards the small man who was now wiping blood from his hands with a handkerchief ' – and a few guards. The others have all gone to the Wewelsburg. A big day tomorrow, you know. Many preparations to make.' A shoe playfully tapped Steadman in the ribs. 'So, for tonight, you're all mine.' Still smiling, Köhner raised his foot to Steadman's shoulder and pushed him down on to his back again. Then he walked away.

Questions crowded the detective's mind. What was the 'Wewelsburg' and why had Gant and the others gone there? What was going to happen tomorrow? Was Gant completely mad, with all his talk of Hitler and this spear? If he was, it was a dangerous madness. But just how dangerous? Were they just a small group of fanatics or were they widespread? Pope had said Gant had influential friends, powerful men. My God – the man he'd seen drive away in the BMW that afternoon, the MP. Was he one of them? And Holly. Why had they taken her? Did they really believe she was a Mossad agent? What would they do to her? Why had they left him with this murderer, Köhner?

His mind stopped churning when he saw his captor standing behind Hannah, his hands resting on her shoulders, fingers kneading the flesh. She was still tied to the chair, but she was conscious. Her eyes were staring at the bundle lying in the corner.

'Come along now, Steadman,' Köhner said, the smile, so pleasant, so sinister, still on his face. 'Come and join us here.' He picked up the empty chair next to Hannah, the chair which had been occupied by Goldblatt, and moved it to a position facing her, a little distance away. 'Bring him over, Craven.'

The small man ran forward, drawing a gun from inside his jacket. Without a word, he grabbed Steadman just above the elbow and yanked him to his feet. With a hard push, he sent the investigator staggering down the room towards the empty chair. Steadman stumbled and fell, but a prod in his back from

Craven's gun encouraged him to rise again. He stood in front of the chair, swaying slightly and was roughly pulled down into it. He looked across at Hannah and there was sadness in her eyes. Regret.

'I'm so sorry ...' she began to say, but Köhner lashed out with his hand, stopping her words abruptly.

'Shut up, you Jew bitch! You'll talk, but you'll talk to me – not him!'

'Let her be, Köhner,' Steadman said wearily. 'She's only a woman, she ...'

Köhner's hand lashed out and again it was the woman he struck. She cried out this time and the regret in her eyes was replaced by fear.

Köhner smiled sweetly at Steadman. 'You see, she is the one to be hurt, not you. You are going to tell me what we need to know because if you don't, it will be the woman who will suffer.' He pulled Hannah's jacket apart, then ripped open her blouse. 'It's incredible how sensitive certain areas of the body are, you know, the erogenous zones, in particular. Ironic, isn't it, how parts that can give so much pleasure can also give so much pain.' He reached inside his jacket and once again withdrew the wicked-looking blade from a sheaf worn like a shoulder holster. Steadman saw the knife was double-edged and still bore the bloodstains of its previous victim. He prepared to launch himself forward as the blade descended towards Hannah's exposed stomach, but Köhner glanced towards him and hesitated.

'Better tie him, I think, Craven,' he said. 'This may be too much for the poor man.'

The cold metal of the gun barrel was placed against Steadman's temple and Craven's rough hand grabbed his shirt and jacket collar, sharp fingernails raking the back of his neck. 'Don't worry, sir, he won't move while I've got him like this.'

Satisfied, Köhner knelt before Hannah and once again directed the knife towards her bare flesh. His other hand reached for the waistband of her skirt and tugged at the material, inserting the blade into the gap, then ripping, tearing the skirt down its middle until the two sides flapped open and hung loosely by her sides. He repeated the process with her panties and tights, then snipped open her bra as he rose again. Now her body was completely exposed to him.

Steadman averted his eyes, feeling her shame, wanting to strike out, but forcing himself to wait for the right moment.

There were tears in Hannah's eyes and she closed them so she would not have to see the three faces before her. Their cause was lost now: David had been murdered and Baruch was probably dead too. Steadman would be killed even though he was an innocent in the whole affair. But they'd had no choice; *they'd had to use him.*

Köhner left them and walked to the end of the room towards the table. He picked up something and as he returned, Steadman was puzzled at the object's familiar appearance. 'A simple hairdryer, Steadman. It doesn't take sophisticated instruments to hurt someone – anything handy will do. This is one of my specialities, actually.' He plugged it into a socket by the door, unwinding the long lead as he rose. Köhner flicked the switch with a thumb and the machine whirred into life. He switched it off again, satisfied, and took up a position behind Hannah.

He grabbed her under the chin and held her head against his body in a vice-like grip. 'The ears, first, I think. It'll do terrible damage to her eardrums. Bad enough when it's cold air, but when it really warms up...'

'There's nothing to tell, Köhner. For God's sake! They hired me to find their missing agent and that was it! That's all I can tell you!' Steadman's hands gripped the sides of the chair, his knuckles white. The hold on his collar tightened.

'Oh, come now,' Köhner said, shaking his head. The dryer was switched on again and air was sucked into its fan and thrown out in a quickly heated stream. 'You can't expect me to believe that, Steadman. You're much more involved. Mr Gant expects quick answers, that's why he left you to me. Pity he was too busy to watch: I think he'd have enjoyed my skill. He has in the past.' He tested the heat by blowing air against his own cheek. 'Ah, yes. Nicely warming up. It's of the more powerful variety, of course – the type used by hairdressers – so it gets a little hotter than usual. Although that isn't really necessary. An ordinary hairdryer is just as good – it takes a little longer, that's all. Let me see, the breasts after the ears. No, perhaps not. I think she'll be too far gone by that time to feel anything there. Maybe the eyes. Yes, the eyes will be good, even with the lids closed.'

'Köhner!'

'And finally, the vagina. That will kill her, of course, Steadman.' The whining machine was pushed against Hannah's ear and she tried to struggle away from it. She screamed as the hot air blasted its way down her ear canal and reached the eardrum.

'Please, stop! I'll tell you everything I know!' Steadman pleaded.

Köhner looked disappointed. He took the dryer away from Hannah's ear but left the motor running. She moaned and tried to twist her head from his grasp, but he was too strong for her. 'Well?' he said.

'It's true what I said about being hired by Mossad to find Baruch Kanaan. I did belong to Israeli Intelligence, but that was years ago. I'd left them.'

'Why would you do that?'

'I – I was sick of the bloodshed. The Arabs killed someone ... someone close to me. I went on the rampage after, killing, killing – until I was sick of it!'

'How traumatic.'

'It's true, fuck you! I'd had too much of it! Too much killing. Too much revenge.'

'And you left them.'

'Yes. I wanted nothing to do with them any more. But they had someone watching me all the time, an old man who'd lived in this country since the war.'

'The jeweller.'

'Yes.' Steadman stared at Köhner. 'Yes, how did you know?'

'It doesn't matter how I know. The old man's dead now – he didn't survive his visit to you last night.' Then he added with a grin, 'Something frightened him to death.'

There was so much happening that Steadman didn't understand. He shook his head and went on: 'They came to me a couple of weeks ago, Goldblatt and this woman, Hannah. I refused to help them find their missing agent, but my partner agreed to without my knowing.'

'Yes, Mrs Wyeth. I had an interesting chat with her. Unfortunately – for her – she couldn't really tell me much. Mr Gant was right: she really didn't know anything.'

'You ... you were the one ...'

'Keep talking, Steadman. No questions, just answers, please.'

Craven made the gun's presence known even more strongly when he felt the investigator tense again. Steadman was nearing breaking point he told himself. Perhaps they should have tied him after all. Pity he was talking so soon, though; he'd have liked to have seen the woman squirm more. She had a beautifully ripe body, the cut clothes accentuating its sensuality; it would be good to see it writhe, see those smooth thighs open wider with agony. Pity to kill her. Maybe Köhner would let him use her first. If he didn't ... well, he would be the one who had to dispose of the body. Plenty of time then ...

The dryer was moving towards Hannah's head again and Steadman quickly resumed talking. 'After Mag ... my partner ... was killed, a man named Pope came to see me. He was from British Intelligence and knew Mossad were operating here. He's also investigating Edward Gant.'

Hannah stopped twisting her head and stared across at the investigator, her eyes wide. 'Steadman, don't ...'

Köhner clamped his hand over her mouth and snarled, 'Don't interrupt, you Jew whore. It's getting very interesting. Go on, Steadman.'

Köhner suddenly yelped in pain as Hannah bit deep into his hand, her teeth drawing blood. He dropped the dryer and reached for the knife again, all in one reaction.

Steadman screamed 'No!' as the blade plunged deep into the flesh of Hannah's stomach, and Craven, whose eyes had been watching the exposed parts of her body, froze at the suddenness of it all. The knife, still embedded, was travelling upwards in a straight line towards her chin when Steadman grabbed the gun barrel and pushed it aside.

The investigator was on his feet, the hand at his neck having no effect on his enraged strength, the chair crashing over behind him. He still held on to the gun and realized the little man hadn't even released the safety-clip. Twisting his body, he brought his leg up and Craven was lifted into the air, his scream piercing the air.

Steadman whirled, forgetting about the injured man for the moment, knowing his agony would keep him out of action for a while. He flew at Köhner, hands outstretched, grabbing for the knife that was now raised against him, its blade red with blood. He was lucky enough to find the knuckles clasped around the knife's handle and he pushed the weapon away as both men went over, dragging the chair holding Hannah with them. They went down in a heap, Steadman pushing the knife-hand to the floor, while Köhner kicked and struggled beneath him, grabbing at the investigator's hair and trying to pull his head back. Hannah, still tied securely to the chair, rolled on to her side, the blood flowing from the long rent stretching from her lower stomach to her breast-bone, creating a dark viscous puddle on the wood floor.

As Köhner pulled at his assailant's hair, he managed to bring a knee up and bring it hard against Steadman's hip, the blow sending the investigator to one side, Köhner rolling with him. The knife came up from the floor and he almost managed to wrench himself from the investigator's grip. But Steadman knew if the knife-hand got free again, Köhner had the speed and experience to kill him easily. Both men were on their sides and Köhner used his strength to carry his body through with the roll so that he gained the advantage of having Steadman beneath him. He let go of the investigator's hair to add strength to the hand pressing the knife towards Steadman. The pointed tip pushed against Steadman's cheek, pressing the skin inward until the flesh broke and a trickle of blood emerged. Steadman had both his hands around Köhner's and he tried to hold the straining blade away, but he felt it slowly sinking into his cheek, millimetre by millimetre, eager to burst through into the cavern of his mouth. Köhner's eyes were above him, staring down, a gleam of triumph and blood-lust in them. He felt no pain; only the relentless force of the cold metal.

He slowly turned his head, feeling the skin tear as the steel blade sliced a shallow red-lined path across his cheek.

He used his whole body to try and squirm away from Köhner and felt his opponent moving with him, endeavouring to keep him pinned. The knife edge was grating against bone now and he knew his head would move no further; metal and bone were locked together. With a roar he changed his direction and heaved upwards, using all his strength against the other man's weight. Köhner resisted but the movement was too sudden; he was forced backwards. When he knew he had reached the point of overbalance and the knife had been pushed clear of Steadman's cheek, he allowed himself to be carried with the momentum, skilfully using his weight and strength to his own advantage. His intention was to continue the roll, using pressure only when the movement would put him on top again. But Steadman still retained enough cunning in hand-to-hand combat to break away at the right moment. He hadn't wanted to release the hands holding the knife, but he had guessed Köhner's reason for withdrawing the pressure. He twisted away from his surprised antagonist and kept rolling, knowing the weapon would be following, striking towards his exposed back.

He felt rather than heard it thud into the floor behind, and swiftly rose to a crouching position while the knife was tugged free. He turned to face his antagonist, hands held poised before him.

Köhner had also risen and both men were silent as they watched one another, each waiting for the other to make the first move. Steadman stared into Köhner's eyes, the blade still in the periphery of his vision but not in focus, the eyes would tell him what the man would do. He could hear Craven groaning and writhing on the floor to his left and he knew he would have to move fast if he were to avoid having two opponents again: Köhner was enough on his own. Köhner's eyes widened slightly before he lunged, but it was enough to give the investigator warning. He threw himself to one side, ducking low, and the blade went on past his shoulder. Their bodies made contact and Köhner staggered, spinning round, but managing to control his movements so that he was balanced and ready to lunge again. Steadman wasn't there though; he was racing towards the black object lying in the centre of the room. Köhner followed, confident that the knife would be deeply embedded in the investigator's back before he had time to use the gun.

Steadman realized the same. He stooped and reached for the back of the overturned chair he'd been held captive in only minutes before and, hearing the footsteps behind, he swung his body round, bringing the chair up as he did so. It crashed against Köhner's shoulder causing him to stumble to one side, and before he could recover fully, the chair was on its return journey, this time aimed at his head. He ducked instinctively and Steadman was momentarily thrown off balance. He recovered quickly enough to swing the chair up again, this time as a shield against Köhner's oncoming rush. It struck Köhner's body and Steadman pushed, the knife waving in the air in a vain attempt to reach him. Steadman exerted all his force and kept pushing, moving the other man backwards. Köhner resisted, hopelessly caught up between the legs of the chair, unable to thrust it aside. He took the only course available: he dropped to the floor pulling the chair with him but lifting it so it sailed over his head. It still left him at a disadvantage, for he was flat on his back, and he struck out at Steadman's legs with the knife as he lay there.

The investigator drew in his breath as the knife's razor-sharp edge slid along his shin-bone, only its angle preventing it from cutting deeply. He tried to leap clear of the thrashing blade as he staggered over Köhner's recumbent figure and fell heavily against the chair which had crashed into the floor just beyond the fallen man's head.

Steadman found himself lying on his stomach, the chair leaning against him and, for the briefest second, he looked into the face of Hannah still trapped in her chair in the centre of the big room. Her eyes were pleading and her lips moved as her life oozed from her. She was looking directly at him. He staggered to his feet, bringing the chair up so it cracked against the advancing Köhner's chin, sending the German reeling back. Köhner raised a hand, reaching for his eyes as if to wipe the dizziness from them. Steadman was on him, relishing his sudden advantage, reaching for the arm clutching the weapon with both hands and bringing it down sharply against his rising knee in an effort to break it. He didn't succeed, but at least the knife flew from Köhner's grasp, clattering uselessly against the bare floorboards.

The investigator used his elbow against the other man's ribs, still holding the now limp arm outstretched with one hand. Steadman heard Köhner gasp, but his satisfaction was short-lived as his opponent twisted and managed to encircle the investigator's neck with his other arm, squeezing hard to cut off his air. Steadman leaned forward and jerked Köhner off the floor, bending almost double so the other man tumbled over his shoulders on to the floor before him.

Lithe as a cat, Köhner was up again and turning to face him. But Steadman's rage at this creature who could destroy lives without remorse, and with an ease that said he was a master of it, drove him on relentlessly. He plunged into the murderer, his fists striking the man's face, sending him staggering back towards the low-burning fire. Fear began to show in Köhner's eyes as Steadman bore down on him. He knew the investigator's rage had made him unstoppable; only a weapon would have any effect. He looked around, desperate for a means of escape or a weapon within reach and saw there was nothing. The knife had disappeared into the shadows, Craven's gun was on the other side of the room. But Craven was beginning to rise now. He was on his knees, his shoulders hunched, his hands still pressed between his legs. But he was beginning to rise! If he would only reach for the gun!

Köhner was about to call out to the kneeling man when another blow sent him reeling. 'Wait, I can help you! Don't ...' Steadman paid no heed to the words. The same hatred he had felt when Lilla had been so mercilessly killed had once again taken over.

Köhner recognized the hate and put up his hands to ward Steadman off, but they were easily knocked aside. He backed away until he could feel the heat behind him. The fire! Oh God, he was backing into the fire! He tried to make a break to one side, but Steadman grabbed his collar and struck him again, a hard, stinging blow that covered his vision with a blinding light. He fell, his arms flailing, instinctively trying to grab the sides of the fire surround. His hands made no contact and he screamed as he fell into the small, dancing flames. As the heat burnt his coat and scorched his body, he pleaded with the investigator to pull him out.

Steadman raised a foot and planted it squarely on the burning man's chest, holding him there, his loathing rejecting any mercy. Köhner screamed again and again, twisting his body, trying to wriggle free while Steadman held him, no expression on his face. It was only when Köhner's hair began to burn that the investigator reached forward, grabbing him by the lapels of his jacket, and pulled him clear. Köhner's screams echoed round the room as Steadman tore the jacket from him, much of the shirt coming away with it, and threw it towards the fireplace. The investigator beat out the smaller flames on the man's clothing with his hands, not even wincing at the sight of the scorched flesh. Köhner's singed hair hung in blackened clumps on the back of his head and his teeth chattered as though he was freezing.

Craven's cry of alarm warned Steadman and he turned just in time to see the little man crawling rapidly towards the gun lying on the floor. The investigator sprang forward, racing towards the scrambling man, who looked up in fear at the sound of his approach. It was that moment of hesitation that lost Craven his chance. He was half up, no longer crawling, reaching down for the gun, when it was kicked from under his grasp. He saw it scudding away into the shadows and felt terror as a hand fell on to his exposed neck. Another hand grabbed the back of his trousers, and then he was being propelled forward, his own rush towards the gun now working against him. He was powerless in the grip that held him and the floorboards sped beneath his feet as he tried to keep his balance. They were gathering momentum, heading towards the table at the far end of the room, towards the twisting body of Köhner. He tried to sink to the floor when he realized Steadman's intention, but the grip was too strong, the pace too fast. He felt himself lifted, skidding across the table's surface – and then beyond.

He felt the glass break around him, yet did not hear the sound. The ground rushed towards him and, mercifully, he felt nothing as his head broke open against it.

Steadman stood with his hands resting against the table-top, breathing in deep lungfuls of the cold night air as it gushed through the shattered window, his shoulders heaving with the exertion. The fury was still in him, hardly dissipated by the violence he had just committed; but it was a cold fury now, his mind working almost dispassionately. He knew the disgust for himself would come later, would torment with the knowledge that he was little better than the men he had acted against. For the moment, though, those feelings would be held in abeyance – there was so much more to do.

He pushed himself away from the table and crossed the room, ignoring Köhner, who lay on his stomach, moaning softly, parts of his clothing still smouldering. Steadman knelt beside Hannah and grimaced at the sight of the terrible wound the knife had inflicted. The floor around her was awash with blood and he turned his eyes away from the long gash when he saw glistening organs beginning to protrude from the opening. He thought she was dead, but as he began to untie her bonds, her eyelids fluttered, then opened. Her lips moved as she tried to speak.

'Don't talk,' he told her. 'I'm going to get you to a hospital.' He knew the words were without meaning, for there was no chance she would live.

Hannah knew it too. 'Steadman,' she said, her voice faint as though she were calling back to him from a distance as her life seeped away. He leaned down towards her, putting his ear close to her mouth to listen. It was difficult to make out the words, but she kept repeating them as though making sure he understood. 'The ... Spear ... for ... Israel, Steadman ... you must ... for Israel ... get ...'

Her voice trailed off as Hannah sank into her death. Steadman drew away from her, closing her eyes with his fingers and arranging her clothing to cover her nakedness and the awful gaping wound. He touched a hand to her cheek, then rose to his feet. He looked towards Köhner, his eyes cold.

The burnt man was on his hands and knees, moving towards the door. He turned his head at the sound of Steadman's approach and his eyes widened in fear when he saw the expression on the investigator's face.

Steadman pulled him to his feet, and pushed him on to the table, Köhner screaming as his scorched back made contact with the table-top.

'You're going to tell me some things, Köhner,' Steadman said, shaking him by his shoulders. 'You're going to tell me what will happen tomorrow.' He brought Köhner's face close to his own and said. 'You're going to tell me where Holly Miles and Baruch Kanaan are being held.'

Köhner tried to pull himself away, but his injuries – and his fright – had weakened him.'I can't tell you anything, Steadman. Please, you've got to get me to hospital.'

'Not until you've told me all I want to know, Köhner.'

'No, they'll kill me!'

'*I'll* kill you.'

'Please, listen. There's nothing you ...'

'Where has Gant gone to?'

'I can't tell you!'

Steadman slammed him back down on to the table. He placed his elbow under Köhner's chin, pushing it up, ignoring his feeble efforts to pull away. He grabbed the German's right hand and held it by the wrist with one hand, then with the other he took hold of one of the fingers. The smallest. He pulled it back swiftly and it snapped.

He closed his mind to Köhner's scream and fought his own revulsion. He had to fight on their own level, evil for evil. For Holly's sake. For Baruch's. He would not let them be taken as Lilla had been taken.

'Tell me, Köhner. Where have they gone? Where are they holding the girl?'

Tears ran down the sides of Köhner's face and Steadman was afraid the man might pass out. It said much for his toughness that he hadn't.

'The Wewelsburg! They've gone there! Please don't!'

The Wewelsburg. That name again. Steadman took hold of another finger. 'What *is* the Wewelsburg, Köhner?' he asked, beginning to apply pressure again.

'Don't! It's a house – an estate. It belongs to Gant.'

'Where?'

'On the coast. North Devon. Please don't hurt me again ...'

'*Where exactly?*'

'Near a place called Hartlands. Further on!' Köhner tried to squirm away and the investigator pressed down harder with his elbow. 'The girl is there, Steadman. She's all right, she's alive!' The words were meant to appease him.

The west coast. Holly had said Gant had a place on the west coast. Was this his Wewelsburg? 'Okay. Now tell me what Gant is up to? What's happening tomorrow?'

'I can't. I can't tell you.'

It was only footsteps on the stairs that prevented another of Köhner's fingers from being broken.

▪ 13 ▪

'We must interpret "Parsifal" in a totally different way to the general conception ... It is not the Christian-Schopenhaurerist religion of compassion that is acclaimed, but pure, noble blood, in the protection and glorification of whose purity the brotherhood of the initiated have come together.'

ADOLF HITLER

THE TWO GUARDS, BOTH ARMED WITH A GENERAL-PURPOSE MACHINE-GUN AND rifle similar to the NATO FN, but of Gant's own manufacture and considerably lighter because of it, raced up the stairs to the room where the prisoner was being held. They were veteran mercenaries who had finally found a binding allegiance – as had all the soldiers in Edward Gant's private army. It was a small army, no more than fifty carefully chosen soldiers, a Guard really – a *corps d'élite*. Some were mercenaries who fought battles for others, their loyalty only bought with money; others were taken from the crack SAS regiments, chosen because of their special skills and aptitudes by Major Brannigan and steered into Gant's organization. Their common bond was their extreme right-wing views and a dislike for the world in general. They admired strength and craved strong leadership: Gant provided them with that leadership. Officially, they were merely employees of Gant's weapons' factory, testing the weapons in practical ways and acting as security for the plant. They wore dark green overalls which somehow succeeded in having a military air without actually being uniforms. There were no insignia, no badges of rank; but each man knew his position and who his superiors were. They enjoyed their secret military ceremonies which took place only on the arms dealer's vast North Devon estate, even grateful for the harsh discipline imposed on them there, and disliked their dealings with the various factions who visited the estate to learn how to use the many weapons they were buying from Gant. They sneered at the groups of Arabs, Africans, Japanese and Irish they had to teach, *wanting to turn the weapons on them*, but patiently went through the exercises, demonstrating, explaining, because they knew it helped the cause of world disunity. These groups of fanatics would help create the world unrest which would succour their own movement. They had learned to obey their orders without question, the fate of their comrades who had failed to do so ever-present in their minds. Hanging may have been abolished in England, but Edward Gant worked to his own laws. They had no title, but sometimes, when they were very drunk and only when they were safely inside the estate's boundaries, they laughingly gave themselves a name. They called themselves the Soldiers of the Fourth Reich.

These two, McGough and Blair, had been left behind with the guard on the gate, the three others of their unit returning to the estate by lorry that night. The rumour was that a special op was planned for the next day, but as yet no briefing had been given and speculation on their part was strictly forbidden. They had regretted being left behind, though did not question it. Nor did they question Gant's particular instructions.

They rounded the bend in the wide stairs and stopped abruptly, aiming their guns at the two figures that had appeared on the landing above them. One of the figures was Köhner, his face contorted with pain and his blackened shirt hanging loosely around him; the other man standing immediately behind Köhner was the prisoner, the private investigator who had been shown through the weapons store at the back of the house that afternoon.

'Don't move!' Blair commanded and resumed his ascent of the stairs, McGough following close behind.

Steadman did not hesitate. There was no time to search for the fallen gun in the room he and Köhner had just left, so he used the nearest thing at hand to stop the progress of the two men below: Felix Köhner. He shoved the injured man hard, sending him careering down the stairs, his arms flailing wildly. Köhner's body struck McGough and Blair with a force that sent all three tumbling backwards until they landed in a tangled heap at the bend. Steadman descended the stairs three at a time and was able to kick the gun from one of the soldier's hands before it could be aimed at him. The other man was scrambling towards his gun which had clattered further down the stairs, and Steadman hooked a foot beneath him, sending the soldier well beyond the fallen weapon.

The investigator lifted the dazed Köhner to his feet and said, 'Come on, I still need you.' He pushed him forward and turned to the soldier who was beginning to rise. Steadman's knee hit him full in the face and the soldier slammed back against the wall, then slid to the floor. The investigator pulled Köhner away from the banister and raced him down the stairs past the disorientated second man lying at the bottom. He dragged Köhner down the hall towards the doorway, knowing only speed would prevent a bullet in his back. If he had tried for one of the guns himself, the men would have been on him before he'd had a chance even to aim it; past experience told him, when outnumbered, keep on the move. He reached the front door and yanked it open, pushing Köhner ahead of him into the night.

On the stairs, McGough had reached his weapon and was automatically sighting it on Steadman's back below, when he caught sight of Blair's upturned face. It was white and the lips were clenched, but it shook hastily. McGough lowered the gun and stared regretfully at the front door as it slammed shut.

Steadman was relieved to find no guards outside and his car still waiting. He hurried the dazed Köhner over to it and yanked open the passenger door, pushing the injured man into the seat. He ran round the front of the car, reaching in his trouser-pocket for the keys, then jumped into the driver's seat, hauling the weakened Köhner back as he tried to scramble out.

'I told you I need you, Köhner. You're going to get me through the gate.'

He gunned the engine, expecting the door of the house to be flung open at any moment and the two guards to run out, machine-guns blazing. But his luck held: there was no movement from the house. They still must have been stunned. The Celica spewed up gravel as it roared away from the building towards the main gate. Steadman switched on full-beam to blind the guard and his dogs, knowing he would have to be through those gates within seconds, for the two soldiers would soon ring the hut from the house – if they hadn't already done so.

As the car sped round the curve in the long drive, the guard, standing before the solid gate with the menacing Alsatians, was frozen in the headlights. The investigator brought the car to a halt ten yards away from him and the guard raised an arm up to his brow to cut out the blinding glare. The dogs strained at their leash.

'Who's there?' the guard called out. 'Turn those bloody lights out so I can see you.

'Tell him to let us through, Köhner,' Steadman said quietly.

Köhner shook his head, his injured hand clasped to his stomach. His smoke-dirtied face was streaked with tears. 'Go to hell,' he managed to gasp.

The guard began advancing on the car, a hand reaching inside his tunic for a gun he kept hidden away from usual visitors to the house. The dogs were excited, instinctively catching the mood of the situation. The guard's arm was at full-stretch as he tried to hold them back and he had to dig his heels into the gravel to prevent himself being dragged forward too fast. The growls of the dogs became barks and then howls as they struggled to break free.

Steadman moved fast. He reached across the injured man and hooked his finger around the door-catch, pushing the door open. Then he shoved Köhner out of the car.

Köhner rolled on to his back, screamed and tried to rise. It was too much for the Alsatians. They broke away from the guard and pounded towards the rising man. They leapt upon him, teeth slashing, sensing their victim was injured and easy prey.

The confused guard was hurrying forward, his gun aimed at the frenzied group, the car's lights still dazzling his vision. Steadman depressed the accelerator and the car shot forward, striking the guard, knocking him over the bonnet and into the gravel. Hitting the brakes immediately, Steadman leapt from the car, snatched the revolver from the stunned guard's grasp and reached for the key to the gate which hung on a chain from the man's belt. It was a huge key and Steadman's shaking hands fumbled at the clasp securing it to the chain for several precious seconds before it was free. He could hear Köhner's screams and the blood-chilling snarls of the dogs on the other side of the car as he fumbled. The guard, whose legs felt numb and lifeless from the blow they had received, raised himself on to his elbows and tried to grab at the gun. Steadman pushed the man's head back on to the driveway with a force that put him completely out of action.

The investigator finally yanked the key free and ran to the gate, keeping a wary eye over his shoulder in the direction of the dogs who, by now, were wild with bloodlust. He inserted the key and twisted, then swung the gates wide. As he returned to the car, holding a hand up against the headlights' glare, he knew he could not just leave Köhner to the mercy of the Alsatians. He stepped out of the beam of light, the gun raised before him, and blinked his eyes rapidly to get them used to the sudden darkness again. The screams had stopped and the snarls were less wild as the dogs pulled and tugged at the inert body. One of the Alsatians sensed his approach and turned its eyes towards him. Its growl was deep-throated and full of warning. The other looked up too, its mouth bloody and drooling pink foam. Steadman saw their muscles tense as they readied themselves to spring at him. He raised the gun and fired two rounds into each body as they leapt, taking a step back as one of the dogs slumped against his legs.

He quickly glanced at the unmoving body of Köhner, then walked around to the other side of the car and climbed in. He drove through the open gateway on to the main road.

Steadman was forced to jam on his brakes once again as he began his turn.

Two figures had emerged from the woodland on the opposite side of the road and were frantically waving their arms at him.

'Sexton! Steve! What the hell are you doing here?' Steadman wound down his window and looked at his two employees with amazement.

Sexton jerked a thumb at his companion. 'Goldblatt and a woman were picked up by three men. Steve followed 'em here. Are you all right, Harry?' he asked, suddenly noticing the fresh blood on Steadman's cheek.

The investigator ignored the question. 'I've got to get to a phone.'

'There's one about a mile-and-a-half down the road, Mr Steadman,' Steve said, excited by the action.

'Okay. Jump in, both of you. There'll be men coming from the house any minute.'

The two men hurried around to the passenger side of the car, Steve nimbly climbing past the front seat into the back and Sexton slumping his cold-stiffened frame beside Steadman.

'It's back that way, Mr Steadman.' Steve pointed. The investigator quickly reversed, the rear of the car almost entering the grounds again, then spun the wheel to the right as it screeched forward. Sexton just had time to see a dark figure sitting in the driveway rubbing the back of his head. He turned to face Steadman as the car gathered speed along the road.

'What's been happening, Harry? We were a bit worried.'

'It's Gant. He's a madman. He had Goldblatt and the woman killed. And Maggie.' There was a weariness in Steadman's voice.

'Christ! What do we do? Get the police?'

'Not yet. I'm going to call a man named Pope. He works for Intelligence – MI5. He'll have to sort it out.'

'But what about this Gant? He'll get away.'

'Already gone,' Steadman replied grimly.

'The helicopter. We saw a helicopter leave and a truck drove out shortly after.'

Steadman dimly remembered the sound of rotor blades as he'd recovered consciousness back in the house. 'Yes, that would be it. I saw one earlier in the afternoon. He's gone to somewhere he calls his 'Wewelsburg". Somewhere in North Devon.

'He's got an estate there where he tests weapons,' Sexton said. 'I found that out this morning. A lot of the country around that area is used by the Military for testing.'

Steadman nodded. 'He's got something planned for tomorrow – I've no idea what. It sounds important to him and his crazy organization, though.'

'What's he up to?'

'He imagines himself as the new Hitler – only stronger. I told you – he's completely mad. Where's this bloody phone, Steve?' There were street lights now, and houses lined the roadside.

'Not far. Just up here a bit on the left.'

'What happened back at the house, Harry?' Sexton asked. 'How did you get away?'

'Gant left me behind – with his special inquisitor. Fortunately for me, neither he nor the few remaining guards were too efficient. I had a lot of luck on my side, though.' He pulled over to the telephone box. 'Wait here,' he told the two men as he left the car, its engine still running. 'Keep an eye on the way we've come. They may decide to look for me.' Sexton and Steve turned their attention to the rear window.

The pips indicating someone had lifted the receiver at the other end began almost as soon as Steadman had finished dialling the memorized number, and he pushed the coin into its slot. A voice said, 'Pope,' and the investigator breathed a sigh of relief.

'Pope,' he said. 'Thank God you're there.'

'Steadman? I've been waiting for your call. Been rather anxious, actually. Now, have you found out any more on Gant?'

There was a hint of relief in Pope's voice, but it was hardly comforting to Steadman. 'I found out plenty, but it's all so incredible. You were right. Gant is the head of an organization called the Thule Gesellschaft.' Steadman quickly told him what had happened at the house and Pope listened patiently, occasionally interrupting with a pertinent question. 'But why did he leave you in the hands of this man, Köhner?' he asked when Steadman explained Gant's departure from the house.

'To get information from me, to find out what I knew and who else was involved. Gant has a big operation to mount and he had no time personally to waste on me.'

'Operation? What sort of operation?' Pope's voice had a keen edge to it.

'I don't know. He's gone to his North Devon estate – somewhere near Hartlands – to carry it out. Do you know anything that's going to happen some time tomorrow, Pope? Anything in that area?'

There was a long silence at the other end then Pope said, 'There is something, but ...' Another silence. 'No, it can't be that, it's nothing to do with that area. Unless ... Oh God, he wouldn't try to do anything like that.'

'What, Pope? Remember, he's a madman. He'd do anything to further his crazy cause.'

'Not over the phone, Harry – I'll tell you later. We'll have to move in. We know this estate – a large part of his weapons-testing takes place there, so it's usually under some sort of surveillance by us.

'There's another thing. He's got the girl there. Holly Miles. He thinks she's working for Mossad.'

'The journalist? Is she working for Mossad?'

'I was going to ask you the same question.'

'I've no idea, dear boy. Rather confusing, isn't it?'

'What about Major Brannigan and the MP I saw down here? What will you do about them?'

'They'll be hauled in when we have Gant. It's all very delicate, though.'

'The murders of Maggie, Goldblatt and Hannah – and maybe Baruch Kanaan – are all very *indelicate*, Pope,' Steadman said angrily.

'Of course, Harry. They'll be accounted for, don't worry. Now listen, can you get to Hartlands?'

'Are you crazy? Why the hell should I go there? It's up to you now.'

Pips began, informing them that their allocated time was up, and Steadman fiercely pushed another coin into the slot.

'Harry, are you still there?'

'I'm here.'

'I need you to go there, Harry. You know Special Branch has to make the arrests – I haven't that power as MI5. You're the only man who knows the full story, and if I order a large force into the estate, I need some verification. Your personal evidence will save a lot of unnecessary official wrangles. Please believe me, I need you there if only to convince my superiors.'

'Why can't I just come over to your HQ now?'

'It's easier this way. It's pointless for you to come back to London when you're already on the way to the west. I want you on the spot, Harry. Do you feel up to it?'

'I'll manage.'

'Good man. There's a town called Bideford not far from Hartlands. Find yourself a hotel and book in. We'll find you there easily enough by checking round.'

'Will you involve the local police?'

'They'll be informed but not involved. Too many people in high places involved for this to be made public, I'm afraid.'

'Listen, Pope, if you're going to protect...'

'Please, Harry, there's no time for discussion now. I've got a lot to do and you have a long journey ahead of you. I'll have to have any calls from Gant's estate in Guildford intercepted for a start. If any of those guards warn Gant before I can get a squad down...'

'Christ, Pope...'

'Please, Harry, there's no time. Remember the girl's in danger. I'll see you tomorrow.'

The receiver at the other end was put down and Steadman stared blankly at the burring earpiece. He slammed down the phone and left the booth.

His two companions looked at him anxiously as he threw himself back into the driver's seat. He ran his hands over his face as though to wipe away the fatigue.

'What now, Harry?' Sexton prompted gently.

'I'll take you back to your cars, then I've got a trip to make. To Devon.'

'Are we coming with you, Mr Steadman?' Steve asked eagerly.

'No, I don't want either of you involved in this thing.'

'We work for you, Harry,' said Sexton. 'If you're involved, we're involved. Besides, we thought a lot of Mrs Wyeth.'

Steadman smiled at them. 'There's one thing you can do, but I'll tell you what on the way back to your cars. Tell me though: have either of you heard of something or someone called "Parsifal". When I was in the house, Gant said something in German to his friends. He said: "Our Parsifal is inquisitive and impatient." He was referring to me and obviously didn't know I understand a little German thanks to my ex-wife. Have either of you heard the name before?'

Sexton shook his head, but Steve leaned forward towards the front seats, his eyes gleaming.

'There is a Parsival, Mr Steadman. He was one of the Teutonic Knights. Wagner wrote an opera about him, but he changed the spelling to "Parsifal" for some reason. It was all about the Holy Grail and the sacred Spear that was stolen from the king, Amfortas, the Keeper of the Grail.'

The two men twisted their bodies to stare at his excited face, lit by a nearby street light.

'A sacred Spear?' Steadman said quietly.

Steve suddenly became embarrassed under their scrutiny. 'I'm a bit of an opera freak – that's how I know the story. I think Parsifal was one of Wagner's greatest. He was...'

Steadman interrupted him. 'You say this Spear was stolen?'

'Yes, by Klingsor, the evil magician. It was Parsifal who had to get it back.'

'What's all this got to do with Gant, Harry?' Sexton asked impatiently. 'Aren't we wasting time?'

Steadman silenced him with a raised hand. 'Tell me the whole story of this Parsifal, Steve,' he said. 'Try to remember every detail. It could be the key to this whole bloody business.'

Steve looked in bewilderment at the investigator, took a deep breath, then began.

▪ 14 ▪

'But are we to allow the masses to go their way, or should we stop them? Shall we form simply a select company of the really initiated? An Order, the brotherhood of Templars round the holy grail of pure blood?'

ADOLF HITLER

STEADMAN RELAXED ON TO THE BED AND REACHED FOR THE CIGARETTES ON THE small side-table. He lit one and drew in a deep breath, watching the smoke swirl in the air as he exhaled. He felt rested now and his mind was beginning to think more clearly. He winced when he crossed his ankles, then drew up a trouser-leg to examine the knife wound inflicted by Köhner the previous night. It wasn't deep, but it was irritatingly painful. Fortunately the hotel receptionist hadn't noticed the torn trousers from behind the desk. After reading the investigator's London address as he filled in the card, she had merely accepted Steadman's somewhat dishevelled appearance as a result of his long drive. In fact, Steadman had broken his journey.

It was just outside Andover that events had caught up with him. He had been forced to stop the car as tiredness overwhelmed him, and a feeling of remorse had had a lot to do with that tiredness. Even the thought of the danger Holly – and Baruch, if he really was still alive – was in could not spur him on. In his present condition, he knew he could not help anyone. Slumping against the steering wheel, he cursed himself for having become involved with such violence, for having broken his vow to himself and Lilla that never again would he become part of such things. It wasn't his fault, he knew. He'd been reluctantly drawn into it; yet he'd used their own kind of violence against them. And it had been perpetrated with a coldness that now disturbed him. Pope had been right at their first meeting. His aggressiveness *had* only been smothered; it was still there waiting to be unleashed.

He felt no pity for Köhner or the little man, Craven – they had deserved to die – but he felt concern for his own actions. He had recovered enough energy after a while to find a motel and there he'd spent the night, surprisingly falling into a deep and dreamless sleep. The following morning, after a shower, then a half-eaten breakfast, and covering the gash in his cheek with a Band-aid obtained from the curious but sympathetic motel receptionist, he had resumed his journey, feeling better for the rest, his mind clear again. The guilt was still there but, he thought cynically, he would wallow in it when matters had been put right. The remainder of his journey had been more relaxed and it had given him time to sort out his thoughts. By the time he reached Bideford he had a new resolve. Before, his purpose had been to protect Holly, to let Pope deal with Gant and whatever he was up to; but now he had decided to take care of the arms dealer himself. After all, wasn't that the reason for his involvement in the whole bizarre affair – the final confrontation between himself and Edward Gant?

The blood on the knife-wound had hardened, forming a natural healing seal. He slid his trouser-leg back down and rested the injured limb; he could bandage it later. He looked at his watch, impatient for Pope's call. Had he missed him because of his unplanned late arrival at the hotel? No, Pope would keep checking all the hotels until he showed. What was keeping him though?

It was strange how it all made a crazy kind of sense: Hitler, the Spear of Longinus, Gant's referring to him, Steadman, as Parsifal. But what was the Wewelsburg? More symbolism, ancient beliefs? Steve had told him about Wagner's opera, and the significance had begun to sink into Steadman's confused brain. It was the reason for his involvement, why it had to be played out to the end. It was the fulfilment of the legend, but this time with a different ending, and that ending would be the omen of their success.

The ringing of the bedside phone startled him from his thoughts. He picked up the receiver.

'Oh, Mr Steadman? Two gentlemen in reception to see you. A Mr Griggs and a Mr Booth. Acquaintances of a Mr Pope.'

'I'll be right down,' he replied and put down the phone.

He stubbed out the cigarette in an ashtray and swung his legs off the bed, groaning at the stiffness of his bruised ribs and limbs, then donned his jacket and left the room.

Mr Griggs and Mr Booth were sitting in the lounge area, a small coffee-table between them, an empty chair awaiting his arrival. He recognized them as the MI5 agents who had taken the collapsed jeweller from his house two nights before. They jumped up at his approach and one said, 'Glad you made it okay, Mr Steadman. I'm Griggs, by the way.'

Steadman nodded and took the provided easy-chair. 'Where's Pope?' he said bluntly.

'Up at the estate. We moved in early this morning without much trouble.' Steadman could not be bothered to register surprise.

'Is the girl all right?'

The second man, Booth, spoke up. 'Fine, sir, a bit confused though.' He grinned at the investigator.

'And you've got Gant?' Steadman didn't grin back.

'Yes, Mr Pope's still interrogating him,' said Griggs. 'He's refusing to say anything even though he knows the game's up. I think the sight of you should unsettle him, though.'

'What about Major Brannigan and the others?'

'Quiet as mice. The whole operation was extremely smooth. Hardly any resistance at all.'

'Have you found out what they had planned for today?'

'Not yet,' said Booth, 'but we think we know already.'

'Can you tell me?' Steadman looked directly at Griggs, who seemed to be the senior of the two.

'Afraid not, Mr Steadman. Not yet, anyway. I'm sure Mr Pope will fill you in on the details, though. In fact, er, I think they're rather anxious to see you out there. Special Branch have co-operated rather well, but they'll be relieved to have some hard evidence to substantiate the allegations against Gant. What we've found is highly suspicious, but not enough to warrant any arrests to be made. It's your evidence that will hang Gant and his friends.'

'But what about the dead bodies of the two Mossad agents at Guildford? That's pretty damning evidence.'

'He denies any knowledge of them.'

Steadman laughed humourlessly. 'They died in his house,' he said. 'Does he deny that.'

'He says he left Guildford early yesterday evening, and you were still there at that time!'

'And I probably killed them.'

'And Köhner. When we told him the man called Köhner was dead he said you must have been responsible.'

Steadman shook his head, a thin smile on his face.

'We'll soon break him, Mr Steadman. We've got too much against him and his organization now. But they do need your help at the estate. The SB boys are hopping up and down with frustration and demanding to see you personally.'

'Okay, let's go then,' the investigator said, rising to his feet. 'I'd like to make a phone call first.'

'Oh, you can do that from the house,' Griggs said as the two men rose with him. 'It really is important that you get there right away. Booth and I just have to check in with the local police to put them in the picture – it's all a bit much for country coppers – so I'll tell you how to get to Gant's estate and you can go on ahead. Mr Pope will be waiting for you.'

And so the game continues, Steadman thought grimly.

Ten minutes later, he was in the Celica driving along the A39 towards Hartlands. It was a cold day, the clouds hanging dark and heavy against the horizon, but Steadman kept his side-window open, wanting to feel the cool air on his face. His mind was clear and resolute.

He turned right when he reached Hartlands, and the banks of the narrow roadway rose up sharply on either side, blocking the view to the surrounding fields. Then the road swung to the left, suddenly widening, and an ancient church confronted him. It was a grey stone building with a high, square-shaped tower that must have offered a fine view over the surrounding countryside. A grotesquely twisted tree stood beside the low, stone wall which enclosed the churchyard, reaching towards the building like a withered and gnarled claw. Then it was gone, the road dipping suddenly, and he saw the sea less than a mile ahead. The road levelled once more, and again the steep banks of undergrowth restricted his vision.

There was no sign at the entrance to the estate, but Steadman knew from the directions he had been given that this was the right place. He stopped before the open gates, feeling very much alone.

His hesitation was brief. He pushed the gear-stick into first and sped through the wide opening, changing up and gathering speed, as though his pace would override too many doubts. The road was well-laid and straight, and he saw the huge white mansion in the distance, surrounded by open fields fringed with deeply wooded areas. The brooding metal-grey sea lay beyond the house, a dark backdrop that seemed to threaten him as ominously as the building he was approaching. The stillness of it all added to his unease. There were many cars parked in the forecourt of the mansion, but no people anywhere. He slowed the car, delaying his arrival at the house, his resolve giving way to trepidation. He could turn back now, swing the car round and race back to the gates before they had a chance to lock them. But where would that leave Holly? And Baruch? He was their only chance.

A rainspot came through the open window and touched his cheek as the threatened drizzle began to soak the ground. His speed was less than ten mph now, and the huge house loomed up before him, giving him the feeling that the black windows were eyes staring. Watching. Waiting for him.

He saw the main door open and a rotund figure step out on to the low terrace that ran the length of the house. A hand was raised in salutation, but Steadman failed to respond to Pope's greeting. He stopped the car, switched off the engine, took a deep breath, and climbed out.

▪ 15 ▪

'One day ceremonies of thanksgiving will be sung to Fascism and National Socialism for having preserved Europe from a repetition of the triumph of the Underworld.'

'That's a danger that especially threatens England. The Conservatives would face a terrible ordeal if the proletarian masses were to seize power.'

'Fanaticism is a matter of climate.'

ADOLF HITLER

The interior of the huge house was clinically clean: it resembled an expensive sanatorium. Pope had stepped aside wordlessly, indicating that Steadman should go ahead of him through the polished wood doors. Once inside, Pope closed the doors almost ceremoniously, then turned to face the investigator.

'I'm glad you arrived safely,' he said. 'We were rather concerned this morning when we couldn't locate you at any of the hotels in town. It was a relief when we went through the list again later on.'

'I broke my journey,' Steadman replied, then added by way of explanation, 'Events kind of caught up with me.'

The hallway they stood in was wide and long, almost a room in itself. An occasional gilt-framed picture broke up the blinding whiteness of the walls.

'It's very quiet,' Steadman commented.

Pope smiled, two cheeks suddenly blooming like rosy apples at each end of the smile. 'Everything's under control, Harry. Things have worked out rather well.'

'No trouble?'

'None at all.'

'And the operation? Did you find out what it was?'

'Oh yes. Come along with me and you'll hear all about it.' The large man took Steadman's elbow and gently propelled him towards one of the doors leading off from the main hallway. He knocked, pushed open the door, and once again invited the investigator to enter before him.

Steadman stopped just inside the room and stared into Edward Gant's mocking eyes, too weary of the game to fake surprise.

'It's good to see you again, Mr Steadman. Unbelievably good.' Gant's artificial but perfectly natural-looking nose was back in its place, disguising his disfigurement. He looked around the room and the sight of Major Brannigan, Kristina, and the old man, Dr Scheuer, gave him a feeling of *déjà vu*; it was like their first meeting in Guildford all over again. But there were some new faces present this time: new, yet familiar. All eyes were on him, and all eyes revealed a strange curiosity, a discerning interest in him.

He swung round as he heard the door close behind him and looked straight into the face of the still-smiling Pope. The Intelligence man was leaning against the door, both hands behind his broad back and clasped around the handle, as though his huge bulk was an extra barrier for the investigator to break through should he decide to run. The smile wavered slightly under Steadman's steady gaze and Pope was relieved when the investigator turned back to face Gant.

'So he's in it with you,' he said to Gant, not having to point at the fat man behind him.

'Yes, Mr Steadman, Mr Pope has been enormously helpful to the cause – as you have.'

'Me? I've done nothing to help you, Gant – or your crackpot organization.'

'Ah, but you have.' Gant walked to a high-backed easy-chair and sat facing Steadman, his hands curling round the arms of the chair like talons. 'We have many men like Pope among the Thulists, men in positions of power who see the hopeless plight this nation is in – indeed, the world is in. Make no mistake, Mr Steadman, we are not a tiny "crackpot" organization existing in this country alone. Our society has a network spread throughout the world, the United States providing us with some extremely powerful members, one of whom will join us later tonight. We have money, influence, and most important, an ideal.'

'An ideal to conquer the world?'

'No, Mr Steadman. To govern it. Look at the men in this room,' Gant said, his arm sweeping outwards. 'I'm sure you recognize most of them. Ian Talgholm, financial adviser to the Chancellor himself – some call him the inner Cabinet's secret member; Morgan Henry and Sir James Oakes – industrialists well-known for their nationalistic pride, envied and feared by the Jewish money-grabbers because of their wealth and power; General Calderwood, a soldier who will eventually govern all the Armed Forces of this country – he is but a representative of many other high-ranking military men who support our Society; and last, but hardly least, Lord Ewing, fast becoming the most vital and powerful man in today's media.

'And these are just a few of our Order, Mr Steadman. The rest will be joining us later today and this evening. Our special council of thirteen, I, myself, being the thirteenth and principal member.'

'Just who are the others, Gant?'

'Ah, you're really interested. Excellent. Well you, of all people, have the right to know. After all, without you, the omens would not have been in our favour.' Gant chuckled, but it was obvious that not everyone in the room shared his humour. Steadman saw several members of the 'Order' give the arms dealer uncertain looks. One of them – Talgholm, the financier – spoke up.

'Look, Edward, do you think this is necessary?' he said, irritation in his voice.

'We've gone along with you on most of this, but he could have been highly dangerous to the whole project. Why tell him any more?'

'Because,' Gant snapped back, 'my dear Ian, because he has played a key part. Because there is no danger from him, nor has there ever been.'

'But the risk last night, letting him go free ...'

'There was no risk, everything was planned. But he had to come here of his own initiative. *It had to be his choice!*'

The financier looked around at his companions as though appealing for support, but they avoided his eyes. He shrugged his shoulders and said, 'Very well, there's nothing he can do now, anyway.'

'Thank you, Ian,' Gant said icily, then proceeded to list the names of the absent members of the Order, one of whom was the racialist Member of Parliament Steadman had seen leaving the arms dealer's estate at Guildford, the day before; the others were important men in their fields – and their fields were greatly diversified.

'We are but the nucleus,' Gant explained, 'the governing body, so to speak. We make quite a powerful group, wouldn't you agree?'

Steadman nodded, but his mind was concentrated on making a quick count of the names. 'You said there were thirteen in the Order and you've mentioned, including yourself, only twelve. Who is the thirteenth member, Dr Scheuer or Major Brannigan?'

'Why, neither, Mr Steadman. They, although extremely important, are only tools. Men like our Major Brannigan and the unfortunate and unstable Mr Köhner – it was his unreliability, by the way, that prompted us to leave you in his hands: a calculated test for you, if you like – these men merely implement our plans. As for the esteemed Dr Scheuer,' he smiled benignly at the wrinkled old man, 'he is our medium, the one who brings our thirteenth member to us. He is the physical voice of our Leader.'

Even as Gant said the name, Steadman knew who the thirteenth member of the Order – the Teutonic Order of the Holy Knights – was. They had rejected Hitler because he'd failed them and switched their allegiance to the SS Reichsführer, founder of the Nazi Occult Bureau, who had encouraged and sustained the Thule Group.

Gant was smiling as he spoke, his eyes radiating a passion felt by everyone in the room. 'He will be with us tonight. Dr Scheuer will bring him to us. And you will meet him, Mr Steadman. You will meet our Führer, Heinrich Himmler, before you die.'

Gant spoke to the investigator for over an hour, laying out his plans for the new Order before him, treating him almost as a confidant; or perhaps a guest to be dazzled by his host's genius. The others had added their own comments, reluctant at first, then swept along by the arms dealer's fervour, realizing Steadman could do them no harm, for he was already a dead man. They needed an outsider they could boast to, impress with the magnitude of their schemes. And Steadman listened, sometimes goading, sometimes visibly astonished at their thoroughness, at the far-reaching effects their fanatical plans would make on the governance of the country. By intricate and brilliantly devious routes, it all arrived at one simple but major conflict: Right against Left. It would be the only choice for the people of Britain. No in-betweens, no fence-sitting. The public would be forced to choose. Civil war would be balanced in favour of the Right, for the majority would be the wealthy, those whose sympathy lay towards nationalistic pride; and the middle classes who had suffered so much between the élite of the country and the working classes, would choose to join them rather than be ruled by the economy-wrecking socialists. The choice would be made easy for them. New leaders would emerge and their ideals would be uncompromising, just as Hitler's had been in the 1930s. Edward Gant had been in the shadows for many years weaving his sinister power behind the scenes. Now he was emerging from those shadows, a new figure to the public, but already powerful enough to repel any attacks from those already in power. Steadman saw how their inner Cabinet – their Order – had been carefully chosen, comprising men already in key positions, all waiting for the right moment to throw off their disguises and unite publicly, and so unite the masses to them. Timing was of the essence, and events to further their cause were manipulated at *exactly* the right time.

Steadman prodded and they eagerly reacted. He drew information from them in a way that made them feel they were merely obliging a doomed man's last wishes to know the reason for his impending death; and their fanaticism, calm though it was, made them try to convert him to their cause and accept his sacrificial role. And all the while, the woman smiled, and the old man gazed at him from shadowed pits.

The Thule Society's next move was imminent. Other actions had already been implemented over the past years, insignificant in themselves, but creating a pattern vital to their cause, subconsciously affecting the climate of the free world's feelings. The worldwide terrorist attacks, the emergence of the neurotic African nations, the ever-present threat of Russia, detente merely used as a cover while they took a further step towards controlling the Western world, the gradual breaking-down of the world's economic structure, the Middle-Eastern countries' sudden strength and bold demands because of their ownership of two-thirds of the world's oil: all these shifts in the world's power balance were creating fear and mistrust on a universal scale which could be easily exploited by those who sought to create a new regime where only the pure-blooded races would rule. Thulists in many countries had contributed to the unrest, working behind the scenes, encouraging, advising, building the strength of their own enemies to the point where other nations would be forced to take action to break that strength lest its greedy eyes look towards them.

Gant, and many like him, secretly sold arms to terrorists not just for profit, but to encourage them on their road to self-destruction. The more outrages they committed, the more they were reviled and feared. And fear was the perfect tool for the new Reich, for fear created revolution.

A strategic move was to be made in the early hours of the following morning – 1.55 p.m. to be exact – when the American Secretary of State would be flying to Britain for talks with the Prime Minister and Foreign Secretary before journeying on to a neutral country in a new bid for peace – reconciliations between the Arab countries and Israel. The world knew that this was the culminative peace-talk, all others – particularly Egypt's, which had begun the fresh moves towards peace in '77 – having led up to this point, both frustrated nations poised for a war that would decide the ultimate victory for either side. But the American statesman's jet would never touch down in England, for the Thulists wanted no such peace between Arab and Jew. The aircraft would be blown to pieces while still over the Atlantic.

No one would know just who had been to blame, although the suspicions and accusations would lean more towards the Arabs than the Israelis, for the PFLP and the PLO had the worst reputation for such atrocities. The responsibility would hardly matter though: civilized countries had had enough. The two opposing nations would be allowed to attempt mutual annihilation, the world would stand by and watch. Of course, certain evidence would be 'discovered' amongst the floating wreckage of the aircraft which would suggest it had been destroyed by a missile of probable Russian make. It was well-known that the Russians supplied their Middle-East friends with such weapons.

The fact that the missile had been produced by Edward Gant's munitions factory and launched from the shores of North Devon would never be discovered; anti-radar devices would ensure its flight path was not traced. Ironically, the RAF had a Radar Tracking Station not far away at Hartland Point, but they would never suspect the missile had been launched from their own area.

At that point, Steadman's probing had been brought to an abrupt halt, for there had been new arrivals at the estate – other members of the Order, Steadman assumed – and details of the operation had to be discussed with them. The assassination of the American Secretary of State was just one of a series of major catastrophes, Gant had explained to the investigator; there were more to follow in rapid succession, each escalating to the next, until world hysteria reached breaking-point. Anarchy by the left-wing had to be nurtured until it could be smashed, terrorism encouraged, until it could no longer be tolerated by the masses.

The door was opened for Steadman and he found the two bogus MI5 men who had come to the hotel in Bideford waiting outside. Neither of them spoke as they led him away, and Steadman felt little inclined to acknowledge their previous meeting; his mind was too busy absorbing all he had learned.

They took him upstairs and along a stark, white corridor, then pushed him into a room, locking the door behind him.

Holly was sitting on a bed facing him, her face white as the walls around them.

'Harry?' she said, not believing what she saw. Then she was on her feet and rushing towards him. 'What's happening, Harry? Why are they keeping me here?'

She raised a hand towards his injured cheek, concern in her eyes, but he held her at arm's length, looking down into her frightened face, unsure, not believing in anything any more. She smiled up at him, her pleasure at seeing him undisguised. It faded as she looked into his cold eyes, and suddenly her mouth quivered as though the toughness had finally been knocked out of her.

'Harry, you're not with them ... ?'

'Do you work for The Institute?' he asked harshly.

'The Institute?'

'Come on, Holly, don't lie to me. You're a Mossad agent. You've been playing me along, like all the others.'

'No, Harry.' She pulled away from him, angry now and defiance beginning to show through the tears. 'They've been asking me the same thing. What the hell's going on, Harry? Why do you all think I'm working with the Israelis?'

Her anger seemed genuine and he wavered for a moment. Could he trust anyone? They hadn't reached the end yet; the Final Act had not been played out. Was Holly part of that?

'Okay,' he said softly, placing his hands on her upper arms. 'Okay. Just tell me what's happened to you, nice and slow. And tell me who you really are, Holly, it's important that I know.'

He led her back to the bed and gently pushed her down, then sat by her side. She looked at him, hurt and confusion showing on her face. But was it all an act? 'You know who and what I am, Harry. I told you, I'm a freelance writer and photographer. I came here to do a feature on Edward Gant, using my family connections with his late wife. That's all there is to it, why should I lie to you?'

He ignored the question. 'And you've never heard of David Goldblatt and Hannah Rosen? You've never heard of Baruch Kanaan? You're not a member of Israeli Intelligence?' She shook her head vehemently, and then another thought struck him. 'Or British Intelligence?'

'No, for God's sake, no! What have I got into, Harry? What have *you* got to do with all this? The other day at Long Valley, the tank – why were they trying to kill you? Who are they and who are you?'

He told her then, not because he believed her, but because if she was with Mossad, then she already knew most of it, and if she wasn't ... Well, what did it matter? But he didn't tell her everything. Just in case.

When he informed her of the plan to assassinate the US Secretary of State at one fifty-five that coming morning, she just sat there, a stunned expression on her face. Then she said, 'So that was why they locked me up.'

He looked at her quizzically.

'The missile launcher,' she said. 'I found it. They caught me taking photographs of it. I thought it was just another part of Gant's testing-ground – the whole estate's riddled with testing-ranges.' She flicked her blonde hair away from her face. 'No wonder they got so mad.' She almost managed a smile.

'Where was it, Holly? Where did you find it?'

'Oh, it's towards the shoreline,' she pointed vaguely in the direction of the sea. 'I'd slipped my guard – Gant wouldn't allow me to wander around free, naturally enough, even though he was anxious I do this article on him – and I pretended I was going to take a nap. It was late afternoon and we'd been trudging around most of the day, so I guess my guide believed me when I told him I was tired. Anyway, he escorted me up here, then disappeared for a while.

I sneaked out and started exploring the areas he'd taken care to keep me away from. This is a strange house, Harry. Did you know the back half is completely different from the front, as though the section we're in now is just a façade?'

He shook his head but remained silent.

'Well, I'd been taken in completely opposite directions before, towards the weapons plant about half-a-mile away, but this time I headed round the back. I was surprised it was so easy, but I guess with Gant away they'd all relaxed a little. Anyway, I got to the back of the house and took a peek in some rear windows on the way. The interior's like a castle back there, very old, dark wood and heraldic symbols, you know? There was no way in, though, all the doors were locked. I heard guards coming – did you know he's got his own private army here? – so I took off away from the house, towards the clifftops.

'I hid behind an old outhouse for a while, waiting for the guards to disappear. It was a little way off from the main house, but was locked and the windows boarded up, so I didn't get a look inside to see what it was used for. When the coast was clear, I took off again, staying away from the road leading to the beach, not looking for anything in particular, but curious enough to keep a lookout for something peculiar. Well, I found something peculiar, all right, but I found it by accident. I'd ducked into some undergrowth about fifty yards or so from the cliff-edge because one of their patrol Range Rovers was heading in my direction – they keep regular patrols all over the estate – and I nearly fell into a huge hole the undergrowth had been disguising. It was about twenty feet wide and had camouflage netting spread over it. I could see through the netting, and the hole looked natural enough except the sides had been smoothed with concrete all the way down, and there was a circular staircase running round the edge. I looked into it and saw it was about forty feet deep and light was coming in from one side below. It was the shaft of a cave, you see, the cave leading up I assume, at an angle from the beach – I could hear the sea down there. The tide wouldn't get into it because the bottom of the well was much higher than the beach. And there, at the bottom of the shaft, was the missile mounted on its launching pad. It wasn't very big, but it looked kind of lethal.'

'They must keep the shaft camouflaged because of all the low-flying military aircraft around these parts,' said Steadman.

'I guess so. Anyway, it was too good to miss. I started clicking away with the Pentax and I became too engrossed in what I was doing. Two guards snuck up on me and all but threw me into the hole. They brought me back here and confiscated my camera. Then the grilling began.'

She put a tentative hand out towards him and rested it on his arm, unsure of his reaction. He let it stay there. 'They asked me about you, Harry: what I knew about you, who you were working for, were we working together. Then they started in on me about Mossad. I told them the same as I told you: I'm a freelance journalist trying to make some bread. They didn't believe me, either.'

She stared earnestly into Steadman's eyes. 'Didn't the other day mean anything to you? Weren't your feelings the same as mine?'

He looked away from her, confused.

'God, you're like a stranger,' she said, anger returning.

'Holly,' he began, trying to come to terms with his doubts, wanting to believe in her. 'So much has happened in the last few days, I swear to God I don't know who I can trust. Those men downstairs with Gant – Christ, they're high-level people. And Pope. He's with British Intelligence! Even one of my own clients has been spying on me since I left Mossad. How can I trust anybody?'

She drew his hand towards her and at that point he wanted to give in, to hold her, to believe. But another part of him held back.

'Okay, Harry,' she said, no longer angry. 'Don't trust me, be as suspicious as hell. But what it all boils down to is that we – just you, if you like – are in big trouble and have to get out. Now, does anyone else know you're here?'

He shook his head, still doubting.

'That's kind of dumb, but okay, we're on our own. So, let's think of a way.' She tried to smile. 'Like the movies, huh?'

'Some movie,' he said, extricating his hand and moving away from the bed and towards the curtainless window. She watched him peering down into the grounds below.

'There's a guard out there all the time,' she said, 'and the window can't be opened – I've tried. You'd break a leg jumping, anyway, and the guard would put a bullet through you before you even reached the ground.'

The guard was looking up at him, face expressionless, but his pose menacing. Steadman looked back at Holly. She seemed calm enough now. Did she have reason to be or was it just a natural facet of her character?

'Any ideas?' she asked, conscious of his gaze.

'We wait,' he said. 'Gant wants me to meet someone later tonight.'

He grinned without humour at her surprise and suddenly felt she had been telling the truth. But still he remained withdrawn. He could be wrong.

Major Brannigan's face was flushed with a brooding sulkiness as he tapped lightly on the door. He wanted to rap hard at the wood with his fist, for he knew she would be laughing inwardly at his mood. He wanted to throw open the door and slap away the smirk she would have on her face. He held his anger in check, however, for he was both afraid and in desperate need of her.

Kristina's voice came to him from inside the room: 'Who is it?'

'It's me – Andrew,' he said, leaning close to the wood, his voice already losing its rancour. 'May I come in?'

'It's open, Andrew.'

He entered and closed the door quickly behind him. He hesitated before approaching, the mere sight of her filling him with the usual desire – *and shame for being in bondage to such a creature.*

She was sitting before a mirror, deftly tucking strands of damp hair beneath a towel worn around her head. The long, white bathrobe she wore was parted around one thigh, and he could not help but stare at the smooth skin, wanting to touch its softness, stroke it, to reach for her and hold her close.

She knew his look, and knew his desire; and laughed at him.

He looked down at her, resisting the temptation to reach out for her elegant neck, the neck he had caressed with his lips so many times, wanting to choke the life from it now, but knowing his hands would never have the strength. They would squeeze until the knuckles were white, until her eyes showed panic, fear, laughter gone from them; then his grip would loosen and his hands would reach down, across the smooth flesh, down until they cupped her hard-nippled breasts – for her very fear would have aroused her, made her want him as much as he wanted her. That was the kind of perverse creature Kristina was. And her fear would have aroused him – *that was the kind of perverse creature he was*. He would sink to his knees and beg forgiveness, his hands still clutching her breasts as though afraid to let go. And Kristina would sink down beside him and they would make love in their unnatural way.

'No, Andrew,' she said, reading his mind. She turned from him and resumed tucking away the damp strands of hair, watching the reflection of his clenched fists in the mirror, smiling at the conflict of desires he was going through.

'Please, Kristina, I …' He fell to his knees and pushed his cheek against the roughness of the bathrobe, a hand resting on her exposed thigh, fingers spreading and moving inwards towards the even softer flesh on the inside of her leg.

She snatched his hand away and drew the bathrobe over her nakedness. 'You know what has to be done later,' she said scornfully. 'We've no time for this.'

'Why?' Brannigan said, almost wearily. 'Why does it have to be you?'

Her eyes flashed angrily. 'You know why. He has to be debased.'

'As I was? As I am now?'

'This is different, Andrew. It's nothing to do …' She stopped abruptly, but he completed the sentence for her.

'Blackmail? No need to blackmail him as you did me?'

'It began as blackmail, Andrew. But you believe in our cause now, don't you? You've told me so many times that you do, and you've done so much for us.'

'Of course. But why Steadman? For God's sake, Kristina …'

'God? What has He got to do with this?'

Brannigan was silent.

'Dr Scheuer says the legend has to be refuted,' Kristina said impatiently.

'And Gant believes all this nonsense.'

'Nonsense? You can say that after all you've seen?'

'I … I don't understand all of it, Kristina. I don't understand how these … things happen.' His voice was pleading. 'You said you loved me. Was that also just for the cause?'

She dropped a hand to the back of his head and stroked his hair. Her voice softened. 'Of course not. You know how much I think of you.' The major could not see her smile at her own reflection in the mirror. 'I have to do this, Andrew. Our Parsifal has to be –' her smile was filled with malice '– corrupted.'

Without force, she pushed Brannigan away, then tilted his head up so she could look into his eyes. 'Now go away and check that everything's secure for tonight. This is the beginning, Andrew, and nothing must go wrong.' Kristina kissed his lips, holding herself back from his passion, restraining him with a gentle hand. 'I must rest,' she said. 'Tonight is important to us all.'

Major Brannigan rose clumsily and, with a last penetrating look at Kristina, left the room. He walked towards the right wing of the house and entered a room next door to the one in which Steadman and Holly Miles were being held. A green-uniformed man wearing headphones, seated next to a tape-recorder, looked up and acknowledged him with a respectful nod.

'Anything?' Brannigan asked.

The man shook his head. 'They've been quiet for some time now. He asked her direct if she worked for Mossad when he first went in and she denied it. Looks like she really is clean.'

'Unless she suspects the room is bugged. What else did Steadman have to say?'

'He told her quite a bit – about Mr Gant and the organization, about tonight's op – but he doesn't know the whole story himself.'

Brannigan nodded briskly and turned to leave. 'Keep listening till he's taken out of there. I still don't think that woman is what she seems. If anything does slip out, let me know immediately.'

'Very good, sir.' The eavesdropper saluted and Brannigan left the room, making his way towards the main stairway and the front entrance. A check on the guards, posted at various spots around the estate's boundaries, then a visit to the missile site to make sure everything was set for tonight's – or more accurately, tomorrow morning's – launching. Things would be moving at last and they'd begin to see some fruition of their dream. The Society had remained in the shadows for so many years, but the time was coming for the strong leaders to emerge. *They* would rule and the military would no longer be the puppets of weak men. No longer would the country's defences be whittled away by the weaklings in government. No longer would the leftists be allowed to dominate. That kind of destructive freedom was to end in England. It had to if the nation was to survive. Of course, the identity of their true leader would never be revealed, for it would be abhorrent to the people who had so misguidedly fought against his great ideals in the last World War. And they would never allow themselves to be ruled by someone they thought had perished so many years before.

Dusk fell and the white house was silent. The drizzle had ceased, but it seemed all life, animal and human, was still sheltering from its dampness. Only the roar from the ocean could be heard, the sound of cruel Atlantic waves breaking on the rocky beaches, their thunderous crashes drifting up the cliff-faces and rolling over the grassy slopes.

The night slowly closed in around the house and its whiteness turned grey, the windows black and impenetrable. A cold wind stirred the grass in spreading ripples and disturbed the tree branches, dislodging the final stubborn leaves.

The darkness became solid and a heaviness, despite the just-fallen rain, seemed to hang in the air. It was as if the very night was waiting, and time was a creeping thing.

▪ 16 ▪

'But the day will come when we shall make a pact with these new men in England, France, America. We shall make it when they fall in line with the vast process of the re-ordering of the world, and voluntarily play their part in it. There will not be much left then of the clichés of nationalism, and precious little among us Germans. Instead there will be an understanding between the various language elements of the one good ruling race.'

ADOLF HITLER

'COME ALONG, HARRY, SEPARATE ROOMS FOR YOU TWO, DEAR BOY.'

Pope's gross figure stood in the doorway, a grin on his face and a gun in his hand. When he saw the investigator was a safe distance away from him and not lurking near the door he returned the gun to his jacket pocket. He always felt ridiculous holding the 'Baby' Parabellum .25 in his immense hand anyway, but it was a convenient and unobtrusive size for his pocket.

Steadman swung his legs off the bed, his hand squeezing Holly's as he stood, his eyes warning her to keep quiet.

'Where are you taking me?' he asked Pope.

'Mr Gant felt that now you've been assured of Miss Miles' well-being, you should be kept apart just in case you should get up to any mischief.' Griggs and Booth leered from their position behind the fat man.

Steadman walked towards the trio crowded in the doorway and Pope stood aside to let him through.

'Harry, don't go with them!' Holly suddenly shouted, leaping from the bed.

Pope turned his huge bulk towards her and held up a hand to keep her at bay. 'He has no choice in the matter, my dear. Now go back to where you were *and keep quiet!*'

Holly glared at him defiantly. 'What are you bastards going to do with him?'

'Nothing, dear lady, absolutely nothing.' The smoothness had returned to Pope's voice. 'Until midnight, that is. In fact, it should be rather pleasant for him until then.' One of the men in the doorway chuckled aloud, but there was no amusement in the fat man's eyes. 'Now, move!' he ordered Steadman.

With a last backwards glance at Holly, the investigator stepped into the hallway and began to follow Griggs and Booth with Pope close behind.

She looked scared, Steadman mused. Genuinely scared for him. Was she really innocent in all this or was it merely an elaborate ploy to get him to talk to her, to make sure he knew only what *they* wanted him to know? And to make sure he was completely alone?

He was led up a flight of stairs on to the next floor, taken along another corridor and finally shown into a room that was infinitely more comfortable than the one he had just left. The decor was still stark, but a fire blazed in the grate, throwing a warm glow around the walls. A small lamp gave the room an intimate atmosphere and a long pin-buttoned couch stood at right-angles to the fire. A four-poster bed dominated half the large room and its soft, inviting quilt reminded Steadman how tired he was. It had been a day full of tension. He fought against the tiredness that suddenly dragged him down.

Turning to the big man, he said bitterly, 'Why, Pope? Why did someone like you get involved in all this?'

The fat man laughed hollowly, then motioned his two henchmen to leave the room. When he and Steadman were alone, he said, 'I've always been *involved*, Harry. The British Secret Service was never much *before* the last war, and after ... just a shambles, a complete bloody shambles.'

Pope crossed the room and gazed into the fire, one pudgy hand resting on the mantelshelf above. 'You were in Military Intelligence,' he said, his face lit by the flames, 'so you must have been aware of the general incompetence that was rife throughout the whole of the British Secret Service.'

Steadman nodded unconsciously, remembering the frustration he had felt over the apparent idiocy of many of his superiors. At the time, he had forgiven their seemingly senseless directives on the assumption that there was some deeply hidden motive behind them, and when he had often later discovered the motive was just as senseless as the directive, he'd almost given up in despair. That was why the Shin Beth had been so attractive to him. Israeli Intelligence had been, and probably still was, the most respected intelligence organization in the world, the British equivalent paling in comparison. However, some sense of loyalty forced the investigator to refute Pope's damning statement.

'But it's changed now – the dross has been cleared out, the "old school tie" network doesn't work any more.'

'Hah!' Pope faced him, amusement and scorn turning him into a jovial gargoyle. 'I *am* part of the "old school tie" network, dear boy. Only *I* do not choose to socialize – ideologically, of course – with my peers at the Ministry. Even after the outrageous attempts by the SIS to protect traitors like Philby in the sixties, the "old boy" network was allowed to go on ruling the roost. Even when Burgess and Maclean defected and it was evident Kim Philby had tipped them off, they went on protecting him – *and were allowed to*. God, it was no wonder the CIA lost all confidence in us after that débâcle – after all, they suffered as much as us through our incompetence. Co-operation between our two organizations has been slight, to say the least, after the sixties. The exposé of spy rings such as Lonsdale's, and the internment of men like Vassal, far from gaining our security service glory has, in fact, cast serious doubts on our reliability in matters of State secrecy. And these are only our publicized defections! You'd be amazed at the disasters that have been swept under the carpet in the interest of national confidence in the department! You can't blame the bloody Americans for not collaborating with us any more!'

Steadman sank down on to the couch. Before he could speak, Pope had continued his tirade against his own organization. 'And when the change comes in this country, dear boy, I'll be directing the new broom as far as my own department is concerned. No more kid-glove treatment for suspect aliens, no more foreign trawlers in our waters. Family connections will mean nothing in the organization. Chinless wonders and nancy boys will be flushed out. Our 'grey' people will be made to earn their keep.'

'You're as insane as Gant,' Steadman said quietly.

'Insane? Am I ranting, Harry? Am I raving? Do I really sound as though I'm mad?'

Steadman had to admit, he didn't. 'But what you're talking about – what you're all talking about – is revolution. That's impossible in England.'

'What we're talking about is *counter*-revolution. The revolution is already taking place. We intend to oppose it.'

'What's to stop your kind of power from becoming corrupt?'

'Our one ideal, Harry. Don't you see, we are a Holy Order? The thirteen men who will ultimately control the country will not be ordinary men. We'll use the corruption around us, we'll fight fire with fire ...'

'And not get burnt yourselves?'

'Our spiritual leader will see we don't.'

'Himmler? A man who's been dead for over thirty years? How can a corpse help you, Pope?'

The fat man merely smiled. 'You must rest now, tonight will not be an easy one for you.' He walked to a large oak bureau to one side of the room, on which stood a tray containing a dark bottle and one glass. He brought the tray over to Steadman and placed it at his feet. 'Brandy,' he announced. 'I'm sure you need it.' He straightened his huge frame, grunting at the effort. 'Compliments of Mr Gant. Now, would you like some food, Harry? I'm sure you must be starving.'

Steadman shook his head. The hollowness in his stomach couldn't be filled by food. The brandy might help, though.

'I'll leave you to rest.' Pope walked to the door and for a brief moment the investigator considered attacking him, smashing the brandy bottle over that obese head. His muscles tensed and he reached down for the neck of the bottle.

'I shouldn't, dear boy,' Pope warned with a pleasant smile. 'Griggs and Booth are just outside; you wouldn't get very far. There is no escape for you, don't you see? You've almost served your purpose, so why not relax and enjoy your final hours?' Before the fat man disappeared through the door he gave Steadman a meaningful look. 'Thank you, Harry, thank you for all your co-operation.' Then, with a deep-throated chuckle, he was gone.

Steadman stared at the closed door for some time before he picked up the brandy. He uncorked the bottle and poured the dark brown liquid into the glass. He raised the glass to his lips and just before he sipped, he wondered if the drink could be drugged. But what would be the point? He was captive here, no chance of escape. Would they need him in a drugged state for whatever was to happen later that night? He doubted it; they had enough strongarm men to keep him passive. He took the tiniest of sips and rolled the fiery liquid around his mouth. He longed to swallow, knowing the brandy would do him good, but the faintest bitter taste held his throat muscles in check. Was it only his imagination or was there really a strange taint to the drink? Because of his danger his senses were acute; but was their sensitivity exaggerating the ordinary bitterness of the spirits?

He spat the liquid into the fire and the sudden flare-up made him jump back. The interior of his mouth burned with the thin coating of brandy left there, and he ran his tongue round it to dilute its strength. He looked longingly at the remaining contents of the glass and asked himself what they would try to drug him with – *if* they were trying to drug him – and his mind ran through the legend, the mythical story of the Holy Grail which had inspired Wagner's *Parsifal*. The mystical opera he insisted be performed only at Bayreuth, the spiritual capital of the Germanic peoples. The opera Hitler had believed was the divine ideology of the Aryan Race!

Young Steve had told Steadman the basic story of the opera, which was a dramatization of the thirteenth-century poet's Grail Romance, and the investigator had begun to understand why Gant – perverse though it was – had referred to him as 'his Parsifal'. The central theme of the opera was the struggle between the Grail Knights and their adversaries, over the possession of the Holy Spear – *the Spear of Longinus which had pierced the side of Christ.*

The Spear had been stolen from them by Klingsor, a castrated evil magician who embodied Paganism, and in so doing, had dealt Amfortas, the leader of the Knights, a wound with the Spear that would never heal. In the hands of Klingsor, the Spear had become an evocator of black powers which only a completely guileless knight could overcome.

In Gant's devious – or was it desperate – reasoning, he had seen himself as Klingsor, for Gant believed more in the powers of evil than in good, despising – as had Hitler – the Christian rituals connected with the myth, and in the arms dealer's strange mind, Steadman had become his Parsifal, the 'guileless' knight who would have to be thwarted if the legend's meaning was to be revoked. Parsifal had become a battle-weary soldier, a man whose mother had died grief-stricken when he had left her while still a boy. Although Steadman had always believed in the cause he had fought for, he would hardly have ascribed any deeply noble instincts to his own character, yet Gant had cast him in the romantic role of defender of the Good. Was it desperation on the arms dealer's part, a need to create an omen where none existed, a megalomaniac's desire to symbolize his own destiny? Perhaps Gant felt time was running out for him, the moment to launch his offensive was at hand, and someone was needed quickly to re-enact the final scene of Good against Evil, with the outcome this time heavily weighted on the side of Evil. A charade, a false ceremony for the benefit of the New Order! Steadman found it difficult to smile at the foolishness of it all. This was why he had been drawn into the elaborate game. Unwittingly, David Goldblatt had provided them with their symbolic knight, a single man to be foiled, then destroyed as an omen of their future success. Gant must have been filled with elation when Maggie, under torture, had revealed she had been sent by Mossad, but only as second choice to her partner, Steadman, an ex-soldier, an ex-Mossad agent. An untainted Englishman.

It would have been easy for Pope to have gained access to the file kept by Military Intelligence on his, Steadman's, past activities, and they had probably gloated on how his background could be compared – albeit loosely – to the mythical Parsifal's. From then on, it had just been a matter of drawing him in. Maggie's vile murder had been committed in order to tear him from the state of passivity he had built up over the last few years; the visit from Pope when he had declined to go against them despite his partner's cruel death; the meeting with Gant at the armaments exhibition to assess his worth as an opponent; and the subsequent test when the tank had tried to crush him (had Holly's life been as expendable as Köhner's, or was this real proof of her innocence in the deadly game?); the revelations at Guildford to ensure his further involvement, and the next test of his worth against the sadistic Köhner, knowing if he escaped, he would contact Pope who would send him off on the last part of the charade without risk to their plans; and his luring to Gant's North Devon estate, the 'Wewelsburg'.

And now the Final Act was drawing near and one last test remained; but they wanted him to fail this one, so that his degradation would refute the outcome of the original legend. In the thirteenth-century *minnesinger's* poem adapted by Wagner for his opera, a woman, Kundry by name, had tried to seduce Parsifal and degrade him as she had so many other knights. How these ancient standards of honour and chastity could compare with today's, Steadman was at a loss to know, but nothing was sane in this whole bizarre plot. Gant and his followers would derive their own meaning from his sexual 'downfall'. Anger boiled up in him and he threw the contents of the glass into the fire, enjoying the searing throwback of heat as the fire flared greedily, almost as though it were an emanation of his own rage. But they had made one small mistake in their elaborate scheme: Köhner had known about the Israeli agent, Smith; he had told Steadman the man had died. How could he have known unless he had been told by the bogus MI5 agents, Griggs and Booth? And that implicated Pope. It was enough for Steadman to have taken precautions before allowing himself to be drawn finally and irrevocably into the spider's web. But had those precautions been enough? He looked at his watch and cursed. Where were they? What the hell were they waiting for? Were *they* part of the game too?

He leapt up and strode briskly to the window. It, too, was locked, and he looked out into the dark night, seeing little but his own reflection in the glass. He had lost track of time standing there, when the sound of a key turning in the lock made him look towards the door. The handle turned and the door opened slowly.

He was almost relieved when she slipped into the room; relieved it wasn't Holly.

■ 17 ■

'And I shall not shrink from using abnormal men, adventurers from love of the trade. There are countless men of this sort, useless in respectable life, but invaluable for this work.'

ADOLF HITLER

HOLLY DECIDED IT WAS TIME TO MAKE HER MOVE. SHE KNEW HER PEOPLE WOULD be reluctant to close in, but her absence would force them to do so. That might be too late, though.

She had been genuinely astounded when she had 'stumbled' on the hidden missile site. She was aware that Gant and his lunatic followers had some pretty twisted plans in mind, but had not realized those plans could involve such overt armed aggression. Even though it was known to her organization that Gant encouraged terrorist activities and supplied these various factions with arms – for a price – it was thought his own methods of undermining world peace were more subtle, more insidious. She had been stupid to get caught taking 'snaps' of the site, but they were still unsure of her. After all, if she *was* a freelance journalist and photographer as she claimed, then it would be perfectly natural for her curiosity to be aroused at such a discovery. Many journalists had been anxious to write a feature on 'Edward Gant, Twentieth Century Arms Dealer', over the past decade, so it was not unnatural that she had been so persistent. The fact that Gant had now begun to seek publicity and that her story of connection with his late wife's family in the States had checked out, had led to her privileged position. Some privileged position, she reflected wryly.

Gant had invited her to his closely guarded estate the day before, promising her an 'exclusive' that would be the envy of the journalistic world. A car had arrived at Holly's flat in the early hours of the morning with the arms dealer's message, and had whisked her away before she had time to inform her own people. She was sure they were keeping tabs on her, though.

When she learned from Harry the purpose of the missile, she had been astounded at the flagrant cunning of Gant's plan. There would be no tracing those who launched the rocket, though both Israelis and the Arabs would obviously be suspected. But the Israelis would *know* the Arabs were the perpetrators, and the Arabs would *know* the Israelis were the perpetrators. It would unsettle all the negotiations for peace between the two nations, and lead to another full-scale war which, in all likelihood, the Israelis would not win this time.

Holly had guessed the room was bugged – why else would they send Harry in to her? – and had had to deny any knowledge of Gant's secret organization. However, she hadn't lied about Mossad. She had wanted to hold him, tell him he wasn't alone in all this, that others knew of the arms dealer's intent. Harry had looked so grim, his mistrust undisguised, and she had wanted to blurt out the truth, to tell him of her government's suspicions and anxiety over this, the most powerful Hitlerite group since the war. They knew its tentacles spread into high places, British Intelligence not the least of those places, and that they had to tread carefully and secretively in this country where the actual nest existed and thrived, for it was not just a threat to Britain, but to world equilibrium in general.

The investigator's sudden appearance on the scene had mystified them at first and Holly still hadn't figured out why he was so important to Gant. Her brief, though unexpectedly emotional, acquaintance with Harry had revealed nothing of any significance apart from the fact he had once been a Mossad agent. So why was he so important to Gant and why had he been allowed to get so close? And why, Holly asked herself, had he become so important to her?

Holly rose from the one easy-chair in the room and moved towards the door. She pressed her ear against the wood and listened: no sound came from the other side. Even if they thought she wasn't involved, Holly doubted that they would leave her unwatched. She tried the door handle, twisting it to and fro.

'Leave it, lady,' a voice commanded from the other side. 'You're not going anywhere.' Holly looked around the room, searching for an idea more than an object. But it was the object that gave her the idea.

Kristina closed the door and smiled across the room at Steadman.

He had to admit she was beautiful, her long, dark hair framing her pale face like a black sea flowing around an ice drift. The deep red of her full lips could have been an imprint of blood on the snow, a curving stain that was as cold as the ice around. Only her eyes were alien in the frozen landscape of her face, for they were alive, deep and glowing as though containing some inner amusement. Yet, there was an excitement in them too, and he felt it was to do with desire.

Her skirt was of the darkest umber, velvet in texture, and ending well below the knee where high and slim-heeled boots clung to her calves and ankles, flowing with the shape of her lower legs as the skirt flowed with the shape of her thighs. A brown shirt, two tones lighter than the skirt, open to a point below the cleft of her breasts, completed the picture of aggressive sexuality and, despite himself, he felt the opening pangs of desire. He caught the sudden flick of her eyes towards the brandy bottle and his passion was immediately stemmed.

'I wanted to see you, Harry,' Kristina said, before advancing on him.

'Why?' he asked bluntly.

She stopped before him. 'To talk to you. Perhaps to help you escape.'

For a moment he was too stunned to speak. 'You'd help me escape from here?'

'I'd help you escape from the fate Edward Gant has in store for you.'

The sudden hope drained from Steadman and he asked, 'How?'

'By persuading Edward to let you live, by convincing him you could be useful to us.' She was close to him now, having imperceptibly drawn nearer as they spoke. He looked down at her, interest more than contempt in his eyes.

'How could I be useful to your Thulists?' he asked.

'You're a resourceful man; you've done well to survive so far. You know much about Israeli Intelligence, a natural enemy to our movement, and any information you could give us would be invaluable. Your past record shows you are a ruthless man, and ruthlessness is something this country will need in the years ahead.'

'But wouldn't I have to believe in Nazism?' Steadman asked scornfully.

'You'd come to believe in time. Not all our members are convinced of our ideals, we're aware of that. They seek power for power's sake, not for race advancement, but for personal gain. Eventually, they'll see it our way.'

'And you think Gant would trust me?'

'You'd have to convince him you could be trusted. I could help you do that.'

'How?'

'If I trusted you I could influence his judgement. I have in the past.' She placed a hand on his shoulder and, inexplicably, a shudder ran through him.

'But why should you believe in me?' he said.

'If we were lovers ...' he almost laughed aloud as she said the words. '... I'd know.'

'And Major Brannigan. Isn't he your lover?'

She smiled indulgently at Steadman. 'You're very observant. Andrew is a weak man. He doesn't have your qualities, your strength.'

'But I bet you helped draw him into all this.'

'It's not important now, Harry.' She closed the gap between them and pressed her body against his. The contact was at once strongly repulsive yet intoxicating. Had the tiny amount of tampered-with brandy he'd allowed into his mouth begun to have some effect? Or was it her eyes? They had a peculiar mesmeric quality and he felt a tiredness overcoming him. He tried to flood any other thoughts from his mind, filling his head with the Parsifal legend, reminding himself of Gant's malignity. Yet when he looked down at the beautiful face before him, it was difficult to imagine any reasonable motive behind the seduction. It would hardly be humiliating to succumb to such a woman, and he had certainly not taken any knightly vows of celibacy. Her dark eyes gazed back at him, unblinking, drawing him down, his head bending towards her, his lips reaching. It was almost as though he was being hypnotized, she exerting a stronger will over his ...

It was then he realized exactly what was happening: she was drawing his strength, sapping his will. Her power was not in her body, but in her mind. It drank in his will, drew him into a mental whirlpool, her deep eyes sucking him in, drowning him. Her hand took his and placed it on her breast, holding it there, making him feel her firmness, the nipple hard and thrusting. Their thighs pressed close, his body stirring, no longer unwilling, oblivious to the legend, subject now only to physical need. Their lips were almost touching, only minimal resistance preventing him from crushing his against hers. But it was the physical stirring in her that suddenly froze his movement, that tore through the overwhelming net of carnality she had cast over him. For her own desire had manifested itself against his lower body, a protuberance that pushed against her clothes, and deemed to match his.

With a cry of rage he pushed her away, driving his fist hard into her face. She screamed with the shock and sudden pain, falling to the floor, and he knew why they'd sent her to seduce him. Why he would have been humbled before them, and more importantly, himself, if he had succumbed. The door flew open and Pope stood there, others behind him with guns drawn. There was anger in Pope's eyes as he looked at Steadman then down at Kristina who lay propped up with one hand against the floor, the other clutching an already-swelling face.

Kristina spat at Steadman. 'You bastard!' she screamed, and her voice had become guttural. 'You lousy bastard!'

Disgustedly, and before Pope's muscle-men could rush him, Steadman took a step forward and aimed a vicious kick at the hermaphrodite lying prone on the floor.

It took two minutes for Pope's men to knock him senseless, but as Steadman sank into unconsciousness, he took relish in the sobs of pain coming from the creature lying only a few feet from him.

Holly Miles stood on the bed and reached up towards the light bulb, a pillow-case cover draped over one hand to prevent her fingers being burnt by the calescent glass. With a deft twist, the light bulb was free of its socket and the room plunged into darkness. She stood still for a few seconds, allowing her eyes to adjust to dense blackness, the hand clutching the light bulb becoming warm with the heat. The full moon outside suddenly broke free from smothering clouds and she was grateful for the increased visibility, although it might work against her in a few moments. She stepped off the bed and moved silently towards the thin bar of light that shone beneath the door from the hallway. Once again, Holly listened with her ear pressed against the woodwork, praying she would not hear sounds of muffled conversation indicating there was more than one guard outside; she didn't think she could tackle two of them. Reasonably satisfied, she tapped lightly on the door with her fingernails.

'Hey,' she called softly. 'Open up. I want to see Gant.'

There was no reply and this time she rapped harder, using her knuckles.

'Hey, you! I've got something to tell Gant. It's important.'

Still no answer, and she began to wonder if there was still someone out there. 'Can you hear me?' she demanded to know, thumping the door angrily.

'Keep it down, lady,' came the surly reply.

'Ah, the zombie speaks,' she said, loud enough for the guard to hear. 'Listen to me, I've got to see Gant.'

'Mr Gant's busy.'

'No, look, I've got information for him. I warn you, it's important.'

'Go fuck yourself,' came the lazy reply.

'Cretin!' she said, and gave the door a powerful kick.

'Cut it out, lady, I'm telling you!' There was menace in his voice now.

She kicked it again.

'I'm warning you, I've got orders to keep you quiet,' Holly heard the disembodied voice say, and she smiled grimly. She kicked at the door again.

'You'd better let me see him, moron. You'll regret it if you don't.'

There was a brief silence as though the guard was pondering, then his voice came through the woodwork again. 'What have you got to tell Mr Gant?'

'That's between me and him.'

'Oh no. There's a meeting going on tonight and I'm not interrupting it just for you.'

'Then let me see whoever's in charge of you – your commanding officer.' She used the description of rank scornfully, refusing to accept that these mercenaries were genuine soldiers. Perhaps if he went to find his superior she would have a chance to work on the door. It was a slim chance, but slim was better than none at all.

'Major Brannigan's busy.'

Yes, probably supervising the missile launch, Holly told herself. 'Okay, your captain or sergeant, or whatever,' she shouted back.

'Leave it out, lady. There's enough going on tonight without you causing problems.'

She swore furiously and began to pummel at the door. My God, what if she really *had* some vital information for Gant? This cluck would still carry out his orders and keep her imprisoned here, no matter what.

'Cut it out!' the guard shouted. 'I'm telling you, I'll come in there and sort you out!'

She nodded to herself and increased the rain of blows on the door.

'Right!' she heard him say. 'You've asked for it!'

The rattle of a key entering the lock was music to her ears. She flew across the room, diving on the bed and rolling over it on to the floor beyond. She crouched there, praying for a cloud to snuff out the moon's brightness. The door opened, slamming back against the wall, the guard's way of ensuring she wasn't lurking behind it. Light flooded in from the hallway and she heard him curse and the light-switch being flicked.

Holly knew if he was professional he would immediately step back into the hallway and to one side, to make his silhouette less vulnerable, so she had to act first.

Without showing herself, she hurled the still-warm light bulb into the corner of the room to the left of the guard. The glass popped and shattered, the noise resembling the blast of a small firearm. The guard whirled towards the sound, his single-hand submachine-gun aimed at the corner.

Holly was like a banshee streaking from the shadows and it was already too late for the guard as he turned to meet her rush. She hurled herself at him, twisting her body as she leapt, so that her back and one shoulder struck him just below chest level. He cried out in alarm, falling backwards, striking the doorframe as he went down, the shock of the blow causing him to lose his grip on the submachine-gun. They sprawled halfway out into the hall and Holly, lithe as a cat, rolled to a crouching position, her eyes already searching the long corridor for other guards. With relief, she realized it was empty.

The guard's gun was lying back through the door, bathed in light from the hall, and she scrambled towards it. A hand grabbed her ankle and tripped her, sending her flat.

The guard, still stunned and wincing at the numbing pain between his shoulder-blades, had seen her intent and was quick enough to snatch at her leg. He pulled her towards him and that was his second mistake.

His first had been to underestimate her because she was a woman. His second was to clutch at one lethal appendage while allowing the other to remain free. Her other foot shot out and struck him just below the chin, snapping his head back so it struck the hard wood of the doorframe once more. The foot struck again with deadly skill as his head bounced back, smashing his nose and hastening his already speedy flight into unconsciousness.

Holly sprang to her feet, the guard's hand falling limply away from her ankles. She cleared the curtain of blonde hair that screened her vision with a toss of her head and peeped back into the hallway, listening for the sound of approaching footsteps. Satisfied that their struggles had not aroused anybody's attention, she reached down for the unconscious guard's ankles and dragged him away from the doorway and further into the room. Flicking his eyelids up, she was careful to avoid the blood flowing from his broken nose, and guessed he would be out for quite some time. Nevertheless, she decided to bind him with bedsheets just to be safe. Within minutes it was done, and his inert body lay beneath the bed out of sight of anyone who should casually check on the room. It was probably an unnecessary precaution, for she knew her mere absence and the sight of the unguarded hallway would set off alarms throughout the estate, but she was a firm believer that in her business, every little detail could sometimes help. Her one concession to the man's condition was to leave him ungagged; with his nose and throat clogged with blood, she knew he could easily choke if air from his mouth was cut off. She even positioned him on his side to help the flow of blood run on to the carpet rather than down his throat, feeling slightly foolish and knowing her past instructors would have cursed her vehemently for her unprofessionalism. But she was prepared to take the small risk of his coming to his senses and calling for help rather than let him die in such a defenceless manner.

Holly straightened, running her hands down her jeans, trying to wipe the bloody stickiness from them. She walked over to the submachine-gun still lying near the doorway, light bouncing off its oily, black surfaces, and noted it was similar to an Ingram. Small and compact, inaccurate over any great distance, but deadly effective at close quarters. She wondered if it had the same firing power of twelve hundred rounds a minute as the Ingram. A small stock was hinged to the main body, providing a recoil buffer when pulled back and held against the upper arm. She picked it up, surprised because it was even lighter than the Ingram: Gant's private army was privileged with the finest equipment.

Once again she checked the hallway, listening for sounds, her senses keened to the atmosphere. All was quiet.

She closed the door, locking it with the key still protruding beneath the handle, and crept stealthily down the long corridor, keeping close to the wall, prepared to use the recessed doorways as cover should anyone suddenly appear. Holly made her way towards the back of the house, away from the main stairway, and towards the curiously castle-like older part.

The wind howled around the ancient church tower, the breeze cold, sweeping over the land from the sea, biting and tangy with salt. As the moonlight struggled through the thick, rolling clouds once again, a group of men was revealed crouching for shelter behind the parapet at the top of the tower. At all times, however, one man remained kneeling, his elbows resting against the cleft in the fort-like wall, night-sighted binoculars held to his eyes, watching the dim white house in the dip of the land almost a mile away.

'Still no movement, sir,' he muttered, ducking his head below the parapet so his words were not whisked away by the wind. 'Reckon they've settled down for the night.'

The man he was speaking to half-covered his watch with a hand so that the luminous dial could function. 'Nearly half-eleven,' he said to no one in particular. 'The last helicopter arrived about ten, didn't it?'

Sexton, crouched next to him, nodded and said, 'Yes, about that time. Look, it must have been the last of 'em. Can't we move in now?'

'Sorry, we can't go in until we've been given the order from the Commissioner.' Detective Chief Inspector Burnett sympathized with the retired police officer, Blake, but there were bigger things at stake here than the safety of one man. He was acting under the directions of the Commissioner *and* the Home Secretary. They were running the show – so if his orders were to wait, then wait he would.

'But what are you hanging on for?' Blake persisted. 'For fuck's sake, he could be dead by now.'

The Chief Inspector turned to him and said patiently, 'Look, Mr Blake, I can appreciate your concern, but this Steadman went in there of his own free will …'

'He said he had to. He had to play it out the way Gant wanted. He was worried about the girl, he didn't know if she was involved or not, whether she was safe or …'

'Holly Miles. Yes,' Burnett said wearily, 'we know all about her now.'

'Why weren't we informed about her before, governor?' a voice came from close by.

'Mistrust, Andy. They played everything close to their chests. Christ, who would have thought Pope was dodgy?'

The Detective Sergeant shook his head in the dark. 'How long have they known about him?'

'God knows. You can bet that's why the CIA were in on it, though – nobody knew who could really be trusted in MI5. If someone with Pope's rank could be part of Gant's group, then who else – upstairs *or* downstairs – could be involved. Aah,' he waved a hand disgustedly, 'makes you sick to think of it.'

Sexton rose to his feet, his cramped position making his bones ache. The wind hit him instantly and he pulled the lapels of his overcoat up around his neck, tucking one point beneath the other to protect his chest. He looked over the edge and could clearly make out the ugly, twisted tree that stood by the roadside at the base of the old church. On the other side of the ancient stone building, groups of cars and Special Branch Land Rovers lay hidden from the road, all filled with cold, bored men, impatient for the action to start.

It had been a frustrating twenty-four hours for Sexton and with every passing minute his concern for Steadman's safety grew. They had done what Harry had told them, he and Steve, continuing their vigil on the house at Guildford, waiting for the police to arrive, trying to keep awake through the night. All that had happened was that the guards had come and locked the gates, seemingly unconcerned with thoughts of escaping, gathering up the bodies of the man and the two dogs, loading them into a truck, and driving back up to the house. He and Steve waited beyond that time because Harry had said to wait a few hours, give this man Pope the chance to act – give him the benefit of the doubt.

Nothing had happened though, and in the early hours of the morning, Sexton had felt sure nothing was going to happen. He had left poor Steve there – the boy had really acted well throughout all this – and driven back to town, straight to New Scotland Yard. It was fortunate he still had good contacts there, otherwise he would have had a difficult time convincing them his story was true. It sounded unlikely even to him as he related it, but eventually the police had been persuaded to make a few enquiries, strictly as a favour – and there were a few of them there who owed him a favour or two – about Pope. Special Branch had been contacted to see if they knew anything of the matter, then the whole thing had taken on a new pace.

When questions are asked by Scotland Yard about a member of MI5, the reaction is swift and tight. Sexton had soon found himself being interviewed by several obviously senior people, one of whom was an American. He told them all he knew, which wasn't much; but it seemed to be enough for them. Events took on a new impetus and a clampdown on internal security was immediate; only a select few seemed to know exactly what was going on.

Steve was brought in and a discreet guard placed around the Guildford house. The house was still under observation, untouched and unwarned. The men inside were probably feeling very smug.

There was much Sexton didn't understand and it was obvious the Special Branch officers he was now with were not fully in the picture either. But one thing was certain: the authorities – those at the very top – were aware something was afoot, otherwise action on such a grand scale would never have happened so promptly. It was as though Harry Steadman was the trigger that had set it off. And the American who had interviewed him earlier that day – did that mean the CIA were involved too? It seemed Harry had uncovered a hornet's nest.

He crouched down again, out of the stinging wind, cursing softly under his breath.

'We can't just sit here!' he shouted at no one in particular.

Burnett placed a hand on Sexton's arm and moved his head closer. 'We've got to wait, Mr Blake. It won't be much longer, I promise. The Commissioner's coming down himself to direct operations. That's how important it is.'

'Then why isn't he here now?' Sexton said angrily. 'Why is he keeping us bloody waiting?'

'I don't know for sure. I think he's got to make arrangements at the other end. The word is that it's not just a bunch of terrorist fanatics we're bringing in, but some very high-placed bastards, men as rich and powerful as Gant himself, maybe even more so. If you ask me, the Commissioner's consulting the PM himself on just how to handle the whole affair.'

'It's wasting so much bloody time, though!'

'We'll be in there in a matter of minutes once we get the word. We're having a force of Marine Commandos flown up from their base in Plymouth by RNAF helicopters. We know Gant's got his own private army, so if he resists there's going to be some bloody battle. Now I'm just as keen to get it over with as you – waiting makes me nervous – but there's nothing we can do until we get the order. So be patient and try not to worry about this Steadman. He hasn't done too bad so far, has he?'

Sexton turned his head away in frustration. No, Harry hadn't done bad so far. But how much longer would his luck last?

▪ 18 ▪

'He clipped him in such a way that he can never more give pleasure to any woman. But that meant suffering for many people.'

WOLFRAM VON ESCHENBACH

'We are more valuable than the others who now, and always will, surpass us in numbers. We are more valuable because our blood enables us to invent more than others, to lead our people better than others. Let us clearly realize, the next decades signify a struggle leading to the extermination of the sub-human opponents in the whole world who fight Germany, the basic people of the Northern race, bearer of the culture of mankind.'

HEINRICH HIMMLER

STEADMAN'S EYES SLOWLY BEGAN TO FOCUS ON THE MOVING FLOOR BENEATH HIM. His head still rang with the blows it had received.

He realized he was being hauled along a corridor, hands gripping him by the armpits and his feet dragging behind on the dark wood floor. He twisted his head to see where he was and recognized the voice that spoke; it belonged to Griggs.

'He's awake. Let him walk the rest of the way.'

The investigator was hoisted to his feet and the sombre face of Pope glared at him.

'I'm very glad you've rejoined us, Harry, though I think you'll wish you never had.'

'Go screw yourself, Pope,' Steadman replied, trying to shake the dizziness from his head. Griggs and Booth on either side prevented him from falling again.

'Ah, still the same arrogance. I could admire it if you weren't such a fool.'

'You're the fool, Pope, to think all this is actually going to happen.' Steadman managed to steady himself, but rough hands still gripped his upper arms.

A deep scoffing sound came from the fat man's throat. 'Look at it this way, Harry,' he said without smiling. 'What's the alternative?'

He turned away, motioning his two men to bring the investigator along. Steadman was propelled forward and felt too groggy to resist. His curiosity was aroused by the long corridor's decorations. It was like being in a medieval castle, for the walls were dark-grey stone, tapestries hanging in the spaces between doorways. The doors themselves were of intricately carved oak, the handles elaborately shaped wrought-iron. His examination of the carving on the doors was perfunctory, but they seemed to be individual coats-of-arms, with an inscription or a title worked into each, and embellished with metal and what looked like precious stones.

They soon reached a point where the corridor opened out on one side and he realized they were now on a balcony overlooking a large, darkened hall. They stopped at the head of a broad stone stairway and Steadman's eyes widened in new alarm at the sight below him.

The huge room was decorated in the style of an ancient banqueting hall, with deep rich carpets, heavily brocaded curtains flanking the high windows; more tapestries adorned the walls. High, thick candles were placed symmetrically around the room, their colour black, providing the only light apart from the fire that raged in the deep, man-sized cavity behind what appeared to be a dais. The design theme throughout was that of a golden spear.

In the centre of the vast floor stood a huge round table, made as far as Steadman could tell, from solid oak, and around it were placed wooden high-backed chairs. He could see from those facing away from him that each had an inscribed silver plate on the back. Every chair – save for two – had an occupant; and the face of each occupant was turned towards him.

'Welcome to our Wewelsburg.' It was Edward Gant's voice and Steadman's eyes darted around the table to trace the source. A figure began to rise and he saw it was Gant in a central position, his back to the curious dais. 'Bring him down!' There was anger in the command.

Steadman was shoved brutally from behind, causing him to lose his balance and reach out for the stout banister to one side of the stairway. It prevented the fall from being too serious, but still he tumbled down, losing his grip and rolling to the bottom. Footsteps behind, then he was again hauled to his feet. He shook the clutching hands off, forcing himself to stand alone.

'It would appear Kristina has failed in her task.' Gant's voice was cold, the familiar mocking tones absent now.

'Did you really believe I could be corrupted by that … thing?' Steadman said harshly.

'Her power is in her mind, Mr Steadman. Yes, I am surprised you resisted that. It seems she still has much to learn from her mystagogue, Dr Scheuer.' Gant made a motion with his hand, and a chair was brought from the shadows of the room to be placed three feet away from the round table. Steadman was shoved into it. A gap had opened up between the seated figures, offering him an unrestricted view of the arms dealer opposite. He had time to notice several uniformed guards situated at strategic points around the room, submachine-guns held across their chests, before looking into the mad, glaring eyes of Edward Gant. The artificial nose was still affixed to the arms dealer's disfigured face, making him at least look human. He was dressed in a charcoal-grey suit, his shirt white, though it looked yellowish in the suffused light, and his tie was black. The investigator was surprised Gant and his cohorts were not clad in robes or medieval costumes, such was the atmosphere in the dark baronial hall. Around the table, neatly placed before each member of the group, was a short ceremonial dagger and he noticed that those whose hands were placed on the table's surface wore curiously designed signet rings. The guests he had met earlier that day were among those seated, and others were familiar to him through the media. Dr Scheuer was there, looking even older and more frail; Steadman felt his eyes boring into him even though he could not see them in their dark caverns. He was distracted as the vast bulk of Pope filled one of the unoccupied chairs.

'You are an honoured person, Mr Steadman,' Gant's voice echoed around the stone walls, increasing its sibilance.

'Honoured? To be part of this?'

'To be one of the few outsiders to visit the Wewelsburg.'

'I'm overwhelmed.'

'Don't mock us, Mr Steadman!' Gant warned, his hand toying with the dagger before him. 'Your death will be painful enough, but it can be made excruciating. The honour bestowed upon you is to see this, almost an exact replica of the Reichsführer's fortress which he had built in Westphalia. A shrine devoted to the Teutonic Knights. Only a select few, twelve in all, were allowed to visit Himmler's domain, all SS officers. There they meditated, remembered their Nordic origins. Each had his own room and that room was dedicated to great kings and emperors such as Otto the Great, Henry the Lion, Frederick Hohenstauffen, Philip of Swabia and Conrad IV. The Reichsführer's own room was in honour of Henry I. Adolf Hitler's belonged to Frederick Barbarossa. But Hitler refused to visit the Wewelsburg! He turned his back on the forces that brought him to power. He would not even allow Himmler to bring the Spear to its natural resting place! That is why the Führer failed, you see. Because at the end, he no longer possessed the Holy Spear – Heinrich Himmler had taken it for himself!'

Gant twisted in his chair and pointed towards the altar-like dais. 'And we have possessed it ever since!'

Steadman saw the leather case resting on top of the dais and guessed at the object lying inside. So the Heilige Lance was here!

The arms dealer turned back to face Steadman across the table, but his eyes flicked upwards to the balcony above.

'Come, Kristina, join us. You have failed, but then so did the original Kundra. It matters little now; the final achievement will be ours.'

Steadman heard the footsteps on the stone stairway behind him and the man/woman came into view. Her face was swollen and bruised where he had struck her, and her beauty now seemed obscene. She scurried around the table, avoiding all the eyes that were on her, and sat in a chair placed behind Dr Scheuer. The old man ignored her, still looking directly at Steadman.

The figure of Major Brannigan emerged from the shadows then, pure hatred in his eyes. He strode towards Steadman, a hand reaching for the revolver strapped to his side.

'Major!'

Brannigan halted at Gant's harsh command. 'Wait outside for our latecomer, Major Brannigan, and take your guards with you. We have no need for them here.'

'But what about Steadman? You know he's dangerous.' The Major's voice was resentful.

'I'm sure Griggs and Booth are capable of taking care of Mr Steadman should he become ... restless. Now go and wait by the helicopter pad. Our visitor should be here at any minute and I want him brought straight in.'

Brannigan whirled and called for the soldiers around the room to fall in after him. They marched out, boots heavy on the solid floor.

'Forgive the Major, Mr Steadman,' Gant said. 'He's insanely jealous over Kristina. Rather pathetic, don't you think, to be so concerned over such an aberration?'

The hermaphrodite's head snapped up and she looked balefully at Gant.

'Unfortunately,' the arms dealer went on smoothly, 'she is of the utmost importance to our cause. She will eventually take over from Dr Scheuer, you see. Our poor doctor's health is failing and I'm afraid he has not much longer for this world. Somehow, I think he will prefer the next.' Gant smiled warmly at the old man.

'Don't you think we should get on with the ceremony, Edward?' Sir James Oakes, the industrialist Steadman had been introduced to earlier that day, said from the far side of the table.

'I agree.' It was Talgholm who spoke, and a few others murmured their approval. 'Time's running out, Edward. The missile will soon be launched.'

'Gentlemen, there is ample time. Our ally from overseas expressed a specific desire to be present tonight and we shall abide by his wish. You all know how necessary he is to us.' Gant held up a hand, warding off any further protests, but when the voices still persisted he banged his fist down hard on the table. 'Enough!' he shouted. 'Have you forgotten what is to happen tonight? The atmosphere must not be disturbed for Dr Scheuer!'

Their protests faded into silence and Gant smiled grimly. 'There is too much tension in the air,' he said by way of explanation to Steadman. 'Our members are – shall we say – on edge?'

'They're as crazy as you, Gant,' Steadman said evenly.

'Yes. And you are the only sane one here tonight.' The mockery was back in the arms dealer's eyes. 'I wonder if you will still be sane before you die?'

Steadman's brain was racing. What had happened to Sexton and Steve? Had they failed to convince the authorities? Were they *still* trying to? Or worse – had they been taken by Gant's men at Guildford? They were his only chance, but now it looked a very poor one.

'Okay, Gant,' he said. 'I'd like to hear more about your organization. You say you're Thulists, but I thought such societies in Germany were wiped out after the last war.'

'Only people are "wiped out" in wars, not ideals. Some of us survived to further those ideals.'

'You were in Germany during the war?'

'Oh yes,' Gant chuckled, enjoying the puzzlement on the investigator's face. 'I was not a common soldier, but I served the Reich in a more meaningful way. I've already told you how Hitler rejected us and how, because of the Führer's final foolishness, the power passed on to Reichsführer Heinrich Himmler. Thanks to plans carefully laid out long before the end of the war, Herr Himmler and I managed to escape the clutches of the Allies ...'

The four men hurried single-file across the field, their feet sinking inches into the mud at each step, their breathing – particularly the third man's – laboured and sharp. It was quiet in this part of the country, for the rumble of guns had been left far behind. But still they hurried, knowing they were near to freedom, near to Kiel where a boat would be waiting.

They had successfully evaded the clutches of the US Ninth Army, abandoning their armour-plated Mercedes early on in their hazardous journey for a less conspicuous grey Volkswagen. The little car had taken them a great distance and they had kept to the smaller roads and away from the jammed autobahns, travelling only when it appeared safe to do so, hiding the vehicle in wooded areas off the road when not. But now they were on foot for, in their haste, they had neglected to bring along extra cans of petrol. It may have been for the best though: the roads were too dangerous and SS Colonel von Köhner felt they had pushed their luck far enough in that respect.

The third man in line suddenly stumbled and went down on one knee in the mud. Von Köhner took him by the elbow and gently helped him back to his feet, asking if he might carry the faded leather case for the Reichsführer. Himmler shook his head and they continued their traverse of the field, eyes wary for any other signs of life.

Heinrich Himmler held the leather case containing the ancient spearhead tightly against his chest, refusing to let anyone else take possession, unwilling to let it out of his grasp, even for one second. The others – Reichskriminaldirektor Mueller, Erik Gantzer, and SS Colonel von Köhner – could carry the money and the valuables that would buy their escape and ensure their freedom. And of course, the secret files, his beloved files kept through the years: documents concerning not only the devious activities of his fellow countrymen, but men, influential men, of other countries. Regretfully, they had taken only the most important, those which could be used again at another time; they would have needed ten trucks to bring all the others along. His three loyal followers would manage those between them but he, alone, would bear the holy relic.

All four wore civilian clothing, Himmler, Mueller and Köhner having discarded their uniforms at the beginning of the journey, Erik Gantzer a civilian anyway. A strange and powerful man, this Gantzer, Himmler reflected, studying the tall figure ahead of him. His grandfather, Otto Gantzer, had been apprenticed to the Royal Prussian Arms Factory in Spandau, near Berlin, working there as a master gunsmith for many years until he left to establish his own business in the port of Rostok, which his son Ernst, also a master gunsmith, had continued. The business had prospered after the old man's death, Ernst developing and diversifying the range of weapons he produced. His son, Erik Gantzer, after graduating from high school, was apprenticed to the arms factories in Suhl and Zella-Mehlis, following the family tradition, and eventually took over the whole Gantzer industry when the father died. Spared from service in the army because of his immense contribution to the war effort, Erik Gantzer had played a great part in introducing the Führer himself into the Thule Gesellschaft, the society in which Gantzer had become a key member. He had proved to be extremely useful, a brilliant young man with no conscience, who fought only for the future of the Aryan race. A man whose eventual disenchantment with the madman, Hitler, had led him to switch his allegiance to the Reichsführer himself. And now, even though their beloved country had been crushed, he would still serve him. It was his connections that would see they survived, his genius that would ensure the furtherance of the cause! It was he who had devised the escape, planned the route, made the contacts, long before it was inevitable that Germany would lose. He had ignored the normal Nazi escape routes, had dissuaded Himmler from making deals with the Allies, had insisted all was not finished, that the new beginning would be better planned, more guile, more subterfuge, would be used. Nothing was lost; only the moment delayed.

From Kiel, the boat would take them through the Kieler Bucht, travelling by night till they reached the rough waters of the Store Baelt, then on to Ebeltoft in Denmark, where they would journey overland to a small landing-strip owned by a contact of Gantzer's. From there they would fly to Iceland and eventually, when world affairs had moved on to more important matters than the hunting down of elusive Nazis, they would go to Canada, then down into America, and finally, the ironic twist – back across the ocean to England. A bitter smile contorted Himmler's lips at the thought and, if he had had the breath, he would have laughed aloud. No South America for Heinrich Himmler! Let the Bormanns and the Mengeles go there!

He suddenly doubled over as pain wrenched at his gut and, once again, Colonel Köhner was there to support him. Himmler waved him away, grateful for his concern but indicating he would be all right in a short while. Franz von Köhner: another good man! A true German, prepared to leave his wife and young baby son – as he, himself, had left his own family, not to mention sweet Hedwig, his mistress – for the good of the cause! It was von Köhner who had secretly replaced the real Heilige Lance with a skilfully made replica which Himmler himself had had made even before the annexation of Austria. The fool Hitler had never realized he possessed only a forgery painstakingly reproduced with metal almost as ancient as the Spear itself! He, Himmler, kept the original spearhead in the Wewelsburg, his mighty fortress in Paperdorn, Westphalia, dedicated to the Teutonic Knights: it was the natural resting place for the legendary relic.

Despite the pain, Himmler smiled grimly. Von Köhner had served him well. And so had Heinz Hintzinger, the corporal in the Feldpolizei who looked so incredibly like him! When it had become an indisputable fact that Germany would lose the war, the hunt for doubles had almost become a game among the Nazi generals and officials, so many of them unwilling to face the wrath of the Allies. Cowards, all of them! For Himmler, it was different. It was his duty to survive! Now that the Führer had lost his mind, someone had to carry on, to rise like the Phoenix when the ashes had settled. He was that man.

Von Köhner had found many who resembled Himmler, but all had been rejected for Hintzinger; this man was prepared to die for his Reichsführer. His zeal for the Nazi cause amounted to fanaticism and the Schutzstaffeln knew how to use fanatics. He had been sent out under an escort who believed him to be their real leader, thinly disguised, and ready to admit he was no less than Heinrich Himmler himself when caught. And ready to crush the cyanide capsule between his teeth when he was sure the officials believed his statement.

Himmler again sank to his knees. He had to rest, just for a little while. The other three gathered round him, but he waved them on. See if it was safe on the other side of the field. Von Köhner could stay with him, help him on when the pain in his belly had subsided.

Mueller and Gantzer turned away, concern on their faces. They began to trot towards the screening hedge at the far side of the field.

Von Köhner squatted beside the Reichsführer and waited patiently.

He had been present when Himmler had received the message from Hitler's successor, Admiral Dönitz, dismissing the SS Reichsführer from the service of the Reich. How could they humble such a great man in that manner, a man who was prepared to fight on when others had given up? He had never looked impressive, this middle-aged man with his paunch, his narrow shoulders and curved back – too many hours hunched over paper-work – but what vision! What stature! The generals – traitors like SS General Wolf – already falling over each other to make deals with the enemy, to save their own necks, were not fit to lick his boots! The untermenschen would never defeat this man!

He wished the mystical masseur, Kerston, was here to ease his master's pain with those strange deft fingers that gave the Reichsführer such instant release. He wished he could provide a glass samovar containing a hot mixture of gentian and dandelion tea, for he knew how it soothed the Reichsführer's stomach pains ...

The explosion shook the ground beneath their feet and mud and stones spattered their clothing. They looked in horror across the field to where two bodies lay, one still, the other writhing and screaming in agony.

They raced towards the two bodies, wondering which one was dead – Gantzer or Mueller? One of them must have trodden on a landmine or disturbed a concealed unexploded bomb; whoever had made the contact would be the dead one.

They reached the twisting body and realized only by the clothing that it was Erik Gantzer. His knees were hugged to his chest, his hands between them, clutching at his lower body. Von Köhner resisted the urge to vomit as he looked at the arms manufacturer's face – or lack of it. Blood spurted from a red hole in the centre of his face, a loose piece of flesh hanging by a thin tendril, the remnants of his nose.

Himmler's stomach was not as strong as the SS Colonel's. He paled and bent over as the contents of his stomach spilled on to the muddy earth. As he looked down, he caught something that made him close his eyes tightly and wheel his body away. Two feet that must have been Mueller's, one still inside a boot, lay on the ground before him. The one in the boot was standing upright, the bloody stump facing up at him, splintered bone showing whitely against the red flesh. His vomit had covered it before he twisted away.

Himmler dropped the leather case containing the Spear and fell to his hands and knees and retched, his whole body shuddering with the effort. He crawled, trying to get away from the grotesque sight of Mueller's dismembered feet, and when he finally found the strength to look up, he saw von Köhner's figure kneeling beside the twitching body of Gantzer, a Luger pointed at the injured man's temple.

Himmler staggered to his feet. Gantzer must not be shot. If there was a chance that he might live, no matter what pain he was in, he must be saved!

He pulled von Köhner's arm away just as the SS Colonel's finger began to squeeze the trigger. The gun never fired, but when Himmler stared down at Erik Gantzer's body and the mass of blood that covered his face and groin area, he wondered if he, the Reichsführer, should not have been more merciful …

'But Himmler was captured. He was identified before he committed suicide.'

Gant laughed and the sound echoed hollowly around the hall. 'That was another man, a double. A good German, prepared to die for his Reichsführer. Of course, his family would have suffered if his courage had failed him at the last moment. Fortunately, that was not necessary.'

'But he was examined, surely? They'd have had to be sure.'

'Can you imagine the confusion that was taking place in Germany at that time, Mr Steadman, with thousands – millions – fleeing? Have you any idea how many Germans the Allies caught trying to escape and whom they thought to be Himmler, Goebbels, Göring or Bormann? Or even Hitler himself? When they found one who confessed to being a Nazi leader and looked exactly like him with his disguise removed, do you really think they questioned the matter in any great detail? And when the chaos began finally to take on some order, it was too late; the body of the Reichsführer had been long buried in an unmarked grave. I promise you, the aftermath of such a war, with each nation fighting over territories like wolves over a dead carcass, is infinitely more complex than the planning of an enemy's defeat. With the removal of the obvious enemy, the allied nations became enemies to each other. It was not difficult for mistakes to be made.'

'But where could a man like Himmler go? Surely he would have been recognized?'

'You forget just how insignificant our great leader looked. I mean this as no disrespect, for this was the wonderful dichotomy of the man. He was one of Germany's greatest heroes, yet his appearance was that of an ordinary man.'

'I've read that he looked like a typical filing clerk,' said Steadman pointedly.

'Exactly, Mr Steadman,' said Gant as though the slight had been a compliment. 'A filing clerk with true Nordic blood.'

'So his very insignificance allowed his escape?'

'It allowed him to exist in another country.'

'Might I ask where? I take it that South America, the obvious place, was out of the question.'

'Of course. We could have fled there, lived among the Nazi colony; but we would have been impotent. No, we needed a country where we could build again, not a place where we could sit in the sun and reminisce over the past glories of the Fatherland.'

'So where, Gant? Where did you choose?'

'Why, England, of course. What better place?'

Steadman looked incredulously at the smiling faces around him. 'But that would have been impossible!'

'At the time, yes,' said Gant. 'Although we had many friends in Great Britain, even then – several were Thulists – many had been interned for the duration of the war because of their sympathies, and were never entirely trusted after.

'No, our first stop was Denmark. It hadn't been our intention, but we stayed hidden there for many months. I had been severely injured, you see. It was the Reichsführer who saved my life.'

The arms dealer paused as though the memory was a precious thing. 'We left Flensburg on 10 May 1945; Reichsführer Himmler, Colonel Franz von Köhner – the father of the inept fool you disposed of last night, Reichskriminaldirektor Ernest Mueller, and myself. Unfortunately, after making good progress towards Kiel, a bomb killed Mueller and almost killed me. It was only the Reichsführer's intervention that prevented von Köhner from putting a bullet through my brain. Herr Himmler insisted that I should be carried to our rendezvous point where my wounds could be treated. He even sacrificed his sacred files for my life. They were buried, along with Mueller, in that very same field. Colonel von Köhner carried me, and the Reichsführer carried our valuables and our talisman, the one object he refused to leave behind: the Heilige Lance!

'I was almost dead by the time we reached our contact near Kiel, but again Herr Himmler refused to allow me to die. They treated my wounds as best they could and then we went on by sea to Ebeltoft in Denmark. The journey was an extraordinary nightmare for me, Mr Steadman, and I pleaded with the Reichsführer a hundred times to put me to death; he would not allow it, though. He saw that some day, I would be the new leader, the Grand Master, in his place. His vision was far beyond human limitations.

'We stayed in an area far inland from Ebeltoft until I had recovered from my injuries; not fully, you understand, but enough to travel on. From there we were flown to Iceland and, a few years later, to Canada. Seven years passed before we dared enter the United States of America. Our contacts, both in America and England, had been renewed long before, and our movement was already beginning to thrive. We kept undercover, for obvious reasons, allowing the more vulgar nationalistic organizations to take all attention from us. Subterfuge and progressive infiltration has been our policy since the setback.'

'You call the last World War a setback?'

'Yes, Mr Steadman. Nothing more than that!' There was silence around the table as though each member was defying the investigator to refute Gant's statement. Steadman shrugged.

'So Himmler was alive all that time,' he said.

Gant nodded solemnly. 'Yes. Colonel von Köhner died in '51 while we were still in Canada. A stroke. Before he died he made us promise to find the young son he'd left behind in Germany, and to indoctrinate him into our cause. We readily agreed. The offspring of a man like Franz von Köhner would indeed be valuable to the Society. Perhaps it was fortunate for the Colonel that he never knew the incompetent his son was to become. The youth, Felix, readily joined us, for in Germany he had nothing. Von Köhner's wife had died shortly after the war and the boy was being raised by relatives. They allowed him to come to us, for they were poor, the war having stripped many such families of their wealth. Felix joined us in England when he was twenty-one.'

'When ... when did you ... and Himmler come to this country?'

Gant smiled and the smile made Steadman shudder. 'In 1963, Mr Steadman. An historic date.'

The others around the table voiced their agreement. 'He was very ill by then. The stomach pains that had plagued him most of his life had finally broken his health, but even at that time, we did not realize how serious his condition was ...'

Steadman was so stunned at the idea of the infamous mass-murderer living in England that he missed the arms dealer's next few words. When he had recovered enough to listen again, Gant was talking of his marriage in America.

'Louise was an extremely rich American, from the Deep South. Our ideals matched, for the Southerners' intolerance towards race impurity was almost on a par with the Nazis'. She never really knew the true strength of our ambitions, and the real identity of our permanent, reclusive house-guest was kept a secret from her. She suspected he was an ex-Nazi, I'm sure, for she knew I was, but I don't think it ever occurred to her she was housing one of the world's most "notorious" men. She was an extraordinary woman who shared our ideals and demanded nothing physically from me. She lived only for the day when our ideals would find fruition, and I cannot tell you how much her wealth and contacts furthered our cause. It was tragic that a road accident should have taken her from us so early in our rising.'

The whir of helicopter blades suddenly drew everyone's attention. 'Ah, that sounds like the arrival of our twelfth member,' Gant said.

'It's about time!' said Lord Ewing, the news magnate.

'The General has had a long journey,' Gant reproached, and the man fell silent.

Astonished by the arms dealer's authority over such powerful men, Steadman looked around the table at each one in turn, then said, 'How can you follow a man like this? An ex-Nazi, a man who helped one of the most evil men in history, a man who fought against us in the war. How can you betray your country for someone like that?'

'Betray? You're the one who's a traitor, Steadman,' said Talgholm. 'You claim to be British, but you'd sit by while the country sinks. What kind of loyalty is that?'

'Look ...' Steadman began.

'Shut up!' It was Ewing who shouted across the table, his face red, his eyes bulbous with rage. 'We're sick of do-gooders like you. Live and let live, that's what you believe, don't you? Do you think *they'll* let us live once they've taken over? Your kind are almost as bad as them!'

'Let's get rid of him now, Edward,' came another cry.

'Yes, we don't need him,' Talgholm agreed. 'The legend will still be fulfilled.'

'Not yet!' Gant's voice was stern. 'You know how it's to be done.'

'We're running short ...'

'There is time.' The pronouncement was made quietly, but the assembled group became silent again.

'Tell me more, Gant,' Steadman said with a calm he hardly felt. 'How ... where did Himmler live in this country.'

'Always in this area, Mr Steadman. He was fascinated by the Arthurian legends. King Arthur's Knights were based on the Teutonic Order, and their activities took place mainly in this part of the country. He was so overjoyed when I had the Wewelsburg built here for him.

'The Thule Gesellschaft was a wealthy organization by then. The arms industry I had set up, aided substantially by the money my dear, late wife had left me, was thriving, and donations from our secret members were flooding in. We had recovered the files von Köhner had buried so many years before and they opened many ...' he smiled and looked at the faces around the table '... so many doors for us.'

Steadman began to realize how blackmail had played such an important part in the rebuilding of their movement.

'The Reichsführer, despite the pain he was in, was very happy in his final days,' the arms dealer said softly. 'He knew this time we would win.'

'He died here?' Steadman asked, somehow – inexplicably – expecting a denial of the Reichsführer's death, for his presence felt so real.

'Yes, Mr Steadman. In a sense. He was sixty-seven when cancer took his life. But even though his body failed him, his spirit did not. Almost a year after his death he sent someone to us.' Gant turned to Dr Scheuer seated next to him. 'Dr Scheuer was a spiritualist living in Austria. The Reichsführer chose the Herr Doktor to be his intermediary.'

At that point, approaching footsteps were heard outside the hall. A door set back in the shadows against the wall opened, and a broad-shouldered figure strode in briskly followed by Major Brannigan.

'Good evening, gentlemen.' The voice was unmistakably American, and when the man drew closer to the light, Steadman groaned inwardly as he recognized him. The assembly stood in deference as he took his place in the empty chair beside Dr Scheuer.

'Is this the man?' He glowered across at Steadman.

'Yes, General, this is our Parsifal,' Gant said smoothly. 'Mr Steadman, I'm sure you recognize Major-General Cutbush, the US Forces Deputy Commander.'

They weren't crazy at all, Steadman realized. They really had the power and influence to dominate a nation's thinking. Over the years, by bribery, blackmail, or sheer mutual agreement on racial ideals, they'd built up an incredible force, a force strong enough to direct public motivation, wavering between the two extremes, towards their own aims. It was just the worship of the dead Himmler and all it entailed that was their madness, and he was puzzled at the necrophiliac devotion displayed by such men. What could instigate such an insanity? Suddenly, he was terrified.

'Okay, Edward, I said I'd go along with all this because *he* wanted it this way.' The American's burly figure and grizzled features looked strange to Steadman, for he had been used to seeing pictures and film of him in full military uniform. 'But I don't like it one bit. It's too ...' he searched for the word '... theatrical.'

'I understand your feelings, General, but it would be unwise not to comply with *his* wishes now,' said Gant.

'Mebbe,' the General said gruffly, 'but I still don't like it. Brannigan!' The British major flinched to attention. 'Shouldn't you be at the launching site?'

'We were just waiting for your arrival, sir. I'm on my way now.' Brannigan marched from the room, his back stiff and his stride determined.

'Goddamn fag,' Cutbush muttered to no one in particular when the door closed. 'Okay, let's get on.'

Gant stood and made to move away from the table towards the dais, but Steadman's shout stopped him.

'For God's sake, General, you're a veteran of the Second World War. You fought against men like him!' The investigator's finger was pointing at Gant and the two guards on either side had stepped forward and clamped their hands on his shoulders to prevent him rising from the chair.

The General looked across at him and his eyes narrowed. 'Now you ... shut ... your ... mouth, mister. Sure, I fought against him and his kind. That was my mistake. I was with Patton throughout the damn war and I saw how his ass was kicked around by the so-called free-thinking leaders of our country. We had long chats, the old war-horse and me, and I know the kind of man he was.

He saw the Russian threat while everyone else was still messing with the Germans. He wanted to march right through Germany and straight on into Moscow itself! It was he who told me the legend of the Spear – even though he was a pragmatist, he had a deep belief in such things – an' I was with him in a Nuremberg bunker when he thought he'd found it. We didn't know it then, but there'd been a switch. "Blood and Guts" never could figure out why nothing had happened for him. Himmler had already vamoosed with it!

'Now I don't mind admitting it: General Patton was my God, an' if he said there was something in the legend, there sure as hell was! I saw what they did to Patton when they no longer needed him. You think the car smash that killed him after the war was an accident? And I see what they're trying to do to me because they think I'm not needed. Old "Blood and Guts' " aggression became an embarrassment to them, and they feel the same about my hard-line views. But unlike the General, I started making plans a long, long time ago and it was our good fortune ...' he waved his hand around the table '... that Edward Gant brought us together. We all believe in the same thing, sonny, and we don't need any crap about who we were fightin' in the last fuckin' war!'

Steadman relaxed back into his chair and managed to stare insolently at Cutbush. 'So they were putting you out to pasture.'

'You fuckin' crud. I'll break ...' Gant checked the General's rising figure with a hand on his shoulder. The General sat but glowered at the investigator. 'I'm goin' to enjoy the next few minutes, jerk,' he said.

Steadman returned the glare.

Gant nodded at Griggs and Booth, and Steadman felt his arms gripped tightly.

'The time has come, Parsifal,' Gant said, walking towards the dais. He reached inside the leather case and turned with a long dark object in his hands. Steadman saw it was the spearhead, the holy relic whose legendary powers had caused the bloodshed of millions and the glory of a chosen few. There was no shine to the ancient black metal, only a dull glow from the section of gold, but the blade still tapered to a menacing point. Gant placed it on the table, its flattened blade pointed towards the investigator.

Steadman looked at the ancient relic and began to tremble inwardly. It was strange, but it felt as if a force were emanating from the cold metal, a force that was already piercing his heart. And then, he knew what was to be his fate: he was to die from a spear thrust. Gant would refute the Parsifal legend by using the weapon itself to kill his adversary.

He closed his eyes, but the image was still there in his mind: the evil tapering blade, the nail driven into an aperture in the blade, the small crosses engraved in the dark metal. He tried to force it from his thoughts but it stayed, a cold, dark object, a dead thing that somehow thrummed with energy. In his mind's eye he saw it was bloodstained.

'Can you feel its power, Parsifal?'

Steadman opened his eyes and now he saw the spearhead only as an aged piece of metal, lifeless and cold. He tore his eyes away and looked into the face of Gant who was leaning forward over the spear.

'Do you know Wolfram von Eschenbach's legend of Parsifal?' The arms dealer's eyes seemed to glow in the darkness of the room. 'The legend which inspired Wagner's mystical opera. Parsifal served the dying king, Amfortas, and sought to regain the Spear of Longinus, the holy symbol, for his master. As you sought to regain it for your masters – the Jews!'

'That's not true!' The hands on Steadman's arms tightened their grip. 'They wanted me to find their missing agent, Baruch Kanaan. You know that!'

'Lies, Parsifal. Their agent came for the Spear and when he failed, they sent you.'

Why hadn't Goldblatt told him of the Spear? Why hadn't he levelled with him from the start? The woman, Hannah, when she lay dying in his arms, had told him to find the Spear. But why hadn't they told him at the very beginning? Did they assume that finding Baruch would lead them to the ancient weapon? Resentment rose up in Steadman. They had used him just as the Thulists were using him. He'd been manipulated by both sides, one side using him as a tool, a lever to uncover a viper's nest, the other using him as a player in a symbolic ritual.

'You were to kill me, just as the knight, Parsifal, killed Klingsor, who held the Spear at his castle. Klingsor, the evil magician whose manhood was cut away by the fool king – as mine was taken from me. A sword took Klingsor's testicles from his body – an explosion took mine. The Reichsführer saved my life and when he saw the damage that was done to me, *he knew* I was Klingsor reincarnated! He knew I would be the future bearer of the Spear of Longinus.'

Gant's shoulders were heaving with the mental stress he was going through. To Steadman, it seemed as though the man was possessed. Abruptly, the tone of the arms dealer's voice changed, and he spoke as if he were revealing a long-kept secret to friends.

'The legend, you see, was neither a myth, nor a prophecy. It was a warning. Von Eschenbach was our guide from the thirteenth century. He was warning us of the disaster that could come if we allowed it. And he warned us again at the appropriate time in this century through Richard Wagner!'

'It's fantasy, Gant. Can't any of you see that?' There was desperation in Steadman's voice now. 'You're just twisting everything to make it seem as if the story is coming true. I'm not your Parsifal and he's not your Klingsor. The Spear has no power. It's all in *his* mind!'

A rough hand was cupped over his mouth and his head jerked back. He tried to twist away, but Griggs held him firmly.

'No, it's not all in *my* mind, Mr Steadman,' Gant said calmly. 'We are led by another. Someone who knows you now. Someone who sent a tank against you as a test. Someone who visited you at your home just two nights ago, but who was disturbed by the meddling old Jew. Someone who wishes to meet you again.' Gant chuckled. 'As it were, face to face.'

There was silence in the vast room, the shadows flickering and weaving with the dancing candle-flames. Gant sat and the thirteen around the table put their hands on its rough surface as though a signal had been given. Their fingers touched and Steadman could see that their eyes had closed and each man's face was creased in concentration. Nothing happened for a while, then suddenly he felt his muscles weakening as if all strength was being drained from them. His head was released and he felt, rather than saw, the two MI5 men step back from their position directly behind. He tried to rise but found he couldn't; an invisible force seemed to be holding him there. He opened his mouth to speak but no sound came. The sudden oppression in the room had become an increasing pressure, weighing down on him like a physical force. He saw that several members of the circle were sagging in their seats, their heads lolling forward as though their energy was being sapped. Dr Scheuer's head was resting almost on his chest.

A stillness had crept into the room. The candle-flames seemed to be frozen solid, their light dimmed. It became cold. A terrible, cloying coldness that closed in and gripped the skin. An odour pervaded the air and the room became even darker, the chill more intense.

Steadman stared hard into the shadows behind Gant and Dr Scheuer, for he thought he had seen something move, a dark shape against a black backcloth. From the balcony overlooking the hall, he had noticed steps set to one side of the room leading down to a door, the top half only, level with the floor. The black shape had seemed to emerge from that point. But now it had disappeared and he wondered if it had been merely a trick of the fading light.

A humming vibration reached his ears and his attention was drawn to the table's surface. Some of the Thulists' heads were sagging, almost resting on the table, but still their fingers touched, trembling and greyish in the poor light. His eyes came to rest on the dark object lying opposite, and somehow he knew that was the source of the vibration. The ancient weapon lay unmoving, yet it seemed to throb with some inner life. He shook his head and the effort seemed almost too much; he felt giddy with fatigue. He knew the humming vibration was only in his own head, yet it seemed to come so definitely from the talisman. He became weaker and for a moment his eyes rolled in his head; he had to fight consciously to control them. He found himself looking across the table at the bowed head of the old man, Dr Scheuer, the scant white hair hanging loosely around his hidden face.

Steadman stared, for it seemed all the energy in the room had been drawn into the old man. The others, those who could, were watching him too, their bodies swaying slightly. The investigator fought against the weariness, trying to build a wall in his mind against the will-devouring force. But he could not tear away his eyes from the bowed head of Dr Scheuer.

As he looked, the white-haired figure began to straighten. The head came up, slowly, smoothly, taking long, long seconds for the eyes to meet Steadman's. And when they finally looked deep and penetratingly into his, the investigator's blood seemed to stop flowing, and the hair on his neck rose as though a cold hand had swept it upwards, for he found himself staring at the hate-filled image of SS Reichsführer Heinrich Himmler.

▪ 19 ▪

'Though he had the mind of an ordinary clerk or schoolmaster he was dominated by another Himmler whose imagination was controlled by such phrases as "The preservation of the Germanic race justifies cruelty", or "Unqualified obedience to the Führer". This other Himmler entered realms which transcended the merely human and entered in to another world.'

FELIX KERSTON

'For us the end of this war will mean an open road to the East, the creation of the Germanic Reich in this way or that ...'

HEINRICH HIMMLER

Holly crept stealthily down the corridor using only the balls of her feet, measuring each step and gently easing her weight on to the solid floorboards. There was a tension in the house that had nothing to do with her own nervousness. The air was heavy with it.

She wondered about the strange building, half-house, half-castle. What was the purpose of such a place? She had found her way towards the back of the house, heading for the baronial-type rooms she had seen only from the outside. There had been only a blank wall at the end of the corridor leading from her room – it was too short to have run the length of the house – and she had been forced to retrace her steps to the staircase near the front of the house.

Guessing it might be a mistake to descend – bound to be more guards around – she had decided to go up on to the next level and make her way back from there. There had to be another way of getting to the rear of the house on the second floor. She moved silently up the stairs, holding the miniature machine-gun ahead of her, wishing she had taken time to search the unconscious guard for the silencer that went with the deadly weapon. She knew that the Ingram MAC II, on which this weapon's design had been based, could be fitted with a lightweight sound suppressor which cut out even the light 'plopping' noise silenced guns usually made. She would have to take her chances without it – if someone discovered her, she would shoot to kill and to hell with the noise.

She reached the top of the stairs and paused: the house was deadly silent.

The long corridor running down the building's centre lay ahead of her, two minor corridors ran to the left and right from her position at the top of the stairs.

She had just begun her long walk down the central corridor when a door ahead opened.

Her reaction was fast. She ducked back into the left-hand corridor, prepared to run its length if the footsteps came her way. They didn't; she heard the footsteps receding into the distance. She stole a quick look around the corridor's corner and caught sight of the woman, the one they called Kristina. She was holding the side of her face as though she had been hurt and Holly caught a glimpse of her leaning against the wall momentarily for support. Holly held her breath, waiting for the footsteps to fade away. She was a strange one, this woman, Holly felt intuitively. She couldn't quite understand why, but was distinctly uneasy in her presence when Gant had introduced her. Not that she'd felt at home with the arms dealer himself.

She took another look and saw that the woman had vanished. Good. She'd definitely walked the length of the corridor, so maybe she was headed for the back of the house. There had to be a way through. Holly stole down the passageway.

There was a T-junction at the end and Holly debated with herself which way to go. She chose the right and at the end of it found a solid-looking oak door, its intricate carving suggesting it wasn't just the door to the broom-cupboard. She tried the wrought-iron handle and discovered it was locked. Okay, the left-hand turn might have a similar door. It did, and this one was open.

It was like stepping into another world: the walls on either side of the dim passageway were of heavy grey stone and the doors along its length again were of delicately carved oak. The lights overhead were deliberately dim so their brightness would not jar against the medieval atmosphere. Holly moved forward, carefully closing the door leading from the new to the fake-old behind her. If anything, the tension was even more acute in this part of the unusual house.

She crept forward, remembering to breathe again. Fainting from lack of oxygen wasn't going to help her any.

Holly stopped at one of the doors on her left and listened: no sounds came from within. She noticed a name was inscribed in the carving of the door and tried to decipher it in the poor light. It looked like Philip of ... somewhere or other ... Swabia? That was it. Where the hell was Swabia? She moved on to the next door which was even more difficult to read. Frederick Hohen ... oh, what difference? She listened again, but still heard nothing. She gently tried the handle and found the door was unlocked. Pushing it open slowly and pointing the gun into the widening crack, she peered into the dark room. Deciding it really was empty, she pushed the door wide and was provided with a soft light from the hallway.

The room was furnished with antiques and smelled musty, unused. A four-poster bed dominated the floor-space and a portrait of someone in cere-monial – or at least, ancient – garb hung over the mantel. Maybe that was Fred what's-his-name. Holly closed the door and went on to the next room. She was able to make out Henry I on this one and sheer instinct told her that this time the room was not empty. The question was: to look in or not to look in? Well, she decided ruefully, I'm not going to find Harry by not looking for him. She turned the handle as softly as she could.

The odour hit her nostrils immediately, vile and unclean; it was as if a malevolent spirit was rushing past her, fleeing through the opening she had created. It was a smell of dust, human sweat – and something else. Rank meat? No, it was indefinable. She pushed the door open further.

Holly saw the rows of books lining the walls first, then, as she cautiously stepped into the room, its other contents were revealed to her. It was a larger room than the one she had just peeked into, containing a long, solid-looking desk, two high-backed chairs, a carpet of richly woven design, the shelves running around the walls on three sides, holding volumes of books. In a break between the shelves to her left, hung a picture – it looked like a portrait in the dim light – and again, the subject seemed to be wearing the clothing of centuries before. Old Henry, presumably. Opposite, on the wall to her right, another picture hung between two bookshelves, its enclosure almost shrine-like. It was a portrait also, but this time the clothing was not as ancient. The man in the picture wore a uniform. A black uniform.

She guessed the identity of the subject: the modern-day Nazis still worshipped their old heroes.

A sudden sound drew her attention towards the desk. Something had moved there, she was sure. She raised the machine-gun, her hand trembling slightly. Above the desk, between the heavy drapes concealing the room's two high windows, hung their symbol – the white circle on a red background, the circle containing the evil black swastika. She felt exposed under its glare and suddenly sensed that the two portraits on either side were watching her. She quickly shrugged off the uncanny feeling.

Again she heard the noise, a slivering sound as if something had dragged along the floor. It came from behind the desk.

She wondered if she should turn and run, but quickly dismissed the thought. If someone was hiding from her, someone who'd seen she had a gun, they would raise the alarm as soon as she left the room. Whoever it was had to be temporarily put out of action. The decision made, she crept towards the desk.

It was a wide-top desk and its base was solid, a panel covering the centre leg-space. It was a pity, for Holly could not duck down to see if anyone was lurking behind. The smell seemed to hit her in waves now, but it was human staleness that dominated the general rancidity of the room.

The natural course of action would have been to move around the desk, rapidly but cautiously, ready to spring away from anybody crouched behind it; Holly believed in unpredictability, though. She smoothly swung her hip on to the desk and slid herself across its surface, ready to poke the machine-gun into any enquiring face. As she peered over the edge she realized she had been mistaken: the noise hadn't come from beneath it, but beyond it.

What looked like a bundle of rags lay on the floor against the wall and, even in the gloomy light from the hallway, she could see two frightened eyes staring at her. The bedraggled figure seemed to be pushing itself away, trying to sink into the wall itself. That had been the sounds she had heard: the slivering of bare feet on the floor, as the figure had tried hopelessly to get away from whoever had entered the room.

Holly slid off the desk and knelt beside the quivering bundle and it was then she realized the figure was that of a man and that he was cruelly tied, a noose-like rope around his neck, biting into the flesh, making it raw; the rope stretched down behind his back to bound wrists and ankles. A shirt hung loosely round him, the front completely open and exposing a chest which bore the marks of severe beatings. His trousers were filthy and stiff with stains as though the man had soiled himself many times. He lay on his side, his neck craned round to see her, and she noticed his wrists and ankles were caked in dry blood caused by the tightness of the ropes. Fresh blood was seeping around the ropes binding his ankles, probably caused by his struggle to get away from her. His hair was completely white, yet, as she looked into his frightened eyes, she realized he was not an old man. His face was lined with strain, heavy dark circles surrounding his eyes, the lips cracked and sore. But even through that, and through the bruises and dried blood that marred his features, she could see he was young. His face had aged not because of years but because of shock. She'd seen the same kind of ageing in released Nam prisoners – the ones who had been returned to their own country, but would probably never return to their own homes. Their minds had deteriorated beyond repair.

'Who are you?' she whispered.

The eyes only watched her in terror.

'Can't you speak? Can't you tell me who you are?'

Still the eyes watched her, but now a wariness had crept into them.

'Look, I'm a friend,' Holly tried to reassure him. 'I'm not with these people, I'm against them. Something's going to happen here tonight that I've got to prevent and time's running out. You've got to tell me who you are.'

She reached forward to touch his shoulder and the figure tried desperately to move away. The sudden movement jerked the noose around his neck tighter and a gurgling noise came from his throat as he began to choke.

'Hey, take it easy,' Holly whispered in alarm. She grabbed his wrists and pulled them upwards to ease the pressure on the noose. He stopped twisting and kept his body still. Holly wondered if his mind was functioning normally again or sheer animal instinct had made him stop moving.

'Look, I'm going to untie these ropes, but before I do, I want you to realize I'm not with the people who did this to you. I'm a friend, okay?' Holly placed the machine-gun on the floor and reached for the ropes binding his wrists. The knots were difficult, obviously pulled tighter by the man's own efforts to free himself. She looked around for something sharp to cut them with. Rising, she scanned the desk-top and found what she had been searching for. The paper-knife had a long point to it and could be pushed between the twists of rope to loosen the knots. She knelt beside the tensed figure again, placing her free hand on his upper arm. This time, he did not flinch.

'I'm going to get you free with this, so just try and relax. If you pull against the ropes they'll only get tighter.'

Holly tossed her hair back over her shoulder and set to work on the knots.

It took several minutes, but eventually she pulled with her fingers, using the knife as a lever, and then his wrists were free, one length of rope hanging loose from his neck, the other from his still bound ankles.

Holly breathed a sigh of relief and relaxed on to her haunches. She examined her broken fingernails and shrugged. 'I hate long nails, any ...' The man pushed her back with a strength that belied his appearance. He grabbed the gun lying on the floor and pointed it at her, using two hands to hold the light weapon steady.

'Do not move,' he hissed fiercely. The three words were thickly accented.

'Hey, I'm trying to help you,' said Holly from her prone position. 'We're on the same side – I think.' She bit her lip when she saw him flick the safety-catch off. 'I was trying to help you,' she said desperately.

'Who are you?' His eyes were burning, all fear from them now gone. 'Why are you here?'

'My name's Holly Miles. I'm a freelance writer.' Better to tell him that, she thought. Better to find out more about him first. 'I was doing a feature on Edward Gant as an arms dealer until I found out he was into something more sinister.'

His eyes darted around the room, wild again.

'Can't you tell me your name?' she pleaded. 'I promise you I've nothing to do with Gant.'

His eyes came to rest on her again. 'How do I know that?'

'I set you free, didn't I?'

He sagged back against the wall as though the sudden effort had drained him of any strength he had left. His bound feet slid out from beneath him and came to rest against Holly's denimed legs. He motioned at her with the gun and murmured, 'Untie them.'

She began to work at the knots again with the paper-knife.

'Why would a journalist carry a gun like this?' he asked, indicating he still had his wits about him even in his weakened state.

Holly threw caution to the wind and told him everything, realizing she had to move fast, had to trust the man. She thought he showed some reaction when she mentioned Harry Steadman's name and that he was also being held a prisoner in the house, but he sat up in alarm when she told him of the proposed plan for the US Secretary of State's jet.

'The missile site – where is it?' he asked, his feet free now. He tried to rise, but the circulation was still not flowing freely.

'At the back of the house, towards the cliffs.' Holly moved closer to him and he waved her back with the gun's barrel.

'You've got to trust me,' she cried out in frustration. 'Someone might come along at any moment!'

He ran a hand across his face, wincing in pain as it touched the bruises. 'I ... I don't know. They've done so much to me. I cannot think.'

'How long have they kept you here?'

'Years ... years. No, it cannot be. I do not know.'

'Let me help you,' she said softly.

'They used me. They used my strength!' The man rolled his head in despair. 'They left me in this room so *he* could take my strength.'

'Who?' Holly urged. 'Who took your strength?'

'Him … him …' He pointed the machine-gun at the picture on the wall behind them. She saw his finger tighten on the trigger and for a moment she thought he would fire at the portrait.

'No, don't,' she said quickly. 'You'll bring the whole house down on us.'

The hand holding the weapon dropped limply to his side and she exhaled in relief. 'How did they take your strength?' she asked him.

'They … beat … me. Kept me tied … in here. That is how … he survives. He draws … power … from others. Used me.'

Holly shook her head, not understanding. She glanced down at her wrist-watch. Twelve thirty-five. 'Look, we have to get moving. You must trust me.'

He nodded, knowing there was no choice. Some of his strength was return-ing, but he didn't know how long it would last. They had barely fed him, just given him enough to keep him alive. Had it been years? Or was it really only weeks? Time had become meaningless to him. He had been able to stand the beatings – for a while, anyway. It was the other things that had defeated him. The humiliation. The abuse of his body by the freak human, the one that was both man and woman. The base things they had made him do with the creature, taking away his manhood, shaming him … Tears clouded his vision and his shaking hand wiped them from his eyes.

He had told them everything they wanted to know, for eventually they had reduced him to an animal state. The man, Köhner, how well he knew the most vulnerable parts of the body, where to apply pressure, where to insert a blade. Even worse were the nights alone in this room where *he* had visited him – the jew-hater – mocking him and existing parasitically on his spirit. Had it all been in his own mind? Had they finally driven him mad with their torture?

But even more terrible than that were the times they had taken him to the strange room below, beneath the great hall. To the room they called the crypt.

It was there that all previous horrors had been surpassed.

He felt the girl shaking him and he opened his eyes to look into her concerned face. He had to trust her; there was nothing else he could do.

'Will you help me?' she was saying. He nodded his head and she gently took the light machine-gun from his loose grip.

'Tell me, then,' she said. 'Who are you? Tell me your name.'

'Baruch Kanaan,' he said. 'My name is Baruch Kanaan.'

The Commissioner looked around the ring of tense faces. Operational HQ had become the interior of the church overlooking the Gant estate. The vicar, who had been roused from his peaceful evening by the fireside in his nearby house earlier that evening, was busy organizing relays of coffee for the bitterly cold men, and had even allowed the ancient church's heating system to be switched on to combat the icy cold. It was no match for the wind that had collected its chill from the ocean and sought to invade any opening in the old masonry it could find.

The Commissioner knew his men were impatient for action; this was always the worst time for them, waiting and praying they'd come out of it all right. It bothered him too; he liked to get things over with. However, the years had taught him to be patient. So much harm could be done by rushing in at the wrong time. Sir Robert had been a great advocator of patience and the Commissioner had learned well from him.

He caught sight of the man called Blake, the retired policeman who worked for Steadman's agency. Blake's face was anxious and he was looking at the Commissioner as though deciding whether to approach him or not. The police chief beckoned him over and Blake bounded forward like a puppy to its master.

'We'll be going in at any moment, Mr Blake, so please try not to worry.'

'I'm sorry, sir. I don't mean to be an old woman, but Mr Steadman has been in there for quite some time.'

The Commissioner nodded sympathetically. 'I know that, but if we move in now we could upset some carefully laid plans.'

'I don't understand, sir,' said Sexton, puzzled.

'We're waiting for one last guest to arrive. The others – those we know about – have already been accounted for. Their movements have been watched for weeks and we're sure they're all down there with Edward Gant. They make a powerful group and we can't just barge in and arrest them purely on grounds of conspiracy. They have to be taken away and broken separately. I've spent most of the day with our American colleagues in Central Intelligence persuading the Prime Minister to let us do so.'

Sexton caught his breath. This really was the big one.

'We've got a fair amount of evidence on this group, but much of it is circumstantial,' the Commissioner went on. 'We need to catch them red-handed and then, as I say, break down their stories individually. Thanks to your employer, Harry Steadman, I don't think that will be too difficult. He seems to have triggered off quite a bit of action.'

'But did you know what Harry – I mean Mr Steadman – was getting into all this time? Did you know about this man Pope?'

The Commissioner raised a hand as if to ward off Sexton's questions.

'We've known about Nigel Pope for some time; his intolerance towards his superiors and his own colleagues could hardly go unnoticed. But he was part of the pattern and we couldn't remove him without destroying the whole framework. It had to be allowed to fester so it could be lanced once and for all – at the right time. Harry Steadman is the instrument we are using for drawing the poison.'

'You could have warned him ...'

'No, Mr Blake. We didn't know his part in the whole business. He appeared out of the blue. For all we knew, he was one of them.'

'But Mrs Wyeth!'

The Commissioner had the good grace to look down at his shoes. 'I'm afraid we weren't aware of any involvement from your agency at that time. It was most unfortunate.' He looked up again and gazed steadily into Sexton's eyes. 'We were only really sure of Steadman's good intent when he sent us the warning through you last night.'

Sexton shook his head wearily. 'I don't pretend to understand all this, Commissioner, but it seems to me no one was really bothered about Harry getting himself killed. He was getting kicked from all sides.'

'Not at all, Mr Blake,' said the American who had just returned from the vicar's house where he had been using the telephone. 'We just allowed him to wander around loose for a while until we could be sure of him.'

'And even if he was straight, he might stir something up anyway. Is that right?'

The American smiled, his chubby face friendly but his eyes steely. 'You got it, Mr Blake. Let me say, though, we had someone watching out for him some of the time.' He suddenly turned to the Commissioner, his manner now brusque. 'We got the word from your man outside on the radio, Commissioner; I said I'd let you know. The last helicopter just landed. The General's in.'

'Right. I'll give the order to move in immediately.'

'Also, there's activity around the estate's perimeter. Gant's private army is keeping the area tightly sealed, I guess.' The American frowned and looked at his watch. 'I'd be happier if we really knew if this meeting tonight has anything to do with the Secretary of State's arrival in the country.'

'They'll be able to tell us that themselves.'

'I wouldn't count on it.'

The Commissioner did not bother to reply. Instead he began issuing orders to the Special Branch officers around him. When his men were moving he turned back to the American. 'I'll be going in immediately after the first assault. Will you be with me?'

'Sure,' the American said, smiling pleasantly. 'I wouldn't miss it.'

'You'll have to stay here I'm afraid, Mr Blake,' the Commissioner said, then he was gone, his officers jumping from his path. He disappeared through the church doorway. The American tucked his hands into his overcoat pockets and headed after the Commissioner. Sexton caught his arm.

'You said someone was looking out for him some of the time. Who was it?'

The American grinned. 'One of our agents. Girl by the name of Holly Miles. We poached her from our Domestic Operations Division when we discovered she was a distant relation of Edward Gant's late wife. She's in there with Steadman now.'

Blake was left standing alone in the empty church.

▪ 20 ▪

'I witnessed for the first time some of the rather strange practices resorted to by Himmler through his inclination towards mysticism. He assembled twelve of his most trusted SS leaders in a room next to the one in which von Fritsch was being questioned and ordered them all to concentrate their minds on exerting a suggestive influence over the general that would induce him to tell the truth. I happened to come into the room by accident, and to see these twelve SS leaders, all sunk in deep and silent contemplation, was indeed a remarkable sight.'

WALTHER SCHELLENBERG

'The Beast does not look what he is. He may even have a comic moustache.'

SOLOVIEV: *The Anti-Christ*

STEADMAN'S MUSCLES WERE LOCKED RIGID.

His mind tried desperately to deny the vision his eyes saw so clearly. Heinrich Himmler was dead! Even if he had not killed himself at the end of the war as the world believed, the arms dealer had said the Reichsführer had died of cancer at sixty-seven. Yet he was here in this room, his eyes burning with life!

Hypnosis, Steadman rationalized. It had to be hypnosis of some kind. It couldn't really be happening.

'Ist das der lebendige Parsifal?' It was a thin, piping voice, completely different to that of Dr Scheuer's, and came from the apparition that had somehow superimposed itself over the old man's features.

'Ja, mein Reichsführer, der ist unser Feind.' It was Gant who spoke, his face shining in a strange ecstasy.

The men around the table were staring at the vision, some rapturously, others in fear. They all appeared unsteady, as though their energy had been drawn. One or two could barely lift their heads off the table. The figure of Kristina lay inert in her chair.

Gant spoke again, a deferential tone to his voice. *'Herr Reichsführer, darf ich ergebenst darum bitten, dass wir uns auf Englisch unterhalten? Viele Mitglieder unseres Ordens verstehen nicht unsere eigene Sprache.'*

'Er versteht sie.' The words were hissed and the apparition glowered at the investigator.

Steadman flinched. The vision was so real: the pudgy white face and small pig-like eyes; the clipped moustache and hair cropped to a point well above the ears; the finely formed lips marred by a weak chin receding into a flabby neck. Was it just a dream? Would he wake soon?

The figure began to rise and it was stooped, still in the shape of Dr Scheuer; its eyes never left Steadman's. It smiled evilly. 'Do you feel weak, Parsifal?' The words were spoken in English. A snigger from the apparition rang round the room. 'They feel it too. But they give me their strength willingly, while you resist.'

The investigator tried to move his arms and found it impossible. It was all he could do to hold his head up. He tried to speak, to shout, to scream, but only a rasping sound came from his throat.

'It's useless to struggle,' said Edward Gant as the macabre creature beside him chuckled. 'You cannot resist his will. This is how the Reichsführer still lives, you see. He draws etheric energies from the living, and feeds upon it. Adolf Hitler could do this when he lived. Heinrich Himmler learned the art, with the help of Dr Scheuer, when he was dead.'

'*Adolf. Ja, der liebe Adolf. Wo ist er doch jetzt? Nicht mit uns.*' The figure swayed and a hand rested against the table-top. The head sank for a moment and the image of Himmler's face seemed to waver, become less distinct. Then the moment was gone and the head rose again, the small eyes piercing into Steadman's, transfixing him.

'It is time, Herr Gantzer. He must die now. His death will signify our beginning.'

'Yes, Reichsführer. It has finally come.' Gant reached forward for the ancient relic lying on the table's rough surface. 'The Spear that protects the Holy Grail, Reichsführer. Take it now and feel its potency. Let its force flow through you. *Use its power!*'

The figure took the Spear of Longinus from Gant and held it in both hands. The weapon quivered in the apparition's hands and Steadman sensed or saw – it was all the same now – the light emanating from it. A blueness seemed to glow from the worn metal and the light stretched and grew, travelling over the gnarled hands that were still those of the old man, up along the arms, spreading and enveloping the frail body.

The figure began to straighten and Steadman could hear a screaming sound tearing around the hall, screeching from corner to corner, an inhuman cry that told of unseen demons. The coldness of the room deepened, becoming so intense that Steadman felt ice stiffening against his skin. His limbs were trembling uncontrollably, his hands a shaking blur. He wanted to cry out against the screaming cacophony of the unseen things, but only frosty air escaped his lips. The sounds tore from wall to wall like birds trapped in a dark room, screeching across the round table, sometimes beneath it, the seated men shying away as though their flesh had been touched by something unholy. The strident pitch grew louder, higher, reaching a crescendo.

Steadman saw the figure was no longer stooped and frail; it stood erect, powerfully vibrant. The etheric glow encompassed the whole body and the Spear was held in arms stretched rigid at chest level. The face of Himmler was directéd towards the ceiling, the eyes closed but movement beneath the eyelids showed that the pupils were active. The lids began to open slowly and Steadman could just see the slits of white between them. Then the head began to lower and the screaming became even more shrill. The investigator pushed himself against the chair, trying to break free of the invisible bonds that held his body and mind. It was no use, his strength was no longer there.

He could not tear his eyes from the face of Himmler even though he managed to twist his head; no matter in which direction he turned, his eyes remained locked on the creature before him.

The face was directed at him, watching his vain struggle with a grin made vile both by its intent and the shiny wetness of the lips. The eyes were watching him, but the fully opened lids revealed only blank whiteness; the pupils were still turned inside the head. The figure laughed aloud and the laughter mingled with the undulating screams. Suddenly the pupils dropped into place and Steadman tried to close his own eyes against their glare.

He had to make himself move! He had to will himself to run!

The figure began to move, the Spear held before it. Around the table it came, moving nearer to the investigator, the wicked point aimed low, ready to strike at his heart.

Gant was on his feet, his face covered with a sheen of excitement. This was the time! This was the time for Parsifal to die, not by the hands of Klingsor, but by the true Master – *the Antichrist*! And the Spear of Longinus would pierce the side of their adversary just as it had pierced the side of the Nazarene two thousand years before!

The figure raised the Spear higher, but the point was still aimed at Steadman's heart. It was drawing near to him now, still walking slowly around the huge table, the eyes always on him, holding him there. And then the figure was looming over him, the blackened spearhead held in two hands, raised above the head, ready to strike deep into his heart.

He was aware that the screaming had reached fever pitch, and the air was being violently disturbed by the frenzied, unseen things. He was aware that he was going to die by the hand of this unclean, drooling demon who bore the features of a man the world had despised. And he was aware there was nothing he could do to save himself.

But as the ancient weapon quivered at its zenith, ready to plunge into his unprotected chest, the table's surface erupted in an explosion of flying splinters. The bullets imbedded themselves in the old wood, then spattered into the soft body of the creature bearing the Spear of Longinus.

▪ 21 ▪

'We shall never capitulate – no, never. We may be destroyed, but if we are, we shall drag a world with us – a world in flames.'

ADOLF HITLER

'I am a strong believer that, in the end, only good blood can achieve the greatest, most enduring things in the world.'

HEINRICH HIMMLER

Jagged splinters from the oak table flew into Steadman's face and the shock galvanized him into action. His strength had returned and with it, old instincts. He threw himself to the floor and lay still, stunned by the piercing sounds around him: the screams of those hit by the deadly rain of bullets; the noise of the bullets themselves, thudding into the table, into bodies, ricocheting off stonework; the agonized gurgling of the old man, Dr Scheuer, as his body was shredded, blood vomiting from his mouth in an explosive stream.

Steadman saw the old man still held the Spear aloft in one hand, but it suddenly skidded from sight as his wrist was shattered. Dr Scheuer fell to his knees, then slowly toppled forward, his head striking the floor inches from the investigator. For the first time, Steadman was able to see the old man's eyes, as they stared into his, wide but with no disturbing force emanating from them; just the inanimate stare of the dead, even though the body twitched and seemed alive.

The hail of bullets continued, spraying the hall at random, a lethal, indiscriminate strafing. Steadman twisted his head and felt a flicker of recognition when he saw the man with the gun on the balcony above. But it couldn't be; it was an old man up there, his hair white, his hate-filled face lined and aged. His mouth was open and he seemed to be shouting, but the investigator could not hear him over the barrage of sound. A figure appeared next to the dishevelled man and Steadman called out her name as he realized it was Holly. He saw her try to snatch the light machine-gun, but the white-haired man held her off with one hand, continuing his vengeful onslaught.

He saw her quickly scan the room, fear in her face, and when their eyes met, he knew that fear was for him. Her lips formed his name.

A wild bullet suddenly stung the side of his hand, close enough to burn, but not enough to tear the skin. Pushing himself forward with toes and knees, he dived beneath the heavy table, drawing his legs after him. There were other bodies crouched there.

He watched the carnage around the hall from his place of safety, saw the running legs, the overturned chairs that tangled and tripped them, the bodies that suddenly slumped into view as they were hit. Booth was crawling towards the table, gun in hand, but staring straight ahead. He almost made it.

As he reached the shadow of the table his head suddenly jerked up, a look of astonishment on his face. A line of bullets had raked across his back, snapping his spine. He tried to turn and fire back, but his body collapsed and he rolled over, the gun pointing at the ceiling, his finger curling around the trigger guard and squeezing it uselessly. He lay there looking into the blackness overhead and waited for the pain to begin.

Steadman began to crawl towards the other side of the table and saw there were at least three others crouched in the darkness. It was the hugeness of the shape before him that told him the identity of one of the cowering men.

There was just enough light for Pope to see it was Steadman moving towards him. The fat man wasn't afraid, only angry that everything had gone so terribly wrong. He had just had time to see it was their prisoner, the Israeli agent, who was causing such havoc, before he dived for cover. They should have killed him as soon as they had captured him. He cursed Gant for his sadism, the sadism he disguised as ritualistic symbolism. Major-General Cutbush was dead – Pope had seen him rise then fall across the table, arms outstretched – and so were many of the others. Talgholm, Ewing, Oakes – he'd seen them go down. Others he could see writhing around the floor, curling themselves into tight balls to avoid being struck again. Griggs had been one of the first to be killed and Booth had not made it to cover, so he, Pope, was on his own. These others – those not dead or wounded – were not fighting men, didn't even carry arms. Where was Gant? What had happened to him? It was only seconds since the firing had begun, but every fragment of time stretched into a bloody eternity. They had been foolish not to have kept some guards in the room. It was Gant who refused to allow them full knowledge of the Order. Now they were paying the price.

Pope reached inside his jacket pocket for the small gun, his hand fumbling in its haste. There would at least be some revenge.

Steadman accelerated his movements when he saw the big man reaching for the weapon. Unfortunately, he was too restricted and, as Pope drew the gun and aimed it at his head, Steadman realized he wasn't going to make it. It was at that moment that another body hurled itself into the table's shelter and staggered between Steadman and the MI5 man. Pope's gun went off and the body in front of Steadman twitched violently but remained poised on hands and knees; the power of the small firearm was not enough to topple its victim even at that close range.

The investigator went barging on, keeping the injured man between himself and Pope. His shoulder hit the man just below his ribs and Steadman shoved hard, pushing him against Pope. Pope pumped bullets into his dying fellow-member, wanting him prone so he could get a clear aim at the investigator. It was no use; the body was pushed into him knocking him backwards.

He struggled to prevent himself from being ejected from the table's protective cover and, as the body finally fell to the floor, he grinned with relief, aiming the gun once more. Steadman had abruptly changed his tactics. As soon as the body he had been pushing had slumped to the floor, he had swivelled his body around in order to strike out with his feet. He lay with his back against the stone floor and kicked with all his strength.

Pope, despite his great weight, went tumbling out into the open, rolling once with the force of the thrust. There was a lull in the shooting from above and the big man had a moment to reach his knees and aim the gun at the figure beneath the table.

The firing began almost at once and bullets flew off the stone around Pope. He whirled, this time aiming upwards at the balcony, but bullets tore into him before he even had a chance to pull the trigger. He keeled over backwards and tiny explosions ripped his obese body.

It was then that Steadman saw the shadowy figure emerge from behind the altar-like structure which shielded the room's blazing fire. The movement was fleeting, and whoever it was had ducked into the shadows of the hall. Steadman realized that the machine-gun fire was now in short bursts rather than the continuous onslaught of before. The shape appeared again, then plunged down into the stair-well that led to the door set in the room's wall. Before it disappeared completely, Steadman had time to recognize the hawk-like features of Edward Gant.

He pushed himself from the protective cover and ran, leaping over Pope's recumbent form, tripping once but rolling with the fall, jumping into the stair-well and crashing through the open doorway below.

Holly screeched Steadman's name and tried to grab the machine-gun at the same time.

The Mossad agent seemed to realize who it was below and his finger suddenly released the trigger and he swayed backwards. Only the screams and moans of the dying filled the air now, but the atmosphere was heavy with the smell of death.

Baruch stiffened as though recovering his senses and once again, he aimed the machine-gun at the twisting bodies below.

'No,' Holly implored. 'Leave them – please!'

He stared at her with uncomprehending eyes.

'We've got to stop the missile from being launched.' Holly held his head between her hands to keep him looking directly at her, desperately wanting him to understand. 'The missile will be launched soon. We've got to stop them.'

A sadness swept over the Israeli. He tore his head from her grasp and surveyed the carnage he had created. When he turned to look at her once again, there was a hardness in his eyes and she knew the sorrow had not been for those he had just killed.

'How ... long ...'

She guessed his meaning and glanced down at her watch. She groaned. 'We're too late. There's only four minutes left.'

He gripped her arm. 'Where ... is the site? Where is it?' His grip tightened.

'Near the cliffs. It's too late, though; we'd never make it.'

'Helicopter. All day ... I have heard ... a helicopter landing and ... taking off. If we can find it ...'

'Can you fly helicopters?' she asked, hope rising in her.

He nodded, then clung to the balcony for support. 'Get me to it, quickly,' he whispered.

Holly gripped him around his back, her shoulder beneath him. 'Give me the gun,' she said, and he handed it to her without any reluctance.

They staggered down the stairs, almost stumbling once but Holly's determined effort saving them. She averted her eyes from the terrible scene below and prayed that those still alive would not try to stop them. She hated to kill.

Once again Holly called out Steadman's name, but there was no answer. She had seen him leap into the stair-well at the side of the hall and knew he had been chasing somebody – why else would he have broken cover? She longed to go after him, but the stair-well would only lead to the lower level of the house, and not to the outside. Her priority was to prevent the US Secretary of State's jet from being blown to pieces. She said a silent prayer for the investigator and ignored the awful wrenching feeling inside her.

'This way,' she said to the Israeli, pointing the gun into the shadows. 'I think there's a door over there. It's in the right direction, anyway.'

The pilot and the two guards who had been patrolling the exterior of the house glanced nervously at each other. They had heard gunfire inside and were making towards the back entrance when a different sound, much further away, had attracted their attention.

'What's that?' one asked, skidding to a halt with the others. Instead of going on towards the back door, they rushed to the corner of the house and peered inland, towards the estate's easterly perimeter. They were filled with dismay at what they saw.

'Oh, fucking hell,' one said in a low voice.

Four helicopters, powerful light beams descending from them, hovered in the distance. They began to fly along the estate's boundaries where Edward Gant's private army was deployed and dropping what looked like small bombs on to the soldiers below. The three men realized they were gas canisters as white vapour erupted from the ground. Lights suddenly appeared on the road leading down to the estate as vehicles began moving in.

'It's the bloody Army!' the pilot exclaimed. 'We're under attack from the bloody Army!'

Even as he spoke, one machine broke away from the action and came racing towards the house. The others began to settle on the ground and the three men saw figures begin to pour from them. Above the whirring of rotor blades they heard the crackle of gunfire.

'I'm getting out!' the pilot suddenly announced, whirling round and racing back to the Gazelle.

The two soldiers glanced at each other, their faces white in the moonlight. Without a word, they turned and chased after the pilot. 'Wait for us,' one of them called out, 'we're coming with you!'

The pilot was already in his seat and had set the chopper's blades in motion, thankful that the aircraft's engine was still warm from its previous flight. The two soldiers had almost reached him when the door of the house behind them opened and Holly Miles and Baruch Kanaan staggered through.

The brightness of the moon gave Holly a clear picture of the two running soldiers and the small four-seater helicopter they were headed for. She and Baruch had the advantage; the men had their backs to them and the pilot was too busy with his controls to notice them.

She freed herself from the Israeli and raised the light machine-gun.

'Hold it!' she shouted and the running soldiers halted dead in their tracks. They turned and one went down on his knee aiming his standard machine-gun at the two figures in the doorway.

Regretfully, she squeezed the trigger and the fast-firing machine-gun spewed its lethal dosage at the soldier. As he fell, his companion threw down his own gun and ran to the right, screaming back at Holly not to shoot. She let him go.

The pilot inside his cabin was frantically increasing his engine's power to give him lift and the machine was trembling around him. Holly shouted, ordering him to cut his motors, but he didn't hear her over the noise of the whirring blades. She bit her lip and said, 'Shit,' then raised the gun in both hands and sighted it at arm's length. Only when she was sure of her aim did she squeeze the trigger; she did not want to damage any of the Gazelle's machinery.

The pilot toppled from his aircraft, the short burst killing him instantly. He hit the hard landing pad with a dull thud.

Holly stole a quick look at her wristwatch, but the moon suddenly vanished behind a heavy black cloud and she failed to see its hands.

'Come on,' she said to Baruch and pulled him towards her. 'We don't have much longer.'

Baruch took a deep breath, then pushed himself away from her and stood erect. 'I will be all right.' The words were spoken singularly, but there was a certain strength behind them. He began to move towards the helicopter, his legs stiff, as though he were consciously willing them to bear his weight.

Holly caught up and the wind tore at their bodies as if to hold them back; she held on to his arm to keep him steady. The moon suddenly burst through again and she took advantage of the light to have another look at her watch.

She swore silently. They would never make it. There were only thirty seconds to go.

▪ 22 ▪

'The German conscience is clear because the blame for everything sinister, contemptible, criminal and horrible that happened in Germany and the occupied countries between 1933 and 1945 rests on Himmler.'

WILLI FRISCHAUER

DARKNESS ENVELOPED STEADMAN LIKE BLACK LIQUID. HE HAD FALLEN THROUGH the doorway at the bottom of the stair-well and continued his descent, for there were more stairs on the other side.

The stone steps had scraped painfully at his limbs as he had tried in vain to halt his tumbling fall. He reached the bottom with stunning force and lay there, gasping to fill his lungs with air again.

He managed to push himself to a sitting position, groaning softly at the effort. He blinked and tried to see into the blackness ahead, but the only light was coming from the doorway above and behind him, and that was very faint. He reached out and felt nothing before him, then waved his hand from side to side. It came in contact with a wall to his left.

The wall was damp and he could feel the velvety smoothness of moss. He rose to one knee, leaning against the wall for support, and drew in a deep breath. Jesus, it was freezing. Cold like a tomb.

He stood, cautious of broken limbs. The plunge had numbed him and he could not be sure he hadn't damaged himself badly. His legs supported him and he could move his arms around, so all he had suffered was some nasty bruising.

Keeping one hand against the wall, he moved out at right angles to it and stretched his other hand outwards. The fingertips touched another smooth surface and he guessed he was in a fairly narrow passageway. He knew what lay behind him, so the only way to go was forward. Dropping his right arm, he inched forward, using his left to feel his way. It was an eerie sensation; at any moment he expected his hand to come in contact with human flesh, Gant lurking there, waiting for him in the dark.

The only sound he heard was his own harsh breathing and he briefly wondered what was happening above.

His hand came in contact with a wall running across the one he was following. He ran his fingers along it and felt it dip forward again. He touched a rough surface; there was a door in front of him. Holding his breath, he felt around for a handle, hesitated, then gave it a twist.

The handle was stiff, rusted by the dampness of the underground passage, but with extra pressure, it gave. Steadman pushed the door open slightly, listening for any sounds before he entered. Then he opened it fully and stood to one side.

A wave of icy air hit him and he shivered against it. It had been cold enough in the narrow passageway, but it was even colder ahead. A faint aroma reached his nostrils and it was familiar to him. Just a waft of – what? Oil, spices? It was too slight to be certain.

There was a diffused light coming from a point in the blackness ahead and the investigator narrowed his eyes to make out some shape or form. The light was too soft though; it was just a dull hue against a black backdrop. For some reason, Steadman felt it was beckoning, inviting him to come closer. He fought down the inclination to go back the way he had come; he had to find Edward Gant. And kill him.

He stepped through the doorway and crept stealthily towards the light source, each step measured and slow. He stretched out his hands on both sides as he walked and neither made any contact with the walls. He was either in a wider passage or in a room of some kind, perhaps an antechamber. He drew nearer to the hazy light and realized it was being diffused by something and, when he was close enough to touch, he reached out, his fingers brushing against coarse material. It was a curtain and the light shone through the tiny apertures in its rough texture. Once again, he stood and listened, controlling his breathing, but unable to still the pounding in his chest. A small voice inside told him not to look, to turn away and run from whatever lay in wait on the other side of that curtain, that some things were better left unseen. The voice persisted, but he succumbed to the compelling fascination that had taken hold of him. It was as if there were no choice; he dreaded what might be there, but there was no denying its lure. Steadman ran his fingers over the rough, mildewed material, searching for an opening.

He found it slightly to his right and manoeuvred himself so his eyes would be directly before it when he parted the curtains. He drew them open and looked into the strange chamber beyond, his pupils shrinking against the unimpeded light.

It was a circular room, the walls of stone shiny with damp. Recesses containing small, black crucibles in which green flames glowed were placed at regular intervals around the room's perimeter. It was these tiny green flames that gave the room its peculiar light, and the colour suggested that chemicals or herbs of some kind were being burnt. It explained the aroma that drifted along the passageway. A stone platform ran around the wall's edges and another door lay directly opposite to where Steadman was standing, steps leading down from it to the chamber's lower level.

The floor area was large even though the ceiling was comparatively low and, because of its shape and the higher-level walk around the sides, it had the appearance of a miniature arena. Twelve four-feet-high pedestals stood around the circumference at well-ordered points like stone sentinels gazing silently towards the room's centre. And there, at the centre stood a solitary, high-backed chair.

It was facing away from Steadman so he could not see whether it was occupied, but kneeling six or seven feet from it was the shadowy form of a woman. The long, black flowing hair identified her as Kristina and Steadman could see she was clutching something rising from between her thighs, like a huge phallus. As he watched, she crawled forward holding the object before her, and placed it on the stone floor two feet away from the high-backed chair. She crawled back to her original position and began to sway on her knees, her arms stiff by her sides.

Steadman knew by its shape it was the Spear of Longinus she had put down before the chair and, as he prepared himself to enter the chamber, a fresh feeling of unease swept through him. Sounds came from the hermaphrodite's lips, but they were unintelligible, a wailing incantation. He closed his mind to his misgivings, forcing himself to ignore his frenzied imagination, and began to slip through the curtain.

It was then he became aware that he wasn't alone in the antechamber.

A sound from behind. A rustle of material? A scraping of a foot against the floor? He couldn't be sure. But as he turned, his back now to the curtain, he heard breathing. It came in jerky rasping sighs, as though whoever it was could no longer control its rhythm; and as he listened, it became even more agitated, louder, the air sucked in greedily and exhaled in short gasps.

Steadman felt momentarily paralysed, wanting to move away from the curtain, knowing the dim light shining through must show his body in rough silhouette. The rasping grew louder and he peered into the darkness, trying desperately to discern a shape. It was no use, he could see nothing. But he could feel the warm breath on his face; and the cold fingertips that reached out to touch his cheek.

He staggered back from sheer reaction and hardly felt the knife-blade slice across his stomach, the tip barely penetrating the skin through his shirt. He went through the curtain and his assailant came after him, the ritual dagger slashing at the air between them. The investigator fell but kept his body moving, twisting to his right, aware there was a drop on to the chamber's floor behind him. The tall figure of Edward Gant lunged and missed again, overbalancing and falling to one knee.

They both crouched, facing each other, Gant's eyes wild with malice and Steadman's cold with hate.

'I still have you, Parsifal. I can still destroy you,' Gant hissed.

'You can try, you crazy bastard,' Steadman replied, rising immediately and aiming a foot at the arms dealer's face.

Gant avoided the blow and rose more slowly, the silver dagger pointing at the investigator's stomach. He inched forward, his manner even more menacing because of its deliberation. Steadman backed away.

'Stay, Parsifal. You can't run from fate.' Gant smiled, his face evil in the soft green hue. 'My soldiers will take care of the Jew and the slut. They won't get far.'

'It's all over, Gant, don't you understand?' Steadman's attention was directed more at keeping the blade at a safe distance than his own words. 'There's too many dead up there. Important men. How will you explain their disappearance?'

'Why should I have to?' The familiar mocking look had returned to Gant's eyes. 'No one knows they were here. Our associations have been quite discreet.'

'But you've lost the power behind your organization.'

Gant sneered. 'They were only the nucleus; there are others equally revered only too eager to take their place. All we have suffered is a setback.'

'Another setback, Gant? Like the war?' The mockery now in the investigator's attitude had the desired effect. Gant screamed with rage and leapt at his quarry, just as Steadman reached for the burning crucible in the recess he had been trying to reach. His hand encircled the hot metal and brought it from its resting place in one swoop, smashing it into the side of Gant's face as he advanced. The arms dealer screamed again, this time in pain, as the hot, burning oil poured into his face and down his neck. The dagger imbedded itself in Steadman's arm and was jerked free again when the arms dealer staggered away.

Steadman cried out with the sudden tearing pain, but he had the satisfaction of knowing his assailant's wound was far greater. Gant had dropped the dagger and was slapping at his face, trying to dislodge the fiery oil that was sizzling into his skin. Small dots of fire were spattered over his jacket and shirt, but he ignored them for the greater pain in his face. Steadman saw oil had splashed on to Gant's nose and it was melting like wax, a pink stream flowing over his tortured lips. The investigator flinched as the naked bone and gristle beneath the artificial organ was exposed, but he felt no pity for the injured man.

Even in his agonized state, the arms dealer's virulent hatred for the investigator and the force he symbolized rose to the surface like a bubbling volcano. He had known great pain before, and had learned to keep one part of his mind secure from its distracting influence. With one eye only, the other seared by the oil, he searched for the fallen dagger. It was lying close to his left foot and he quickly stooped, screeching against the intense heat in his flesh.

Steadman saw his intention and stepped forward, his right arm outstretched, reaching for the weapon.

Gant was faster. He picked up the silver dagger and began to bring it up, the wicked point aimed at the stooped investigator's chest. Steadman grabbed at the wrist holding the knife and deflected its direction, using his own strength to continue the upward arc. The blade sank up to the hilt into a point just below Gant's breastbone. He stared disbelievingly at Steadman, his fingers still curled around the dagger's handle, the investigator's hand still gripped around his wrist, and there was a moment of absolute silence between them. One side of Gant's face was popping and blistering, a scorched eyelid covering one eye; the gaping wound where his nose had once been was weeping fresh blood. And then the arms dealer screamed and fell forward, his chest coming to rest against his knees, the dagger's hilt between them, his forehead touching the cold stone floor as though he were paying homage to the victor. Blood gurgled up from his throat and created a thick, red pool around his head, and he died in that position, his body refusing to topple on to its side, escaping gas from his abdomen taking any last shred of dignity from his dying.

Steadman stepped away to avoid the spreading pool and leaned against the wall, shock and weariness overcoming him. He looked down at the slumped body and felt no regret nor any gladness that the man was dead; only relief that it wasn't himself crouched there.

The throbbing in his arm reminded him of his wound. He touched a hand to his injured limb, flexing it at the elbow and wincing as the pain flared. It wasn't too bad, though: he could still lift his arm so no muscles had been torn. He glanced back at the dead arms dealer. Was it all over? Had the death of Gant signified the end of the new Reich, or was the net too widely spread, already too powerful to falter just because its leader had been killed. There would be chaos upstairs, the injured and the dying screaming for attention, Gant's soldiers searching for Holly and the man she had been with – had it been Baruch? Perhaps they were already dead. The idea that Holly might have been shot filled him with a new desperation. He knew she had lied to him, that somehow she was deeply involved in the whole affair, and he was angered by the deception; but stronger feelings overrode that anger, feelings he had thought burned from him with the death of Lilla long ago.

He had to go back and find her even though it was probably hopeless. He turned towards the curtained doorway. It was finished down here. The arms dealer was dead, there was nothing left. It was over.

But the sudden stillness, the sudden thick, cloying odour, the sudden drop in the already cold room's temperature, told him it was not over. Not yet.

The presence seemed to be everywhere, filling the gloomy underground chamber, and it was a familiar thing to Steadman now. The same feeling of intense pressure, the awareness that something unseen had manifested itself. Unconsciously, the investigator had backed himself against the curved wall, his eyes darting from left to right, searching the chamber, trying to see the presence and not just perceive it. They came to rest on the figure in the centre of the room.

The hermaphrodite was rigid, no longer swaying, no longer moaning. Kristina's lips were open wide as though mouthing a silent scream of agony; her eyes were tightly closed. She was still in a kneeling position before the high-backed chair, and the ancient spearhead lay on the stone floor where she had placed it. It seemed to quiver slightly, as though a current were running through its black metal, and Steadman felt, rather than heard, its vibration. He knew he had to take it from her, away from that dark room, away from the forces that were using its power … and he wondered at himself for believing such things.

Sounds seemed to be swirling around the circular chamber, soft voices that laughed and called, building to a crescendo as they had in the room above. The crucibles were burning black smoke and the wind swirled the smoke around the room, weaving dark patterns in the air, and Steadman imagined the shapes were lost spirits, twisting and writhing in a secret torment. Cold air brushed against his face, ruffling his hair, tearing at his clothes, seeming to beat against him, forcing him to raise an arm to protect his eyes, willing him to fall, to cower against the wall. Abruptly it ended, and silence returned to the underground chamber.

Only *the* presence remained.

The investigator forced himself away from the wall, dropping to the lower floor-level, crouching for a moment. He retched at the overpowering stench, the terrible smell of corruption, and his body felt leaden, the weakness spreading through him, drugging his brain, dragging him down. He tried to rise and staggered against one of the small pillars set around the arena. He saw the metal plate on the stone pillar, bare of any inscription, and he suddenly knew the reason for the twelve pedestals facing the room's centre: they would bear the ashes of the members of the new Teutonic Order as each member died. How he knew was no mystery to him: the presence had made him aware. It was telling him the truth of the Spear's legend, the power the holy relic held, the power that could be used for good or evil. It taunted him, cursed him, reviled him. And it feared him.

The knowledge that he could be feared drove Steadman on. He stumbled across the room he now knew was a place of the dead – a crypt – feeling his energy draining from him, forcing himself onwards to reach the Spear, resisting the urge to lie down and rest, just for a moment, just for one sweet second.

He fell, and began to crawl, one hand before the other, one knee forward then the other, one hand, one knee, one hand, one knee ...

Kristina watched him, a tremor running through her body with a ferocity that made her shape blurred. Her mouth was still wide, and black smoke from the low flames in the crucibles entered her throat, descending into her lungs, filling her.

Steadman was near the spearhead, his hand reaching out, meeting a force that pushed his grasping fingers away. He looked up at Kristina and her eyes were straining against their sockets as she stared down at him, the pupils glazed yet strangely filled with life. Her body convulsed once, twice, became rigid again, her back arching but her gaze still on him. One more convulsion, this time even more violent, her hair crackling with the tension, her grimace stretching her lips and tearing them in several places. Then, with a long rattling exhalation of air, she fell backwards, and life was drawn from her body.

Steadman closed his eyes and rested his head against the cold floor for a brief moment, wanting to stay there, to sleep and so take himself away from the malevolent force in the chamber. He resisted, knowing to succumb would mean his death. Forcing his eyes open again, he saw the slumped form of the hermaphrodite, her tortured face mercifully turned away from him. He twisted his head, not wanting to look at the miscreation, and his eyes fell on something far worse. He faced the husk sitting in the high-backed chair.

The rotted corpse wore the faded uniform of the Nazi Schutzstaffeln: the brown shirt and black tie, the tunic with three silver-thread leaves enclosed in an oak-leaf wreath on each lapel, the sword-belt with ceremonial dagger attached, the cross-belt passed beneath silver braiding on the right shoulder, the swastika armband on the sleeve, the breeches tucked into long jackboots.

On its head was the silver-braided cap with the Death's Head emblem at its centre. The whole uniform was covered in a fine layer of dust and hung loosely over the still form, as if the body had shrivelled within it.

It sat upright as though locked in position, and Steadman's horrified gaze travelled up from the jackboots, across the body, to the shrunken head that stared sightlessly across the dark chamber. The flesh on its face was stretched taut, greyish cheekbones showing through clearly, huge, festering rents in the skin alive with tiny, white moving shapes. The yellow skin at the throat sagged over the shirt collar, a shrivelled sack resembling a balloon that had been punctured. The lower lip had been eaten away revealing an uneven row of teeth stumps, and white, wispy hair clung sparsely to the upper lip. The face appeared chinless, as though the jawbone had receded back into the throat. One ear was missing completely, while all that remained of the other was a remnant of twisted, dried flesh. Thin strands of white hair hung from beneath the cap, whose peak fell low over the forehead, several sizes too big.

Peculiarly, pince-nez glasses were stuck firmly against the bridge of the nose as though permanently glued there, and one eye had escaped from its retaining socket and pressed against a lens. The tip of the nose was missing but the rest, although wrinkled and pitted, was intact. As Steadman watched, something black crawled from a nostril and scurried down the lower lip into the gaping mouth, disappearing from sight.

The investigator's stomach heaved and he could no longer control the bile that rose in his throat. It poured from him in pain-wracking convulsions, steam rising in the deeply cold air. He pushed himself away, away from his own sickness and away from the vile, stinking creature they had kept embalmed in the underground crypt.

He knew, without any doubt, whose mummified body it was: the Gestapo uniform, the pince-nez, the remnants of a moustache – their Reichsführer, Heinrich Himmler. The stupid, demented bastards had kept his body all these years!

He shook with the horror of it. They had continued to worship not just his memory, but his physical body as well, hiding it here, a corrupted husk of dried flesh, an abomination which they could idolize as though he were still there to lead them!

He looked at the skeletal hands resting on the cadaver's lap, withered and yellow, conscious that they had written the orders which had sent millions to their deaths: the hands of a clerk, the hands of a murderous butcher. And as he looked at them, the fingers began to move.

'Oh, sweet Jesus,' he said as the head slowly swivelled round to look down at him.

▪ 23 ▪

'And the devil that deceived them was cast into the lake of fire and brimstone, where the beast and the false prophet are, and shall be tormented day and night for ever and ever.'

THE REVELATION OF ST JOHN THE DIVINE: 20:10 (RSV)

'QUICKLY. IN WHICH DIRECTION IS ... THE LAUNCHING SITE?' BARUCH'S VOICE was raised so it could be heard over the sound of the Gazelle's engine and the whirring blades overhead.

'It's too late, Baruch. There's less than twenty seconds left,' Holly shouted. She sat next to the Israeli in the small cockpit, tugging at his arm to make him understand.

'Just point,' he commanded, and she did so immediately.

'Towards the cliffs ... there, you can just make it out in the moonlight ... that bushy area!'

Baruch weakly moved the collective pitch lever upwards and the helicopter began to lift; he pressed the foot pedals, changing the pitch of the tail rotor blades to swing the machine round so it faced the direction they wanted to go. It was a jerky ascent and the Israeli concentrated his mind on controlling the engine power with the twist-grip throttle, thinking only of flying, shutting the nightmare from his mind. The machinery around him, the smell, the noise, brought him back to the world of the normal and he adjusted the cyclic control stick to speed the helicopter towards the clifftops.

Dark clouds scurried through the night, hiding the bright moon for long seconds, blacking out the land below them.

'I've lost it!' Holly cried, her head craned forward to look through the cockpit's perspex dome. 'I can't see a bloody thing down there!'

Baruch felt himself spin and he knew he had hardly any strength left. 'It ... it must be somewhere ... below us. I will keep to this area.'

'It's no good, Baruch. Even if we find it, what can we do? They'll be under cover down there. This gun won't stop them.'

The Israeli was silent, his head beginning to loll down on to his chest. The helicopter began to weave dangerously close to the ground. Suddenly, the moon appeared again and the grassy slope below was bathed in its silvery light.

Holly gripped the Israeli's shoulder. 'Over there! The small building – the outhouse! It's near there. Yes, I can see it, that circle of undergrowth. They've cleared the opening.'

Baruch's head jerked up and he looked in the direction the girl was indicating.

The helicopter veered towards the spot and Holly was thrown back against her seat. They reached the shaft within a matter of seconds and Baruch hovered the machine before it.

Without turning towards his companion he yelled, 'Jump!'

Holly regarded him with astonishment. 'What are you going ... ?'

'Jump!' His voice had reached a screech and he shoved her roughly towards the door at her side. Then she realized his intention and knew it was the only way.

'Get out! Now!' Once more he pushed her, and this time she reached for the handle and threw the small side-door open. She tumbled to the soft grass eight feet below and lay flat, unhurt but the wind knocked from her. She raised her head just in time to see the helicopter surge forward, hover for a brief second, then plummet down into the deep, brush-surrounded hole in the grassy slope.

Major Brannigan waited patiently for the second-hand to reach the appointed time, his body and brain keen with the excitement of a military operation that would alter the course of history. He and his staff were tucked away in a small alcove set in the side of the deep circular shaft, a thin metal partition erected at the alcove's entrance to protect them from any back-blast of the missile. The sound of crashing waves was driven up from the beach by the wind, along a winding tunnel, and the sea tang was strong in Brannigan's nostrils.

He quickly looked over the metal barrier's top to check visually that everything was in order. The stone staircase built around the shaft's circumference was free of personnel, the missile, bathed in a dim red light, was poised, waiting for its thrust into the sky. The surface-to-air missile stood only ten feet high and resembled the Soviet Goa in design, but it had been manufactured in Edward Gant's own weapons' factory, and to his specification.

'Broad Band Jamming in action?' he asked over his shoulder.

The technician seated at the control unit gave him a thumbs up and was immediately relieved that the Major had his back to him: such informal gestures were frowned upon by the stiff-backed officer. 'All's fine, sir,' the technician answered quickly. None of the nearby radar stations dotted along England's south-west coast would pick up the missile's flight path.

'Target on screen?'

'On screen and our beam locked in.'

Brannigan grunted with satisfaction. Their missile would home in on the US Secretary of State's jet like a needle drawn to a magnet. They knew the exact flight path and time schedule thanks to Cutbush. He looked up at the circular area of sky, the inconsistent moon a silver bright circle encompassed by the larger black circle of the shaft's entrance. He listened intently for a moment. He thought he had heard the whirring sound of rotor blades, but the crashing sea echoing up the long cave and swirling around the shaft's walls made it impossible to be sure. He glanced down at his watch. No time for pondering now. Only five seconds to go.

'Right,' he said, crouching down.

The technician was intent on the dials in front of him, his finger poised over a particular button. He had his own timer and that alone would give him the signal to press the button and not an order from the Major. Two of Gant's special militia stirred uncomfortably behind the technician; they didn't like their confinement with the missile, even though they had been assured there was no possible danger.

'Three. Two ...' Brannigan's index-finger ticked the seconds away on his knee ' ... One. Let her go!'

The technician's finger stabbed at the button as Brannigan spoke and, on the other side of the metal screen, the surface-to-air missile roared into life, vapour pouring from its base and filling the sunken cavern with its flames.

Just as it began its ascent, Major Brannigan looked up through the gap between the top of the screen and roof of the alcove, and had time to frown and wonder what the huge object blocking out the round circle of moonlight was before the helicopter plunged down the shaft and met the missile on its way out.

There was not even time for the men inside the deep well to scream their terror as the explosion created a massive ball of fire which swept around the shaft, filling it completely, and searing their flesh and bones to charcoal.

Steadman stared at the obscenity in the chair and felt every hair on his body stiffen, a coldness running up his back and clamping itself against his neck. His skin crawled with revulsion and the urge to urinate was almost irresistible. He tried to push himself back, to get away from the decayed creature, but his strength was drained, there was no power in his muscles. Kristina's energy had been taken completely by this dead thing; she had not had the power to control its ravenous demands and now it was feeding off her psyche, had become a living entity. Now it was drawing on his, Steadman's, spirit, sucking the life from him as it had sucked Kristina's.

The head leaned forward, and Steadman shuddered as tiny white crawling worms were dislodged from the cavities in its cheeks. He saw one shaking, skeletal hand reaching down, flesh flaking from the fingers, and he drew in his breath at the thought of being touched by it. But the hand was stretching down towards the stone floor and he realized it was reaching for the ancient spearhead lying near the jackbooted feet. Steadman knew, beyond all doubt, that if the monstrosity grasped the Spear it would derive more strength from its strange power, and the weapon would once again be used against him, used to take his life.

With a cry of desperation, the investigator lunged forward and grabbed the spearhead just as the corpse's fingers curled around it. As he pulled the ancient weapon away, one of the creature's fingers fell to the floor, the rotted skin and brittle bones unable to resist the sudden movement.

Steadman drew the Spear to him, clasping it to his chest in both hands. He felt new strength coursing through him and though the pressure still drugged his brain, he was able to fight against the sensation, was able to rise from the floor and stagger away from the moving carcass. He backed away, stumbling over the dead body of Kristina, losing his grip on the spearhead, feeling the weakness again, crawling after the talisman, gripping it tightly, turning to see the dead thing rising from the chair and walking towards him, one arm raised, mouth gaping open, willing him to return the Spear, urging him to come back and be embraced.

Steadman screamed and staggered to his feet. He found the stairs on the opposite side of the chamber's curtained entrance and clambered up them, the weakness making his movements slow, his footsteps leaden. He reached the door and slammed against its rough surface, one hand scrabbling madly for the handle, sensing the figure was behind, mounting the stairs, reaching for him.

He pulled at the handle, but the door was locked. He half-collapsed against it and, as he sank to his knees, he saw a rusted iron key projecting from the lock. He tried to twist the key, but it was jammed and his strength was useless. A shadow fell over him and he refused to turn round, too frightened to look into the corrupted face again, knowing the sight would paralyse him with its closeness. The foul smell swept over him, drawing his senses with its stench, and he wanted to close his eyes, to roll himself into a ball and hug himself tight.

Instead, he dropped the Spear and used both hands to turn the key, praying to God the mechanism would be released. His hands and arms shook with the exertion, but he felt the lock give, slightly at first, only a half turn, and then completely. He swung the door open as a hand grasped his shoulder and he pulled himself away from the deathly grip, scooping up the ancient weapon as he stumbled through into the black passage beyond.

There was no light. Only the freshness of the air drew him on, for it had to come from above ground, from the world of the living. He had no idea how long the passage was for he could see nothing ahead, only total darkness. Soft, tenuous material clung to his face and he thrashed wildly at the unseen cobwebs, smashing through them, revolted by their touch. His flesh crawled as tiny legs scurried across his cheek, and he slapped the spider away, shuddering at the sensation as its fragile body popped against his face. The floor was wet and he slipped, crashing painfully to his knees, his hand reaching out and scraping down a slimy wall. He turned his head as he rose and saw the corpse silhouetted in the doorway, a black shape growing larger as it moved forward. Then the door, urged by the breeze flowing along the passageway, slammed shut, and he knew the husk was in the darkness with him.

A sudden muffled sound came to his ears, the noise of a distant explosion, and the earth beneath his feet seemed to tremble with its force. He slipped again before he had fully risen, and heard the metal of the spearhead clang against the wall, nearly falling from his grasp. He gained his feet and forced himself on, a sudden thought bringing him to an abrupt halt. He wasn't sure in which direction he was headed. In the panic-stricken moment of rising he had lost his bearings; for all he knew he was running straight back into the decomposed arms of the corpse. He held his breath and listened.

A shuffling noise to his left sent him scuttling away, once again using his hand as his only guide forward. The slowness of his actions taunted him, but he could not make his limbs move any faster. It was only his greater fear of what stalked him that made him progress at all. When he stumbled into the stone steps ahead, it was his own lethargy that prevented any serious injury. The freshness of the air drifting down seemed to confirm that the stone steps led outside. Steadman began to climb, his breath escaping in short, sharp sobs.

As he climbed, the effort became greater, as though the creature below were using a stronger force to prevent him from reaching the surface. He fell against the stairs, too tired to move, too exhausted to try, and the shock of clammy, cold fingers entwining themselves around his exposed ankle made him scream again, sending the blood pounding round his system, releasing the adrenalin that sent him crawling upwards, tearing himself free from the loathsome grip.

The husk that had once been a living being followed.

The stairs ended abruptly and Steadman knew he had reached ground-level. A thin silvery bar lying horizontally before him made him halt; then he realized it was moonlight – beautiful, silver moonlight – shining beneath a door. With an exclamation of hope, he rushed forward, crashing against the wooden structure in his haste. But this door, too, was locked. And this time, there was no key in the lock.

He looked around the room, searching for something with which to prise open the door, but the silver bar suddenly vanished as clouds obscured the moon's rays. He groaned with frustration and footsteps made him look towards the stairway he had just emerged from. Even though he could not see in the dark, he knew the corpse was mounting the steps, was near the top, its head level with the room's floor. He turned back to the door and banged against it with the spearhead, striking out in anger, fear, dread. The sound of the metal against wood brought him to his senses: he was holding the tool for his escape in his own hands.

He felt again for the lock, then moved his hand to the right, feeling for the gap where door joined frame. He found it and inserted the spearhead's tip into the narrow gap, pressing his whole body against the rest of the blade, praying it wouldn't snap with the force. Fortunately the wood was rotted and the lock none too strong.

The door flew inwards with a sharp cracking sound and fresh night air flew in as though to do battle with the nauseating stench of the thing that was now on the top step. Steadman rushed through the door and the cruel wind whipped at his body, unbalancing him in his weakened state. He went down and, in a night of bizarre sights, his eyes focused uncomprehendingly on yet another. In the darkness ahead, huge flames leapt into the sky, flames that seemed to spring from the very earth. It acted like a beacon to him, for it was light among total darkness.

He clutched the Spear to his chest as the corpse appeared in the doorway of the strange, vault-like building, the black uniform now blood-red in the glow from the fire. Steadman sensed that this creature – this abomination – wanted not just him but the Spear also. It needed the Spear to exist.

He lurched to his feet, the drugging sensation making his head reel. He staggered towards the flames, the corpse of the Reichsführer following, the wind tearing strips of parchment skin from its body, revealing the bones beneath.

The grass beneath Steadman's feet was soft, sending new life into him as though the earth was trying to help him escape the unnatural thing. The fire was close and he swayed like a drunken man towards it, feeling its heat, welcoming its attack on the abnormal coldness behind him. His legs were in quicksand, but he forced them on, each step a single battle, each one taken, a new victory. He finally reached the brink of the pit, swaying dangerously before it, the heat singeing his hair and eyebrows, his skin reddening and beginning to scorch. He turned his back to the inferno and faced the advancing demon, knowing he could run no further, that if he could, he would drag the thing down with him into the depths below, back to the hell it had risen from.

Then the creature was before him and he was gazing into one sightless eye, the pince-nez torn away by the wind, the eye that had rested against the lens hanging down on to a fleshless cheek. The mouth was open wide as though the creature was screaming at him, but no sounds came from the lipless gap. Loose skin hung in flaps, breaking away, flaking into swirling dust. The corpse of Heinrich Himmler raised its withered arms to take Steadman in its embrace, the skeletal hands reaching behind the investigator's neck to draw him forward, to touch its face to his. And Steadman was powerless to resist, mesmerized with horror, feebly trying to twist his head away as the skull came forward, a small cry of terror his only sound.

He felt his senses swimming and though he turned his head, his eyes refused to look away from the terrible face. For a moment, he thought he saw the images of Edward Gant and Kristina in the hideous features, screaming out at him from their new-found torment. The skull seemed to grow larger, to fill his vision completely, the eaten-away features sharp in detail. He knew the creature wanted to drag him back to the crypt, to take his will and exist on it. The thing pulled at him and Steadman was powerless to resist.

The ravaged head suddenly burst apart in a hail of bullets, exploding into a fine powder, the remnants toppling from the corpse's body and rolling in the grass at its feet. Steadman drew back and felt his strength return, surging through his body till every nerve-end tingled with the sensation of it. He saw Holly on her knees no more than four yards away, her arms stretched before her, the gun she held in both hands aimed at their swaying figures. He called out her name, the relief of seeing her alive almost too much for his battered emotions, and her face was a mask of fear and incomprehension.

Inexplicably, the headless corpse remained erect, the hands having dropped from Steadman's neck to its side. It stood like a statue, the howling wind whipping at its clothing and threatening to disintegrate the frail body completely. Lights in the distance distracted Steadman for an instant and the crackle of gunfire came faintly to his ears, telling him it really was all over for Edward Gant's macabre New Order. He saw figures scurrying around the house and heard shouted commands, the breaking of glass as they forced their way into the building. Other figures had broken off from the main body and were hurrying towards them, towards the blaze.

He felt the vibration running through the spearhead and looked down, the power from its black metal seeming to course along his arms, penetrating his bloodstream. Then he felt the weakness again, the dragging sensation of energy being drained from him, syphoned from his body by a magnetic force. He fought against the sensation, against the power from the Spear. The headless figure before him reached out, the withered fingers grasping his wrists, and Steadman felt the strength in his arms begin to leave him, to flow from the Spear into the body of the dead Reichsführer.

Steadman screamed in rage, pulling away from the corpse, twisting his arms to break the grip. He staggered and the corpse lurched forward, almost toppling on to him. The investigator turned his body, the heat from the fire burning into his face again, his eyes narrowing with its intensity. In a last desperate effort, and with the agonized cry of the near-defeated, Steadman raised the ancient weapon and plunged it down at the figure's chest, aiming at the heart that had long ceased to beat. The spearhead sank deep, seeming to melt into the rotted flesh. The screech that tore into Steadman's mind was from a tormented creature, a piteous soul suffering the final torture.

Steadman pressed the spearhead in even deeper, pushing the body back towards the flames, ignoring the fresh screams that came from it, closing his mind to its beseeching, wailing cries. They were at the edge of the pit and he saw smoke rising from the black uniform as it began to smoulder. The pain was too much; Steadman knew he would soon collapse with it. But then the body was over the edge, the jackbooted feet scrabbling against the shaft's side, falling away from him, a black shape disappearing into the inferno below, to be devoured by the fires. Consumed into non-existence.

Steadman swayed on the brink, the full power of the Spear now flowing through him. Something had made him cling to the holy weapon as the corpse had fallen away from it, something that had told him he was now the bearer of the ancient talisman, that he now held the key to revelations sought by those who yearned for power and glory. In the flames he saw a mighty battle taking place, a cosmic war between hierarchies of Light and Darkness, a mighty struggle between Good and Evil powers to control the destiny of mankind. It waged before him, a battle that was eternal, neither in the past nor in the future, but always in the present.

Holly screamed his name, seeing his body sway on the edge of the pit, knowing his skin was already being seared by the fire. She tried to reach him but found it impossible to move. She could only watch as he raised his arms above his head, holding something that had a tapering point, something wicked. A blue glow seemed to effuse from the object, an energy she could see clearly against the background of roaring yellow flames. It moved down his arms, flowing like incandescent water, encompassing his body, spreading to his lower limbs, and she saw his body quiver with some strange elation.

Holly called his name again and tried to crawl towards him in an attempt to drag him back from the fire. His body became rigid, and she wondered if he had heard her. She heard him shout as though in anger. He stretched his body back and with an effort that seemed to take all his strength, he hurled the object into the pit.

The flames swallowed the Spear, and Steadman knew it would melt in the inferno. He prayed its powers would melt with it.

The fire suddenly lost its intensity, became cold, frozen yellow tentacles rising from the deep shaft, the wind scarcely influencing their straight path into the sky; and it was the chill that drove Steadman back from the edge, not the heat.

Holly ran to him and for a moment his eyes were strange, looking down at her as though he did not know her, as though he did not know the world she was in. Then recognition flooded back and he held her to him in a grip that threatened to crush her; but she held on to him, returning the pressure, loving him and feeling his love.

The blazing heat returned, pouring from the pit like an explosion, and they moved back, away from its scorching blast. He leaned against her, now feeling the pain in his blistered face, the wound in his arm. But it was welcome pain, for it was real. It was something he could understand.

They held each other close as the first of the soldiers reached them, watching the flames rise into the sky, and they were suddenly aware of the distant droning of an aircraft in the deep, night air. The Marine Commando wondered why the dishevelled couple's upturned faces were smiling.

SEPULCHRE

There are no absolutes . . .

THE SUMERIANS

Three thousand years before the birth of Christ, the first real moves towards civilization emerged from southern Mesopotamia, around the lower reaches of the Euphrates and Tigris rivers. Because the land was between two rivers – *Sumer* – the people there were called Sumerians.

Their ethnic origins have never been explained.

This race of people made three important contributions towards our advancement – four if you count the establishment of firmly governed communities.

The first two were these:

The measurement of time in hours, days and months; and astrology, the study of the stars' influences, which eventually led to the science of astronomy.

But the third was most important of all, for the Sumerian high priests discovered a way of making man immortal. Not by eternally binding his spirit to its earthly shell, but by preserving his knowledge. These high priests devised the written word, and nothing invented since has had a greater effect on mankind's progression.

Yet little is known of these people themselves.

By 2400 BC they had been swallowed up by surrounding, less enlightened tribes, who absorbed the Sumerian culture and spread it to other lands, other nations.

So although their achievements survived, the Sumerians' early history did not. For the kings, the princes, and the high priests destroyed or hid all such records.

Possibly they had good reason.

· 1 ·
MORNING DUES

THE MAN WAS SMILING. HALLORAN WAS SMILING AND HE SHOULDN'T HAVE BEEN.

He should have been scared – bowel-loosening scared. But he didn't appear to be. He seemed ... he seemed almost amused. Too calm for a sane man. As if the two Armalites and the Webley .38 aimed at his chest were of no concern at all.

Well, that wisp of a smile on his unshaven face would spirit itself away soon enough. This 'eejit's' reckoning was coming, sure, and it was a terrible unholy one.

McGuillig waved his revolver towards the van parked in the shadows of trees just off the roadside.

'Your man's in there.'

The harshness of his tone made it clear he held scant patience with Halloran's manner.

'And your money's here,' Halloran replied, nudging the bulky leather case on the ground with his foot.

McGuillig watched him coolly. When he'd spoken on the phone to the operative, he'd detected a trace of Irish in Halloran's voice, the merest, occasional lilt. But no, he was pure Brit now, no doubt at all.

'Then we'll get to it,' McGuillig said.

As he spoke, rays from the early morning sun broke through, shifting some of the greyness from the hillsides. The trees nearby dripped dampness, and the long grass stooped with fresh-fallen rain. But the air was already sharp and clear, unlike, as McGuillig would have it, the unclean air of the North. Free air. Uncontaminated by Brits and Prods. A mile away, across the border, the land was cancered. The Irishman regarded the weapon he held as the surgeon's scalpel.

Just as McGuillig, brigade commander of D Company, Second Battalion of the Provisional IRA, watched him, so Halloran returned his gaze, neither man moving.

Then Halloran said: 'Let's see our client first.'

A pause before McGuillig nodded to one of his companions, a youth who had killed twice in the name of Free Ireland and who was not yet nineteen. He balanced the butt of the Armalite against his hip, barrel threatening the very sky, and strolled to the van. He had to press hard on the handle before the backdoor would open.

'Give him a hand,' McGuillig said to the other provo on his left. 'Don't worry about these two: they'll not be moving.' He thumbed back the Webley's hammer, its *click* a warning in the still air.

All the same, this second companion, older and more easily frightened than his leader, kept his rifle pointed at the two Englishmen as he walked over to the van.

'We had to dose up your man,' McGuillig told Halloran. 'To keep him quietened, y'understand. He'll be right as rain by tomorrow.'

Halloran said nothing.

The backdoor was open fully now and a slumped figure could be seen inside. The older provo reluctantly hung his rifle over one shoulder and reached inside the van along with the youth. They drew the figure towards themselves, lifting it out.

'Bring him over, lads, lay him on the ground behind me,' their commander ordered. To Halloran: 'I'm thinking I'd like to see that money.'

Halloran nodded. 'I'd like my client examined.'

McGuillig's tone was accommodating. 'That's reasonable. Come ahead.'

With a casual flick of his hand, Halloran beckoned the heavy-set man who was leaning against their rented car twenty yards away. The man unfolded his arms and approached. Not once did Halloran take his eyes off the IRA leader.

The heavy-set man strode past Halloran, then McGuillig. He knelt beside the prone figure, the Irish youth crouching with him.

He gave no indication, made no gesture.

'The money,' McGuillig reminded.

Halloran slowly sank down, both hands reaching for the leather case in front of him. He sprung the two clasps.

His man looked back at him. No indication, no signal.

Halloran smiled and McGuillig suddenly realized that it was he, himself, who was in mortal danger. When Halloran quietly said – when he *breathed* – 'Jesus, Mary ...' McGuillig thought he heard that lilt once more.

Halloran's hands were inside the case.

When they reappeared an instant later, they were holding a snub-nosed sub-machine-gun.

McGuillig hadn't even begun to squeeze the .38's trigger before the first bullet from the Heckler and Koch had imploded most of his nose and lodged in the back of his skull. And the other provo hadn't even started to rise before blood was blocking his throat and gushing through the hole torn by the second bullet. And the Irish youth was still crouching with no further thoughts as the third bullet sped through his head to burst from his right temple.

Halloran switched the sub-machine-gun to automatic as he rose, sure there were no others lurking among the trees, but ever careful, chancing nothing.

He allowed five seconds to pass before relaxing. His companion, who had thrown himself to the ground the moment he saw Halloran smile, waited just a little longer.

▪ 2 ▪
ACHILLES' SHIELD

THE SIGN FOR ACHILLES' SHIELD WAS AS DISCREET AS ITS BUSINESS: A BRASS plaque against rough brick mounted inside a doorway, the shiny plate no more than eight by four inches, a small right-angled triangle at one end as the company logo. That logo represented the shield that the Greek hero Achilles, if he'd been wiser, would have worn over his heel, his body's only vulnerable part, when riding into battle. The name, with its simple symbol, was the only fanciful thing about the organization.

Situated east of St Katharine's Dock, with its opulent yacht basin and hotel, the offices of Achilles' Shield were in one of the many abandoned wharfside warehouses that had been gutted and refurbished in a development which had brought trendy shops, offices and 'old style' pubs to lie incongruously beneath the gothic shadow of Tower Bridge. The company plaque was difficult to locate. To spot it, you had to know where it was. To know, you had to be invited.

The two men sitting in the third-floor office – a large, capacious room, because space wasn't at a premium in these converted warehouses – *had* been invited. One of them had been invited many times over the past six years.

He was Alexander Buchanan, a suitably sturdy name for an underwriter whose firm, Acorn Buchanan Limited, had a 'box' on the floor of Lloyd's of London and company offices near Fenchurch Street. Acorn Buchanan's speciality was K & R insurance. Kidnap and Ransom.

The person with him was his client, Henry Quinn-Reece, chief executive and deputy chairman of the Magma Corporation PLC. He looked ill at ease, even though the leather sofa on which he sat was designed for maximum comfort. Perhaps he did not enjoy the scrutiny he was under.

The scrutineers were three, and they were directors of Achilles' Shield. None of these men did or said anything to relax their prospective client. In fact, that was the last thing they wanted: they liked their interviewees to be on edge, and sharper because of it.

The one behind the large leather-topped desk, who was in charge of the meeting, was Gerald Snaith, Shield's managing director, officially titled Controller. He was forty-nine years old, a former major in the SAS, and had trained soldiers, British and foreign, all over the world. His main service action had been in Oman, his exploits largely unknown to the public because, after all, that particular conflict – or more accurately, the British Army's participation in it – had never been recognized officially. A short man, and stocky, his hair a slow-greying ginger, Snaith looked every inch a fighting man which, in truth, he still was.

In a straight-backed chair to the side of the Controller's desk sat Charles Mather MBE, a keen-eyed man of sixty-two years (those keen eyes often held a glint of inner amusement, as though Mather found it impossible to treat life too seriously all the time, despite the grim nature of the business he was in). Introduced to clients as Shield's Planner, or sometimes Proposer, staff within the organization preferred to call him 'The Hatcher'. He was tall, thin, and ramrod, but forced to use a cane for walking because of a severe leg wound received in Aden during the latter stages of that 'low intensity' campaign. A jeep in which he was travelling had been blown off the road by a land mine. Only his fortitude and an already exemplary military career had allowed him to return to his beloved army, sporting concealed scars and a rather heroic limp; unfortunately a sniper's bullet had torn tendons in that same leg many years later when he had been GOC and Director of Operations in Ulster, hence the stick and early retirement from the British Army.

The only non-English name among a very English assemblage was that of Dieter Stuhr, German-born and at one time member of the *Bundeskriminalamt*, an organization within the German police force responsible to the Federal Government for the monitoring of terrorists and anarchist groups. Stuhr sat alongside Snaith at the desk. Younger than his two colleagues and four years divorced, his body was not in the same lean condition: a developing paunch was beginning to put lower shirt buttons under strain, and his hairline had receded well beyond the point of no return. He was an earnest, over-anxious man, but supreme at organizing movement, finances, time-tables and weaponry for any given operation, no matter what the difficulties, be they dealing with the authorities in other countries (particularly certain police chiefs and high-ranking officials who were not above collusion with kidnappers and terrorists) or arranging 'minimum risk' life-styles for fee-paying 'targets'. Within the company he was known very properly as the Organizer.

He bore an impressive scar on his face which might well have been a sword-scythed wound, perhaps the symbol of machoism so proudly worn by duelling Heidelberg students before and during Herr Hitler's rapid rise to infamy; but Stuhr was not of that era and the mutilation was nothing so foolishly valiant. It was no more than a deep, curving cut received while falling off his bicycle after free-wheeling down a too-steep hill outside his home town of Siegen. A truck driver ahead of him had been naturally cautious about crossing the junction at the bottom of the hill and Stuhr, an eleven-year-old schoolboy at the time, had neglected to pull on his brakes until it was too late. The bicycle had gone beneath the truck, while the boy had taken a different route around the tailboard's corner catching his face as he scraped by.

The scar stretched down from his left temple, and curved into his mouth, a hockey-stick motif that made his smile rise up the side of his head. He tried not to smile too much.

Gerald Snaith was speaking: 'You understand that we'd need a complete dossier on your man's background and current life-style?'

Quinn-Reece nodded. 'We'll supply what we can.'

'And we'd have to know exactly how valuable he is to your corporation.'

'He's indispensable,' the deputy chairman replied instantly.

'Now that is unusual.' Charles Mather scratched the inside of one ankle with his walking stick. 'Invaluable, I can appreciate. But indispensable? I didn't realize such an animal existed in today's world of commerce.'

Alexander Buchanan, sitting by his client on the leather sofa, said, 'The size of the insurance cover will indicate to you just how indispensable our "target" is.'

'Would you care to reveal precisely what the figure is at this stage of the proceedings?'

The question was put mildly enough, but the underwriter had no doubts that a proper answer was required. He looked directly at Quinn-Reece, who bowed assent.

'Our man is insured for £50 million,' said Buchanan.

Dieter Stuhr dropped his pen on the floor. Although equally surprised, Snaith and Mather did not so much as glance at each other.

After a short pause, Buchanan added unnecessarily, 'A sizeable amount, I'm sure you'll agree.'

'I dread to think of the premium involved,' Mather remarked.

'Naturally it's proportionate to the sum insured,' said the underwriter. 'And I'm afraid the discount on the premium to Magma, even if you accept the assignment, will be accordingly low. Ten per cent instead of the normal twenty.'

'I imagine, then,' said Mather to Quinn-Reece, 'that we are discussing the safety of your chairman.'

'As a matter of fact, no,' came the reply. 'The person to be insured doesn't actually have a title within the company.'

'We can reasonably assume that he doesn't serve the tea, though,' Mather said dryly. 'I'm sure Mr Buchanan has already informed you that a "target's" name never appears on any document or insurance slip concerning such a policy, even though documents will be lodged in various vaults – we demand total secrecy for security reasons, you see – but can you at least tell us your man's role within the Corporation? We'll come to his name later, if and when there is an agreement between us.'

Quinn-Reece shifted in his seat, as if even more uncomfortable. 'I'm afraid I can't tell you that either, not at this stage. Once a contract is agreed, then Magma will give you all the necessary information – on a "need to know" basis, of course.'

'We're well used to such discretion,' Snaith assured. 'In fact, we encourage it. But so long as you understand that nothing – absolutely nothing – must be withheld from us should we decide to take on the job.'

'I understand perfectly,' the deputy chairman replied, nodding his head gravely.

I wonder if he really does, thought Snaith. That every part of the 'target's' life would be delved into – his wife, family, friends, his habits, recreations.

Whether or not he has a mistress. Especially that. A mistress (or mistresses) was always a weak link in any operation of this sort, because usually the target himself tried to cover up that particular side of his activities, would even endeavour to elude his own protectors for the occasional tryst with his woman. Shield would also have to know how the target was regarded as a man – stubborn, soft, fit, unfit, loving, harsh, conformist or otherwise, and so on (intelligence was assumed if he was worth insuring in this way). If married and had children, what kind of husband was he, what kind of father? Snaith and his operatives would need to know his precise movements, every hour, every minute of the day and night. Were these movements regularly reported both inside and outside the Corporation? Would the media ever be informed in advance? He was already aware of the employee's value to Magma – an incredible £50 million – but what was the nature and value of his function? All these questions, and many more, would have to be answered before Shield could begin to devise a specially-tailored security cover. Even then, no such protective system could ever be foolproof, not where terrorists were concerned. But one question had to be answered at the outset.

Snaith leaned forward on his desk, his fingers interlocking, thumbs turning circles around each other. 'Why now?' he asked. 'Why do you feel this member of your corporation needs protection at this point in time?'

'Because,' Quinn-Reece replied blandly, 'he told us so.'

This time Snaith and Mather did not refrain from looking at each other.

'Your man has received a warning, a threat?' asked Mather.

'Not exactly.'

Dieter Stuhr, who had been jotting down odd notes throughout the proceedings, rested his pen. 'Is Magma involved in some venture that could put your employee at risk?'

'Not at this moment.'

'It has been in the past?' Stuhr persisted.

Buchanan quickly spoke up. 'Gentlemen, I'm sure you're all well aware of the Magma Corporation's undoubted prominence in the commercial world. It has widespread international interests in the mining, industrial and energy sectors, with assets of over £6,000 million and an annual turnover of something like £45,000 million. It would take you a whole day to study the list of subsidiary companies the Corporation owns.'

'Thank you for the information, Alexander, but what the hell has that to do with what we're talking about?' Snaith enquired bluntly.

'Only that you may rest assured that Magma is not involved in any enterprises that might be considered, er …'

'Shady?' Mather obligingly finished for him.

Stuhr smiled way past his left eyebrow.

'Questionable,' Buchanan allowed.

'I'm sorry, I didn't mean to imply …' Stuhr, still smiling, began to say.

'That's quite all right, I understand,' said Quinn-Reece. 'You need to be fully in the picture, as it were. Let me put it this way: the man we are discussing has certain … abilities …' he stressed the word '… that companies whose commercial activities are similar to our own might well envy. In that respect, he could always be at risk should one of those rival companies, shall we say, become *over*-envious.'

'They could always pay more than you for his services,' suggested Mather, becoming somewhat intrigued by their prospective client.

'If,' Quinn-Reece replied almost slyly, 'they knew of his existence.' He smiled at the three men facing him, pleased with their rapt attention. 'I'm sorry to sound so mysterious but, you see, our man has unique skills that would be virtually impossible to match. Not that our competitors would ever have knowledge of them – those skills are kept secret even within our own organization.'

Mather rested his hands over the handle of his cane. He glanced towards the room's huge window, a gull catching his eye as it swooped by, wings dazzling white in the cold sunshine. 'This sounds, uh, quite interesting,' he said, returning his gaze to the deputy chairman. 'Yes ...' the word drawn out '... interesting indeed. Would you care to elaborate?'

Quinn-Reece held up his palms. 'Again, I'm afraid not. At least, not until you agree to the assignment. I know that puts you in an awkward position, but we have our own security requirements. There is also one other matter that might not meet with your satisfaction.'

Stuhr's pen was poised once more.

'The man we're discussing,' Quinn-Reece went on, 'already maintains a strong protection unit around him.'

'Ah,' said Mather.

'Bodyguards?' enquired Stuhr.

Quinn-Reece nodded.

'Are they well-trained?' asked Snaith.

'Reasonably so, I believe,' replied Quinn-Reece.

'Then why does Magma need our services?'

The deputy chairman looked at Buchanan.

'That's a priority condition of Acorn Buchanan if we're to take on the risk,' said the underwriter. 'These personal bodyguards may well be proficient, but my company would feel more comfortable if Achilles' Shield were running the show.'

'It's no problem,' commented Stuhr. 'I can work out an effective operation into which they can be absorbed. First though, we would have to ascertain just how good these men are, and how trustworthy; and they would have to recognize implicitly our authority over them.'

'Naturally,' agreed Quinn-Reece. 'Your company would have complete control.'

'That's fine then,' said Snaith. At least, he thought it was fine.

Buchanan cleared his throat. 'There is yet another factor, Gerald,' he said.

The tone of his voice hinted that Snaith and his colleagues were not going to like this one.

'I've already explained to Mr Quinn-Reece and his chairman that it's Achilles' Shield's practice to have at least three operatives in direct contact with the target, so ensuring a too-friendly relationship never develops between protector and protected.'

'It's our way of making certain,' Snaith told Quinn-Reece, 'that if our precautions fail and our client is abducted then negotiations between the kidnappers and our man won't be hindered by personal involvement.'

'I can appreciate that,' the deputy chairman responded.

'Unfortunately,' Buchanan went on, 'the Magma Corporation will allow only one of your men to cover the target on a close basis.'

'Good Lord,' said Mather, while Stuhr muttered under his breath, 'Verflucht!'

'That's impossible,' Snaith quickly asserted.

'Please understand that the condition only applies to internal security,' said Quinn-Reece anxiously. 'Whatever outside arrangements you care to make are entirely up to you. You see, we're dealing with a matter of utmost secrecy here – the nature of our man's role within the Corporation – and the less people who know of it the better as far as Magma is concerned.'

'I can assure you of absolute confidentiality,' Snaith insisted.

'I've no doubts on that score. But this person is one of the prime reasons for the Corporation's success throughout the world. Our secret weapon if you like. We have no wish for that secret – nor even the fact that we *have* a secret – to be exposed beyond key executives within the organization itself. If you are to take on this job, your man must be governed by that same secrecy.'

'You mean even we in this room are to be excluded from this knowledge?' a surprised Stuhr asked.

'That is the case.'

'It's highly irregular,' huffed the German.

Quinn-Reece was no longer ill at ease. He actually enjoyed laying down this last condition, because it reminded him of his position and how strong was his Corporation: imposing Magma terms was part of normal business negotiations and home-ground to him. He began to feel less intimidated by these three Shield people, more bullish. Besides, he was a shrewd judge of atmosphere and knew they were already hooked. Perhaps the talk of 'secrecy' was close to their own clandestine hearts. And obviously, the financial inducement was irresistible, for Achilles' Shield fees would be in direct ratio to the premium paid.

'Irregular,' he admitted, 'but as far as the Chairman and myself are concerned, fundamental.'

A silence followed in which the Controller, Planner, and Organizer considered the implications of such a condition.

'For what period of time is the insurance cover?' Mather finally enquired.

'No more than a few weeks at the most,' Buchanan promptly answered.

'Reason?' asked Snaith.

Buchanan turned to Quinn-Reece, who replied: 'Our man feels there will be no risk after that.'

'He's somewhat remarkable,' said Snaith.

'Yes, that's quite true. Are you interested in the assignment, gentlemen?' Quinn-Reece searched each face.

'You'd be making our task very difficult,' Snaith told him. 'But yes, it sounds like an interesting job. Finding the right operative might be tricky, though – our people are used to working as a team.'

'Oh no,' said Mather mildly. 'I don't think there's any problem at all in that respect, Gerald. I think we have exactly the right chap, don't you?'

Snaith stared blankly at his Planner for a moment. Then understanding dawned in his eyes. He opened his mouth, but before he could speak, the other man nodded his head.

'Yes,' Mather said. 'Yes, I think he'd be ideal.'

A shade reluctantly, Snaith had to agree.

▪ 3 ▪
MAGMA

HALLORAN STOPPED FOR A MOMENT TO GAZE UP AT THE TWENTY-FOUR-STOREY building. Impressive, he thought, and impressive it was, rearing up between staid, grey City blocks like a massive glass and bronze sculpture, tinted windows impenetrably black, its metal structure reflecting the morning sun so that multi-faceted surfaces glowed a deep gold. Exterior elevators slid up and down the smooth walls, pale faces staring out from the capsules, watching the human patterns moving below. All corners – and there were many – were gracefully curved, the outermost buttresses adding a fort-like strength to the architecture, an image abetted by the different levels of the main building, some recessed, others outcropping.

Magma's headquarters was not a place to be easily stormed, Halloran mused. Yet for all its stunning grandeur, emphasized by the mostly uninspiring drabness of London's financial sector, there was something ... something brooding about this edifice. Its surfaces dazzled a metallic lustre which seemed almost overpowering, too forceful for the surroundings.

He stood there a while longer, studying the Magma building, oblivious to the office workers scurrying around him, before crossing the road and going inside, to leave the crisp coldness of the early-spring air for the sterile coolness of the air-conditioned foyer.

Mather was already waiting for him, seated in the middle of a row of beige lounge chairs and facing a huge circular reception desk. Men in light-blue, epauletted shirts roamed inside the circle, banks of television monitors behind them, monochrome offices and corridors displayed on the screens. Other screens were imbedded in square pillars around the vast concourse, these providing a variety of information for anyone passing through: foreign exchange rates, the general market report, company news, active shares, leading shares, traded options, USM, new issues index and even BBC news headlines.

The area bustled with life. Escalators carried visitors and staff up to and down from the floor above, while lifts around the glass walls took passengers to the heights. Digital payphones were mounted on low tables set before the rows of lounge chairs, there for the convenience of waiting businessmen. Lush palms and plants together with kinetic sculptures constructed from the same material as the outside walls, strove to de-formalize the concourse, succeeding only in part. Long glass display cases contained examples of rock strata, while others held samples of ore and minerals, crystals, even semi-precious stones, all exhibits of the earth's contribution towards the Magma empire.

Halloran noticed several informal meetings taking place around the floor, discussions conducted *sotto voce*, the undertones adding to the complex's general buzz. Who'd need an office with a set-up like this? he wondered. Maybe the roving security guards who were very much in evidence were also there to discourage non-company personnel from such practices.

A marble-cladded wall, the large rectangular slabs needing no other decoration than their own subtle-hued textures, brought the wide reception area to an end; several doors and a central lift system (obviously provided for those whose vertigo somewhat reduced the joy of viewing the City panorama while rising above it) spaced themselves along the wall.

Mather had spotted him and was rising from his seat, one hand pushing against his cane for support. Halloran went forward to meet him.

'Rather splendid, isn't it?' said Mather as they drew near.

'Even better than Changi airport,' Halloran replied, shaking the Planner's hand.

'Good to see you, Liam. Sorry about the Irish operation.'

Halloran nodded, said nothing.

'Let's check in and get our instructions,' suggested Mather, turning away and limping towards the circular reception desk. Halloran followed, still taking in the scene around him.

A receptionist watched their approach and, when they reached him, said with no curiosity at all: 'Can I help you?'

'Mather and Halloran – to see Sir Victor Penlock. Ten o'clock appointment.'

If the uniformed receptionist was impressed that they were there for a meeting with the Corporation's chairman he gave no indication.

'Company?' he enquired.

'I think you'll find that information isn't necessary,' Mather told him.

The receptionist, a youngish man with spectacles and a distinct lack of charm, sat at his desk and tapped computer keys. Green lines of type reflected in his glasses and soon he appeared satisfied, although there was no noticeable change in his demeanour.

'You'll need ID tags,' he told them and punched more keys on a machine concealed from view beneath the counter. When his hand appeared once more it was holding two yellow strips with Mather and Halloran's names typed individually in capitals on each. He slipped them into plastic clips and passed them over.

'Attach these to your lapels, please. You need to go up to the eighteenth. You can take the scenic route to twelve, then transfer to an interior lift for the rest of the way. Or if you prefer, you can take the interior express straight up to the eighteenth.' He pointed at the lifts beyond the reception circle.

'I rather fancy the scenic route,' said Mather brightly. 'What d'you say, Liam?'

Halloran smiled as he clipped on his name tag. 'Fine by me.'

They crossed the busy floor to one of the capsule elevators, Mather chattering like a child looking forward to a funfair ride. They saw one of the lifts discharging its load and headed towards it, Mather quickly pressing the 12 button once they were inside so that they would be alone.

The older man's mood became serious, although he peered through the thick glass, looking for familiar landmarks as the lift rose above the streets.

'What went wrong, Liam?' he asked.

Halloran, too, watched the shrinking streets, the broadening view. 'My guess is that our client died at the time of kidnap or soon after. We already knew from his company's medical report he had a weak heart. He'd suffered a minor heart attack two years before.'

'But you didn't know he was dead before you went in with the money.'

Halloran shook his head. The Thames was coming into view, its surface silver in the bright sunshine. To the west was St Paul's, to the east, the Tower of London; other landmarks, grey in the distance, were beginning to appear. 'I had the notion. They would never let me speak to him on the phone, told me I had to take their word for it that he was in good shape. There was little choice.'

'Thugs,' said Mather. 'Murdering IRA thugs.'

'They consider themselves to be at war.'

'Kidnap and murder? Indiscriminate bombings? A strange war.'

'There's never been a normal one.'

The older man glanced at Halloran. 'I know you too well to imagine you have any truck with the IRA.'

Halloran watched a dragonfly helicopter inching its way along the river, keeping strictly to its assigned route where an air accident could cause the least damage, heading for the Battersea heliport.

'I read your report,' Mather said to break the silence. 'Why the Heckler and Koch? An Ingram is more compact, easier to conceal.'

'Our own man had to examine the client – I needed accuracy so that he wouldn't get hit. And I didn't know how many I'd be up against, so I had to have the choice of switching to automatic. It was a pity for them their victim wasn't a well man – their organization could have been a lot richer.'

'And a pity his company didn't call us in earlier as more than just negotiators. He might not have been abducted in the first place under our protection.' Mather shook his head with regret. Then: 'At least publicity was avoided.'

Halloran smiled grimly. The last thing Achilles' Shield wanted was attention from the media, always preferring to remain anonymous, not only in name but in role also. Too many Members of Parliament were fighting to introduce a Bill banning K & R organizations such as Shield, condemning them as an inducement to kidnap rather than a deterrent. He had removed their client's corpse from the scene of the shooting, leaving it by the roadside in another county to be discovered by others. Because of that, the two incidents hadn't been connected – at least, not by the public. The authorities on both sides of the border who had cooperated with Shield before on similar K & R operations, had turned a blind eye (although the Garda naturally hadn't been happy about the killings on their territory).

'Here we are,' Mather said as the elevator glided to a smooth halt. The doors sighed open and the two men stepped out.

They found themselves in another reception area, although this was far less impressive than that on ground-level, and much quieter. Through the windows to their right they could see a wide, open terrace, white tables and chairs placed all around, the building itself recessed here to provide a spectacular viewing platform over the southern half of London. It was empty of observers at the moment, the sun too feeble to take the chill from the breeze at that altitude.

A few people sat inside, though, waiting in the beige loungers, while Magma staff wandered through, some carrying documents, others collecting the visitors and leading them off to second-stage lifts or into corridors branching from the lobby.

The desk on this level was set into the wall and stationed by only two blue-uniformed men. A girl was standing by the counter talking to one of them. On seeing Mather and Halloran emerge from the lift she broke off conversation and hurried over.

'Mr Charles Mather?' she asked, smiling engagingly.

The older man raised a hand. 'And this is Mr Halloran,' he said indicating.

'I'm Cora Redmile. Sir Victor sent me down to fetch you.' She shook hands with both men.

She was slender, dark-haired, her eyes a muddy brown flecked with green. Mid or late-twenties, Halloran guessed. Her smile was mischievous as she looked at him.

'I hope you enjoyed the journey up,' she said. 'Some visitors are quite unsettled by the time they reach the twelfth.'

Halloran only smiled back, and for a moment, uncertainty flashed in her eyes.

'Absolutely splendid, m'dear,' Mather answered. 'Marvellously clear day for spying the landscape. You should make people buy tickets.'

The girl gave a short laugh. 'Compliments of Magma. If you come with me I'll take you to the eighteenth. Mr Quinn-Reece is waiting with Sir Victor.'

'Up to the eyrie. Splendid.'

Still smiling, the girl turned away and they followed her to the row of interior lifts.

Inside and on their way, Mather said: 'You'd be Sir Victor's personal secretary, I take it.'

'No, not Sir Victor's,' she replied, and made no further comment.

'Ah,' murmured Mather, as if satisfied.

Halloran leaned back against the wall, feeling the slight headiness of blood pressured by high speed. He caught the girl looking at him and she quickly averted her gaze.

'My goodness,' said Mather. 'We're fairly shifting, aren't we?'

'I can slow us down if you prefer,' Cora told him, anxiously reaching for a button on the console.

'Not at all. I'm rather enjoying the experience.'

She smiled at Mather's glee, her hand dropping back to her side. Once again, her gaze strayed to Halloran. In his dark tweed jacket, with its leather elbow patches, his check shirt and loose-knitted tie, he should have resembled a country squire; only he didn't. Far from it. And there was something about his eyes ... He looked like a man who could be cruel. Yet there was a quiet gentleness about him too. Cora was puzzled. And interested.

'How many security men does the building have?'

Halloran's question took her by surprise. There was a softness to his voice also, the slightest trace of an accent. West Country? No, Irish. With a name like Halloran it had to be.

'Oh, I think Sir Victor has all those details ready for you,' she answered quickly, realizing she had been lost for a moment.

He looked at her steadily. 'You know why we're here?'

Now she wasn't sure if there was an accent at all. 'Yes. I'll be assisting you.'

Mather raised his eyebrows at Halloran.

A small *ping* as the elevator came to a halt. The doors drew back like stage curtains to reveal a sumptuous lobby, its thick carpet a deep mauve, hessian walls, the palest green. Ceiling lights were recessed so that soft glows puddled the corridors leading off from the open area. Strategically placed lamps and spotlights compensated for the lack of natural light. A wide chrome and glass desk faced the elevators and the girl sitting behind it rose as soon as their feet sank into the lush carpet.

'Good morning. Sir Victor is ready to see you. May I arrange some tea or coffee?'

'Tea would be very nice,' said Mather.

'Any preference?'

'I'll leave that to you, m'dear, though I'm partial to Earl Grey.'

'Earl Grey it is.' She raised her eyebrows at Halloran, who said, 'Coffee, black, no preference.'

'If you'll follow me,' said Cora, and led them into the corridor beyond the hi-tech desk.

There were no doors, but display cases were set into the walls on either side, each depicting the Corporation's worldwide industrial and mining activities, either photographically or as models: a vast borate minerals open-pit mine, Mojave Desert; a hydrofluoric acid plant, UK; a pyrite mine, Spain; gold, silver, and emerald mines, Zimbabwe; open-pit copper, South Africa; oil and gas wells, UK and global. And more: tin, uranium, diamonds, coal, low-grade ores, all manner of base and precious metals, some, like molybdenum (a silver-white metal), that the two men had never even heard of. Towards the end of the corridor was an encased back-lit map, bright red circles indicating areas of exploration and research around the world; there were a lot of red circles.

It was something of a relief when they arrived in a wide area flooded by daylight, both men feeling that they had just emerged from an educational passage in a geological museum. If visitors to Magma's chairman were meant to feel over-awed, perhaps even intimidated by the time they reached his office, then the ruse was effective.

'Nothing like flaunting it,' Mather quietly remarked to Halloran.

'The Magma Corporation is very proud of its many interests,' said Cora with no hint of reprimand in her tone.

'So it seems.' Mather smiled sweetly at her.

Broader corridors stretched left and right, glass-walled rooms with vertical blinds, most of these open, on either side. Sounds buzzed from them: muted conversations, ringing telephones, clattering typewriters. But Cora crossed the open space before them, going to a wide double-door which looked so solid that Halloran wondered if she had the strength to push it open.

It opened with ease. She stood back to allow them through.

Now they were in an office shared by two secretaries; one could have modelled for *Vogue*, while the other, with her heavy-framed spectacles and wire-frizzed hair, might have looked well on the cover of *Science Today*. Both were busily involved with word processors; they barely glanced up.

Another large door directly ahead. Cora went to it, tapped once, entered. A brief announcement, then she turned and beckoned Mather and Halloran through.

▪ 4 ▪
THE NEED FOR SECRECY

THE CHAIRMAN'S OFFICE WAS HIGH-CEILINGED, THE WALL AT THE FAR END MOSTLY tinted glass; it looked disconcertingly easy to step off the edge into open space. The chairman's oak desk was almost as wide as the room and the only traditional piece of furniture present. The rest comprised black leather and chrome, with dark ash units around the walls. The chairman himself was as imposing as the rest of the Magma building.

Sir Victor Penlock was tall and slim, with silver and grey hair in plenty, and no sign of relaxed stomach muscles. He wore a grey, double-breasted suit, the material of which had a subtle sheen. His face was sharp, light blue eyes keen. His grip was firm when he greeted them.

First Mather, then Halloran, shaking their hands, studying their faces. He spent a second longer studying Halloran's. 'I understand you haven't yet met Quinn-Reece,' he said to him.

The deputy chairman came forward. 'I'm told you'll be particularly suited for protection cover of this kind. You prefer working on a one-to-one-basis.'

'We'll see,' Halloran replied, disliking the clamminess of Quinn-Reece's hand.

'I beg your pardon?'

'We'll see if I'm suited after I've spoken to the target. We don't appear to know much about him.'

'My apologies for that,' cut in Sir Victor. 'But there are reasons.' He indicated chairs. 'Please, won't you sit down, then perhaps we can put you fully in the picture.'

The chairman took his place behind the desk and the others found themselves seats around the room. Cora, Halloran noticed, sat in a chair by the wall as though she were an observer of the meeting rather than a partaker.

'By the time most new visitors to Magma reach my office,' Sir Victor began, 'they've become aware of the Corporation's numerous activities throughout the world, so it should be unnecessary for me to give you a detailed lecture on our size and strength. Suffice it to say that we're recognized as a major force as far as mining, industrial and energy interests are concerned. No doubt you've taken note of the various companies that form our Group, and the reason they have their own identity is because for the past twenty years we've practised a decentralized system of management which encourages the profitable development of individual companies inside their own industries and locations. Between them, they either produce, process and fabricate most prime metals – anything from aluminium to zinc – as well as manufacture industrial, construction and engineering products and chemicals; or they may supply raw materials for energy, principally coal, oil, gas and uranium.'

He paused. 'I said I wasn't going to lecture, didn't I? No matter – I *am* leading up to an important point. So, you have an idea of what Magma and its companies are all about. We employ over eighty thousand people throughout the world, twenty thousand of those in the UK.'

There was a light tap on the door and a woman in a pale blue uniform shirt and dark blue skirt brought in a tray of tea and coffee. Sir Victor waited for the beverages to be distributed and the door to close again before continuing.

'As a corporation involved in enormous investments both here and abroad, we have two considerable problems. One is that large fluctuations in currency exchange rates give us immense difficulty in predicting the economic environment in which long-term investment decisions will come to maturity.'

Halloran caught Mather's eyes glazing over and hid his grin behind the coffee cup. Sir Victor's diction was crisp and clear, yet nothing could prevent the words themselves entering the brain as a drone.

'Unfortunately, the lengthy lead times from feasibility study to commercial operation mean that decisions have to be made today concerning the next generation of mining projects. In other words, we have to decide now what will be best for Magma in, say, seven to ten years' time. You'll appreciate just how difficult that might be.'

'Yes, yes,' Mather appreciated. 'I should think you'd need to be a fortune-teller to do that.'

Mather smiled broadly, but Sir Victor and his second-in-command regarded him soberly.

'You're nearer the truth than you might imagine,' said the chairman.

Mather's eyebrows arched and he shot a look at Halloran.

Sir Victor leaned back in his chair and swivelled it sideways, his head turning away from them to examine the view outside. It was an odd gesture, almost as though he was suddenly reluctant to face them directly. Yet his manner was uncompromising when he spoke.

'What I'm about to tell you, gentlemen, must not go beyond these walls.' He turned back to them, his eyes boring into theirs. 'I must have your solemn promise on that.'

Mather was quick to respond. 'My company has already given assurances regarding confidentiality.'

'I'm not referring to Achilles' Shield. I mean Mr Halloran and yourself. This matter cannot even be discussed within your own organization. May I have your word?'

'That would be highly irregular. If our assignment is to be water-tight, we must have every cooperation from – '

'You will have that. In full. But there are certain details which are not essential to your planning that must not become common knowledge ...' He held up a hand against Mather's protest '... even among a select few. In fact, there aren't many inside the Magma Corporation itself who are privy to this information. I can promise you, though, your security arrangements will not be affected to any significant degree.'

'I shall have to confer with my senior colleagues,' Mather said dubiously.

'Let's agree.'

All eyes went to Halloran who had spoken.

'It can't do any harm.' He placed his empty coffee cup on a small table by his chair. 'But there are conditions. If anything illegal is involved here, then we're out. And you must tell us everything – no little details held back. If we don't like what we hear, Shield withdraws. Simple as that.'

Quinn-Reece looked set to bluster, but his chairman smiled.

'That sounds reasonable,' Sir Victor remarked. 'Thank you for being so direct, Mr Halloran; it saves time. Are you in accordance with this?' He aimed the question at Mather.

Who smiled too. He was used to Halloran's bluntness. 'I suppose I have no objections,' he answered as if wondering to himself.

'Very well.' The chairman appeared to relax a little. 'A moment or two ago you suggested we might need a fortune-teller to predict safe investments for the ongoing profitability of the Corporation . .'

'A mild joke,' put in Mather. 'I noticed you didn't laugh.'

'Nor would we. Would you be surprised if I revealed that despite all the highly sophisticated research methods, our extensive statistics for forward planning, explorations of new territories, satellite surveys using micro-wave, ultra-violet and infra-red radiation, structural analyses, advanced computer calculations – all that, and more – much of our new growth depends almost entirely on the special ability of one person?'

'I'd be very surprised,' Mather replied without hesitation.

'As our competitors would be if they knew. As would the Press, and of course, our shareholders. Yes, I suppose such a revelation would create amusement in some quarters. And great personal risk to our man from others.'

'Your rivals? Surely not?'

'When the stakes are so high, with discovery of fresh raw materials diminishing so rapidly, access to new fields proving more and more difficult and expensive, there develops over the years a competitively cut-throat situation – and I use that term literally.'

'Is this why you want your man so heavily insured?' asked Halloran. Sir Victor nodded.

'He's already received threats?'

'Not exactly.'

Mather interrupted. 'Look here, can we slow this down for a minute? I'm not clear at all on just what this employee of yours does for Magma. Are you saying he's some kind of exploration wizard? And isn't it time we were told his name? All this non-identity business is only serving to compound my confusion.'

Halloran knew the older man's mind was far too sharp to be fogged by anything said so far; this was merely the Planner's way of drawing out basic information that so often prospective clients were reluctant to convey.

' "Exploration wizard" is not entirely correct, although "wizard" might be appropriate in some respects.' Sir Victor allowed a small laugh between himself and his deputy chairman. Again Halloran found the girl, Cora, watching him closely.

'Gentlemen,' said Sir Victor, his tone serious once more. 'It's time you met your – how is it you refer to them? Target? – yes, it's time you met your target. I think then all will be made clear. At least, I hope that will be the case.'

With that, he stood and indicated a door leading off from his office. Mather and Halloran rose too, both more than a little curious.

· 5 ·
THE WHITE ROOM

HE WAS TIRED. HE'D HAD TO LEAVE IRELAND DISCREETLY, TRAVELLING SOUTH BY road to Wexford, hiring a boat to take him from there across to a point just outside Newport, Wales, the journey made in the dead of night. The sea had been rough, but that hadn't bothered Halloran unduly. No, it was disappointment that had dragged his spirits down, exhausted him.

He hated to lose a man. The negotiations for the release of the kidnap victim had gone on for weeks with Halloran using all the techniques he had learned over the years dealing with terrorists such as these: when to play tough, when to appease, when to hedge; when to sound innocently confused. Anything to gain more time and information. The first priority was always to retrieve the client unharmed – unharmed as possible, anyway, the capture of his or her abductors a minor consideration. If that wasn't possible, then it was vital that the kidnappers did not get their hands on the ransom money. That would make them too careless with their victims' lives in future snatches. It would also upset whoever was supplying the money.

Terrorists, as opposed to the normal criminal (if there was such an animal), were always tricky to deal with, because they were invariably neurotic, unpredictable, and given to bouts of violence towards their captives and quite often those negotiating the release. The IRA were different. Oh, they had all those faults, and others not mentioned, but they could be cool and calculating – and sometimes more cruel because of it. There was no trust in them, and no trusting in them. They were a conscienceless and dangerous entity.

Which was why Halloran was so often chosen to deal with them.

But this current assignment with Magma puzzled him. Not as to why *he* had been chosen to handle it – he worked best alone, when he didn't have to rely on others – but more specifically, why the Corporation had allowed only one protector working on the inside. For the incredible amount of money for which the target's life had been insured, he should have had a small army around him, even though he had four bodyguards of his own. Could keeping secret his function for Magma be that important? Apparently so.

They were in yet another lift, the access to which had been in a small ante-chamber next door to the chairman's office, and were rising towards the twenty-second floor. Quinn-Reece was no longer with them, having excused himself to attend another meeting elsewhere.

'Two floor buttons only,' remarked Mather, looking at the panel set by the doors.

'This is a private lift and only travels between the eighteenth and twenty-second,' Sir Victor explained. 'A limited number of employees are allowed to use it.'

'And the twenty-third and fourth?'

'Living quarters and machinery rooms, the latter being at the very top.'

What price a sky-high penthouse in the heart of the City? Halloran silently mused. And whose penthouse? The chairman's? Maybe the target's, if he really was that important to the Corporation. There were a lot of questions still hanging in the air.

The lift walls were a glossy black, the occupants' reflected figures like shadowy ghosts around them. The overhead light was subdued, and it would have been easy to imagine they were travelling below the earth's surface rather than up towards the clouds.

Movement stopped, a subtle sensation, and the doors parted. The corridor beyond was as gloomy as the lift's interior.

A heavy-set man stood opposite, close to the wall, as if he had been awaiting their arrival. His arms were folded across a broad chest and they dropped to his sides in a token gesture of attention when he saw the chairman.

'He's ready for us?' asked Sir Victor, stepping from the lift first with no deference to Cora's gender or courtesy towards his guests.

The man nodded. 'He's waiting.' Just a hint of civility in his voice, his accent American.

From his thick-set stature and how uncomfortable he appeared in his business suit, it was easy for Mather and Halloran to surmise that this man was one of the bodyguards. His hair was long, incongruously (considering the staid suit) tied into a tail behind. Sullen eyes set in a pudgy face flicked over the visitors. At first, Halloran had thought the man's cheeks were unusually ruddy, but when he moved closer he realized that a patchwork of thin, livid scars emblazoned both sides of his face. Without further words the bodyguard led the way along the corridor, keeping at least six feet ahead of the entourage. The walls on either side were bare and dark and Halloran brushed fingers against one side, feeling a coarse material: the covering was black hessian. It was unusually cold in that corridor, yet the gloom was beginning to feel stifling.

A turn to the right, a large double-door facing them. Its surface, like the lift walls, was glossy black, and for one startling moment Halloran had the impression of apparitions approaching them. As the bodyguard leaned forward, extending both hands to grip the separate doorhandles, his spectral reflection leaned closer as if to snatch him. Both sides of the double-door were pushed open, the bodyguard standing aside to allow the party through.

The room was huge and almost blindingly white.

'Welcome to limbo,' a voice said.

· 6 ·
FELIX KLINE

THE MAN WHO HAD SPOKEN WASN'T WHAT MATHER OR HALLORAN EXPECTED AT all.

He didn't look worth £50 million. He didn't seem like someone whom a multi-national, first-league corporation could possibly be dependent upon. He looked nothing like a genius, and nothing like a wizard.

He was something of a disappointment.

At first their eyes had been stung by the unexpected dazzle, the abrupt contrast between gloom and astonishing brightness. But as they blinked away the irritation, they were gradually able to take in their new surroundings. There were no windows, and there was no furniture apart from a low, moderate-sized dais in the centre of the luminously white floor. If there were other exits around the room, they could not be discerned against the white walls, at least not until their eyes had become accustomed to the glare. Even the high ceiling was of white light. The whole effect was of vast and empty space which served to make the figure sitting on the edge of the dais seem even more insignificant.

He was wearing jeans and a blue sweatshirt chopped off at the elbows, his legs stretched out before him, ankles crossed, his hands behind him and flat against the small platform's surface. He grinned at the group standing in the doorway.

'The sudden change wipes your mind clean, doesn't it?' he said. Then he laughed, a peculiar high-pitched giggle. 'That's the idea, y'see. A blank mind, a clean slate; a white sheet, waiting to be filled with images. I can make everything black if you prefer?' He looked at them with eager expectancy.

'Not just now, Felix,' said Sir Victor quickly. 'Not if you don't mind. I want to introduce you to Mr Mather and Mr Halloran from Achilles' Shield, the company I discussed with you.'

The man addressed as Felix stood and ambled over to them, hands tucked into the back pockets of his jeans. He was well below average height, about five-three, his shoulders slightly rounded so that he appeared to stoop. His age could have been anywhere from twenty-five to thirty-five. His curly hair was dark and unkempt, his complexion swarthy, almost yellowish. And his eyes, above a hooked nose, were large and pitchy, as deep and shiny as oil pools.

'Let me guess,' he said, grinning again, and looking over their heads.

There was something odd about his eyes and Halloran couldn't quite figure out what.

He stepped before them, lowered his gaze. 'You,' he said, stabbing a finger at Mather. 'You're Mather. You're the Organizer – no, no, the *Planner*, that's what you're called, right? Am I right? Course I'm right. Damn right. And you …' He faced Halloran.

His grin dropped away for an instant.

The grin was back, but humour was lacking. 'And you are Halloran,' he said more slowly, less excitedly. 'The Muscle. No, no, not just that. A bit more than that. Shit, you're a cold bastard.'

Halloran returned his stare and realized what was bothering him about the smaller man's eyes. The pupils were unusually enlarged. With all the dazzling brightness around them, they should have been almost pin-points. Smack? Could be. He seemed hyped up.

'This is Felix Kline,' Sir Victor interposed. 'The person you've been engaged to protect.'

If Mather was surprised he didn't show it. 'I'm very pleased to meet you, Mr Kline.'

'That you are,' agreed Kline. 'How about you, Halloran? You pleased to meet me?'

'You might grow on me,' replied Halloran.

The girl stepped in quickly. 'There are lots of arrangements to make, Felix. These gentlemen will have to know your day-to-day movements, your plans in advance, how best their people can cover you twenty-four hours a day.'

'People?' snapped Kline. 'We agreed only one. Halloran's it.'

'He'll need back-up,' said Mather, beginning to get annoyed with this volatile young man. 'He can't keep his eyes on you every minute of the day and night. There has to be outside protection.'

Kline was still watching Halloran. 'All right. You take care of that, Cora – you know my movements better than I do. Give the details to Mather, he's the brains. I want to be alone with Halloran for a while. If he's going to be my constant companion we'd better get to know each other a little. What d'you say, Halloran? D'you have a first name?'

'Liam.'

'Yeah? I'll call you Halloran. It's okay for you to call me Felix.' He smiled then, and suddenly looked like an innocent. He turned to the chairman of Magma. 'Listen, Victor, I need to see you later about Bougainville.'

'Copper?' asked Sir Victor.

'Uh huh. Think so. A source we haven't tapped yet.'

'That's good news if you're sure.'

Kline was irritated. 'I can't be sure. You know I can't be *sure!*'

'No, I'm sorry, of course not,' the chairman appeased. 'We'll discuss it later. When you're ready.'

'Okay, okay. Now leave me alone with Halloran. We've got things to discuss. You come back when you're through, Cora.'

They left, only the bodyguard lingering by the door. Kline snapped his

fingers, then pointed, and the heavy-set man followed the others, closing the
double-doors behind him.

'Mystified, Halloran?' said Kline, walking backwards, away from him,
towards the low dais at the room's centre, his white sneakers squeaking against
the shiny floor. 'Yeah, I bet you are. How come a little creep like me can tell a
big wheel like Sir Victor what or what not to do?' He hopped onto the platform
and stood with legs apart, thin arms folded across his chest.

'I'd be interested to find out,' said Halloran, remaining where he was. His
voice sounded hollow in the empty space around them.

'Yeah, and I'd be interested to find out about you. You bother me, Halloran,
and I don't like that.'

Halloran shrugged. 'You can always ask for someone else. There are plenty
of good operatives at Shield who could take my place. But if I bother you, you
might be more prepared to do as I say. It's your life I'll be protecting, remember.'

'Could I forget?' He dropped to the floor again and sat on the dais' edge,
elbows on knees, his body hunched. 'You got questions you want to ask?'

Halloran walked over and sat next to him. 'Tell me exactly what you do for
Magma. That'll be useful for beginners.'

Kline laughed, a quick explosive sound. 'You mean the old boy hasn't told
you? Probably wanted to lead you into it gently. Okay, Halloran, sit there and
listen – you're about to be educated.'

He was on his feet again, skittishly pacing up and down before his one-man
audience.

'I welcomed you to limbo, right? Well, that's what this room represents.
Nothingness. A void. Nothing to distract, nothing at all to interest. Not unless
I do this!'

He darted towards the dais, reached for something behind Halloran. He held
the rectangular object in one hand and Halloran saw it was a plain white remote
control unit, even the buttons colourless and unmarked so that it had been
almost invisible against its resting place. Kline aimed the sensor cells and
thumbed a button.

The room was instantly plunged into total darkness.

Halloran moved instinctively, changing his position on the dais, going to his
left. He heard a dry chuckle from somewhere in the inkiness, an eerie scratching
sound that stiffened the muscles of his back.

'A different kind of void, isn't it?' came Kline's voice.

Halloran twisted his head, hopelessly trying to locate the source in the pitch
black.

'It's full of things,' Kline said, and this time he sounded close, almost by
Halloran's shoulder.

'Bad things,' Kline whispered in his ear.

Halloran rose, reached out. Touched nothing.

'And now we do this,' said the voice.

Halloran squeezed his eyes shut against the burst of light from one of the
walls. He opened them cautiously, giving his pupils time to adjust. Some
distance away an unmarked relief map of South America glowed.

Light reflected off Kline who stood six feet away to Halloran's right. His hand, holding the remote, was extended towards the brightly lit map. He shifted his aim.

'Now this,' he said. *Click.* Another map. North America by the side of South.

'This. This. This.' Kline used his arm as a pointer, turning slowly, maps of different countries appearing one after the other, lining the upper halves of the walls, all the way around. India, Africa, Spain, Australia, Indonesia, Alaska, many more, plus sections of land or islands he didn't immediately recognize. They illuminated the room, large, detailed murals in greens and browns, with seas unnaturally blue.

Kline was grinning at him, his face and body a kaleidoscope of soft colours.

'Satellite photographs,' Kline told him. 'We're looking down at Mother Earth from outer space. Now look at this.' He carelessly aimed the remote at one of the relief maps. A button clicked. The map became an incredibly detailed flat study, exactly in scale to the one it overlaid, but with towns, villages, rivers, and mountains clearly marked. 'Something else, right, Halloran? I can tell you're impressed.'

Click.

The pictures around the wall disappeared, shut off together save for one. An island.

'Know this place, Halloran? New Guinea.' The relief zoomed up, the left side growing out of frame. The map froze again. 'Papua New Guinea, a steamy hell-hole. But rich in certain things.'

He watched Kline return to the dais, a shadowy, back-lit figure that somehow exuded electric energy. The small man squatted in the middle of the low rostrum, ankles crossed, crouching forward towards the screen.

'Copper, for one,' Kline said, his eyes intent on the bright picture. His voice became dulled as he concentrated. 'My deed for the day as far as Magma's concerned. It already has a copper mine down there, but it's running low. Did you know the demand for copper is up ten per cent after the long recession? No, guess you didn't. Why should you? Shit, I hardly care myself. But old Sir Vic does, him and his cronies. Big money to them, y'see. Well, looks like I found 'em a new source, quite a ways from the established mine. Did that this morning, Halloran, before you arrived.'

Halloran stared. 'You found them copper? I don't understand.'

Kline laughed gleefully, smacking the platform beneath him with his free hand. 'And who can blame you? You're like the rest: no concept of the mind's real power. Reason is mankind's disease, did you know that? A wasting away of senses. So what do you care? A dumb bodyguard is all you are.'

'So educate me a little more.'

Click.

Total darkness once again.

Halloran softly walked to a new position.

Kline's disembodied voice came to him. 'All this black worry you, Halloran?'

He didn't answer.

'Make you wonder what it's concealing? You know you're in an empty room, you saw that when the lights were on. But now you're not so sure. Because you can't see anything. So your own mind invents for you.'

A chuckle in the dark.

'You can hear me, so you know I'm here, right, Halloran? 'Bout six or seven feet away? But if I touch you ...'

A cold finger scraped Halloran's cheek.

'... now that scares you. Because reason tells you it doesn't make sense.'

Halloran had instinctively gone into a crouch. He shifted position again, heard his own feet scuff the floor.

'Scares the shit out of you, right?'

A finger prodded his back.

Halloran moved again and kept moving, reaching out for a wall, something solid on which to get his bearings. His stretched fingers touched a face.

Then brilliant light forced his eyes shut.

'You were helpless. I had you cold.'

They were on the platform once more, Halloran steadily forcing his jarred nerves to settle, Kline sitting beside him, grinning, his oil-slick eyes watching. Halloran could smell the other man's sweat, could see the damp patches beneath his armpits.

'Sure, you had me cold,' he agreed. 'What was the point though?'

'A tiny lesson about the unreality of reality. You asked me to educate you some more.'

'That wasn't what I had in mind.'

Kline giggled. 'Fear was something I put into you. And you did feel fear.'

'Maybe.'

'Yet you knew it was only me and you in here. A little guy like me up against a trained heavy like you. Unreasonable, wouldn't you say? The darkness overcame your reason, don't you see? Made you vulnerable.'

'I admit I was disorientated.'

'Much more, I think.'

'It hasn't helped me understand anything. I don't see what it had to do with finding copper on a map.'

'Perhaps it was a demonstration and a test at the same time.' The coarseness had left Kline's voice and his manner had subtly changed, the banter all but gone to be replaced by a cool mocking. 'A silly game, yes, but I wanted to gauge your reaction to, as you put it yourself, disorientation. My life appears to be in your hands, after all.'

'Let's get on to that later. Talk to me about copper in New Guinea. How did you locate this new source?'

'Through my mind, of course. Intuition, second sight, sixth sense, extrasensory perception – call it what you will. I look at maps and I perceive hidden minerals and ores. Even stores of raw energy. I can tell where they can be found beneath the earth's crust. Oh, I don't mean to boast – I'm not always right. Seventy-five per cent of the time I am, though, and that's good enough for

Magma. Oh yes, that's more than good enough for Sir Victor Penlock and his board of directors.'

Halloran slowly shook his head. 'You find these ... these deposits with your mind? Like a diviner locates underground springs?'

'Huh! Finding water beneath the soil is the easiest thing in the world. Even *you* could do that. No, it's a bit more involved. Let's say scientific geological studies and even carefully calculated estimations point me in the right direction. I'm given an area to look at – it could cover thousands upon thousands of square miles – and I totally shed irrelevant matters from my thoughts. This room helps me do that: its emptiness cleanses my mind.'

He waved a hand around at the room. By using the remote control a few moments before, Kline had dimmed the light considerably, rendering the walls and floor a pale, cheerless grey. Halloran could now see faint lines where the screens were imbedded. He also noticed tiny sensors strategically and discreetly positioned to pick up commands from the console held loosely in the other man's hand. The room was ingenious in structure and design.

'Can you understand why I'm so valuable to the Corporation?' asked Kline, gazing down at the floor and massaging his temples with stiffened fingers as though easing a headache. 'Have you any idea how fast the developed countries are using up our resources – fossil fuels, minerals, metals, timber, even soils? We're rapidly running them down. Worldwide we're searching and digging and consuming. We've got greedy. The big corporations don't believe in restraint: they've always done their utmost to supply the demand, with no cautions, no warnings, nothing to upset the flow of cash into their silk-lined pockets.'

He raised his head and there was something sly about his smile when he looked at Halloran.

'Now they're getting scared. The harder new sources of raw materials are to find, the more concerned they get; the more expensive it is to scour those materials from the earth, the more jitterish they become. That's what makes me Magma's biggest asset, why I'm so precious to the Corporation. Even £50 million would hardly compensate for my death.'

Halloran rose and walked away, his hands tucked into his trouser pockets, head bowed as though he were deep in thought. He turned, looked back at the small watching figure.

'That's some story you're asking me to swallow,' Halloran said.

Kline's cackled laughter shot across the room. 'You don't believe me! You don't believe I can do it! All I've shown you and you think this is some kind of game. Wonderful!' He pummelled his feet on the white floor with the joke of it.

Halloran spoke calmly. 'I said it's hard to believe.'

Kline became still. 'You think I give a shit what you believe? All you have to do is protect me, nothing more than that. So maybe it's time I found out how good you are.'

His thumb worked the remote control unit once more and a buzzer or a light must have alerted the man outside the double-door, because one side opened and the bodyguard stepped through.

'Halloran here doesn't think you're up to much, Monk,' said Kline. 'You want to give him a little workout, introduce yourself?'

Monk wasn't smiling when he approached.

Halloran still faced Kline. 'I don't do auditions,' he said.

'In that case Monk's liable to break your arms.'

Halloran sighed and turned to meet the other man who was ambling forward as if he intended to do nothing more than shake the operative's hand. But there was a certain, recognizable, gleam in Monk's eyes.

He took the last two yards in a crouching rush.

To find Halloran was suddenly behind him.

Monk felt Halloran's foot planted squarely against his rear end, a hard shove propelling him further forward, the action one fluid movement. All balance gone, the bodyguard skidded to his knees, reduced to a clumsy scrabbling figure. He came up in a crouching position.

'Bastard.' The curse was high-pitched, almost a squeal, as though his voice-box was squeezed somewhere too low in his throat.

'Jesus, it speaks,' said Halloran.

The bodyguard ran at him.

'Felix, call him off!'

It was Cora's voice, but Halloran didn't bother to look towards the doorway. He had no wish to hurt this lumbering apeman, but at the same time it was too early in the day to be playing silly games. He stepped aside from the charge again and brought his knee up into the bent man's lower ribs, using only enough force to bruise and upset his victim's breathing for a while.

Monk went down with a *whoosh* of escaping air and spittle from his open mouth. To give him credit, he immediately began to rise again, his face red and glowering. Resignedly, Halloran prepared to jab a pressure point in the man's neck to bring the contest to a swift and relatively harmless end.

But Cora strode between them to confront Kline. 'Put a stop to this, Felix,' she demanded. 'Right now.'

Halloran caught the brief flash of rage in the small man's eyes before it was suppressed and Kline beamed a smile of the innocent.

'Only a test, Cora,' he all but simpered. 'No harm done. I needed to know how good this guy was, that's all.'

'He wouldn't have been recommended to us if he wasn't any good,' she replied, her tone modified by now. She turned to Halloran. 'I'm so sorry, this should never have happened.'

Monk was clutching his sore ribs with one hand, looking from Halloran to Kline, awaiting further instructions.

'Wait outside,' Kline snapped, obviously displeased with his man's perfor-mance. Then, to Halloran as Monk left the room with less ease than he had entered: 'You move pretty fast.'

'If he's your best, you've got problems,' said Halloran.

'Oh, he's not my best; he's my ox.' Kline rose from the dais, a quick feline movement. His eyes seemed even darker than before, and glistened with some inner thought. 'No doubt there are matters you will have to discuss with Cora concerning my future safety. She's my PA – no, much more than that – so feel free to confide in her absolutely. Now I need a shower; I'm beginning to stink.'

'You and I have a lot to go through,' Halloran said to him.

'Tell it to her. I need to rest.' It was a command and Halloran frowned.

The girl touched his arm though, and he looked down at her. Kline was already walking away, heading towards a far corner of the room. He clicked a button on the unit he was still carrying and a door that had been virtually invisible before slid back.

'Felix really does need to rest for a while,' Cora said as they watched him disappear through the opening. 'His special gift often leaves him quite exhausted.'

Halloran had noticed the perspiration stain low at the back of Kline's sweatshirt as well as those beneath his arms, and his frown deepened. It was cool in the room, almost uncomfortably so. And when he had touched the small man in the darkness, Kline's skin had been cold.

He remembered that moment, remembered the shudder that had run through him.

For when his fingers had reached out and felt Kline's face in that total darkness, they had touched ridges and creases, dry, wrinkled skin that had no place on the features of a comparatively young man.

Reason told him he must have been mistaken, the shock of the moment creating an illusion, the sudden blinding light instantly wiping the image from his mind.

But now that thought – that *feeling* – had returned. And Kline, himself, had warned against reason.

▪ 7 ▪

KLINE'S PREMONITION

CORA PICKED AT THE SALAD, HER INTEREST CENTRED ON HALLORAN RATHER THAN the food before her. The riverside terrace was beginning to fill with office workers on early lunch break, the fine weather after such a dreary winter proving an attraction. A pleasure-boat filled with pink-faced tourists cruised by, the Thames a slatey-blue again after months of sluggish greyness. New buildings lined the bank across the river alongside old decaying warehouses. There was still an edgy chill in the air, but it only served to make the new season more fresh, a cleanness in the breeze sweeping away the dregs of winter.

Halloran was winding his way through the circular tables, holding the two drinks chest high to avoid nudging heads and shoulders of other diners.

She watched and she was just a little afraid of him. The casual way in which he had dealt with Monk's aggression made her wonder how lethal he could be if the situation were desperate. Yet at first glance he seemed anything but a violent man. He was tall, but not massive, his body lean, certainly not muscle-bound. Even his clothes were casual, nothing sharp or self-conscious about them.

That was at first glance. Take another look and notice the pale blue eyes, the warmth in them that could turn to a bleak coldness in an instant. She'd seen that happen when he'd been introduced to Felix. And Felix had been aware of it, too.

That worried her, for Felix might need this enigmatic man, no matter what mutual dislike had already sprung up between them. There was something about Halloran's quiet strength that was totally reassuring: he was a man to feel safe with – unless you were his enemy.

Cora thanked him with a smile as Halloran placed the gin and tonic in front of her; she deliberately left it there, aware that she'd taken the first one too fast (to Halloran's surprised amusement). His own was a whisky with ice and he put it to one side as he tucked into his ham salad. She tried a dismal attack on her own food once again, but gave up after a few mouthfuls.

'I don't seem to be very hungry today,' she said, and wondered why it sounded like an apology. She lifted her glass and drank, finding the gin more sustaining than lettuce and cucumber.

Halloran nodded and took a healthy sip of his whisky to keep her company. His smile was gentle.

'What part of Ireland were you born in, Mr Halloran?' Cora asked, the sinking warmth from her second drink already beginning to relax her.

'Call me Liam,' he replied. 'I wasn't born in Ireland. My parents were Irish, but I was born here in London, although I grew up in Kilkenny. My father was a captain in the British Army, and spent much of his time abroad while Mother and I stayed on my grandfather's farm.'

'And did you eventually join the army?'

'It was a natural enough thing to do.' He put down his knife and cut pieces of cheese with the edge of his fork. 'I need to know a good deal about your employer, Miss Redmile. His private life as well as business.'

'Cora.'

'Okay – Cora. Tell me about him. Tell me how long he's been your boss.'

'I joined Magma about five or six years ago, but I haven't worked for Felix all that time.'

He encouraged her with a nod.

'Felix took me on as his PA three years ago. I don't know why. He saw me when I was delivering some documents to Sir Victor's office one day from my department on the sixteenth. The documents were urgent and I interrupted their meeting. Apparently he asked about me and the next thing I knew he'd put in a request to have me as an assistant. I wasn't even sure who he was at that time, although I'd heard rumours.'

'Rumours?'

'Yes. No more than office gossip. Felix Kline's presence at Magma has never been official; you won't find his name mentioned in company papers, not even on a pay slip or P.45.'

'Isn't that illegal?'

'Not if he's never been employed by the Magma Corporation. As far as the outside world is concerned, he could just be paying rent for the penthouse suite.'

'Except I bet even that isn't on record,' suggested Halloran.

'The official resident is Sir Victor himself.'

'So Kline's role for the Corporation really is that secret? Your board of directors is afraid that he'll be nabbed by the competition?'

'More than that. There are over a hundred thousand shareholders of Magma, most of them UK registered: imagine their reaction if they found out their Corporation was guided by a mystic.'

'It's a relief to hear you say that. I was beginning to wonder if I was the one who was out of touch with modern business practices.'

Cora laughed and he was glad. She had been tense ever since she'd taken him away from the white room, as if the minor tussle she'd witnessed between himself and the heavy had upset her. Later, in the daylight, he'd noticed a faint darkness beneath her eyes, like smudges under the surface skin, the look of someone who'd recently found sleep difficult. Maybe she was concerned for her employer, worried because the danger to him was considered serious enough to warrant hiring a K & R agency, despite the fact that Kline already had his own bodyguards.

'I gather – and this might sound naïve given all I've learned so far today – that Kline has achieved fantastic results for Magma.'

'That's an understatement.' Cora smiled at him before sipping from her glass.

'When did the Corporation discover his talents?' Halloran left his fork on the plate and leaned forward, resting his folded arms on the table's edge. 'I mean, just who approached who?'

Now she avoided his eyes. 'I'm not at liberty to say. I'm sorry, Liam, but my instructions are to supply you with information relevant only to your protection plans.'

'Is there a reason for that?'

'The same reason that just one person – you – will be allowed to stay close to Felix: secrecy, discretion, call it what you like. The less people who know about Felix Kline, the easier Sir Victor and others will feel.' She was suddenly anxious. 'I'm not assuming too much, am I? You have accepted the assignment.'

'Oh yes,' he replied softly and again, there was something disconcerting in his eyes when he smiled. 'But there are certain ground rules he'll have to agree to.' Halloran reached into the inside pocket of his jacket and drew out a folded sheet of paper. 'A simple list of Do's and Don't's,' he said, handing it to Cora. 'Make sure he reads through it today. If Kline's willing to go by them, call Shield later this afternoon, talk to Mather.'

'And if Felix isn't willing?'

'Then we've got problems. Possibly Shield will turn down the assignment.'

'May I see the list?'

'Of course. You'll be part of the set-up.'

Cora unfolded the sheet of paper and ran her eyes over the lines of type. She nodded her head. 'It all seems straightforward enough.'

Halloran reached over and tapped the corner of the paper. 'Point three there. Does Kline have a chauffeur?'

'Yes. One of his bodyguards. Janusz Palusinski.'

'Is Palusinski familiar with anti-kidnap driving techniques?'

'I ... I don't know.'

'It's important.'

'I'm sorry, I really have no idea. Palusinski has been with Felix a lot longer than I have.'

'Okay. If he isn't he'll have to spend a day or so with one of Shield's drivers. He'll need to learn the handbrake turn, the reverse turn, how to break through a road-block – that kind of thing. None of it's too difficult to master for an experienced driver. Until then, I'll do any driving for Kline.'

Cora looked down at the list again. 'Covert signals?' she asked.

'We'll work out a system of identifying each other with code-words. Handy for telephone conversations, knocking on doors and the like. We'll arrange non-verbal signals too for emergencies where words either won't help or might put us at risk. Nothing fancy, just simple signs. There'll be other key words for use in a kidnap situation, words that will let us know if Kline is hurt, the number of abductors, maybe even clues to his location if he's aware of it himself. If he sticks to the rules there shouldn't be any need for those.'

Cora shivered, caught by a breeze skimming off the river. 'This is scary,' she said.

'Sure it is. But that's how it should be – scary enough to keep you both on your toes.'

'That isn't very reassuring.'

'You're hiring my company for Kline's protection, not for giving false comfort. I've got to be frank with you, Cora: if an organization, be it terrorist or hoodlum, is out to get someone, it's virtually impossible to prevent them from at least making the attempt – and that's usually when people get hurt. We can only do our best to minimize the risk. But if it's any consolation, it's far easier to assassinate someone than it is to kidnap them.'

She visibly paled.

Halloran leaned forward again and gripped her lower arm. 'I didn't mean to alarm you. We *are* only talking about a kidnap and ransom situation here, aren't we? Nobody's threatened his life?'

Cora slowly shook her head and Halloran withdrew his hand.

'What is it, Cora? What's upsetting you? As I understand it, all we're going on is a "feeling" Kline has that he's in some kind of danger, with no hard evidence of that really being the case.'

'You don't know Felix, you've no idea of his psychic ability. He has powers ...' Her voice trailed off.

'Yeah, I know – powers that are secret.' Halloran looked away from her, towards the river. 'Well that's between Magma and Kline. My only interest is protecting a man made of flesh and blood, someone as vulnerable as the rest of us. But if he knows something about this particular predicament he's in – or imagines he's in – he'd better tell me. What is it that's frightened him so much, Cora?'

She bowed her head for a moment. Her fingers curled around the base of her gin glass, which was now empty; she twisted the glass, sunlight glistening off its rim. A group at a nearby table laughed at a shared joke. The microphone-voice from a pleasure-boat guide drifted over the terrace parapet. Cora's fingers became still.

'For the past week,' she began, her voice low and hesitant, aware of the people around them, 'Felix has been troubled by some kind of premonition. Nothing substantial, nothing he can recognize. A dream, a nightmare, one that he can never remember when he wakes. But he knows it's a warning to him, a precognition of sorts that won't fully reveal itself to him. It's made him distraught. No, more than that – Felix is terrified.'

'He didn't look that way to me,' commented Halloran.

'He'd never show those feelings to an outsider. Felix is a very private man.'

'You're telling me he's had a premonition of his own death?'

She gave a shake of her head. 'No. No, something worse than that.'

A shadow fell across the table startling them both. A barman collected their empty glasses, transferring them to a tray of others.

'Lovely day,' the barman said, turning away without waiting for a reply.

The girl looked across at Halloran. She said nothing more.

▪ 8 ▪
BODYGUARDS

SNAITH WASN'T HAPPY.

'You mean Magma is going to all this bother because their man – this chap Kline – has had a premonition of some sort?' He glared at Halloran as though it were his fault.

Halloran, himself, seemed preoccupied. He scratched the back of his fingers against his jaw. 'That's how it is,' he said.

Snaith rested back in his chair, one hand still on the desk, fingers drumming a beat. 'Ludicrous,' he pronounced.

'Not to the Corporation,' said Mather, sitting in an easychair opposite

Halloran, his bad leg stretched out before him (now and again during the briefing and planning meeting he would absent-mindedly rub at his kneecap as if to ease the pain of the old wound). 'They have great faith in this man's ability; I don't think it's for us to dismiss his foreboding so lightly.'

Dieter Stuhr, sitting at one end of the Controller's desk, tapped the blunt end of his pencil against the large notepad in front of him. 'Personally, I don't see how that affects us anyway. What goes on between Kline and the Magma Corporation is their affair. We should treat this like any other job.'

'Of course you're right,' agreed Snaith, 'but this business bothers me. It's ...' he shook his head, frustrated '... it's not logical. What kind of man is he, Liam?'

'Changeable,' came the reply. 'I'd say he's highly unstable – neurotic, in fact. He's going to be a problem.'

'I see.' Snaith's expression was grim. 'Well, we've dealt with prima donnas before. And his personal bodyguards? What's your opinion of their worth?'

'I was only introduced to one. He wasn't very effective.'

Nobody in the room asked him how he'd reached that conclusion; they accepted his word.

Mather consulted a notebook. 'I have the names of the other three here. Let me see now, yes – Janusz Palusinski, his driver, then Asil Khayed and Youssef Daoud. They're described as "personal attendants", which I suppose could imply anything.'

'Good Lord,' exclaimed Snaith. 'Arabs?'

'Jordanians.'

'And the first? Czech? Polish?'

'Janusz Palusinski – Polish.'

'And the one you met, Liam?'

'Monk. He didn't say much.'

'Theodore Albert Monk,' Mather supplied from his notebook. 'According to the Magma files, he's American.'

'That's some mixed bag,' commented Snaith.

'Apparently Felix Kline picked them up on his travels. They've all been with him for years.'

'The driver might need some training,' suggested Halloran.

'That's being taken care of,' Snaith told him. 'Kline's PA, Miss, uh – Redmile, rang me earlier this afternoon to arrange it. Dieter?'

'I've got him booked in for tomorrow. We'll lease Magma one of our own specials – for Palusinski to train in and to use afterwards. Kline's own vehicle doesn't have enough protection facilities; body and windows are bulletproof, but that's about it. I'll want to keep Palusinski for at least two days, Liam, to make sure he really knows what he's doing when he leaves us, so it looks like you're Kline's chauffeur until then.'

Halloran nodded.

Snaith spoke: 'Miss Redmile also confirms that her employer agrees to the list of conditions regarding his own actions in the forthcoming weeks. I understand you had lunch with her today?' He was looking directly at Halloran. 'Apart from their business relationship, what is she to Kline? Is she his mistress?'

Halloran took time to consider the question. Finally, he said, 'She could be.'

'She's that type?'

'What type?'

'The type who beds her boss.'

'I wouldn't know.'

'But she's a looker.'

Halloran nodded.

'Let's assume that's the case, then.'

Mather noticed the brief flare of anger in Halloran's eyes and was puzzled by it. Liam usually held his emotions totally in check. 'I don't see that it's entirely relevant, Gerald,' Mather put in. 'After all, Kline isn't married, and there's no mention of other girlfriends – or boyfriends, for that matter – in the dossier from Magma.'

'She could be a weak spot,' Snaith replied. 'He might put himself at risk if he knows she's in danger. There could be other possibilities, also. Has she been checked out?'

'I have her file right here,' said Stuhr. 'Charles brought it back from Magma earlier today, so I've only managed to glance through it. She sounds pretty solid to me. Raised in Hampshire, an only child, father a university lecturer, mother a local GP, both now deceased. Attended private school until eighteen, bright – seven Os and three As – but never went on to university. Rents an apartment in Pimlico, has a substantial sum of money in her bank account – what's left of the proceeds from the sale of her parents' home, plus a little of her own savings. Magma is her first and only job apart from a bit of summertime temping when she was still a student; she worked her way up in the organization and I think she is wonderful.' He took a black and white photograph from the file and held it up for the others to see.

Snaith didn't smile. 'Dig deeper over the next few days. Find out who she socializes with, boyfriends, lovers, her politics, religion – you know the kind of thing. She's close to the target, so we can't take chances.'

Snaith paused, ran fingers through his short ginger-grey hair.

'Now,' he said, looking round at all of them. 'Our friend Mr Kline. Just what the hell do we know about him?'

'Hardly anything,' answered Stuhr. 'It took me all of half-a-minute to read through his file.'

'Hmn, that's what I was afraid of. This bloody secrecy can be taken too far.'

'Oh, I don't think Magma is to blame,' said Mather. 'When I spoke with the chairman this morning it became very apparent that the Corporation doesn't actually *know* too much about Felix Kline's background. I got the impression that so long as the man continues to make them money, they're not particularly bothered.'

'Would somebody please tell me just what it is he *does* for Magma?' complained Stuhr.

'Sorry, Dieter,' said Snaith, 'that isn't necessary for you to know. Their terms, I'm afraid, so don't sulk. What does his file tell us?'

Stuhr made a snorting noise, but didn't argue. 'Like I said – there isn't much.

He was born in Israel, arrived in England eleven years ago, began working for the Magma Corporation almost immediately – '

'A Jew with two Arab companions?' interrupted Snaith.

'They're not all bitter enemies. He moved into the penthouse suite of the Magma building when it was completed about five years ago. He also has a country home in Surrey, by a lake, two thousand acres of pastures and woodland. I need hardly say that's a huge amount of land to own in the Home Counties. He's obviously a very wealthy man. Unmarried, doesn't drive, doesn't smoke, drinks a little, no mention of drugs – but there wouldn't be – doesn't gamble. That's about it.'

'What?' said Snaith incredulously. 'There must be more.'

Stuhr reached for a file lying beneath Cora Redmile's. He opened it and indicated the single sheet of paper inside. 'I told you there wasn't much to read.'

'It must give his birth date, where he was educated, his employment before Magma. Isn't there anything about his social activities? It's essential that we at least have some idea of what those are.'

'He doesn't appear to have any if this document is anything to go by.'

'Charles?' Snaith appealed.

Mather waved a hand. 'That's the situation I'm afraid. Even in conversation the chairman gave nothing away. Naturally I probed, but got nowhere. As I said, they seem to know little about the man themselves, and I think that's of Kline's choosing; perhaps part of his own terms of employment was his complete privacy on all personal matters. If he'd already demonstrated how good his abilities were, I don't suppose the board objected too much.'

'All right. I'm not happy, but let's accept the situation for what it is.' Then Snaith asked hopefully, 'I suppose his salary isn't in there somewhere?'

Stuhr grinned and shook his head. 'Not even a hint.'

'We could find out from other sources, but let's not waste our time. In fact, there's a lot more information we could uncover if we took the trouble, but we'll take the assignment at face value. Our contract will be signed later today – we're moving fast on this one. Liam, you'll be Kline's constant companion as of eight o'clock tomorrow morning. Dieter, I want a report from you on terrorist and kidnap activities during the last year. Obviously anything relevant to Magma or its subsidiary companies is what we're after.'

Stuhr made a note. After the meeting he would spend some time at the data processing machine, using a special access code to link up with another company which specialized in maintaining and updating the activities and whereabouts of known worldwide terrorist groups on computer.

'I'll do some checks on Magma's rivals, also,' the German said, 'see if there are any areas where competition has become over-fierce.'

'Good. We're looking for enemies, business or otherwise. But if Kline is as neurotic as Liam says, this whole affair could well be a waste of time and effort. The man might be suffering from a severe case of paranoia.' The Controller managed a grim smile. 'Still, that's his and Magma's problem – Achilles' Shield gets paid either way. What do you have for us, Charles?'

Mather stopped rubbing at his knee. 'It's all fairly straightforward. For the time being we'll allocate four operatives to work with Liam, our inside man. Two to a team, working six-hour shifts around the clock. We'll also keep a back-up here on alert. Any preference as to whom you want, Liam?'

Halloran shook his head.

'Very well. As requested by Magma, our teams will keep at a distance. They'll maintain a constant patrol around the Surrey estate's boundaries – as usual, we'll inform the local police to save them from getting into a tizz.'

'Will our people be armed?' enquired Stuhr.

There was a pause. Snaith preferred his operatives to be 'kitted' against 'severe hostility', but it was illegal for private bodyguards to carry weapons in England (a law which was constantly abused, particularly by foreign visitors to the country). The Controller came to a decision. 'Liam will take with him to the estate whatever hardware he feels is necessary. I'm reluctant to sanction anything that will harm our special relationship with the police and Home Office, so our patrols will be unarmed for the time being. However, should there be any definite moves against our client, then the situation will be reconsidered. Although we'll have to rely on Liam and Kline's own bodyguards to take care of internal surveillance, we'll need a detailed report on the security system of this place ...'

Stuhr made another note.

'... and the Magma building itself. The latter worries me considerably. Too many people in and out all day. However, we can plant an extra couple of our men in the lobbies of the ground and twelfth floors; naturally Magma's own security people will have to know they're there. We'll have a surveillance team outside at night, front and back, when Kline's in residence.'

'The building worries me, too,' said Halloran, and all eyes turned towards him. 'It's a glass and metal fortress, but it's vulnerable.'

'Then let's hope nobody tries to get at the target before we're operational,' commented Mather. 'Now that would be amusing.'

Snaith didn't find that prospect amusing at all. Not one bit.

• 9 •
ENTICEMENT

AH GOOD, AT LAST HE IS APPROACHING THE BOY.

The boy is nervous but he speaks with bravado. He is pale, the boy, and looks unwashed; no doubt the rumpled plastic bag he carries contains all his worldly goods. He is perhaps sixteen, perhaps seventeen. The English believe that is too young to be without family, without a home; would that they knew of the orphans who freely roam the streets and market-places of Damascus, boys who wander alone, others who prowl in packs, stealing, begging, and joining lost causes because they will supply them with guns. Pah! The self-important British knew nothing of such things.

The boy is smiling. An unsure, nervous smile. He is lost in this huge railway station with its throngs of blank-eyed strangers. He would be even more lost in the city itself should he step outside. Now he assumes he has found a friend. If only he realized. Hah, yes, if only the boy understood.

Ajel, be quick, Youssef, do not linger on this plain of shuffling travellers and vagrants. Policemen patrol, they search for runaways such as this one.

Now he is hesitant. The boy is uncertain. Perhaps it is the dark skin he does not trust. The English nurture such intolerances, instil them in their young.

Talk smoothly, Youssef, my friend. He looks around, the movement casual, nothing more than a glance at arrival and departure times, a constantly changing pattern high on the station wall: but Youssef really looks to see if he and the boy are being observed. You are not, my friend; I, Asil, have already looked for you. I am the only one who is interested. Besides, a man talking to a *shab* is familiar to these surroundings. Nobody really cares. Life is too personal.

He places a reassuring hand on the runaway's shoulder and the boy does not flinch away. Perhaps money is mentioned. Ah, I see the boy nods. He has all the boldness and the stupidity of the unworldly.

My friend turns away and the boy follows. They walk side by side. Not close, not like lovers, but like associates in sin. I see it in your eyes, Youssef, the gleam that shines from your dark soul, even though outwardly you are calm. And the boy swaggers; but this is a self-conscious posturing, an arrogant affectation.

I must quickly go to the car. I must be ready in the darkness of the backseat. The boy will hardly feel the needle's sting; he will only sense my presence when it is too late.

Then, for him, sleep. A long, deep sleep.

And when he wakes – our pleasure and the master's sustenance.

Hurry, Youssef, *ajel*. I suspect that same gleam is now in my own eyes. My body is already aching.

▪ 10 ▪
INTRUDER

MONK WAS SURPRISED. NOBODY WAS DUE THIS TIME OF NIGHT. LEASTWISE, nobody'd told him.

The elevator was humming though. Faint, but it was on its way up. Sounded like the one from the chairman's suite. No way could it be Felix's elevator, the one that slid all the way down to the basement. Nobody else had the code for that. Even the chick, Cora, had to wait 'til it was sent down for her.

Monk was momentarily distracted by Cora's image. The image was naked from the waist down.

Sound's stopped. It'd travelled no more'n four storeys. Yeah, from Sir Vic's den. Who the hell – ?

Monk heard the doors open.

But no one stepped out.

The bodyguard laid down his magazine and rose from the chair at the end of the corridor. He released the restraining hoop on his shoulder-holster, but stayed where he was, awaiting developments.

No mood for fuckouts tonight, he told himself. It'd been a bad day already. He'd been shown for a jackass that morning, a clumsy meatloaf, and he was in no mind for surprises tonight, even if some jerk had made a mistake in coming up to the twenty-second. Just step outside, lessee the colour of your teeth.

Still no one. But the doors weren't closing, and that wasn't right.

Monk crept down the corridor, one hand on the butt of his pistol, a big lumbering man who nevertheless approached the lift silently, soft carpeting helping his stealth. The corridor was gloomy-dark – the way Felix liked it – and mellow light from the opening ahead stained the floor and opposite wall.

The door should've closed by now. Unless someone had a mitt on the O button.

Monk drew out the Smith and Wesson.

He paused, the opening only two feet away. There were no shadows in the glow that spread from it.

He braced himself, readied to spring forwards and sideways, gun-arm pointed into the lift. But he thought better of that tactic. Monk wasn't stupid. His bulk was too good a target.

So he got down on his hands and knees and crawled forward, gunbarrel almost alongside his nose, elbows digging into the deep-pile. No one expected to see a face appear below knee level.

He was at the very corner, easing his massive head past the shiny metal ridge, the lift's interior coming into view. His gun hand was no more than a few inches ahead of him.

Nobody there. It looked like there was nobody there after –

A hand grabbed his hair and yanked him forward onto his belly. A leg straddled him and crushed his gun into the carpet. Iron fingers still dug into his hair making the roots scream. Something slammed hard into his neck and his thoughts became unsettled dreams.

Janusz Palusinski sat at the kitchen's breakfast bar slapping butter on bread with a carving knife whose blade was at least nine inches long. Beside his plate was a tumbler half-full of vodka.

He checked his wristwatch, parts of tattooed numbers showing at the edge of the broad strap, then sawed off chunks of roast beef, the red meat rare almost to the point of being raw. As he cut he wondered if Felix – *mój Pan*, he mentally and with more than a degree of cynicism added – would scream in his sleep tonight. A terrifying sound that stilled the blood of anyone who heard it. What did the man dream of? What fears possessed him when he slept? How close to total madness had he come? But no. Janusz must not even have a negative *thought* about his master. Felix would know, he would sense.

Felix, Felix, Felix.

Just the name could cause an ache in Palusinski's head.

The Pole wiped the back of his fist across his forehead, the knife he held catching light from overhead in a sudden flare. Normally the kitchen lights, like all the others in the penthouse, would be kept low by dimmer switches, but at present Felix was sleeping, he wouldn't know. Yet sometimes he did ... Sometimes he would accuse them all of things that he should never have been aware of, and they would cringe, they would cower, they would be craven before him. Still Felix – O lord, master, and oppressor – would make them suffer, sometimes the punishment cruel, other times involving a mere few hours of discomfort. Palusinski often felt that the two Arabs enjoyed that part of their servitude. Monk's brain was too curdled to care either way, *blazen* that he was.

But Janusz was different, he assured himself. Janusz was aware of certain things ... The others were fools. No, the Arabs were not fools. They believed ...

Palusinski gulped neat vodka, then unscrewed the mustard jar lid. He dug in the tip of the carving knife, sunk it four inches, then spread the dollop it came out with across the cut meat. He slammed another thick slice of bread, also lavishly buttered, on top, pressing down with the flat of his hand so that yellow goo oozed from the sides.

Twenty minutes before the gorilla was to be relieved, he told himself as he raised the overflowing sandwich and barged his mouth into it. Monk – a good name for an animal such as he. Hours of sitting watching an empty corridor was a fitting task for such an *idiota*. But for Janusz, it meant five hours of misery to look forward to. A torment. Another torture imposed by Felix. Even pain was better than boredom.

What was it that had made Felix so nervous? The man was mad, there could be no doubting that. But a genius also! No doubting that, either. *Gówno*! No doubt at all. But why afraid now, *mój szef*? You, who lives in shadows, who distrusts the light unless it is for your purpose. What fresh fear haunts you now, *mężczyzna* of many dreads?

Palusinski chomped on meat and bread, lips glistening from the surplus of butter. He stilled his jaw to gulp vodka, seasoning the mushed food in his mouth with fire. His eyes were small behind the wire-framed spectacles he wore, their lids never fully raised, like blinds half-drawn in a room where secrets were kept. They were focused upon the rim of the open mustard jar, everything else a soft periphery; yet his eyes were not seeing that rim with its sliver of reflected light, for his thoughts were inwards, perhaps examining those very secrets within that room of his mind. He sat, slowly munching, as if mesmerized.

Something snatched him from the introspection, though. And he didn't know what.

A sound! A movement? Palusinski was puzzled. He was sensitive to intrusion. Months of living rough, sleeping in ditches, eating raw vegetables dug from the earth, always with his eyes darting left, right, afraid he would be seen, what would happen to him if they found him... all that, even though it had been many years since, had attuned his senses for the slightest shift in atmosphere.

His grip tightened on the knife. Someone was in the room beyond.

Monk? He would never disobey Felix's orders to watch the corridor one floor below until Palusinski took over. Unlikely, then, that Monk would desert his post. Youssef and Asil? No, they were not due to return that night, they had the country house to prepare for their precious lord and master's visit. Then who?

Palusinski slipped off the stool and reached inside his jacket, which was draped over a chair back. His hand came out with a thick, round metal bar, its length matching the blade protruding from his other fist. He crept over to the lightswitch and extended finger and thumb to turn it anti-clockwise. The light in the kitchen faded.

From where he stood the Pole could see a broad section of lounge beyond and he cursed the shadows out there, the darkness of the furnishings, the blackness of the walls. He could wait; or he could venture out. He had the patience – skulking and hiding in the old country had instilled that in him – but he also had a duty. To Felix. He must *never* fail in that.

He held his breath and armed with the weapons moved towards the open doorway.

The danger – *if* there was someone out there – would probably be from either side of the doorway where a person could lurk safe from view. Which side?

Always the dilemma. Which side would an assailant strike from? *If* there was someone there ...

He crouched low and ran through, counting on surprise, the knife held at hip level, tip pointing upwards, ready to plunge or swipe. Palusinski turned immediately he was clear, thrusting one leg back for balance and for leverage, so that he could spring forward or withstand an assault.

There was no need. Nobody hid outside the kitchen doorway, not on any side.

But somebody was behind the long black couch nearby. Only Palusinski, sensitive to intrusion though he was, neither saw nor *felt* the shadow that rose up from it.

He may have felt fingers tilt his head to one side so that certain nerves in his neck were exposed, but if so, he didn't remember later. He definitely did not feel the edge of the stiffened hand chop down, fast and silent, to deaden those nerves. Nor would he have felt the shock travelling along their roots towards a certain terminal inside his brain. The journey was too swift for that.

Kline was within himself.

He swam in blood vessels amid cells which changed from red to scarlet around him, through narrow passages, breaking out into round caverns, swept on by a bubbling tide that never stilled, towards a source that was no more than a distant rhythmic echo somewhere ahead in the labyrinth of busy tunnels, the rush to the sound as exhilarating as it was terrifying.

There were other things racing with him that were alien to these passages, black misshapen forms that were there only to disease and destroy; but these parasites themselves were steadily destroyed, attacked by globules which engulfed, swallowed, digested. And these defenders decided that he, too, was foreign, had no place alongside healthy corpuscles, that he was an interloper, a danger, up to no good. Even though it was his own body he journeyed through.

He screamed at the giant lumps to get away, to leave him alone, he meant no harm. But they were programmed to fight to the death all that was not right in the system and had no minds of their own. Two attached themselves to him as he was flushed through into a wider tunnel, and he felt the burning of his own back, his arm, acid seeping into him.

Yet he was so near, the rushing even faster, moving in contractions, the steady beat louder, louder still, becoming a thunder, the rapids leading to a fall, the fall to be mighty and devouring. And that was his desire, no other yearning possible to him now: he wanted to be consumed by the mountainous heart.

Instead these blind, ignorant creatures, organisms that knew nothing of other things, were eating him. His body was decomposing under their chemical excretions.

Nearly there, nearly there.

He could hear the hysteria of his own laughter.

Nearly there.

The noise ahead – *THUD-UP THUD-UP* – deafened him, filled him with dread. *Elated* him.

Nearly there.

Nearly swallowed.

It wasn't too late.

He would make it.

Be absorbed by the heart.

THUD-UP THUD-UP

There ... !

But not there.

Drifting back, drawn away, consciousness the carrier. Floating upwards, a soft retreat ...

An abrupt awakening.

There was someone with him in the bedroom. Kline opened his mouth to call out, but something clamped hard over it. A hand. A strong, threatening hand. He felt the extra weight on the bed. Somebody, a shadow among shadows, kneeling over him.

Another hand encircled his throat.

'Someone else and you could be dead,' Halloran whispered close to his ear.

· 11 ·
A DANGEROUS ENCOUNTER

HALLORAN GLANCED INTO THE REARVIEW MIRROR.

The blue Peugeot was still there, keeping well back, at least four or five other cars between it and the custom-built Mercedes Halloran was driving. His own back-up, in a Granada, was directly behind him.

He reached for the RT mounted beneath the dashboard and set the transmit button.

'Hector-One,' he said quietly into the mouthpiece.

'Hector-Two, we hear you,' came the reply through the receiver. 'And we see the tag.'

Kline leaned forward from the backseat, his face close to Halloran's shoulder. There was a bright expectancy in his eyes.

'Turning off soon,' said Halloran. 'Stay close 'til then. Out.' He replaced the instrument.

'We're being followed?' Kline asked, nervousness now mingled with expectancy.

Cora, next to him in the backseat, stiffened, and Monk, who occupied the front passenger seat – riding shotgun, as he liked to think of it – shifted his bulk to look first at his employer, then out the tinted rear window. His fingers automatically went to the revolver at his waist.

'No need for that,' Halloran warned. 'And use the side mirror if you want to spot them.'

'Nobody can see in,' Monk protested petulantly, already aggrieved with Halloran for having made him look so useless twice the day before.

'They can see shadows through the glass. Face the road and take your hand off that weapon.'

'Do it,' snapped Kline. Then to Halloran: 'Which one is it?'

'The light blue. A Peugeot, a few cars back. It's been on our tail since we left London. My guess is it took over from another car that picked us up in the City, probably close to the Magma building.' In fact, Halloran had felt uneasy long before he'd arrived at Magma early that morning to take Kline down to his Surrey home for the weekend. Yet he'd been unable to spot the 'tag' until they were into the outskirts.

'Are you sure?' asked Cora, resisting the urge to look over her shoulder at the traffic. 'This road is a main highway south – most of these cars have probably been with us for miles.'

'Cora,' said Kline, 'if he says we're being followed, that's it – I believe him.' Halloran's easy penetration of Magma's security system the night before had impressed him. By wearing clothes that had merely resembled the security guards' uniforms, Halloran had strolled into the basement carpark, hidden until most of the day staff were leaving that evening, then found his way to the upper floors using the outgoing rush as cover. Nothing more than a stroll against the tide. Then a vacated room, a broom closet, or a toilet – Halloran hadn't given him details – until night time, then through to the chairman's suite, locked doors only slowing him down, not barring him. Observation cameras? No problem. Only certain corridors and halls were monitored that late at night and, at an agreed time, Shield had created a minor diversion. No more than a motor-bike messenger thumping on the glass main door to attract the attention of the two security guards on the monitoring desk. The messenger had waved a package in his hand and one of the guards had gone to the door while his colleague watched from the desk, poised to press an alarm button which would alert the other two security guards patrolling the building as well as the local police station should anything untoward occur. So his eyes had been on his partner and the messenger outside (the latter insisting that delivery forms had to be filled in and signed before he released the package) and not on the screens behind him. The ruse had allowed Halloran to negotiate the more exposed locations without being seen. Naturally a risk was involved, but human reaction being what it is, the risk was slight. The rest of the journey had been simple (simple that is, for someone like Halloran): the private elevator, the 'pacification' of Monk and Palusinski, the entry into his, Kline's bedroom. No big deal (and heads were already rolling in the Corporation's office that morning as specialists from Achilles' Shield revised Magma's security arrangements).

Someone else and you could be dead. Kline remembered Halloran's words. Not quite that simple, Halloran, he thought. No, not *quite* that easy.

He smiled and Cora was puzzled by the sudden burning intensity in his eyes.

The Mercedes was slowing, the left indicator blinking. Halloran turned the car off the main road, then picked up speed again, their surroundings soon vignetting into green fields and hedgerows, with few houses between.

Cora noticed Halloran occasionally glancing into the rearview mirror, but his reflected eyes betrayed nothing. He had warned Monk not to look back and she, herself, followed the instruction. Their car maintained a steady speed and still Cora could not detect from Halloran's manner whether or not they were being followed.

Several minutes passed before he reached again for the radio transmitter.

'Hector-One.'

'Hector-Two. Over.'

'Tag's still with us, keeping well back.'

'Yeah. We made out three occupants. Want us to block them?'

'No. No offensive until we're sure. There's a village ahead. Pull in somewhere and let 'em by. Follow at a distance and come up fast if they make a move. Out.'

'Will do. Out.'

Houses quickly loomed up, then they were into the village, a hamlet really, only a few houses on either side of the road. Halloran saw the small filling station and knew where his back-up would pull into. He checked the mirror as the Granada slowed into the forecourt. The blue Peugeot soon came into view and he put his foot down a little to give them cause to hurry.

He had taken a more circuitous route than necessary to Kline's country house, but now they couldn't have been more than fifteen minutes away. If these people were hostile, he wanted them to make their play soon, before they were too close to home. He preferred to keep trouble off the doorstep.

He eased up on the accelerator, inviting in the possible pursuer. The Peugeot increased speed, coming up fast, beginning to fill the rearview mirror.

Halloran had faith in the 'hardened' vehicle he was driving. The door panels, trunk, roof, and engine compartment were armoured with Kevlar, aluminium oxide ballistic ceramic tiles, which was lighter than the old-style heavy steel plate that tended to render a vehicle clumsy and so impede its performance. The windows were of layered bullet-and blast-resistant glass and the tyres were compartmentalized and self-sealing so that speed need not be reduced should they be punctured by bullets. Even the fuel compartments, main and reserve, consisted of separate cells which would limit the outbreak of fire should they be pierced.

The French car was directly behind now, only feet away from the Mercedes' reinforced bumper.

'Sit back,' he told Kline, whose face was still close to Halloran's shoulder. 'And keep low, legs against the back of the front seat, as though you're resting. Cora, they'll be coming up on your side, so brace yourself. You'll be okay – they'd need a bazooka to dent this tub.'

'Speed up,' Kline urged. 'Don't let them get alongside us!'

'Stay low,' Halloran calmly repeated. 'They may be no threat at all.'

'Why take the chance? I don't like this, Halloran.'

'Trust me.'

Cora wasn't sure if Halloran's tone was mocking.

Monk had drawn his revolver by now. Halloran didn't even look his way, but said, 'Keep that bloody thing tucked into your lap and don't even think of using it unless I tell you.'

They were rounding a bend and the Peugeot was straddling the middle of the road ready to overtake.

Halloran continued to instruct the bodyguard. 'Put your elbow on the sill and keep your left hand in sight. You know how to act nonchalant?'

The American grunted something.

'Okay,' said Halloran. 'Here they come. See that church steeple in the distance? I want you all to keep your eyes on that. No watching our friends here.'

The road had straightened, a clear stretch ahead for at least half a mile. The Peugeot drew level with the Mercedes' rear wheel and Halloran deliberately glanced over his shoulder and touched his brakes, a gentlemanly gesture to allow the other vehicle to pass by. His hands tightened on the steering wheel, holding it steady, as the Peugeot inched its way alongside. He could feel the occupants' eyes on him and his senses sharpened to such a degree that he could smell new-cut grass under the petrol fumes, even though all windows were closed, could hear the Mercedes' tyres rumble over the road's hard surface, could feel the pounding of machinery beneath the car's bonnet. The acuteness of danger overlaid all those sensings.

Halloran smiled at the other driver, nodding at the deserted road ahead, an indication that he was leaving the way clear.

The Peugeot suddenly accelerated even more, then was by them, tail rapidly receding into the distance.

'Hogshit,' grumbled Monk.

'You scared us for nothing, Halloran,' Kline complained. 'Bastard, you scared us for –'

'Keep down,' Halloran warned.

There was yet another bend ahead and the blue car had disappeared around it.

Kline's mouth dropped. He snapped back into his seat and said, 'You're right. They're there.'

The Peugeot was parked across the road, blocking it completely. A fence lined one side of the road, trees the other. The occupants of the car were outside, crouched low behind the bodywork.

Halloran slammed on the Mercedes' brakes and the car screeched to a halt, rubber burning off into the concrete in straight black lines. He immediately shifted into reverse and stabbed down hard on the accelerator pedal, throwing his passengers forward then back into their seats.

Monk's revolver had slid onto the floor and he doubled over, restrained by his seatbelt, podgy hands scrabbling at the floor to reach the weapon. Cora felt herself propelled forward again by the reverse motion of the car. Kline had already scrambled down into the well between backseat and front.

Halloran increased speed, looking over his shoulder through the back window, both hands still on the steering wheel. The bend in the road loomed up fast. He began the turn, hardly slowing down at all, the passengers hurled to one side. Round the curve and out of sight from their attackers. He straightened the car, increased speed.

Suddenly Halloran stamped on the footbrake, rapidly winding on full lock as he did so. The Mercedes responded beautifully, making a 180-degree turn so that it faced the direction in which it had been reversing.

Hard on the accelerator again, and they were away, scorching road, using its full width.

The back-up Granada was hurtling towards them and Halloran swerved over to the left-hand side of the road, both cars screeching to a halt beside one another. He was already snapping orders before the electric window was fully down.

'Hostiles just around the bend. Stop them following.'

'You want us to engage?' the other driver shouted back.

'Not if you can help it – I saw guns in their hands. I'll use another route to Home.'

The cars took off at the same time, the exchange taking no more than seconds.

'Am I safe?' came Kline's querulous voice from the back.

'Not yet,' Halloran replied, looking into the rearview mirror in time to see the Granada disappear around the curve. He returned his attention to the way ahead, on the alert for possible support for the 'hostiles'. A van was approaching, two more cars behind that. He pressed the button to raise his window and made ready to accelerate or slam on the brakes yet again, whichever course of action might prove necessary. The line of vehicles passed without incident and he checked the mirror once more. Still nothing coming up from behind, the van and cars continuing to travel away from the Mercedes. He felt some of the tension ease from him.

Kline was back by his shoulder. 'Why didn't you tell your guys to shoot the bastards?' he demanded angrily.

'This is Surrey,' Halloran told him, 'not the Middle-East. Gun wars are frowned upon here. Besides, they're not armed at present, a condition that'll have to be changed, I think.'

'Listen to me, Halloran ...' Kline began to say when the radio transmitter interrupted.

'Hector-Two.'

Halloran reached for the hand-set. 'Hector-One. Give me the news.'

'They were gone before we rounded the bend. We drove on, but there was a junction not far ahead – they could've gone off in any direction. Our guess is that they'd spotted us earlier, so didn't hang around or try to follow when you got away.'

'You made out the number?'

'Sure, when they passed the garage.'

So had Halloran, but there was no need to repeat it to his operatives: they were too well trained to have made any mistakes. 'Call Base, get them to use their influence to run a check.'

'Will do. As it was a Peugeot, it's probably been stolen, not hired.'

'I agree. Check it out though. Scout the area for a while, then make your way to Home. Out.'

'Catch you later. Out.'

Halloran drove on, moving briskly without breaking any speed limits, using the roadway to the full when he could, ever-watchful at sideroads and bends, even though instinct told him they were now safe.

'Who were they, Felix?' he heard Cora ask from the back, nervousness still in her voice.

'How should I know?' was the reply. 'Thugs, lunatics!'

'Take it easy,' Halloran soothed. 'It won't be long before we reach your place.'

Kline peered out the windows. 'Oh yeah? Well this isn't the fuck the way.'

'No, but it'll get us there eventually. I worked out various routes this morning before I collected you. My team will use another way and meet us there. Monk, you can put the gun away, you won't be needing it.'

The pony-tailed bodyguard reluctantly obeyed.

'I told you, Cora,' Kline said, his words rushed, his breathing excited. 'I said I was in danger, I told you all.' He was once again the Felix Kline Halloran had first met, nervous, arrogant, too many words spilling from his lips. 'I sensed the danger, I just damn knew didn't I? Bastards! Halloran, I need more of your men to protect me. I could've been hurt back there.'

'Wasn't it your idea that we limit our forces?'

'Yeah, yeah, you're right. You'll do. You got us out of a tight spot. No more manpower required. Right. I don't feel too good.'

Cora immediately reached for him.

'Leave me alone!' Kline snapped, sinking back into his seat. 'I'm tired, I need to rest. You all want too much from me, you all expect too much. Let me rest, will you?'

Halloran heard a clasp being opened, a rattling of pills in a container.

'Felix,' said Cora, 'take them, they'll calm you.'

'You think I want drugs at a time like this? You trying to make me weak?'

There was a slapping sound and the pills sprinkled onto the seat and floor.

'I've got to stay alert, you stupid bitch! Those bastards want to hurt me and you're trying to dope me up.'

'They're only Valium, Felix, that's all. You need to calm down.'

Monk's seat jerked as Kline kicked its back. The bodyguard continued to watch the passing countryside as if he hadn't noticed.

Kline's voice had risen to a high pitch. 'You know what I oughta do with you, Cora? You know what? I oughta dump you right now, out of the car into the road. Leave you here. How would you like that, Cora, huh? How would you get by then? What fucking use are you to me?'

'Don't, Felix.' There was a mixture of misery and low panic in her voice. 'You've had a bad scare, you don't mean what you're saying.'

'Don't I? Oh don't I? You think I give a shit about you?'

Halloran heard the smack of flesh on flesh, heard the girl's small, startled cry. He brought the Mercedes to a smooth halt by the side of the road and turned round to face Kline, one arm resting casually on the back of the driver's seat. Cora was leaning her forehead against the window, eyes closed, a watery line slowly seeping onto her eyelashes; there were red marks on her cheek.

'Kline,' he said evenly, 'you're beginning to irritate. I can do my job better if you don't. I want you to sit quietly so I can think, observe, and get you to our destination unharmed. If by the time we arrive you're sick of me too, you can make a phone call and have me replaced. It's no skin off my nose, know what I mean? Do we have an arrangement?'

Kline stared open-mouthed at him and for the merest instant, Halloran saw something in those liquid eyes that he couldn't recognize. He'd faced killers and fanatics before and each had a distinctly similar and identifiable glint adrift in their gaze; he'd looked upon gunmen, abductors, and extortionists – child-murderers even – and a certain mien linked them all, setting them apart from others of the human race. But there was a glimmer shining from deep inside this man that was like nothing else he'd witnessed before. Kline's stare was almost mesmeric.

Until whatever held him became dulled, or at least was veiled by a creeping normality. Kline laughed, and it was a full, rich sound, unexpected and unlike his usual cackling.

'Whatever you say, Halloran,' he said good-humouredly. 'Yeah, whatever you say.'

Halloran turned and shifted into D. The Mercedes pulled away, heading into the winding country roads. And during the last part of that journey, Halloran frequently checked the rearview mirror. But this time he was mostly studying the man who was resting, with eyes now closed, in the backseat.

While Monk, from the corner of his eyes, watched Halloran.

MONK
A PILGRIM'S PROGRESS

IT WAS A LOUSY NAME ANYWAY. BUT NONE OF THE OTHER KIDS EVER ADDED THE 'ey'. MONKEY. Nah, too easy. They called him Ape. Up until he hit fourteen, that is. That was when the ape pissed right back out of the cage.

Theo was never gutsy (or Theodore Albert, as his mama always called him – 'Theodore Albert you wuz baptized, and Theodore Albert you be called, honey mine' – as she parted his hair right down the middle, slicking either side with a licked palm, every fuckin' morning afore she pushed him out the door and along the path to where good ol' Uncle Mort waited in the pick-up – 'You'd look real purty, boy,' Uncle Mort often observed, 'if you wunt so porky' – to take him down to Coatesville Junior High where the boys bent their knees and dragged their knuckles along the ground behind him, lumbering from side to side in an ape waddle, imitating his high wheezy voice (another affliction which didn't help none) until he finally flipped his lid and whirled around and *knocked them squat* – no, a lie: he cried, he always fuckin' cried, 'cos he was a mama's boy, he knew it and they knew it and they all knew he'd never raise a pudgy fist, he was too chickenshit to hit back, but …) but he hadn't been chickenshit those few years later at West Chester High when he struck the fire under the assembly hall on prize-giving (no prizes coming to him anyway) morning, when all those turds had been up there nudging and sniggering and whispering, but soon wailing and screaming and punching, falling over each other to break out of that burning hell-hall, where only three were really roasted by the fire, but fifteen (no teachers damaged – the parents hated *them* for that) kicked off from chokin' and crushed rib-cages.

That day was the turning point for Theodore Albert Monk, 'pissin'-out day', the day he discovered every person had a power, anyone – big, small, fat or skinny – could decide for someone else when their Pay-Off Time (POT) had arrived. You didn't need to be Einstein or Charles Atlas (or even Charlie fuckin' Brown) to choose their day for 'em. Point a stubby finger and raise a meaty thumb like a cocked gun and that was it. Bingo. Not right there and then, of course; but that was decision time, that was as good as. After that you waited for the right moment. Could take days, weeks, maybe months. Thing was, it always came. You gottem when they and nobody else expected it. When *you* were safe.

He'd shown it to insects first, his power, graduating to animals – mice, frogs (slice 'em, dice 'em), Grandma Kaley's old cross-eyed cat (weed-killer in its milk bowl), a stray mutt (lured by half a salami sandwich into a rusted freezer left to rot on the town's rubbish dump – he'd opened it up two weeks later and the stink had made him throw up). Then on to the big time.

Four of 'em he'd wasted (he enjoyed the macho sound of *wasted*), two boys, two chicks. And nobody the wiser.

When he'd moved on to Philly, there'd been two more – three if you counted the spic. In LA almost – *almost* – one (the hooker had fought like a wildcat when, on the spur of the moment – maybe just to get hisself excited – he'd decided to cancel her subscription, and the stiletto-heeled shoe she'd been treading him with for his pleasure had nearly taken out his left eye, hurting him so bad that he'd had to leave her there moaning and hollering in a way he'd thought nobody could with a snapped neck and a belly-full of bruises).

Things had gotten a mite tricky after that. The Pigs had a description, they knew who they were looking for. Hooker had seen him around before, that was the piss-puller, seen him hanging loose with Glass-Eye Spangler (an inch to the left with that stiletto heel and they'd have been calling *him* Glass-Eye, too). And good 'ol boy Spangler knew his drinking buddy's name, where he was from. Turned out there was a small matter of an unsolved crime and a missing delinquent back there in Coatesville. Nah, not the two boys, two chicks – one drowning, one car burning (the lighted rag stuck into the gas filler had blown the tank right under the backseat which the boy and girl were using for a make-out pad at the time), and one rape with strangling as the dessert (or maybe the main course, it was hard to remember now), not those. There was the little mystery of Mama and Uncle Mort, brother and sister, found locked together in bed (joined at the loins, that is) with bed bugs buddying up with maggots on what must have been one sweltering, rotten feast-week, and Rosie Monk's sixteen-year-old, the one they figured was semi-imbecile because he never talked much and lumbered around like … like … *say it* … like one of them fuckin' orangy-tans and just about as smart (this was in the days before Mr Smith), had lit out, making him Number One suspect, since no one in his right brain would even *think* about kidnapping the big fucker (oh yeah, Theodore Albert *aka* Ape had filled his fat with muscle in the two years after POT power), after bludgeoning Mama and that groin-groping bastid Uncle Mort with his battered old Jim Fugosi baseball bat in the bed where they'd grunted and heaved and made the springs sing along.

So the Pigs were on his tail again, years after the event, hot for his ass. And maybe now those cops were finally figuring the big galoot had something to do with those other unexplained homicides, and if not, why not? Neatened up things to hang them on Monk too. Yeah, let's go for it, let's nail the mother-killer, the uncle-pounder, let's hand him the check for them all. They recalled nobody'd liked the fat creep anyway.

Escape. To Vegas. Some stuff on the way, most of it a blur now. Teaming up with Slimeball and Rivas in the glitz city, rolling drunks and mugging hookers for their purses nights, dealing crack days. Fine until the pimps ganged up (a pimp posse no less), sorely aggrieved that their take margin was down because three stooges from outa town hadn't yet learned their place in sub-society. This very point was explained to Monk one night by a big buck who had razor blades glued to the insides of the fingers of one hand so that when he slapped – palm or backhand, made no difference, the blade edges stuck out from either side – neat red lines would criss-cross your cheeks until the cuts got closer and closer to eventually become one huge open wound, while five other hoods crushed Slimeball and Rivas' fingers and toes before chopping off an ear from each and making the boys chew on it (each other's ear, that is). They were saving him for something else, because he was the muscle and he had badly altered one of the girls' features two months ago, turning her into an asset loss, no good to no muthuh.

But what the razor-toting buck hadn't counted on – he had a crazy grin to match his crazy eyes – was that pain hardly meant a pig's ass to Monk (it took extreme and prolonged agony to give Monk any pleasure, even in those days), so the slicing steel could have been chopping cheese for all he cared. Monk did what he had come to know best. POT – Pay-Off-Time – had arrived for the nigguh and introduced itself in the form of Monk's hawked phlegm in his eyes (ol' Uncle Mort, in between feeling him up, had taught young Theodore Albert how to do that to dogs straight out of the pick-up windows) and a grinding of the black's privates by Monk's raised knee. The buck's own razor-blade fingers were used to sever his own jugular.

This last upset had proved too much for the rest of the vigilante squad who, pissed enough already by the cash loss, decided that what they'd had in mind for the ape-walking creep (their girls' description had pin-pointed Monk nicely) wasn't quite special enough. This bozo required something more permanent.

They came for him with open switch-blades and surgeon's hatchets (that season's in-weapon) and Monk would have been chopped ape if he hadn't used the still-gurgling black man as a battering ram.

Oh yeah, he'd gotten away, but had been damaged in the getting (but not as damaged as the two dead he'd left behind). A knife stuck firmly in his shoulder-blade had proved uncomfortable as well as a bad feature for walking the streets. Fortunately, a shithead who knew him on a supplier/client basis and whom he ran into several blocks away obliged him by tugging the knife free after much jiggling and muttering 'man-oh-man' and some giggling. Jiggle and giggle. The junkie had paid for the enjoyment with a windpipe so badly flattened that he talked like Popeye for the rest of his short years.

Once again, Monk was on the hoof, and this time both Pigs *and* Mob were after him. He robbed a drugstore for some travelling money (no gun necessary for a crude dude like Monk), leaving the druggist seriously splattered among his pills and potions.

The old flaky Dodge he stole only took him as far as the outskirts of town before coughing oil and chunking to a permanent demise.

Shoulder all fiery and already beginning to fester in the heat, ragged oozy cheeks like fast-food counters for flies, Monk legged his way down US95 (maybe he had Boulder City in mind – he wasn't thinking straight by then), a fat thumb hoisted (all fingers fisted, no POT sign this) every time he heard an engine motoring up from behind. But who would stop for a hiker with a dark bubbly stain on his back and tomato-ketchup spread across his face? Right. No fucker. Nobody normal.

Except one car did stop.

The black car, its windows all tinted dark and mysterious, glided to a soundless halt beside him, the movement as easy as a vulture landing on a carcass.

Monk shifted his bulk so that he was facing the silent car (no grace in *his* movement, none at all), pain and fatigue stooping him by now (he'd left the dead Dodge at least five miles behind), his clothes and pony-tailed hair powdered with dust, his face, with its scarlet-rose cheeks, puckered up into a shit-eating grimace. For a few moments, he wondered if the occupants were Big Guys who kept Small Guys down (to keep the law in your pocket you had to maintain a certain law yourself) and he waited for a snub-nose to poke through a lowered window like some black viper sliding from its hole.

But a window didn't sink down. And no gun was pointed towards him when the rear passenger door was opened wide.

He squinted to see into the big gloomy interior and could only just make out the dark shape sitting in there among the shadows.

Then a voice said in a persuasive way: 'Need a lift, Theo?'
(That was the first and only time Kline had called him by his first name.)

• 12 •
NEATH

'NOT FAR, LIAM,' SAID CORA, LEANING FORWARD SLIGHTLY IN HER SEAT. 'LOOK
for the gates, just ahead on your left.'

Kline, beside her, opened his eyes and for a moment that seemed no less than
infinite, he and Halloran stared at each other in the rearview mirror. It was
Halloran who averted his gaze and he was surprised at the effort it took to do
so.

Thick undergrowth and trees crowded either side of the road, the greenery
even more dense beyond, the few gaps here and there almost subterranean in
their gloom; these were woodlands of perpetual dusk. The high, old-stone wall
that appeared on the left came as a surprise: it looked firmly rooted as though
having grown with the trees, a natural part of the forest itself, organic life
smothering much of the rough stone and filling cracks. Twisted branches from
trees on the other side loomed over, some reaching down like gnarled tentacles
ready to snatch unwary ramblers.

He noticed the opening in the near-distance, the forest withdrawing there,
allowing the smallest of incursions into its territory. Halloran slowed the
Mercedes, turning into the drive, the roadway here cracked and uneven. The
rusted iron gates before them looked impregnable, like the forest itself. Letters
worked into the wrought iron declared: NEATH.

'Wait for a moment,' Kline instructed him.

Halloran waited, and studied.

Tall weathered columns hinged the gates, stone animals mounted on each
(griffins? he wondered. Too decayed to tell), their blank eyes glaring down at
the car, their lichen-filled mouths wide with soundless snarls. The gates would
be easy to scale, he noted, as would be the walls on either side. No barbed wire
and, as far as he could tell, no electronic warning system. And all the cover
between wall and road that any would-be intruder could desire. Security was
going to be difficult.

Then he noticed, beyond the gates, the lodge-house.

A two-storey building, its stone as seasoned as the walls. Its windows were
as black as the Devil's soul.

Halloran frowned when the thought sprang into his mind.

... *as black as the Devil's soul.*

A phrase remembered from early years in Ireland, only then it had been: *The Divil's owhn soul.* Father O'Connell, thrashing the living daylights out of him, had said it. Thrashing Liam because of the heinous wickedness he had led the two Scalley boys into (the younger one had confessed, fearful of the mortal jeopardy in which his soul had been placed because of Halloran's leadership). Thrashing him because of the sacrilege against St Joseph's, breaking into the church in the hush of night, leaving the dead cat – the boys had found it crushed at the roadside – inside the holy tabernacle, the animal's innards dripping out onto the soft white silk lining the vessel's walls, its eyes still gleaming dully when Father O'Connell had reached in for the chalice the next morning. Beyond redemption was Liam's soul, the priest had told the boy with every sweep of his huge unpriestlike hand, beyond saving, his spirit as graceless and *as black as the Divil's owhn soul.* A creature spawned for Hell itself, and a rogue who would surely find his way there with no problem at all. His troublesome ways would ...

Halloran blinked and the memory was gone; but the disquiet lingered. Why think of boyhood iniquity at that moment? There were worse sins to remember.

'The gates are locked?' The trace of Irish in his voice once more, the unexpected reverie tinting his speech.

'In a way,' replied Kline.

Halloran glanced over his shoulder and the psychic smiled.

'Wait,' Kline repeated.

Halloran turned back and looked through the bars of the gate. There was no movement from the lodge, no one leaving there to come to the entrance. But then his eyes narrowed when he saw – when he *thought* he saw – a shadow shift within a shadow inside one of the lodge's upper windows. His sharpened focus detected no further movement.

'Open up, Monk,' Kline ordered his bodyguard.

With a low grunt, the heavy-set American pushed open the passenger door and hefted himself out. He ambled towards the gate and indolently raised a hand to push one side open, taking it all the way back, its base grating over the road's uneven surface, until foliage poked through the struts. He did the same with the other half, then stood to one side like an unkempt guardsman while Halloran drove on through. He closed the gates once more when the Mercedes drew to a halt inside the grounds.

Halloran had been irritated by a simple procedure which had been dramatized into a ritual. He could only assume that an electronic device in the gate's lock had been triggered by whoever was inside the lodge; yet when driving through, he hadn't noticed any such mechanism.

'I take it there's someone inside ...' he nodded towards the lodge-house '... capable of stopping any uninvited visitors from coming through?'

Kline merely grinned.

Halloran was about to put the question again, more pointedly this time, when he heard the sound of a vehicle braking sharply on the road outside the grounds. He turned swiftly to see the other Shield car reverse back to the opening then turn in.

'Tell Monk to open the gate again,' he said.

'I'm afraid not.' Kline was shaking his head. 'You know the rules, Halloran.' There was a hint of glee in his voice, as though the psychic were enjoying the game now that he was safely home.

'Have it your way.' Halloran left the Mercedes and walked back to the gate, Monk grudgingly opening it a fraction to allow him out. The two Shield operatives waited for him beside the Granada.

'Nearly missed this place,' one of them said as he drew near.

Halloran nodded. 'No bad thing. How about the Peugeot, Eddy?'

'Clean away. No sign at all.'

Halloran wasn't surprised. 'Response from Base?'

'As we figured. The car was stolen from Heathrow's short-term carpark some time last night. As usual the owner had left his exit ticket inside.'

'Should we inform the Blues?' asked the other man, who had been keeping a wary eye on the road.

'That's for Snaith to decide, but I don't think our client would want the police involved at this stage. If things get serious, we might have to insist.'

Both operatives grinned, aware of how much it would take to render a situation 'serious' as far as Halloran was concerned.

'D'you want us to check the grounds?' enquired Eddy, gesturing towards the gate.

Halloran shook his head. 'Off-limits for you two. Patrol the roads around here and keep an eye out for that Peugeot. You never know, they might chance their luck again later. I'll keep my RT with me at all times so you can warn me if you spot anything suspicious. From what I've seen so far this place is high-risk, so stay sharp. Be back here by the main gate in three hours so the next team can take over.'

'Body cover's a bit thin, isn't it?' the second operative remarked, never once allowing his observation of the main road to stray, 'particularly now we're sure the contract's positive.'

'We've no choice. It's how our target wants it. Maybe Snaith and Mather will convince him otherwise through the insurers, but 'til then, we do it as briefed. I'll be back here for changeover, so we'll compare notes then.'

He turned away and the two operatives shrugged at each other. Halloran was never forthcoming with finer details, but they trusted his judgement implicitly; if he wanted the operation to proceed in this way, then they wouldn't argue. They climbed back into the Granada and reversed from the drive.

Once inside, the gate closed behind Halloran with a solid *thunk*, leaving him with an absurd feeling that the estate had been sealed permanently. Monk glowered resentfully at him as he passed and he realized there were going to be problems between them. That was unfortunate; if outsiders had to be involved in an operation, Halloran preferred them at least to be dependable. Ignoring the big man, he went to the Mercedes, gunning the engine as soon as he was inside. Monk's leisurely stride became more brisk when he realized he might be left behind.

'How much of the perimeter does the wall cover?' Halloran asked as the bodyguard lumbered in beside him.

It was Cora who answered. 'Most of the estate's northerly border. Wire fencing and thick hedgerows protect the other aspects.'

None of it was adequate, Halloran thought, but he said nothing. Before moving off, he looked past Monk towards the lodge once more, curious to catch a glimpse of whoever watched the gate from there. The windows could have been painted black so darkly opaque were they.

The car rolled into motion, crunching stones beneath its tyres, gathering moderate speed as it travelled along the winding road through the estate's woodland. The lodge-house shrunk into the distance, then was cut from view by the trees, and it was only at that point that Halloran was able to concentrate on the road ahead without constantly glancing into the rearview mirror.

He pressed a button and the window on his side slid down; the scent of trees wafted through as he inhaled deeply, relishing the air's sharpness, only then realizing how cloying the atmosphere inside the vehicle had become; fear, and excitement, left their own subtle odours, neither one particularly pleasant. The woodland itself was an untidy mix of oak, willow, beech and spruce, no species more dominant than another. Here they canopied the roadway, creating a gloomy tunnel, the air inside cool, almost dank. Ferns stirred on either side, disturbed by the Mercedes' passage.

A sudden stab of colour ahead startled him. It was instantly gone, the angle of vision through the trees changed by the moving car. Then again, a flash of redness among the green shades. The route was curving gently, winding downwards into a small valley, and soon the house was in sight, a wide area of grass and then a placid blue lake spread before it, while wooded slopes framed its other sides. Those hills disturbed Halloran, for he realized it would be easy for intruders to slip unseen down through the trees to the very boundaries of the house itself.

His attention was irresistibly drawn back to the building itself, which appeared to be a curious jumble of irregular shapes. Principally Tudor in period, various sections had apparently been added on during its history with no regard for symmetry. The two gables were of unequal height and pitch, and the twisted chimneys were scattered almost inconsequently over the various roofs. There were different levels of turrets and a wing had been built onto the far side that stood higher than any other part of the building. Yet the overall image was not unpleasing and much of that had to do with the rich colouring of its brickwork, for the walls fairly glowed in the sunlight, the aged stone mottled a warm red, that same redness even within the roof tiles; the gables were half-timbered and the many turrets fringed grey, serving to complement the ruddiness of the main walls.

Although the building as a whole was compact, Neath was nevertheless hugely impressive, its position alone, between the small hills and lake, supplying its own special grandeur. Halloran began to re-assess Kline's worth in terms of personal wealth.

They were moving on level ground again, the expanse of water on their right, the entrance porch to the house looming up on their left; across the lake Halloran could see the muted hills of Surrey. He drew the car to a halt outside the stone entrance, and just behind a white Rover, the porch itself jutting from the building, wide and dented pavings inside leading up to the main door. Both sections of that door were already opening; two robed figures appeared together, dashing forward with heads bowed. They ran to the Mercedes' rear door, one of them eagerly pulling it open for Kline.

The two Arabs bowed even more deeply when Kline stepped out. '*Marhaba, Mouallem,*' they welcomed.

Halloran heard one of them mutter something further as he, himself, climbed from the Mercedes, and he saw Kline smile, the glitter of his dark eyes containing some kind of satisfaction, but no warmth.

'*Youssef meeneeh,*' Kline said quietly.

Halloran opened the other rear door for Cora, while Monk walked around to the back of the car. The bodyguard caught the keys tossed by Halloran against his chest and opened the boot, reaching for the luggage inside. Cora seemed unsteady and Halloran gripped her arm.

'You okay?' he asked. He thought there was apprehension in her expression when she looked towards the house, but it may only have been nervousness, a delayed reaction perhaps to their experience earlier.

'What? Oh yes. Yes, I'm fine.' She stiffened, finding her strength, and he let go of her arm. 'Thank you for what you did back there. You acted quickly.'

'We'll discuss it inside. You look as though you could do with a stiff drink.'

Kline was watching them across the roof of the car. 'Cora needs no excuse for that, Halloran. I bet even you could use one after that nasty little business.' He was smiling gleefully, his earlier panic obviously forgotten.

'Let's move inside as quickly as possible,' said Halloran, scanning the road they had just travelled as well as the surrounding area.

'No need to worry,' Kline assured him. 'Not here, not inside the estate.'

'I wouldn't be too sure of that,' Halloran replied.

'Oh, but I am. Completely. Nothing can touch me here.'

'Then humour me. Let's go in.'

The Arabs and Monk followed behind with the luggage, although Halloran retrieved a black bag himself. They crossed the uneven paving inside the porch and entered the house. Halloran found himself inside a large hall, a coolness rapidly descending upon him as if it had pounced; directly opposite the main door was a screen of linenfold panelling, above that a minstrels' gallery, stout oak beams set in the walls and rising to the high bowed ceiling. A broad stairway led to the floor above from where diamond-paned windows provided inadequate light.

'Refreshments in the drawing room, Asil,' Kline snapped, stone floor and walls creating a hollowness to his words. 'Not for me, though. I've got things to do. Cora, you'll take care of our guest, show him around the place.'

'We need to talk,' Halloran said quickly to Kline.

'Later. We'll talk all you want later.' He skipped up the stairway to their right, soft shoes almost silent against the wood. He turned back to them at the stairway's bend and leaned over the balustrade.

'Can you feel Neath's welcome, Halloran?' he said. 'The house senses you, can you feel that? And it's confused. It doesn't know if you're friend or foe. But you don't really know that yourself yet, do you?' He sniggered. 'Time will tell, Halloran. You'll be found out soon enough.'

Kline continued his ascent leaving Halloran to stare after him.

▪ 13 ▪

CONVERSATION WITH CORA

FROM THIS LEVEL NEATH RESEMBLED A SMALL MONASTERY, THOUGHT HALLORAN. Except that there was nothing godly about the place. The day had become overcast, clouds hanging low and dark over the Surrey hills, so that now the redness of Neath's stonework had become subdued, the floridity deepening to a tone that was like ... the notion disturbed him ... like dull, dried blood. The house *looked* silent, as though it could never contain voices, footsteps, life itself. It might resemble a monastery, but it was hard to imagine invocations inside those walls.

He and Cora were on one of the slopes overlooking Kline's home, Halloran's brief reconnoitre of the estate confirming his doubts about its security. The two thousand acres were enclosed well enough to keep stray ramblers out, but there was no way any interloper of serious intent could be deterred. Kline's confidence in his own safety within the bounds of the estate was surprising, to say the least.

Immediately below them was what once must have been a splendid topiary garden. Now its bushes and hedges had become disarrayed, their sculptured shapes no longer maintained; where once there had been carved animals, cones and spheres, there were protrusions and distortions, the vegetation neither natural nor engineered, but tortured and bizarre. At present these green deformities served only to provide random screening for anyone approaching the house.

'Can we sit for a while?'

Halloran turned to Cora again, the fragile anxiety behind her gaze puzzled him. She had changed into jacket and jeans for their tour of the grounds, the transformation from city lady into country girl both easy and pleasing. Even so, that slight darkness beneath her eyes seemed more pronounced, tainting some of her freshness.

'We've covered quite a distance in a short space of time,' he said. 'I'm a little breathless myself.'

'It's not that. It's ... just peaceful up here.'

He caught the hesitation and wondered at it. He also caught her glance towards the house as she'd spoken. She sank to her knees and he followed suit, lounging back on one elbow while his search roved the grounds below. The lake had become leaden and grey, no breeze stirring its surface, no sunlight dappling its currents.

'Tell me about him, Cora.'

She looked startled. 'About Felix?'

He nodded. 'Is he as mysterious as he pretends? Is he as crass as he pretends? I'll accept that he can do these wonderful things for Magma – why else would they insure his life for so much? – but what is his power exactly, where does it come from?'

Her laugh was brittle. 'Perhaps even he doesn't know the answer to that last question.'

'Why are you afraid of him?'

Her look was sharp, angry. Nevertheless she replied. 'Felix commands respect.'

'Fear and respect aren't the same thing. You don't have to tell me, but is he much more than an employer to you?'

'As you say, I don't have to tell you.'

There was something moving from the trees on a slope at the far side of the house. Halloran watched without alerting the girl.

She mistook his silence for something else. 'I'm sorry,' she said. 'I understand you're only doing your job. I suppose it's important that you know as much as possible about Felix.'

The shape had slunk back into the trees. Too small, too low to the ground to be a deer. Too big and dark to be a fox. Why hadn't it been mentioned that there was a dog on the estate? Maybe it was a stray.

'It isn't quite that important, Cora,' he said. 'I think the reason I ask is that I want to know more about you, not Kline.'

A subtle flaring of her pupils, the movement noticed by Halloran. His words had roused emotions in her. Those dark spots within the brown quickly retreated. 'I suppose that's part of your job too. You obviously think I could endanger Felix in some way.'

'It's possible, but it isn't why I'm interested.'

She gave a small shake of her head, her expression confused. 'Then why ... ?'

He shrugged. 'It's bothering me too. Let's say I don't feel we're strangers.'

Cora stared at him. He wasn't smiling, but there was humour in his eyes. At first she thought he was mocking her, but then he did smile and its warmth was enveloping. That warmth spread through her, seeping into her body as if to purge the coldness there. Yet paradoxically she sensed a chilling danger in this man and she was afraid of how much he would discover about her, about Kline – about Neath itself – before this affair was through. She had sensed Kline's fascination with his newfound protector at their first meeting and it frightened her, for there might be unguarded moments they would all regret. There was a perceptiveness about Halloran, a *knowingness*, that was intimidating as it was reassuring. There was the dichotomy of the man and perhaps that was part of his allure.

'I ... I think we should return to the house,' was all she could think of to say.

He caught her wrist as she began to rise and the touching startled her. 'I'm here to see that no harm comes to you,' he said.

'To Felix you mean,' she replied, staying there on the ground when he took his hand away.

'You're part of it. Your safety is just as important.'

'Not as far as Magma is concerned.' She managed to smile.

'You're part of it,' he repeated, and Cora was unsure of his meaning. 'You still haven't answered any of my questions,' he persisted.

'I'm not sure that I can. I'm not sure that I know.'

He watched her confusion and realized he had delved too soon. Cora could never accept him so quickly: an instinct told him she held secrets that bound her to Kline in some way.

'All right,' he said. 'For now.'

He stood, then reached down to pull her to her feet.

At first Cora thought he was angry, so forceful was his grip; but he held her to his chest for a moment longer than necessary, looking down into her face, a quiet intensity to his gaze.

'Liam ...' she said, but he had already released her and turned away. She watched him for a few moments before following, an unsteadiness to her movement that threatened to make her slip. She caught up with him and Halloran noticed her awkwardness; this time he reached for her arm and held it gently, lending just enough support to help her walk more steadily. Cora's breathing was shallow, nervous, and she felt something had drained from her; not her strength, and not her resolution – Felix Kline had subjugated those a long time ago – but perhaps her fear of Halloran himself.

'Who are you?' she could only whisper.

'Nothing more than you can see,' he replied.

But she felt that was not quite true.

· 14 ·
ROOMS AND CORRIDORS

THERE WERE DARK PLACES IN NEATH, CORNERS, NICHES, WHICH SUNLIGHT COULD never touch, rooms gloomed in permanent dusk, corridors where dust motes seemed to clog the air, halls where footsteps echoed in emptiness. Yet there were also areas of dazzling light, the sun bursting through leaded windows with a force intensified by thick glass; these were cleansing places, where Neath's dank chill could be scoured from the body, although only briefly as other rooms, other corridors, were entered, brightness left behind like some sealed core.

Halloran explored and found many locked doors.

Tapestries adorned hallways. Fine portraits hung in main rooms and on stairways, meaningless to anyone other than direct descendants of the subjects themselves. Curved giltwood furniture displayed itself in arrangements that precluded comfortable use. Ornaments and sculptures were set around the house like museum pieces, there for admiration but perhaps not out of love – or so it seemed to Halloran. The house was a showcase only, full of history, but oddly devoid of spirit, Kline's attempt (presumably) at presenting an aesthetic side to his nature revealing nothing more than an indifference to such things (or at the most, pretensions towards them). The giveaway was the separateness of each item, the lack of relationship to those nearby, every piece of furniture, every sculpture or painting, an isolated entity in itself, set-pieces among other set-pieces. Fine for a museum, but not for a home.

Yet spread among them, as if at random, were curios from a vastly different and more ancient culture: an encased necklace with thinly beaten gold pendants shaped like beech or willow leaves; stone statuettes of a bearded man and a woman, their hands clasped over their chests as though in prayer, their eyes peculiarly enlarged so that they appeared to be staring in adoration; a board game of some kind, its squares decorated with shell and what appeared to be bone, two sets of stone counters of different colour laid alongside; a silver cup with a robed figure in relief. Perhaps these, thought Halloran, along with other similar items, were a clue to where Kline's real interests in art lay, for they provided a consistent thread, a continuity that was missing in the other, later, antique pieces. It would seem that his client had a penchant for the older civilizations.

The room allocated to Halloran was at the front of the house, overlooking the lawns and lake. Furnishings were functional rather than pleasing to the eye: wardrobe, chest of drawers, bedside cabinet – utility fare with no heritage to boast of. The wide bed, with its multi-coloured, lumpy quilt, looked comfortable enough; bedposts at each corner rose inches above the head- and foot-boards, the wood itself of dark oak.

He had unpacked his suitcase before exploring the rest of the building, and placed the black case he'd also brought with him on a shelf inside the wardrobe.

His inspection had taken him to every section of the house – save where the locked doors had hindered him – even out onto the various turrets from where he had surveyed the surrounding slopes with considerable unease. The frontage, with its lawns and placid lake, provided the only point of clear view; the rear and side aspects were defence uncertainties. And worse: there was no alarm system installed at Neath. It was difficult to understand why a man who was evidently in fear for his own safety hadn't had his home wired against intrusion, particularly when his penthouse in the Magma building was a place of high, albeit flawed, security. Well at least conditions here could soon be rectified. Halloran had wandered on through the house, examining window and door locks, eventually becoming satisfied that entry would prove difficult for the uninvited.

Another surprise was that Neath had been built around a central courtyard with a disused fountain, its stone lichen-coated and decaying, the focal point.

Halloran walked along the first-floor corridor overlooking the courtyard and made his way downstairs, quickly finding a door that led outside. The house was quiet and he realized he hadn't seen Cora nor any of the others for over an hour. He stepped out into the courtyard; the flagstones, protected on all sides from any cooling breeze, shimmered with stored warmth. Brown water stains streaked the lifeless fountain, fungus crusting much of the deteriorated stonework; the structure appeared fossilized, as if it were the aged and decomposed remains of something that had once breathed, something that had once moved in slow and tortuous fashion, had perhaps grown from the soil beneath the flagstones. He walked out into the middle of the courtyard, circling the centre-piece, but his interest no longer on it. Instead he peered around at the upper windows.

He had felt eyes watching him, an instinctive sensing he had come to rely on as much as seeing or hearing. From which window? No way of telling, for now they were all empty, as if the watcher had stepped back from view.

Halloran lowered his gaze. There were one or two doors at ground-level other than the one he had just used. No risk these, though, for there was no direct entry into the courtyard from outside the house.

He crossed to the other side of the enclosure and tried a door there. It opened into a kitchen area, a large, tiled room he had come upon earlier. Closing the door again, he moved on to the next, looking into windows as he passed. The house might well have been empty for all the activity he saw in there. The second door opened into another corridor – Neath, he'd discovered, was a labyrinth of such – which was closed at one end by yet another door.

This was a passageway he hadn't discovered on his exploration of the interior and, curious, he stepped inside. To his left was a staircase leading upwards, yet he could not recall finding it when he had circuited the first floor. Probably a staircase to one of the rooms he'd been unable to enter. He decided to investigate that possibility after he'd tried the door at the other end.

He walked down the passage, noting that the door looked somewhat more formidable than any others inside the house. The lock was of sturdy black iron and there was no key inserted. He reached for the handle.

And turned quickly, when he heard a creak on the stairway behind.

One of Kline's Arabs was smiling at him. But just before the smile, Halloran had glimpsed something else in the robed man's expression.

There had been anger there. And apprehension.

• 15 •
A STROLLING MAN

He walked along the pavement blank-faced, his eyes meeting no others, a plainly dressed man, suit as inconspicuous as his features. His hair was thin on top, several long loose strands tapering behind indicating the slipstream of his passage. One hand was tucked into his trouser pocket, while the other held a rolled newspaper.

Occasionally he would glance into a doorway as he went by, no more than a fleeting look as though having care not to bump into anyone on their way out. Not once did he have to slow his already leisurely pace though, his journey along the street unimpeded. On he strolled, perhaps a clerk returning home after the day's work and, judging by his appearance, someone who lived in one of the older houses that hadn't yet succumbed to developers' mania for wharfside properties.

After he had passed one particular doorway he casually tucked the newspaper under his left arm, his pace even, still unhurried.

He walked on and some way behind him two men in a parked car looked briefly at each other, one of them giving a sharp nod. The driver started the engine and gently steered the vehicle away from the kerbside. It came to rest again after only a hundred yards or so further down the street.

The two men settled back to watch and wait.

▪ 16 ▪
A DIFFERENT KLINE

DINNER WAS OBVIOUSLY OF LITTLE INTEREST TO KLINE LATER THAT EVENING. To
Halloran he seemed drained, listless, his sallow skin tight over his cheekbones,
hollowed beneath them. His dark eyes had lost much of their lustre, and his
usual banter was less sharp, as though his thoughts were elsewhere. His
youthfulness had unaccountably vanished, or so it appeared to Halloran, the
man before him looking at least ten years older than the one he had first been
introduced to at Magma.

Maybe the incident earlier in the day had taken more out of Kline than
Halloran had realized. He'd witnessed delayed reaction many times in the past,
had even suffered it himself – the abrupt recognition of what might have been,
the leadening of spirit, the swift evaporation of energy followed inevitably by
a further apathy. True, his client was unpredictable, but Halloran was surprised
at the abrupt change.

Only three had sat for dinner, Cora, Kline and himself, the two Jordanians
serving, Monk off somewhere keeping watch or, more probably, reading his
comic-books. Kline had barely touched his food, which was solid English fare
and not the exotic dishes Halloran had half-expected the Arabs to prepare
(Khayed and Daoud ran the kitchen as well as the rest of the estate for their
employer, with Monk and the Polish bodyguard, Palusinski, sharing the task
of maintenance, both inside and outside Neath itself, with apparently no
outsiders at all allowed within the boundaries).

Opposite him at the long and rough oak table that could easily have seated
two dozen, Cora tried dutifully to engage both Halloran and Kline in conversation.
But more than once she averted her eyes when Halloran spoke directly to her. He
found her demeanour perplexing, yet so were many other aspects of this operation.

'You still haven't explained why there's no alarm system inside the house,'
he said to Kline, putting thoughts of Cora aside for the moment. 'It's hard enough
to understand why there's no system around the grounds, let alone inside.'

Kline sipped wine and his tone was dulled when he replied. 'I have locks, I
have bodyguards. Why should I need anything more?'

Again that different manner of speech, an older man's intonation, the words
themselves more considered.

'I think adequate alarm protection will have to be a condition of contract.'

Lethargy gave way to irritability. 'The contract has already been agreed and signed. You have to take my word for it that I'm quite safe here. Nothing can reach me within these walls, nothing at all.'

'That isn't very sensible.'

'Then consider me stupid. But remember who calls the tune.'

Halloran shook his head. 'Shield does that when we offer our services. I want you to understand that this place is too vulnerable.'

The other man's laugh was dry. 'I'll make a deal with you, Halloran. If you still feel this way about Neath when the weekend is through, we'll discuss your proposals some more. Perhaps you'll be able to persuade me then.'

Halloran rested back in his chair, suspecting that Kline was too arrogant to be swayed by reason alone. He looked over at Cora for support, but again she gazed down at her plate to toy with her food.

'I think we'll need more men patrolling the perimeter,' he said finally.

'That's entirely up to you,' Kline replied. 'As long as none of them stray into the grounds. That might prove unpleasant for them.'

'You didn't tell me there were dogs roaming the estate.'

Both Cora and Kline seemed surprised.

'I saw one of them earlier today,' Halloran continued. 'Just how many are there running around loose out there?'

'Enough to see off any intruders,' answered Kline, his smile distracted.

'I hope you're right. Let's talk about these people who tried to stop us today: you must have some idea who they were.'

'That's already been discussed. Jealous rivals of Magma, or hoodlums who want me for my ransom value.'

'You knew you were in danger, that's why Magma is paying for my company's services. It follows that you're aware of where that danger's coming from.'

Kline wearily shook his head. 'If only that were true. I sense the threat, that's all. I sense many things, Halloran, but sensing is not the same as knowing.'

'You can be pretty specific when you're locating minerals.'

'A different matter entirely. Inert substances are nothing compared to the complexities of the mind.'

'Aren't thought patterns easy to pick up by someone like you?'

'But difficult to decipher. Take your own thought-waves – what am I to deduce from them?' Kline leaned forward, for the first time that evening his interest aroused. A slight gleaming even came back to his eyes.

Halloran drained his wine. One of the Arabs immediately stepped forward and refilled his glass.

'I look at Cora,' Kline said without taking his eyes off Halloran, 'and I feel her emotions, I can sense her fear.'

A small sound from the girl, perhaps a protest.

'Her fear?' questioned Halloran.

'Of me. And of you.'

'She has nothing to fear from me.'

'As you say.'

'Why should she be afraid of you?'

'Because I'm … her employer.'

'That's reason enough?'

'Ask her.'

'This is ridiculous, Felix,' Cora said, her manner cold.

Kline leaned back in his chair, both hands stretched before him on the table. 'You're quite right, of course. It's utterly ridiculous.' He smiled at her, and there was something insidious in that smile.

For an instant, Halloran caught sight of the man's cruelty, a subtle and fleeting manifestation; it flitted across his face like some shadowy creature from its lair, revealing itself to the light momentarily, almost gleefully, before scurrying from sight again.

The moment was swiftly gone, but Halloran remained tense. He saw that Cora's hand was trembling around the stem of her wine glass.

Kline waved a hand towards the two manservants who stood facing one another on opposite sides of the room. 'I can feel Asil and Youssef's devotion,' he said, the smile less sly, weariness returning to weaken his expression. 'I can sense Monk and Palusinski's loyalty. And of course I'm very aware of Sir Victor's avaricious need of me. But you, Halloran, from you there is nothing. No, a coldness that's worse than nothing. Yet perhaps that very quality – can it be called quality? – will protect my life when the moment comes. Your reaction today showed me your skill, and now I'm anxious to know your ruthlessness.' He drew a thin finger along his lower lip as he pondered the Shield operative.

Halloran returned his gaze. 'Let's hope it won't be necessary,' he said.

A void seemed to open up in those sombre eyes of Kline's. His breathing became shallow and Halloran realized the man was somehow afraid.

'Unfortunately it will be,' said Kline, his words no more than a murmur.

• 17 •
A DREAM OF ANOTHER TIME

SECURE AS KLINE FELT WITHIN HIS OWN GROUNDS, MONK HAD THE TASK OF closing up the house completely each night when they stayed on the estate; Halloran, however, had little faith in the big man's diligence, and patrolled the house twice after dinner, on both occasions testing doors and windows. He arranged three-hour shifts with the bodyguard, taking the first until one in the morning himself.

Dinner had been cut short, Kline's evident fatigue finally overwhelming him. He had left the dining room without apology, the two manservants shuffling anxiously in his wake, leaving Cora and Halloran to themselves. Halloran had gently probed in an effort to discover more about her employer, about Neath itself, why certain rooms were inaccessible, who was it that guarded the gates by the lodge-house, where were the dogs kept? But Cora had been unforthcoming, steering the conversation towards matters that had nothing to do with Kline or the estate. It was frustrating for Halloran, as well as puzzling, and he eventually excused himself so that he could phone Mather at home to report on the situation so far and to find out if there was any news on the would-be abductors. He learned that the Peugeot had been found abandoned by the police in a London suburb, and there were no clues as to who had stolen the vehicle. Naturally they had wondered at Shield's curiosity over the theft but Dieter Stuhr, who had made the enquiry through a personal contact on the Force, had promised that all would be revealed at some later date. That statement had, of course, aroused even more interest from the police, for they were all aware of the kind of activities Achilles' Shield was involved in. Mather had warned that total discretion might be difficult to maintain as far as the police were concerned.

At precisely one a.m., Halloran made his way up to the second floor and knocked on the door of Monk's room. The silence around him was occasionally disturbed by the creaking of aged timbers as they settled after the day's heat. Corridors were poorly lit as though power was low. He waited and heard movement from inside the room, heavy but dulled footsteps – no shoes on those lumbering feet – approaching. The door opened only a few inches and a section of the bodyguard's face peered out, his eyelids drooping as if sleep was reluctant to lose its claim. The sour odour of sweat drifted out and it was as unpleasant as Monk's stare.

'Your watch,' Halloran informed him.

'Uh?' came the reply.

'Time to earn your keep. Check exterior doors and all windows first, then settle down in the main hallway. Take a walk round every half-hour, more often if you get bored.'

The door opened wider and he saw that Monk was dressed in vest and loosened trousers, his belly pushing outwards so that the hem of his vest was stretched to its limit, the flesh between it and open belt buckle matted almost black. The hair on his head was no longer tied back, hanging loose around his broad flat face, strands curling inwards to touch his stubbled chin, while the hair on his arms, thick and dark, reached up to his sloping shoulders and splayed there like pubics.

The day of the Neanderthal wasn't quite over, mused Halloran.

Monk moodily turned away, revealing the shambles of his room in the wedge of light from the open door. Magazines and comic-books littered the floor, a tray filled with dirty plates and a beer can rested by the bed – a surprisingly small bed considering the man's bulk. Halloran had no desire to see further.

'Monk,' he said quietly, and the bodyguard looked back. He stood there as if rooted, his shoulders hunched so that his neck seemed sunken into his chest. He glowered at Halloran, who told him, 'Any disturbance at all you come straight to me. Is that understood?'

'You're shittin' me,' was the response.

Halloran shook his head. 'You come and get me. Not Kline. You warn me first.'

'That ain't the way.'

'You find me first or I'll break *your* arms when the fuss is over.'

The bodyguard turned back all the way, squaring himself at Halloran. 'I'm paid to watch out for Mr Kline,' he said, his piping voice as low as he could register.

'I'm being paid more to do the same. You want to discuss it, take it up with Kline in the morning. Tonight you do as I say.'

Monk might well have rushed him there and then and Halloran didn't think it was the memory of what had happened last time that prevented him from doing so: no, it had more to do with getting into trouble with his employer. Monk flicked his tongue across his lips, glistening them, his mind still not made up.

'I want you downstairs in two minutes,' Halloran told him curtly. Then he walked away, hearing something shatter in the room behind. Monk's bedroom must have been even more of a shambles with his dinner things scattered across the floor. Halloran smiled, knowing that a score would have to be settled when this affair was over; he, himself, was prepared to let it lie, but he knew the other man wouldn't share the same view. That was going to be Monk's misfortune.

He returned to his bedroom on the first floor, pausing to look out over the centre courtyard on the way. The moon palely laminated the flagstones, the fountain throwing a misshapen shadow across the whiteness, an irregular stain on a pattern of rough squares. He searched to one side of the fountain, wondering about the sealed door he had found in the short corridor there. It had been Youssef Daoud who had disturbed him as he tried the door.

Halloran had asked where the door led to and why was it locked, but Daoud's comprehension of the English language (it was mentioned in their files that both Arabs spoke good English) had suddenly become very poor, and he could only grin at Halloran and shake his head. Halloran had gone back outside to the courtyard. Later Cora told him that the staircase the Arab had watched him from led to Kline's private quarters.

Darkness crept over the rooftops and down into the well below, thick clouds claiming the moon for their own, dim lights from windows around the house asserting little influence over the blackness. He moved away, going to his room and quietly closing the door behind him, relieved to shut the rest of Neath away for a short while. He shrugged off his jacket, hanging it on one of the posts at the foot of the bed. Taking the Browning Hi-Power from its waist-holster, he placed it on the bedside table, then set his soft-alarm clock for ten minutes to four. With one last scan of the grounds outside the window – there wasn't much to see save for the black humps of hills and an orange glow over a nearby town – he lay on the bed, undoing two more shirt buttons, but leaving his shoes on and laced. He put one pillow on top of its mate and rested back, his eyes closing immediately, the dim light from the bedside lamp no bother at all.

Sleep was not long in coming. And with its dream came a memory ...

... *He could hear the harsh breathing from behind the wood latticework, as though drawing in air was an uncomfortable process for the priest ... Bless me, Father, for I have sinned... Liam wondered why he did not feel the shame he was supposed to. He recounted his 'crimes' against the Holy Father in Heaven and smiled in the unlit confessional, feeling no resentment even in having to reveal secrets to a man whom he had no liking for, and worse, no respect for ... I've lied, Father, I've stolen things ... the bow of the priest's large head in the diamond holes of the struts, a nodded acceptance of the confessor's iniquity... I've abused my own body, Father – that's how the boys were taught to say it, 'abused' instead of 'pleasured' ... and I've called God dirty names ... movement stopping in the adjoining cubicle, the priest's breath momentarily held... Liam's smile widening... I've asked God why He's a wicked bastard, Father ... the bulky head turning towards him, the priest's eyes, unseen but felt, burning through the latticework. He took him from Mam an' me ... the boy's smile hard, his eyes staring ahead, seeing nothing ... Liam, gunmen took your father's life, not God ... why He ... why He made me Mam ... why He made her ... the boy's eyes moistened, the smile still there ... do things ... mad things ... why she's to go away ... Liam – the priest again, gentle now ... why ... the boy's first sob, the hunching of his shoulders, hands reaching up, fingers sinking through the black diamonds of the grille, curling round, clutching and pulling as if to wrench away a barrier against truth... the shadow beyond moving, light thrown to show emptiness there ... the door beside Liam opening, Father O'Connell reaching in, touching the boy's shoulder... Liam pushing him away, shrinking down into the booth's corner, forcing his head hard against his raised knees, tears uncontrolled, thin body jerking with the outflow ... the priest, a burly and dark silhouette, bending forward, arms outstretched ...*

... A tapping on the door.

Halloran's eyes opened immediately, consciousness returning almost as fast. The dream remained as an image, one that could be put aside for the moment. He was moving towards the door, gun tucked into holster, before the tapping resumed. He opened up, one foot rigid against the base of the door so that it couldn't be forced wider.

Outside stood Cora.

• 18 •
UNHOLY COMMUNION

THERE WERE CANDLES ALL AROUND HIM, TALL THICK-STEMMED CANDLES, CANDLES that were black. They hardly lit the chamber, though his wretchedly thin naked body glistened highlights under their subdued glow; the two dark-skinned men had used oil on him, their excitement enhanced by the slippery smoothness of his skin.

And there were eyes watching him constantly. Large, unblinking eyes, grouped together at the far end of the room.

The youth moaned, twisted his head, movement weakened by the frequent injection of fluid into his veins. They kept him passive. But not all the time. Sometimes the Arabs liked to hear him screaming.

No sound could escape this room, they had said, grinning at him, holding each other's hand. This was a secret place, one of worship, where the walls were strengthened by the very earth itself. Scream, they had urged him. Shriek, for our delight, they had said as long needles pierced his flesh. Let us see you weep, they coaxed as sharp things were imbedded in his genitalia.

They had taken the hair from his body, even pulled free the eyelashes, plucked his nostrils clear, so that he remained only gleaming colourless flesh, a languid, loose-muscled object one moment, a fitful shivering creature the next. And sometimes, perhaps because of the drugs, the pain was exquisite.

They had removed his tongue when they grew tired of his words, suspending his body so that he would not suffocate on his own blood, sealing the wound with liquid that blazed more than the cutting. Then they had mocked his gibbering as they used his body with their own, thrusting into him with a force that tore and bloodied him inside.

The youth attempted to move his limbs, but they were restrained, not by drugs but by manacles. He lay on the hard flat surface, arms and legs stretched outwards, body punctured by wounds, many needles still protruding, metal dull in the poor light, thin rivulets of blood, now dried and crusted, on his skin. Every part of him seared pain and, had his senses been more lucid, the agony might have checked his heart. While one channel of his mind struggled for reason, others closed down, refuting the hurt to his body, the degradation it had suffered, instinctively knowing that full acknowledgement could only mean insanity. The remaining dregs of morphia were an ally to their cause.

The low flames wavered, caressed by a breeze. He raised his head from the cold slab he was chained to, the motion sluggish, taking all his strength, and looked down along his own body. The slender spikes in his chest were huge to his fuddled brain, rising like crooked metal poles in a greasy snow field, and their undulation as he breathed became mesmerizing. But light from above was seeping into the chamber. He struggled to keep his head raised, but it was too heavy, the strain was too much. It fell back onto the stone with a sharp crack. He had seen the figures emerge from the passageway though, grouped together at the top of the stairs as if their bodies were joined. The youth moaned aloud, his dread even more acute.

He tried to call out when he heard their footsteps on the stairs, wanting to plead with them, and could only manage an incoherent wailing sound that became a whimper when his head lolled to the side and he saw them approach.

The two Arabs, as ever, were grinning down at him and between them stood – no, sagged, for the others were supporting him – a small man whose ravaged face was so old and so wicked that the youth tried to turn away. But it was impossible – the strength wasn't there; the side of his face could only rest against the stone and his eyes could only stare.

The dark-haired man, whose features were wizened and cruel, skin flaking away as though diseased, gazed on the youth, and his tongue flicked across dry, cracked lips. He extended a tremulous hand, index finger pointing, and trailed a yellow fingernail along the white stomach, bringing the nail up towards the sternum. As it travelled, the finger sank into the flesh, with no apparent effort, leaving a shallow rent behind.

Once more a syringe found a vein in the youth's spindly arm and fluid was pushed into him. The glow rapidly spread through him and he almost smiled his gratitude. Now he could turn his face towards the black, limitless ceiling above.

He was conscious of, but did not feel, the pulling apart of his skin, and the vapour that rose from his stomach into the cool air was no more to him than a light cloud rising from a warm dampness.

The dark-haired man shuffled away, aided by one of the Arabs, the other disappearing to a different part of the room.

The youth lay there on his blood-soaked slab, his body opened, and dreamily wondered why they had gone away. He didn't mind, not at all. It was pleasant lying there, watching steam gently curl upwards from a source near him, but just out of sight. He wanted to drift away, to sleep, but for some reason his mind wouldn't allow him. It was nagging, trying to tell him something, something desperately urgent, but he didn't want to know, the peace after so much pain was too intoxicating. Now the needles were like birthday candles, their heads gleaming as tiny flames. Was it his birthday? He couldn't remember. Any celebration was nice though.

He heard nearby sounds and turned and craned his neck as far as it would go. Nerve-ends twinged only a little. The dark-haired man was inside an alcove, opening something, a cabinet of some kind. No, not a cabinet. One of those … what were they called? The sort of thing they had in churches, a box-thing priests were always poking into. Funny, this place was like a church with all the candles, even though they were black. The stone he lay on was like an altar.

The youth giggled, although the noise he made was more like a gurgle.

The three men converged on the pale, prone body, the dark-haired man carrying a dish of black metal, a veil, black again, draped over its edges. Blood was spilling over from the long scission in the youth's body, spreading in pools on the stone's surface, beginning to trickle down the sides. The youth had scant life left in him.

The veil was drawn away, revealing the dish to be more like a wide-brimmed chalice, for it had a base which was clutched in one trembling hand. With his other hand, the dark-haired man removed the contents and placed it inside the youth's stomach, gently pressing down, soaking it in blood, smothering it in slithery organs.

Now the youth did scream, a piercing screech that echoed around the stone walls of the chamber, for no drugs could deaden the pain nor the horror.

He was alive, but barely, when the Arab on the other side of the stone raised the tool he had collected and began cutting into the youth's outstretched limbs.

And still those myriad eyes stared, never closing, never wavering.

▪ 19 ▪
CORA'S NEEDS

'I NEED COMPANY,' SHE SAID SIMPLY. 'I GET … FRIGHTENED WHEN I'M ALONE IN this house.'

Halloran had opened the door wider and she'd hurried by him, glancing back over her shoulder as if someone had been stalking her along the corridor. He looked out to make sure there really was no one there.

He turned and she was putting the bottle and glasses she'd brought with her on the bedside cabinet.

'I remembered you liked Scotch,' Cora told him, and there was no confidence in her voice.

He shook his head. 'I'm on watch again in …' he checked his wristwatch '… a couple of hours. You go ahead if you want.'

She did. Cora poured herself a stiff measure, turning slightly away from him to avoid his eyes, and he wasn't sure if she felt guilty at coming to him in the middle of the night or because she needed a drink. He closed the door.

Cora wore a white bathrobe against the night chill. 'You must think me silly. Or …' She let the sentence trail away.

Halloran walked towards her, lifting the big automatic from its holster and laying it beside the bottle and empty glass. 'We all have fears,' he had said.

Halloran began to move into her, taking care, even though she dug her fingers into his naked back, urging him on. Her teeth nipped his neck, his shoulder, as she squirmed beneath him, thrusting herself upwards. Cora still wore the bathrobe and he pushed it open so that he could caress her breasts. She moaned and there was a desperation to the sound. He lifted himself so that he could see her flesh, could kiss her breasts. He bent to a raised nipple and softly drew on it with his lips, moistening the tip with his tongue. She caught her breath, then let it escape in an unsteady sigh. He pulled the robe from her and tossed it over a chair, then turned back to her welcoming naked body.

He let his fingertips trail away, touching her side, her hip, his hand moving inwards so that it was between them, his palm smoothing her stomach, fingers reaching down into her hair. Her thighs rose around him and he was inside her, pushing inwards, meeting only slight resistance. Cora's hands were low on his back and they pulled him tight so that he lost control of the movement. He was drawn into her sharply, causing her to give a little cry of pain.

Every part of her seemed stretched, her muscles stiffened as if she had been pierced rather than entered. Halloran's demand now matched hers as he felt the familiar floating sensation, the incredible tensing of his own muscles, the swift rise towards the breaking of that tension. He gasped air and the low moan came from him this time.

But it changed. Her clutching altered in intensity, became fraught rather than encouraging; her cries became those of frustration rather than passion. Halloran slowed his rhythm, aware that he was losing her.

Cora's legs straightened and her motion subsided, then became still. She turned her face away from him. Perplexed, Halloran raised himself and looked down on her. A tear gathered in the corner of her eye, welling there and finally spilling.

'Cora... ?'

'Please, Liam. Help me.'

He frowned.

Her eyes closed. 'In my robe,' she said so softly he scarcely heard.

When Halloran left the bed and found the thin coils of leather inside the bathrobe's pockets, he began to understand ...

• 20 •
ABDUCTION

They had watched the man with the strange scar that looked like the continuation of a smile leave the building and the observer in the passenger seat of the car nodded his head in affirmation. The man who had earlier ambled down that same street carrying a rolled-up newspaper leaned forward from the back, resting an arm on the top of the driver's seat, his face keen with interest.

The balding figure had turned in the other direction to where their vehicle was parked and they allowed him to get some distance away before the backseat passenger reached for the doorhandle. The man in front stopped him with a motion of his hand. Their quarry was unlocking a car parked by the roadside.

The driver switched on the ignition and waited for the other car to pull out. When it did so, they followed.

They came for him before dawn, easily and quietly forcing the lock on the door to his basement apartment without causing damage. He awoke only when they were at his bedside, his cry of '*Wer ist da?*' quickly stifled by his own bedclothes. Several blows were dealt to his head, the first two stunning him (the second breaking his nose in the process) but the third, delivered with impatient strength, rendered him unconscious. The fourth blow was just for the satisfaction.

His limp body was removed from the bed and dressed, wallet placed in an inside pocket, watch strapped to his wrist. The bloodied sheet was then stripped from the bed and folded into a neat square. It would be taken with them. The bed was remade and, first checking that everything was in order, they carried Stuhr into the hallway, then up the short concrete stairway to the street where a car was waiting. The last man carefully closed the front door behind him. There was no wife, no lover, no one at all to witness the German's abduction.

• 21 •
BENEATH THE LAKE

MORNING HAD BROUGHT WITH IT A LOW-LYING MIST, THE NIGHT'S DAMPNESS evaporating as the earth slowly warmed again. Trees in the distance appeared suspended in the air; low bushes nearby were like spectral animals crouching in the whiteness, waiting for prey.

Halloran scanned the slopes above the mist as he walked through the neglected gardens, looking for any sign of movement on them, studying one spot for a while, going back to it seconds later to see if anything had altered. He also kept an eye out for the dogs that apparently roamed the estate, even though Cora had told him they never came near the house itself – he had little faith in that particular notion, wondering just how they could be trained to keep away. He thought of her as he walked, confused by the ambivalence of his feelings towards her. The bondage and the harshness of their lovemaking had helped satisfy Cora, but his own pleasure had been limited. True, his arousal had been enhanced to begin with, but the satisfaction afterwards had not been so complete. Prudish guilt, Halloran? Was the Catholicism of his youth still intrinsic to his attitudes? With all he had been through, all he had done, he doubted it. Maybe he'd been mildly disappointed in her; and yet her inclination, her weakness had made Cora more vulnerable to him. After, when she had risen from the bed to find her robe, he had noticed marks across her back and buttocks. He made no comment, aware that they could only be faded whipmarks. But he couldn't help wondering what else there was to discover about her.

He rounded the corner of the house and saw the mist shrouding the lake, slowly rolling across its surface, shifted by a mild breeze. His feet crunched gravel as he approached the dew-stippled Mercedes. Halloran dropped flat to inspect the underneath of the car, searching with a pen-torch for any object that could have been attached during the night. He quickly checked all underside parts, then the wheel wells, shock absorbers and brake lines. Satisfied, he walked around the vehicle looking for grease spots, pieces of wire, hand prints, even disturbances on the gravel near the car doors. Before opening each door fully, Halloran ran a credit card around the tiny gaps to check for wires. This done, he sniffed the interior before entering, seeking the smell of bitter almonds or any other odd odour. Wary of pressure detonators, he checked the dashboard, glove compartment and ashtrays without putting any weight on the seats. He then looked under the seats. He examined the engine, using the credit-card check once more before lifting the hood completely; afterwards he did the same with the trunk. Only when this ritual was complete did he start the engine and let it run for a few minutes, moving the car backwards and forwards a few feet. Sure that the Mercedes had not been tampered with during the night, Halloran switched off and climbed out, locking up again before leaving it.

'Was all that really necessary?' a voice asked from the porch.

He turned to find Felix Kline watching from just inside, his arms folded as he leaned one shoulder against the stonework. He was dressed casually once more – jeans and loose-fitting jacket, a sweater underneath. And he had a grin on his face that dismissed all the fatigue Halloran had noticed the night before.

'I'd have done the same even if the Merc had been locked away in a garage overnight,' Halloran replied. 'I'll check out the Rover if it's unlocked.'

'So you really didn't believe me when I told you I was safe here.'

Halloran shrugged. 'It isn't Shield's policy to take chances.'

'Nope, I suppose not.' Kline emerged from the shade, stretching his limbs and looking up at the sky. 'It's going to be a good day. You want to take a trip, Halloran? A little pre-breakfast exercise, huh? Something to keep you in trim.'

'What've you got in mind?'

'Follow the leader and you'll find out.'

He strode off in the direction of the lake and Halloran was surprised at the briskness of his step. Only last night Kline had appeared overcome by exhaustion, his features haggard, all movement wearied; this morning the man exuded energy.

'C'mon, forget about the other car,' Kline called back cheerfully.

Halloran walked after him at a more leisurely pace, although he was far from relaxed: all the while he kept an alert eye on their surroundings, looking for any sudden change in the landscape, any glints of light that might be sun reflecting off binoculars or a rifle barrel; he paid particular attention to the road leading from the estate's entrance.

Kline was well ahead, almost at the lake's edge. Occasionally he would wind his arms in the air or skip full circle, and Halloran half-expected him to do a cartwheel at any moment. It was as if the small man had too much energy to spare.

The ground dipped slightly towards the water and Kline was stooping, only his head and shoulders in view. Halloran hurried his pace and found his client on a low jetty; moored to it was a rowing boat.

'This'll set you up for the day,' Kline said as he untied the mooring rope.

'No outboard?'

'I like the quietness of the lake, its stillness. I don't like engines upsetting that. Monk or Palusinski usually do the rowing for me, but you can have that privilege today.' Kline hopped into the boat and settled at its stern. 'Let's get going.'

'There won't be much to see with this mist,' Halloran remarked, stepping onto the jetty.

'Maybe,' Kline replied, turning away to look across the cloud-canopied surface.

Halloran climbed aboard, using a foot to push the boat away from the landing-stage. Sitting on the middle bench, he used one oar to set the boat further adrift, before sliding both into their rowlocks. Turning about, he set course for the middle of the lake, soon finding an easy rhythm, their passage through the curling mists smooth and unhurried. His position gave Halloran an opportunity to study his companion at close range and he realized Kline's change had little to do with any physical aspect, but was linked with the man's volatile nature, his puzzling split-personality, for nothing in his features had altered. There was just a brightness to him, a shining in those dark eyes, a sharpness in his tone. Not for the first time, Halloran wondered if his client was on drugs of some kind.

Kline, whose face had been in profile, suddenly swung round to confront him. 'Still trying to figure me out, Halloran?' He gave a short laugh. 'Not easy, is it? Nigh on impossible, I'd say. Even for me.' His laughter was longer this time. 'Thing of it is, I'm unlike anyone you've ever met before. Am I right?'

Halloran continued rowing. 'I'm only interested in your safety.'

'Is that what your bosses at Shield instruct you to tell your clients? Is that in the handbook? You can't deny you're curious though. Wouldn't you really like to know more about me, how I got so rich, about this power of mine? You would, wouldn't you? Yeah, I know you would.'

'I admit I'm interested.'

Kline slapped his own knee. 'That's reasonable.' He leaned forward conspiratorially. 'I can tell you I wasn't born this way. Oh no, not *quite* like this. Let's call it a late gift.' His smile was suddenly gone and, although his eyes bore into Halloran's, Kline seemed to be looking beyond.

'You make it sound as if your psychic ability was handed to you.' An oar had dredged up some rotted weeds and Halloran paused to free the paddle end. The tendrils were slick under his touch and he had to tug several times to clear the wood. When he dipped the oar back into the water he found Kline was smiling at him, no longer preoccupied with distant thoughts.

'Did you sleep soundly last night?' the dark-haired man enquired.

Was his smile really a leer? And why the abrupt change in topic? 'Well enough for the time I had,' Halloran replied.

'You weren't disturbed at all?'

'Only by Neath's lack of security. You're taking unnecessary risks here.'

'Yeah, yeah, we'll discuss that later. Cora's an interesting lady, don't you think? I mean, she's not quite what she seems. Have you realized that?'

'I don't know much about her.'

'No, of course not. Has she told you how she came to be working directly for me? I decided I wanted Cora the first time I laid eyes on her in old Sir Vic's office about three years ago. Recognized her potential, y'see, knew she had … hidden depths. Know what I mean, Halloran?'

Halloran ignored the insinuations, but had to hold his rising anger in check. 'She obviously makes a good PA.'

'You're right, she does. Aren't you curious though?'

Halloran stopped rowing, resting the oars in the water, letting the boat drift. 'About what?' he said evenly.

'Hah! You are. Me and Cora, what goes on between us. Does she do more for me than just arrange schedules, type letters? Maybe you want to know if she and I are lovers.'

'That's none of my business.'

Kline's smile was sly. 'Oh no? I'm an extremely aware person, Halloran, and it isn't hard for me to sniff out something going on under my nose. I don't mind you having your fun as long as you remember who Cora belongs to.'

'Belongs to? You're talking as if you own her, body and soul.'

Kline turned away, still smiling. He squinted into the low white mist, as if to pierce it. The trees and slopes were faded along the lake's edge, the haziness of the sky belying the sharpness of the early morning air.

'Can you feel the weight of the water beneath us?' Kline suddenly asked, still looking away from the other man. 'Can't you feel the pressure underneath these thin wooden boards, as if all that liquid down there, all the slime and murkiness that lies on the bottom of the lake, wants to break through and suck us down? Can you sense that, Halloran?'

He almost said no, a total rejection of the notion. But then Halloran began to feel the potency beneath his feet, as if the water there really could exert itself upwards, could creep through those tight cracks between the boards like some glutinous absorbing substance. Kline's suggestion had somehow turned the lake into something less passive. Halloran shifted uncomfortably on the rowing bench.

A ripple in the lake caused the boat to sway.

Kline's attention was on him once more and his voice was low in pitch, less excitable, when he spoke. 'Look over the side, look into the lake. Notice how silky is its skin beneath this mist, and how clear. But how far can you see into the denseness below? Come on, Halloran, take a peek.'

Although reluctant, Halloran did so. No big deal, he told himself, no reason to be churlish. He saw his own shadow on the lake.

'Keep watching the water,' came Kline's quiet voice. 'Watch how it swells and falls, as soft as anything you could ever wish to touch. Look into your own shadow; how dark it makes the water. Yet somehow the darkness allows you to see more. And what if the whole lake was shadowed? What depths could you perceive then?'

Halloran was only aware of the blackness of his own reflection. But the blackness was spreading, widening in tranquil undulations, forcing away the mist as it grew. Kline's voice coaxed him to keep his eyes fixed on the lapping water, not even to blink lest that merest of movements disturb the placid surface, to stare into the darkness until his thoughts could be absorbed ... absorbed ... *absorbed* by the lake itself, drawn in so that what was hidden before could now be viewed ...

'... *There are monsters beneath us, Halloran* ...'

He could see the shapes moving around, sluggish, lumbering patches of greater darkness, and it seemed to him – it was *insinuated* to him – that these were grotesques who knew nothing of light, nothing of sun, creatures who slumbered in the depths, close to the earth's core. Among them were sleeker denizens, whose very tissue-like structures prevented pulverization under such pressure; they glided between their cumbersome companions, two opposite natures co-existing in a nocturnal underworld. There were others with them, but these were less than fleeting shadows.

Halloran sensed their yearning, the desire to ascend and make themselves known to the world above, weary of perpetual gloom but imprisoned by their own form. Yet if they could not rise, perhaps something of what they sought could be lured down to them ...

The boat tilted as Halloran leaned further over the side.

'*Touch the water,*' he was softly urged. '*Feel its coldness* ...'

Halloran stretched his hand towards the lake that had become a huge liquid umbra, and there was a stirring below at his approach, a kind of quivering expectancy.

'... *sink your fingers into it* ...'

He felt the wetness and its chill numbed more than his flesh.

'... *deeper, let it taste you* ...'

The water was up to his wrist, soaking his shirtsleeve.

'... *reach down, Halloran, reach down and* ...'

He heard laughter.

'... *touch the nether-region* ...'

Halloran saw the shapes rising towards him, mutations that should only exist in the depths, mouths – were they mouths? They were openings, but were they *mouths*? – gaping, ready to swallow him in ... to *absorb* him ...

The laughter was sharper, startling him to his senses. Halloran pulled his hand clear, standing in the boat as if to push himself as far away from those rearing, avaricious gullets as possible.

Still they surged upwards, climbing as a single gusher, an almost solid stream of misshapen beings, terrible unearthly things without eyes but which had limbs that were stunted and as solid as their bodies, while others were only tenuous substances housed around jagged needle-teeth ... coming closer, rushing as if to shoot above the surface itself ...

... Until they began to disintegrate, to shatter, to implode, for they were never meant for the fine atmosphere of the upper reaches.

He heard their anguished screams though there were no sounds – their torment was in his mind only. All around the boat the water was bubbling, white foam spouting upwards as if the lake were boiling. Here and there geysers appeared, jetting into the air and carrying with them – or so Halloran imagined – remnants of flesh, all that was left of the abyssal creatures.

The boat pitched in the ferment and Halloran quickly sat, both hands gripping the sides for support, staying that way until the turbulence began to subside, the lake becoming peaceful once more.

The two men were in an area of clarity, for the mist had been driven back to form a wide circle around the boat. Everything was still within that clear area, the boat now barely drifting.

The only sound was Kline's low chuckling.

• 22 •
FOOD FOR DOGS

CHARLES MATHER WAS KNEELING AMONG HIS SHRUBS WHEN HIS WIFE CALLED him from the terrace steps. Always used to rising early, he had found the habit hard to break after leaving military service. So nowadays, rather than disturb Agnes, who did not share his fondness for early-morning activity, he would creep from their bedroom, dress in the bathroom, take tea in the kitchen, then wander out into the garden, which had become his second love (Agnes would always be his first). Whatever the season, there was always work to be done out there, and for him there was no better way to start the day than with lungs full of sharp – and at that time of the morning, reasonably untainted – air. The only negative factor was that the chill (always a chill first thing, be it winter, spring *or* summer) played silly-buggers with the metal in his leg.

He looked up from the bed he had been turning over with a short fork. 'What's that, m'dear?'

'The telephone, Charles. Mr Halloran is on the telephone. He says it's important that he speaks to you.'

Agnes was a trifle irritated because she'd had to climb from a bath to answer the phone, knowing that her husband would never hear its ringing in the garden. Here she stood shivering with the morning freshness and catching pneumonia by the second.

Mather pushed himself up from the padded kneeler and, the tip of his cane sinking into the soft earth, he hobbled towards the terrace.

'I should get back inside if I were you, Aggie,' he said as he awkwardly climbed the steps. 'You'll catch your death of cold standing around like that.'

'Thank you for your concern, Charles, but I'm sure poking around in the damp grass for a couple of hours hasn't done much for your leg either,' she replied more tartly than she felt. 'I think you'd better take a bath right after me.'

'Mother knows best,' he agreed with a smile. 'Now you get yourself back indoors before I whip off your dressing-gown and chase you naked around the garden.'

She quickly turned to hide her own smile and walked to the patio doors.

'That might give the neighbours a breakfast thrill,' she said over her shoulder.

'Y'know,' he murmured, limping after her and admiring her rear with almost as much enthusiasm as when they were younger, 'I really believe it would.'

He took the call in his study, settling down into an easychair first and waiting for the click that signalled Agnes had replaced the upstairs receiver. 'Liam, Charles here. I hadn't expected to hear from you today.'

There was no urgency in Halloran's voice. 'I've been trying to contact Dieter Stuhr since eight this morning, but had no luck.'

'As we have an ongoing operation he'll be at Shield all weekend,' said Mather. 'I assume you've already tried to reach him there though.'

'I thought I'd probably catch him at home earlier, then I rang the office. No answer from there either.'

Mather checked his wristwatch. 'H'mn, just after nine. He'd have one other coordinator with him today and she should have arrived by now.'

'Only Stuhr would have a key.'

'Then she might be waiting outside at this moment. It's not like Dieter to be late, but perhaps he's on his way. That could be why you missed him.'

'I rang his apartment over an hour ago.'

'Well, he could have been delayed. Look, I'll get on to Snaith – don't see why his Saturday shouldn't be disrupted – and between us we'll see what we can find out. No doubt it'll prove to be something trivial – his car's probably had an upset.' With his free hand, Mather rubbed his aching knee. 'D'you have a problem there at Neath, Liam?'

'I wanted to arrange for extra patrols outside, that's all. And I think our men should be armed. Security here is virtually nil.'

There was a pause, but Mather sensed that Halloran wanted to say more. When no further words came, the older man spoke up: 'Anything else bothering you, Liam?' The question was put mildly, but Mather knew his operative well enough to understand something was wrong.

More silence, then, 'No, nothing else. Our client is unusual, but he can be handled.'

'If there's a problem between you two, we can switch. No need for added complications, y'know.'

'Uh, no. Leave things as they are. Let me know what's happened to the Organizer, will you?'

'Surely. Soon as we know something ourselves. Perhaps Stuhr stayed somewhere else overnight – I understand it frequently happens to single men. Could be whoever he's with has found ways to detain him.'

'It's not like him to be out of touch.'

'I agree, particularly when there's an operation in progress.' Mather was frowning now. 'We'll keep you informed, Liam, and in the meanwhile we'll organize some extra cover for you. I assume last night went without incident?'

'It was quiet. Anything more on the stolen Peugeot?'

'Still drawn a blank there, I'm afraid. Police can't help. You're sure our client doesn't know more than he's telling?'

'I'm not sure of anything.'

Mather stopped soothing the ache in his knee. Again he waited for Halloran to continue, but all that came through was atmospherics on the line. 'It might be an idea if I paid Neath a visit myself,' he suggested.

'We'll be back in London on Monday. Let's you and I meet then.'

'If you say so. Look, I'll get back to you as soon as I've got some news.'

'Fine.'

He heard the click as the line was disengaged and he held his own phone close to his ear for several seconds before putting it down. Mather was thoughtful for several more moments before he lifted the receiver again.

Halloran stood by the telephone in the large open hallway, his hand still resting on the receiver. He was concerned about Dieter Stuhr's absence, well aware that it was out of character for the German to go missing during a major assignment (or even a minor one, for that matter). Maybe, as Mather had suggested, he was having problems getting into the office that morning. Less likely was that he'd been detained at some other address; the Organizer didn't run his life that way – he'd have at least let Shield know where he could be contacted no matter how impromptu the situation. Halloran ran his fingers across his as yet unshaven chin. Maybe Kline – and Neath itself – was getting to him. He was beginning to feel uneasy about everything.

There were footsteps on the staircase behind him. He turned to find Cora approaching, her descent faltering momentarily when he looked into her eyes, her hand touching the wide balustrade for balance.

'Good morning, Liam.' Her greeting was subdued, as if she were not sure how he would react towards her.

'Cora,' he responded. He moved to the foot of the stairs and waited. Neither one smiled at the other and both were conscious that this was not the usual way for lovers to say hello after a night of intimacy.

'Have you had breakfast?' she asked, the question put to break the awkwardness between them rather than out of any real interest.

'I'm on my way in,' Halloran replied. He touched her arm to stop her from walking on. She looked up at him, startled. 'Cora, why didn't you warn me about Kline?'

She could not conceal the tiny flicker of alarm that showed in her eyes.

'Why didn't you tell me he had the – I suppose you'd call it 'power' – to hypnotize? We took a little trip this morning, out on the lake. He made me see things there, things I never thought possible. Creatures, Cora, monsters that seemed to be living in the slime beneath that water. I don't know whose imagination he dredged them from – his or mine – but they scared the hell out of me even though common sense told me they couldn't really exist. He froze me, and it's been a long time since anyone did that.'

'He was playing games with you.' She had moved closer and her voice was quiet, almost mournful. 'It was Felix's way of showing you how manipulative his mind is, how sometimes he can direct images into the minds of others.'

Halloran shook his head. 'Thought transference – it's the same as hypnosis.'

'No. No it isn't. He can't make you *do* things, control your actions. He can only suggest images, make you *feel* something is happening.'

Halloran thought back to the white room at the Magma building, remembering his first encounter with Kline, the finger prodding him in the darkness when no one was near, reaching out and touching withered skin when only he and Kline were in the room ... 'At least it makes a kind of sense,' he said aloud, although it was more a rationale for himself.

Her laugh was brittle. 'Don't look for sense in any of this,' she said. Cora slipped from his grip and made her way towards the dining room.

A creak from the balcony above. He looked up sharply and was just in time to see the bulky shape of Monk stepping back out of sight. Halloran was sure the big man had been grinning.

'Well, I can see your appetite hasn't been spoilt by this morning's little upset.' Kline waved away the Arab who had been pouring him more coffee.

Halloran glanced up from his plate and returned his client's smile. 'It takes a lot to do that.'

'Oh yeah? For a moment there in the boat I thought you were going to puke. Couldn't figure it – there was hardly a ripple in the lake. Unless all that mist out there disorientated you – that can often make you giddy, y'know, that and the drifting sensation. You had me worried.' He sipped from his cup. 'Youssef, give Miss Redmile some more coffee. She looks as if she needs it. Make it strong, leave the cream. Cora, you've got to eat more than you do, you're going to waste away otherwise. Don't you think she looks kinda drawn, Halloran? You not sleeping well, Cora?'

Halloran had to agree: she looked pale, the dark smudges under her eyes even more pronounced.

'I think that business yesterday is having some effect on me,' Cora said. 'Delayed reaction, I suppose.'

'The attempted kidnapping?' The incident sounded pleasurable to Kline. 'There was no problem, not with our hero along to protect us. Those bastards didn't stand a chance, am I right, Halloran? Not with you around. I bet they couldn't believe their eyes when they saw our car reversing away like a bat outa ...' He didn't complete the sentence, gulping coffee instead.

'Hopefully your own driver, Palusinski, will have learned the technique by now. That and a few others to get away from a road-block fast.' Halloran continued eating, a surprisingly good English breakfast provided by the two Jordanians. He noticed that Kline, for all his jibes at the girl, hadn't eaten much either. Monk probably made up for the pair of them in the kitchen.

'Were you an army man, Halloran?'

The question from Kline was unexpected.

'Most of your outfit are ex-military, aren't they?' Kline went on. 'You ever killed anybody? Shot them dead, knifed them? You ever done anything like that?'

Cora was watching him, along with her employer. Halloran leaned back
from the table. 'What makes you ask?' he said.

'Oh, curiosity. Wondered if you had the capability. Can't be an easy thing
taking someone else's life away. No, got to be the hardest thing in the world to
do. Or is it? Maybe it's easy once you have the know-how, the experience. Have
you had the experience? Could you do it?'

'It would depend on the situation.'

'Hah! Let me give you a situation then. Suppose those creeps yesterday had
managed to stop our car. Suppose they came at me with guns – which,
presumably, given the chance they would have. Would you have used your
own weapon?'

'That's why I'm here, Kline.'

'Okay. Let's change the scenario a little. Say they held a gun at Cora's head
and threatened to blow it off if you made a move towards them. You got your
own gun in your hand and it's pointed in their direction. They're dragging me
into their car and the guy with Cora is blocking your way. What would you do
in that situation? Would you risk her life to protect me? I'd be interested to
know.' He smiled at Cora. 'I'm sure she'd like to also.'

Halloran looked from one to the other, Kline grinning, enjoying the moment,
Cora uncertain, as though the question was more than academic.

'I'd let them take you,' he replied.

Kline's grin faded.

'Then I'd negotiate the ransom for your release.'

His client's fist hit the table. 'That's the wrong fucking answer! You're being
paid to look after me, Halloran, nobody else! Not her, nobody!'

Halloran kept his tone level. 'By shooting the one who held Cora – and I
could probably do it without her being harmed – I'd be endangering your life.
Everyone would get gun-happy, and undoubtedly you'd be the second target
after me. It'd make sense to keep things peaceful, bargain for your release later.'

Kline was noticeably quivering. 'Bargain for my release? You crazy fuck.
They could take the money and then kill me.'

'It doesn't work that way. These people are normally professional in what
they do – to break a negotiated contract would mean they'd lose credibility next
time.'

'You talk as if the whole thing is nothing more than a business.'

'That's just what it is, a multi-million pound business. Kidnap and ransom
has become one of the world's few growth industries. Sure, every once in a
while you get amateurs trying their hand, but they're few and far between, and
generally frowned upon by their own but more competent kind – their bungling
makes successful transactions more difficult for the professionals. It doesn't
take organizations like mine, or the police, to discover which type we're dealing
with, and I have to admit I prefer to be up against professionals – they're more
predictable.'

'And that bunch yesterday? How would you classify them, Halloran?'
Kline's fists were clenched on the table-top and his lips were drawn tight.

'I'd say they knew what they were doing. The car they used wasn't traceable, they were patient and waited for exactly the right moment. Fortunately for us we had them spotted before they made their move.'

'They weren't that good. They failed, didn't they?'

'Only because we were better. And the fact that they managed to get clean away confirms my belief that they were competent. Once the first attempt failed they didn't compound their mistake by giving chase. That could have been too messy. My guess is they'll be patient a while longer, wait for the right opportunity to come along. Or, at least, engineer that opportunity themselves. Now they know we're on the alert they'll be even more cautious.'

'They'll try again?' It was Cora who had asked the question.

Halloran looked at her in surprise. 'Of course. But at least we have the slight advantage of knowing our client is a definite target.'

'I already told you that!' Kline was glaring at him, but although his words were spoken angrily, the shrillness had gone from them. 'Why d'you think Magma hired your company in the first place? You think I'm on some kind of ego trip? Or suffering from paranoia? This is a *real* situation, Halloran, I told you that from the start.'

'Okay, so let's go back to an earlier question: who or what organization do you think is behind it? I still can't accept that you've no idea.'

'Have any of your previous so-called targets known just who was out to get them? Why d'you expect me to?'

'Because you were aware before an attempt was ever made.'

Kline's sigh transmuted into a groan. 'After all I've shown you, you still don't believe.'

'It's precisely because of what I know about you that I don't understand why you can't sense who your enemies are.'

For the first time Kline looked unsure. His eyes went to Cora, then back to Halloran. 'There's the mystery, Halloran,' he said. And then, as if to himself, he repeated, 'Yeah, there's the mystery.'

Once more Halloran was checking through the house, prowling the corridors, ensuring that no outside door or window had been left unlocked. Even in daytime he wanted Neath shut tight. It was when he was passing along the first-floor hallway overlooking the inner courtyard that he paused. A door was opening on the other side of the decayed fountain.

He waited by the window and watched, curious, as Khayed came through. The Arab was carrying a round metal container with handles on either side and by the way Khayed's body leaned backwards the burden had some weight. He scuttled across the yard, calling out to someone behind. Youssef Daoud appeared at the same doorway and he, too, dressed in the robes of his country as was his companion, carried a similar metal container. Both men were laughing and apparently joking as they went through another door leading to the front of the house.

On impulse, Halloran hurried downstairs and went out into the courtyard. He quickly crossed over and went through the door the two Arabs had emerged from. He was in the short passageway he had entered the night before, at one end the stairway, at the other the sturdy closed door. He walked to the latter and tested the handle. It was still locked. Or, if the two men had brought the containers from there, locked again.

Halloran stooped to examine the lock and immediately felt cold dank air from the keyhole on his cheek. He touched the stone floor at the door's base and the chill draught was even more noticeable. It had to lead to a cellar of some kind, perhaps where Kline kept his best wines.

Noises outside. The Arabs returning. Halloran straightened, taking one last look at the lock as he did so. Old and strong, large keyhole needing a long key. Shouldn't prove too difficult to open. But he wondered at his own curiosity. And why not ask Kline or Cora what was down there? He also wondered why he was reluctant to do just that.

The voices outside were louder, approaching.

He quickly went down the short length of the passage and stepped through the open doorway. The two Arabs stopped when they saw him. The one called Khayed was the quickest to regain his composure, his friend's look of hostility dissolving a fraction later.

Khayed gave a small bow and regarded Halloran questioningly. '*Assayed*?'

'I found it open,' Halloran said, indicating the doorway behind.

'Ah,' said Khayed, then spoke to his companion in their own language. '*Sadi koona hashoor.*' Daoud smiled at Halloran, who offered no more explanation than he'd already given.

A smell of spices drifted towards him from the two men. They waited there and he guessed they'd stay all day without saying another word until he went on his way. It was in his mind to ask them again what was beyond the locked door, but he doubted he'd receive a reply. He noticed Khayed held a long key by his side.

Halloran waved them through, but they remained where they were, politely indicating that he should pass them. '*Min fadlak, assayed,*' said Khayed.

With a shrug, he cut back across the yard, this time making for the corridor leading to the main hall and the front of the house.

Coolness and gloom after the brightness of the yard struck him as soon as he entered and his footsteps were hollow on the stone flooring. He frowned when he saw that the double-doors of the entrance were open wide and guessed that Khayed and Daoud were the culprits. He went to the door and passed through into the porch area.

Outside he saw that the Rover's tail was up, and inside were the two metal containers. He walked over to examine them more closely, tapping them both at first, the sound heavy, indicating they were full. The tops were tightly sealed.

He was prising at one with his fingertips when he heard the crunch of gravel behind him. Now there was no quick disguising of the alarm in Khayed's expression. He was alone, obviously having followed Halloran out while his companion went on about his business.

'*Kala, assayed,*' the Arab said, recovering well enough to smile.

Halloran raised his eyebrows. He indicated the containers. 'What's in them?'

he asked.

'Nothing to concern the good sir,' came the reply.

'I'd like to take a look.'

'Oh no, sir, there is nothing of interest for you in them. It is food, you see.'

'What?'

'I said it is food inside the bins.'

His companion appeared on the porch and he was holding yet another container. He halted to look at both men, then hurried over to the back of the car, politely edging past Halloran to place his load inside with the other two. He straightened and grinned at Halloran, his eyes full of amusement.

'For the dogs,' he said. '*Akel llkaleb*. They will eat well tonight.'

His snigger became laughter. Khayed joined in that laughter.

▪ 23 ▪
THE LODGE-HOUSE

DUSK WAS AIDED BY A CLOUDED SKY, THE FINE DAY HAVING CHANGED ITS MIND mid-afternoon, becoming overcast and broody, yet shedding no rain, as if sulking without tantrum, leaving the air warm and muggy. Halloran took off his jacket as he strolled away from Neath's front gate, no longer having to worry about exposing his waist-holster now he was away from the public road.

He had just completed briefing the two sets of Shield operatives, keeping them no more than ten minutes so that the roads around the estate would not be left unpatrolled for longer than was necessary (he realized even double the number of observer cars would still be inadequate, because it would be easy enough for intruders to enter the grounds during surveillance 'gaps'; nevertheless, even two cars could usually spot potential trouble – parked vehicles, loiterers, anything out of place or suspicious – and two were better than one, one better than none). Halloran wasn't happy with the situation, but knew that only a small army would really be adequate in the circumstances and at least the operatives were now discreetly armed; he could only hope that Kline's faith in his guard dogs was justified.

It had been an odd day (no reason it shouldn't have been, Halloran told himself, considering the whole affair was odd), beginning with his hallucination on the lake that morning. But that had amounted to no more than Kline flexing his psychic muscles, showing Halloran his psyche's strength, a mild 'frightener' to let him know he was dealing with a man who had a genuine ability, one that could be used in any direction Kline chose. Fine. The experience had been unnerving, but at least had given his client some satisfaction, and that in turn might make him more amenable to following Halloran's strictures on security.

Kline's outburst at breakfast had left the operative unperturbed: he already knew the man was an ego-maniac, as well as being somewhat eccentric, so it wasn't surprising that he was concerned solely for his own safety. How Cora tolerated her employer's boorishness Halloran couldn't understand at all. The question had been in his mind most of the day: why was she so dependent on Kline?

Halloran had wanted to talk with her alone, but she had avoided his company, disappearing to her room immediately after breakfast. He had gone to her, and she had opened her bedroom door only slightly, her eyes downcast, almost as if she were ashamed of what had happened the night before. Cora had told him she was suffering from a migraine headache, that she needed to lie down for a few hours, curtains drawn, if it were to pass. He'd left her, disappointed in her lack of response to him, for even though her sexual preference had surprised him (and, if he were to be totally honest with himself, dismayed him a little) a tenderness between them had followed the lovemaking. Cora had wept when he untied her, and had clung to him, body trembling, tears dampening his chest, for a long time before falling into a troubled sleep.

Somewhere in the distance he heard the faint sound of church bells, evensong in some nearby parish, and his thoughts drifted back to the country of his childhood. The small town in Kilkenny, where the priest's authority was irrefutable, his word law, his temple the court, his judgement final ... Halloran checked himself. It wasn't the time for such reflection – he needed to be alert, aware of what was going on around him at the present moment, not having his thoughts wandering around the past. That was happening too much of late.

Adding further to the day's discord was the news that Dieter Stuhr had disappeared. Mather had rung Halloran before lunch to inform him that Shield's Organizer couldn't be located, but everything at his apartment appeared to be in order. Key members of Shield had been recalled to the office to try and track him down, and Gerald Snaith had decided it was far too soon to involve the police. Besides, out of keeping though it might be for the German, there might just be a rational explanation for his absence. Mather would ring Halloran the moment he had more information.

He was before the lodge, a building of similar but darker stone to Neath itself, its grey-slated roof full of holes, windows dulled by grime. It looked unlived in. Yet someone inside had somehow allowed him to open the front gates (he'd had a better chance to examine the lock and still hadn't detected any electronic device installed within), for on first try the gates wouldn't budge. He studied the lodge a while longer before leaving the road and walking the short track up to the front door. The best he got when he stretched a hand to the rusted bell was a dull clunk. He rapped on the wood.

There were no sounds from inside the house. No one came to open the door.

He knocked louder, then tried the handle; it was as though the door were solid to the stone itself, for it did not even jar in its frame. Halloran stepped back to look up at the first floor windows and saw nothing through the smeared glass. He walked back to the edge of the rutted road for a better view, but the angle merely rendered the windows an opaque black. He took one more backward step.

Halloran was suddenly cold, as if he'd stepped into a pocket of wintry air. He was being observed.

Such an awareness was not unusual for him – experience in his particular profession brought with it a certain sensitivity towards prying, unseen eyes – yet never before had the sensing been so acute for him. The coldness, he realized, was due to the crawling sensation of his own skin, as if it was undulating in small ridges. He shifted his jacket to his other arm so that his gun hand was free.

Nothing stirred inside the lodge. At least, not as far as he could tell. But the urge to run from there, to put as much distance between himself and that uninviting abode, was immense. A whisper, whose source was somewhere deep in his own mind, cautioned him against further investigation. Irrational, he told himself. Are you sure? his sub-conscious taunted.

He raised a hand to his forehead as if to dispel further insinuations that had gathered, warnings that something nasty, something unclean, was waiting for him inside the lodge-house, and that contained within its walls were secrets that should remain secrets; but physical action was useless against the tenacity of the psyche. The thoughts continued.

Halloran almost sagged under their force. He willed their dispersion and it was only gradually that his mind became calmer, that his own consciousness became dominant.

For those other thoughts had not been his. He was certain they had not originated from some sub-level of his own mind, but had been implanted by another. He turned his head, searching the woods behind, the roadway leading to Neath. *Kline.* Those thoughts had been Kline's. He had the gift: Kline had shown him that very morning. But the psychic was still at the main house. Or should have been. Again Halloran scanned the area around him. Did distance bother someone like Kline, could ideas be directed no matter how far away the recipient? *Or was Felix Kline inside the lodge?*

The coldness was still with him and Halloran slipped his jacket back on. He took a step towards the building.

And the thoughts intruded once more, stabbing at him, bringing with them not only fear but a curious reluctance to discover what was inside the old house. He remained where he was.

Halloran could see no one at the windows, but he sensed a presence beyond those walls. He had lost the inclination to enter the house, though, no longer wanting to find out who the occupant was. Not at the moment. He'd return when he was ... prepared.

Halloran backed away.

With a last lingering look, he turned from the lodge and began the long trek to the main house where earlier he had decided to leave the Mercedes, preferring to make the journey to the estate's entrance on foot. Too much could be missed when viewed from a moving car and Halloran had wanted to get the *feel* of the surrounds, with particular regard to the private roadway which was a natural place for an ambush, safe from public gaze, out of sight from anyone in Neath itself. Now, with the evening gloom taking a firmer hold and the unease left by the uninvited thoughts, Halloran regretted his decision. At once he berated himself, a little astonished by his own trepidation. But then, as he'd already acknowledged, it had been an odd day.

In the stillness around him his footsteps seemed louder than normal. Ahead the road narrowed, trees on opposite sides linking leafy arms to form a tunnel. It was twilight inside that tunnel.

He was too warm suddenly, the air almost too heavy to breathe. The clouds were swollen and dark and he relished the idea of rain, or even a storm. But it was as though the dampness was sealed into the masses above. He walked on, at irregular intervals glancing from left to right, occasionally checking the road behind. All was quiet. The lodge-house was a distant image, rendered small and impotent. The road in front of him had begun to curve, no exit visible inside the tunnel.

A stirring of ferns by the roadside, no more than a transient breeze. A faint crash further within, merely a dead or broken branch shed from a tree.

Light faded as he passed beneath the canopy of leaves. It was cooler, although not much, and Halloran quickened his pace. The more he progressed, the dimmer became the light. Soon it was as though night had fallen prematurely. His senses sharpened and he allowed his vision to wander, never focusing on any particular section of forest for too long, constantly shifting his attention from one dark area to another.

At first he thought he had imagined the snuffling, for it had been barely audible over the sound of his own footsteps, but then it came again. He stopped to listen. Nothing now. And that in itself was unusual, for the woods were always full of noises of some kind, small scufflings, the flapping of wings, an owl settling in for the night's vigil. Over many years he had learned to discern nature's disturbances from those that might originate from stealthy humans, the difference being that animal or natural noises generally continued even if for no more than a second or two, whereas those caused by humans – be they hiding or stalking prey – had a tendency to cease immediately.

He resumed his journey, the tension in his stride indicating an extra alertness. Keeping his steps as quiet as possible, Halloran moved into the curve of the tunnel. A rustling to his right, a definite movement. He carried on walking, a hand reaching under his jacket to the butt of the Browning. More movement, something keeping pace with him. He began to suspect what that something might be.

He had assumed that the dogs were controlled during the daytime and allowed to run free at night. Perhaps it was at dusk that their keeper set them loose on their own.

Snuffling noises again, and then a louder rustling through the undergrowth as though the animals were hurrying to get ahead of him. Initially the sounds had come from some distance inside the woodland, but now they were drawing close, as if the dogs were cutting in at an angle. Halloran deliberately maintained his own steady pace.

For one brief moment he caught sight of a shadow loping through the trees, low to the ground. It was followed by another, then another ... he watched a stream of shadows slinking through the undergrowth.

Strange that they didn't come straight at him, but maybe that was part of their training, to cut off and intimidate rather than attack. He sincerely hoped so. Could be that they'd also been trained to keep silent while they tracked their quarry. Halloran resisted the urge to break into a run, knowing he would never outpace them: there was no point in turning back either – they'd only follow. He slid the gun from its holster and held it down by his side.

It could have been midnight, so dark had it become under the trees. The disturbance to his right had settled as though the procession of dim shapes had passed on its way, having had no real interest in the solitary walker. Halloran did not relax his guard.

Something moved out into the open ahead. He could hardly make out the dog's form so mantled was the roadway, but he could hear the soft panting. The animal loitered there, making no other sound. Waiting for him. Soon others joined it, slinking from the undergrowth to create an undefined obstacle across the roadway. Their combined breathing seemed to take on a rhythm.

Halloran aimed the weapon in their direction. He moved forward again, his step slow and steady, his body erect, offering the beasts no fear.

He heard their base, scratchy snarling. Drawing near he sensed rather than saw those closest tensing themselves to pounce. He was within seven or eight feet of the nearest shadow. His steps did not falter.

Until there was a different sound, and this from behind, growing louder by the moment. He stopped, but dared not look away from those looming shapes lest they take advantage of a brief second's distraction. The trees and the road were becoming brighter as lights approached, rounding the bend. Illuminating what lay ahead of Halloran.

He drew in a breath, his grip tightening on the automatic. Eyes, yellow-white in the glare from the car's headlights, were watching him. The rest of their lean bodies became brighter.

They were indeed dogs, but of a special loathsome breed.

They stole back into the woods, soon swallowed by its inkiness, and he listened to their quiet retreat until the sounds had faded completely.

The car drew up behind him and he slid the gun back into the holster. He turned around to face the vehicle, shielding his eyes with an arm and, save for the dazzling lights and the soft purr of its engine, the car might never have been there, for its blackness blended perfectly with the darkness of the forest. As he walked around to the driver's side he heard a window descending. A broad face appeared, barely recognizable in the dimness.

'It is better that I drive you back to the house, *mój kolega*,' said Palusinski. 'The jackal can be a ferocious beast, particularly against the defenceless.'

JANUSZ PALUSINSKI
A PEASANT'S SURVIVAL

HIS FATHER, HENRYK PALUSINSKI, HAD BEEN A HERO OF THE PEOPLE, A PEASANT farmer who had joined the march to Zamosc to do battle with the much-feared General Semyon Budenny of Russia's First Cavalry.

So fiercely did the tiny ragbag army of Polish cavalry, peasants and gentry fight there, sheer desperation their driving force, that General Budenny had no other choice but to order a retreat and flee back to Russia with his defeated and humiliated troops.

The year was 1920, and Janusz Palusinski had not yet been born.

Henryk returned to his village wearied but triumphant, the sabre slash wound in his side never to heal completely, weeping small amounts of blood mixed with foul-smelling poison for years to come. The villagers were proud of their man and, still mourning for those who had not come back from battle, pledged their help to Kazimiera, their hero's devoted wife, in running the small farm until Henryk was well enough to cope for himself. Unfortunately it was two years before he was able to plough his field again, and then only with his faithful Kazimiera by his side to lend support. Still his neighbours offered assistance, but less so than before; hero-worship is difficult to sustain when danger has long since passed. Besides, Henryk was no longer the solid and pleasant individual they had once respected and liked: his disability and reliance on others had soured him considerably.

So by the time little Janusz was born some three years later, conditions in the Palusinski household (which had always been less than comfortable anyway) had somewhat deteriorated. Nevertheless the couple were happy to have been blessed with a son; he would grow broad and strong as his father had once been, and in time would work the farm, rebuild it to its former (modest) glory. Providing they didn't all starve before he came of working age.

Due to Kazimiera's fortitude and the continuing kindness of others – albeit a dwindled kindness – the Palusinski family survived. But the father became more morose as the son grew older, for Janusz was not the kind of boy Henryk had in mind when he had dreamt of the offspring he would eventually raise. The boy was sturdy enough, no disappointment there, but there was a sly laziness to him, a reluctance to offer more than was required of him. Janusz's mother despaired, and she herself often did extra work her husband had ordered the boy to do, always taking the greatest care that Henryk would not find out. They ate poorly, selling what they could of their meagre produce and, because theirs was a farm without livestock, turnips, beetroots and potatoes became their staple diet. The boy craved something more.

Then one night his father, out of desperation and perhaps even bitterness, stole a neighbour's pig. It was a young pig, not yet plump, but one that could be dealt with quickly and easily in the dead of night. Henryk felled the animal with one sharp blow of a *mlotek*, not even its sleeping mother rousing to the short squeal of pain. He yanked the pig from its pen, concealing it beneath his coat even though there was no one around to see, then scurried back to his own home.

The family did not wait for morning to cook their prize, for their stomachs groaned at the sight of the pink flesh. The small animal was quickly gutted and set over the fire to roast, liver and kidneys set aside for later consumption. Henryk's wife chopped vegetables, adding to them dried mushrooms picked from the forest weeks earlier. Some would be cooked for the feast they could not deny themselves that night, while what was left would be used for the soup they would make from the pig's bones and trotters. Any guilt Kazimiera felt over her husband's dishonesty vanished as soon as the first aromas from the roasting meat wafted towards her.

Young Janusz was impatient. And there was something about the pink nakedness of the uncooked pig that had its own allure. His father brought out a bottle of the cheap wine he had taken to consoling himself with of late, filling tin mugs for himself and Kazimiera, even allowing his son one or two sips. It had been a long time since Henryk had felt in such hearty mood and his wife enjoyed his suddenly restored robustness. While they toasted each other, Kazimiera almost coy under the leering looks she received from her man, Janusz's gaze kept wandering towards the liver and kidneys that lay neglected on the table.

The harsh wine on empty stomachs took no time at all to lighten heads and Henryk, after warning his son to watch the roasting pig as if his life depended on it – the slightest charring would mean the severest beating for the boy – pulled his not-unwilling *kochankę* into the bedroom.

Janusz obeyed, turning the pig on its spit every few minutes. His mouth was wet with juices as the meat cooked. Yet his eyes kept returning to the raw meat glistening on the table at the centre of the room.

Making sure that the bedroom door was closed, he approached the table as stealthily as his father had approached their neighbour's farmyard. With trembling fingers he picked up the liver, finding its clammy softness not at all unpleasant. He sniffed the meat like a nervous mongrel. The smell wasn't strong, yet somehow it prevailed over the roasting pork. He bit into it.

He discovered that devouring raw meat was not so simple. It stretched and stretched, its shininess preventing a firm grip. He laid it down once more and lifted the kitchen knife. Janusz carefully cut off a thin sliver of meat (some enjoyment there, cutting into the moist softness, blood staining the blade), then pushed it into his mouth. To begin with the taste was repugnant, but the more he chewed the more he became used to it. And soon he began to appreciate the raw freshness.

Janusz, aged just nine years, swallowed the meat and cut off another sliver.

The whole family feasted in the early hours of the morning, eating the pork and vegetables in enraptured silence, Henryk swilling wine until the bottle was empty, occasionally winking at Kazimiera and grinning lewdly. The very fact that the meat was so clandestine added its own special flavour.

It was a feast that the young Janusz would never forget. Indeed the memory would taunt his tastebuds many, many times in the years to come.

Neither of his parents mentioned the missing liver the following day – perhaps Henryk's improbity towards his good neighbour subdued any anger he felt against his own son for stealing the meat, and Kazimiera could only feel shame that circumstances had driven her little Janusz to such a hungry state. Conditions did not improve when suspicion for the loss of the pig fell on the Palusinski family, although no accusations were made. Help from others came less and less.

Janusz grew, his frame sturdy enough, but his flesh lean and undernourished. He was disliked by the other boys of the village (who had no particular regard for the senior Palusinski's ancient act of valour) for Janusz could best be described as shifty, always on the edge of any group, constantly seeking ways to better his own lot (he was hungry most of the time, a discomfort that can easily shape a person's character). As the years passed and the boy was able to take on more man's work (albeit unenthusiastically), conditions for the Palusinskis improved. They were still impoverished, true, but then so were many of their neighbours, and Henryk's old wound continued to make prolonged labour difficult: yet food for the table slowly became less of a problem and occasionally there were *zlotys* enough to spend on other things, usually new farming equipment. Poland itself was establishing a more benevolent governance, initiating land reforms that were beneficial to the small farmholder, creating a social security system and organizing health care for its population. Janusz Palusinski might well have grown into a relatively normal young man had not yet another unfortunate chapter in Poland's history begun.

On 1st September 1939 Germany invaded, bringing a reign of terror that would eventually lead to the total subjugation of the Polish people. Important officials, potential troublemakers, men of learning were to be eliminated under the new order of the *General Government*. The Polish workers were to be intimidated into submission: the murder of countless numbers saw to this. Failure to obey the edicts of the Third Reich meant immediate execution or being sent to a concentration camp (which usually resulted in a more lingering death). All Jews were to be exterminated.

For Poland it was a return to the bad old days of rule by fear. For Janusz Palusinski, then sixteen years old, it meant a return to the bad old days of permanent hunger.

The Nazis had set the Polish farmers working for the sustenance of the German people, each district commander ensuring that no produce was withheld, only the most meagre amount left for the farmer and his family so that they had the strength to work the fields. To hide food from the occupying forces meant punishment by death.

The people of Janusz's village, both men and women, young and old, were decimated during the terrible years that followed, for the Polish people are a proud and defiant race (not to mention stubborn) and the village was no more, and certainly no less, than an encapsulation of the country as a whole. Many of the younger men became partisans, hiding in the surrounding forests by day, venturing forth to sabotage where they could by night.

Henryk Palusinski saw this as a time to redeem his former glory. Age and his old wound prevented any active part in resistance operations, but he endeavoured to supply the hiding groups with what little food he and the other villagers could spare. He also fed them any information on German troop activities that came his way. He urged his son to join the partisans many times, but Janusz was even more reluctant to do that than he was to plough the field, and Kazimiera, when her son complained to her, forbade Henryk to persist with such suggestions. The risk in providing food for the cause was enough, she scolded, without exposing their one and only son to more danger than already existed for them all. Besides, who would work the farm if anything happened to the boy? Although disappointed in his son's lack of spirit, Henryk was forced to listen to reason.

Events took their own course when the older Palusinski fell ill in the winter months with a severe respiratory condition. In the early hours of one morning when he lay wheezing in his sickbed, there came an urgent rapping on the frontdoor. Kazimiera feared it was German soldiers making a spot check on the farms around the village, a frequent occurrence in those dark days, searching for hidden food stores, perhaps hoping they might discover a partisan or two skulking on the premises. She opened the door with much trepidation and it was with relief that Kazimiera recognized the woman standing outside, hair dampened by drizzling rain: she was from the village, her husband a member of the resistance. The woman held a small bundle in her arms.

'Food, *Pani* Palusinska,' she told Kazimiera, 'for my husband. The Germans watch me, they suspect my Mikolaj is with the resistance. But our men are starving in the forest, *Pan* Palusinski must take this to them.' Kazimiera explained that Henryk was too ill for such a journey. 'You have a strong son,' she was reminded, the woman's tone cold.

Henryk had heard the conversation through the open door of his room and he called out for his wife to bring the woman inside lest by chance she were seen by their enemy. The villager rushed to Henryk's door and pleaded with him to send Janusz into the forest with the food. The older Palusinski began to rise, prepared to undertake the mission himself despite his poor health, and Kazimiera pushed him back again, agreeing that their son should go, afraid that such an effort would surely kill her husband.

Janusz had no other choice. If he refused he would be pilloried by the villagers and neighbours, branded a coward, and his own father would make his life even more unbearable for him than it was already. Besides, the risk should be minimal at that hour of the morning.

His father gave him detailed instructions on where to find the partisans' forest hideaway, and the youth set out, pulling his coat tight around his neck against the chill rain. It was one of those few occasions when Henryk Palusinski felt truly proud of his son. Unfortunately that pride was to be short-lived.

Janusz was captured in the forest by German soldiers who had always been aware that there was a supply line between the partisans and the villagers and farmers. As fate would have it – and as perversely ironic as fate often is – a patrol had chosen that morning to watch a particular section of woodland in which the young Palusinski crept. He was caught within ten minutes of leaving his home.

To his credit, Janusz did not instantly break under the Nazi threats and beatings which followed. However, it took less than a day at the dreaded Lublin interrogation centre for that to happen.

He gave the names of partisans, revealed where their encampment in the forest was hidden, mentioned which villages assisted them (much of this was guesswork on his part and he strove to make it sound convincing to his tormentors) and who among the farmers supplied the underground movement with food. It was not until they took him to another room and completely immersed his body in water, pulling him up just before he lost consciousness, repeating the process several times, that he admitted his own parents were involved with the partisans. Only when lighted cigarettes were pressed against his testicles and no more information babbled from his broken lips was the Gestapo sure there was nothing left for him to tell.

The next day Janusz was driven to Zamek Lublin, a hillside castle that served as both prison and courthouse. There, in an old chapel that had been transformed into a courtroom, the dazed youth was sentenced to imprisonment. He was lucky: others with him found guilty were dispatched to a room next door and instantly shot.

From Zamek Lublin he was taken to Majdanek, a notorious internment centre just east of the city where many thousands of Poles, Hungarians and Czechoslovaks were being held, and it was here that Janusz received the tattooed number on his wrist that forever would identify him as the unfortunate victim of a Nazi concentration camp.

Once he had recovered from his injuries, he began to realize he had certain advantages over many of the other inmates which might possibly help him survive: he was young and had learned to exist on a limited amount of food for a number of years (on this point he was soon to discover that at Majdanek 'limited' meant hardly any at all); he was cunning, already a natural scrounger; he held scant remorse for any personal misdeeds (the thought of what had befallen those he had betrayed – including the fate of his parents – hardly disturbed him); he was not Jewish.

And there was one particular aberration of character that would eventually ensure his survival under the worst of circumstances, but that was not to be appreciated until much later.

His clothes were of a black-and-white striped material, thin and coarse and loose-fitting; his bed was a plank of wood on damp ground. His companions were the starving.

Janusz became used to raving hunger once more. He dreamt of great plates of sauerkraut, sausages, boiled pork and pickles, with coriander seeds mixed in. And often he dreamt of when he was nine years old, of the night his father had stolen the tiny pig, how his family had feasted, the pork lasting for days, thin soup made from the bones lasting even longer. He would wake from the dream in the darkness of the night, his sunken eyes wide and staring, the succulent memory vanquishing the moans and smells around him in the rough hut. He would remember other details of that clandestine night, and juices would run from his open mouth.

Time passed and Janusz mentally sank into himself just as his flesh physically sank into his bones. Yet there was ever one bright, although tormenting, light for him. Unlike many of his fellow internees for whom food had become almost an abstract thing – they still craved it, still licked their bowls which had often contained only watery, meatless soup, a piece of black bread and sawdust; but the less they were fed, the more unreal to them became true sustenance – he never relinquished that one glorious memory of his family's night feast all those years ago. It became an obsession with him. And oddly, a driving force. Where others slowly drifted down into their own private abysses of despair, Janusz's thoughts constantly stretched towards his vision, perhaps as a drowning man might reach for a swooping seagull.

He worked as hard for his gaolers as his enfeebled body would allow (and with considerably more eagerness than on his father's farm) and was never averse to mentioning any subversive talk he might hear in the barrack huts during the night, always willing to point out potential troublemakers to the German guards. He became a pariah among the prisoners for, although they could only guess he was an informer, it was his readiness to serve the Third Reich beasts that he was hated for. Fortunately for him, there was too much dread in their hearts and too much passion sapped from their souls for them to take vengeance.

Then one day, Janusz and two dozen or so others were marched from the camp to a hillside that was used for mass executions. They were instructed to wait beside several open pits. The number of *Unerwünschte* – 'undesirables' as the Nazis referred to Jews – was too many to count (years after the nightmare Janusz could not remember if there had been hundreds or if there had been thousands) as they were lined up before the pits in groups. There they were machine-gunned, most of the bodies toppling into the open graves. It was the task of the working party to throw in those who had fallen the wrong way, then arrange the bodies so that the next batch could be heaped in on top. When the pile reached a certain level, they were to cover the pit with lime and soil. Before that was done though, there was a special job to perform for a chosen few. Janusz was one of the chosen.

An SS captain provided Janusz and three companions with pliers and short blunted knives; their orders were to pull any gold teeth they could find among the corpses and to cut off any rings that had not already been confiscated.

This was no shock for Janusz, because his mind had long since decided to protect him from such traumas. He crawled among the still warm corpses, giving them no more regard than if they were freshly slaughtered livestock. Dead meat. That's all this great tumble of arms and legs was. White carcasses. Some still pink-coloured. Like the little pig ...

No one was watching as he lifted the hand of the plump woman, the flesh of her finger swollen over the rim of her gold ring. The Gestapo had been merciful: they hadn't cut the jewellery from her while she was still alive. He sawed at the finger. No one was paying any attention. He slid the ring off. And drew meat from the fingerbone with his teeth. He swallowed. The woman's eyes opened. She looked at him and he fought to keep the bloodied morsel down. It lodged in his throat as life went from the woman's eyes. He swallowed again, once, twice. The meat was accepted.

That was the real beginning of Janusz Palusinski's survival. He had found a food supply. He was filled neither with joy nor shame, merely relief that he had a means to exist.

Exist he did, even though he was violently ill for days after that first eating of human flesh; his stomach was not accustomed to such richness. He was lucky to recover, for his general weakness might have allowed permanent damage. But Janusz was resilient, if nothing else. From then on he was more cautious about how much he cut from the piled corpses, often concealing small segments in his loose clothing to be consumed late at night beneath his thin blanket. The amount he was able to eat was never enough to have any marked effect on his physique, and that was fortunate, for such a change would have been easily noticed amidst the walking skeletons of the Majdanek concentration camp. But it was sufficient to strengthen him and thus renew his desire to survive.

Disaster, for him, came months later when for no apparent reason he was taken off the burial detail. Perhaps the German soldiers themselves had grown sick of his eagerness to crawl among the dead, or perhaps they felt he had become too privileged. Whatever the reason, Janusz's specialist services were no longer required. His condition deteriorated rapidly with no regular sustenance.

He became as the others of the camp, a shuffling corpse, eyes enlarged as his skin shrivelled, his bones jutting with deep hollows between. He began to have fits of coughing that drained him of any strength he had left, and bloodspots speckled his palm when he took his hand away from his mouth. Delirium soon followed. Finally he was moved to a hut where those who were dying were left without food or care, their passing hastened by lack of both.

He had no idea of how long he had lain there, it could have been days, it might only have been hours. But something had drawn his senses towards one focal point. It was a smell. Familiar. From the past. He stared into the greyness above and his tongue ran across dry, cracked lips, failing to moisten them. He drew up his knees as hunger cramped his stomach and his head lolled listlessly when the pain passed. That faint smell, what was it? So familiar. He was a boy again, and he stood in the centre of the room watching a door. *Mamusia* and *Tatuś* had shut him out. They always did when they did things to each other, unless they thought he was sleeping. He could hear them laughing, and then he could hear them moaning as if they were hurting one another. But one night, when they thought he was asleep, he had watched them across the bedroom ... and hadn't liked what he saw ... but had wanted to be part of it ... to enjoy the game with them, to be hurt in the same way ... but he knew it was forbidden ... The faint smell. The boy looked towards the table, towards the source. The meat was dark red, blood seeping onto the rough wooden surface. He moved closer.

Janusz recognized the odour of raw liver. But it wasn't possible. He was no longer a child and this place was not his home. No, this was the death hut. The smell though. It was here. There was raw liver somewhere nearby. His smile made his lips bleed.

For the first time he heard the dull moans and they were around him, not from behind a closed door. And the smell was with the moans.

He let his head fall to one side and in the pre-dawn light saw the shapeless bundle next to him. There was hardly anything left of the man, and he barely moved. But the smell was from him and it was mouth-watering. Janusz's arm trembled when he reached towards the figure.

The man was not sleeping, nor was he really conscious. He was near death and that proximity was comforting for him. Most of the pain had gone to some distant point, so far away it could scarcely be felt. He sunk further within himself and realized that the journey inwards was the way to final peace. Yet something was moving him, interrupting his floating descent. Something was caressing his stomach. Pain was coming close once more, and the man did not want that. He tried to protest, but a murmur that was only a sigh was all the sound he managed. Sharp agony now. And something hard covering his mouth and nose, stopping any more sighs, any more breathing. The agony increased as something gnawed into his belly and he was too feeble to protest further. But the pain was becoming dulled, bliss was washing through him, for his senses were leaving and he, at long last, was leaving with them and it was good, so ultimately good.

No one went near the hut that day, nor the next. No corpses were taken away, no more of the dying were dumped inside. It was to be five days before the door of the Majdanek death hut was opened again, and then by Russian soldiers, for this was the summer of 1944 and the German invaders were being driven from Poland.

The Russians, already hardened by their own suffering in the terrible war, and by the atrocities they had witnessed during the march across their neighbouring country, were sickened by what they found inside the hut. Only one man was still alive and he, understandably, was demented by what had happened around him. He lay on a floor that was filled with corpses. Many had been mutilated, for it seemed rats had found their way inside and fed off his dead and dying compatriots.

Unfortunately for the Polish people, once the Russians had occupied their country they felt no compunction to leave. Poland came under Communist control, and oppression, although never as severe as under Nazi rule, remained the norm. Again farmers and factory workers found themselves working for the State rather than for themselves, with the government dictating at what rates produce should be sold.

Janusz Palusinski, who bore the indelible mark of German brutality on his wrist and never failed to let the tattoo show on any occasion that sympathy might help better his cause, came to thrive under the system, for scrounging and self-interest was the ideal apprenticeship for a black-marketeer. It took him a full year to recover from his treatment by the Nazis (although a whole lifetime would never erase the damage to his psyche) but his will to survive at all costs had been enhanced rather than depleted. He did not return to his father's farm for two reasons: he was not sure of the reception he would get from the villagers who must have known that it was he who had betrayed the partisans and those who helped them; he had no desire to become a farmer once more. During the year of recuperation, most of which took place in a small hospital just outside Lukow, he read through the published crimes of the Nazi regime, always searching for mention of his own village, and one day he came across what he had been looking for. Listed were the names of locals and villagers who had been shot for giving aid to the underground movement. A hundred and thirty-two people were on that list, his parents among them. Even now, when concern for his own well-being was no longer acute, he felt no remorse, not even for the fate of his own mother. Such emotion, never strong within him anyway, had been entirely eradicated over the last few years.

As time passed, life began to flourish for Janusz, who took to the illegal trade he dealt in as if born to it. He supplied goods-hungry farmers and food-hungry manufacturers with what they desired, trade between the two factions being lucrative for the middle-man. But he always operated in a small way in those early years, never wishing to rise in fortune so much that he became visible to the authorities.

Janusz could have survived very comfortably under the Communist system, except that the older he grew the more he prospered and the more he prospered, the greedier he became. He bought a four-storey house in the suburbs of Lodz and, as a front which legitimately enabled him to visit farmers around the country, he maintained a small farm equipment spare-parts workshop. Middle age had softened his caution though, and he went against his own basic rule. He had gained too much and was no longer invisible.

The authorities began to take an interest in the activities of Janusz Palusinski. His spare-parts business was discreetly investigated and it was found that the profits derived from it by no means accounted for the relative luxury the owner appeared to be living in. His movements were watched. Party officials came to his house to question him. His answers were not entirely satisfactory. They took away all documents found in his home, warning him they would return as soon as the papers had been thoroughly studied and that he was to keep himself available until such time. Janusz stole away that same night, taking with him what little cash he had and leaving behind his automobile, knowing how easy it was for the authorities to trace any vehicle on the roads of Poland. He left the city on foot, sleeping in cheap lodging houses at night, travelling by bus during the day, too afraid even to take trains. His journey led him towards the north, in the direction of the great forests. He had no idea why, panic and self-preservation driving him onwards without calculation, only instinct telling him that the dark forests were a place to lose oneself and to be lost to others. He was aware of the severe punishment dealt to those caught trading on the black market and was sure that his mind would never stand another term of imprisonment – too many dreadful memories would have been rekindled. There was no grand plan to his escape, no considered scheme for invisibility once more. Janusz fled merely because he had no other choice.

Because of the furtive manner in which his journey progressed, it took him several weeks to reach the mediaeval town of Grudziadz, and by then his money had nearly run out. A basic plan had formed though, an idea that took no details into account. He would make for the Baltic seaport of Gdynia, avoiding nearby Gdansk where too many merchants knew him. There he would bribe his way onto a boat. He didn't care where his passage took him, just so long as it was far away from this accursed country and its oppressively authoritarian government which constantly hindered entrepreneurs such as he. The problem now was money. He had barely fifty *zlotys* left and such a secret voyage would prove expensive.

Late at night Janusz went to the home of Wiktor Svandova, in Grudziadz, a particular businessman with whom he'd had many dealings in the past.

But Janusz had not reckoned on Svandova's respect for (or fear of) the State. The business associate ordered Janusz from his home, threatening to call in the police if he didn't leave at once. The fugitive reasoned with Svandova, cajoled, pleaded, even wept before him; he only produced the short metal bar he carried inside his greatcoat when Svandova strode to his desk and reached for the telephone. The first blow struck the businessman across the left temple, but amazingly he was able to stagger to the door, with Janusz following and beating at the back of his head and shoulders as he went. He threw open the door and even managed to scream out his wife's name before collapsing to his knees while his assailant continued to rain blows on him. At last, and to Janusz's great relief, Svandova pitched forward onto his face, blood from his broken head instantly flooding the hallway. Janusz ran from the house when the dead man's wife began screeching from the top of the stairway. He knew she had recognized him and he had it in mind to climb the stairs and silence her forever too; but other figures had appeared behind her, presumably Svandova's sons, and Janusz had no desire to battle it out with them.

He left the city, heading north once again, cursing his bad luck and his business associate's foolishness. He was now a fugitive from a far more serious crime and every endeavour would be made by the police to capture him.

For nearly three months Janusz eluded them, the northern forests swallowing him up completely, bestowing upon him the invisibility he craved. But autumn was turning to winter and even the extra clothing he had stolen to wear under his greatcoat could not prevent the chill reaching his bones. Food – the roots and nuts he found, the turnips and beetroots, and potatoes he dug from farmers' fields late at night, the small animals he occasionally was able to trap and kill – already scarce was becoming even more so. Yet again Janusz became intimately acquainted with terrible hunger. When stealing from farms – odd items of clothing came from outside washing lines – he yearned to come across a pig pen, dreamt of reaching in and pulling out a piglet, just as his father had all those years ago. When he slept he dreamed of his family's feast, when he had watched the roasting pig, making sure the meat wasn't burned black. He awoke many times with the delicious smell still in his nostrils and before reality edged it away, a more subtle aroma would become dominant ...

His heavy beard was matted and dirty and Janusz may have appeared plump, but only layers of clothing created the illusion, for beneath them his flesh was hollowed between the bones, just as it had been in the years when Germans had occupied his country. He had plodded for two days through the snow-laden forest, sheltering where he could, cramming any foliage he could find into his mouth and chomping until it was mulched enough for him to digest. He even pulled pieces of bark from trees to gnaw on.

The *policjanci* had been waiting for him at the last farmhouse he had attempted to rob; he had remained in one area for too long, the stealing becoming more than just an annoyance to the locals. A trap had been set for him and only blind panic had lent him the strength to outrun his pursuers. Now it was only stomach pains that drove him on.

Janusz saw the column of smoke rising above the treetops and stumbled off in that direction. He came upon a small, log house in a clearing. His weary legs barely got him to the frontdoor. His fist made the faintest of sounds when he pounded on the wood.

The woodsman caught him as he fell inside and dragged him over to the fire. He called for his wife to warm some *sok* and bring it to the half-frozen man while he loosened the unfortunate's clothing. They were kind to this wretched wayfarer, even though suspicious, and they did their utmost to revive him. After a while, when he was able to sit at the table and sip more of the warm brew, they tried to question him, but his replies were incoherent, his voice rambling. They soon realized the man was crazed with hunger and exhaustion. And the wife was uneasy at the way he kept staring at their twelve-year-old daughter who sat quietly in the corner watching everything with a wide-eyed expression on her plump little face, her skin pink and unblemished in the glow from the fire.

Janusz repaid their kindness by killing them all. He used his trusty metal bar to batter the man unconscious as he stooped to put another log on the fire, and a breadknife quickly grabbed from the table to cut all their throats.

When the two *policjanci* who had been following his tracks through the forest burst in less than an hour later, he had already started to eat the woodsman's daughter.

In one respect Janusz was lucky. The officers were fresh enough in their careers not yet to have witnessed the worst of criminal brutality and nor were they old enough to comprehend the true barbarism of the Nazi occupation during the last World War. When they saw what had become of the woodsman and his wife, when they *realized* that what their quarry was stuffing into his mouth was from the child's open belly, they were too shocked – too *revolted* – to move.

The madness in Janusz, further incited by the excitement of his deed, overcame the fatigue that was still with him; he threw the breadknife at one uniformed intruder and rushed screaming at the other. The vision of this wildman, his body puffed up by the layers of clothing he wore, mouth and beard daubed with blood, eyes huge and crazed, would have frozen the bravest of men, and the two *policjanci* had thus far won no service awards for gallantry. Neither of them could help but cringe away.

One was pushed back against the wall while the other scrambled to retrieve his rifle, dropped when he had dodged the thrown knife. The thief they had tracked so many miles was through the door and out in the snow again, scurrying back into the trees as a single shot was fired at him. The bullet chipped the top of his right collarbone but, despite the agonizing jolt, he did not stop running. Nightfall helped cloak his escape.

Soon the gunshots behind him grew fainter and Janusz was both laughing and weeping as he scrambled up a slope. He toppled over the ridge and rolled down the other side, giggling and crying out as he went. He came to rest at the bottom of the hill, spreadeagled on his back, half-buried in snow and his chest heaving with exertion.

He stayed that way for some time, his breathing gradually slowing as he listened for his pursuers. Their voices came from high above him and soon drifted away again, the darkness now concealing the trail of disturbed snow he had left behind. He had lost them. He had got away. He giggled once more and licked his lips, the taste still strong on his tongue.

Janusz waited a little while longer before rising to his knees.

He was instantly blinded by dazzling white light.

Russian tanks were strategically positioned in many sectors of Poland, never obtrusively, but usually in areas where their threat could be felt rather than continually observed. The soldiers who manned them were highly disciplined and never mingled with the community; but they were always on standby, ready to move against insurgence at a moment's notice. Perpetually bored by their low-profile assignment, the tank crews were eager for any distraction that might come their way. They had observed the dark figure tumbling down the hillside and patiently waited for it to move again once it reached the bottom. When it did, they switched on their tank lights as one.

Janusz screamed in terror. He stumbled away, not caring in which direction he ran, his only thought to be out of that intense glare as quickly as possible. The two *policjanci*, alerted by the abrupt flaring of light, turned back.

Never had Janusz felt so naked, so visible. There was nothing he could see, nothing but blinding light, and he felt like a specimen exposed on a scientist's slab. He crashed into a tree, tasted his own blood rushing into his mouth. He staggered away, hands to his face. Then onwards, refusing to allow pain to stop him, too afraid to let it.

He was hurtling downwards again, over and over, this slope much steeper than the previous one. He shrieked when his damaged shoulder struck something solid. He was no longer falling, the surface flat and hard beneath him.

Janusz sobbed with self-pity. He was lost now. He no longer had the strength to run. They had him and they would punish him for the wicked things he had done.

He raised his head. The lights had found him. They were coming close, exposing him in the roadway as if he were some helpless animal, broken-limbed and prey to anything that should come along. Janusz tried to shield his eyes against the blaze, but there was no strength left in his arms.

The light was almost upon him. He waited in despair.

But now the bright beams were passing him, shining beyond. He blinked and it took an eternity for his eyes to discern the big black car that had drawn up alongside his prone body. The engine was still quietly running and nothing happened for a while. Then a rear door opened.

'*Mogę cię zrobić niewidzialnym, Janusz,*' a soft voice said from within. 'I can make you invisible.'

(And in a way, Kline did make him invisible.)

· 24 ·
CORA'S ANGUISH

'Why jackals, for God's sake? There are plenty of other breeds that make better guard dogs.' Halloran had craned his neck round to look through the black limousine's rear window, half-expecting to see shadowy shapes back on the roadway.

Palusinski shrugged, then gave a short laugh, his eyes becoming small behind the wire-rimmed glasses he wore. 'Perhaps Felix cares for the underdog.' He laughed again, enjoying his joke.

Halloran faced the front. 'I've never heard of trained jackals before.'

'All animals can be trained, *mój kolega*. As can all men.'

'I thought they were nocturnal, yet I saw one roaming in daylight yesterday.'

'They prefer night hunting, but even inherent habits can be changed. The dogs obey their master.'

'Kline?'

'Ah no.' Palusinski's foot gently touched the brake pedal as they gathered speed on the hill. The lights of Neath were like a beacon against the leaden slopes behind. 'Even an old dog such as I has learned some new tricks over the past two days. Your driving instructor teaches well.'

'Let's hope you never have to use those techniques.'

The older man nodded. 'I am informed that you, yourself, had to do so yesterday.'

Halloran made no comment. 'How long have you been employed by Felix Kline, Mr Palusinski?' he asked instead.

'Please, you may call me Janusz. Rest assured, I bear you no ill-will for your rough treatment of me two nights ago. I appreciate that you were merely pointing out the weakness of our defence. And there was no pain at the time, only an aching of the neck muscles afterwards. A skilful blow, sir, if I may say so.'

'Pity your partner can't forgive as easily.'

'Monk? An animal. A beast. It would be prudent to watch yourself with that one. Now, as to your question, I'm sure your company has access to the files on all of us. You must know how long I have been in Felix's employ.'

'Those files are pretty vague. They give no account of length of service.'

'I see. And you are curious, naturally.' The car pulled up behind the silver Mercedes at the front of the house. 'Felix brought me from Poland some years ago,' Palusinski said as he switched off the engine. 'Fourteen or fifteen years ago, I think.'

Halloran was startled and about to question the Pole further, but Palusinski was already getting out of the car. 'Wait,' he said, and the bald-headed man bent down to look back inside. 'How old is Kline?' Halloran asked.

Palusinski smiled, his eyes narrowing behind the spectacles. 'Felix is older than you would imagine, sir.' Then he was gone, walking around the front of the car towards the house.

Halloran quietly tapped on the door and waited. He was tired and that was due to more than just the lateness of the hour. There was a tension about this house that had little to do with any kidnap threat. Yet the day before there had been a stillness in Neath, a brooding heaviness which dragged at the spirit. That had now given way to a peculiar atmosphere of instability and he could almost feel a charge in the air, as if the building itself had been roused by the visitors like some slumbering monolith disturbed into a tensed wariness. He pushed the fanciful idea aside. A house was a house, bricks and mortar, timber and glass. The events of the day and the unpredictability of his client were having an adverse effect on him. That Dieter Stuhr was still missing – Mather had phoned Halloran an hour before to inform him of this – added to his general unease for, as the Shield Organizer, the German was at the hub of an ongoing operation. Nothing seemed right about this particular assignment.

He raised a hand to tap on the door again, but stopped when he heard the lock click from the inside. Cora looked out at him.

'I wondered if you were okay,' he said, then added: 'You weren't at dinner.'

Her hair was damp around her face as if she'd just stepped from the bath or shower. 'I wasn't hungry,' she told him.

'Nor was anyone else. I ate alone.' He was silent for a moment, waiting for some response from her. When none came, he said, 'Can we talk?'

Hesitation, then: 'I'm sorry, I'm acting like a stranger to you.' She opened the door wide and stood aside so that he could enter, their roles reversed from the previous night.

He rested a hand against the doorframe. 'I didn't know ...'

'Come in, Liam. Please.'

He entered the room and saw that it was bigger and more comfortable than his own. One half contained a small sofa and armchair, a coffee table in between, an antique writing bureau by the wall; the other side was occupied by a four-poster bed, bedside cabinet and dressing table, and a wardrobe of cavernous proportions. An open door led off and he assumed this was to an *en suite* bathroom. The curtains at the windows were drawn closed, which seemed unnecessary considering Neath's remote location.

Cora shut the door behind him and went to a table. 'Can I offer you a drink?' she asked, adjusting the belt of the white towelling robe she wore. 'Oh no, I forgot. You're always on duty, aren't you? I suppose you won't be surprised if I have one.' She poured herself some wine from a bottle on the table and settled back in the sofa, drawing her legs up under her.

'Why the antagonism, Cora? After last night –' He stopped when she bowed her head as if the words had stung her.

'Have I disillusioned you?' There was scorn in her voice. 'I drink too much, I make love in an odd fashion, I'm subservient to a man who's half-mad, half-genius. I can imagine what you think of me.'

Halloran sat next to her, their bodies touching. 'The only thing I can't figure out is what you really drink.'

Cora had to smile. 'Whatever happens to be on offer,' she replied with only a hint of sullenness. She sipped the wine and he noticed the bottle level was down to the last quarter. 'Did I shock you last night?' Cora asked, looking into her glass.

'Sure,' he answered.

She looked up sharply.

'I'd be a liar if I said I didn't enjoy it, though,' Halloran added.

'He made me do it.'

'What?'

'He made me go to your room.' She reached for the bottle and topped up her wine glass, even though it was still half-full. 'Felix told me to go to you last night.'

Halloran was stunned. 'I don't understand.'

'He ordered me to seduce you. I don't know why. Perhaps he was testing you in some way. Or testing me. Perhaps he got some kind of kick out of it, finding another way to degrade me, turn me into a whore.'

'Why should he want to do that?'

'Felix enjoys corrupting people. But it's too soon for you to have realized that.'

'Cora, this doesn't make sense.'

'You already know there's no sense to any of this, Liam. Why persist in looking for it? I'm sorry if I've bruised your ego, but the truth is I was merely obeying instructions last night.' Her hand was shaking and she quickly drank to prevent the wine spilling over. She glanced at him and was surprised to find him smiling still, but this time that coldness was there, the glint of cruelness that somehow was constantly lurking beneath his surface manner.

'Maybe Kline wanted me kept busy,' he said.

She caught her breath. He was right. For reasons of her own – reasons that were unclear even to herself – Cora had wanted to hurt Liam, to break through that aura of sureness. But there was more to it than that. She had wanted him, had wanted him to make love to her, had gone to him willingly as if ... Cora struggled to crystallize the thought ... as if he might be her ... saviour? Redeemer? Oh God, what a fool she was. Even then, when he had been inside her, it wasn't enough. She'd needed something more, much more. And they'd had to make love a different way so that she could achieve her own satisfaction. Felix had reduced her to that, made her a creature of sensations rather than emotions. And she'd despised Liam for this also, for she had allowed him to see her for what she was. Tonight she had tried to hurt him, but he had turned it around. It was she who had been humiliated further.

'Please go, Liam,' she said, her voice brittle.

'Oh no, not yet. Not yet, Cora.'

That faint Irishness to his voice again. How strange that it should make him sound so dangerous.

'I want you to leave.'

Instead he took the glass from her hand.

'I don't know what game it is you all think you're playing,' he said quietly, 'and honestly, I don't much care. But at least there's something more to you, Cora, something that megalomaniac hasn't touched yet. I don't know how he's managed to bring you to this point, but I do know you've kept a part of yourself away from him. You were different the first time I saw you, and I think it was because I was seeing you the way you used to be, the way you can still be.'

'There's nothing left for –'

He touched his fingers to her lips. 'You're wrong.' His own lips replaced his hand and she tried to turn away. He held her firm and kissed her, hurting her.

Cora sank into the sofa and pushed at his chest. She didn't want this. He wasn't the man to take her from Felix. They were alike, Felix and Liam. Cruel men. Vicious men. That was why Felix was fascinated by him. They were akin.

He was hurting her, and there was pleasure in that. But she mustn't let him, she couldn't let him ...

Halloran grabbed her wrist and pulled it aside. She was lying on the sofa now, the robe open beneath the belt, exposing her thighs. He continued to kiss her, his mouth hard against hers, and when she finally wrenched her head away, his lips sank to her neck and he bit, but used no strength. Cora moaned, partly out of self-pity and partly out of self-disgust, for feelings were being aroused in her.

'Please don't,' she tried to say, but Halloran had pulled the robe away from her breasts. He lowered his head to them. 'I don't want this!' she hissed, but his hand was on her thigh, pressing firmly, then gliding down to her knee, reaching behind, touching delicate nerve-points. His weight was on her, pinning her, and he used his body to part her legs. Still she protested, squirming against him, her fingers clenched on his shoulders. She could have clawed him, or pulled his hair, or bit him. But she didn't.

He sank to the floor, kneeling before her, keeping his body between her legs. Her robe had fallen open completely, the belt loose around her waist, and Halloran deftly undid his own clothing. He entered her, the movement hard and quick, causing her to cry out even though she was moist, ready for him despite her resistance. His lips found hers once more and this time she did not refuse him; the force of her kiss matched his.

Her arms reached around him, drawing him tight, and now Halloran groaned, a soft murmur that excited her. Cora's legs were rigid against his hips and she thrust herself forward, letting him fill her, wanting more, crying for more, her breathing tight and her arms trembling. Cora's cries turned into gasps and Halloran's hands went under and around her shoulders so that he could pull her down onto him, his own thrusts controlled and rhythmic. But that restraint was soon overwhelmed and he twisted his face into Cora's wet hair and she arched her neck, pushing her head back into the cushions, her hips almost rising off the sofa, clutching at him as their juices surged to mix inside her body. Her cry was sharp, trailing to a whimper, their bodies shuddering together, slowly calming to a trembling, eventually relaxing to a stillness. They lay there, neither one willing to separate.

Halloran felt the wetness on his cheek and lifted his head to look at Cora. She was weeping and when he tried to speak she pulled him down against her. His arm slid beneath her neck and he held her tightly.

They stayed that way until her weeping stopped, neither one saying anything, feeling no need to, content to rest with each other. Cora loved the feel of him inside her, even though he was soft now, and she ran her fingers beneath his shirt, caressing his spine. Halloran raised himself without withdrawing and lifted her legs onto the sofa. He lay on top, brushing his mouth across her face, kissing her eyes, her temples, her cheeks, passion subdued, replaced by tenderness.

'You don't know what he's done to me,' she said.

'None of that matters,' he soothed.

She sighed, a sweet sound, when she felt him becoming hard again. They made love slowly this time, their movement sensuous, almost languid, sensing each other in a different, more perfect, way. Their passion grew but was unleashed easily, a flowing then gently ebbing release.

As before, they remained locked together for some time and, when at last Halloran withdrew, it was with reluctance. He adjusted his clothing, then sat on the floor, an elbow resting on the sofa where Cora was still stretched. He leaned forward to kiss her lips, his hand smoothing away the damp hair from her face.

'Liam ...' she began to say, but he shook his head and smiled.

'No need, Cora. We'll talk tomorrow. Tonight just think about what's happened between us.' He stroked her body, fingertips tracing a line over her breasts down to her stomach, running into the cleft between her thighs.

Her arms went around his shoulders and she studied his eyes, her expression grave. 'I need to know more about you, can't you see that?'

'In time,' he said.

'Is it possible for me to trust you? There's something ...' she frowned, struggling to find the word '... *dark* about you, Liam, and I can't understand what it is. There's a remoteness in you that's frightening. I felt it the first time we met.'

He began to rise, but Cora held on to him.

'I told you yesterday,' he said. 'I'm what you see, no more than that.'

'It's what I *feel* in you that scares me. '

'I often deal with violent people, Cora. It can't help but have an effect on me.'

'You've become the same as them? Is that what you're saying?'

He shook his head.'It isn't that simple.'

'Then try to explain.' There was exasperation in her demand.

He began to rise again and this time her arms dropped away. 'In my trade violence usually has to be met with violence,' he said, looking down at her. 'It's sometimes the only way.'

'Doesn't that corrupt you? Doesn't that make you the same as them?'

'Maybe,' he replied.

She pulled at her robe, covering her nakedness.

Halloran walked to the door and paused there. 'It's when you start to enjoy the corruption that you know you're in trouble.' He went out, quietly closing the door after him.

Leaving Cora to weep alone.

Halloran washed himself in a bathroom along the hall before returning to his room. Once there, he hung his jacket over a bedpost and took the gun from its holster, placing it on the bedside cabinet. He removed his shoes this time, set the small alarm clock, and lay on the bed. The curtains were apart, but moonlight was feeble again that night and barely lit the room. Despite the fact that there was an extra bodyguard on duty inside the house, Halloran would only allow himself four hours' rest, intending to check on Monk and Palusinski during their individual watches, scouting Neath and the immediate outside area in between. Cora had taken up nearly an hour of his rest period. And a lot of energy.

He shut his eyes and remembered the hurt on her face as he'd left the room.

A brightness flashed beyond his eyelids.

Halloran opened his eyes again. The room was in darkness. Had he imagined the sudden flare?

It came once more, filling the room like a lightning flash. Yet no rumble of thunder followed.

He quickly moved from the bed, going to the window. He peered out into the night. A muted white glow marked the moon's presence behind a bank of clouds, the ragged-edged, mountainous shapes barely moving, the landscape below blurred and ill-defined. The lake was a huge flat greyness that appeared solid, as if its depths were of concrete.

Halloran blinked as the light flared again. The source was the lake itself, an emanation from its surface. And in that brief light he had seen forms on the water, black silhouettes that were human. Or so he assumed.

He rolled back over the bed, pulled on his shoes, and grabbed his gun. Halloran headed for the stairs.

▪ 25 ▪
LAKE LIGHT

MONK SHOULD HAVE BEEN ON GUARD DUTY. BUT THE MAIN HALL WAS EMPTY.

Halloran wasted no time searching for him; he switched off the hall lights, then opened one side of the frontdoors just enough to slip through. He was disturbed that the door had been left unlocked. His steps were barely audible as he hurried through the stone-floored porch, and he stopped only briefly once out in the open.

The lake was nothing more than a broad expanse, slightly lighter than its surrounds.

Halloran holstered the Browning and moved off, quickly edging along the frontage of the house, using it as a dark backdrop against which it would be difficult to be seen, his intention being to approach the lake from an angle rather than in a direct line from the main door. Once at the corner he made a crouching dash towards the lawn. Instinctively he dropped to the ground when light flared from the lake again. He blinked his eyes rapidly, feeling conspicuous and vulnerable lying there on the damp grass. But imprinted on his mind was the image the sudden brightness had exposed.

There was a boat out there, three or four figures huddled together in its confined space. They were watching something that was outside the boat, on the lake itself. Something that was not in the water but *on* the surface.

The vision dissolved as his eyes adjusted to the darkness once more. He stiffened when a howling came from the shoreline to his right, an eerie, desolate cry in the night. It was followed by a collective ululation, the baying of wolves – or *jackals* – a fearful sound wending across the water. He narrowed his eyes, hoping to see them among the indistinct shapes of trees and shrubbery that edged the side of the lake.

He thought he could make out the jackals, although it might only have been a clump of low foliage, for there was no movement. Halloran rose to one knee.

And again was temporarily blinded by a fulguration from the lake.

It had come from below the water, expanding across the surface, a silvery-white luminance swiftly expanding across the flat surface, its extremities shading to indigo and the deepest mauve. The illumination lasted only a second or so, but there was time for Halloran to observe the jackals gathered there at the water's edge. The glare had frozen them. Their heads, with long pointed muzzles and erect ears, stood high from their shoulders, cocked in alertness and perhaps puzzlement. At least a dozen pairs of glowing orbs, set in irregular pattern, reflected the light.

Darkness, total after the glare. But again an impression lingering. Halloran had seen someone standing among the beasts. A bent figure, a cowl concealing its features. Whoever it was had been watching the lake.

Halloran heard a voice – no, laughter – and his attention was diverted to the boat. He had recognized the dry cackle of Felix Kline, the sound amplified across the water. Halloran rose to his feet and moved forward at speed, keeping low, taking the gun from its holster as he went.

He could make out the landing jetty ahead and noted that the boat he and Kline had used that morning was no longer moored there. Did Kline enjoy a night-time boat-ride as well as an early morning one? Or had he been forced into a trip not of his choosing, the lake making an obvious route to avoid the guard dogs? But he had heard Kline laughing, hardly the attitude of someone being kidnapped. Nevertheless, Halloran did not relax. If they moved any further away he would get to a car and be ready to meet them on the opposite bank at the estate's border. He would also have a chance to call in back-up on the journey.

There was no cover this close to the shoreline, so Halloran moved back a ways, then spreadeagled himself on the ground, his gun pointing towards the dull shape on the lake. He waited and yet again was dazzled by another vast spasm of light. The intervals between had not been regular in length, so there was no way of preparing himself for each surge. The light vanished instantly, neither fading nor receding, snuffed like a candle flame. He rubbed at his eyelids, disbelieving what he had seen, telling himself there had to be a simple explanation, that he hadn't been able to take in everything during that short burst of light. Reason reassured him, but the after-image refused to compromise.

Halloran had seen four men in the boat – Palusinski, Monk and the two Jordanians. Kline had not been with them.

He was several yards away. He had been standing on the calm surface of the water.

Halloran shook his head, resisting the urge to laugh at the absurdity. There had to be something else out there just below the water level, a sandbank, a submerged platform, perhaps even a large rock. There was a logical explanation. Had to be. It was in Kline's nature to play such childish games. But surely they would have come across such an obstruction when he, himself, had rowed out there that very morning?

In the distance the jackals howled, the sound further away this time, as though they were leaving the shoreline to slink back into the wooded slopes. He heard oars swishing on water. Voices. Drawing close to the jetty. He waited for them all to disembark before getting to his feet and going towards them.

Moonlight squeezed through the merest rent in the clouds and the group came to a halt when they caught sight of Halloran.

'No need for weapons,' Kline said, humour in his voice. 'No enemies among us tonight, Halloran.'

'What the hell were you doing out there?' The question was quietly put, Halloran's anger suppressed.

'I'm not a prisoner in my own home,' Kline replied jovially. 'I do as I please.'

'Not if you expect me to protect you.'

'There's no danger tonight.'

Moonlight broke through with greater force and he saw that Kline was grinning at him.

'The light from the water ...?'

Khayed and Daoud, dressed in the robes of their country, grinned as broadly as their master, while Palusinski glanced anxiously at Kline. Monk remained expressionless.

Kline's eyebrows arched uncomprehendingly. Then: 'Ah, the lightning flashes. Yes, there seems to be quite an electrical storm raging above us tonight. With thunder soon to follow, no doubt. And then, of course, a deluge. Best not to linger out here, don't you agree?'

Once again his manner had changed. Kline's disposition had become that of an older, more reasoning man, the insidious mocking still in his voice, but his tone softer, less strident. His persona was vibrant, as if brimming with energy, though not of the nervous – and neurotic – kind that Halloran had become used to.

'You weren't in the boat,' Halloran said almost cautiously.

There was elation in Kline's laughter. 'I'm not one for moonlight dips, I can assure you.'

Palusinski snickered.

'I saw you ... on the water.'

'*On* the water?' Kline asked incredulously, continuing to smile. 'You mean *walking* on the water? Like Jesus Christ?'

Halloran did not reply.

'I see you've been hallucinating again, Halloran. Something in this lake obviously doesn't agree with your mental processes.'

The Arabs chuckled behind their hands.

'I really think you should be resting,' Kline went on in mock-sympathy. 'The strain of the last couple of days is apparently affecting your judgement. Or should I say, your perception? I can't say I'm not surprised, Halloran. After all, you did come highly recommended as a bodyguard. I wonder if your employers realize that stress is getting the better of you.'

At last even Monk smiled.

The clouds resumed their dominance and the landscape darkened once more.

'I think we should talk,' Halloran said evenly, ignoring the stifled sounds of mirth coming from Kline's followers (for that was what they were, he had decided, not just employees, but in some way, disciples of this strange man).

'But you should be sleeping. Isn't this your off-duty period? That's why we chose not to disturb you – we are perfectly aware that someone under your kind of pressure needs his rest.'

'Monk and Palusinski had instructions to alert me to any activity, no matter what time it was.'

'A late-night excursion on the lake was hardly worth rousing you for.'

'I gave them orders.'

'And I countermanded those orders.'

'My company can't function under those conditions. Tomorrow I'll recommend the contract is cancelled, or at least that I'm taken off the assignment. There's too much going on here that I don't like.'

'No.' At least the mood had been broken; Kline's tone was sharp, urgent. 'You mustn't do that. I need you with me.'

'You might need Shield, but you don't need me. There are other operatives equally as good.' He tucked the automatic back into its holster and turned to walk away.

'Wait.' Kline had taken a step after him and Halloran paused. 'I suppose I'm being a little unfair,' the smaller man said, and immediately something of his 'other' self was in evidence, almost as though it were another guise. 'You're right, we should have let you know we were coming out here, should've brought you along for safety. But it was a spur of the moment thing, y'know, something I felt like doing. I didn't see any need to worry you.'

'That doesn't explain why you went on the lake. Nor does it explain the light. Or what I saw.'

'Look at those clouds. Just study them for a while.'

'That isn't nec –' A flash of light stopped him. He gazed skywards. Another, fainter, discharge of energy, but enough to throw the tumbled cloud into relief. 'That isn't what happened before. The light came from the lake.'

'Reflections, that's all. It bounced off the water's surface. The lake's calm tonight, just like a big mirror.'

A stuttered glare from above lit the group of men standing before him, hardening them into statues, bleaching their faces white. In the distance, as if to confirm Kline's explanation, came a deep rumbling of thunder.

'Let's get inside before the rain comes,' Kline suggested.

'I saw –'

'You were mistaken.' There was a firmness to the statement. 'We'll go back to the house, Halloran, and I'll tell you a few things about myself, about this place. You'll find it interesting, I promise you that.'

Halloran was tempted to advise his client to go to hell, but part of him was intrigued. The man was an enigma, and unlike any person he'd had to protect before. 'One condition,' he said.

Kline lifted his hands, palms towards Halloran. 'Whatever.'

'You answer all my questions.'

'Can't promise you that.'

Light blazed the land again.

'I'll answer as many as I can, though,' Kline added, and the thunder was nearer this time.

'Tell your Arab friends to go on ahead.' Halloran indicated Monk and Palusinski. 'You two follow behind. And don't watch us – keep your eyes on those slopes and the road.'

'Ain't nothin' here to worry us,' Monk protested.

'Just do as I say,' Halloran snapped.

Palusinski slapped a hand on the American's shoulder as if to warn him not to argue. 'You go,' the Pole said to Halloran. 'We'll follow. Everything is fine.'

As the group started walking towards the house, fanning out so that Kline and Halloran were at the centre of a square formation, the first raindrops spattered the grass. Kline grinned at his protector. 'I told you it was about to rain,' he said.

The deluge broke as though by command and within seconds the men were soaked through. That didn't appear to worry Kline at all. He laughed and suddenly ran free of the formation, twisting his body around in the air, raising his arms high, fingers stretched outwards. He came to a stop facing the hurrying group, his face turned up towards the sky, mouth open wide to receive the pelting raindrops. He slowly lowered his head and arms and something in his gleeful expression brought the others to a halt.

Kline pointed behind them. 'Look at the lake!' he shouted over the downpour.

They turned to look back.

The broad expanse of water, suddenly lit by another flickering of lightning, was a churning mass, the rainfall exploding into the surface and creating millions of tiny geysers.

After the light was spent, Halloran was left with the unnerving impression of a million fingers pushing through the surface from the other side.

▪ 26 ▪
AN ANCIENT CULTURE

THEY SAT OPPOSITE EACH OTHER IN THE DRAWING ROOM, KLINE FURIOUSLY rubbing at his dark curly hair, grinning across at Halloran as he did so.

'Refreshing, huh?' he said. 'I love the rain. It purges the flesh. Pure and fresh, uncontaminated by human effluence. You ought to get dry. Don't want my bodyguard coming down with pneumonia.'

'I'll take a bath before I turn in.' He realized ruefully there would be scant time for sleeping if he were to keep to his own schedule.

The room was like most others at Neath – sparsely furnished and cold in atmosphere, even the roaring fire Kline had ordered to be lit infusing little spiritual warmth to the surrounds. Save for the fire glow there was no other light source in the room, for Kline had switched it off moments before. On a pedestal in one corner, its face animated by dancing shadows, stood the stone figure of a robed woman; the eyes were wide and staring, her hair swept back in almost mediaeval style. Above the mantel over the fireplace was a frieze depicting chariots and soldiers on the march; its colours, almost lost in the shadows, were of blue and white with the palest of reds for contrast.

'Made of shell and limestone,' Kline said when he noticed Halloran studying the frieze while Khayed tended the fire and Daoud went off to fetch a towel. 'Part of the Royal Standard of Ur. See one of the enemy being crushed by a chariot? There was plenty of gore in art and literature even in those distant days. People's taste doesn't change much, does it? You know anything at all about the Sumerians, Halloran?'

With the feeling he was about to find out, Halloran shook his head. 'History was never one of my strong points.'

'Not even ancient history? I think you'd have found it fascinating.'

'I'm more concerned with what's going on right now. You agreed to answer some questions.'

'Sure. Just relax. Let me tell you something about these Sumerians first, okay? Never too late to learn, right?'

Daoud returned with a towel at that moment, which he handed to his employer.

'You can go ahead and feed Palusinski,' Kline told him. 'Our Polish friend has been drooling all evening.'

The Arab grinned. 'I have kept for him some tasty morsels,' he replied and beside him, having completed his task at the fireplace, Khayed chuckled. Halloran noted that, unlike yesterday, Daoud had not bothered to disguise his understanding of the English language. Both Arabs gave a slight bow and left the room.

Kline dried his hair with the towel, his rain-soaked jeans and sweater apparently not bothering him. Halloran watched his client, tiny orange glows fluttering in Kline's dark eyes, his features sharp as if he were eager for conversation, with no thought for the lateness of the hour. One side of the psychic's body was in shadow, the side close to the fire warmly lit, shades of yellow dancing on his skin. His chair and body cast one corner of the room into deep, wavering gloom, but from its midst Halloran could see and feel those enlarged eyes of the stone woman staring at him.

Kline draped the towel over his head like a shawl so that only the tip of his nose and chin caught the glow from the fire. 'Did you know they invented the written word?' At Halloran's quizzical expression he added, 'The Sumerians.'

'No, I didn't know that,' Halloran answered tonelessly.

'Yep. And they were the first to count in units of ten and sixties. That's how we got sixty minutes to an hour and sixty seconds in a minute. They applied it to time, y'see. It's why we divide a circle into 360 degrees, too. Not only that, but those old boys invented the wheel. How about that?'

'Kline, I'm not really – '

'*You might be.*' The retort was sharp, but a hand was immediately raised, palm outwards, to indicate no offence was meant. 'They knew about algebra and geometry, even had some idea of anatomy and surgery. I'm talking about 3000 *BC*, Halloran, 3000 BC and earlier. Can you beat that? Shit, the rest of the world was barely past Neolithic!'

'You haven't told me why you went out on the lake tonight.'

'Huh? I thought I had.'

'No.'

'Okay, okay. Look, would you believe me if I told you that the lake acts as some kind of conductor to my psychic power? That my psyche draws strength from certain physical sources. You know how a divining rod in the hands of special people is attracted towards an underground spring or subterranean lake, how it vibrates with energy and bends towards the source? My mind does the same thing, only it also absorbs psychic energy from these places.'

'That's impossible. You're mixing the physical with the psychical.'.

'And you naturally assume there's no connection between the two. Never heard of kinetic energy, Halloran? How d'you imagine certain gifted people can move inanimate objects through the power of their own minds? It's that very connection I'm talking about, the link between the physical and the psychical. There's energy in everything around us, but energy itself has no form, no substance – it's an incorporeal thing, just like our own mindwave patterns. Is it getting through to you, or are you the type that never wants to understand?'

Kline was leaning forward so that his whole face was in the shadow of the cowl. Halloran did not respond to the last question.

'It's the reason I bought Neath,' Kline went on. 'In these grounds I have my own psychic generator – the lake itself, one huge receptacle for spiritual force. You saw for yourself tonight how the lightning was drawn to it, and how those mysterious properties of the waters reacted. There are hundreds, maybe thousands, of such fields on our earth, places that different races have worshipped from, built their shrines on, paid homage to, since man first became aware of the other side of his nature. They still do to this day. And very few really understand why.'

He sat back and the towel swung away from his jaw. He was smiling.

'In some locations, metaphysical and physical deposits become almost one, and that's because both kinds of energy are related. The moon affects the minds of men, ask any psychiatrist or psychologist, as well as influencing the earth's tides. Vast mineral deposits – ores, oil, gas or whatever – have that potential because they're all sources of energy. How d'you think I locate them for Magma? My mind's attracted to them because it's from these sources that it draws sustenance, the same way an animal can sniff food from great distances, a shark can sense blood in the water from miles away. Instinct or mind-power? Or is it all the same thing?'

Halloran understood what he was being told, could even appreciate that there was some kind of weird logic to it, but Kline's dissertation was difficult to accept. 'Are you saying the lake has particular properties, minerals that – '

'I don't know what the fuck it has, Halloran. Nor do I care. Maybe there's something underneath the lake itself, or in the sludge swilling on the bottom. None of that matters to me, I'm just happy to have my own private supply.' Kline rubbed at his hair again with the towel. 'I still have to search out sources in other parts, though. Like the Bedouins have their secret water-holes all over the desert, always handy when one dries up, I have my own wells. It involves some travelling, but like they say, travel broadens the mind. Right?'

'Is that how you picked up your bodyguards, passing through various countries?' Halloran asked, keen to lead the conversation away from such 'mystical' overtones.

Kline was reflective. 'Yeah. Yeah, I did a lot of travelling. Found suitable people along the way.'

'People and animals. How did you get the jackals back into the country?'

Kline shook his head. 'They were bred for me here. Unusual pets, huh?'

'You could say. I can't help wondering why you chose such a breed.'

'Because they're despicable, Halloran. I like that.' Kline chuckled as he gazed into the fire. 'And they're scavengers. But an underestimated species, all the same. Scavengers, yes, but not cowardly as popular belief would have it. Oh no, they'd fight off eagles and hyenas for food. And they'd snatch a morsel from under a lion's nose.'

He shook his head as if in wonder. 'Cunning, too. You know, one will distract a mother antelope while another grabs the baby. They'll tear off pieces of a kill and bury them in different places for another day to foil rival scavengers. They'll even swallow food and regurgitate it later to avoid the risk of it being stolen by swooping eagles on the journey back to their young. Wonderful survivors, these creatures, Halloran.'

'As you say, they're scavengers.'

'True, their main diet is carrion, but they appreciate other delights. The jackal is very partial to the afterbirth of the wildebeeste, for instance. They'll follow a herd for miles sniffing after the pregnant cows.'

'There was someone with them tonight. He was standing by the lakeside.'

Kline turned back to Halloran. 'So?'

'I assume it was the person who controls the gates.'

The other man nodded.

'Someone else you picked up abroad?'

Kline ignored the question. 'I haven't finished telling you about the Sumerians. Did I say they were the first astrologers? No, I don't think I did. They built ziggurats, massive square towers, as temple observatories. That was the start of astronomy just in case you're unimpressed by zodiac predictions.'

He draped the towel over his head again and rested back in his chair, watching Halloran from the shadows.

'Their nation sprung up between the Rivers Tigris and Euphrates in what these days is called Iraq. A green, lush area, desert all around. It's the traditional site of the Garden of Eden, where that bad old angel called Serpent got Adam and Eve into deep trouble, and had his wings clipped – his legs too – for the rift he'd caused. Serpent was forced to spend the rest of his existence crawling on his belly, and when you're immortal, as all angels are, that's a long time. Anyway, the Sumerians knew how to govern themselves, with laws and organization of labour forces and rates and taxes and coalitions between the different cities. The smaller towns and villages even had their own mayors and municipal councils. Thing is, they took their farming seriously and because whole communities could be fed by a few, others were left to get on with developing new skills and professions. The beginning of real civilization, Halloran. For better or worse, the start of the whole cultural shebang.'

'Look, right now there are more relevant matters to discuss. Like the lack of security on this estate, for instance.'

It was as if Kline hadn't heard him. 'They even had their own sure-fire method of dealing with crime. On an eye for an eye basis, y'know? A son who raised his hand against his father would have that hand cut off, same with a doctor who fouled up an operation. An unfaithful wife would have a breast cut off. A man who set fire to a house, or maybe looted a burning home, would be roasted alive.' Kline sniggered. 'Rough justice, but effective. And oh boy, their death penalty. As well as roasting, there was beating, strangulation and being thrown from their highest temples. Oh yeah – and mutilation. Anyone who really pissed them off was mutilated, had their arms and legs chopped off. The idea was to make sure that particular evil would never rise up against them again. Literally. So they turned these sinners into limbless creatures, snakes – like the Serpent of old, you see – only fit to crawl on their bellies in the dirt. Nasty way to die, left all alone, unable to move, the only hope being that death didn't take too long.' Kline visibly shuddered.

'You said they were civilized.'

'They found a way to make their system work. A cruel regime in many respects, but they taught the rest of the world something. Strange thing is that, as a race, they vanished from the face of the earth. Can you beat that? Just died out, absorbed into other cultures. You have to wonder why, don't you, considering all their achievements?'

'Yeah,' Halloran replied wearily, 'you have to wonder.'

'Even their language died with them.'

A burning coal cracked, a gunshot sound that made both men glance towards the fireplace.

After a moment, Halloran said: 'I want to ask you about Cora.'

Kline settled back in his chair and slowly pulled the towel from his head. There was a curious mixture of innocence and wickedness in his expression, perhaps because while his smile was ingenuous, there was a glint of maliciousness in his eyes.

'This on a personal basis, Halloran, or to do with my protection?'

'Maybe both. Why is she so ...' an apt word was difficult '... dependent on you?'

The other man giggled, a childish outburst. Halloran waited patiently.

'She isn't,' came the reply. 'Nobody's ever truly dependent on another person, didn't you know that? It's only their own weaknesses that they're servile to. An indulgence on their part. Self-inflicted. The tendency is to use someone else as a focus for their own deficiencies, maybe even as a patron to them. Surprised you haven't figured that out for yourself.' Kline leaned forward as if to make the point. 'We all have total governance over our own will, Halloran. Ultimately, no one can interfere with that.'

'People can be corrupted.'

The reply was swift. 'Only if that's what they secretly want.'

Halloran realized that he was now reluctant to pursue the matter. 'We, uh, have to make arrangements for tighter security around the estate.'

Amused, Kline studied his protector for several seconds. 'Why so interested in Cora? You haven't become involved in anything that might be construed as "unprofessional", I hope. After all, you've been contracted to take an interest in my well-being, no one else's.'

He knew his client was mocking him and wondered, not for the first time, why Kline had sent Cora to him the night before. 'There's a difference between loyalty and dependence.'

Kline looked genuinely surprised. 'You suggesting Cora would betray me?'

'Not at all. I just need to know the full picture.'

'Well let's talk about her some more.' Kline interlaced his fingers over his stomach, his elbows resting on the arms of the chair, eyes closed as if picturing Cora in his mind. 'She's intelligent, works hard, is super-efficient at her job. She's also some looker, wouldn't you agree? A little jaded nowadays, though, like she's got deep-rooted troubles. D'you feel that? Yeah, it's pretty obvious. What do you suppose those troubles are?'

He was being taunted, but Halloran refused to take the bait. 'Let's get on to other things.'

'I think she's agonizing over some terrible moral dilemma, don't you? You can see she's losing sleep over it. Can't be anything to do with the job, otherwise she'd leave, wouldn't she? No, it's got to be something in her personal life. She's a sensual woman, so maybe sex is involved, huh? What d'you think, Halloran? Stupid of me – how would you know?'

The urge to wipe the leering grin from Kline's face was almost overwhelming. 'We need chain-link fences topped by barbed wire erected at all access points to the grounds,' Halloran said calmly, 'with vibration sensors attached. Intruders can always cut their way through hedges, but at least we'll slow them down and make it easier for patrols to spot them.'

'Maybe Cora likes things she's been taught not to. She had a strong moral upbringing, you know. I understand her parents were pillars of society, so maybe they wouldn't have approved of her little ways. You think that's what's bothering her? Parental disapproval, even though they're dead and gone? Guilty conscience on her part? Destructive thing, guilt.'

'I'm not in favour of moving searchlights – they're too easy to dodge – but a good lighting system close to the house and pointing outwards would be useful. That and low-frequency audio scanners or magnetic fields would provide a good cover. You need intrusion-detection sensors between the house and the lake, too, with sonar equipment directed onto the lake itself.'

'Still, none of us are infallible, are we, Halloran? We all have our weaknesses and foibles that make us vulnerable. We wouldn't be human without them. Can't help wondering what yours are.'

'Along the inside road you could do with one or two access control points where vehicles can undergo thorough checks. Closed-circuit television is essential for the main gates, incidentally, with a guardhouse by the side. That'll have to be built with hardened walls and glass, and will require a telephone line direct to the house. Reliance on your man at the lodge isn't good enough.'

'What makes you so inscrutable, Halloran? What goes on behind that mask of yours?'

'As well as CCTV points on entrances to Neath, you ought to have bars mounted on all windows that provide easy access. It goes without saying that intrusion alarms will have to be installed on all windows and doors, too.'

'Do you believe in God, Halloran?'

He stared back at Kline. 'I'll draw up a list of firm recommendations and submit copies to the Magma Corporation and Achilles' Shield,' he said evenly. 'If we don't receive yours or Magma's consent to carry out these precautions, there's not much my company can do for you.'

'My question rattle you? You should see your face. I thought all the Irish were God-fearing, no matter what particular brand of religion they followed.'

'I'm not Irish.'

'Your old man was. And you may not have been born there, but you were raised in the ol' country.'

'How did you know that?' He realized immediately that Cora must have told Kline.

'You still haven't answered *my* question.'

'Information about myself isn't part of the contract. All you need to know is that I'm capable of doing a good job.'

'Just curious, that's all. You suddenly look even more dangerous, d'you know that?'

There was an abrupt vision between Kline and himself. Father O'Connell's big, ruddy face was contorted with anguish, his tear-soaked cheeks catching the flames from the fire. Only these reflections were of flames from another time. Halloran cleared the image from his mind. But the sounds of the priest's wailing as he ran into the burning church were more difficult to erase.

'You still with me, Halloran? You look as if you've seen a ghost.'

The Shield operative blinked. Kline was watching him intently and the slyness of his smile somehow suggested he had shared Halloran's vision.

'The Sumerians had lots of gods – lots of goddesses, too,' Kline went on as if nothing unusual had occurred. 'A whole team of 'em. Anu, god of the Heavens, Su'en, the Moon god, Enlil, god of Water, Markuk, god of Babylon, Ea, one of the good guys, and the goddess, Inin, later known as Ishtar – now she was something else. She was a whore. Then there was Bel-Marduk, the one they came to despise.' His smile had become venomous. 'They misunderstood his cruelty, you see. But there was always someone – excuse me, some *deity* – to pray to for any cause, or to blame for any wrong. Delegation was the idea, spreading the load. Don't put too much pressure on the one god or goddess in case they get vexed and turn nasty. Or was it because they didn't believe in putting all their trust in one master? Maybe a lesson learned from their past. And that's the weird thing about these people, Halloran: we know hardly anything at all about their origins. Now, like I said before, that's odd, considering the Sumerians invented the written word.'

Halloran scarcely heard, for he was still numbed by the strength of the vision of moments before. And tiredness also was beginning to weigh heavily upon him.

'It seems,' Kline continued, his enthusiasm not curbed by lack of interest from his audience, 'that kings, princes – maybe even the high priests – hid or destroyed all records of Sumerian early history. Yet they'd been setting things down as cuneiform writing on clay tablets since 3000 BC! What d'you suppose they needed to hide? I mean, to wipe out centuries of their past like that, they must have had some terrible dark secret they wanted to keep from the rest of the world, don't you think?' He was leaning forward again, hands resting on his knees, his face bright in the glow from the fire.

Halloran struggled to rouse himself, the room's warmth and Kline's almost mesmeric tone abetting the weariness. 'There's something more I need to ask you,' he said, and then had to concentrate to remember what it was. In the gloom of the far corner, the stone woman's eyes seemed larger.

'Even one of the greatest archaeological finds ever failed to turn up any evidence of what went on in Sumerian society much before 2500 BC,' said Kline, ignoring the pending question. 'That was when Sir Leonard Woolley discovered a gigantic grave site near the city wall of Ur in the 1920s. Thousands of the graves had been plundered, but something spurred on the old boy to dig deeper, and what he found *underneath* that cemetery staggered historians all around the world.'

Halloran pinched the corners of his eyes with thumb and forefinger. What the hell was Kline rambling on about?

'Know what was there?' Kline gripped the arms of the chair as if unable to contain his excitement. 'Stone tombs. Sepulchres! Can you believe it? Woolley's team got to them by ramps leading into deep shafts. Inside those chambers they found intact skeletons of Sumerian kings, queens, princes, princesses, and members of the high priesthood, all decked out in full regalia of gold and semi-precious stones – and that's why it came to be known as the Royal Cemetery. Around them were golden cups, stelae and statues, beautiful vases, silver ornaments – all kinds of valuable stuff.' Kline gave an excited laugh. 'And know what else, Halloran? All their servants and attendants were buried right there with them. Court officials, soldiers, priests – even oxen with their wagons. No signs of violence, though. Those people had accepted their fate without argument. They'd taken poison and allowed themselves to be sealed in with their masters and mistresses.' He grinned. 'How's that for loyalty?'

Halloran experienced a peculiar sense of relief when the other man turned away from him to gaze at the fire, as though Kline's intensity was a parasitical thing. Some of his tiredness lifted and he remembered the question he had meant to ask.

But Kline was speaking once more. 'For twelve years Sir Leonard worked that site, delving, dusting, probing, digging, yet nowhere did he find anything that told him of the early Sumerians. Some historians surmise that everything was destroyed at the time of the Great Flood – *if* there ever was such an event. No one's ever been sure whether or not that was only a myth, and one borrowed by another religion, incidentally. For Noah, read Utnapishtim, a hero of Sumerian legend. Anyway, no matter, flood or not, something should have survived from that catastrophe – unless those old boys didn't want it to. But what could be so bad, so *diabolically* awful, that they'd want the knowledge of it obliterated from their history? Answer me that.'

His head slowly came around so that he was facing Halloran again, and there was a meanness to his smile. The flames of the fire had died down, the room considerably darker. Halloran felt oppressed by the shadows, as though they were drapes closing around him. And the weariness had returned, resting on his eyelids so that they were difficult to keep open.

The question. Not Kline's but his own. What was the question? Kline had reminded him. *Underneath* the cemetery. Under. Neath. Kline had even emphasized the word. He thought of the sturdy oak door that led to the cellar.

'Curious about what's down there?' said the other man. 'Under the house? Down in the cellar?'

But Halloran hadn't voiced the question. His head sagged with tiredness.

'Not falling asleep on me, are you?' said Kline. 'Ah well, it's been a long day, so go ahead, close your eyes.'

He didn't want them to, but his eyes closed. Halloran stirred in the chair, his limbs leaden. Sleep was approaching and it was irresistible.

'Not just a cellar,' he heard Kline say from a great distance. 'Something more than that. Down there is where I have my very own sepulchre. Did you hear me, Halloran?'

Barely. Kline must be a long way away by now …

'… *My sepulchre, Halloran* …'

… yet the words were suddenly near, a whisper inside Halloran's mind.

▪ 27 ▪
A DREAM AND BETRAYAL

'*Liam*. WAKE UP.'

He felt a hand shaking his shoulder and consciousness quickly drew him away from the unreality of his dream. Halloran's body was tensed and ready before his eyes opened, his fingers instinctively curling around the butt of his gun. Cora was leaning over him, her face anxious.

'Liam, we have to go back to London immediately.'

He looked past her at the empty chair opposite. Only grey ashes were in the fireplace and daylight did its best to penetrate the heavy curtains over the windows. Stone eyes still watched him from the corner of the room.

'Liam,' Cora urged.

'It's all right.' He stood, all drowsiness gone, his senses fully alert. He was angry with himself when he glanced at his wristwatch and saw that it was nearly 8.40. Why the hell had he allowed himself to fall asleep in this room, and why hadn't one of the bodyguards woken him at the proper time? 'What's the problem, Cora?' he quickly asked.

'Felix has just had a call from Sir Victor. He has to return to Magma right away.'

'On a Sunday?'

She nodded. 'It's serious.'

He made towards the door, but her hand on his arm stopped him.

'Last night …' she said.

So much had happened the night before that it took him a second or two to understand what Cora meant. Her expression was so solemn, her eyes so grave, that he couldn't help but smile.

'We'll talk later,' he told her, then kissed her cheek. They left the room together.

The streets of the City were empty, save for the few tourists who took the occasion of such quietness to view London's financial sector. Light drizzle soaked the pavements and roadways, freshening them for the onslaught they would take during the rest of the week. Glass towers glistened as though newly varnished, while older buildings hued darker as they soaked up the dampness.

A convoy of three cars, a black limousine, a Mercedes and a Granada, sped through the deserted streets, the drivers of each checking their surrounds and rearview mirrors each time they were halted by traffic lights.

Halloran was in the back of the second car, the silver-grey Mercedes, sitting next to Felix Kline, prepared to cover his client with his own body should anything untoward occur. Janusz Palusinski was driving the armoured vehicle, and Cora sat beside him in the passenger seat. Monk was the driver of the car ahead, Khayed and Daoud, who never ceased looking back to satisfy themselves that their master was not far behind, were his companions. In the Granada, the last in the procession, were two Shield men who had been taken off patrol duty around the estate.

Kline had been unusually silent throughout the journey, mentioning neither the events of the previous night, nor the reason for the summons to the Magma building that morning. Halloran realized he was witnessing yet another facet of this strange man's nature, a quiet brooding stillness that was in sharp contrast to Kline's irritatingly animated and talkative side. This mood was more akin to the soft-spoken, cultured role that Kline sometimes adopted, although again it was different, for there was no mocking in his gaze and no air of secret knowledge. The small man was withdrawn, thoughtful, seemingly unaware of any danger he might be in, with no agitation in his movements, no nervousness in his scrutiny. Yet Halloran could sense a deep anger burning inside him.

The Shield operative remembered the dream Cora had roused him from, for Kline had been part of it. They had walked together, he and Kline, Halloran allowing himself to be led by the other man through a great blackness, his hand in Kline's as though they were lovers. Although nothing could be seen, he had felt a frightening vastness of space around and above them, as if they were inside a cathedral or a huge subterranean cave. Now and then something light would waft across his face, so that he recoiled, fearing there were long trailing cobwebs on all sides. Kline's whispered voice assured him that there was nothing to be afraid of, they were merely passing through thin, unseen veils. There was something in the distance, a tenuous mass that was blacker than the blackness around them, and Halloran could hear the sound of his own heartbeat as they drew nearer to that ultimate darkness, the thudding growing louder, joined by the beating of another's – Kline's – their life-surge keeping time, becoming as one. And then, all about the darkness, eyelids were opening in slow, drawn-out movements, so that a multitude of stone eyes stared as the two men drew closer to the void, the nucleus of the blackness itself. Kline had released his hand and was stretching his arms towards the core, creating an opening within its shell, their combined heartbeats becoming thunderous, joining – or so it seemed – with yet another whose loudness grew so that soon, very soon, it smothered their own, and although the rising sound appeared to emanate from the void before them, it was everywhere, filling the infinite space, deafening the two men. Kline was reaching inside that pitchy nothingness, arms trembling, his mouth gaping in a silent ecstatic scream and Halloran had moved close to see what it was that the other man grasped, but he was blind in such blackness; he could feel a terrible heat, sense something there, something he was glad he could not see. Yet still he reached out with Kline, the two men joined in an unholy alliance, compelled by the mystery ...

'*Liam.*'

And Cora's voice had recalled him from the dream.

'Liam.'

The Mercedes was passing the Mansion House, the Magma building not far away, towering above others around it. Cora had turned in her seat and was looking directly at him.

Halloran blinked. He'd been completely lost in his own thoughts and once again was angry at himself for his negligence.

'Should we drive straight down into Magma's underground carpark,' Cora said, 'or do you want us to be dropped by the front entrance?'

'The carpark,' he replied. 'I arranged for it to be checked out by Shield before we left Neath. If there were problems they'd have contacted us.'

'Was there any news of those people who tried to stop us on Friday?' she asked.

Cora's face was still pale, her actions skittish, the weekend in the country apparently having had little calming effect, Halloran thought wryly. 'Nothing's turned up so far. Something'll break soon though, it usually does. We'll be okay so long as we're prepared.' He had addressed the last remarks to Kline, but the psychic's attention was averted; he was watching the streets, though Halloran had the feeling his client's vision was directed inwards.

The Magma Corporation's headquarters came into full view, and Halloran was once again impressed by its grandeur. The rain had intensified the lustre of its bronze surfaces, the deep shade of the windows defining and enhancing the metal sections so that the building's complicated structure was drawn in bold and deliberately simple lines. The curved buttresses and various levels added to the forcefulness of design, a formidable edifice amidst staid and less aggressive architecture.

The limousine ahead pulled into the kerb outside the main entrance and Halloran instructed Palusinski to keep moving until they reached the garage entrance around the corner in a narrow side-street. A member of the Shield team saw their approach and signalled for the entrance barrier inside the building to be lifted. The Granada followed the Mercedes down the ramp, the limousine now in the rear of the convoy. The Pole reversed their vehicle into a bay and Halloran stepped out immediately it came to a halt. He quickly went around to Kline's side, right hand inside his jacket. A figure was already limping towards them as Palusinski opened the passenger door for Kline, and Halloran raised a hand in greeting. Mather's countenance was unusually grim.

'A word, Liam,' he said as he drew near.

'Go on ahead to the lift,' Halloran told the others. 'I'll join you there.' He went towards Mather, who ushered him a short distance away so that they would not be overheard.

'How have things been at your end?' the Planner said, stopping by a concrete pillar. At the top of the ramp the Shield operative who had signalled the car's approach stood with his back to them, observing the street outside.

'Not good as far as security's concerned,' answered Halloran. 'Neath is wide open.'

'But you've had no more trouble?'

He hesitated before giving a shake of his head. 'What's wrong, Charles?'

'It's Dieter, I'm afraid.' Mather looked down at his cane, unconsciously tapping it twice on the ground. 'His body was recovered not more than an hour ago.'

Halloran saw the others were walking towards the lifts, Monk and the two Arabs following close behind. The two operatives from the Granada were standing by their car, waiting for further instructions. 'What happened?' he said to Mather.

'Shot through the back of the head. Gerald is with the police finding out a bit more at this very moment. What we do know is that Dieter was tortured before being killed.'

'Jesus, Mary ...' breathed Halloran. 'Who?'

Mather shrugged. 'I haven't a clue, Liam. No trademarks that we're aware of as yet.'

'Where was he found?'

'Floating in the Thames. Whoever did it didn't even bother to weigh down the body.'

'Anything to do with this operation?'

'We can't discount that factor. If there is any logical reason for his murder, and providing it isn't the work of some outraged husband, then torture obviously suggests information was being sought. Nevertheless, it's somewhat drastic to go to such lengths just to gain details of our plans for Felix Kline. It's reasonable to assume that any would-be kidnappers have sufficient knowledge of their target without resorting to that kind of violence. Another theory is that someone with a grudge from Dieter's past hated him enough to inflict such injuries before ending his life.'

'There's another possibility,' suggested Halloran. Kline and his entourage were at the lifts and looking round to see what was delaying him. 'It could be a way of warning us off.'

'From protecting Felix Kline?'

He nodded. 'It's our only major assignment at the moment.'

'Hmn, it's a thought, I suppose,' voiced Mather. 'Unlikely, though. In the event of a successful snatch, kidnappers would rather negotiate with K & R people than the authorities, who're invariably against payment of ransom money.'

The lift doors were opening. 'We'd better join the others,' said Halloran. 'I assume we keep this to ourselves.'

Mather limped alongside him, the group ahead beginning to enter the lift. 'No need to cause undue anxiety as far as our client is concerned. We may have to issue some kind of public statement once the Press gets hold of the story, but even then there's no reason why Dieter's death should be linked with the Magma contract.'

Halloran signalled the two Shield bodyguards to wait in the carpark, and stepped ahead of Monk and the Arabs before they could follow their employer into the lift. 'Take the other one,' he ordered and before they could protest, Kline nodded his head in a gesture of assent.

Mather endeavoured to promote conversation during the swift journey to the eighteenth floor, but the psychic refused to be drawn from his brooding silence and Cora's replies were perfunctory although polite.

Sir Victor Penlock himself was waiting to greet them when the lift doors opened again. He wore a navy-blue double-breasted blazer over a fawn turtle-neck jumper, sharply pressed beige slacks adding to the casual elegance. Halloran realized that Magma's security guard in the booth by the carpark entrance must have reported Kline's arrival. It seemed unusual, though, that the chairman of such a vast corporation should be waiting so anxiously for one of his own employees.

'Sorry to have dragged you back to town, Felix,' Sir Victor apologized, 'but as I explained over the phone, the situation is serious.'

Apparently a day for bad tidings, mused Halloran as Kline swept by Sir Victor with barely a glance. The tall chairman nodded towards the two Shield men before walking after the psychic. 'Henry is waiting for us in my office,' they heard him tell Kline as they, too, followed behind along the mauve-carpeted corridor. As they passed the display cabinets set in the walls on either side, Halloran rubbed a hand across his stubbled chin and wondered what the fuss was about. Kline had not been forthcoming on the drive up to London, and Cora appeared to know no more than he, himself. Judging by the gravity of Sir Victor's tone and by the fact that the matter could not be fully discussed over the telephone, the cause for concern was not only serious but extremely confidential, too. The corridor widened into the broad hallways and whereas previously he had heard normal office hubbub from the offices to his left and right, now there was only silence. The big double-door opposite was already open and the chairman ushered them through. Once inside, however, he asked Mather and Halloran to wait in the outer office.

Then Kline spoke up. 'No. Halloran can listen in on this. But not Cora.' Without another word he disappeared into Sir Victor's office.

The chairman raised his eyebrows at the girl, then indicated that Halloran should follow him. He went after Kline.

'Seems you're to be privileged,' Mather remarked lightly. 'Well, Miss Redmile, shall we see if we can brew up some tea for ourselves? Perhaps you'll remain on guard here, Mr, er, Palusinski?'

The Pole sat at one of the two secretaries' desks. 'I will keep good watch,' he assured them and frowned, his eyes narrowing behind his spectacles, as he regarded the computer screen on the desk top. 'Such knowledge inside this tiny window,' he said distractedly.

Before Halloran went through to the main office, he caught Cora's surprised expression; she was obviously bewildered by her employer's blunt dismissal. He closed the door behind him, curious himself about Kline's motive.

Quinn-Reece glanced up briefly from the papers neatly spread on a low table in front of him, but gave no sign of welcome. Kline was standing with his back to the room, staring out of the huge floor-to-ceiling window, the rain outside stippling the glass. Sir Victor vaguely waved towards a chair and Halloran lowered himself into it. Kline then did something quite unexpected: he whirled around, walked across to the chairman's broad, oak desk and took the seat behind it. He looked directly at Quinn-Reece and asked, 'How is it possible?'

The vice-chairman cleared his throat before answering. 'Obviously we have a leak within the Corporation.'

Sir Victor sat in a chair close to his own desk and tugged at the crease in his trouser leg. 'But who? How could such information be divulged so quickly unless its source was from a very high level.'

Halloran shifted in his seat, puzzled but intrigued by the conversation.

'That isn't necessarily so,' said Quinn-Reece. 'Someone in the field team could be selling us out.'

'You mean that every single time that Consolidated Ores has negotiated exploration rights before us one of our agents in that particular area has gone over to them?' Kline spoke as though the notion were not feasible.

'It's hardly likely, is it?' Sir Victor agreed. 'The betrayal must be from these offices.'

Halloran interrupted. 'Does what you're discussing have any bearing on my company's assignment for Magma?' As Kline, himself, had insisted that he 'listen in', it was a reasonable assumption to make.

Quinn-Reece's reply was brusque. 'This matter doesn't concern Achilles' Shield in any way. As a matter of fact, I don't understand why your presence is required in this room.'

'I invited him,' Kline said quietly. He was staring at the vice-chairman, his dark eyes unblinking, and Quinn-Reece appeared uncomfortable under his gaze. 'Halloran has been hired to protect me, and this morning I feel in particular need of that protection. Strange how betrayal can leave you feeling so vulnerable.'

'You can't seriously imagine that Consolidated would be behind an attempted kidnapping?' the astonished Sir Victor protested. 'They may be formidable business rivals, and admittedly we've fought some fierce battles with them in the past, but it's always been purely on a competitive business basis. I can't honestly believe that they would resort to any kind of physical violence.'

'Someone has,' Kline snapped back.

'It might help if I know what's happened,' Halloran suggested.

'What's happened, my friend,' said Kline 'is that over recent months, practically every new source of mineral deposits I've discovered has been laid claim to by Consolidated Ores before our field agents have had a chance to make tests. It doesn't take an Einstein to figure out someone from within our own organization is tipping them off.'

'If that's the case and they're getting their information anyway, why bother to kidnap you?' Halloran commented. 'Wouldn't that in effect be killing the golden goose? Besides, industrial espionage may be illegal, but it's nowhere as serious as abduction.'

'That's a fair argument, Felix,' put in Sir Victor. 'Why should any rival company take that risk when it doesn't appear to be necessary?'

'Because sooner or later the informer will be exposed.' Kline's reply was calm, his demeanour having changed yet again, his normal (normal? Halloran had to wonder at the term) excitability subdued.

'But what good would kidnapping you do?' queried Quinn-Reece.

'Maybe the idea's to eliminate me permanently.'

Sir Victor and his vice-chairman exchanged astonished glances.

'I think that would be too extreme, particularly if Consolidated really is involved. I know the chairman personally and although he's something of a scoundrel, I cannot believe he'd sanction murder. No, no Felix, that really is beyond the bounds of reason.'

'Then why do I feel so threatened?' Kline coolly retorted.

'Uh, perhaps, Felix, perhaps you're overwrought,' Sir Victor suggested cautiously. 'After all, so much reliance on your psychic ability must eventually take its toll. You know, you haven't had a proper break for quite some time now.'

Kline smiled. And Halloran's eyes narrowed. Despite everything that had happened over the past few days, he hadn't realized until that moment that there was so much danger in the man.

'Yes,' the psychic admitted, 'I do feel in need of some rest. A few more days at Neath, maybe. And then some travelling. Yes, it's time I ventured abroad again.' His smile withered. 'But that doesn't resolve our current crisis.'

'How often has this other company managed to beat you to these new locations?' asked Halloran, genuinely interested in Magma's problem.

Quinn-Reece provided the answer. 'Three times in a period of five months.'

Halloran raised his eyebrows. 'That doesn't seem an awful lot.'

'I can assure you,' Sir Victor said, 'that in a world of diminishing natural resources, it is.'

'Couldn't it be coincidence?'

'We were prepared to accept that on the first two occasions,' replied the chairman. 'But Felix indicated to us only last Thursday that an as yet untapped source of copper could be found in a certain region of Papua New Guinea. By the time our agent had arranged to see the appropriate authority dealing with land exploration rights, negotiations were already well underway with Consolidated Ores. These matters are usually dealt with on a first-come, first-served, basis – provided contracts are favourable to the country of origin, naturally. But no, Mr Halloran, this time we're certain that confidential information is being disclosed outside almost as soon as we, ourselves, learn of new deposits.'

'Could be they use a psychic of their own.'

Sir Victor received the suggestion gravely. 'There is no other person on this earth who can match the sensory ability of Felix Kline.' It was a statement not meant to be argued with, and Halloran saw no point in doing so.

'How many Magma personnel knew of this recent find?' he asked.

'Not many,' replied Quinn-Reece, leaning forward and shuffling the papers before him. 'Myself, the chairman, and of course, Felix and Miss Redmile. At the other end, only the agent whom I contacted. The news hasn't even been announced to our board of directors, and only one or two of our executives have become involved since, although we now know that wasn't until after Consolidated made their move.'

'Don't forget me,' said Halloran. 'It was mentioned to me on the first day I visited Magma.'

Sir Victor turned inquiringly to Kline, who nodded. 'As you've only been associated with the Corporation for less than a week, I think we can sensibly discount you as a mole,' the chairman reasoned.

'Well, your range of suspects is mercifully limited,' said Halloran. 'But before you point a finger at anyone, I suggest you investigate these offices for electronic listening devices and make sure your phones aren't being tapped. You ought to check that your computer codes haven't been cracked also. Shield can make a thorough sweep, if you like.'

'Anti-bugging searches are carried out every week by our own security,' Quinn-Reece assured him.

'In an irregular pattern? I'd hate to hear, for instance, that you search the offices every Monday morning at nine o'clock.'

'Our security people aren't that naive, Mr Halloran.'

'Let's hope they aren't disloyal, either. And your computer codes?'

'We've no reason to suspect they've been broken.'

'Might be an idea to find out if there have been any recorded but unauthorized admissions over the past few months.'

'That wouldn't have any bearing on our immediate problem,' Sir Victor remarked.

'No, but locating a hacker might help direct those accusing fingers.' Halloran stared across the room at Kline, who seemed almost dwarfish behind the broad desk, the high, rain-spattered window at his back increasing the effect. 'Aside from that,' he said, 'you're the psychic: don't you have an idea who's giving away company secrets?'

Kline returned the Shield man's stare. 'Oh yeah, Halloran,' he said, 'I'm sure I know who's the traitor in our midst.' He looked at each person in the room and his face was expressionless when he spoke.

'It's Cora,' he told them.

· 28 ·
HALLORAN

'IF I MAY SAY SO, M'DEAR, YOU DON'T LOOK AT ALL WELL.'

Cora had taken Shield's Planner to one of Magma's smaller conference rooms on the eighteenth floor, a place used for private meetings with business associates rather than full-scale executive gatherings or board meetings. Cora had disappeared for a few minutes, returning with tea for them both. Rather than sit at the room's long table, they had relaxed in easychairs that were spaced around the walls. As Cora sipped her tea, Mather noticed a slight tremble in her grip.

'I sincerely hope this kidnapping business isn't upsetting you too much,' he said soothingly. 'We have you well guarded, you know. And I promise you, Liam is the best operative we have in this kind of situation. He has an uncanny instinct for striking before being struck.' He caught her sudden glance at him with the mention of Halloran's name. Ah, he thought, our man is having an effect on her.

'I suppose it's made us all nervous,' Cora said.

But you look as though you haven't slept properly for several weeks, Mather thought to himself. 'Yes, I can appreciate that. Perhaps the blackguards will be flushed out soon and then we can all get some rest. Our job isn't only physically to protect the target; we spend a great deal of time searching out those who are the threat.' He deliberately refrained from saying 'or assassins', unwilling to worry the girl any more than was necessary. 'We've been working on that since we agreed to the assignment.'

'But without any success.'

'True, but it's early days. We'll find out who's causing these problems soon enough, never fear.' He placed the empty teacup in the saucer by his feet.

'Would you like some more?' she asked.

'No thank you, one's enough. Of course, these villains might well have cried off after their unsuccessful attempt the other day. Nothing like a show of strength to make such thugs turn tail and run.' He smiled, doing his best to reassure her.

Cora merely stared blankly into her teacup. Her question was tentative. 'Liam would kill anyone he considered to be a danger, wouldn't he?'

Mather was slightly taken aback. 'Why, yes, if that was the only way. However, he isn't a murderer, Miss Redmile. He'll only take what measures are necessary to retrieve a situation. I can assure you that Achilles' Shield is a law-abiding organization which doesn't employ reckless hit-men. All right, it must be confessed, we sometimes bend the rules here and there, but our operatives are trained to control a situation rather than be pressured by it.'

'He ...' Cora looked up and Mather saw the anxiety there '... he frightens me.'

Mather's short laugh was meant to be encouraging. 'There's nothing *you* need fear from Liam,' he told her.

'What makes such a person deal in violence? He can be so gentle, and yet ...'

Oh dear, mused Mather, it's gone deeper than I'd imagined. 'Liam is essentially employed to deter violence,' he said.

'You know it's there inside him, a terrible coldness. Sometimes, when he smiles, you can see it in his eyes. I could easily believe he has no conscience.'

'Perhaps you've mistaken that coldness for an immunity against ... well, it's difficult to put a word on it, but you might consider it as an immunity against ... forgiveness. Liam is unremitting, relentless even, when he, or others in his charge, are threatened. I don't believe he's a man who would ever seek vengeance, but nor is he one to turn the other cheek.'

Mather tapped his cane against the shoe on his outstretched foot. 'Let me tell you something of his background, then perhaps you'll understand him a little more.'

She appeared apprehensive, as though uncertain that she really wanted to know too much about the man.

'Liam's father, Pat Halloran, was a captain in the British Army, who met Siobhan, his future wife, while on leave in Southern Ireland – apparently he was a keen walker and angler, so what better place to spend his free time? He was also of Irish descent himself, so felt a natural affinity to the country. He returned some months later, proposed to the girl, was promptly accepted, and both came back to London where they were married. Within a year, Liam was born.'

Mather reached down and retrieved his cup from the floor. 'Perhaps I will have more tea, m'dear.' He watched her as she walked to the table and refilled his cup. She's confused about Halloran, he thought, and could hardly be blamed for that. Even to Mather, who knew him better than most, Halloran was still something of an enigma. But it was Felix Kline and his strange cohorts that the Planner had misgivings about, doubts which he could not explain rationally; the girl could be an ally to his operative, an insider who could give warning of any odd business going on that might affect Halloran's course of action. The Planner had voiced his growing unease concerning the Magma assignment to Gerald Snaith that very morning, after the discovery of Dieter Stuhr's mutilated corpse. Naturally, the Controller of Achilles' Shield, a pragmatic individual to say the least, had demanded evidence of any link between the two matters. Which Mather could not provide.

He thanked Cora when she handed him the fresh tea, and waited for her to sit before proceeding.

'His father's army career involved a fair bit of travelling that did not, unfortunately, require any long-term overseas duty whereby the family could stay with him. He took them when he could, but more often than not, Siobhan and the boy were left at home. Eventually it was decided that they might be better off living with Liam's grandfather back in Ireland.'

The girl had remembered that Mather favoured Earl Grey, and he sipped gratefully before continuing. 'I mention these early details, Miss Redmile, because I believe they, for good or bad, helped shape the man.'

He received no response.

'The captain spent as much time as possible with his wife and son, but their marriage had created a rift between Siobhan and other members of her family. You see, she had cousins who had links – strong links, as it turned out – with the IRA, and they suspected that her husband was no more than a British plant, put there to seek out information on rebel activities in the area. It was sheer nonsense, of course, but fanatics can rarely be bound by common sense. And who knows? Perhaps over the years, Captain Halloran did innocently hear of certain nefarious goings on that he felt duty-bound to report to his superiors. Whatever, suspicion alone was enough for the terrorists.

'Liam, just eight years old, had gone fishing with his father, who had been home on leave for only a few days while serving in that bloody, if discreet, war in South Arabia. God knows, the man needed the rest.'

Cora regarded Mather curiously.

'They were both standing in the middle of a shallow stream, father and son, no doubt enjoying each other's company after so many months apart, when the gunmen struck. Liam saw his father shot dead before him. He told the Garda later that his father had struggled to the bank and had tried to crawl from the water. The boy was frozen with fear and could only watch when one of the masked gunmen kicked his father down into the stream again, then stood with one foot on the dying man's back holding him beneath the water. The boy said the stream had already turned crimson with blood when the man pointed his revolver into the water and shot Captain Halloran in the back of the head.'

Cora closed her eyes, but the ghastly image became sharper in her mind. She quickly opened them again.

'Siobhan knew her cousins had been involved, otherwise Liam would have been murdered, too, as a witness. That's why the assassins had taken the trouble to wear masks, so the boy wouldn't recognize any of them. But there was nothing she could do. If she were to voice her suspicions, not only would she be at risk, but so too would her son, and possibly the grandfather. It's my opinion that her silence partly contributed to her eventual breakdown. Grief did the rest.'

The girl was staring at him. 'How ... how do you know all this? Did Liam tell you?'

'Pieces,' he replied. 'Even as a youth, Liam was never one to reveal his inner feelings. I made enquiries, I talked to his grandfather. You see, I was Captain Halloran's commanding officer in Aden. He was an excellent soldier, one I had a high regard for, and his death was a great loss for my unit so early in the campaign. I took a personal interest in the family he'd left behind, and that's how I learned of the boy.'

Mather finished the tea and again placed the cup on the floor. When he straightened, his hand began to soothe the ache in his knee. Talk of the war in Aden somehow always revived that pain.

'As Liam grew older, it seemed he was always in some kind of trouble, as though a wildness in him had been unleashed. Perhaps that was his way of smothering the sorrow, disguising it with anger. I've no idea, to be honest. The wildness grew out of hand when his mother, unhappy and unstable for all those years, finally committed suicide. I'd kept track of them both since the death of Captain Halloran, made sure the widow received full financial compensation from the British Army, but lost touch for some time when I had difficulties of my own.' He tapped his aching knee to indicate the precise nature of those 'difficulties'. 'Thought I was going to lose it, but managed to convince the medics the leg would come good again after a little tinkering with their scalpels. Nowadays, I wonder if I did the right thing,' he added as if to himself. 'Anyway, I received a letter from the grandfather informing me of Siobhan's death, and when I was well enough, I travelled to Ireland myself to see what could be done for the boy.' He smiled wryly. 'I believe I arrived just in time.'

It was difficult for Cora to picture Liam as a boy, angry, probably frightened, grief-stricken again with the loss of his mother, her death a direct consequence of his father's murder. How could she equate that image with the man who had come to her room the night before, had taken her against her will, that very act of ravishment stirring the familiar pleasure such defilement had for her, so that she could not help but respond? But then the quieter passion afterwards, the lovemaking that was gentle, so tender, arousing purer emotions that eclipsed mere desire. It had left her stunned, unsure, as though he had deliberately enacted both sides of passion with her, the cold harshness lacking any caring, and then the simple joy which came without abuse or pain, a fulfilment she'd almost forgotten. But then Cora had to wonder if Halloran was someone on whose actions others put their own interpretations. Was she presuming too much of him? Was he really only a man of violence?

Mather's voice broke into her thoughts. 'Liam had been getting into scrapes. No, more than that – his mischievousness went beyond the bounds of natural boyhood hooliganism. From what I heard on my arrival, he was in serious danger of being taken into youth custody. Several incidents around the small town where he lived with his grandfather had been attributed to him, although on the worst occasions no damning evidence of his involvement could be laid absolutely on his doorstep. There were particular problems with the local priest. Whether or not it was because the Church represented the nearest authority against which he could rebel, I've no way of knowing. One particular incident ... but no, as I say, there was no definite proof, it would be wrong for me to speculate.'

The Shield Planner interlocked his fingers, his elbows resting on the arms of the chair. He pressed his forefingers against his lip, momentarily lost in thought. 'I felt it was time to take Liam away from that environment; Ireland held too many tragic memories for him. So I arranged for him to board at a school in England, the least I could do in honour of his late father. The school had close connections with the army, turned out many fine cadets. I'm afraid I was rather preoccupied with my own career, which was starting afresh after my leg injury, but I tried to keep an eye on things as much as I could. The boy appeared to settle down – perhaps a strict regime was what he needed all along. I suppose because of what his father had been, the type of school that had educated him, and the fact that his grandfather had passed away and that there really was no other place to go, Liam eventually decided that soldiering was the profession for him.'

Mather's face wrinkled with pleasure. 'Damn good at it, too, by all accounts. Oh, he was still somewhat reckless, never quite losing that touch of Irish wildness; but the army has ways of channelling that kind of spirit. Liam took to that way of life as if ordained for it, and was good enough to make the SAS.

'Unfortunately, he was involved in an incident in 1972 that I believe was the root cause of Liam's later cynicism. Still not into his twenties, he was stationed with a small British Army training team at Mirbat in Oman – about ten of 'em in all. A civil war was going on between the monarchy of Oman and its left-wing opponents, and the SAS unit had spent three months in that dreary little town of Mirbat attempting to drill some kind of order into the loyalists. They held two forts, thirty Askaris in one, around twenty-five Dhofar Gendarmerie in the other, with an unruly bunch of counter-guerrilla irregulars billeted in the town itself. The only artillery of any real weight they had was a Second World War 25-pounder, a .50-inch Browning and an 81mm mortar.

'One morning, just after dawn, they were attacked by nearly three hundred rebels armed with machine-guns, mortars, anti-tank rifles and a Russian rocket-launcher. It should have been an outright massacre, but the SAS commanding officer, an absolutely fearless individual, and only a few years older than Liam himself, organized his own men and their Arab allies into a fighting force to be reckoned with.

'I won't bore you with all the battle details, m'dear, but the officer, a captain, was here, there and everywhere, screaming orders, directing what meagre artillery they had, shaping his defence so that the attackers couldn't take a hold. Under enemy fire, he crossed four hundred yards of open ground with a medical orderly to reach the fort where the Gendarmerie was holed up. He'd already radioed his HQ for a helicopter to evacuate casualties, but enemy fire-power was so fierce the damn thing couldn't even land. The captain took over the second fort's gun position, the guerrillas no more than thirty yards away, and nearly had his head chopped off by machine-gun fire. Men were being cut down around him, but not for one moment did the captain consider giving the order for surrender. No, no chance of that. From his position, he was able to site targets for two Strikemaster jets that had arrived to lend support, but still the battle raged.

'At last, a relief squadron flew in from Salalah to assist, and the rebels, already stopped in their tracks and their numbers considerably depleted, gave up the ghost and fled. A quite remarkable resistance by the commanding officer and his men, and the rebel forces never really recovered from the defeat, although it took another four years for the war to end.

'I believe that battle affected Liam in two ways, the first being that he was involved in a carnage of mindless ferocity, and he, himself, had dealt out much of it; and the second was that he was shown an example of outstanding courage by his commanding officer – a captain, don't forget – which I'm sure he imagined his own father had been capable of. Yet the battle was never "officially" recognized by his own government, even though he was awarded a Military Medal for his actions, and the captain a DSO. That and the fact that he was unclear in his own mind as to whether he was on the side of the "goodies" or the "baddies" made him rather cynical about war itself. Worse was to follow.

'Seven years later, that same captain, a man he had come to admire and respect, by then promoted to major, died from exposure during an SAS exercise on the Brecon Beacons. A totally wasteful death which so filled Liam with disgust that he resigned from the army shortly after.

'He became a mercenary, using conflict for his own ends, which were purely financial, rather than allowing it to use him. I observed from a great distance, learning of his activities through contacts I had in various countries and, it must be confessed, I was saddened, appalled even, by what I heard. Although it was never said that he killed indiscriminately, or ever used violence when it could be avoided, he had a reputation for being utterly ruthless as far as his enemies were concerned – and enemies were defined as those being on the side of those *not* paying his wages.'

Mather noticed that Cora did not appear shocked, nor even surprised; it was as though he had merely confirmed her own suspicions about Halloran.

'A few years ago I began recruiting for Achilles' Shield,' he went on. 'Ex-SAS officers make extremely good operatives, so they were my prime targets. I'd lost all contact with Liam by then – it may be that I was afraid of what he'd become – but something inside urged me to seek him out, a niggling guilt perhaps, a feeling that it was *I* who had let him down. It may possibly have been nothing more than a nagging curiosity.

'I eventually located him in Moshupa, a small township in Botswana, very close to the border of South Africa. He was training ANC guerrillas for incursions into their homeland where they would wreak as much destruction as possible before stealing back across the border to the neighbouring state. But Liam was a far different person from the young man I had come to know. He seemed … empty. As though what he was doing, the killers and saboteurs he was training, the awful conditions he was living in, meant nothing at all to him. He didn't even register surprise when I turned up, only a chilly kind of amusement. When I spoke with Liam it was like talking to someone drained of emotion; but gradually I began to realize he possessed an inner seething that frightened me more than anything else about him. God knows what he'd been involved in after resigning from the British Army, but its mark had been left. No, he hadn't been brutalized; it was as though he'd become immunized against outrage, wickedness, against *caring*. As I said, that was on the surface: inside, emotions were being stifled, held so firmly in check that I suspect even he was unaware they were there. Or perhaps he glimpsed them now and again, yet refused to let them rise, refused to be influenced by them. I was sure I'd come at exactly the right time, couldn't help but feel I'd been nudged by some inner instinct of my own, because I could tell that Liam had had enough, he was ready to break. Those suppressed emotions – his own self-hatred – were about to erupt.

'He wouldn't admit it, not even to himself, but I think he saw me as some kind of lifeline, a means of dragging himself from that moral squalor he'd sunk into. As for me, I was only too happy to throw down the rope.

'Liam told me he had discovered there were no absolutes. No absolute right or wrong, no absolute good or evil. There were degrees of everything. Once you accepted that – truly accepted it, he insisted – you were able to set your own balance, you understood the bounds within which you could function without guilt clawing at you, tainting your thoughts and so hindering your actions. And he said that virtue, righteousness, whatever you like to call it, often held little sway over evil, because its own rules inhibited. Sometimes only evil could defeat another evil. Degrees, he kept repeating, the lesser against the greater.

'None of it made much sense to me, but it indicated the slough of despair he was wallowing in. No, perhaps despair suggests self-pity, and the man I spoke to was too hardened for that. Pessimism might be a more appropriate word, cynicism even better. Anyway, he agreed to return to England with me and work for Achilles' Shield, protecting lives instead of the opposite. In my opinion, that change was vital for Liam, because it pulled him back from the brink.'

Cora, who had been listening quietly throughout, finally spoke. 'He was that close ... ?'

'In my opinion,' Mather reasserted. 'It may be an old-fashioned notion on my part, but when all probity is lost, total degradation is swift to follow. It seemed to me at the time that Liam had almost lost all reasonable values.'

The girl looked down at her hands and Mather wondered if he had embarrassed her. Were his ideas too rigid, or too 'quaint' for these racy times? Probably, but no less valid for that, he reassured himself.

'And has he changed?' Cora asked softly.

'Well, he's been with Shield for over six years now, and in many ways he's the best operative we have. Yes, he has changed.' Mather smiled. 'But just how much, I really can't say.'

·29·
RECONNOITRE

THEY DROVE PAST THE GATES, ALL THREE OCCUPANTS OF THE CAR PEERING ROUND, looking along the uneven drive to see where it led. Unfortunately it curved into woodland which obscured any further view.

With a nod of his head, the front passenger indicated the old lodge-house set to one side of the big iron gates. The car did not slow down.

They studied the high wall as the car picked up a steady speed once more, and then the dense trees and undergrowth when the weathered brickwork ran out. They travelled a long way before a narrow lane came up on the left. The driver steered into it, the other two occupants continuing to study the hedges that bordered the left-hand side of the lane. Presently they were able to catch brief glimpses of downward slopes, woodland, a lake. The man in the backseat told the driver to stop the car.

Although their view was restricted by the trees closest to the lane, they could just make out what appeared to be a red-stoned building on the far shore of the lake, nestled beneath low hills. Reluctant to linger too long, the back passenger instructed the driver to move on.

The lane joined a wider road and again the car turned left, maintaining a casual speed, neither fast, nor slow. There were bends and dips along the route, but the observers' attention rarely wavered from the heavily wooded countryside on their left. Through his rearview mirror, the driver noticed another vehicle approaching from behind. It was a Granada and he mentioned the fact to his companions. It slowed down, keeping a distance of forty or fifty yards away, following without pressurizing the lead car into hurrying.

The driver of the first vehicle watched for a road to come up on his right. One did, and he drove on by. Soon another appeared, again to his right, and this one he took.

In his mirror he saw the Granada pass along the road they had left, its two occupants staring after them. It quickly vanished from view, but the driver of the first car kept on going, picking up speed.

Only when they had travelled a mile or so further did he pull in by the side of the road and turn to look at his companions.

The passenger in the back nodded. From what they'd seen so far, the scar-faced man (when they had finally broken him) had been quite correct: the estate was large, very large indeed.

▪ 30 ▪
RETRIBUTION IN DARKNESS

QUINN-REECE WAS ALONE IN HIS OFFICE ON THE EIGHTEENTH FLOOR OF THE Magma Corporation.

The tiniest smile of satisfaction twitched his lips as he completed the last paragraph of the report concerning the Papua New Guinea copper situation. A report that Felix Kline had requested he provide before leaving the building, so that the chairman could call a forward planning meeting after he had broken the news to the board of directors on Monday morning.

Did they really hope to retrieve the situation? Exploration rights for that particular area of land had already been granted to Consolidated Ores, and not even if Magma's bribe to the government officials involved out-matched their rival company's could the agreement be rescinded.

He gathered the papers together on his desk. They would be ready for his secretary to type first thing in the morning. Rarely a happy man, Quinn-Reece allowed his smile to broaden. He was pleased with the wording, for it emphasized, in all due modesty, of course, his strenuous efforts to secure those rights before anyone else got wind of the find, continuously trying to contact their agent on the island by telephone, telex and even personal messenger to his hotel. Unfortunately, the man could not be located (or so Quinn-Reece indicated in his report) and in the meanwhile, Magma's biggest rival had learned of the 'find'.

He allowed himself to chuckle.

Time to go home, he decided. Enough is enough. The report could indeed be more full, but why the hell should he put in any more hours on a Sunday? It was late afternoon and the skies were already darkened by clouds and drizzle. Before he went, though, a stiff gin and tonic to celebrate yet another successful deception.

He left his desk and went to a wall cabinet, opening it to reveal his private liquor stock, there for entertaining business associates or, more often than not, for the frequent 'nips' that got him through the day. The small ice bucket was empty, but who needed ice? He poured a good measure of gin into a glass tumbler and added an equal amount of tonic. He raised the glass to his lips when the noise outside his office door stopped him.

He shrugged. Security on their rounds, checking all offices. Your excellent health! he silently toasted himself, and took a large swallow of the drink. The mixture warmed him, lightening his mood even further. Just a few more months' subservience to that obnoxious, stunted oaf, then home and dry, working for a company who would appreciate his business acumen, and who would be extremely grateful for past services. The risk had been worth it. And what could the Corporation do anyway even if they had discovered he was the source of the leaks? Take him to court? Oh no, he knew too much for that. The shareholders would be unhappy if they were to learn of Kline's true position at Magma, and the financial Press would have a ball. Even Consolidated were unaware of the psychic's presence within Magma – they merely assumed that the Corporation's field agents were more astute than their own. No, the worst that Magma could do would be to dismiss him. And pay him off for keeping his mouth shut, of course. Instead they were sacking the girl, Cora.

He was smiling again.

Quinn-Reece turned his head. Was someone still outside? He was sure he'd heard movement in the outer office. Leaving the glass on the corner of his desk, the vice-chairman walked to the half-open door.

He pulled it open all the way and looked through. 'Anyone there?' he called out, feeling rather foolish.

There was no response.

He stepped forward and caught a whiff of spices just before something soft fell over his head and blocked out the light.

Hands shoved him from behind and he staggered forward, fell, lay sprawled on a hard floor, his head still covered.

Quinn-Reece remained prone for a few seconds, regathering his senses, terribly afraid to move. He heard the click of a door closing. He was trembling badly.

The brief, stumbling journey had been one of the worst experiences of his life (so far), for it was a brutally rushed trip towards a fate unknown. He now knew how murderers must have felt in the old days when they were taken hooded from their cell and hurried to the gallows, giving them precious little time to consider the eternity waiting for them at the end of the corridor (except there was *always* time to consider that prospect, no matter how fast they took you, no matter how roughly they treated you, because part of your mind was quiet, entirely remote from the rest of your feverish thoughts, numbingly and so fearfully aware …). He had been held down – by two of them – even though no words were spoken, no one answered his demands, nor his pleas, he was sure there were two of them – yet he had felt himself rising. The lift. They must have bundled him into the lift. But why? Where were they taking him? Oh God, was it true then? Were these people after Felix Kline? Had they made a mistake, thinking that he was the psychic? That had to be it! So perhaps it was safe to look up, to show them, convince them they'd got the wrong man. He had no allegiance to Kline, far from it: he could tell them all they wanted to know. No need to harm him, he wasn't the one they were after.

Quinn-Reece hesitantly raised his head and saw the whiteness of the floor below the edges of the cloth. Tentatively, expecting to have his hand knocked away at any moment, he lifted the hem. He could see the room now. Slowly he pulled the fluffy material away (it was a large towel, he realized, probably from one of the executive bathrooms) and looked around.

He was in the white room. Kline's white room.

And he was alone.

He pushed himself to his knees, his eyes half-closed against the brilliant glare. What was happening, what the hell were they playing at? Was the idea only to keep him out of the way for a while? The notion came as a relief. It emboldened him enough to rise to his feet.

Quinn-Reece went to the double-door and listened with his ear flat against the glossy surface. No sounds without. He tried one of the doorhandles. Locked.

Stepping back, he surveyed the entrance for a while, gradually becoming used to the assailing brightness. He turned and began walking towards the smaller door on the opposite side of the room, his footsteps loud because of uninterrupted acoustics. He had reached the low central dais when the harsh whiteness around him collapsed into utter darkness.

Quinn-Reece cried out, as if the abrupt change had come as a physical blow.

There was nothing to see, absolutely nothing to focus on. Even the floor beneath his feet had somehow lost substance. His hands – unseen – waved in the air before him, as though grasping for light itself.

'What are you doing?' he shouted, a feeble entreaty to the blackness.

Naturally there was no reply.

So disorientated was Quinn-Reece that he had to will one foot to go forward. The thought that he might be stepping over the brink into an abyss was difficult to dismiss. He moved his other foot, arms still outstretched like a blind man's (which, in effect he was), even though he knew there were no obstacles in his way.

Another step.

His breathing was fluttery.

Another step.

He could not see them, but he was aware that his fingers twitched like insect antennae.

Another step.

And he touched flesh.

So unexpected was the sensation, and so tense had Quinn-Reece become, that he shrieked like a woman. He fell away, a leg coming into sharp contact with the dais. He slumped across it and lay shaking.

Wondering why the fingertips of the hand that had touched whatever – no, he meant *who*ever – stood in his way were tingling, he brought them closer to his face, disregarding the fact that he was unable to see. He felt something clinging to them.

He rubbed his fingers together and whatever had been there flaked away. It had been tissue-thin.

'Who's there?' he managed to say, and was uncomfortable with the sound of his own voice.

The silence was more frightening than any reply.

A warm breath brushed his cheek. He spun around on the platform, scurrying to its furthest edge, away from whoever had leaned over him.

But a sigh close to his ear sent him scuttling back.

The men who had dragged him into this room must have slipped inside somehow after the lights had gone out! Yet he hadn't heard the opening and closing of a door, there had been no sudden shaft of light. How *could* they be in there with him? He remembered the spicy smell before he had been hooded. The smell was familiar. From where, from when?

A low chuckle. From someone close by. And then a hand caressing his cheek.

Quinn-Reece flinched violently and quickly squirmed away. The touch against his cheek had been roughened as though the other's skin was crispy with age. When he tried to wipe off the mark he felt had been left there, he discovered flaky tissue hanging to his own skin. He slapped it off in revulsion.

He twisted his head, this way and that, sightless but attempting to perceive. His whole body was quivering uncontrollably now. He sniffed, for there was a peculiar aroma in the air. Nothing to do with spices, this. Something different, vaguely unpleasant. Like a faint moulding dampness. Decay.

Light lashed out at him.

He cringed, covering his face with his hands. Peeped through open fingers at the rectangle of vivid colours high on the wall. One of the screens was lit.

It depicted a relief map of an island. A recognizably irregular shape. New Guinea. The colours merged, became a muddy blur. Faded to white. Became black.

A new map lit up. He forced himself to look. Was it? – yes, it was. Brazil. There had been a recent find, a low-grade gold deposit. Not by Magma, though. No, by Consolidated.

As the colours merged, Quinn-Reece looked around the room. The brightness from the screen should have revealed anyone else present. But he was the only occupant.

Blackness again.

Another screen came alive, and this time he could guess the location without recognizing it. Namibia. Yes, there had been a new discovery of uranium there. Again, not by Magma. He began to understand some of what was going on.

'Felix?' he ventured.

Total blackness. Still no reply.

'Felix, you're making a mistake. The girl, you said yourself ...' His words trailed away. Kline wasn't in the room. Why was he talking as if he were?

Quinn-Reece began to slide his legs off the dais. He stopped when he heard a soft chuckle.

This time not only three screens lit up: they all did. And the colours ran together, from one screen to the next, frames no longer divisive, blues and greens and browns beginning to streak, to flow around the room, a swift-moving stream, faster and faster, a kaleidoscope of colour, dazzling him, mesmerizing him, melting together, faster now, merging, gradually becoming white, an absence of colour, a broad pale strip circumscribing the room.

Things began to break through that white band. Creeping things. Black and shiny. Like giant cockroaches. Although their limbs, three on either side of their glossy shells, were like human arms. But scaly, and dark.

They hatched from the whiteness, wriggling through, dropping to the floor and into the shadows where only muted reflections on their curved backs could be observed. They scuttled across the floor towards him.

Quinn-Reece moved to the centre of the platform, drawing up his legs, denying to himself that this was happening, certain it was a nightmare, wondering why he could not wake.

The cracked band of white vanished.

Terrible blackness around him once more.

Nothing at all to be seen.

But he could hear those things tapping towards him.

'Felix, *please!*' he implored, for he knew that Kline was responsible, that Kline was punishing him for his betrayal. But he didn't understand how *this* could happen, for he realized it was no nightmare, the pain in his lower lip, where his teeth had clamped down, too sharp to be dreamt. He shrieked this time. '*Please!*'

A chuckle from somewhere behind.

And a clicking close by as the first of those creatures scrambled over the edge of the dais.

Some time later, the doors to the white room opened and Khayed and Daoud slipped in. They went straight to the dead but unmarked body spread across the low dais, lifted it between them, and carried it out.

When the doors closed behind them, the room swiftly regressed to black.

KHAYED AND DAOUD
DISPLACED AND FOUND

THEY WERE NOT TRULY JORDANIANS. ASIL KHAYED AND YOUSSEF DAOUD WERE, in fact, displaced persons, their families having fled Palestine when the Independent State of Israel was declared in May 1948. Their parents were of the same clan and came from the same village, which was close to Jerusalem. They had been led to believe by those who had their own political motives that the Zionist forces would destroy their homes and meagre crops, would slaughter their children and livestock, would rape their women, would torture and murder the men. Flight to the River Jordan was their only hope.

They came to the refugee camp at Ein es Sultan, one of many such sites scattered around the city of Jericho and along the West Bank. The two Arab boys had been born within weeks of each other, to be raised in the squalor of a vast tent city containing tens of thousands of grieving migrants, where there were no toilets, kitchens, or medical facilities, and where most days were spent awaiting the arrival of water trucks and supply convoys from Damascus and Amman. The tents provided by the International Red Cross were of thin canvas which, unlike the tough Bedouin tents of animal skins and furs, were virtually useless against the rains and sandstorms. Their beds were nothing more than light sleeping mats. Running, open sewers and hills of rotting garbage were everywhere, attracting flies and mosquitoes by the millions. Severe dysentery was rife. Cholera, typhoid and other diseases claimed thousands of lives. Fierce rainfalls and then intolerable heat brought in by hamsin winds from the desert weakened all.

The muktar of their old village, whom the clans gathered around, could offer no comfort, for his spirit had been broken by the ignoble flight of his people and the hopelessness he saw all around. Hate with all your heart, he could only tell them, despise the Zionist dogs who have brought you to this. Nurture the hatred, live for revenge against the Jews.

Typhoid took Youssef's father, along with his two older brothers and a sister. That the young baby and his mother survived was no miracle, for death was indiscriminate. The widow and her child came under the protection of Asil's father, there being no energy for jealousy among the women. And the Koran, which spoke severely against adultery and fornication, also preached the blessedness of caring for cripples, idiots, blind men and widows. The boys grew up together and became closer than natural brothers.

Although rough hovels of mud bricks gradually replaced the tents, a form of rough villages taking shape along the Jordan, the rule of *kaif* – a passivity that might be described as idleness – prevailed. Few businesses were set up, no industries were started. There were no schools for the younger exiles, no games or activities organized for them. The demoralized Palestinians relied on the charity of others, as if content to wallow in their own hatred for the Jews and the foreign powers that had betrayed them. The Moslem Brotherhood were eager to exploit the persecution and never tired of stoking the fires of vengeance against these infamous 'invaders', while at the same time extolling the virtues of martyrdom for the great Arab cause of repatriation.

Asil and Youssef were children of a rubbled ghetto, existing on whatever was sparingly given, thriving on bitterness which was generously supplied. When Asil's father was killed in a riot against the reviled Arab Legion of Jordan's King Abdullah who, along with certain leaders of other Arab states, saw the political advantages in keeping the Palestinians a nation in exile rather than welcoming and absorbing them as true brothers (acceptance of the State of Israel would be a threat to his own power in the Middle East), the boys took on the responsibility for their family. By then the United Nations had taken charge over the welfare of the refugee camps and at least some progress was taking place in these humble villages. In Ein es Sultan there were mosques, a ritual slaughterhouse, stores, warehouses and food distribution centres. The boys were lucky enough to find jobs as coffee vendors, passing from shop to kiosk with their trays bearing coffee finjans, cups and sticky sweets, often trekking out to the lines of lorries awaiting customs clearance at the Allenby Bridge.

For pleasure they hung around the cafés and listened to the elders reminiscing about the old life in their villages, of the main square always awash with the aromas of pungent spices, cardamom in coffee, incense, and camel, donkey, sheep and goat dung. They spoke of important feasts, sighing over the exotic foods once served, while the boys would drool at their mention.

The elders' conversation would turn to memories of the houses they once dwelled in, solidly built with mud bricks and dung, brightly whitewashed to deflect the sun's rays, with a single colour outlining doors and windows, the roofs flat for collecting water during the rainy season. They spoke of village tradesmen, the potter, the carpenter, the sandal-maker, the basket and cloth weavers. Their eyes brimmed with tears as they remembered what had been lost to them. How life once centred around the village square with its well and ovens, the store and café where they could listen to the radio all day while they watched the passing activity, the cameleers, the pedlars on their loaded donkey carts, the knife and scissor grinders – the veiled women going about their daily tasks.

Eventually, when nostalgia held them in its soft-edged grip, they would boast of their feats in battle, their bravery, their cunning. And they would dismiss the Arab defeat by the Jews as a misconception, for they had been tricked by the agents of the devil, *jinn* – evil spirits – in human form. The Jews were not a worthy enemy. The Jews had an alliance with unholy forces. Mohammed, himself, had declared that the Jews had been led away from the edicts of Allah, and for that their punishment would be burning.

Asil and Youssef listened and absorbed. They wept for their homeland and for the life they had never known but missed dearly. They seethed with hatred for these people who called themselves Israelis.

The boys grew and became wise in the ways of survival. Schooling, even under the auspices of the UNRWA, was little more than a revolutionary training ground, the Arab tutors organizing their students into cells, each with its own aggressive title, incitement against the so-called State of Israel and its treacherous allies the main lesson of every day. Physical education included weapons training, knife fighting, tracking and the negotiation of assault courses.

Black-marketeering became the most profitable occupation, stealing and intimidation a second best. Asil and Youssef became the runners for dealers in hashish, then lookouts for raids on supply depots.

Crude and boastful chatter between the two boys of the sexual delights they would bestow upon females soon faded when awareness took on physical actuality and they discovered their true yearning was for each other, their experiments resolving in glorious consummation. Asil and Youssef could imagine no other form of lovemaking surpassing the pleasure they had given one another. Although males were allowed to hold hands and kiss in public, homosexuality was frowned upon generally in the Arab world; Asil and Youssef kept the intimate side of their relationship to themselves, the illicitness adding to its deliciousness.

As with other Palestinian youths, they were pressured into joining the fedayeen when they were old enough, its members' violence and unruliness directed towards the *jihad*, the holy war, and against the oppressor. The Jordanians encouraged guerrilla raids into Jewish territory, the killing and maiming perpetrated in the name of Allah, and the more youths lost in such expeditions, the more martyrs the Arabs had to hold up to the world. A mark of manhood for the fedayeen recruits was to bite off the heads of live chickens and snakes, or to strangle puppies and cats.

Never considered outstandingly bright by their superiors, Asil and Youssef's performance in the field and their cunning in fighting was impressive. And the elders were suitably struck by the youths' cruelty.

Their missions into enemy territory became more frequent – and more hazardous. It was on one such expedition that they discovered for themselves the extent – and the true nature – of their own barbarity.

Avoiding Israeli patrols, they had slipped across the border, their venture more of a test than a serious assault (the fedayeen were considering the two youths for important work in the revolutionary movement), their destination a kibbutz some miles from Bira. Dunams of marsh and swampland there, as at countless other settlements in this relatively new state, had been skilfully irrigated and cultivated, so that what was once barren land had become areas of rich soil suitable for vines, orchards and grain. The fields were protected against incursion with nothing more than fences of cactus and thorny jujube, although the living quarters themselves were behind a tall stockade. Asil and Youssef's intention had been to blow up one of the kibbutz's water towers located outside the compound with explosives readily supplied by their Jordanian hosts. But as they broke through the crude boundary under the cover of darkness, they came upon a young Israeli couple, a youth and a girl, who had found a remote spot where they could make love without being disturbed.

The couple were lying beneath a eucalyptus and it was their murmurings that caught the attention of the two Arab intruders. Asil and Youssef looked at each other in surprise, their eyes wide and clear in the star-lit night, then crept closer to the source of the breathed sounds. The things they saw the youth doing to the girl sent shivers of excitement running through them, for never in their lives had they witnessed such wantonness, and never before had a female's hidden flesh been exposed thus. Because of the urgency of their lovemaking, the young couple did not hear the Arabs' approach.

Asil quickly disposed of the girl who, apart from curiosity over her secret places, held little interest for them. He slit her throat while Youssef rendered her lover unconscious with a hefty stone picked up from the ground. Between them they dragged him back through the opening they had made in the rough perimeter fence. Once they were a safe distance away they tore strips from the Israeli's clothing to tie and gag him. Then they enjoyed themselves with his body.

But they did far more to him than they had ever done to each other.

Their sadism was spoilt only by his abrupt finish, a lesson well learned by them, for in later years they practised curbing their extremes so that the exquisite pleasure would last for hours, if not days. The corpse was barely recognizable as human when they had done, and their *coup de grâce* was to cut off their victim's private parts and bring them back in a goat-skin pouch to their masters in the fedayeen (who, although irritated that their orders to destroy the water tower had not been carried out, realized the dismemberment and castration of a Jew held true significance).

Asil and Youssef had proved they were worthy soldiers of the *jihad*, as well as revealing their skill in passing through well-guarded enemy lines without detection. It wasn't long before they were sent to a terrorist training camp in the Bekaa Valley of Lebanon. There they lived in a cement shack and were taught how to use Russian firearms, rocket-launchers and mortars, how to make bombs and use them with altimetric, movement and time detonators, assassination techniques, how to enter locked buildings quietly, stalk their prey through the streets, and methods of escaping pursuit. They ran six miles every morning, then did four hours of physical training. All this was followed by daily indoctrination classes.

They were taught that their destiny (not merely their duty) was not only to kill Zionists and their close allies, but members of any nation showing friendliness towards the non-State of Israel. Within a year or two, Asil and Youssef were travelling to other countries as an efficient and respected assassination team. However, they had a weakness they strove to keep from their associates (although not as cleverly as they thought; fortunately their masters allowed certain indulgences as long as operations were never jeopardized). That ecstatic thrill of their first sadistic murder of the Israeli youth at the kibbutz near Ofra had never been forgotten. They sought to relive and refine that excitement time and time again in the foreign capitals they visited. There are many hundreds of missing persons reported in cities all over the world every year, and most of them never appear again. At least not alive. It was relatively easy for Asil and Youssef to pick up men or boys, or sometimes even girls (for the two terrorists, the latter was a perversion of a perversion), and lure them to some quiet place where they could abuse, torture, and finally kill their prey. And sexual crimes, where there is no other motive involved and no previous connection between victim and murderer, are perhaps the most difficult to solve.

The bomb had gone off prematurely.

Asil and Youssef had left the package with its quietly ticking contents beneath a bench at the Gare du Nord, leisurely strolling away from it through noisy and earnest-looking travellers towards the arches that led out to the streets of Paris. The explosion from behind stunned everyone into an eerie three-second silence (or perhaps the roar had deafened ears to the screams). Pandemonium broke loose, commuters and tourists curling up against walls, running out into the streets – incredibly, some going towards the source of the explosion – or clutching at each other and waiting for the worst to happen.

The two terrorists knew that the European clothes they wore and the fact that they were among a cosmopolitan crowd would not help if they panicked and rushed from the scene, even though others around them were doing precisely that. At that particular time, Parisians were regarding any Arab or Algerian 'type' with suspicion, for the French authorities had arrested a known PLO activist a few weeks before under a charge of conspiracy; an ultimatum had been delivered by Al-Fatah that unless the 'hostage' was released and allowed to leave the country, then France could consider itself at peril. The French authorities had a reputation in those days for 'going soft' under such pressure, and the bomb planted at the Gare du Nord was meant to show how serious the terrorists were.

Asil and Youssef forced themselves to walk calmly away from the train station. Unfortunately it was their apparent coolness that gained the attention of an astute *gendarme* who was making his way into the station. The police, including the CRS and CSP, had been put on special alert since the arrest of the terrorist, and this particular *gendarme* had taken note of his pre-duty briefing on exactly what to look out for before and after an outrage such as this. He hurried after the two smartly dressed Arabs, stopping them with a sharp, '*Alors, messieurs!*' when he was close.

The mistimed blast had considerably shaken Asil and Youssef, for if the bomb had exploded just a few moments earlier, it would have been their own bodies spread across the station concourse. Now they were being apprehended by the police! Without even waiting to be questioned, Asil drew a knife from a hidden sheath in his jacket and stepped towards the uniformed man. He was expert with the blade, as Youssef had become expert with the garotte, and knew that the policeman's belt and buttoned tunic might prevent a clean thrust into the stomach. The heart was equally as difficult, because their pursuer had raised his left arm across his chest, intentionally or unintentionally blocking a lunge. Asil went for the next best target, aware that it would take his victim a minute or so longer to die, but at least he would drop instantly and lose consciousness within fourteen seconds. The knife slashed across the *gendarme's* upper left arm, the thrust outwards and deep, severing the brachial artery. The wounded man stared in disbelief, then fell to the pavement.

A woman screamed, but in the hubbub of similar cries and the blaring of sirens, no one took much notice. The Arabs fled, no longer concerned whether or not they were more noticeable. They ducked into the *métro*, hastily purchasing tickets and anxiously waiting on the *quai* for a train – any train – to come in, expecting shouts from the barrier at any moment. When one arrived, Youssef shuffled along beside it, pulling at the latch which opened the compartment door before the train had fully stopped. They collapsed into seats, praying to Allah that the doors would shut and the train move off before any blue-uniformed men tumbled in after them. They changed at the next station, Gare de l'Est, going on to Chaussée d'Antin, and from there to Montmartre. They had journeyed no great distance, but enough to throw off any pursuers and not long enough for the police to set up checks at *métro* exits (even if that were possible with so many stations). They emerged into the soft glow of evening and the distant sounds of sirens.

They strolled down the wide, tree-lined boulevard towards the river, mingling with tourists, their hearts still beating wildly, although outwardly they managed to appear nonchalant. They passed streetside restaurants, sniffed at roasting meat and spicy sauces, politely declined when approached by smiling prostitutes, not stopping until they reached the Seine where.they watched the passing *bateaux-mouches* crammed with sightseers.

Only then did they look slyly at each other and giggle.

They had a 'safe house' to go to, an apartment in one of the small courtyards in the Rue Mouffetard area close to the outdoor market just across the river. But there was no need to make their way back yet; indeed, training had taught them it was often better to stay lost in the crowd for as long as possible.

They wandered along the river bank for a short while, then headed back into the streets towards St Denis, taking their time and watching the street entertainers – buskers, dancers, jugglers, even fire-eaters. They felt frightened but exhilarated. They felt alive. The operation had been successful, and there was the bonus of one dead *gendarme*. Their clothes were too nondescript for easy identification, even if witnesses to the stabbing had come forward; and at the height of the tourist season, with students of all races gathered in this city of culture and romance, two young Arabs of murderous natures would be almost impossible to wheedle out.

The only disappointment came when they were seated at a streetside café drinking white wine (so wonderful to be away from the strictures of a Moslem society) and learned from the conversations around them that nobody appeared to have been killed in that day's bomb blast at the Gare du Nord, although five people, a child among them, were seriously injured.

Asil and Youssef drifted on, soon finding a crêperie where they took delight in decadent European cooking. As they consumed the food and wine, it was with each other they flirted. The bustle and the festive atmosphere (despite the bombing) around them heightened their excitement; the killing and maiming served as a stimulus for their passion.

Eventually they crossed the river at the Ile de la Cité, going towards the market quarter and their apartment, but stopping once again to take more wine at one of the cafés on the Place de la Contrescarpe. After two more glasses they decided that the night still held further adventures for them. The crowds had dwindled, most of the tourists having tottered back to their hotels and *pensions* leaving the streets mostly to students and winos, the *clochards*. Asil and Youssef finally went in search of yet another victim, one who would fulfil a certain need in them.

They rejected the first two male prostitutes because they looked too old – in their twenties at least – and too tough. The third was an effeminate boy who looked no more than seventeen. He led them into a dark *cul-de-sac* where he assured them they would not be disturbed. Youssef did not have his beloved garotte with him, but the tie he wore would do; prolonged torture would not be possible here, but Asil would have fun with his blade while the boy's skin turned purple and his tongue swelled from his mouth.

Unluckily for them, the 'boy' was neither as young as he appeared, nor what he claimed to be (and certainly not effeminate).

Light from a distant lamp glinted on the pistol he produced from beneath his jacket. 'Police,' he informed them, holding up an ID in his left hand.

The bullet scraped along the bone of Asil's lower arm as he lunged with the knife, this time his victim's stomach exposed and an easy target. The fake prostitute dropped like a stone, the gun firing into the pavement before falling from his grasp.

Asil screamed with the pain in his arm, the knife slipping away, lodged in the policeman. Somewhere not too far away a whistle blew for the *gendarmerie* were out in force that night because of the bomb outrage, and the gunshots had been heard. Youssef dragged his friend away, hurrying him through the narrow streets in the direction of their apartment. A car screeched around a corner ahead of them, its lights blazing.

The two terrorists ducked into an alleyway, breaking into an awkward run, convinced they had been spotted. They had. The police car came to a halt at the alleyway entrance; doors flew open, uniformed men jumped out. They shouted, '*Arrêtez!*' before aiming their weapons and firing.

Bullets smacked into the walls around the fleeing Arabs and one ricocheted off cobblestones to tear through the outer edge of Youssef's calf. Both men were handicapped, although they were able to keep on the move. Youssef was weeping as he limped along, the whole of his leg numbed with the shock, pain not yet registering.

They emerged into a wider street and saw other uniformed men coming towards them. There were still a few pedestrians around, one or two cars crawling close to the kerbs. All came to a standstill as the shouting *gendarmes* weaved through them. Asil and Youssef started in the opposite direction, running as fast as their wounds would allow, cursing themselves for their foolishness, knowing how angry their masters would be at the risk they had exposed themselves and the organization to. They silently implored Allah to lend them wings.

Rounding another corner, they stumbled over the bodies of three *clochards* huddled on a *métro* vent (these raggedy men relished the underground warmth whatever the season). Asil struck his head against the pavement, stunning himself. The complaining winos kicked out and Youssef rolled into the gutter. He quickly sat up and was horrified when he saw the inert body of his friend. Running footsteps drawing near, headlights and blaring sirens approaching fast. He scrambled to his feet and pulled up his dazed companion, urging him to run.

Into an alleyway opposite they went, the smell of an underground river that had been turned into a sewer strong in the confines of the narrow space. A saxophone played bluesily overhead, the musician uninterested in the commotion below. Garbage piled up in heaps against walls near the backdoors of restaurants. Run, Asil, run, Youssef! But to where? Paris was not familiar, and now they were disorientated. They would never find their way to the apartment that night.

The numbness had left Youssef's leg. It felt as though it was on fire. Asil's head had not yet cleared, and all he was really conscious of was the searing pain in his arm. He had to rely on his lover to lead him onwards.

Out into another street, this one wider than the last, but with little cruising traffic. Across the road, into a courtyard, shouts and footsteps behind. Both men were near to exhaustion, their wounds draining strength. They knew they could not go much further.

Akhoo sharmoota! No way out! The courtyard was a closed trap! Beloved Allah, show mercy to loyal soldiers of the *jihad*!

Shouted commands outside. Whistles blowing. Tyres screeching to a halt. Doors slamming.

But Asil was pointing and Youssef could not understand how his dazed companion had seen the tiny opening between the buildings, a dark cleft as if the houses had been eased apart.

Yatamajad ism al rab! The way had been shown!

They staggered across the courtyard, where lights from windows were coming on to throw reflections like searchlights down on them, and entered the pitch-black opening, just enough room inside for them to lope along helping each other. A dim glow seemed to rise from the ground ahead, and they soon found themselves at the top of a steep flight of stone steps. A single streetlamp lit the exit a short distance away.

Voices in the courtyard behind. No time to linger. Down they went. But blinding pain gnashed through the muscles of Youssef's calf and he slipped, grabbed for Asil as he fell, taking him along, over and over, the edges of the worn steps scraping skin, jarring bones, as they plunged then slid, slowing to a tumbling roll as they neared the bottom.

They lay there, tangled together, sobbing and moaning, with no strength to carry on, and no will either.

The exit was not far away. Yet it was too far.

Echoing footsteps from above. The policemen would punish them severely for killing one of their own. And when they realized they had killed yet another earlier in the day, that they were responsible for the bombing at the station, what then? Asil and Youssef shuddered, the thought shared. They reached for each other's hand and waited, shivering with hurt and fear.

But something was moving across the opening in front of them. A shiny blackness. Sleekly slow. They thought it would pass by, but the vehicle stopped when the rear door was level with the passageway.

The door opened. A voice whispered to them down the close walls of the alley.

'*Ta al maee wa sa ta eesh lee taktol mara sani ya* – come with me and you'll live to kill again,' it said.

The promise gave them enough strength to crawl into the black limousine.

(And it was a promise that Kline certainly kept.)

▪ 31 ▪
RETURN TO NEATH

KLINE STIRRED, SHIFTING IN THE SEAT SO THAT HIS FACE WAS AWAY FROM HALLORAN.

The Shield operative watched him, his attention momentarily away from the passing countryside. The psychic had hardly moved since the Mercedes had left the Magma building an hour or so before, yet he had seemed too still to be sleeping. No rhythmic breathing, no total limpness; it was almost as if he had gone into some kind of self-induced trance. Maybe he had, Halloran considered. Wasn't that what psychics did?

Not for the first time during the journey, Halloran looked over his shoulder through the rear window. A couple of cars behind but, as far as he could tell, nothing to worry about: they weren't being followed. The Granada containing his own men came into view, keeping well back, ready to accelerate into action should a problem arise. He checked ahead before settling back into the seat, remaining alert, but reasonably sure there were no immediate worries. Although Monk and the Jordanians had been left back at Magma, evidently to collect some items for Kline from his penthouse, he considered it no great loss of manpower. If the Mercedes were to come under attack, then he could rely on himself and the two Shield men without the blunderings of untrained bodyguards to hinder his own counter-tactics. The fact that his own men were armed now added to his confidence.

Halloran ran a hand over his eyes and across his rough chin. He was tired, the dream last night obviously having disturbed what little rest he'd had in the armchair. A shower, a shave, and something to eat wouldn't come amiss. An inspection of the house and grounds and then, with luck, a couple of hours' sleep. There was an unsettled feeling in the pit of his stomach that had nothing to do with hunger, but which told him he would need all the rest he could get if he were to cope with the next day or two. An instinct he had come to depend on through the years made him aware that something was imminent. It was a feeling he couldn't explain even to himself, but there was a familiar tension building inside him, honing his senses, sharpening his reactions, preparing him for what was to come. Fear had always mingled with that sensing, and that was natural; but this time a deep foreboding was involved, a disquieting dread, and that was new to him.

A muffled sound from Kline. The psychic's shoulders rose and slumped. His breathing became regular. Now he was sleeping.

Cora, next to Palusinski in the front of the car, turned to look at her employer. Her eyes caught Halloran's and her smile was tentative. A moment went by before he returned the smile.

She faced the front again and Halloran, on the opposite corner of the Mercedes, was able to study her profile. He wondered if she really had it in her to give away company secrets. Unlikely. She was too closely linked to Kline and, Halloran was sure, too much afraid of her employer to betray him. Yet Kline had had no doubts. He'd denounced her before Magma's chairman and vice-chairman. Surely there had to be good reason for that?

Halloran checked the windows again. All clear, with only the Granada behind them. He realized they would soon be at Neath.

So what plans *did* Kline have for Cora? Would she be accused once they arrived at Neath, or would he set a trap for her, catch her in the act of betrayal? Kline's paranoia suggested the former, his sly vindictiveness the latter. Halloran made up his mind that he would get to her first, warn her of what was to happen. To hell with Kline and the Magma Corporation. To hell with the assignment. He'd continue to guard the target, but he would also keep the girl from any harm. Halloran had already suspected that Kline's four bodyguards were more than just that; he was sure they were well used to meting out punishment – particularly Monk, in this respect – whenever their employer pointed a finger. It was an unnecessary complication to the situation but, guilty or not, Cora wasn't going to suffer in their hands. He intended to keep a good watch on her.

As the car rounded a bend, Kline's hand flopped down by his side, its fingers curled into a claw. Halloran noticed that small sections of skin were whitish, as if about to peel off.

'Is good to be away from city,' came Palusinski's voice from the front. 'Air is cleaner here. My father was farmer, Mr Halloran, *rolnik*, so countryside is my love. Cities are bad place for me.'

'Where in Poland d'you come from?' Halloran asked with no real interest.

'Ah, it is of no importance.' Palusinski tapped the steering wheel. 'I am here now, is all that matters. He ...' the Pole inclined his head towards the sleeping man and Halloran was surprised to catch the hint of a sneer in his tone '... bring me here many years ago, take me from my beloved country.'

'You could always go back,' Halloran suggested, watching the road which was becoming familiar as they neared the estate.

'Back?' Palusinski uttered a bitter chuckle. 'To what go back? To Russians who bleed Poland dry? I stay here, I think. Yes, I stay here where everyone is friendly, and food is good!' He laughed aloud and thumped the steering wheel.

The gates to the estate were not far away and Halloran checked the front and rear windows yet again. Only the Shield vehicle was bringing up their rear. The Mercedes swung in towards the iron gates and stopped no more than a foot away from them. Kline stirred but did not awaken.

Halloran opened his door and stepped out, walking to the edge of the road, and waited for the Granada to pull up beside him. He leaned forward, one hand on the roof, as the passenger lowered the window.

'Contact the patrol and make sure everything's okay. I'll meet you back here ...' he lifted his wristwatch '... in three hours.'

'Anything extra we should do?' the driver called across his passenger.

Halloran shook his head. 'Just patrol, the full tour. Don't come into the grounds.'

'What if we spot someone?' the man nearest said, plainly irritated.

'Use the RT to let me know. Don't come in.'

'Why the hell not?'

'You wouldn't like it.'

Halloran straightened, examined the roadway in both directions, then walked to the gates. He heard the Granada speed away as he reached out and grasped one of the thick iron struts. There came a dull, heavy click and he pushed against the metal. The gate swung open, a grating of rusted hinges accompanying the sluggish movement. Halloran took it all the way back, then did the same with the other half, feeling observed from the lodge-house as he did so.

Another resolution for Halloran: he was going to confront whoever it was inside that place, the person who guarded the gate, who was master of the dogs. He would visit the lodge later, and this time he would find a way inside. Before leaving Magma, he had discussed the vulnerability of the Neath estate with Charles Mather, and the Planner had promised to raise the matter with Gerald Snaith, after which an ultimatum would be delivered to Sir Victor Penlock: either adequate defences were installed around the house and grounds, or Shield would be forced to relinquish the contract. The enormous sums of insurance money involved would ensure the alliance of the Lloyd's underwriters. Mather had been horrified to learn there were jackals roaming the estate, and perplexed when Halloran had told him that he had not yet met the lodge-keeper to discuss any emergency measures. A rum business altogether, Mather had voiced in his dry manner. Time to lay down stricter ground rules.

Halloran waved the Mercedes through, then closed the gates. There was a solid permanence about the thudded clunk as they locked together.

He climbed back to the car and as it pulled away Palusinski said cheerfully: 'No dogs to bite you today.'

Halloran frowned. 'Where are they kept?'

'Kept?' came the reply. 'You mean caged? Hah! These beasts wander freely, they go where they please.'

'They're not much in evidence.'

'We are not hostile.'

'Yesterday … ?'

'You were alone. And perhaps they sensed …'

Halloran wondered why the Pole did not complete the sentence.

'They tend to keep under cover in the daytime,' said Cora, twisting in her seat. 'They dislike people, they keep away from them. But at night they prowl.'

'And search out intruders,' Palusinski finished.

'Have there been any?' asked Halloran. 'Intruders?'

Palusinski giggled. Cora said, 'There have been one or two trespassers, but they've always been frightened off.'

'They were lucky they weren't savaged,' Halloran commented.

'No, the jackals didn't touch them. They were frightened off by … other things.'

'I don't understand. What things?'

Palusinski giggled again. 'Wood devils, *Pan* Halloran. You have not heard of the wood devils?'

The house, its walls a deeper and duller red under the overcast day, came into view. Cora turned away from Halloran, as if unwilling to continue the conversation, but he leaned forward and grasped her shoulder.

'What does he mean, wood devils? What's he talking about?'

'It's nothing, Liam. Really it's nothing.'

'But explain to him,' said Palusinski, his tone bantering. He snatched a quick look at Halloran, eyes small and squinted behind his wire-framed spectacles.

'They're only images, no more than that,' Cora said quickly. 'Felix can project mental images, make a person see what isn't really there.'

Oh yes, Halloran knew that. He had seen such visions for himself in the lake.

'Felix senses when the dogs are alerted. I don't know how – it's as if there's some kind of telepathic link between himself and the animals. He doesn't even have to hear the jackals to know there are trespassers in the grounds.'

Halloran started to understand why Kline felt so secure within his own territory. The man had his own inbuilt alarm system, according to Cora, and his own defence weapon. With such power, no wonder his subordinates feared him.

The car drew up outside the house and Cora leaned over the back of her seat to rouse Kline. 'Felix,' she said, quietly at first, then again, louder, when there was no response.

'Felix, we're here.' Cora reached down and tapped his knee. The dark-haired man, curled up into the corner of the Mercedes, twitched but did not awaken. She shook his leg this time and repeated his name more sharply.

Kline stirred, his legs stretched. He mumbled something and began to push himself up in the seat.

'We're home?' he asked, voice slurred with tiredness.

'Yes, Felix, we're at Neath,' Cora told him.

'Good,' he said, 'good.' He turned, sitting upright, one hand touching the door lever.

Cora's gasp stopped him. Her eyes were wide as she stared.

Halloran had become still.

Puzzled, Kline looked from one to the other and, as he did so, flakes of skin shed from his face. A face that was bubbled and broken, thin tissue hanging loose in layered scales.

As he frowned, more pieces fell away, falling lightly onto his chest and lap. He began to tremble.

▪ 32 ▪
A SHEDDING OF SKIN

THE GUN WAS IN HALLORAN'S HAND BEFORE THE BEDROOM DOOR WAS FULLY OPEN.

Cora stood in the doorway, frightened by the weapon. 'I'm sorry,' she said. 'I should have knocked.'

He waved her in, swinging his legs over the edge of the bed and sitting up. He put the Browning back on the bedside cabinet.

'How's Kline?' he asked.

Cora closed the door and leaned against it, her hands behind her. 'He hasn't left his room since we got back.'

'Have you sent for a doctor?'

She shook her head. 'Felix won't allow that. He told me he suffers from psoriasis, a rare type of skin complaint that recurs every few years, but it's nothing to become alarmed about.'

'Some complaint. And he wasn't too relaxed about it when Palusinski helped him into the house. Have you seen him like this before?'

'No.'

'We really ought to get a doctor to take a look at him.'

'He insists that we shouldn't. His orders are that we let him rest and send Khayed and Daoud to him as soon as they return from London. They have special lotions that can help.' She seemed uncertain. 'I didn't want to disturb you. You must be very tired.'

'A clean-up and a change of clothes helped. I even managed to grab a sandwich.' He extended a hand. 'Cora, I need to talk to you. Please come over.'

For a moment he thought she might leave. But then she walked to the bed. 'Sit by me,' he said.

She obeyed, and immediately leaned into him, her head against his chest. He held onto her, surprised, but glad her reserve had broken.

'Liam,' she whispered, 'I have such strange feelings, such a sense of dread ...'

'I can understand why. I get the same feeling about this place.'

She looked up at him. 'You too?'

'Maybe it's a neurosis we're catching from Kline. You know he's mad, don't you?'

'In a way I wish that were true – insanity would be easier to deal with. Felix is unstable and, as you say, neurotic; but not mad, Liam, not totally mad.'

'He thinks you've been giving away company secrets.' Halloran had been deliberately blunt, the unexpectedness of the remark meant to throw her off balance so that he could judge her reaction.

'You're not serious,' she said incredulously.

He took her hand, now having no doubts about her loyalty to Kline. 'I'm afraid so. That's why all the fuss at Magma this morning. New locations of untapped resources have been leaked to one of your rival companies.'

'It's happened again?'

He nodded. 'Kline put the finger on you.'

'But why? I wouldn't –'

Halloran shrugged. 'You're closest to him.'

She seemed to shrink within herself. 'How could he even think that? Liam, I –'

He pulled her to him again. 'I know it isn't true, and maybe Kline will see reason. Who can tell with someone so unpredictable?'

'I still don't understand why he should accuse me.'

'*I* don't understand what makes you so loyal to such a bastard.'

She didn't answer right away. Then she said, almost sorrowfully: 'I depend on him. He ... he's like a drug to me. I need him, Liam.'

'Then you're as crazy as he is.'

'No, don't say that, you don't know ...'

'What is there to know, Cora?' he said angrily. 'Just what the hell goes on between you and Kline?'

She began to weep. 'Help me, Liam,' she said quietly. 'Please help me.'

'How can I when you won't tell me what's wrong?'

Cora began to fumble with the buttons of her blouse. 'Make love to me. Hold me and make love to me, but gently, like last night, after you ... Let me feel how good it can be again.'

Baffled, Halloran stood up and crossed to the door. He locked it.

*

The room's thick curtains were drawn against outside light, so that scattered artefacts of another age stood as dark shapes in the gloom. The smell of burning incense came from one corner, filling the air with a heavy and faintly acrid musk. Zodiac signs and symbols, drawings of horned beasts, of winged creatures, of single eyes, were roughly etched into walls and woodwork, obscure and patternless in the poor light. Books lay scattered around the floor. A canopied bed dominated the room, its four stout carved posts supporting layers of sheer drapes, the material hanging in loose folds.

A dry, rasping breathing came from within.

Kline lay on the bed, the skin of his naked body broken and ravaged, creating new fissures, causing paper-thin tissue to dislodge and fall away.

He feebly lifted an arm, but the darkness was even greater inside the shroud and all he could see was a myriad of interjoining cracks. His arm fell back to his side and a sob escaped him.

It couldn't be, it wasn't time. The ritual had been enacted, the psyche strengthened. The sacrifice made. This shedding of the outer layer had come too soon, and with it there was pain. But why, what did it mean?

His unsightly body spasmed as another sob burst from him, and he felt the breaking of delicate tissue with the violence of the movement.

Must lie still. Must not move until Asil and Youssef arrive with their salves. It was too soon, too soon! He was not prepared! And the pain had never been like this before. Hurry, my friends, bring me your soothing oils! Spare me from this wretchedness!

Kline tried to steady his breathing, for even the rising and lowering of his chest was loosening the dead skin. He moaned, a self-pitying sound, and salt from his tears stung the sensitive grooves around his eyes.

And as he lay there, his mind absorbed in his own suffering, something inside the sepulchre that was hidden away in the blackest depths of Neath, throbbed once.

▪ 33 ▪
INSIDE THE LODGE

From his position by the main entrance, Monk watched the Shield operative descend the broad staircase and wondered what was inside the black case he was carrying. The bodyguard's thick lips set in a sneer, his heavy-set body tensing as Halloran approached.

'I'm taking a look around the grounds,' Halloran told him.

'You'll get your ass bit off.'

The hope in Monk's high-pitched voice did not go unnoticed by the other man. 'I intend to stay in the car,' Halloran replied. 'Did the Arabs let you know how Kline is?' Khayed and Daoud had returned some hours earlier, rushing up to their master's room immediately they learned of his condition.

'They ain't been down,' said Monk, shaking his large head.

'All right, let's assume it's nothing drastic. Lock the door behind me when I go out and don't open it for anybody until I return. I'm taking a spare key, but I'll let you know it's me before I come in just so you don't get over-excited. If I knock a regular three times it means there's trouble and I'm not alone. I'll repeat that knock after a pause so you'll know it's for real. You got that?'

Monk smirked rather than reply.

'Check around the house every fifteen minutes, test windows and doors each time. And I mean test them – try them, make sure they're properly locked.'

'What the fuck for?' Outrage accompanied the bodyguard's hostility now.

'Just do it. I'll be back in about an hour. Any calls for me and you write down the message. Don't try and remember.'

'You think I'm stupid, Halloran?'

'We both know it.'

Monk's shoulders visibly straightened and he almost took a step forward. Only Halloran's hard-eyed smile stopped him.

The Shield operative went by the American and unlocked one side of the double-doors. A breeze of cold air from the lake made him shiver as he stepped outside. It was like the first chill of winter out there instead of the coming of summer. He called back to Monk: 'Lock it and take out the key.' Then he walked through the porch to the outside.

Although cold, the night had temporarily cleared, the moon, an edge sliced off, still low in the sky. There were thunderous clouds on the horizon. The slopes around the house and lake were of deep-toned greys, trees and shrubbery the darkest patches. The lake itself appeared smooth and unbroken, even though a wind ruffled the grass before it.

Halloran climbed into the Mercedes, placing the black bag on the passenger seat beside him. He switched on the engine and lights and pulled away, gravel crunching beneath the tyres, bringing the car round in an arc. As he did so, he glimpsed the neglected topiary garden at the side of the house, the tortured shapes resembling surrealistic figures, misshapen limbs twisted towards Neath like a frozen tableau of anguished souls.

He left the house behind, heading uphill towards the main gates, the woods soon closing around him, the car's beams seeming to swathe a path through the trees. Halloran kept a vigilant eye on either side of the road, searching for low shapes slinking through undergrowth, but saw nothing that moved. A sharp *crack* on his left startled him. A thin branch had snapped against the side window. Halloran eased over the road's centre, realizing he had drifted too close to the edge.

The Mercedes rounded a curve and from there the roadway became a straight line running up to the gates. Halloran eased up on the accelerator, approaching the beginning of the drive at a cautious speed. The headlights picked out the iron gates, and he dipped the beams to reduce the glare. His foot touched the brake pedal, slowing the car even more so that he came to the lodge-house at a smooth glide.

Halloran pulled over onto the rough verge in front of the old building, switched off the lights and cut the engine.

The lodge was in darkness, not even a glimmer showing from the grimed windows. Halloran sat there for several minutes, watching for any sign of life. There was none. But that didn't mean the house was empty.

Without using the interior light, Halloran unzipped the black bag by his side. He lifted out the stubby weapon an inch or so, loosening it, making sure it wasn't snagged on the inner lining. He carefully lowered the sub-machine-gun again, then reached for the doorhandle.

A breeze ruffled his hair as he stood outside the vehicle studying the upper windows of the lodge. The moon was rising behind the building so that its frontage was an unlit void, the windows merely black shapes, barely distinct against the brickwork.

Again the unshakeable feeling of being observed. Carrying the gun bag in his left hand, Halloran walked into the shadow of the house.

The ringing of the telephone came almost as a relief. Mather laid the newspaper on the pile of Sundays, foreign as well as English, by his feet, exhausted with reading of yet more terrorist outrages and despairing of various governments' weakness in dealing with them, despite the vowed joint intention to do so over the past decade. Unfortunately it was the price paid for a world without major conflicts, the major evil giving ground to the lesser evil, a fact recognized by those same governments. Nevertheless, the atrocities committed in the name of so-called freedom or religious beliefs were hard to stomach and the time was coming when 'official' war would have to be declared on those countries and states who overtly supported and encouraged the multifarious terrorist groups. And even then the problem would never be eradicated.

He stood up from the dining table on which more journals were spread and limped out into the hall.

'I'm here,' he called out to Agnes, who was in the sitting room, no doubt indulging herself in the current television trivia with her evening sherry.

'Mather,' he announced into the phone, first removing the pipe from his mouth.

'I'm sorry to disturb you. It's Sir Victor Penlock here.'

'Sir Victor?' Mather's brain stepped up a gear, alerted by the gravity in the Magma chairman's voice.

'I'd like you to meet me at my office once again. My apologies for calling on you twice in one day, particularly as it's a Sunday, but I'm afraid I had no other choice.'

'That's perfectly all right. Do I take it Mr Kline and my operative will also be there?'

A pause first. 'No. No, this will be strictly between you and me. It's rather serious, so do you think you could come immediately?'

'Shouldn't take much more than twenty minutes this time of evening.'

'It's very much appreciated. I'll let Security know you're on your way. One other thing: no one else must know about this. Can I have your word on that?'

'Naturally, although I don't understand why.'

'I'll explain when you get here.'

When Mather replaced the receiver he went into his study and, as a precaution, wrote a note of his destination and whom he was to see, then sealed it in an envelope on which he scribbled his wife's name. He left the envelope propped up on his desk.

The stench at the back of the lodge-house caused Halloran to catch his breath. No doubt this was where the jackals were kept when they were not prowling the grounds. He shone the thin beam of the penlight around the yard, expecting to find kennels or a stockade of some kind. There was none, and no animals either. But the light reflected on something shiny.

With a twist of the torch's head, the beam was broadened to take in more. Halloran recognized the three metal containers Khayed and Daoud had carried from the house the day before. All were lying on their sides, the lids close by, as though the contents had been spilled out. He moved closer, using the light to guide himself through the mounds of excrement scattered around the yard. Drawing near to one of the bins he bent low to shine the light inside. His foot crunched something beneath him. He shifted to see shattered bone where he had been standing, and realized that there were many more pieces around him, clean and meatless. At the bottom of the container there were clogs of maggot-infested meat, the jackals obviously having been unable to reach them. Much of the yard's putrid stink came from these containers.

Halloran straightened, relieved at least that the beasts themselves were nowhere in evidence. He flashed the beam up at the windows, heedless of giving anyone inside warning of his presence; he had, in fact, already pounded on the front door, knowing that his approach in the Mercedes would not have gone unnoticed by anyone supposedly guarding the estate's entrance. The lodge-keeper might have been roaming the grounds with his pack, of course, but Halloran could not rid himself of the notion that there was someone inside. Even now he sensed he was being watched.

He lowered the torch, finding the backdoor, then manoeuvred his way through the faeces and bones towards it. As expected, this door, like the front, was firmly locked. He moved along the wall to a window and, although also locked, this was less of a problem. Placing the bag on the windowsill, Halloran slid a knife blade up alongside the catch, then forced it aside, its movement stiff but yielding. He closed the blade into its handle, dropped it into his jacket pocket, then heaved at the lower frame. The window resisted at first before, with a groan followed by a squeal, it opened upwards.

Halloran lifted the bag, switched off the torch, swung a leg over the sill. Once inside he quickly stepped away from the window, where moonlight had silhouetted his shape. He leaned back against the wall and waited, holding his breath, listening for sounds.

The room smelled musty, damp, unlived in. Light from outside revealed sparse furniture: an armchair, its cushions lumpy, arms threadbare, a nondescript cabinet, neither antique nor modern, against one wall, a curled rug, and nothing else. Apart from the small rug, the floorboards were bare. Halloran flicked on the penlight once more, the beam still broad, and waved it around the room. Wallpaper hung away in strips and black fungus grew in the corners and near the ceiling. There were ashes in the ancient iron fireplace, but they looked solid, as though they had set many years ago. There was an open door to the right.

Halloran listened for a while longer before allowing himself to breathe normally. He swept the light across the floor to make sure there were no obstacles in his path, then crossed the room to the door, unconcerned with the creaking of floorboards. Narrowing the torch beam, he peered out into the hallway, shining the light along its length. Moonlight glowed through the grime of the tiny windows above the backdoor. The hallway had a turn in it and he surmised that it straightened again and led towards the lodge's main door. The stairway would be in that direction too.

He eased himself from the room, holding the torch away from his body. Keeping close to the wall opposite the door he had just left, Halloran slowly walked towards the front of the building. He passed another door on his right, but did not try the handle, guessing it would lead to a cellar.

He reached the point where the hallway turned, and hesitated, listening intently for a few seconds. Only silence. But the smell of oldness was even stronger here.

Halloran noticed a lightswitch close to where he stood and he reached out, pushing it down with one extended finger, the thin torch gripped with the others. Nothing happened, and he was not surprised. Whoever lived in the lodge-house enjoyed the darkness.

He went on, rounding the bend, and pointed the torch at the front door. There were large bolts, top and bottom, rusted fixtures that looked as if they hadn't been shifted for decades. Another door on his left, the staircase rising above him on his right. Halloran made his way towards the door.

Slipping the straps of the bag over his left shoulder and changing the penlight to that hand, he used an elbow to push open the door. Its creaking was explosive in the silence of the house.

Before entering, he shone the torch through the crack by the hinges, satisfying himself that nobody lurked behind the door, and only then did he step into the room. It was empty, devoid of any furniture, its curtains colourless with age and filth. The mustiness prevailed and here the mould festered in thick clusters. Ceiling struts could be clearly seen where plaster had fallen away. Halloran left the room, leaving the door open wide.

The staircase loomed up before him.

And it was from there that the worst of the smell wafted down.

Halloran began to climb.

Mather parked directly outside Magma's main entrance, disregarding the double-yellows. As he limped around the bonnet of his car, he could not help but gaze up at the towering building, its glass and bronze façade brooding under a sky that was quickly filling with leaden clouds from the east. He felt a charge in the atmosphere, the coming of an electrical storm.

The two security men inside had noticed his arrival and one was crossing the concourse towards the closed entrance while his companion at the circular reception desk lifted a phone. Mather started forward again, an urgency in his stride.

The security guard had come to a smaller door beside the main entrance and had already opened it a fraction by the time the Shield Planner was outside.

'Mr Mather?' the guard enquired, and Mather opened his wallet to display his Shield identity. 'Sir Victor's waiting for you. I'll take you right up.'

The guard said nothing as the lift swiftly ascended to the eighteenth floor, but he appeared tense, as much on edge as Mather himself. They trudged the thick-carpeted corridor to the chairman's outer office, passing through, waiting when the guard rapped on the inner door. The guard opened the door after a voice on the other side responded, then stood aside to allow the older man entry, still not uttering a single word: Mather heard the door close behind him.

Sir Victor did not rise from his seat. In front of him was a tumbler half-filled with Scotch.

'Good of you to get here so quickly,' the Magma chairman said, waving Mather forward.

Although on first glance Sir Victor appeared his usual immaculate self – grey, double-breasted suit, thin-striped shirt and navy tie – there was an indefinable dishevelment about him. Perhaps it was the weariness in his eyes, the slight sagging of his jowls, a few loose strands of silver hair hanging over his forehead that gave the impression, the Shield Planner mused. As well as the unexpected laxity in manners, for Mather had not been offered a seat, nor had Sir Victor risen when he had entered the office. Hardly a return to Stone-age etiquette, but surely an indication of the stress this usually most civilized of men was under.

Now the chairman did rise, but not in deference to the other man. 'I want to show you something,' he said, 'after which we must discuss our course of action.'

Curious, Mather followed the tall man back into the corridor, and then into another office which, like Sir Victor's, bore no title on its door. They walked through an outer room where the chairman unlocked a further door into the main office itself.

Mather drew in a sharp breath when he saw the figure slumped forward across the glass and chrome desk. He hurriedly crossed the room to examine the body.

'Quinn-Reece?' he asked, already sure that it was.

'Security discovered the body earlier this evening,' the chairman replied grimly.

Mather moved around the desk and leaned close to the prone man's face. He was prepared to feel for a pulse in Quinn-Reece's neck, but realized it was pointless. The blueness of the vice-chairman's lips, the yellowish tinge to his skin, his very stillness, told him all he needed to know.

'Heart failure?' he ventured.

'I believe so. But lift him into his seat, look at his face.'

Even more puzzled, Mather slid an arm beneath Quinn-Reece's chest and pulled him backwards. He was stunned at what he saw.

'My God, he looks as if he ...'

'Died of fright?' Sir Victor finished for him. 'He was sitting upright like that when he was found. I ordered security to lay him on the desk. I couldn't bear the thought of him staring that way, his mouth locked open ...'

Mather frowned. 'I think you'd better tell me what's going on. I assume your people haven't yet called for a doctor or an ambulance?'

The chairman's guilt was barely apparent. 'Our security guards are under strict instructions never to bring outsiders onto the premises unless someone in authority sanctions it. We regard anything that happens within the walls of Magma as company business, and only I or my executive officers may deem otherwise.'

'Good Lord, man, this has nothing to do with your business. It's possible that medical attention might have saved him.'

Sir Victor was adamant. 'No, I can assure you he was quite dead. Nothing could have helped him, nothing at all.'

'Well I suggest you call for an ambulance now.'

'Yes, of course. But first we must talk. Please allow me a few minutes.'

'Is there good reason?'

The chairman looked away from the corpse. 'I believe so,' he said quietly.

The stairboards groaned under his weight. He thought one or two might break altogether and quickly shifted his footing. It seemed a long climb to the bend in the stairs, as if time itself were being stretched, and at any second he expected someone to appear above him, so strong was the feeling of another's presence inside the lodge-house.

He stopped for a few moments when his head came level with the landing, and listened again, depending on hearing rather than seeing in such poor light. There were three doors along the upstairs hallway, one to the left of the staircase, one directly in front, the last further down. The latter would have a view overlooking the entrance gates, but it was not for that reason alone Halloran chose to inspect it first: he knew, as surely as if someone were calling him, that he would find what he was searching for inside there.

As with the rest of the house, bare boards was the only flooring along the landing and he saw no reason to avoid making noise as he walked its length – it was too late for that. Nevertheless, his movement was stealthy and his right hand was kept free, ready to snatch the gun from its holster at the slightest provocation, even though he was there in his role as Kline's protector, not as an enemy.

The smell of rotting was nauseating as he drew close to the door and he swallowed the wetness rising in his throat.

Halloran went on by the door, going to the window at the far end of the hallway. He pushed aside half-drawn curtains, the coarse material stiffened with dust, and rubbed a palm against the dirt on the glass, clearing a section to see out. Moonlight glimmered from the roof and bonnet of the Mercedes below; the iron bars of the entrance gates looked blackly solid; the undergrowth opposite seemed impenetrable. Light withered as a cloud rolled over the moon.

Halloran returned to the door, his torch haloing the handle. He pressed his ear close to the wood, but heard no sounds from the other side. Hitching the bag so that it was secure on his shoulder, he reached for the doorhandle.

He was sure the door would be locked. It wasn't.

He expected to use force to push the door open. It opened smoothly.

He thought he would confront the lodge-keeper, the guardian of the gates. Instead he met his past.

▪ 34 ▪
INTO THE PIT

KLINE MOANED AS KHAYED MINISTERED THE LOTION TO HIS RUPTURED SKIN. THE burning would soon pass, the Arab assured him, and Kline knew the truth of what he said; his loyal servants had soothed him with their oils many times before. But that was when the sloughing of his skin had been expected, had become a ritual, a ceremony to be indulged in, to be celebrated, for it was the outward sign of spiritual rejuvenation. And a continuance of his own servitude.

He uttered a cry, more in fear than in pain. Daoud misunderstood and hurried forward with the syringe. 'Mouallem?'

Kline saw the needle and raised a hand to deny the morphine, for the drug would dim his thoughts, euphoria would blunt the danger that was so close. Yet his senses were already hindered, for dread gnawed at them like some avaricious parasite. The killing that day of the enemy within had not calmed his unease, as he thought it would; instead the mental effort had further drained his psyche, and weakened him physically. The death of Quinn-Reece had not resolved his own anguish, but had merely contributed to his present condition.

He beckoned Daoud forward again, speaking to the Arab in his native tongue. 'A moderate amount, Youssef. Enough only to soften my ...' he almost said *fear* '... my pain.'

The needle was like a blade heated by fire, but Kline's scream swiftly relaxed to a sigh as his senses began to float. Soon he dreamed, but in truth, it was a memory ...

... he lowered himself into the pit, terribly afraid. It was so deep, so black. But for that reason, it would yield even greater treasures. Why else should it be so skilfully concealed from the other sepulchres? The reward for his courage would indeed be great! The Jewish merchant in Jerusalem had promised him that. Journey to Ur, find employment with the English archaeologist. He needs men of education, people who can direct the lazy and treacherous labourers, and who will appreciate and understand the cultural value of his great discovery. The Arabs will obey because the Englishman will put his trust in you and they will have little choice. You are clever, you are cunning. Bring back to me what small treasures you can easily steal and I will make you a rich man, for I have collectors who will pay kings' ransoms for the most meagre of items from the fabulous and glorious era! These Arabs are plunderers, destroyers, scum of the earth, and care nothing for their heritage. They will allow their own history to be taken from them by foreigners. But we will profit by their stupidity, my young friend. And we will bring great joy to those who honour such relics.

The journey to the Royal Cemetery of Ur had been long and wearisome and he had worried that the dig would be over by the time he arrived there; but no, there was still much work to be done, many more tombs that lay at the bottom of deep shafts beneath thousands of surface graves to be revealed. And the merchant had been correct: the team of foreigners needed several of his ilk to organize the transient labour force, arrange permits and payroll, maintain supplies and medicines, as well as securing the site against thieving infiltrators. He had worked diligently, never becoming too greedy with his own finds, taking only those objects small enough to be smuggled safely from the camp to the single room he had rented inside the city, a place where he could hide his private cache and where every so often the merchant from Jerusalem would arrive to relieve him of the treasures. The system worked well and when all was complete, the merchant assured him, the profits would be admirable.

He had not come upon the secret tunnel leading to the pit by accident, for he had always had the gift, the seeing in the mind, the ability to predict a death before it was claimed, a birth before conception, to judge beforehand good fortune for some, tragedy for others. Even when he was a child, should his mother lose a needle, it was he whom she urged to find it; should his father misplace an article, it was the boy who sought out its hiding place. Later, when his gift became known to others, it was he who was taken into arid territories to locate a source of water beneath the soil so that new settlements could be built around it. Rewards for that rare inner knowledge had paid for his welfare and education after his entire family had been taken by disease (strangely a tragedy he had not been able to predict). So it was that the merchant realized the young man's potential when the great find outside the distant city of Ur in the land where the ancient Sumerians had once reigned became world news. Who better then to seek out those exquisite but concealed antiquities that would end up as mere exhibits in some stuffy London museum unless re-directed elsewhere?

On his very first day inside that vast labyrinth of shafts and corridors, hidden rooms and sepulchres, he had become confused and almost overwhelmed by mourning voices of the dead, whose spirits were locked beneath the earth, for their human vessels had taken their own lives to be with their deceased kings and queens, and their high priests. Over the weeks that followed he had learned to shut out those incorporeal murmurings from his mind; yet one sensing persisted throughout, something that was not a spiritual utterance, but a kind of pulse, a split-second shifting of atmosphere, as if time itself had hiccuped. He would feel it but once or twice a day, never more than that. At first he had believed it was a physical phenomenon, a faraway subsidence, but no one else ever noticed the brief disturbance. The deeper he worked his way into the complex layers of tombs, the louder – or more sensed – the unheard 'sound' became. Then one evening, when the day's labour was done, the workmen returned to their tents or hovels outside the city walls, and the foreigners retired to their lodgings, he had wandered alone through the lowest chambers, drawn by he knew not what, but compelled towards a destiny he had never dreamed of.

The secret tunnel was behind an empty room at the furthermost extremity of the Royal Cemetery, a square space that had puzzled the learned archaeologists, for it seemed to have no purpose: its walls were bare and there were no casks or ornaments within. It was merely an isolated chamber, one that was reached by crouching low along a lengthy corridor which had many turns and dips.

The pulse had come as he had stood in that soulless room, and this time it was as though he had really heard the sound. The walls themselves had seemed to tremble. Startled, he had swung his lamp around and the light had caused a shadow on one wall. He moved closer to inspect the shadow and found a mud brick jutting out a fraction from its neighbours. He had used the trowel he carried, standard equipment along with brushes for the diggers, to cut round the brick and ease it from the wall. The stench of released gases sent him reeling backwards.

He approached again more cautiously, and the smell was still strong but less of a shock. Other mud bricks easily came loose and soon a passageway was exposed. A dreadful fear had overcome him then and he had almost run from that place. But a curious fascination stayed him.

He crawled into the narrow passage, holding the lamp before his face.

The passage led downwards, so steeply at certain points that he had to use his strength to prevent himself tumbling forward.

Before long it opened out into a wide circular chamber, at the centre of which was a gaping hole, an open pit. Around the opening lay human bones, their rotting robes those of high priests and priestesses. Resting against the walls were clay tablets of cuneiform writing, wedge-shaped signs that represented words or syllables. He trod carefully to the edge of the pit and stared down at the blackness. That was when his fear became too much to bear, for something was urging him to descend, an inner compulsion inviting him to leap.

And the mind-sound was a sound, disgorging from the pit.

THUD-UP

He had fled.

Despite his terror, he had resealed the opening to the secret passageway, using dirt from the floor to cover the cracks (not that the room was of any interest to Sir Leonard and his team of archaeologists, who had treasures in abundance to drool over without bothering with empty chambers). This discovery would be his alone.

Four days went by before he gained enough courage to venture down to that pit again, four days of nagging agitation and four nights of feverish nightmares. He knew he would go back; the difficulty was finding the will to do so.

He waited until evening once more when all digging had stopped, only a few guards that he, himself, had helped organize left on duty above ground. This time he returned to the pit with rope and stanchion ...

... Kline wailed as he slept and Khayed and Daoud leaned over him anxiously ...

... and fearfully, his limbs trembling so badly that he almost lost his grip, lowered himself over the edge of the pit. He descended slowly, drawn by an allure he could not comprehend, his lamp dangling below him, attached to his waist by thick string. He was aware that something evil awaited him, something ancient and cruel, for his dreams over the past few nights had revealed that at least to him, although no images, no visions of what it was, were presented. For in his sleep he had tasted the joys of carnality, had been seduced by the delights of depravity, had been pleasured by the thrill of vileness. The dreams had promised that those glories would be his if ... if ... if ... he would but claim them. And to claim them, he would have to descend the pit.

THUD-UP!

The pulse was thunderous, reverberating around the shaft, causing a tremor, dislodging dust. His grip on the rope slipped and he plunged.

But not far.

For the pit was not deep at all. Its very blackness had created that illusion.

His legs buckled and he crashed onto his back, the lamp toppling over, fortunately still burning. Without pause to regather his breath, he reached out and righted the lamp lest he be cast into complete darkness. Only then did he suck in the foul air and feel the pain of his jarred body.

He pushed himself into a sitting position, his back against the crumbling wall, his chest heaving, his eyes wide and frightened.

Opposite was a niche. A square hole that was no more than two foot high, cleverly concealed in shadow so that no one above would ever realize it was there.

It was some time before he was able to crawl towards the niche.

The lamp revealed a closed receptacle of some kind inside, its surface dulled by centuries of dust. He brushed shivery fingers across the front and felt metal; bumps and ridges that might have been symbols were embossed on what must have been a door, for set in one side was a small projection that served as a handle.

He stared. He did not want to open it. He knew he was going to.

His hand shook so violently he could barely grasp the handle. Squeezing his fingers tight around it, he tugged.

The door opened easily.

And his scream threatened to bring the walls of the pit down on him ...

... Kline's scream caused Khayed and Daoud to leap away from the bed in surprise. They quickly ran forward again and babbled soothing words to their master, assuring him it was only a nightmare, that he was safe under their watchful protection, nothing would harm him while they lived and breathed.

He looked from one to the other, his face a cracked mask of seams and ruptures. Suddenly he understood.

'*He's dying*,' Kline rasped.

▪ 35 ▪
THE WAITING GAME

HE WATCHED THE GRANADA CRUISE BY, ITS HEADLIGHTS BRIGHTENING BOTH sides of the narrow road. Keeping low and pulling aside minimum foliage so that he could observe but not be seen, he checked that there were still only two occupants in the patrol car. When it was gone, he stood and held up his wristwatch, waiting a moment or two for the moon to re-appear from behind rolling clouds. Just under twenty minutes this time. The driver varied his speed during the circuit around the estate so that there was never a regular time interval between certain points. The driver of the second patrol car did the same.

The man sank into the undergrowth, making his way back through the thick woods, only bringing out a flashlight when he was well clear of the road. Soon he arrived at a lane, one that eventually joined the route he had been watching; he continued his journey away from the estate.

Two vehicles were waiting in a picnickers' clearing a few hundred yards on, their occupants sitting in darkness. He flashed his torch twice, then switched off before climbing into the back seat of the first car.

'Well?' the passenger in the front said.

'Two patrols. Professionals, as you'd expect. We could easy take them out, though.'

'Shouldn't be any need.'

'No. It'll be no problem to get into the place. We only have to wait for them to pass, then make our move when they're out of sight. The fence'll be easy.'

'We'll wait awhiles, give them time to settle in for the night.'

'It's been a time coming, Danny.'

His expression couldn't be seen, but the man in the front was smiling. 'It has that,' he said, the softness of his accent hardened by the intent of his words. 'But all the sweeter for it.'

· 36 ·
A ROOM OF MEMORIES

Halloran's senses reeled.

It wasn't a room he was standing in but a kaleidoscope of memories. They spun before him, some merging so that yesterday mixed with yesteryear, experiences of childhood confused with those of later times, scenes superimposed upon others. It was as if screens or veils fluttered in front of him – he thought of the veils he and Kline had passed through together in the dream of last night – thin, transparent layers, older images on those new.

He turned, ready to run from there, but the doorway was no longer behind him. Instead there were more visions, closing around him, the colours vivid and fresh, the details perfectly defined, as though they were being lived at that moment.

Slowly some began to dominate the others, dispersing weaker memories – less *significant* memories – to the peripheries of his mind.

He saw himself slicing the tendons behind the black tracker's knee, the man a volunteer of South Africa's Special Service Brigade who would have followed Halloran and his small raiding band of ANCs back across the border to their camp, later to lead his own forces there, had he not been put out of action. Fading in over this was the church, moonlight through the high stained-glass windows revealing the three boys creeping along the centre aisle, Liam hugging the dead cat wrapped in old rags to his chest, its body mangled, opened by the wheels of a speeding car, the other two boys giggling nervously as he approached the altar and reached up to the tabernacle, opening its gilt door, pushing the bloodied corpse inside, running for their lives, laughing and piss-scared of the consequences. *He whirled.* Now he was with the girl, Cora, taking her forcibly, ignoring her struggles, her protests, thrusting into her until she submitted, wanted him, her lust as intense as his, the rape no longer so, becoming a mutual desire which had to be satiated. And here he was with his father, and Dadda was being torn apart by bullets, his eyes bulging with disbelief while his son, Liam, urinated unknowingly into the stream, the father falling then looking up at the boy, pleading – or was it warning? – telling him to run, to get away from there before the gunmen turned their weapons on him, too, only unable to speak, his own blood choking his words. His father crawling to the bank, collapsing there, the masked Irishmen stepping on him, drowning him, shooting Dadda again. *Halloran blinked, long and hard, but the visions would not disappear*. Scenes from his military service, the killings, the terrible battle at Mirbat, the disillusionment with it all, the women who had drifted in and out of his life, the mother he had come to revile because of the craziness inside her head, the beatings he had dealt to others of his age who dared mock her affliction, and who dared spit the word 'Britisher' as a curse at mention of his father, even though Dadda's birthplace was County Cork – and the beatings Liam received when his anger and frustration were no use against the gangs who taunted him. *Halloran staggered with the intensity of it all*. A blurred figure appeared, walking towards him through the hallucinations, the recognitions, arms out to him, calling his name beseechingly, and he could feel his Mam weeping, although she was but a spectre, not yet clear in his vision. She drifted through the eidetic imagery, coming closer, her voice faint, begging for his embrace. And as she drew near, dissolving in and out of projections of his past, her head was distorting, becoming bent and twisted, as were her hands, pulping and spurting blood, as they had when she'd deliberately walked into the threshing machine on a neighbour's farm, her arms and upper body churned by the machinery, her head smashed and almost lopped off ... as it was now, tilting, collapsing, hanging by bloody threads on her chest. *Halloran screamed*. But the memories were relentless. There was the big priest, Father O'Connell, warning Liam that the wildness had to stop, that the Good Lord Jesus would punish the boy for his wickedness, that his cankered soul would be damned eternally into Hell. The priest came at him, unbuckling the thick strap he wore around his waist, winding the buckle end around his fist, raising his arm to flail the boy, *the man*, pity as well as fury raging in his eyes. Then gone, before the black-robed priest could bring down the leather scourge. Replaced by one of the gunmen who had murdered Liam's father, the cousin of Liam's mother. A man she had accused all those years ago, her accusations laughed off, sneered at. And here he was, sneering at Halloran again, a ghost not exorcized, even though the man had blown himself up a few years after the killing, along with a companion, the homemade bomb they had been carrying in the back of their car towards the border too delicate – or too faulty – for the rough, pitted lanes they had chosen to travel, the jigging and jogging causing wires to touch or to dislodge so that the boyos were blown sky-high, and the only person to celebrate the occasion was Liam, who could not understand how the assassin of his father could be venerated as a hero by the local townspeople, blessed by the Holy Roman Catholic Church when his bits and pieces had been returned for burial on consecrated ground, Father O'Connell himself pleading God's bountiful mercy for this poor unfortunate's soul, speaking of him as a martyr to the Cause, this killer who had robbed Liam of Dadda, who had laughed and sneered Mam to her death, who sneered at him now in this very room. *Halloran yelled his outrage at the apparition, shaking with the emotion, every muscle and cord in his body stiffened rigid*. Then it all began to darken and fade, the memories slipping away, fresh ones barely glimpsed until one bright spot remained; it seemed a great distance away, too far to be within the walls of the house itself. It grew in size, coming forward, the movement steady, a gliding, the object soon recognizable, its surrounds slowly filtering through, misty at first, but gaining substance. The tabernacle was on an altar, the altar itself raised above three broad steps, before the steps a Communion rail, the kneeling cushions and then the pews on either side of the centre aisle. Liam, a youth, creeping towards the front of the church, in one hand a metal can from his grandfather's workshed, in the other a lit devotional candle. He swung over the low rail, leaving the candle on top, and mounted the steps. Doubt, guilt – fear – urged him to open the tabernacle, to save the chalice containing the Communion wafers he knew Father O'Connell always prepared the night before early Sunday mass; but he didn't, too afraid to do so, for it would be like opening the door to God, Himself, inviting Him to witness the sacrilege Liam was about to commit, and perhaps God – *if* any such creature really existed – might take away the hatred, the one emotion Liam did not want to lose, because it gave him his life objective, it overcame grief and insecurity, if only for a short while. He tipped the can and poured petrol over altar and steps, retrieving the candle and holding it aloft, well away from the inflammable liquid he splashed along the aisle. Eyes almost blinded with tears, Liam dropped the candle into the puddle near his feet. The fire sped away from him and now he was outside, face bathed in a warm glow, gazing in stupefied awe with the other townspeople as their beloved church perished in flames that might have been sent from Hell itself. And Father O'Connell could not be held back. He broke away from his flock and ran into the church, was gone for long minutes, an eternity, while the men outside moaned, the women wailed, and then he was bursting through the doors, the Holy Chalice clasped in his seared hands, but he was alight, his clothes, his hair, his skin on fire. He staggered on the church steps, and the people – *his* people – were afraid to go near, as if they would be contaminated, the flames would engulf them too. The priest screamed and he shrieked and he raised his arms up to the night, the chalice falling to the concrete, spilling its contents. The crowd moaned as one when Father O'Connell slumped to his knees. They cried aloud when he pitched forward onto his face. His body flared, a fireball without shape, and Liam's screamed Noooooooo *became Halloran's as he stood in the centre of the room, hands striking the air as if to erase the memories, to banish the dreams.*

He stumbled back against the wall, the open doorway beside him. The worst of the stench came to him then, a smell so malodorous it was almost choking. He cupped a hand to his mouth and nose, blinking away wetness in his eyes. His whole body was damp, his clothes clinging, and it was only with considerable effort that he kept his legs straight. The urge to sink to the floor had to be fought against, for he was overcome with weariness and confusion; he resisted, acutely aware that there was danger all around him in this room, in this house.

The torch was lying several feet away, its thin beam pointed at the wall opposite, revealing only a strip of torn wallpaper. He could just make out the shape of the black bag he'd also dropped lying close by.

In a crouch, his senses still not recovered from the onslaught they had received, Halloran moved forward and grabbed both items, then scrambled backwards so that he leaned against the wall once more. He broadened the light beam to take in a bigger area.

The floor was littered with rubbish and filth, a threadbare carpet, corners curled, covering a minimal section of bare boards. The walls were stained, the faded paper hanging in tatters; to one side were cupboards, the wood cracked and dull. A small table and chair were to his left, a few paces away, on the table-top a plate on which remains of a meal had furred green. He noticed that the ceiling light socket had no bulb, the ceiling itself bulging in places, and pockmarked with dark fungi. Mustiness from that fungi contributed to the room's pungency; the rest was a mixture of urine, stale faeces, and ... and something else. A sickly sweetness.

The wide beam lingered around the room's single window, whose curtains were rendered grey by dust. A high-backed armchair faced the window. Wiry stuffing, like internal organs, spilled from holes in its upholstery. He knew that it was from here that the lodge-keeper watched the estate's gates. But Halloran could not see if the chair was occupied. Several seconds went by before he determined to find out.

He edged past the doorway, keeping to the wall, moving to a position from where he could shine the beam directly into the chair. Shadows shifted also, stirred by the changing light. The angle improved as he drew closer, yet somehow he was reluctant to discover who sat there, his mind scarcely coping with the hallucinations it had already been bombarded with; he knew, though, that he could not leave the room without confronting the lodge-keeper.

He reached the corner, his shoulder brushing mould and dust from the mildewed wall, and raised the torch so that it shone directly into the seat. Both relief and disappointment swept through him when he found it empty.

But a faint disturbance was coming from elsewhere in the room. A sighing of air. A breathing.

Halloran slowly swung the beam into the furthest corner, from where the sound came, the light passing an iron fireplace, this one too filled with hardened ashes, before coming to rest on a misshapen bundle of rags lying on the floor.

As he watched, the bundle began to move.

▪ 37 ▪
JOURNEY AROUND THE LAKE

THERE WERE FIVE OF THEM IN ALL, LYING LOW IN THE UNDERGROWTH, FACES pressed into the earth as the car lights drew near. Only one of the men looked up when the brightest moment had passed, and he waited until the rear lights had become pin-points in the distance before speaking.

'That was it, all right. The Granada. Ten minutes at least 'til the other one comes along.'

Next to him, the man named Danny grunted. 'Across the road, quick as you like, and as little noise as possible. There might just be a foot patrol inside the grounds.'

They rose as one, brushing through the foliage and around trees, sprinting across tarmac to reach the wire fence on the other side of the road. They were trained men, and one immediately turned his back and rested against the mesh, cupping his hands between his thighs as a stirrup. He hoisted his companions over, then threw the two rifles left lying in the grass to them. The weapons were deftly caught and he scrambled over after them.

The group melted into the shadows of the trees, then regrouped when they were well out of sight from the road.

The leader whispered loud enough for them all to hear. 'Round the lake, boys, an' no talking on the way. We'll keep to its edge in case there's an alarm set-up in the woods. Eyes sharp, lads, an' single file. Make your mothers proud.'

He went forward, the others following down a slope that led to the water's edge. They crept along the shoreline until the moon emerged from clouds like an all-encompassing searchlight; the group dropped to the ground. They crawled back into the undergrowth and waited to find out if they had been observed. Their leader eventually gave the order and they rose as one to move silently through the trees.

'Look out,' one exclaimed.

The others stopped, crouching low, hands reaching for weapons. Hammers clicked on revolvers.

'What was it?' the leader demanded when there was no movement nor sounds for several seconds.

'I saw something ahead,' the subordinate replied. 'A shape.'

'What the hell are you talking about? Was it man or dog?'

'Neither,' came the nervous response. 'Just a shape. I swear it disappeared in front of me.'

'You're going soft in the head, McGuire. Let's get the job done.'

They moved off again, but soon it was the leader himself who brought them to a halt. His scalp prickled as he watched the wavery mist that drifted in and out of the trees a few yards away. A cry close by distracted him.

One of his men had raised his Armalite and was about to fire.

'No,' he hissed urgently, grabbing for the barrel. 'What the hell are you playing at?'

'Jesus, God, I saw them there.' He pointed into the grass a short distance away. 'A goddamn nest of 'em. Snakes. They just faded away.'

The leader shook his head in disgust. His men were behaving like old folk, frightened of their own shadows. He returned his attention to the spot where the mist had curled through the trees almost like arms reaching towards them. No mist now. God Almighty, he was as bad as the others.

'Danny, will you look over there.'

'Keep it down,' he growled, but turned to where the man was pointing. Through the woods he could see the lake. The water was choppy, stirred by a breeze that grew stronger by the moment, the moonlight tossed by undulations. But it was the far bank to which his man was directing him. There was movement there, a flowing stream that had nothing to do with water.

'What is it?' someone whispered.

'Can't you tell?' said the leader. 'It's dogs, man.'

'Coming for us?'

He could feel his men's panic.

'Not at all. They'd be across the water at a sniff of us. No, they're on their way somewhere else, an' thank God for that.'

He watched the tiny, ghostly forms skirt around the lake, their low bodies catching the light so that in parts they looked silver. Clouds consumed the moon once more and he could follow their journey no longer.

He frowned, wondering where they were heading for with such haste.

· 38 ·
THE KEEPER

THE BREATHING BECAME LOUDER, A HISSING THAT EACH TIME ENDED IN A THICK, muciferous sigh.

It faded again, became almost a whisper, and Halloran strained to listen. The heaped bundle of rags was still, having moved only once.

His own breathing was unsteady and Halloran realized that never before had he felt such debilitating trepidation, for a peculiar virulence seemed to poison the very air in the room. His inclination was to flee, to bolt through that doorway and get out into the night where the breeze was pure. But the curiosity that had led him to this place had become something more: an obsession, perhaps even a quest. Revelations from his own life had spun before him here, things that were bad, his worst sins recreated, and there had to be a reason why. He felt shame, a guilt he had always suppressed rising inside; yet it was his fascination that was stronger. It was that which prevented him from taking flight, for it prevailed over the fear, subjugated the exposed guilt.

Halloran tentatively made his way towards the tangled rags.

He saw the edges of a thin mattress, dried stains overlapping its sides, spreading where fluid had once seeped into the wood of the floor. The mound on top could have been anything – blankets, piled clothing, assorted pieces of material. That there was someone beneath, there was no doubt, for the whispered breathing came from here and the jumbled covering quivered slightly with the exhalation. Halloran leaned forward and gripped the rags. He pulled them away.

A face, partially concealed by a cowl, turned towards him.

Halloran released the covering and stepped back, horrified at the countenance that stared up at him.

The skin was withered and deeply rutted, like wrinkled leather left in the sun; and its colouring, too, was of old leather, except where there were festering scabs that glinted under the torch light. Most alarming of all were the eyes. They were huge, lidless, bulging from the skull as if barely contained within their sockets; the pupils were cloudy, a fine membrane coating them, and the area around them that should have been white was yellow and patchworked with tiny veins.

From this thing came the sickly sweet smell of death's corruption which dominated all the other scents of the room.

Something seemed to shrink within those globular eyeballs when they came to rest on the shadowy form of Halloran, and the figure tried to rise, its scrawny neck arching backwards as if the weight of its head was too much to bear. The hood fell away from a hairless skull whose surface was mottled with deep brown blemishes; incredibly, the skin there, which should have been smooth, was also wrinkled and ridged, as though the bone beneath had no firmness, no substance.

Repulsed, Halloran took another step away. The impression of gazing down at an enormous lizard-like creature was enhanced when the figure's mouth opened and a tongue, so darkly red it seemed black, protruded and rolled across cracked, lipless flesh. Only the lidless eyes refuted the reptilian image.

The figure attempted to speak, but no more than a gasped sigh escaped. The head sank back into the rough bedding with a finality that suggested the body, itself, had expired. Only then, and with reluctance, did Halloran advance again. Those bulbous eyes were fixed on him and he shone the light directly into them. They did not blink, nor did the pupils, behind their mist, retract.

'It's you,' came the sibilant whisper.

Halloran froze.

The figure gasped in air, as though the effort of speaking had caused pain. Even deeper rents furrowed its skin and the mouth puckered inward.

Halloran struggled to find his own voice. 'Who are you?'

The slightest inclination of the withered head, a gesture that the question was of no importance. And then the whisper: 'Death comes.' Its grimace might have been a smile.

Halloran leaned close, ignoring the fetid air that rose from the rumpled head. 'I can get help,' he said and the thought of touching this person almost made him retch.

Again that toothless, puckered expression that could have been a grin. 'Too late for me,' came the whisper. 'Come closer.'

Halloran shuddered inwardly and made no effort to comply.

'I must speak ...' it said '... with you.'

He knelt, but still could not find it in himself to bend near the hideous face. 'Tell me who you are,' he repeated.

This time there was an answer, perhaps an inducement to draw him in. 'The... Keeper.' The voice was stronger, and that, he thought, of a man.

'The gate-keeper?' Halloran said. Surely it wasn't possible. The person before him was too ancient and too infirm to bear the responsibility.

The man's laugh was a choking sound, and his head shook with the exertion. 'The Keeper,' he said again, the last syllable an exhaled breath. A silence between them, then: 'And you ... you are Kline's guardian.' The dark tongue flicked out, the movement quicker this time as it swept across his mouth. The skin was hardly moistened. 'I understand now,' he murmured so softly that Halloran wasn't sure if he had heard correctly.

Those staring eyes with their veiled pupils were disconcerting, and he wondered how much the old man could really see. 'I'm going to bring a doctor to you,' he said, questions racing through his mind.

'Too late, too late.' The words were drawn out as a sigh. 'At long last ... it's too late.' His head lolled to one side.

Not anxious, but curious, Halloran reached out to feel the pulse between the still man's neck and chin. He jerked his fingers away when the face turned back to him.

'Do you understand why you're here?' he was asked.

'Felix Kline is a client,' Halloran answered.

'Do you know why you came to this house?'

'Here, the lodge-house?'

There was no reply.

'I came to check it out, to find out who was inside, who handled the ... the dogs.'

'Now you've seen me.'

He nodded.

'But it seems you understand nothing.' The wrinkled face creased even more. 'I wonder what you sense.' There was an accent in the soft-spoken words.

'What did you see when you entered ... this room?' the old man whispered.

How could he know? Unless he had caused them, just as Kline had caused hallucinations out on the lake.

'Things past, but never quite forgotten?' A catching in the throat, perhaps a snigger. 'Your account has been brought up to date. I wonder why?'

'Is Kline still playing stupid games with me, putting thoughts into my mind?' Halloran felt anger overwhelming his abhorrence.

The shaking of the old man's head was feeble. 'No ... no ... the thoughts came from you. They are yours alone. Memories. You brought yourself... to this point.' Those disturbing, milky eyes watched him, the ragged gash of a mouth curled in what could have been a grin.

'Tell me about Kline,' Halloran said at last.

A sighed whisper, a slow releasing of breath. 'Ahhhh.' The ravaged head shifted slightly so that his eyes looked into the blackness of the ceiling.

Halloran waited, uneasy in the stillness, wary of this person whose decomposition seemed to precede his death. Halloran was wary, too, of the lodge-house itself: there was movement in its shadows, as if spectral shapes weaved and danced there. Things perceived not with the naked eye but through the mind. Halloran checked himself, tried to throw off such crazy notions. Yet still they asserted themselves.

The old man was murmuring and, despite his repugnance, Halloran edged closer, wanting to catch every hushed word.

'A cunning boy. With powers ... powers valuable to us... us Jews. But he was... foolish, too. He imagined ... he had claimed his deity, not realizing that he was the one ... to be claimed.' He groaned and clutched at himself.

Halloran held out a hand to steady him, but could not find it in himself to touch the thing lying there, not even though it was covered by rags.

When the worst of the pain had subsided, the aged and crumpled man spoke again. 'Almost three thousand years of waiting before the ... the Christ ... two thousand years after ...'

He was rambling, and when he coughed, there was a pinkiness to the spittle dampening the corners of his mouth. He gasped, as though anxious to tell. 'We searched the world for disciples ... our kind. And we found them. It wasn't difficult. And Kline caused havoc wherever we went. All for the glory of Bel-Marduk ...' He drifted away once more.

Kline had spoken that name before. Halloran shivered, for the air was very cold. He looked around at the shadows; the torch beam was frail.

A stirring of the makeshift bedclothes, then a shrivelled hand, more like a claw, fingernails long and curled, stained brown with age, appeared. It reached for Halloran's arm and the operative shuddered when it came to rest on him.

'He ... Felix ... used me ...'

He was drifting away. The trembling hand flopped from Halloran's arm. 'No longer afraid ...' came the hushed words. 'No worse Hell than ... here ... ahhhh ...' Life seemed to flow out from him.

Overcoming his revulsion, Halloran shook the covering over the old man's chest. 'Tell me who you are,' he demanded, both angry and frustrated. 'How can you guard this estate, control the dogs? How do you keep the gates locked? You're old, you're sick ...'

A dry, reedy chuckle. The remnants of life flickered. 'I have ... power, too. Kline ... working through me. My mind holds the ... gates. My ... mind controls ... the beasts, the demons ... But no more ... too weak. He needs another ... Someone corrupted to his ways ...'

'Who are you?'

'I am nothing.'

'Tell me!'

'Nothing. Although once ... I was a merchant.' He drew in a grating breath. 'He ... he is vulnerable.' Again he clasped Halloran's arm. 'Is it you? Are you the one?'

'To take your place? Is that what you mean?' A different kind of fear in Halloran now.

The slightest inclination of the wizened head. 'No ... no ... something more ... than that ...'

There were noises from downstairs. A soft rushing. Halloran remembered he had left the window open.

He felt a tightening of the clawed hand on his arm. Then the fingers uncurled and the hand fell away.

A scuffling in the hallway below.

There was a liquid rattling in the old man's throat as a long exhalation of air escaped him.

Pattering on the staircase.

Halloran scooped up the black bag as he rose and leapt for the door in a desperate bid to close it before the jackals came through.

But he was too late.

▪ 39 ▪
A TERROR UNLEASHED

THE FIRST OF THE BEASTS BURST INTO THE ROOM, A GLISTENING ON ITS JAWS caught by the beam of light.

To Halloran's surprise, the jackal bounded past him. He quickly stepped behind the door, using it as a shield as others, snarling and yelping, their fur bristling, streamed through. They made straight for the bundle of rags in the corner of the room.

Halloran drew in a sharp breath as the first jackal reached the lifeless figure and tore into the bedding, its jaws snapping and rending material. He heard a feeble cry above the frenzied yapping and realized that the disfigured old man was not yet dead. The puckered skull suddenly emerged from the rags, its mouth a toothless, jagged hole, the eyes now totally white. The second jackal buried its teeth into the scrawny throat.

And still more poured through the doorway.

Halloran reached into the bag and pulled out the MP5AZ, not bothering to yank out its retractable stock as he aimed at the welter of shoving and tumbling bodies. Blood suddenly gushed upwards to drench the agitated backs of the jackals, its smell, its taste, driving the animals into even greater frenzy. They ripped into their broken victim, shaking him in feverish rage.

Halloran loosed fifteen rounds of 9mm bullets into the pack, aware that the old man would also be hit and knowing it really didn't matter any more.

The jackals screeched, some leaping into the air, others thrown against the wall by the impact. In little more than a second, the room was a carnage of convulsing bodies, a redness coating the floor and running down into the cracks. But not all the beasts had been killed outright. Several had just been wounded. Others had only been frightened.

These turned towards their attacker.

Halloran quickly switched the weapon to single-shot, unwilling to waste the rest of the magazine on one short burst.

The howling subsided to an agonized whimpering, the sound piteous but invoking no pity from Halloran. He pointed the gun at the nearest advancing jackal. The animal leapt, carnassials bared and already stained. The bullet entered its neck and exploded from the other side, taking fragments of flesh and spine with it into the ceiling.

Halloran was pushed back against the wall, the torch he had kept locked against the weapon falling from his grasp as the contorting body struck him. The dead animal dropped away, head loose from its shoulders, and Halloran, crouched now, heard rather than saw the rush of another jackal. He raised the weapon and fired blindly.

The first bullet did not stop the animal, merely creasing its flank, and teeth sank into the operative's wrist. He scarcely felt the pain.

The next bullet, the weapon itself directed downwards by the jackal's weight, scythed along the creature's underbelly. The piercing yelp set off a renewed howling from its injured companions and Halloran cringed under the cacophony. He tugged his arm free, the brute's teeth scraping across the skin of his wrist as it slid to the floor. He reached for the torch, swiftly turning the beam into the mass of juddering scavengers. Those that were still able were crawling towards him, some limping badly, others squirming on their stomachs. The mattress and bedrags behind them were sodden with dark, seeping liquid.

Sub-machine-gun held in one hand against his hip, Halloran stooped to retrieve the bag, which contained extra magazines, never once letting the light beam waver away from the creeping bodies. The howling had died, to be replaced by a low, menacing growling. He edged around the door.

A limping jackal suddenly made a dash at him. Its legs gave way and it slumped at Halloran's feet, jaws weakly snapping the air, a low snarl coming from deep within its throat. He backed out the door as the others gathered their strength and staggered forward. Halloran pulled the door shut with a jarring thud and heard the jackals scratching at the wood on the other side.

He leaned against the frame, forehead resting on a raised arm, breathing slowly, giving himself time to recover from the horror.

But a scuffling on the stairs would not allow that.

He stiffened, then moved to the rail overlooking the stairway. More jackals were bounding up the steps, their backs to him. Halloran leaned over and took them one by one, shooting at the base of their skulls, shattering the bone there. The first jackal stopped dead, as if stunned, then toppled downstairs, the one close behind becoming entangled with the falling body. The third, startled by the gunfire and trying to avoid its companions, dodged to the side and received a bullet in its shoulder. The jackal howled and tumbled out of sight.

Halloran swiftly walked along the landing and paused at the top of the stairs, shining the light down. Only two corpses lay at the bottom.

He descended cautiously, anxious to get away from the charnel-house, but wary of what might still be waiting below. Hopefully these were the last of the stragglers. From above came the continued scratching against the door and a kind of mewling whimpering.

Halloran stepped over the dead bodies at the foot of the stairs and backed away to the frontdoor, keeping his eyes on the corridor leading to the rear of the lodge-house. Slipping the bag over his shoulder and gripping the pen-torch firmly between his teeth, he tried the doorhandle. It resisted his pressure at first, the mechanism obviously rusted, then grudgingly turned. But the bolts, top and bottom, were rusted solid and would not budge.

He guessed the entrance hadn't been used for many years, but was reluctant to leave through the backway. Instead he went into the room on his right.

Halloran was halfway across the floor heading for one of the windows, when something dripped onto his extended arm. He stopped, curious. Liquid spattered against his cheek. He pointed the beam upwards and saw the blood dripping through the ceiling. That was when he heard the throaty snarling from behind the door.

The jackal was on him before he had time to aim his weapon. He went down, dust rising in great clouds as he hit the boards. The torch flew from his grasp, striking the wall and blinking off when it fell to the floor.

The slathering animal was only a dim form above as Halloran clenched its fur and tried to keep the snapping jaws away from his face. He was forced to release the sub-machine-gun so that he could fend off the attack with both hands. Its long legs were sturdy, much more powerful than they appeared, and they raked his clothes, scratching the skin beneath. Halloran felt blood trickling down his wrist, but realized it was from his attacker's own wound. Using one hand again to hold the jackal off, with his other he reached for the blood-soaked shoulder and squeezed hard. With a sharp, high-pitched yelp, the jackal sprang away, but Halloran went with it, keeping the pressure on the wound. Because of their skeletal structure, he knew dogs or wolves were virtually armour-plated, their vulnerable points few; but a sharp blow to the jackal's neck, just before the shoulders, numbed it into immobility. Halloran followed through before it had a chance to recover by slipping both arms beneath its shoulder, joining hands behind the creature's neck, and bringing up his elbows while pressing down his hands in one fast, vigorous action. The jackal's breastbone split with a sharp crack, the shock killing it immediately.

He let the limp body fall away and without taking time to recover his breath, Halloran searched around the floor for the weapon. When he had it in his hands, as well as the black bag carrying the extra ammunition, he returned to the door and closed it, a barrier against any other jackals not dealt with. He went to the window, felt for the catch and, with some difficulty, forced it open. When he attempted to lift the window, however, he discovered it was stuck solid.

Wasting no further time, he covered his eyes with one hand and used the stubby butt of the sub-machine-gun to smash the glass. Halloran squeezed through the opening and dropped to the ground outside. The Mercedes waited in the gloom a short distance away.

He had taken only a few paces towards it when a window above shattered and screeching shapes rained down on him.

He stumbled when one landed on his shoulder, tripped when another jackal fell at his feet. There was no way of telling how many there were around him and he knew there was little chance of recovering the weapon in the darkness. He pushed an animal away, its resistance weak because of its wounds, kicked out at another when he had risen, sending the beast tottering backwards on legs that were already unstable. Something tugged at his ankle and he lifted the jackal off the ground, hurling it away from himself. He ran for the car drawing the Browning from its holster, just as a section of moon appeared.

Throwing open the door, he leapt inside. He changed gun hands to close the car door, pulling at the handle as another jackal launched itself at him. The animal became wedged and Halloran leaned away to avoid its gnashing teeth. With his left hand he touched the automatic to the jackal's head and squeezed the trigger. The beast jerked once, then slumped lifeless. Halloran pushed the body away from the car and pulled the door shut.

He sat there, chest heaving, his arms and forehead against the steering wheel. When he raised his head again to stare back at the lodge, the moonlight revealed a macabre scene: the wolf-like creatures were staggering around in circles, shocked by their wounds as well as in pain, baying at the moon, their stumblings almost a ritual dance.

Halloran reached for the RT, intending to alert the patrol cars of the estate's loss of inner security. It had been unfortunate that neither car had been passing the gates a minute or two earlier when gunfire from the house would have brought them in to assist, but that was always a problem if manpower was stretched; not for the first time he cursed Kline for his faith in his own security. Static blared out at him when he pressed the transmit button. He switched off, then on again, hoping that interference would clear. It didn't. He spoke into the mouthpiece anyway, but the static became even worse as he waited for a reply. Glancing up at the sky, he saw that the clouds were big and thunderous, the atmosphere itself muggy-close, charge-filled. With a muttered curse, he returned the RT, holstered the gun, and switched on the Mercedes' ignition.

Something was calling him back to Neath, a certainty that there was trouble there, that not only was Kline in danger, but so, too, was Cora. And it was her safety he cared about most. After what had happened inside the lodge-house, reason or logic was of minor importance. Sensing – intuition – was all.

He flicked on full-beam and swung the car towards the gates, turning in a tight circle that threw up earth and gravel, cutting through undergrowth on the far side of the road. Instead of setting a straight course for the main house, Halloran veered to the left, bumping across the rough piece of ground, in front of the lodge. He ploughed into the dazed and dying jackals, crushing them beneath the Mercedes' wheels, smashing into those that tried to run so that they hurtled into the air. Only then did he make his way towards Neath.

The car tore down the road, headlights throwing back the darkness, dust curling in its wake. He saw the first flash of light silver the clouds, a strobe effect that reminded him of the fulguration on the lake the previous night. Into the tunnel of trees he sped, the low-hanging branches never more threatening than now. Around the curve, tyres screeching as they gripped. The road somehow seemed narrower, as if the trees on either side conspired to join together, only the searing lights forcing them to retreat. Yet the feeling that the path behind him had closed up was uncanny.

The road began to dip and the car burst clear of the woods. He could not help but wonder if the trees behind had finally linked.

In the distance was the brooding shape of Neath, only a few of its windows lit. Halloran eased up on the accelerator, training taking over from impulse. So wary was he that he switched off the lights completely, trusting his judgement until his eyes had adapted to the night, following the blurred strip of road down to the house.

Lightning brightened the sky again and a jagged but almost perpendicular streak shot from the clouds to strike the lake.

Halloran jammed on the brakes, the Mercedes slewing to one side before coming to a halt. He stared at the water in astonishment as flashes stammered in the clouds for a second or two longer. The after-image was clear in his mind as he sat in the darkness, the car's engine still running. The lake was a turbulent storm of waves and erupting geysers, its foam as white as any ocean's.

The car reverberated with the sound of thunder directly overhead.

▪ 40 ▪
A TERRIBLE DISCOVERY

THE DELUGE STRUCK AS HE ENTERED THE PORCH, A TORRENT OF RAIN SO FIERCE it seemed unnatural. He turned briefly and saw bits of gravel tossed into the air with the pounding. The mass of rainwater looked almost solid, cutting off the view of the lake. Halloran ran along the flagstones towards the entrance of the house itself, reaching for the key in his pocket as he went.

At the double-door he knocked twice and called out his name. He inserted the long key into the lock, the dull porch light lending little assistance, and swung one side of the door open.

The hall was empty.

He moved to the centre of the stone floor, looking up at the minstrels' gallery, the landing, searching the shadows, turning round full circle to study every door on ground level. Lightning outside frosted the windows. Thunder followed almost immediately and it was as though Neath itself trembled.

Halloran drew the gun from its holster once again.

He took the downstairs first, swiftly going through every room, opening each door suddenly but quietly, the automatic held out before him. He switched on lights wherever he went, hating Neath for its darkness; the library, drawing room, sitting room – all were empty save for sparse furniture and ornaments. The dining room, kitchen, corridors, other rooms – all lifeless and feeling as if they had been that way for many years. He trod cautiously, even though rain drumming against the windows covered the sound of his footsteps; but he felt a rising desperation.

Halloran paused to listen, leaning back against a corridor wall opposite a leaded window overlooking the courtyard. Lightning flooded the air.

He drew in a sharp breath when he saw the defunct fountain at the yard's centre now bubbling dirty, viscid water clotted with black slime.

The piercing light stuttered away and thunder rattled the window-panes. Halloran moved on, finding his way back to the main hall.

He took the stairs two at a time, his step agile despite the draining ordeal he had already been through. He hurried from room to room, pushing open doors and peering in, gun always at chest level, safety off. He even looked into his own bedroom.

He thought he heard a cry from somewhere in the house, but thunder cracked deafeningly a moment after so that he couldn't be sure. Halloran headed for Kline's quarters, his stride fast and light. This time he was certain he heard a cry. A woman's. Cora's. He broke into a run.

The door leading to Kline's rooms was open. Halloran went through, slowing to a walk; a glow spread from a doorway near the end of the corridor. He heard a whimper, its source from inside that doorway. A smell of incense tainted the air.

He crept forward, knowing it was Cora who had uttered the small moan of pain. Halloran forced himself to remain emotionless. He neared the door, stopped, waited a moment.

A sharp, slapping sound. Against flesh. Cora's gasp, then her whimper.

Halloran gently pushed back the half-open door.

It was a large room, the walls covered in symbols and rough drawings. He did not take time to study them. Scattered around the floor were untidy piles of books, maps and folios of some kind. He did not pay them much attention. In front of him was a four-poster bed, the posts knotted with carvings, curtains of sheer lace draped between them. He hardly noticed the fine work. Halloran could only stare at what was on the bed.

The drapes were gathered and tied to the posts, revealing a crouched, naked figure, head hanging low between the shoulders so that the back was arched. The flesh was red and wealed. Cora's face was half-turned towards Halloran, but she did not see him, for her eyes were closed, her hair falling over her forehead. Her mouth was open in a slight smile.

Monk had his broad, sloping back to the door, his gaze too intent on the girl to notice anyone in the doorway. The bodyguard was naked too, a mountain of obese, loose flab, covered in wiry hair that was thick around his lower arms and legs, and splaying over his shoulders so that the skin was merely a dullness beneath.

The short, multi-thonged whip he held dropped to the floor as he pushed the girl over on the bed. He grabbed her ankles and yanked them towards him so that Cora was flat on her stomach. Halloran caught a glimpse of her manacled wrists.

Her groan was of pleasure, not of fear.

All calmness, all self-imposed remoteness, left Halloran in a gushing of rage. The anguish he felt was as deep and as painful as on the day he had witnessed the gunning down of his father so many years before. Or when he had learned of his mother's terrible death. It seared him and blinded all other senses.

He roared as he rushed forward and reached for the bodyguard's hair, which had been loosened from the band Monk usually wore. He wrenched hard, hauling the gross man away from the girl, bringing the butt of the Browning down hard against the side of Monk's head, his anger, unleashed like rarely before, spoiling the accuracy of the blow.

Monk cried out and toppled over the tailboard onto the floor.

Cora turned, drawing her legs up. Her glazed eyes looked into Halloran's uncomprehendingly. He raised the gun towards her, his hand shaking, wanting to kill her, wanting to punish her for breaking through to him, for making him care again, then for mocking those feelings. He cursed himself for allowing it to happen.

Cora smiled at him, an idiot's welcome. Then fear finally melted through her drug-induced haze.

Halloran lowered the pistol and closed his eyes against the sight of her.

A meaty arm closed around his neck from behind, a hand reaching round and grabbing his wrist. He was lifted off his feet as Monk heaved.

His windpipe was being crushed by the pressure and Halloran knew it would only be a matter of seconds before he blacked out. The automatic was of no use to him in a situation like this, so he opened his fingers and let it fall, Monk's grip on his wrist still not slackening. The bodyguard was gurgling close to his ear, an animal sound. With his free hand, Halloran reached down behind him and found the fleshy part of Monk's inner thigh. He pinched with thumb and bent knuckle, squeezing with all his strength so that his assailant screamed, a high-pitched woman's cry. The hold on Halloran loosened and he wrenched the arm away.

He whirled and grabbed for the other man's throat, both of them going down slowly as he exerted pressure. Monk tried to pull the hands away, but Halloran's rage could not be opposed. Monk's small eyes began to bulge. The two men's faces were inches away as they sank to their knees, Monk making snorting noises as his face reddened. His thick lips curled back, the tip of his tongue quivered over his teeth. He spat mucus into Halloran's eyes.

Surprised and blinded, the operative's grip weakened fractionally. A blow to his stomach doubled him over, his fingers raking down Monk's chest. A swipe to his head sent Halloran scudding across the floor.

The other man rose and lumbered towards him, hurling himself forward the last few feet, intending to crush Halloran's chest with his bent knees. Halloran sensed the move as he wiped the stickiness from his eyes, and rolled backwards, scattering books. His naked opponent landed heavily on empty space. They rose together, but Halloran was faster. His toecap smashed into Monk's groin. The bodyguard collapsed to his knees again and Halloran moved behind him. Again Halloran pulled Monk back by his long hair, holding him upright. Lightning flared outside, freezing their bodies momentarily. The operative's other fist clenched, middle knuckle raised slightly. His aim was straight and powerful as the fist cracked into a certain vertebra at the back of the kneeling man's neck.

Thunder drowned the cracking of bone.

Halloran reached out to a bedpost for support as the stiffened figure below him swayed, then slumped to the floor. He drew in deep lungfuls of incense-filled air, anger still raging inside, revulsion at Kline and the corruption around him heaving at his stomach.

In that distraction – his rage, his disgust – he failed to notice the figure that had watched everything from behind the door. He heard, or perhaps he sensed, a footstep though, but it was too late.

As he began to turn, Janusz Palusinski brought a short, metal bar down against his temple. The oblivion was almost a relief.

· 41 ·
THINGS FROM THE LAKE

THEY COULD HARDLY BELIEVE THE POWER OF THE RAIN.

It pounded, weighing heavily on their shoulders and backs, making progress slippery and slow. At least the downpour rendered them less visible, their commander thought as he urged them along.

'What the hell is this, Danny?' McGuire yelled close to his ear. 'I've never known the likes!'

A truer word never spoken. The man called Danny looked out at the lake and shivered, not from the cold. The water was as fierce as St George's Channel in the worst winter months, a crossing he had made with loathing many times in the past. God in Heaven, it was eerie what was happening out there.

From the bank they had watched lightning strike the water more than once, sheening its tossed surface a silvery green, the froth on the shoreline luminous in the dark. The thunderclaps that followed had made their ears ring, caused them to throw themselves against the soaked earth as if mortar shells had dropped among them. His men were frightened, wanted to turn back. But that was not to be and greater fear of their commander held them steady, kept them mindful of their duty.

They had been caught by the downpour on a steep embankment, the drenched soil slithery beneath their feet, the only handholds a few tree roots here and there. Two of the men walked along in the water itself, arms stretched out to the bank for support when the going got particularly tricky. Danny cursed the freak storm, wondering at it at the same time.

They had come this far and there was no turning back. Their man, their bastard target, was in the grand manor house they had glimpsed from afar, now but a few minutes away, and he was going to pay dearly for what he'd done. He was going to suffer for the suffering he had caused others. No doubting that, no turning tail now.

An alarmed shout from nearby. One of his men was sliding deeper into the churning water, his Armalite raised high. His companion, who had been wading behind, reaching out to pull him up.

A jagged lightning streak pierced the lake, a startling irradiation instantly spreading outwards. The crack of thunder overhead cowed the group, and in the white glare the leader saw the terrified expression of the two in the water, as if they had both received a shock.

They began to go under.

He slid down the embankment, shouting to the others to help their companions. But when he reached the edge of the water, his boots enveloped, anorak smeared by mud, he stared in horror across the lake.

There were shapes out there.

Canescent, hazy, almost lost in the sheeting rain, but nevertheless, discernible rearing shapes that were part of the storm itself.

It was impossible. He wiped wetness from his eyes, doubtful of what he saw. But they were there, growing like grey amorphous monsters out of the waves.

Something bumped into him and he turned with a start. McGuire – he *thought* it was McGuire in the dismal light – was also watching the lake, his mouth working loosely as though he had lost the power of speech.

A scream and they saw their two companions were in the water up to their shoulders.

'*Help them!*' Danny yelled, scrabbling forward. He noticed that the Armalite was gone and swore at the frightened subordinate who had dropped it. Another of his men was closer and was leaning over, stretching an arm out to the two in the water.

But everyone stopped when whiteness flooded the sky and another discharge channelled itself to the lake, the shifted air booming. It was what they suddenly saw beneath the surface that had frozen them.

Vague, nebulous forms filled the water below, massing together, squirming spasmodically, tendril-like appendages waving in the currents, occupying the lake as though the content was not water but moving, liquid beings.

A waterspout erupted then swooped down, like a tentacle, curling round the two men who clawed at the bank. It drew them into the lake and their screams became a bubbling froth. It seemed, although it was too dark to be certain, that other smaller tendrils of fluid pulled at them too.

The leader shuddered incredulously, then gasped when something tightened around his own ankle. With a frightened cry, he jerked his leg clear, and perhaps it was merely overwrought imagination that caused him to think a watery claw had risen with his leg to plop shapeless back into the choppy lake.

The two men were gone, he knew that. There was no helping them at all. He scrambled up the embankment, digging toes and hands into the slimy soil, afraid he would slide back into the water to lie among those things stirring there. His two remaining men were following suit, scrambling away from the foamy lake where waterspouts resembling misshapen creatures burst upwards into the stormy night.

Waves hurled themselves at the climbing men as if to drag them back, but they plunged their fingers into the mud, using tree roots whenever their fumbling hands chanced upon them, grateful for every inch they could gain.

They collapsed on the grass at the top of the embankment, rolling over and over into the bushes, putting as much distance between themselves and the water's edge as possible. At last they settled among the trees, trembling and panting, the rain's force tempered by the leafy canopy above them.

'*For God's sake, let's away from here!*'

Danny recognized McGuire's voice, distorted by terror though it was.

'No,' he said, loud enough to be heard over the storm. 'Whatever it was back there can't harm us now.' He was shocked, stunned by what had happened and the loss of two good men. But Danny Shay was a determined man. An executioner who had already tortured and killed one person to locate his intended victim.

He rose and grabbed the shoulders of his exhausted companions, hauling them to their feet.

'Get yourselves moving,' he told them. 'The house isn't far and there's a bastard there deservin' to die.'

▪ 42 ▪

SEPULCHRE

As in the dream, there were large, staring eyes watching him. Unnatural eyes. Stone eyes.

Halloran held his breath as pain ached through his head. He raised a leaden hand to his forehead and held his temples, exerting soft pressure with fingers and thumb. The ache eased only slightly. He blinked, taking in the statues, a gathering of them, thirty at least, standing a few yards away. Observing. A few were in groups, man, woman and child. Some were at least five foot high. Their fixed gaze was inescapable.

Among them in a high-backed ornate chair was a figure, this of flesh and blood, for it shifted slightly when Halloran pushed himself up onto an elbow. The figure settled back, a formless shadow amidst the sculptures.

The floor was wet where Halloran lay, grimy water seeping through the cracks in the flagstones. The dampness brought with it a putrid smell, a different odour underlying that. Melting wax. The chamber was lit by hosts of black candles, their glow soft and unsteady.

'Help him to his knees,' a voice said. It might have been Kline's except its rasping quality reminded Halloran of the lodge-keeper.

Hands pulled at him roughly and his mind was too dulled for him to resist. As he knelt, something passed around his throat, and a sudden sharpness there jerked him erect. He tried to twist away and the pressure increased. His hands went to the cause, but there was nothing they could grip.

'Struggle and the wire will bite deeper,' the same voice warned.

Halloran couldn't see the person behind him, but he could feel whoever it was leaning into his back. A spiciness wafted down among the other smells.

'Youssef is master of the garotte,' came the voice again, and this time he was sure it was Kline sitting there in the shadows, even though the tones were roughened. 'Try to resist and you'll find out for yourself.' There was a weariness to his words that made Kline seem very old.

When Halloran took his hands away they were smeared with his own blood.

'Let him see, Youssef. Let him see where he is.'

The pressure slackened and Halloran was able to look around, although his view was restricted. The room was long and high-ceilinged, and the walls glinted in the candle-light as if water was trickling through the brickwork. A solid stairway led upwards and Halloran saw there was a passage but no door in the darkness at the top. There were archways around the sides of the chamber as though the place might once have been used as a wine-cellar; there was no way of knowing what was inside those cavities now, for they were cast into the deepest shadows. As well as the candles, there were oil lamps here and there helping to light the place, these close to pedestals on which stood delicately worked statues and effigies in shiny metals. On one near to where Halloran knelt there was what appeared to be a goat rearing up on hind legs against a tree of gold, the animal's fleece of deep blue stone and white shell. The small statue was exquisite, but Halloran's eyes did not linger on it for long.

At one end of the room was a large rectangular slab of stone which rose up from the floor, its surface a matt-black. A parody of an altar. Spread across it, and lying perfectly still, was an obese, naked figure, thick curling hair covering its body. Halloran wondered if Monk were dead.

The rasping voice broke through his thoughts. 'Impressive, Halloran. You paralysed him, he can't move, can't raise a finger. Useless to me as a bodyguard, but valuable in another way ...'

From outside came a belly-rumble of thunder, the sound muted, a long way away.

The shadow stirred again, shifting in the seat. 'A bad night up there,' Kline said, something of his old, excitable self in the remark despite the distortion in his voice. 'Hope your knees aren't getting too wet, Halloran. So many underground streams running through the estate, you see, with all these hills around. When the lake swells, so do they –'

'What is this place, Kline?' The question was quietly put, but Halloran's tone stopped the other man.

Kline studied the operative for a while before giving an answer. When he drew in a breath the sound was wheezy, as though his throat was constricted. 'A hiding place,' he said finally. 'A sepulchre, Halloran, my very own sepulchre. A room no one would ever find unless they knew of it, and even then they'd have problems. Oh, it's always been here at Neath, I didn't have to *create* it. I had to disguise its existence, though. This place is a sub-cellar, you see. A passageway extends to the real one, but I had it bricked off so no one'd ever know.' His giggle was dry, a scratchy sound. 'Ingenious, huh? Just like the old Sumerian tombs. Impossible to get in, and impossible to get out unless you know how. You could rot in here, Halloran, and no one would ever find you.'

Halloran tried to rise, but the wire around his neck tightened instantly.

'Two, maybe three, seconds, is all it'd take for Youssef to kill you, so don't be bloody stupid.'

'For God's sake, why, Kline? I'm here to protect you.' Still Halloran did not raise his voice. A coldness was in him, one he knew so well. A deadness of emotion.

'God? God has nothing to do with this. Not your God. Only mine.' The wheezing breath, a movement in the shadows. Then he said: 'You killed the Keeper.'

'The gate-keeper? He was dying, he'd lost control of the dogs – the jackals. They tore him to pieces. But how did you know he was dead ... ?'

'You still doubt my abilities?' Kline was shaking his head. 'More than just our minds were linked, Halloran. He was surrogate for my ills, my weaknesses. He took my years. Through him I was allowed to live without blemish, without ageing, free to use my faculties without hindrance.'

'The old man said you'd used him.'

'I was allowed that gift.'

'Allowed?'

'The power to discharge those physical things we all dread, the disadvantages that come with the years and with debility, was bestowed upon me. Now that power is waning. Something has happened and nothing is right any more. You killed my Keeper, you broke the link.'

'I told you he was dying before the jackals got to him. The strange thing is he seemed glad to be dying.'

'He was a fool.'

'Listen, Kline, I want you to tell this idiot to take the wire away from my neck.'

'After what you did to Monk?'

'I'm going to hurt him if he doesn't.'

'I don't think so, Halloran. I don't think you're *that* good. Besides, you want your curiosity satisfied, don't you? You want to learn some more history. Last night I only meant to whet your appetite.'

'Kline ...' Halloran warned.

'*Be quiet!*' Kline's hands clenched over the chair arms. He shuddered, as if it had hurt to raise his voice. 'You're going to pay for what you've done. You're going to help stop what ... what's ... happening to me.' He slumped back, and Halloran could see the rise and fall of his narrow shoulders, could hear the squeezing of his breath.

When he spoke, Kline's voice was low again, the sudden verve gone. He sounded ancient, like the old man in the lodge-house. 'Be patient and listen, Halloran, because I want you to understand. You deserve that at least. Let me tell you about the god who walked this earth three thousand years *before* the Christ God. I'm sure you're no devotee of the Scriptures, but no doubt you had them drummed into you by your Catholic priests when you were a boy in Ireland. Let me make some sense of their fairy-tales, allow me that.'

'Do I have a choice?'

'Yes. Youssef could kill you now.'

Halloran said nothing.

A dry snigger from Kline. 'How precious time becomes when there's little of it left, even for those who have lived so long ...'

The candle flames swayed as though a draught had swept in.

'The man-god was called Marduk by his chosen people, the Sumerians,' Kline began, while Halloran wondered how long the Arab could keep the garotte tensed. 'He civilized the Sumerians, advanced them, taught them the written word, revealed to them the secret of the stars, instilled order into their society. It was from him that they learned to cure by cutting into the human body, how to forge metals dug from rock, to make tools and instruments, to use vehicles for carrying. Was that evil? How could it be? It was knowledge. But for those mortals who ruled, such learning was regarded as a threat, because it usurped their power. That was the fear of the Sumerian kings and certain high priests. And hasn't that always been the fear of your Christian God?'

The question was put slyly, Kline's tenor changing constantly, a shifting of character that Halloran had become used to, but the change never before as abrupt as this. It was as if Kline had little control over himself.

'But perhaps it was the other knowledge that these rulers feared most, because that *gave* power. I mean the knowledge of magic, the ways of alchemy, the understanding of the Cabala, the art of witchcraft.

'For more than a thousand years he influenced them, and how the Sumerian people enjoyed his control. All he asked in return was their worship, their veneration of his ways. Burnt offerings pleased him, the roasting of men, women and children. Defilement of the other gods he demanded. The torture of innocents was an appeasement to him, for they also feared Marduk as much as their rulers did. The kings and princes, the other high priests, were powerless to act against him. Until King Hammurabi, that is, who united all the state leaders against Marduk, whom he declared was an evil god who should be known forever more as *Bel*-Marduk.'

Halloran glanced up at the stairway. He thought he had heard movement in the passage.

'The king denounced Bel-Marduk as a fallen god,' Kline went on in a voice that lurched with anger. 'Much later the Jews referred to him as the Fallen Angel.'

Halloran frowned.

'Ah, I see a glimmer of understanding,' Kline remarked. 'Yes, I do mean the Fallen Angel of the Bible, later to become known as the Devil.'

The lilt of Irish was in Halloran's mild comment. 'You're crazy, Kline.'
A silence.

Then a low chuckle.

'One of us might be,' said Kline. 'But listen on, there's more to tell.'

The staring eyes of the stone effigies around the shaded figure seemed threatening. Halloran tried to close them from his mind.

'Bel-Marduk was destroyed for preaching the "perverted message". His limbs were torn from him, his tongue cut out, so that his immortal soul would be trapped inside a body which could only lie in the dirt. The priests rendered him as a snake, and they called him Serpent.'

The dark figure leaned forward. 'Does it sound familiar to you, Halloran? Didn't your Catholic priests teach you of Lucifer, the Fallen Angel, who was cursed to crawl in the dust as a snake for his corruption of the innocents, for revealing the secrets of the Tree of Life to the unworthy? Don't you see where those stories of the Bible come from? I told you last night that the traditional site of the Garden of Eden was the land between the Rivers Tigris and Euphrates in Sumeria from where, according to tablets found in Mesopotamia, the Jewish race originated. It was from Ur of the Chaldees that Abraham led his tribe north into Syria, then through Canaan into Egypt. They took with them stories that later became the myths of their Bible. The Great Flood, the baby Moses found among bulrushes – borrowed history! The Hebrew account of the Creation and the first chapters of Genesis – they were based on old Sumerian legends. Legends because the old kings had ordered all records of their early history to be destroyed, their way of ensuring Bel-Marduk's corruption would not be passed on to other generations. But they didn't understand how evil can be inherited, not learned from the written word.'

There were figures at the top of the stairs, but Kline appeared not to notice.

'We Jews even adopted the Cabala as our own, claiming it was passed on from Noah to Abraham, from Abraham to Moses, who initiated seventy elders into the mysteries during their years of wandering in the wilderness. Bel-Marduk's teachings were never discontinued, nor was his revenge on mankind! Even the other man-god, Jesus Christ, who chose the Jews as his people, couldn't stem the flow! He came to undo the Serpent's work, the only way of redeeming earth's people. And look what happened, Halloran. He was executed, just like his predecessor, Bel-Marduk! Makes you wonder why he bothered, doesn't it? Look around you today, Halloran, and you'll see the conflict still goes on. You're part of it, I'm part of it.'

Kline leaned forward once more. 'The question is,' he said craftily, 'on which side of the struggle are *you*?'

Halloran could give no answer.

Kline pushed himself back into the chair. '*Bring her down!*' he called out.

There was movement from above and Halloran raised his eyes to see Cora, flanked by Palusinski and the other Arab, descending the stairway. She wore her bathrobe, its belt tied loosely at the front, and her step was unsteady. When she reached the bottom and looked around the soft bewilderment in her eyes was obvious. He wondered if the drug had been forced upon her.

'Liam ...' she began to say on seeing him.

'Concerned for your lover, Cora dear?' came Kline's voice from the shadows. Now there was fear as she looked towards the source.

'What are you going to do with her, Kline?' Halloran demanded.

'Nothing at all. Cora won't be harmed. I haven't groomed her for that. But I need a new ally, you see, someone who'll watch for me. I always knew a replacement would be necessary one day; I just didn't realize how imminent that day was.'

'You can't make her take *his* place.'

'Oh, I can. She's filth, Halloran, degenerate. You must understand that by now. She's become – no, she's *almost* become – what I've always wanted her to be. The final depravity is about to happen.'

'You made her like this?'

'Of course. Cora was a sweet little thing when she first came to my attention, much too good for the likes of you and me. An English Rose, you might say. It was an interesting exercise turning her into something else.'

'With drugs?'

'At the beginning. She never even realized. A few drops of something mixed with her food or her drink, enough only to soften her inhibitions. A gradual process, an extremely slow journey into degradation. Eventually the drugs were hardly necessary – I'd helped Cora develop certain "tastes". There was more to be achieved before she became mine completely, but now time is too precious, the process has to be hastened if she's to fulfil her role.'

The wire was cruel against his throat as Halloran tensed. 'You can't make her into something like that.'

'Like my Keeper? Why not? Who would know, who would care? She'll merely leave the employ of the Magma Corporation to become my private assistant. These kind of relationships develop all the time in business, surely you know that?'

'This is insane.'

'That's a stupid assertion you keep making, Halloran. You don't believe anything I've told you.'

Despite his anger, Halloran smiled.

'You confuse me,' Kline said, weariness heavy in his voice. 'For a while I thought you could be of use to me, like the others. I searched the world for men such as Palusinski and Monk, Khayed and Daoud, seeking out wickedness wherever it might lurk. They're indebted to me, these men, because I gave them a channel for their evil – and such a fine evil it is. There are more, many more, as these four, and I use them on my journeys. You could have joined us because you're not unlike them. Yet I can't know you, and that makes me wary. You saved me from assassination – my dreams and my senses have told me the threat is near – but still I can't bring myself to trust you. You're an enigma, and while that may have its fascination for me, I see no reason to have an unknown quantity so close, particularly at a time when things are not as they should be. No, you'll have to be disposed of.'

The wire bit deeper as the Arab behind Halloran giggled.

'Aren't you forgetting something?' the operative managed to say despite his throat's constriction. The wire loosened once more and he swallowed hard.

'Tell me.' It came as a sneer.

'My organization knows where I am, who I'm working for. I can't just disappear.'

'Tut, tut,' Kline said flatly. 'What a fool I am for overlooking that.' The mocking ceased just as abruptly. 'Don't you see? You put up a valiant fight against intruders, but they murdered you before my own bodyguards drove them off. How's that? Convincing? Who can prove otherwise? And incidentally, Monk was one of them, a traitor in our midst. He went with them after we fought them off. In fact, he was the swine who murdered you.'

Halloran ignored the laughter. 'Cora –'

'She won't be saying anything against me after tonight!' Kline snapped. His hands thumped the side of the chair. 'Time to press on. All this talk is wearying. Help me, Asil.'

The Arab brushed past Cora and Palusinski and hurried to where his master sat among the effigies.

'Let Halloran stand, Youssef, but watch him, keep him harnessed.'

The wire brought Halloran to his feet and he had to concentrate to keep himself steady, for his head was still groggy. Cora took a step towards him and Palusinski grabbed her to hold her back. She looked dumbly at the Pole's hand as though wondering what it was doing on her arm.

Kline, assisted by Khayed, was rising from the shadows. He came forward, movement slow, an old man's shuffle, his servant close by his side. Part of the darkness came with him, for he was wearing a black robe whose hem swept along the floor. He left the statues.

He came into the light.

'Jesus, Mary ...' Halloran breathed.

▪ 43 ▪
THE OPEN GATES

RAIN LASHED THE WINDSCREEN, THE WIPERS BARELY ABLE TO KEEP THE GLASS clear. Charles Mather peered over the steering wheel, his whole body tensed, the aching in his leg bad.

He was close, he was sure of that. The entrance to Neath had to be nearby. Unfortunately, the rain made it impossible to see too far ahead. Damned incredible night, he mused irritably. The storm was as fierce now as when it had first begun nearly an hour ago, with no sign of abating. The clouds were black and ragged with inner strife, the thunder they threw out rattling his very bones.

Lightning lit the way, white-washing the landscape. The earth threatened to split under the explosive *crack* that accompanied the light.

It would have been safer – and more sensible – to have pulled over by the roadside and wait out the storm, but Mather would not consider doing that. He was too concerned for Liam Halloran. Something had been wrong with this assignment all along and the revelation by Magma's chairman earlier that evening had furthered Mather's disquiet. Snaith himself had given the go-ahead to bring out their operative, although he had not personally felt Halloran was at risk. No, the Controller was more unhappy with the Magma Corporation's unreliable conduct, for deceit could easily jeopardize an operation of this sort. 'Negative factor' was the term used by Achilles' Shield when carefully laid plans could be put at risk by deliberate misinformation. Under such circumstances, a commission could be resigned at once, and every Shield contract contained a get-out clause covering this particular area. As Magma had been quite prepared to withhold certain vital information, they could not be regarded as a trustworthy client.

Mather had agreed with his Controller on that score, but it was Sir Victor Penlock's insinuation which bothered him more.

Felix Kline was not an employee of the Magma Corporation. Far from it. He *was* Magma. Many years before, Mather had learned, he had taken over an existing mineral and energy research and development company, acquiring fifty-two per cent of the stock through various other worldwide companies which had no connection with Magma. The secret of ownership had been kept because of 'credibility' in the all-important City market – no financial adviser would recommend investment in a company whose major shareholder was a so-called 'mystic'. The world of high finance was not known for its sense of humour.

If Shield had been made aware of Kline's true role within the organization, then a much more comprehensive plan of action would have been undertaken and a larger protection force, with even more stringent restrictions, employed. As it was, Magma had used a blindfold on the agency.

But what concerned Mather most, though, was Sir Victor's suggestion that Kline might have been responsible for Quinn-Reece's death in some way. The deputy-chairman had succumbed to heart failure, surely. But there had been others in conflict with the psychic in the past who had also died of sudden and, in two cases at least, inexplicable cardiac arrests. Three others, to be precise. One inside the Corporation, a board member who had constantly opposed plans for development put forward (albeit surreptitiously) by Kline; another had been from a rival company, whose persistent investigations were slowly unravelling Kline's real worth to Magma; the third had been a communications magnate who had instigated a take-over bid for the Corporation. This man had a known heart condition, but when he had been found dead from a massive coronary in his bed one morning, a look of sheer horror had been frozen into his features. It was concluded that a nightmare had aggravated his diseased heart to the point of killing him. But both Sir Victor and Mather had seen the horror-struck look also on Quinn-Reece's face.

There had been other incidents through the years, and the chairman had confessed to Mather that he, himself, had begun to live in fear of Kline's strange powers. Although nothing could be proved, Sir Victor realized there had been too many mysterious 'happenings' to be ignored.

Why Quinn-Reece? Mather had demanded. What on earth could Kline have against his own deputy-chairman?

Sir Victor had explained that for some time Kline had suspected Quinn-Reece of leaking news of possible mineral sites for development to another company. Indeed, he and the chairman had discussed those suspicions on more than one occasion. However, this time, Kline had accused his personal assistant, Cora Redmile. But the chairman was accustomed to the psychic's deviousness and Quinn-Reece's subsequent death was too much of a coincidence to be taken lightly. Yet there was no proof, none at all. Only misgivings.

That was enough for Mather. He already had doubts about the assignment, a gut-feeling that things weren't quite right. The torture of Dieter Stuhr had added to his concern, for torture, unless perversion was involved, usually meant information was being sought of the victim. That information might well have been to do with Shield's security arrangements for Felix Kline. Somewhat drastic perhaps, but where huge sums of ransom money were involved kidnappers had few scruples. And then there was always the possibility that more than just abduction was in mind. Kline might well be a target for assassination – God only knew what enemies the man had.

Mather had left the Magma building and had gone straight to the home of Gerald Snaith with the recommendation that the contract be declared null and void. That had been over two hours ago, but he felt he had been driving for much longer.

Mather used the booster fan to clear vapour from the windscreen, his own breath, because he was so close to the glass, contributing to the mist. For a few moments he was driving blind and he slowed the car almost to a halt. He pushed another button and the driver's window slid down. Raindrops pounded at his face when he looked at the road ahead. There was a wall to his left, set back, undergrowth thick before it; on the opposite side of the road was forest. He ducked his head back inside and wiped a handkerchief across his face.

A light behind, dazzling in the rearview mirror, coming up slowly. A car's headlights.

They blinked once, twice. He grunted with satisfaction when they blinked a third time.

Mather touched his brakes twice in acknowledgement, then pulled over to the side of the road, bringing the car to a halt. He waited for one of the two men in the vehicle behind to come to him.

'Didn't expect you, sir,' the operative said loudly enough to be heard over the storm. He crouched at the open window, collar up against the rain. 'Gave us a surprise, seeing your number.'

'I've been trying to reach you on the radio,' Mather complained.

'The storm's fouled up communications. Never known one like this before. We've kept in touch with the other patrol by stopping each time we meet en route. What's up, Mr Mather, what brings you here?'

'We're pulling out.'

'Shit, you're joking.'

'I'm afraid not. Anything occurred tonight that you're not happy about?'

'Only this bloody weather. Visibility's down to twenty yards.'

'Where's the entrance to the estate?'

'Gates are up ahead, on the left. You're nearly there.'

'Follow me down, I'll brief you off the road.'

The operative shrugged, then ran back to the Granada. Mather set his car in motion, going slowly, looking for the gates. An open area swept back from the roadway and he turned into it, driving right up to the tall gates. There should be ... yes, there it was. A dark, bulky shape that had to be the lodge-house. No lights on. Well you'll have to get out of bed, chum, if that's where you are.

Mather flashed his headlights, beeping the horn at the same time.

Lightning blazed the sky, thunder rent the air, and the lodge-house appeared as a bright, flickering image. Mather's eyes narrowed. Had there been something moving in front of it?

The patrol car came to a halt beside his and Mather reached for his cane before stepping out. Both men joined him at the gates.

'Is there anyone inside?' he asked, pointing at the building with his cane.

'There's supposed to be someone there all the time to operate the gates,' one of the men replied. 'Never seen the bugger, though.'

Mather reached and pushed at an iron strut. That half of the gates swung open a few inches.

The three men exchanged glances.

'Something's wrong,' Mather said.

'Could be an oversight.'

The Planner shook his head. 'I'm going in. I want you to find the other patrol and follow.'

'We're not allowed in –'

'Forget about that. You just come after me as fast as you can. Phil, you'll come with me.'

'Right, sir.'

'Why not wait for the other patrol?' the second man asked, suddenly anxious.

Mather had no adequate answer, only a sense of urgency pressing him. 'Just get on with it!' he barked. 'Open them up, Phil.'

He limped back to his car as the operative swung the gates wide. The other man climbed into the Granada and reversed into the road.

Mather settled uncomfortably into the driver's seat, his clothes soaked. He dreaded to think of the agony his leg would give him tomorrow. He took the car through the entrance, pausing just long enough for his operative to jump in beside him.

'Christ, what's that over by the house?'

Mather looked towards where the other man was pointing. Blurred shapes were moving slowly in the rain.

'Dogs,' the operative said. 'Must be the guard dogs. Funny, it's the first time I've laid eyes on them.'

'Can you see how many?'

'Difficult in this rain. I can only make out a couple. Oh shit, there's others lying on the ground.'

Mather wasted no more time. He pushed down hard on the accelerator and the car sped down the drive. Soon it entered a tunnel of trees.

▪ 44 ▪
A SACRIFICE

Halloran was stunned by the change in Felix Kline.

This was an old and bent man emerging from the shadows, one whose skin was cracked and scaly, ruffles of tissue hanging loose, pieces flaking away as he shuffled forward. Oil glistened over fissures in his flesh, dulling the rawness beneath. His hair trailed flatly over skull and forehead, whitish seams cross-hatching under the blackness, and his hands were mostly vivid pink, their outer layer all but entirely shed. Kline's breathing was husky with the effort of moving.

He came to an unsteady halt before Halloran and even his grin seemed corroded.

'Scary, huh?' Kline said, none of his mocking arrogance lost. 'It isn't irreversible, though. It isn't too late, Halloran. Maybe it's worse than ever before, but at least now I understand why.'

The hideous face was close, eyes red-rimmed and bloodshot. With Daoud behind him, Halloran could not pull away. Kline had the same smell of decay as the old man in the lodge-house.

'You took my surrogate,' Kline hissed. 'You killed him and upset the balance. I should only slough my skin once a year, that's part of the deal, my price for immortality. Like a serpent, you see, Halloran. Bel-Marduk made me like a serpent.'

He gasped, a pain reaching him somewhere inside. Blood squeezed from a crack in his disfigured face to mix with the oily gel.

'There's a way to stop this deterioration. You'll see, Halloran, you'll see. You'll be part of it.'

He turned away and with Khayed's help hobbled through the puddles on the floor, passing by Palusinski and Cora, the Pole stepping back as if the shambling figure were a leper. The girl seemed mesmerized. Candle-light reflected from the glistening on Kline's head.

It took a long time for him to get to the slab of stone near the end of the room and he reached out for it, staggering the last few feet despite Khayed's help. Kline eased himself around the stone so that he faced the others. An impatient hand beckoned them to him.

Palusinski led the girl and it took only slight pressure from the wire to make Halloran follow. His eyes darted left and right as he and the Arab passed the archways, searching for possibilities, a weapon perhaps should he manage to break free of the stranglehold. All he could make out in the shadows were stone tables, scored with symbols similar to those he had seen around the house itself.

Then he found himself looking down at the bloated body lying on the slab. And Monk's small, inset eyes stared back at him, his fat fingers twitching as if he were trying to move his body. Those eyes showed no pain, only hatred.

Halloran was surprised that the man was still conscious. He glanced over at Cora, who was frowning, at last some sensibility returning to her gaze.

'Do you see him, Monk?' Kline's voice was all the more insidious for its guttural roughness. 'He did this to you, made you nothing. How you'd like to kill him. But no, my friend, that's impossible for you now. But I have a use for you.'

Fear replaced the hate in the bodyguard's eyes as they darted towards Kline.

'Another injection, Asil,' Kline told the Arab. 'I don't want the pain to kill him. The cutting will do that.'

The Arab ghosted away.

'The correct dosage is important,' said Kline, touching his skinless hands to Monk's body. 'Enough so that he doesn't feel the shock of the blade, but not enough to allow dreams to take him from us. Fortunately Asil has become something of a specialist over the years.'

Anger surged in Halloran, but he held it in check, biding his time. 'You turned Cora into an addict,' he said.

'Oh no, not an addict, not in the true sense. Not yet. She'd be useless to me if she were. I told you, Asil is expert in such matters. Cora is dependent on me, not on any drug.'

The Arab had returned to Kline's side, in his hand a syringe filled with liquid. He smoothed away hair on Monk's arm and pierced a vein with the needle. He emptied half of the liquid into the bodyguard.

Within moments, the bodyguard's eyes took on a dull glaze and the corners of his mouth flickered.

'What are you going to do with him?' Halloran asked sharply.

Kline drew in a long, gravelly breath and gripped the stone to support himself. Still he managed to grin at Halloran, his peeled lips blood red against the yellow decay of his teeth. 'I'm going to feed off him,' he replied simply.

In a night of gross horrors, when nightmares were living, Halloran was further repulsed.

Although delighted with the obvious discomfort his words had caused the operative, Kline shook his head. 'Not his flesh, Palusinski can fill himself with that afterwards. I need something more, Halloran, something that has no substance, no materiality. The part of him that will be set free at his moment of death.' A luminescence glittered in the darkness of Kline's eyes. 'The ethereal energy that's the source of our existence. The psyche, Halloran, the soul. Can you understand that?'

Again Halloran felt a loosening of the pressure around his neck. Daoud's concentration was wavering. 'If I understood, I'd be crazy like you,' the operative replied.

Kline straightened, his look fixed on the operative. The bodyguard lying on the stone between them moaned, either with pleasure or trepidation, the emotion was not clear.

'You're still a mystery to me,' Kline said to the operative. 'My psychic faculties are dimmed where you're concerned. Why is that, Halloran? What is it about you ... ?'

'I'm just a hired bodyguard, nothing more than that.'

Kline's stare did not shift. 'But you're a danger to me.'

'No, I'm here to prevent any harm coming to you.' Halloran tensed the muscles of his arms, preparing himself to strike, concentrating his strength. 'Tell me, Kline, tell me what this is all about.'

'I've already explained.'

'I'd like to know more. How can you ... ?' He couldn't find the words; it felt too ridiculous to try.

'Tap into someone's soul?' the psychic finished for him. 'Absorb its vitality?' He laughed, a choking in his throat. 'The secret was left for me.' His eyes closed, the lids hideously raw, but his smile was rapturous. 'I learned from the ancient cuneiform writings of the Master himself. They were hidden away with his remains, spread around him to give sustenance during his long wait. He drew me to them, so many years ago, a time of ignorance for me, when I was a shell waiting to be filled. I found his works in a chamber, a sepulchre beneath the Royal Cemetery of Ur, and piece by piece I smuggled them out, and piece by piece I had them deciphered so that no one else would understand their full message. Only then did I assemble them once more, when I knew the power contained within their symbols. They told of how potent were the powers of the mind, how they could be developed, channelled ... how they could *create*!'

He swayed, his eyes remaining closed. Khayed reached out as if to steady him, but seemed afraid to touch.

Kline's voice became deeper in tone. 'They taught the delights of perversity, the superiority that comes from corruption. I learned, you see, learned well, became an avid student. They instructed me in the ways of terror, they showed me how to seek out the evil in others and use it for my own ends. They revealed how I could escape the degenerating process, the wearing away of flesh and muscle, the shrivelling of body and mind, how the decay could be transposed to others. They spoke of the secret link between the mind and the earth's own energy, how they could be coupled, and used together. And I feasted upon the knowledge!'

Kline's eyes sprung open, and the blackness in them almost filled the sockets.

'The price of it all was easy to pay,' he whispered. 'Dissension, wherever it could be spread. Atrocity, wherever it could be encouraged. Malevolence, wherever it could be nurtured. I learned to disperse my disruption, took it to many countries and let it fester. Because that was *his* way, and I am his disciple!'

Kline's hands were raised to his chest, palms upwards, fingers curled into claws. He shuddered, a movement that threatened his collapse. But he righted himself, his mouth open in an agitated grin.

'There was another part to this bargain.' Now he was stooping, twisting into himself. 'An alliance between us. I was to keep Bel-Marduk forever with me, to sustain his bodily self, to keep it living.'

A shiver ran through Halloran. There was nothing here of the Kline that he knew. The thing before him was unrecognizable in voice and body. Halloran felt weakened.

'You'll see,' said the form opposite. 'You'll understand how we breathe together.'

Kline moved away, tottering as if about to fall. Yet still the Arab by his side was reluctant to take hold of him. Kline walked awkwardly to an alcove behind the altar, and the others watched, all of them motionless.

He entered the shadows.

Halloran heard something being opened.

Shuffling footsteps.

Kline returning, carrying something clutched to his chest, into the candle-light ...

· 45 ·
NETHERWORLD RISING

AWAY FROM THE BUBBLING LAKE THEY RAN, THROATS ROUGHENED BY HARSH breaths, disarray in their stride. Two of their companions had been lost to the lightning-seared cauldron, and these remaining three had no intention of joining them; clumsy their flight may have been, pounding rain rendering earth and grass slippery beneath their feet, but their progress was determined, panic lending its own pace.

Despite himself, a terrible fascination tempted Danny Shay to look back over his shoulder and he uttered a single alarmed cry at what he saw; he stumbled, went down, the man at his heels sprawling over him so that they both rolled in the soaked grass, kicking out at each other.

Shay sat up, rain streaming into his open mouth, while the other man, Flynn, beat at the earth in pain. McGuire realized he was alone and stopped, searching behind for the others.

'Glory God ...' he moaned when he saw the lake.

Shay scrambled to his knees and Flynn reached out to grasp his shoulder. 'I've done me ankle, Danny!' he shouted over the downpour. 'Give us a hand up!'

But Shay stayed motionless, staring into the rain. Flynn followed his gaze and collapsed back into the grass.

A shining came from beneath the water's boiling surface, a milky greenness that spread to the shoreline. A curling mist rose from it, turning in on itself like vapour reaching cooler air. Geysers popped and spouted, foamy liquid showering down to create ripples, more turmoil. But something else was disturbing the broad lake's centre. A great mass, hindered by its own weight, was slowly emerging like some huge sunken wreck pushed to the surface by an eruption on the sea bed.

This was nothing manmade, though. It might have been regurgitation of a long-lost island, the waters finally relinquishing their claim. Except it was a living, pulsating thing. A mass that swelled and writhed, a gathering in oozing mud of all those nebulous creatures the men had glimpsed earlier beneath the lake's unsettled ceiling, the forms clinging together as if congealed. Pieces – *living things* – dropped away as this ill-shaped mountain grew; lake-water drained off to fall with the rain. Monsters of immense size were among that curling, viscous mass, while leaner shapes wriggled and clung like parasites, the ascending heap never still, constantly bulging and quivering as it rose.

As the three frightened men watched, a bolt of lightning struck the top, sizzling and charring its uppermost layer as if it were flesh. Steam rose as the whole mass shrunk in spasm. It stretched once more, continuing to ascend. They thought they could hear a shrill wailing beneath the roar of thunder.

'What is it!' Flynn shrieked close to Shay's ear, the grip on his leader's shoulder tight.

Shay could only shake his head in a stupefied gesture.

'Let's leave this heathen place, Danny! There's no good for us here!'

The leader climbed to his feet, bringing Flynn up with him, his eyes never leaving the monstrosity growing from the lake, this seen through a screen of driving rain. McGuire joined them, afraid to be left standing alone. He clutched at Shay's other arm.

'There's no turning back!' the leader yelled. 'Whatever devil's work this is, it doesn't matter! It'll not stop us doing our job!'

'No, it's a bad business, Danny!' McGuire protested.

Shay hit him, a back-swipe of his hand. 'You'll do as you're told! The house is close, an' he's in there! We'll not leave until it's settled!'

He shoved both men from him, forcing them to turn their backs on the lake with its phenomenon that could only be some kind of illusion – there couldn't be any reality to such a vision. Although … although didn't he see for himself two of his own men dragged down into its terrible depths?

Shay began running, cutting out further thought, intent on one purpose alone, urging McGuire and Flynn to follow. They did for, scared though they were, disobedience was unthinkable.

They did their best to ignore the squishy gurgling of the sinuous island as it heaved itself from the water, resisting the temptation (it was as though there were whispered entreaties in their minds to do so) to turn round and watch. They kept their eyes on the manor house which was now but a short distance away.

Most of the lights were on, a welcoming relief despite the duty they were bound to perform, a glorious beacon in the darkness they had travelled through.

They found themselves on firmer ground, gravel crunching under their feet as they dashed forward, no caution in their untidy gait. There was a porch at the front, an entrance like a darkened cave. Flynn strove to keep up with the others, the pain in his ankle a handicap, his hand tucked into his anorak pocket touching the revolver there for comfort. He suddenly slid to a halt.

There were headlights coming towards them!

A car on the road, moving fast, freezing them in its searching beams. It skidded to a stop twenty yards away. Doors were opening. Someone was shouting.

· 46 ·
TOWARDS DESTRUCTION

CANDLE FLAMES FLICKERED AND DIMMED MOMENTARILY, SMOKE CURLING FROM them, as Kline came closer, his hands livid against the blackness of the robe he wore. In them he held a black chalice, a cloth draped over the top.

All eyes were on the shuffling figure emerging from the alcove and instinct told Halloran that this was the time to make his move. Yet he could not. Like the others, he was mesmerized.

Kline faltered, as though the weight of his burden was too much. But after drawing in a deep, grating breath, he continued to approach.

Thunder grumbled in the distance and it seemed to come from below, from the earth itself, rather than the atmosphere above.

At last Kline, or the disfigured thing that Kline now was, reached the stone slab. He attempted to grin, perhaps in triumph, but his lips merely wavered, his stained teeth bared only partially. His hands were trembling when he placed the chalice on the altar. He removed the cloth, allowed it to fall to the floor. Then Kline dipped both hands into the vessel, the object he removed still unseen by the others. He held out his prize across the furred belly of the paralysed bodyguard.

A husky whisper. 'His disciples, his loyal priests, preserved his poor muti-lated body. They hid Bel-Marduk away, a deep place where no one could find him. Hidden in darkness, his secrets around him, waiting out the centuries for one such as I ...'

He placed the object on the stone beside the bodyguard, and there it rested for the others to see.

A blackened, crisped shell. A thing almost rotted away, shrivelled stumps that had once been tubes, but which now had no function, protruding.

And as they watched, the ancient withered heart pulsed.

Just once ...

Mather had jammed on the handbrake and was opening the driver's door even before the car had rocked to a halt.

'*Stop there!*' he shouted, but the three figures either did not hear him over the storm or had no intention of heeding his command.

'Draw your weapon, Phil,' he ordered. 'Whoever they are, I don't want them to get inside the house.'

Both men used the car doors as shields, the operative clenching a Browning with both hands, using the triangle between passenger door and frame as an armrest.

'*Hold it!*' he warned, but one of the figures, someone who appeared to be limping, whirled round, bringing something from his anorak pocket as he did so. Flame spat out into the rainy night.

'*Pacify him!*' Mather yelled at his man as a bullet scythed sparks off the car roof. The operative would have preferred to have 'retired' the gunman, a more permanent condition, but he knew better than to disobey an order. He took quick aim at the enemy's shoulder; unfortunately the target had changed position, had tried to follow his companions. The Shield operative knew by the way the man violently jerked, then dropped like a stone, that the bullet had taken him in the head or neck.

He muttered a curse, but didn't take time to shrug an apology at Mather, for the other two intruders were disappearing into the porch.

He gave chase, skirting around the vehicles parked in front of the house, flattening himself against the outside wall of the porch, keeping out of sight until he could position himself. Realizing Mather had not followed, he looked back at their car. The Planner was facing the opposite direction, towards the lake.

They had noticed a strange shining from that area when they had broken free of the woods moments earlier to descend into the valley, but the rain had been too heavy to see clearly. Even this close it was difficult, for there was a mist rising from the peculiar incandescence that was the lake itself, creating a swirling fog which the rainfall failed to disperse. Mather tore himself away and began limping towards his companion, body crouched, cane digging into the gravel.

'What is it out there?' the operative asked when the older man reached him.

'I've no idea,' came the breathless reply. 'Some kind of disturbance in the lake, that's all I can tell. Let's worry about our immediate problem.'

'Here comes the other patrol.' The operative nodded towards the lightbeams descending the hill at a fast pace.

'We can't wait for them. Check inside.'

The other man ducked low, quickly peering into the tunnel of the porch and drawing his head back almost immediately.

'Shit,' he said. 'The door's open. They're inside the house.'

It was a dream. It could only be a bad dream.

Yet Cora knew it wasn't. The nightmare around her was real. She tried to focus her mind, desperate to understand what was happening, why Monk, that bloated, repellent creature, was lying naked on the stone, and ... and ... Shock broke through the haze.

The black-robed figure standing on the other side of the prone bodyguard was obscene in its deformity. Only the eyes allowed some recognition.

'Felix …?' She imagined she had said the name aloud, but in fact it had been no more than a murmur.

She held up her hands to her face, not because of the unsightliness in front of her, but to clear her thoughts …

… While Halloran's mind was sharp by now, all grogginess gone. He stared disbelievingly at the blackened object lying on the stone altar.

'It can't be,' he whispered.

'But it is. The only part of Bel-Marduk that survived his mutilated body's entombment. His heart.'

'Impossible.'

'Naturally.'

'Kline, let's stop this nonsense. Let me walk away with Cora –'

Kline screamed across at him, a furious cry that might have been anguish. The wire noose around Halloran's neck jerked tight and he was dragged backwards by Daoud, away from the altar, his legs giving way so that he fell to the wet floor, the Arab crouching behind him, maintaining the pressure. Cora took a step towards them, then collapsed back against the stone.

'*There's still more to be done, Halloran!*' Kline screeched. 'Especially now, in this era of awesome power, when we hold the very weapons of our own genocide. *Don't you understand that he directed mankind towards this point, he set us on this road!* A few more decades, that's all it will take. A micro-second in earth's lifespan. A few more years of disruption and dissent, of famine and disease, of wars and violence. A culmination of evils, when the balance between good and bad has been tilted irrevocably towards *his*, Bel-Marduk's, way! I showed you the lake, Halloran, allowed you to see its contents. A residue, like many others around the world, of our own corruption, a manifestation of our evils in living form. *You saw them, you recognized your own culpability, your own vileness!* We're not unalike, you and I, Halloran. You just have a little further to travel.'

Kline was leaning over Monk's body, sucking in air, exhausted, drained by his own beliefs. 'I could have made you one of mine, Halloran. A little encouragement, that's all it would have taken. But I can't trust you. I don't have time to.' He calmed himself, or perhaps weariness did it for him. 'She'll join us in our communion, Bel-Marduk's and mine. Cora will help us and be one of us.' He levered himself up from the body. 'Asil …'

The Arab stepped forward and from beneath his robes he drew out a long blade, one edge thickened for weight so that it resembled a machete. The metal glowed in the candle-light.

He raised it over Monk's chest and the bodyguard's hands twitched frantically. His lips parted. A sobbing came from them.

Khayed brought down the blade with a short, sharp movement, minimum effort in the blow, for he needed only to pierce the breastbone so that the paralysed man's ribs could be pulled apart, his heart exposed.

Monk shuddered. His hands and now his feet quivered as the finely-honed blade was drawn down his stomach. The cutting stopped when muffled gunfire was heard from above.

• 47 •
ACROSS THE COURTYARD

'Hold 'em there, McGuire. Don't let anyone through the door.'

McGuire looked at his leader apprehensively. 'An' where the hell will you be?'

'Finding our man. He'll not escape.'

'Are you fuckin' insane, man? There's nothing we can do now except mebbe get away ourselves.'

'You'll do as I tell you, or it'll not only be me you'll answer to.'

'An' what if he's not here?'

'Oh, the bastard's here all right, I can feel it in me piss.'

'I'll give it five minutes, Danny, no more than that.'

Shay decided it was pointless to argue. McGuire had always been the yellow one, enjoying the killing only if he was mob-heavy or guaranteed a safe getaway. Besides, five minutes should be enough; then he'd leave McGuire to his own fate. He turned away from the main doors, one side of which remained open, and quickly scanned the hall, taking no note of its grandness. It was a damned cold house, to be sure. And there was nothing good inside these old walls.

Shay ran across the stone floor, expecting someone to appear at any moment through one of the many doors that opened out onto the hall. He kept an eye on the stairs and landing too as he went, sure that anyone in the house would have heard the din outside.

Into a corridor he ran, revolver held before him like a pointer. He stopped and listened. Gunshots from the hall. McGuire was keeping whoever had driven up to the house at bay. Had they nabbed Flynn? he wondered. Things were going bad. He almost smiled. Things were fucking terrible.

A door was open at the end of the corridor, rain pouring in. What was this? The house couldn't be that narrow. He hurried to the doorway and looked outside, suddenly understanding the layout. A courtyard, filling up with rain by the looks of it. And what was that?

Light from another doorway opposite. Somebody there, like him, peering out.

Shay did not hesitate: he was through the door like a shot, racing across the courtyard towards the other man. Something was bubbling to his right, but he paid it no mind, realizing it was a fountain, the storm causing its basin to overflow.

He kept running and the other person had spotted him, was backing away.

The fool's attention must have been on the fountain before, not on the shadow bearing down on him through the storm. It had been Shay's luck that lightning had not struck during those few seconds.

He burst into the hallway and was able to reach out for the man who, too late, had attempted to flee. He pulled him round, clamping a hand over the man's mouth, then ramming the barrel of the gun beneath his captive's wire-rimmed spectacles so that they rose off his nose, the weapon hard against his closed eyelid.

▪ 48 ▪
BLOOD RITES

THE ARAB WAS MURMURING AN INTONATION THAT WAS BREATHLESS, HIS excitement conveyed through the wire which vibrated against Halloran's throat. Daoud watched the figures at the altar, fretful that he was unable to join them, but chanting the incantations learned from the cuneiform writings, so that he was at least part of the ceremony.

A breeze swept down from the corridor above, bending the candle flames as it swirled around the underground chamber, ruffling the light so that shadows danced and weaved as though they also belonged to the rite.

At the stone slab that served as an altar, Felix Kline, aware that his strength was fading, his will weakening with it, urged Khayed to hurry. Tissue was breaking from him, falling onto the robe he wore, onto the open body lying below on the stone. He could feel fresh lesions forming, the flesh ulcerating and rupturing beneath his clothing, skin weeping pus, dribbling wetness. The pain was intense, as though every joint in his body was on fire, and his scalp was tightening around the skull, splitting apart as it shrank. This agony was like never before, and it was the significance of that which frightened Kline more than anything else. The torments of his sleep, the panic that had lingered afterwards, the sense of deep foreboding – these were feelings he had not experienced since discovering the hidden tomb so many years before. *Why now, O Lord? Have I failed you in some way? Are you failing me, Bel-Marduk?* The questions were silent, his spoken invocations uninterrupted, for those ancient words were important to the ritual, their tonal values an inducing cadence for affinity between the psyche and the spiritual realms.

Khayed's hands were bloodied beyond the wrists as he pulled at the sliced sides of the body to expose Monk's innards. The bodyguard's eyelids fluttered as life dwindled, receding within him so that it could expand outwards through another dimension. The Arab tugged at Monk's exposed sternum, bending the ribs upwards, then pushed sweating organs down towards the gut, reaching for the heart and dragging it clear, stretching arteries and breaking veins until the feebly pulsing organ was revealed. All a familiar and well-practised ritual.

Kline took the other heart, the old shrivelled husk that represented – that *was* – the existence of his deity. With one hand he lifted this shell, while with the other he reached for Cora's wrist. She was too numbed to resist, incomprehension still misted in her eyes.

But when Kline plunged both their hands into the gaping wound, the dried, withered thing held between them, she whimpered. When he settled the remnant organ against the fresh, bleeding one, using their hands as a vice, she screamed.

Cora felt her whole self being drawn down into the huge open wound, blood spurting along her arm, her hand disappeared into the quagmire. And it was the ancient petrified heart that sucked her in.

Kline was lost in a delirium of sensations, a euphoric rebirth without trauma, a vigour beginning to pulsate through him. All this ceased for him when the girl pulled her hand free, bringing with it the parasite heart.

Cora held the relic in her bloody grasp and stared loathingly at it for but a moment. Turning away, she cast it from her, a violent and sudden movement that neither Kline nor Khayed could prevent.

The brittle shell scudded across the stone floor and came to rest in a puddle of blackened water.

Now it was Kline who screamed, a piercing cry that echoed around the walls of the chamber.

And it was Halloran who took his chance.

Daoud's attention was on the dark, blood-soaked mound lying in the water only a few yards away, his grip loosened on the wooden handles of the garotte. Halloran, half-kneeling below the Arab, swiftly brought the point of his elbow up into the other man's groin. Daoud hissed, releasing one of the handles to clutch at himself, the wire cutting across Halloran's throat. The operative grabbed the Arab's ankle and pulled, sending his opponent crashing onto his back.

Despite the pain, Daoud kicked out at Halloran, toppling him as he tried to rise.

They came up together, but tears blurred the Arab's vision. Halloran's stiffened fingers jabbed at the front of Daoud's neck, striking for the thyroid cartilage. If his balance had allowed a greater force to the blow, the Arab would have been killed instantly; as it was, Daoud crouched over his knees, choking and gasping. Halloran half-rose, turning as he did so, ready to launch himself at the Arab's companions.

Cora had sunk down against the altar, blood from the open body above spilling over the edge to stain the shoulders of her white robe. Kline was stumbling around the stone slab, one hand against it for support, the other stretched out, fingers spread, as though reaching for the relic lying in the wetness of the floor some distance away. Khayed's gaze was fixed on his choking lover. Rage burned when it shifted to Halloran. Khayed lifted the long and broad chopping knife.

But others had entered the chamber.

Janusz Palusinski, whom Kline had ordered to investigate the earlier sound of gunfire, had returned. A man in a rain-drenched anorak gripped the Pole's collar from behind; in his free hand was a revolver pointing at Palusinski's head.

Danny Shay was dismayed by what confronted him in the gloomy, candle-lit room. Dismayed, then fiercely angry. There were robed figures below him, one wielding a long, blood-stained knife, another in black wearing a hideous mask of some kind. There was a girl resting against a stone slab, her legs exposed, blood soaking her clothing. And the stone resembled an altar, and on that altar – oh dear God in Heaven! – there was a mutilated body, blood pumping from it like red springwater. There were moving shadows, dark alcoves that might have hidden others involved in this atrocity. Shay thumbed back the hammer of the .38.

And then his eyes came to rest on the man he had been seeking.

'*Halloran!*' he yelled.

The operative looked up towards the top of the stairway, as did the others in the chamber. Khayed became still, while Kline leaned heavily against the stone, a wildness in his eyes. Cora barely reacted, for the moment too disorientated to care.

The man with the gun shoved Palusinski away from him, and the Pole staggered down a few steps before cowering against the wall, folding himself up so that he was small, a poor attempt to make himself invisible. The weapon came around to point at Halloran.

'You've given the Organization a lot of grief, man,' Shay said.

Halloran straightened slightly, his body remaining tensed. The man above him had spoken with a thick, southern-Irish accent and a hint of the truth began to dawn in Halloran's mind.

'You killed three good men, Halloran. Valuable men to the Cause, they were. Shot 'em before they had a chance. You should have known we'd find you, you must have realized the IRA would never stand for that!'

Halloran was stunned. So it was *he* who had been the target all along. This bastard had tortured Dieter Stuhr to find *him* ...

The man on the stairway felt uneasy with the strange smile that had appeared on Halloran's face.

Shay spoke to cover his own inexplicable fear. 'There'll be three Provos, good an' true, smiling in Heaven this night,' he said, raising the .38 so that it was aimed directly at Halloran.

'There's no such place for killers,' the man below said, and his voice was mild, the lilt of Irish there as if he'd not been gone too long from the ould country.

'That you'll be knowing yourself,' Shay replied. 'God only knows what Divil's worship you're involved in here. Ask His forgiveness, if you've a mind to, an' do it now.'

Thunder rumbled as his finger curled against the revolver's trigger.

'*Liam!*' Cora screamed, and just for an instant the gunman was distracted.

That was all the time that Halloran needed to make a grab for the collapsed Arab.

The gun roared deafeningly in the confines of the underground room, but Halloran had already hoisted up the Arab to use as a shield. Daoud shuddered as the bullet struck his forehead and lodged inside. The operative fought to control the twitching body, his hands beneath the dead man's shoulders, holding him upright. The second bullet entered Daoud's stomach, and the third went through his side. Halloran felt this last one nick his hip as it emerged and, although most of its force was spent, the shock was enough to make him drop his cover.

More screams filled the air, but these were from Khayed who had witnessed the slaying of his lover. He ran towards the stairs, the long blade raised high, a continuous screech now rising from deep inside his throat.

Shay was obliged to turn to meet the attack, and he was hardly aware of the person who had led him to this ungodly place brushing past. Palusinski was too afraid for his own life to tackle the gunman; he made for the safety of the corridor at the top of the stairs.

Khayed was almost on the bottom step when Shay fired the gun at him. A hole appeared in the Arab's chest, its edges immediately spreading blood. He staggered backwards, his arms waving as if for balance, then came forward once more, his face not contorted with pain but with outrage. He reached the second step and seemed to sense he would never get close to the one who had killed his beloved Youssef.

The huge knife was already leaving his hand as the next bullet tore away his throat.

Shay fell back against the stairs, the blade imbedded at an angle in his stomach, the heavy anorak he wore no protection at all. His vision was already beginning to dim as he turned his head towards the man below, his target, the Irishman turned traitor whom he and his group had been sent to assassinate as an example to others of how the Organization always avenged themselves. His hand wavered as he raised the Webley .38, for the weapon was suddenly very heavy, almost too heavy to lift.

Once again he aimed the gun at Halloran.

· 49 ·
RETURN TO THE DEATH HUT

'WE CAN'T WASTE ANY MORE TIME WITH THIS ONE,' MATHER REMARKED.

'Find another point of entry?' his operative suggested, looking up from his kneeling position against the porch wall.

'No need,' Mather replied, raising a hand to the other two Shield men running towards them. He went to meet them, keeping out of sight of the main doors inside the porch from where the gunman held them at bay. He tightened his coat collar around his neck against the drenching rain.

'In the mood for target practice, Georgie?' he asked when the two men reached him.

'Always, sir,' came the answer, as all three moved in close to be heard over the storm. 'What's the problem?'

'We're being refused admittance. You see the Mercedes parked in line with the porch? You'll have a clear view of the house doorway from the rear passenger seat, or at least you can see some of it in the darkness – our friend appears to have switched off some lights. The vehicle's ours, so use your spare key if it's locked.'

'How much damage?'

'Just hit the bugger.'

Mather limped away, followed by the second operative who crouched low and used the Mercedes as a screen to reach the opposite side of the porch. The man named Georgie doubled over also, going to the car and trying the doorhandle. Halloran must have left it in one hell of a rush, he thought, when he discovered the doors were unlocked. The keys were in the ignition. Georgie switched on the system, then crawled over to the backseat and pressed the button to lower the passenger window. He raised the Browning, keeping it clear of the rain that spattered in, and waited.

He watched as the operative with Mather crawled on his belly into the tunnel, keeping to the shadow of one wall. The Planner reached inside with his cane to tap the floor, hoping to attract the attention of their quarry.

It worked. Georgie squeezed the Browning's trigger as flame flashed from the doorway ahead. All he heard was the bark of his own weapon, but he assumed Phil, inside the porch, had fired at the same time, aiming slightly left of the gunflash. They waited a few seconds then, as lightning seared and thunder shook the sky, he saw Mather rush inside, Phil rising to accompany him to the doorway. He bundled out of the car, taking up position on the opposite side of the porch to his other colleague, their weapons pointing inwards at the entrance.

Mather pushed the door back further and flicked the Armalite away from the motionless gunman with his cane. Soft light from an open door across the spacious hall and from the landing above lit the area and Mather breathed a sigh of relief when he ascertained that no one else guarded the main doors. Rushing forward like that so soon after the enemy was hit had been a calculated risk, but it had saved some time.

Mather pointed at the slumped figure with his cane. 'Check him, then send one of the others after me while you search upstairs.' He was already limping across the hall making for the lit doorway as he gave the orders.

He entered a corridor at the end of which was a door swaying with the draught that blew in from outside, rain puddling the floor beneath it. He hurried forward glancing into other open doorways as he passed.

From ahead, Mather thought he heard a scuffling.

Palusinski came out into the courtyard, the pounding rain welcome on his face and head, even though huge droplets spattered his glasses and distorted his vision. Lightning pearled everything before him, dazzling him through the water-spots on his lenses so that he blinked rapidly. Whipping off the spectacles, the movement accompanied by a peal of thunder, he hurried across the flagstones. The Pole had no desire to find his way through Kline's private rooms in order to reach the main doors of the house: this way was more direct and the sooner he was away from the madness inside Neath, the better he would like it. His own acute sense of survival told him some kind of reckoning was at hand for Kline – *mój Pan*, oh Lord and Master! – and he, Janusz Palusinski, did not want to be around for the consequences.

But as he passed the centre fountain, a burning liquid sprayed his face. When he stopped to brush at the stinging with his hand, he felt a stickiness on his cheek. He could feel it eating into his skin. He peered short-sightedly at the fountain and there seemed to be shapes contorting from the stonework, rising from the brimming basin, writhing among the ornamentation.

Palusinski uttered a startled cry and began to back away. *Gowno!* This couldn't be! The fountain was a dead thing, defunct, slimed and blocked, an extinct spring! Yet he could discern a bubbling outflow catching reflections from window lights around the yard. And liquid dribbled sluggishly from the carved spouts which, in their decay, resembled gargoyles. And these monsters themselves were *moving*, twisting as if to tear themselves free from the stone-work, hatching from wombs of masonry, spitting their bile of burning substance, the whole structure gushing unnatural life.

Palusinski slipped as he turned to run, his knees smacking sickeningly against the flagstones. His spectacles flew from his grasp, one lens cobwebbing fine cracks as it struck.

The Pole scrabbled away on hands and knees, too much in haste to search for his broken glasses, and too afraid to look back at the quivering fountain. He sobbed when something touched his leg, a curling caress that somehow scorched even though there was no firmness, no strength in its grip. He pushed himself up, moving forward all the time, blundering towards the open doorway on the other side of the courtyard where light was shining outwards.

He blinked away wetness. There was someone else in the corridor, limping towards him. Palusinski reacted instinctively and with his natural sense of self-preservation. He drew out the metal bar he always carried inside his coat and launched himself at the advancing figure.

Mather noted the crazed wildness in the other man's eyes, and saw light catching the shiny weapon being raised, ready to strike. He came to a halt and pointed his cane at the bald man's chest.

Palusinski sneered at the other's ineffectual weapon, realizing there was nothing to fear in this old man confronting him, the only real terror being out there in the courtyard and the underground chamber he had just left. He grabbed the end of the cane and pulled it towards himself, sure that it would be easy to wrench it from the frail grasp. The metal bar had reached its zenith, was trembling in his hand, ready to plunge downwards against the man's skull. He barely heard the faint *click*.

Mather had pressed the tiny button in the cane's handle and the wooden casing slid from the long, slender blade, his would-be assailant unsheathing the sword himself. The Shield Planner took no chances, for he could see the murder in this wildman's eyes.

He lunged forward, the sword piercing the bald man's chest, melting through, entering his heart and still not stopping.

Palusinski looked in surprise at the other man. The pain only came when the sword was swiftly withdrawn.

He sank to the floor, a casual gesture as if he merely wanted to rest for a moment. Janusz Palusinski lay down and, as his mind wandered towards death, he felt he was among other recumbent bodies. He was no longer inside the corridor of the house, but in the dimly lit hut a long, long way from there, and a long time ago.

Those skeletal forms around him were sitting up and grinning their welcome, for they had been waiting many years. One even crawled over to touch the young Janusz's face with bony fingers. Janusz lay there, unable to move, and he wondered why unseen hands were pulling at his clothing. And he wondered why there was no pain when teeth gnawed into his plump belly.

No, there was no pain at all.

Just the nightmare that he knew would go on forever ...

· 50 ·
SHADOWS AND IMAGININGS

HALLORAN REMAINED PERFECTLY STILL, STARING UP INTO THE EYES OF THE DYING gunman.

The weapon wavered in the air, trying to home in on its target. But the exertion was too much, and too late. Danny Shay rolled onto his side to make one last determined effort, but the gun was far too heavy for someone with only seconds to live. For a moment his arm hung over the stairway, the weapon loose in his grip. Then Shay's eyes closed and he knew he would never open them again.

'Dear God ...' he began, the plea cut short when even his voice lost its strength.

He toppled from the stairs onto the damp floor, his landing relaxed, for he was already dead.

Wind tearing in from the passageway above ruffled Halloran's hair. The light stirred, juddered, many of the candle flames snuffed by the breeze so that shadows stole forward from the alcoves. The ancient worshippers watched on, stone eyes dispassionate. And there seemed to be other onlookers within those darkened arches, but these were forms of no substance, observers that could never be defined by light for they were of the imagination even though they existed outside the mind. Halloran was intensely aware of their watching.

He turned towards the altar where the bloated corpse continued to pump blood. Cora had moved away, her shoulders soaked a deep red; she looked imploringly at Halloran, as if silently begging him to take her away from this madness. When she saw the coldness in him, Cora became inert.

Halloran would not allow emotion to hold sway. Not for the moment. He was confused, uncertain of his feelings for Cora. She had touched him, made him vulnerable once more. And naturally, he had paid the price. He told himself she was an innocent used by someone who existed only for corruption. Yet ... the thought persisted ... yet there had to have been some part of her that was susceptible.

'Don't dare to judge me, Liam.' She spoke quietly, but with defiance. 'Not you, not someone like you.'

He understood her meaning.

Thunder rumbled through the passageway, the sound spreading out into the chamber, seeming to tremble the walls. Dust sifted down from the ceiling to congeal in the puddles on the floor.

And in one small slick of black water lay the dried husk that was an embalmed heart.

And those unseen but fearfully imagined forms were emerging from the alcoves.

Halloran sensed their movement at first and only when he looked did they take on a nebulous kind of reality. These were as the things from the lake, and they shuffled forward, eager to embrace. Because they were of him, the creatures mere reflections of the dark side of his inner self, manifestations of his own frailty, his own corruption. Hadn't Kline, himself, explained that to him?

He felt weakened. He staggered as if struck. He spun round.

More of these creations of the subconscious were slipping from between the statues, winding their way through, advancing on him. Yet each time he focused on one, it became formless, a swirling, vaporous nullity. His mind seemed squeezed, as though invisible tentacles had insinuated themselves into the orifices of his body, clogging them, sliding inwards to capture his thoughts.

He clapped his hands against his temples, shaking his head to free himself of these tenuous intruders. He twisted, bent under their weight. Cora was trying to reach him, but something had hold of her, something not visible that tore at her robe, exposing her shoulders, her breasts that were smeared with blood. She was screaming as she struggled, but he could not hear her.

Halloran stumbled forward, desperate to help her, wanting that more than anything else, heedless of his own plight, the invasion of his own body. But it was useless. He was being dragged down by these seeping infiltrators who sought their own origins.

He could not hear her screams. But he could hear Kline's laughter.

Its cracked sound mocked him, tormented, as Kline overwhelmed him with imaginings, the thoughts swelling with all the badness that had been drawn into that underground room, the malignancy that had dwelled inside the dead men, released now by someone who acted as instigator and catalyst, someone who knew the ancient secrets of the Cabala, who understood their potency. Felix Kline ...

Where was he? Where *was* Kline?

Where else but inside your head? came the silent reply.

'That can't be,' denied Halloran aloud, his hands over his ears as though they could cut out the sly voice that was, indeed, inside his head.

Oh, but it can. A familiar snigger. *I can be anywhere. Didn't I demonstrate that the first time we met?*

'I can stop you!'

You can? Please try. A good-humoured invitation.

Halloran's legs buckled as white-hot irons pressed against the back of his eyeballs.

There. Painful? I can do more than that. You deserve to suffer more.

Halloran looked up from his kneeling position. Kline was standing a short distance away, facing him, eyes closed, scarlet hands tight against his own head. A head whose skin was all but gone, the flesh that had been beneath exposed and livid. He was unsteady as shadows that were something more than shadows writhed around him. Kline's mouth was open, an agonized grimace.

'It's too late!' Halloran managed to shout. 'You're weak. Your power isn't the same.' And as he said the words, Halloran felt the slightest easing of pressure, the merest cooling of the fire. Pain immediately came back to him.

You're so wrong, Halloran, whispered the insidious voice inside his head. *My only problem is whether I finish you quickly or take my time, enjoy myself a little.*

But there was a gasp, a sound only in Halloran's mind. Kline was reeling, his hands leaving blotches of scraped flesh as they ran down his face.

'*Halloran!*' A piercing scream, and from Kline's lips.

The psychic's eyes opened, blackness filling them. They rested on Halloran's. 'I can hurt you,' Kline rasped. 'I can make your heart seize up with the horrors I'll show you.' His eyes closed once more and the snigger was back inside Halloran's mind.

Nightmares began to form, and gargoyles drifted from them. But these were tangible, on the outside of his thoughts, for when they touched him their fingernails were like razor blades, and he could smell the stench of their breath, dank and foul, like old sea caves where mammoth creatures of the deep had been abandoned by the tide to die. They clung to him and their lips – not lips, they had no such things as lips – their *openings* pressed against his face to kiss.

He felt the aching in his arms. The tightening of his chest, as fear began to win through. No! They were in his mind – in *Kline's* mind! They couldn't hurt him!

But they could.

For where they touched him, so they drew out his life. He could feel living beings inside his veins, blocking the flow, expanding so that they burst the tubes and his life's liquid poured uselessly into the cavities of his body. He sagged, slumped on his haunches, and he acknowledged Kline's assertion that he could coax a victim's mind to murder its own host. Halloran was unable to resist, the images of Kline's creation were too strong, too *real*! His forehead bowed to the wet stone floor.

This time the roar was not thunder.

It jolted Halloran into awareness. A confusion of senses muddling his brain, a bedlam of emotions causing him to cry out. Now the worst of his pain was from his hip where the bullet that had passed through the Arab had scraped his own flesh. Blood there was soaking his torn jacket. And the soreness around his throat was a relief rather than a discomfort, for it was, like the throbbing pain in his side, an indication of true reality.

Halloran opened his eyes and looked up. The monsters had fled. The shadows were but shadows.

Kline was lying on the floor and there was no movement from him.

Halloran pushed himself to his feet and stood for a while, his body bent forward, hands resting against his legs, waiting for his strength to return. He searched for Cora.

He found her crouched over the dead gunman, her robe in tatters around her waist, marks and bloodstains on her pale skin. In her shaking hand was the revolver, smoke still curling from its barrel. She was staring at Kline, eyes wide, her expression lifeless.

'Cora ...' Halloran said as he staggered towards her. He knelt on one knee and took the gun from her, laying it to one side. 'I think you used his last bullet,' he told her as he gently pulled the remnants of her robe around her shoulders. She turned her face to him and apprehension filtered through the numbness. She murmured something he didn't quite catch, but it did not matter. He raised her to him and held her close, kissing her matted hair, his arms tight around her.

'It's done, Cora,' he assured her quietly. 'Finished. I'll get you away from this place, as far away as possible.'

She sank into him and the wetness from her eyes dampened his collar. He ran a hand beneath her hair and his fingers caressed the back of her neck.

He felt her stiffen.

He heard the slithering.

Halloran turned.

Felix Kline was sliding on his belly through puddles on the floor, leaving a trail of decayed skin and blood in his wake, the raw flesh of his skinless face and hands puckered and cracked, a glistening redness oozing from lesions. Facial muscles were clearly defined in grouped ridges, and tendons stood proud on his hands, with veins stretched as bluish rivulets. His breathing came as a strained animal-like coughing as he pushed himself towards the blackened lump which rested in filthy water at the centre of the room.

He was almost there, one hand extended, quivering as it reached for the relic that once was a heart within a body, his breath becoming harsher, a drool of spittle sinking to the floor from his gaping mouth.

Three feet away from the pool in which the ancient heart lay.

Push.

Two feet away. A piteous moaning from him as his pain-wracked body scraped against the flagstones. Tears as the suffering became too much to bear.

Push.

Through the wetness.

Halloran rose, softly taking away Cora's hand from his arm as she tried to cling to him.

Push.

Not far now.

Desperation gleamed in Kline's dark eyes.

A few more inches.

Push.

Nearly there.

His fingers stretched, sifting through the dirty water, almost touching the withered husk.

A shadow over him.

A lifted foot.

Kline sobbed as Halloran crushed the heart into the stone floor.

▪ 51 ▪
END OF THE STORM

MATHER PEERED OUT INTO THE COURTYARD.

Thank God the storm's easing, he thought. Lightning flashes were mere reflections, with thunder following long moments after as distant rumblings. The rain had lost its force, had become a pattering. He could just make out what must have been an impressive fountain in an age gone by, its structure now misshapen, worn by time. It glistened from the rain, but had no vitality of its own.

He was naturally concerned over the dead man lying behind him in the corridor. Mather realized that the man he had just killed was Janusz Palusinski, one of Kline's own bodyguards. The Planner had met Palusinski earlier that day, but the mad-eyed creature who had rushed at him in the corridor bore scant resemblance to that person: without his distinctive wire-framed spectacles and because of his drenched condition and the sheer lunacy of his expression, the Pole was another character entirely.

Why the devil had the man tried to attack him? He surely must have known who the Planner was. Unless, of course, the reason was that Palusinski was in league with the intruders, yet another traitor within the Magma organization. There had certainly been no doubt about his murderous intent – Mather was too experienced in the ways of combat not to have recognized it. Well, the matter would be cleared up soon enough.

There was activity across the courtyard. An open door there, vague light glowing from it. Shadows, figures. Someone was coming through the doorway.

Mather's grip tightened on the sword-stick. He ducked back inside when he heard footsteps behind him. One of his operatives was hurrying along the corridor. The Planner raised a finger to his lips and the operative slowed his pace, approaching quietly. He examined the bald-headed man whose chest was weeping blood.

Mather returned his attention to the two people who had stepped out into the courtyard, one of them apparently supporting the other.

'Wait there,' he instructed the operative when he recognized the couple as they made their way through the drizzle. Mather limped out to meet them, movement awkward without his cane; he quietly called Liam's name.

'Oh good Lord,' he said when he realized the state they were in.

Halloran expressed no surprise at finding Mather at Neath. In the light from the courtyard window, his face betrayed no emotion at all.

'Get her away from here,' Halloran said curtly, pressing Cora into the Planner's arms.

'What's happened, Liam?' Mather demanded to know. 'I've just been forced to kill one of Kline's bodyguards, the Polish fellow.'

There was the slightest hint of a smile in Halloran's eyes. 'Trust me like you've never trusted me before,' was all he said. 'It's over now, but I want you to take Cora out of the house. Wait for me by the main gates.'

'Liam, that's – '

'Please do it.'

Mather paused. 'And you?'

'There's something I have to take care of.'

With that, he turned away from Mather and the girl to walk back through the soft rain to the doorway from where he and Cora had emerged.

▪ 52 ▪
THE BATTLE OVER

HALLORAN CLOSED THE DOUBLE-DOORS OF NEATH, THEN STRODE ALONG THE gloomed porchway out into the cleansed night air. The clouds had broken up, the moon dominated. Dampness still lingered, but there was no violence left in this night. Across the lawn he could see the lake, a low-lying mist hovering over its calm surface.

He climbed wearily into the Mercedes, switching on engine and beams. He looked back at Neath once more, studying it for several moments before swinging the car around and heading up the road into the trees.

As he drove, he wondered about Felix Kline and his terrible and unique powers. He wondered about the story the psychic had told him, of the Sumerians, of Bel-Marduk, their devil-God, the Antichrist who had *preceded* the Christ. He wondered about the truth of it. And Halloran wondered about himself.

He thought that perhaps he understood.

They waited for him by the big iron gates, the four operatives puzzled and somewhat agitated by the abrupt ceasing of action, while Charles Mather stood with the girl, who wore one of the operatives' jackets draped over her shoulders.

Although barefooted and cold, Cora had refused to wait inside one of the cars; her eyes never left the drive leading to the house. She hadn't spoken a word since Mather had brought her away from Neath, despite his questions. Had Liam instructed her to remain silent? Mather wondered.

Cora caught her breath and Mather, too, saw the approaching lights, the car emerging from the tunnel of trees in the distance so that moonlight struck its silver bodywork. It came towards them at a leisurely pace, an indication that the danger really was past.

They watched as the Mercedes drew near, its headlights brightening the road.

But it stopped. By the lodge-house.

They saw Halloran lean out of the car window and drop something onto the ground in front of the two strange-looking guard dogs that had been prowling around their dead companions as though disorientated.

One of the animals warily came forward and began to devour whatever it was that Halloran had offered.

He watched the jackal chew on the crushed, blackened meat and waited there until the ancient heart had been swallowed completely.

Only then did Halloran start up the car again and drive onwards to the gates themselves.

He climbed out of the Mercedes and Cora took one hesitant step towards him. He raised his arms and she came all the way. Halloran pulled her tight against him.

Mather was bemused. Such a demonstrable show of emotion from his operative was unusual to say the least.

'Liam ...' he began.

Halloran nodded at him. 'I know,' he said. The Planner wanted answers, and what could he tell him? Halloran's tone was flat when he spoke. 'His bodyguards had turned against him. Monk, Palusinski, the two Jordanians – he'd treated them too badly. He's quite insane, you know. They finally had enough of him. None of it's clear, but I think they worked out a deal with the Provisional IRA to kidnap him. I guess they didn't want to live out their lives in servitude, and the proceeds from the ransom – or maybe just a Judas fee from the kidnappers – would have ensured that they no longer had to. And they got away with it. All except Palusinski and those two outsiders I saw you'd put down. You can alert the police, get them over here, have them watch air and seaports.'

'Wait a minute. The IRA ...?'

'They were responsible for Dieter Stuhr's death. I suppose the idea was to make sure no one suspected it was an inside job, that information on the Shield cover was tortured out of our own man. Incidentally, Kline's gate-keeper was attacked by those animals back there. What's left of him is inside that lodge-house.'

There was disbelief in Mather's eyes, but Halloran steadily returned his gaze.

'They took Kline,' Halloran continued evenly. 'But he was badly injured. I think he'll die from his wounds.'

'We'll see if we get a ransom demand. We'll insist on having evidence that he's still alive.'

'Somehow I don't believe that'll happen.'

'Shall I get on to the police now, sir?' one of the other men asked briskly.

'Uh, yes,' replied Mather. 'Yes, I think that would be appropriate, don't you, Liam? God knows how they'll take all this shooting, but we've been in similar predicaments before. Such a dreadful thing that all our efforts failed.'

Not once had he taken his eyes off Halloran.

'Let's sit in the car until the police arrive, shall we?' Mather suggested. 'Miss Redmile is shivering. And then you can tell me more, Liam. Yes, you can explain a lot more to me.'

There was something chilling in Halloran's smile. He looked back at the brooding lodge-house. Then along the road that disappeared into the darkness of the smothering woods, winding its way to the house itself. To Neath.

'I'm not sure you'll understand,' Halloran said finally. He took Cora's arm and helped her into the car.

SERPENT

Lights all around. Soft-hued glows.

Shadows, pretty, never still, constantly weaving their secrets.

Ah, the bliss of lying here. A fitting place, this altar. Peaceful. And no pain. Not yet.

Is this how it was for you, O Lord? Did your priests minister drugs to suppress the hurting? Or was your cask, your vessel, dead before it was entombed, your spirit trapped within to wait out the years, the centuries? Your heart had not died, I know that.

So tired, so exhausted. Sleep will be welcome. Yes, yes, even eternal sleep.

It's cold in this chamber beneath the earth. And damp. Yet why can't I shiver? Why can't I move?

Oh yes. I know why.

So finally he believed. Halloran finally accepted the truth of it all. A triumph in some ways, wouldn't you say?

But why didn't I understand that he was the one conditioned to ruin me? Why, with all my perceptive powers, didn't I realize it was Halloran who was the threat? Is that the one weakness that comes with the gift of seeing, O Lord? The vulnerable point, the blindness to one's own destiny, the unforeseeableness of one's own fate? Is that your answer to me? Quite a joke really, don't think I don't appreciate it.